W9-AZR-360

"A bang-up job, a sharp, satisfying read. Resnick has done her homework, and created a quasi-medieval world with a long history, many different ethnic groups, some long-standing empires, and a conquered country desperately seeking to be free once more. Resnick provides her main characters with sufficiently complex psychologies, and a number of intriguing plots of desire and betrayal. It's a lot better, and a lot less clichéd than most, and should satisfy every fan of the genre. They'll be waiting for a second volume."
—*The Edmonton Journal*

IN
Legend
BORN

LAURA RESNICK

TOR®
fantasy

A TOM DOHERTY ASSOCIATES BOOK
NEW YORK

This is a work of fiction. All the characters and events portrayed in this book are either products of the author's imagination or are used fictitiously.

IN LEGEND BORN

Edited by James Frenkel

Map by Ellisa Mitchell

A Tor Book
Published by Tom Doherty Associates, LLC
175 Fifth Avenue
New York, NY 10010

www.tor.com

Tor® is a registered trademark of Tom Doherty Associates, LLC.

ISBN: 0-812-55547-3
Library of Congress Catalog Card Number: 98-14529

First edition: August 1998
First mass market edition: October 2000

Printed in the United States of America

0 9 8 7 6 5 4 3 2 1

For my grandfather

VALDANIA

NORTH

KINTISH

KINGDOMS

Palace of Heaven

Cavasar

Shaljir

Zilar

Illan

Lake Kandahar

Zilar River

Emeldar

Mt. Dalishar

Gamalan

Alizar

Mount Darshon

Britar

Adalian

Liron

SILERIA

Prologue

"I COME TO SERVE. SHOW ME MY DUTY."

The Beckoner came for her in the night, while the others slept. Lying on her narrow pallet in the dark, Mirabar's chest tightened with fear when she sensed his presence. The other Guardians never heard the Beckoner; it was she alone whom he sought out and tormented.

Knowing the Beckoner was here now, hearing him call to her in the familiar, silent language of the dead, but with a song uniquely his own, Mirabar ground her teeth together to keep from showing her terror. She had learned long ago that predators became more dangerous the moment they sensed fear.

When she finally felt ready to face him without flinching, she opened her eyes and turned her head to seek him out. Moonlight flowed through the mouth of the shallow cave where she and her mentor, Tashinar, both slept. Relief mingled with disappointment as Mirabar's gaze swept the shadows; as always, there was no sign of the Beckoner. Nevertheless, the song inside her head was growing stronger and more compelling with each passing second.

Tonight, she thought, *it will be tonight.*

She glanced briefly at Tashinar's sleeping form, softly outlined in the moon glow, then pushed aside her woolen cloak and sat upright. Tashinar obviously did not hear the song, and Mirabar knew with certainty that no one else heard it either, not even the most gifted Guardian in these mountains.

Come, the Beckoner called her silently, urgently. *Come.*

She was afraid. She pushed herself off the ground and grabbed her cloak, whirling it around her shoulders to go out into the chill night and boldly confront this thing which wanted her for reasons no one could divine; but her chest burned with fear. She set her features in a challenging glare, strode out of the mouth of the cave, and emerged onto the moon-drenched hillside, following the Beckoning even as her heart pounded with dread. It was a twin-moon night, and the snowcapped peak of Mount Darshon gleamed brilliantly in the distance. At the sight of it, she muttered a brief prayer to Dar, the goddess that she, as both a *shallah* and a Guardian, worshipped.

Come to me, come . . .

Mirabar stopped in her tracks and whirled around, seeking the Beckoner. The increasing urgency of his call reached out to her, stirring a response, inciting a compulsion that was almost sexual in its allure.

Come to me, run to me . . .

He had been calling to her like this for months now. Sometimes he would come two nights in a row, and sometimes many quiet days would go by before he would suddenly come again without warning and then fade away without explanation. But the song had never before been so strong, so urgent. Tonight, perhaps tonight, she would see him at last. And perhaps upon seeing him, she would finally know whether or not he meant her harm.

Come . . .

"Who are you?" she asked aloud.

Come to me, come . . .

No one understood what was happening to her, why this thing was seeking her. Guardians summoned shades of the dead, but the dead did not summon Guardians. Not even Tashinar knew whether Mirabar was in danger from this strange, unseen visitant.

You must come . . .

She resisted the pull, the urge, the desire. Her will was strong, and she felt a tremor in the air as the Beckoner redoubled his efforts to lure her away from the mouth of the cave where Tashinar slept.

Come, come to me . . .

"No!"

She drew in a startled breath when something stirred in the gossamer forest at the edge of their camp. All Guardians lived in hiding and with the continual threat of betrayal and death. Could Outlookers be circling the camp? Or was this another kind of predator altogether?

"Who's there?" she said sharply.

A wind stirred, tugging at her cloak, teasing her hair. The low-hanging branches of the gossamer trees parted, their shifting, veil-like leaves teasing her vision with glimpses of something deeper in the woods. A hand, an arm, the flash of eyes as golden as her own. Mirabar stumbled backwards, stifling a scream.

No, you must come . . .

She heard sharp, panting breaths—her own. Her limbs trembled with ancient, superstitious fear as he emerged from the veiling branches of the gossamer trees and she saw him revealed in the brilliant moon glow.

He reached out to her.

She backed away, her eyes watering with horrified recognition. *"No!* Stay away! Stay back or I'll . . . No! You're a . . . Stay *away!"* she choked in breathless, broken terror.

His fire-golden eyes, as clear to her now as his demonred hair, filled with pity. "No," he murmured, "no, don't be afraid. Not like this."

He spoke aloud now, the song of the dead having faded to reveal the face and voice of a man. But Mirabar knew the look of one from the Otherworld; the mystical glow of the afterlife shimmered over his skin, his voice echoed through the woods, and his feet did not touch the ground.

"Who are you?" she demanded, staring into those orange-yellow eyes with mingled fear and suspicion.

He stared back. "Do you believe it, too? *You?"*

She lowered her own golden eyes briefly, conscious of the fiery red of her own hair. The *shallah* superstitions which had made her an outcast in her childhood still ruled a dark corner of her heart. Ashamed, she lifted her chin and glared at him again.

"That you and I were burned by the fires of Dar in the womb?" she said. "That we are accursed, half-demon creatures who must be hunted down and destroyed?" She shook her head slowly, feeling her breathing steady a little. "No, but I have never seen another like me."

"There have never been many," he conceded.

"Even fewer now," she pointed out bitterly.

"Rare and special." He gestured gracefully to her.

"Who are you? What do you want with me?"

"I am sent to lead you to them."

A chill seized her. "To whom?"

He smiled. It didn't reassure her. "Come. They have waited a thousand years. Don't keep them waiting any longer."

"*Who* has—" she began, but he had already turned away and was disappearing amidst the moon-drenched gossamer leaves.

Come, you must come . . .

"Damn you, I asked you a . . ." She swallowed the rest of her words and scowled. How often had Tashinar told her that the dead told you only what they wanted you to know?

Mirabar, come, they are waiting . . .

Mingled shame and anger sent her into the whispering trees in pursuit of her vision. Living in hiding amidst the highest mountains of Sileria, she seldom saw anything as luxurious as a looking glass, but she knew full well how strongly she resembled the Beckoner. Yet she, of all people, had nonetheless recoiled at the sight of those burning eyes and that burning hair; *she,* who had been wounded by such reactions—and endangered by much stronger ones—her whole life. How could she have been so cowardly and superstitious, even when caught off guard like that?

Besides, he would obviously continue to cut up her peace if she didn't follow him now and learn his purpose. Wishing she had thought to put on her worn leather shoes, she plunged into the forest, following the silent insistence of the Beckoning.

Come . . .

He lured her deep into the woods, so deep that even she, who had grown up wild in these mountains and possessed the instincts of an animal, soon lost all sense of distance or direction. The overhead branches grew ever thicker, until their arms entwined like lovers and blocked out the brilliant light of the two full moons floating amidst the stars.

Using Guardian fire magic, Mirabar blew a flame into her palm, intending to use it to light the way. A fierce wind came up and extinguished her fire. She glared unseeingly into the night while the Beckoner urged her to hurry. Then, walking blindly, she stubbed her bare toes hard against a rock and stumbled to one side, cursing impatiently.

Come, they are waiting . . .

"*Where* are they waiting?" she snapped, nursing her foot. "On the other side of the world?"

You must come . . .

"This is ridiculous," she growled, gingerly picking her way through the darkness. "I'm a Guardian." After a lifetime of being an outcast, there was a wealth of pride in those words. "The dead come to *me,* you fool."

She screamed a moment later when her foot encountered thin air where there should have been earth, and she plunged headfirst into an abyss. Instead of the quick, painful end she expected, she simply kept falling, ever falling, as if she really *might* find the other side of the world, as if this black, bottomless emptiness would simply keep swallowing her until she arrived there.

Then, after a long time, tiny pinpricks of light penetrated

her dazed senses. As she neared them, she thought they might be stars. It seemed as if the night sky itself had opened its gaping maw and sucked her off the face of the earth.

Mirabar.

As suddenly as she had fallen, she now found herself floating effortlessly in a celestial whirlwind, surrounded by a swirling chaos of unformed seas and unborn stars. Water and fire, she realized dazedly; the two most ancient and powerful forces in Sileria.

Mirabar.

"What?" she gasped, wondering if she had been taken to the Otherworld. "What?"

They are here. Can you hear them?

"Hear who?"

You must try!

There was no need to hide her fear now. She was beyond fear. She was in a place where no feeling had weight, a place far beyond life and death, thought and fear.

She didn't *hear* him, but she could see him now. She thought he might be a god, but she had never seen one and so wasn't sure. He was enormous, filling the expanse of emptiness that surrounded her whirling nest of fire and water, of unborn stars and borning rivers. His face was stern, but not frightening. His long black hair melted into the night, and his eyes were golden. *Golden,* she saw, as golden as her own, churning and shining with fire.

And she knew then who he was, knew that the stories the Guardians had passed down for a thousand years were true, truly *knew* for the first time in her life that she was no demon.

Humbled and awed, she crossed her fists over her chest in the traditional salute, then bowed her head. "Daurion," she whispered.

Yes! the Beckoner said, his exultation trembling around her.

Daurion, the last great ruler of Sileria, chosen by the Guardians to hold this vast, mountainous island with a fist

of iron in a velvet glove. Daurion, the golden-eyed Yahrdan who had died a thousand years ago and whose mon-
uments and painted image had been systematically
destroyed by his enemies after his death, until only half-
remembered stories and forbidden songs remained.

When Mirabar could move, she lifted her head to look
at him again, her eyes misting as they met his vast ones.
It was true! Those fiery eyes, which now meant almost
certain death in Sileria, had once, centuries ago, been birth
signs which brought respect and even greatness.

But so long ago . . .

The voice was new, and it shivered through her blood
like ecstasy. She saw two others sharing the sky with him
now, one dark-eyed and dark-haired like most Silerians,
and the other golden-eyed and crowned by a mane of flaming red hair: the long-dead rulers of a once-great land, the
forgotten leaders of a proud people enslaved by the Conquest a thousand years ago.

Mirabar . . .

"*Sirani,*" she choked in dialect. *My masters.* "I come to
serve." She searched the sky. "Show me my duty."

He is coming.

She sought Daurion's face, which was already changing;
no longer a face, but something else now. "Who, *siran?*"

The sky twisted and heaved with new images. She fell
into them, and they wrapped around her and flooded her
senses. She saw weapons, sharp blades breaking heavy
shackles, swords gleaming in the harsh Silerian sun. She
sensed a ferocity which threatened even itself, tasted a dark
pool of shame which stained a pure heart, and then choked
on her own longing.

He is coming.

Blood and courage dripped through the stars, and her
heart filled with an emptiness worse than starvation, a bitterness worse than hatred.

"Who is coming?" she cried, torn by this pain, frightened by this terrible courage, shamed and exalted at once.

Prepare the way.

"What must I do?"
He is coming!
"How will I know him?" she pleaded.
And then the sky caught fire.

TASHINAR FOUND MIRABAR at sunset the next day. Old, small, frail, and maimed from some long-ago torture by the Outlookers, Tashinar's strength had been worn down by hardship over the years. Now she nearly collapsed under the weight of her own relief. Her young apprentice was willful, foolishly brave, and gifted with powers she didn't yet know how to control. When Tashinar had awoken to find Mirabar gone and then discovered her cloak caught on some branches just beyond the edge of camp, she had feared the worst.

The strange, unidentified visitant whom Mirabar called the Beckoner had worried Tashinar for months. She knew that several other Guardians had even begun to doubt Mirabar's sanity, but she was primarily concerned with the young woman's safety. Nothing like this had ever happened among the Guardians—a persistent, mysterious vision which no one else could hear, see, or explain. Who could say where it came from or why it wanted their sharp-tongued initiate? For all they knew, this was some strange sorcery of the Society, even though it bore none of the usual signs.

They had searched for Mirabar all day, and Tashinar, who loved her, had grown increasingly desperate. No answers came from the Otherworld, and no explanation presented itself. Tashinar had no doubt that Mirabar had finally heeded the call of the Beckoner, and she was beginning to grieve with the certainty of loss when she literally stumbled over the girl's body in some leafy gully far from camp.

"Mirabar!"

She scooped the young woman into her arms and laughed with relief. Despite the chill in her skin, Mirabar's lifeblood flowed through her with vivid energy, pounding with urgency and force.

She was damp and muddy, her thin sleeping robe was torn and streaked, and her bare feet were cut and bloody. Tashinar looked around her but could find no sign of what had drawn Mirabar to this spot in the middle of the night, alone and half-naked.

Knowing she didn't have the strength to carry Mirabar all the way back to the small Guardian encampment, and unwilling to leave her here long enough to summon help, Tashinar began the unpleasant task of waking her. She had occasionally seen other Guardians in this heavily unconscious state and knew what it signified. It was the body's response to a profound contact with the Otherworld, a contact which had nearly left the individual stranded there. Awakening even under the best of conditions would be physically and emotionally painful; and these, Tashinar reflected resignedly, were hardly the best of conditions.

She struck Mirabar's damp, cold face, then propped the girl upright. Mirabar keeled over sideways and lay facedown in the leaves. Tashinar sighed, turned her over, and hit her again. Mirabar moaned; a promising sign.

The girl was a little on the small side, perhaps as a result of her wild, underfed childhood, but she was strong and lithe, and her skin was as bronzed as any other *shallah*'s. But her *hair* . . . It marked her as an accursed demon from one end of Sileria to the other, from the exotic port of Cavasar to the sacred rainbow-chalk cliffs of Liron. Even in the great city of Shaljir, where every race from the three corners of the world roamed the crowded streets and where one might easily see some hennaed Kintish courtesan, copper-haired Moorlander, or half-caste Valdan . . . Yes, even *there* Mirabar's flame-colored locks would make her a figure of suspicion and superstition.

Thick and untamed, the girl's hair glowed with almost supernatural intensity, shining beneath Sileria's merciless sun like the molten lava inside Mount Darshon. If one could ignore superstition, which Tashinar certainly could, one could eventually adjust to the sight of that vivid mane of flame dancing around Mirabar's face. Even Tashinar, however, occasionally found herself recoiling from Mirabar's gaze; even to one who knew better, there often seemed to be something wholly inhuman in those watchful fire-gold eyes.

"Mirabar!" she shouted, shaking the limp body.

Mirabar moaned and rolled away. Pleased, Tashinar gritted her teeth and struck her again. A small, strong-fingered hand shot out and grabbed her wrist. A pair of dazed eyes gazed into hers; they glowed almost yellow with some strange ecstasy. Tashinar felt an unwelcome chill of fear.

"Ah. You're awake," she said prosaically.

"He's coming," Mirabar sighed, sounding as if she was still half-lost in her visions.

Tashinar frowned. "Who's coming? The Beckoner?"

Mirabar shook her head slowly. Dead gossamer leaves crinkled beneath her red hair. "A great warrior of . . . terrible courage. A man of . . . stained honor . . . bitter yearning . . ."

"A warrior?" Tashinar sat back on her heels and stared at her. "*Why* is he coming?" she asked at last.

"To break the shackles which bind us to the Valdani," Mirabar murmured dreamily. "To set us free."

"He will drive out the Valdani?" Tashinar asked incredulously. The vision. The Beckoner. Tashinar's mind whirled. Was Mirabar insane, or had she been chosen for something they did not yet understand? "How do you know this?"

"My feet."

"What?"

"Ohhh . . ." Mirabar scowled as physical sensation started creeping into her consciousness. "My *feet*. What happ—"

"Mirabar!" Tashinar shook her impatiently. "A warrior is coming to free us?"

"Yes. Ow! My *head*."

"Who? Who is he?"

"I don't know. Stop shaking me, damn you!"

Seeing the pain in her face, Tashinar guiltily let go of her shoulders. Trying to calm herself, she took a deep breath, feeling her chest hammer as she did so. "Are you sure of this?"

Mirabar sat up slowly, rubbing her aching head. "I'm sure of what I saw. What I heard."

"This warrior . . ." Tashinar paused, torn between hope and doubt. "Will he succeed?"

"He will succeed." Mirabar looked to the sky. "And he will fail."

Then, for no apparent reason, she lowered her head and started weeping.

Part One

"FROM ONE THING, ANOTHER IS BORN."

1

THE OUTLOOKERS ARRESTED him less than an hour after his boat docked in Cavasar, the westernmost port of Sileria. It was a poor welcome home after nine years in exile, but Tansen supposed he should have counted on it. Despite his Moorlander clothes and his Kintish swords, he still bore the unmistakable signs of a *shallah*—and bore them proudly: the long mane of dark hair, the cross-cut scars on his palms, and a *jashar,* the intricately woven and knotted belt which declared his name and history.

Under Valdani law, which had ruled Sileria for more than two centuries, *shallaheen* were forbidden to bear weapons. And so the two slender Kintish swords Tansen wore aroused considerable interest; indeed, judging by the speed with which the Outlookers had singled him out, *alarm* would not be too strong a word. Realizing the Outlookers were after him, Tansen ruthlessly suppressed the fear which pricked him at the sight of those fair-skinned Valdani in their anonymous gray tunics following him through the crowded, narrow streets of Cavasar. He was no longer a helpless, ignorant boy, and he would not act like one by racing through back alleys and over rooftops with a pack of clumsy Outlookers in hot pursuit, destroying the fragile peace and abusing innocent city-dwellers.

Perhaps he should have hidden his swords, but he really couldn't afford to have them out of reach. There was no telling when the attack he expected would actually occur; he only knew that he must be prepared for his enemies at all times now that he was on Silerian soil. If a Society assassin came for him, he wouldn't have time to fumble through concealing folds of cloth for his swords. He needed to be as ready as he had ever been in his life.

Now, however, he'd have to do something about these Outlookers. The long years of his exile, the skills he had acquired, and the battles he had won now stiffened his spine and gave weight to his voice as he halted on the rough cobblestones and turned to confront one of the men he'd spotted out of the corner of his eye.

"Did you want something?" he asked blandly. Valdan, the official language of Sileria for over two hundred years, rolled smoothly off his tongue.

Momentarily caught off guard, the Outlooker now swaggered forward. "Hand over your weapons," he ordered.

Tansen arched one brow. "No," he said simply.

The Valdan glanced briefly at another Outlooker who came forward to flank him, then said with a snap in his voice, "By order of the Emperor, no native dogs may carry swords."

Tansen gazed impassively at the two uniformed Outlookers for a moment, then looked around casually, estimating how many more were with them.

"I am no dog," he replied. It had been a long time since anyone had dared to speak to him so; but he was in Sileria now.

The Outlooker studied him for a moment, doubt weakening his expression. "You *are* Silerian, aren't you?"

He didn't bother to answer. He'd spotted two other Outlookers; that made four in all. He could take them; but did he want to? Killing these Valdani would undoubtedly complicate his plans.

"I'll say it once more," the Outlooker snapped.

"Must you?" Tansen asked in a bored voice.

The Outlooker's face screwed up with hatred. Mistaking the odds as being in his favor, he leaped forward and grabbed Tansen's embroidered tunic.

Tan clapped his left hand over the man's fist, trapping it, and then sharply rolled the edge of his right forearm down into the Valdan's wrist, as he had once been taught

by a man whose name he had not spoken aloud since his
boyhood. With a gasp of mingled pain and surprise, the
Outlooker sank to his knees. Deciding not to break his
wrist, Tan seized the man's short hair and, before anyone
had even seen him pull his sword from its sheath, pressed
the blade against the Outlooker's throat.

"These fine Moorlander clothes cost me dearly," Tansen
explained, "and I would not like them soiled by your
hands, *roshah.*"

The word *roshah*—"outsider"—bore a wealth of possible nuances in *shullah* dialect, but Tansen's tone made
his meaning clear; outsiders were generally loathed and
distrusted by the *shallaheen.*

The citizens crowding the street lost no time in reacting
to this sudden development. The fascinated crowd made a
wide circle around the scene almost as quickly as Tansen
had made his move.

"Don't do it!" Tan warned the Outlooker directly before
him as the man reached for his sword. "Move over there
by the fountain." He nodded toward the other two Outlookers. "All of you!"

A dozen women quickly hoisted up their clay water jars
and moved away from the fountain. Water gushed forth
freely from the mouth of a ferocious dragonfish carved in
marble; the people of Cavasar obviously paid their tribute
to the Society waterlords in a timely and generous fashion.

Seeing the Outlookers' hesitation, Tansen added, *"Now,"*
and twisted his blade just enough to make his sweating
captive squeal a little.

Turning red with fury and humiliation, the Outlookers
slowly moved toward the fountain, where Tansen ordered
them to drop their sword belts. The Outlookers in Sileria,
Tansen had learned in his travels, were among the worst-
equipped soldiers in the entire Valdani Empire. The Silerians, a long-ago conquered people, stripped of their
weapons and too busy quarreling among themselves to
rebel against the Valdani, were considered the least of the
Emperor's worries. So the oldest weapons and greenest

troops were sent to keep the "peace" in Sileria.

Tansen watched the Outlookers' short, heavy swords fall to the ground and recalled the gleaming, seemingly invincible weaponry he had seen the Valdani use to crush an army in the Moorlands only last year. When they sought to seize the misty green hills of those blue-eyed giants, they brought all their might to bear. But to hold the jagged, golden mountains of Sileria and the ancient ports along her coasts, the Emperor sent corrupt commanders, inexperienced troops, and weapons that any Kintish mercenary would be embarrassed to be seen carrying. And the great pity of it was that, for two centuries, the Valdani had needed no more than this to rule Sileria.

With the three Outlookers now disarmed and slowly kneeling as ordered, Tansen was considering his escape when a gnarled old fisherman, his arms bearing the intricate indigo tattoos of the sea-born folk, pointed at Tan's hostage and cried, "Kill him!"

"Hmmm, what *is* the penalty for killing an Outlooker these days?" Tansen asked, dragging his captive away from the fountain and toward a dark alley.

"Death by slow torture," the Valdan warned him in strangled tones. "You will have your parts cut off one by one for this, you motherless c—" His threat ended on a gasp as the sharp Kintish blade drew blood.

"I'm only motherless," Tansen growled into his ear, "because Outlooker pigs murdered her, you pus-eating bastard."

"Kill him!" the old fisherman urged, following them.

"Go away, old man," Tansen warned. "This isn't your—"

"Your mother, my wife . . ." The old man pointed to people around them. "Her son, their father . . . Who has not suffered because of these dung-kissing swine?"

"Yes, kill him!" a woman cried.

The crowd took up the chant, some in Valdan, some in dialect: "Kill him, kill him, *kill* him!"

"Some homecoming," Tansen muttered, amazed at how

fast things had gotten out of hand. Since when had people in Cavasar done more than simply turn their backs on a stranger's business?

"My father did *nothing!*" a boy suddenly screamed, running headlong into the Outlookers by the fountain. "And you killed him, you *killed* him!"

One of the men hit the boy. Between one breath and the next, the crowd descended upon them in a fury. A woman raised her water jar high, then brought it crashing down on an Outlooker's skull. Fists and elbows made dull, thudding sounds as they hit flesh. Breathless grunts and outraged screams filled the air. Tansen smelled bloodlust and was so astonished by the suddenness of the riot that he nearly forgot his hostage, who made a clumsy attempt to escape.

"If you won't kill him," the fisherman shouted above the noise, "then let me!"

"Wait, old man! There's—"

Tansen's words were cut off as a group of flailing bodies tumbled straight into him. He crashed backwards into stacks of dried fish, then slipped on spilled oil as he surged back to his feet. The Outlooker he'd used as a hostage was already crawling away, pursued by the old man, who was brandishing a small fish-gutting knife. Tansen heard the horn being blown in one of the city's watchtowers and realized the alarm had been sounded. This sudden brawl was about to be raided by more Outlookers, who would imprison everyone present, if not execute them on the spot. He had to stop the fighting while everyone still had time to get away; he had caused it, after all.

Keeping one sword unsheathed, he seized a dull copper bell from the tumble of what had been a market stall only moments ago, then climbed atop a peddler's cart and started ringing it.

A donkey was the first living thing to take the slightest notice of him. Slapping its rump with his sword as it clattered past, he shouted to the crowd, "Go! The Valdani are coming! *Run!*"

A few people realized what was happening and fled the scene. Most still seemed more intent on killing the Outlookers than on saving their own skins. Exasperated, Tan rang the bell more insistently, wondering when everyone in Cavasar had gone insane. Above the noise of the rioting crowd, he could already hear the hoofbeats of the approaching Outlookers; it sounded like there were a lot of them.

"*Run*, damn you!"

He threw the bell aside and unsheathed his second sword. These bloodthirsty fools obviously wouldn't leave until all four Outlookers were dead, and they were making damned slow and messy work of it. He'd have to kill the remaining ones himself if he wanted the crowd to disperse. He just hoped he could get past these raving Silerians fast enough to do it before all of them were set upon by—

An agonizing shock of pain pierced his back, ripping a harsh grunt from his throat. He was pushing himself off the hard cobblestones before he even realized he had fallen. *An arrow,* he thought, drawing harsh breaths as additional waves of pain started washing over him. As he had been taught long ago, he had not let go of either sword, but his left arm was already growing numb. The Valdani, he knew, often coated their arrow tips with strange poisons. Some mixtures could kill a man if the dosage was strong enough; others merely put him to sleep for a few hours.

More arrows flew into the fray, and then Valdani horsemen were clattering across the stones, sweeping their short, heavy swords through the crowd. Screams assaulted Tansen's ears as his left hand relaxed against his will, letting his sword fall to the ground. Someone ran straight into him, jarring the arrow which stuck out of his back; the pain made his vision go black. Dizzy from the poison seeping into his blood, he whirled toward the clatter of hooves, but his remaining sword encountered nothing. Light flashed before his eyes and figures danced in and out of focus. He held off attacking, unable to distinguish between Outlookers and Silerians. The rasp of his own breath and the desperate thumping of his heart grew so loud that, in the end, he never even heard the rider who rode up and seized his long, single braid to drag him along the hard stones while he clumsily tried to keep away from the horse's prancing feet.

The last thing he was aware of was someone prying the sword out of his useless right hand before he finally lost consciousness.

EVERYTHING HURT.

Someone was dipping a red hot poker into the wound in his back, over and over again. Someone else was kneading his muscles with steel claws. And *someone* was driving a herd of horses through his head. The Fires of Dar scalded his eyes when he tried to open them. With a muttered curse, he gave up the effort.

"He's awake!"

Tansen felt a sharp blade at his throat. It seemed reasonable to assume he was not among friends.

"If you make even one move," someone warned him, "I'll slit your throat like a sacrificial goat."

"I've never understood that." His voice sounded raspy and weak. He wondered how long he'd been unconscious. "What makes your priests think that slaughtering a *goat*, of all things, will—"

"Shut up, barbarian!"

He swallowed, trying to ease the dryness in his throat, and felt the bite of the blade against his skin. "I suppose a drink of water is out of the question."

The sharp slap across his face indicated that it was indeed out of the question.

"Tell Commander Koroll that the prisoner is awake and ready for questioning," the now-familiar voice ordered.

Tansen's stomach twisted with secret fear. He had often seen the results of Valdani "questioning." His mother had died from it. He made a silent vow to Dar, and to all of the other gods under whose protection he had sojourned these past nine years: *If I must die in this place, then I will take as many of them with me as I can.* He was deadly even without his swords. Of course, with his hands and feet manacled, even he was at a distinct disadvantage. He had just recognized the heavy weights around his wrists and ankles: the iron finery of a prisoner.

All right, maybe he *should* have hidden his swords; he had little to fear from Society assassins if the Valdani killed him before the next sunrise, after all. But how was he to have known the Outlookers had become so vigilant? There was a time you could have smuggled a whole cart-load of weapons past the Outlookers and bought them off with an easy bribe if they caught you. There was also a time, he realized as the Outlooker's hot breath brushed his face, that no citizen of Cavasar would have attacked an Outlooker in broad daylight.

Things had indeed changed.

Eyes still closed, he heard the door swing open. He tensed slightly, waiting for what would come next.

A new voice spoke. "Commander Koroll says to bring the prisoner. *Now.*"

KOROLL HAD BEEN stationed in this godsforsaken land for four years. A vast, wild, mountainous island floating in the Middle Sea, Sileria was peopled by violent, ungovernable barbarians who were making his life a misery. He'd already lost four years in this backwater, and if he couldn't crush this new threat, there was every chance he'd spend the rest of his life here. And it might well be a very short life, too, if the next assassination attempt against him succeeded.

Standing at the window of his command chamber in the military fortress, Koroll looked out over the main square of Cavasar as the sun set upon the city. Jugglers, acrobats, and fire-eaters used to come out to replace the merchants, craftsmen, and fishmongers who packed up at the end of the day. Not anymore, however. Koroll had banned such amusements as punishment for the last major riot. Then he had instituted a curfew after the attempt on his life. The trouble had all begun with the murder of two Outlookers in the mountains, and Koroll had so far been unable to stop their killer from wreaking havoc in the mountain villages and inciting the people of this district to violence.

Today's hideous events were becoming all too typical. Four of his men had tried to disarm a stranger in a crowded marketplace. The stranger had resisted, and the crowd had descended upon the Outlookers like hungry dragonfish. Two of the Outlookers were dead, the other two badly hurt, and the city was seething with rebellion. The fiery belly of Mount Darshon was surely a quieter place than Cavasar these days.

The stranger who had apparently been the focus of today's riot was the most puzzling part of the whole event. One of Koroll's officers had immediately singled the man out from the crowd and had the sense to disable him and bring him back to the fortress for questioning. They'd already searched him and his possessions quite thoroughly, and what they'd found only added to Koroll's curiosity about the man.

Although his fine clothes were clearly from the Moorlands, and his swords were unmistakably Kintish, the stranger wore the traditional knotted belt of a *shallah*. One might excuse that as mere vanity, since some people— even some Valdani—found the intricately woven, beaded, knotted work of the *shallaheen* quite beautiful and occasionally used imitations as ornamentation; but the man's palms also bore the deep cross-cut scars typical of most *shallaheen*. Although he wore his hair in the long, oiled, single braid of a Kintish mercenary, the hair was too wavy and the dark-lashed eyes too round for him to be a full-blooded Kint, and he looked a little too fair-skinned for most of the other races living in the Kintish Kingdoms or in Valdani-ruled Kintish lands. It seemed most likely that he was at least part *shallah*.

All of which led Koroll to wonder what a *shallah* was doing bearing the brand of a Kintish swordmaster. They had found the mark on his chest when stripping him to remove the arrow; the scar, which looked like two crescent moons flanking a Kintish hieroglyph, was far from new.

Koroll turned away from the window and looked at the items which now lay on the polished table: two slender Kintish swords, the supple harness in which they were usually sheathed, an old leather satchel with faded Kintish calligraphy on it, and the now-stained but very fine Moorlander tunic they had stripped from the stranger's unconscious body.

The slender Kintish swords were longer than the swords of Koroll's men, but much shorter than the heavy, hacking weapons of the Moorlanders—weapons now also carried by the Emperor's best troops. These were obviously a very fine pair, thin and light, the steel beaten into perfect balance and harmony. Each sword had elegant Kintish hieroglyphs engraved upon it. They were beautifully polished and so sharp that Koroll cut his thumb gently testing one of the blades.

It was often said that there was no fighter anywhere in the three corners of the world to equal a Kintish swordmaster; such a warrior had a special Kintish title which Koroll could not immediately recall. A Kintish swordmaster used two blades where others used one, and used them so fast that he could kill two armed men before either could even draw a sword. Of course, the training was said to take five years, and half the students reputedly died in the process. Therefore, it wasn't something the average Kintish soldier undertook; and so the Valdani beat Kintish armies as thoroughly as they beat everyone else's. Indeed, the ancient Kintish Kingdoms had lost much territory to the Empire in recent centuries.

However, regardless of the stranger's origins or identity, the most intriguing item among his belongings was undoubtedly a single dagger, carefully wrapped in a finely painted silk scarf and hidden in a tightly laced pocket inside the satchel. After four years in Sileria, Koroll recognized the workmanship of both items. The scarf was a

particularly fine example of centuries-old Silerian crafts-
manship, covered with delicately painted flowers native to
the island. Koroll had never seen a man carrying one, and
it seemed incongruous for the stranger to have such feminine finery. However, it was the dagger which truly interested Koroll.

He knew instantly what it was, though he had never
actually seen one before. Having heard such weapons described for years, there was no mistaking this one. It was
a *shir,* the exquisitely deadly, wavy-edged dagger of a Society assassin. *Shir* were made only by the waterlords,
those unpredictable and secretive Silerian wizards who
controlled the Honored Society and, if truth be known,
much of Sileria, too. The Emperor had sworn to destroy
the Society in his lifetime, and most of the waterlords now
lived in hiding. Their power was not to be underestimated,
though; they could bring Cavasar to its knees if they didn't
receive their tribute from the people. They controlled water, the most precious commodity in Sileria, as easily as a
man controlled the fingers of his own hand. While Koroll
remained skeptical about the many whispered stories told
about them, he had learned to regard them with respect.

Moreover, he had just learned that at least one of those
whispered stories was apparently true. It was said that only
three people in the world could touch a *shir* with impunity:
the waterlord who fashioned its deadly blade out of water,
the assassin for whom it was made, and the man or woman
who killed him. Having unfolded the delicate silk which
hid the *shir* from view, Koroll found that it was bitterly
cold, colder than anything he'd ever known, and the brief
touch of it against his fingers made them ache with fierce
pain long after he dropped the thing.

Had the stranger killed a Society assassin and taken his
shir? If so, then he just might be the right man to solve
Koroll's problems. Surely killing one Silerian peasant
would seem a small enough price to a mercenary who
would otherwise be charged with inciting a riot and causing the deaths of two Outlookers. Of course, releasing such

a man and giving him his weapons back was risky, but Koroll was counting on an extra incentive to ensure the warrior's cooperation; the final item of unusual interest among his possessions was a hefty bag of gold. If Koroll held on to that until the swordmaster brought him proof of the *shallah*'s death . . .

He heard a knock at the heavy door to the chamber. "Enter!"

Four Outlookers, young and arrogant in their smooth gray tunics, leggings, and new boots, escorted the swordmaster into Koroll's presence. Koroll studied the shackled prisoner closely as he shuffled into the room. Now that the stranger's eyes were open, Koroll saw that they were the deep brown color typical of most Silerians; they were watchful and intelligent, and they gave away little as the warrior surveyed his belongings spread out on the long polished table. His skin had the rich olive tones of a typical *shallah*, and his facial bones were strong and faintly exotic looking compared to the Valdani around him. Still a young man, he was lean and lithe, with whipcord muscles that looked honed to make him an agile fighter of great endurance.

Even shackled, he looked fierce. Koroll rather marvelled at the courage—or sheer foolhardiness—of the young Outlooker who had demanded this man's weapons this morning, and who had seized his tunic upon being denied. A pity the lad was dead now, gutted with a fish knife.

"I am Commander Koroll, military governor of Cavasar and its district. One of my surviving men says that although you resisted a direct order and broke the law," Koroll began without preamble, "he thinks you did not intend to kill anyone, but merely to escape."

The stranger's bland, closed expression didn't change. "That's true."

"Why did you resist?"

"I'm a *shatai*."

"A swordmaster?"

"Yes. How am I to earn a living without my swords?"

Koroll hefted the bag of gold he'd found in the man's satchel. "You wouldn't have starved."

"I was thinking of my future."

"You could have applied to me to have your weapons returned to you."

Despite his chains, the prisoner managed to look arrogant. "No *shatai* permits his swords to be taken from him."

"I have seen *shatai* give up their swords. At the Emperor's palace in Valda."

"We may choose to give them up, to show respect or to honor a truce. But *no one* is permitted to *take* them away."

"And you didn't deem it appropriate to show respect and voluntarily relinquish them today?" Koroll challenged.

"I was . . . not asked nicely," the stranger replied, lifting one dark brow.

Koroll's lips twitched. "And you are accustomed to being asked *nicely?*"

"Most men treat a *shatai* with more courtesy than I was shown today."

"Yes, I imagine so. We don't see many *shatai* here, you understand," Koroll said cordially. He narrowed his eyes. "And you're not Kintish anyhow, are you?"

"No."

"I didn't know there were any *shatai* who weren't Kintish."

"There aren't many."

"But a Kintish *shatai* trained you?"

"A *shatai-kaj.* One who trains *shatai.*"

"Why did he train *you?*"

The stranger shrugged, then winced as the motion pulled at his wound. "He wanted to."

"A better reason, if you please."

This time the stranger smiled slightly. "The *shatai-kaj* give no better reasons. They are men who need explain themselves to no one."

"But you . . ." Koroll's gaze lowered to the man's hands, to where he had seen the distinctive scars. "You're part *shallah,* aren't you?"

The stranger hesitated for only a moment. "Yes."

"What are you doing in Cavasar?" He saw sweat on the prisoner's face and guessed he was in pain; certainly nothing about the man suggested nervousness.

"I had only just arrived when your men—"

"You came here on a boat?"

"Yes."

"From where?"

"The Moorlands."

"What were you doing there?"

"Working."

"What kind of work?"

The warrior's gaze flashed to the two swords which lay unsheathed upon the table. "The kind of work I do."

Pleased by the answer, Koroll dismissed two of the guards. "He may be seated," he said to the other two, noticing that the prisoner was starting to look a little lightheaded. He had lost enough blood to miss it for the next few days. The guards shuffled him over to a chair that was near Koroll but strategically distant from the weapons on the table, then positioned themselves on either side of him, their swords drawn. Even wounded and shackled, Koroll suspected this *shatai* could take advantage of the situation if permitted.

Koroll picked up one of the Kintish swords and noted that the stranger didn't like him touching them. "What is your name?"

"Tansen."

"Are you from here?"

A brief nod. "I was born in Sileria."

Koroll looked him over for a moment, then decided to try another tactic, for the stranger seemed more concerned about his swords than about himself. He traced his finger down the flat of one blade. "What are these inscriptions on your swords, these Kintish hieroglyphics?"

Tansen's gaze rested possessively on the swords as Koroll handled them. "The left one . . . That's my teacher's motto."

"What does it say?"

"Why do you care?"

"I'm curious." Seeing that Tansen intended to stay silent, Koroll pointed out, "You have caused the deaths of two Outlookers today. Normally, you would already have been sentenced to death by slow torture in a public execution."

"Why haven't I been?"

"Because I may have a better use for you," Koroll snapped, a little annoyed that his warning apparently aroused no concern, let alone fear. "Now answer the question. What does the inscription say?"

Quietly, almost reflectively, Tansen answered, "Draw it with honor, sheathe it with courage."

"Can you read?" Koroll probed. Very few *shallaheen* could. "Or did you memorize that?"

"I can read the inscription," was the oblique response.

"Why is the sword inscribed? A sentimental gesture?"

For a moment he thought the question would be ignored. Finally, as if having decided that the information wouldn't profit his interrogator, Tansen said, "It identifies a *shatai-kaj*'s students to each other, so when we meet, we will not fight each other."

"Not even if you are opponents who have been *paid* to fight each other?"

"We will not fight each other," Tansen repeated.

"How noble," Koroll said dryly. "Does anyone ever cheat?"

"If he did, then all *shatai* would be ordered to kill him on sight, and his *shatai-kaj* would lay a curse upon him."

"Yes, I suppose that would make one think twice." Koroll picked up the other sword and noted that the hieroglyphics were different. "And what's written on this one?"

"My own motto."

"Ah! Which is?"

Tansen's gaze met his and, for the first time, Koroll had a glimpse of the man who dwelt in this *shallah*'s skin. "From one thing, another is born."

"And what thing gave birth to the *shatai*, Tansen?" Koroll asked, held by that dark, steady gaze.

"What 'better use' do you have for me?" Tansen countered.

Deciding this was the right moment, Koroll shoved aside the empty satchel to reveal the *shir* which lay in a pool of painted silk. Tansen's expression gave away little; of course he would have guessed that Koroll had found it when searching his things.

Bypassing the questions he had originally intended to ask, Koroll simply said, "Pick it up."

Finally! He was rewarded with a look of genuine surprise.

"Pick it up?" Tansen repeated.

"Yes. Pick it up."

Tansen glanced significantly at the guards to his right and left. At Koroll's order, they both held their blades to Tansen's throat. Tugging at the silk scarf upon which the *shir* lay, Koroll moved it within Tansen's reach.

Koroll warned, "Just pick it up. If you try to use it, they will slit your throat like—"

"A sacrificial goat. Yes, I know." Looking rather contemptuous of them all, Tansen lifted his hands and, moving awkwardly because of his shackles and his wound, took hold of the *shir*. His expression darkened as he looked down at it, resting in his scarred palms. Very quietly, almost as if he were unaware that he spoke aloud, he said, "It's an evil thing, this."

"Then it's true," Koroll breathed. "You killed a Society assassin."

Tansen's gaze remained fixed on the dagger. "I killed him." His voice was soft, and he seemed lost in the memory for a moment.

"Why did you keep the *shir?*" Koroll asked; Tansen clearly didn't relish possession of the thing.

His bare, branded chest rose and fell with a deep breath. "Because that's what you do when you . . . do what I did. You take the *shir*. That's . . . the way it's done."

Koroll had a feeling there was more to it than that, considerably more, but he didn't really care about the details of yet another bloody and pointless Silerian feud. These people relished killing each other so much that the Outlookers seldom had to bother doing it. Until recently.

Tansen lay the *shir* back upon the table and asked, "Have I answered all of your questions now?"

"There's just one more: Do you want to live?"

"Are you offering me a choice?"

"Yes."

"Ah. I see." A slow, cynical smile spread across Tansen's face. "Tell me, then: Who do I have to kill?"

Recognizing a man with whom he could do business, Koroll smiled in return. "His name is Josarian, and I need him killed soon. Very soon."

2

A SINGLE CRESCENT moon hung like a jewel in the night as Josarian stole through the shadows. Gossamer trees grew in abundance this high up in the mountains, and the brush of their soft leaves against his face reminded him of Calidar's caress. Although his wife had been dead for a year, bleeding away her life as she fought to give birth to their first child, sometimes he could swear he still caught her scent when he first awoke in the morning, or heard her soft whisper when he sat alone to watch the moons rise over Mount Darshon.

He missed her as much as he would miss his own heart if it were torn out of his chest. He missed the child who had never even been born. He missed the future he and Calidar had planned together and which now would ne~ take place.

Young and in love, they had longed only for a child to complete their happiness. But, after their marriage, many seasons went by without Calidar's conceiving. Finally, she went to the Sisters, but their remedies didn't help. After that, she went to Cavasar to consult the tattoo-covered fish-wives who were said to possess the secrets of fertility; but their advice also produced no child between Josarian and his wife. At last, Calidar even made Josarian take her to see the *zanareen*, the strange mystics who lived at the icy summit of Mount Darshon and awaited the coming of the Firebringer.

They had given up after that, and Josarian had convinced Calidar that, in their love, they were already blessed enough for this life. Then one season, to their astonishment and fervent joy, their union suddenly produced a life. When Josarian looked back, he was glad that he hadn't known, had never once guessed that their joy and anticipation would end in a blood-drenched night of horror and grief. If Calidar had ever feared it, then it was the only secret she had ever kept from him.

Since the first time he had seen her, sitting outside her mother's tiny stone house, her face modestly turned away from the street so that only her profile showed, he had never gone an hour without thinking about her. A boy and girl's infatuation had turned into passion, and finally into abiding love, and they had married young. Although they both came from poor families, since all *shallah* families were poor, he had paid a bride-price of twenty sheep. Her father would have accepted much less, of course, knowing how Calidar's heart was set on Josarian; but Josarian had wanted to honor her.

He had never imagined any future other than being her husband and the father of her children. Under the harsh rule of the Valdani, who were starving Sileria to finance their wars of conquest and feed their vast armies, he and Calidar had sought a peaceful life as best they could. And since the road Josarian had chosen all his life was so different from the one he found himself upon these days, he now groped his way blindly, hoping each step would be the right one, knowing full well it could be the wrong one.

The wound in his side was healing well, thanks to the Sisters, but it still stretched and hurt when he breathed too deeply, as he was doing now. The Guardians lived so high up, even a goat might find the climb a little tiring, and Josarian was carrying a heavy load. Outlawed by the Valdani who had seized Sileria from the Kintish some two hundred years ago, all Guardians now lived in hiding. Once the most powerful sect in Sileria, their numbers were now dwindling and they lived like scavengers in these mountains. A thousand years ago they had graced the chambers of the Yahrdan's palace in Shaljir and claimed an altar in almost every town and village of Sileria. Now they lived a nomadic existence in tiny, scattered groups, ever on the move lest their tents and cave-dwellings be discovered by the Outlookers.

The Guardians were secretive, yes, but few events in these mountains were unknown to the *shallaheen*, the mountain-dwelling farmers, shepherds, and craftsmen of Sileria, the most numerous—and the poorest—of the vast island's diverse population. And while many *shallaheen* were likely to die under torture before revealing a secret to the Outlookers, interesting news tended to spread pretty quickly from one mountain village to the next. Thus Josarian had heard the rumors for many days now that there were Guardians hiding in the old caves above the gossamer forest on Mount Niran. He had grown up in these wild, savage mountains and was confident he could find the remote place even in the dark.

Indeed, his intimate knowledge of these rocky hills had saved his life after killing those two Outlookers. He'd been living in hiding ever since then and had made a couple of narrow escapes during the Outlookers' desperate and increasingly extensive search for him.

With no wife to worry about him now, Josarian had grown reckless this past year and had finally joined his cousin Zimran in smuggling black market food through the

mountains. He knew it was illegal, but he didn't believe
for a moment that it was wrong. Why should Silerian peasants break their backs harvesting grain under the merciless
sun, only to watch the Valdani confiscate most of it to feed
their fat citizens and voracious soldiers, leaving Sileria
with barely enough food to survive? Although he believed
a man should have a family, and although he still mourned
his, there had been moments these past few months when
he'd consoled himself with the thought that at least he and
Calidar had never known the pain so many others knew,
that of seeing their children go hungry.

No, he didn't regret the smuggling. It was sheer bad
fortune that had brought him face-to-face with the Outlookers one night. One of the donkeys had gone lame that
night, and he and Zimran had tossed a coin to see who
would have to hang back with it. Zim had lost, and so he
was far behind when Josarian rounded a bend in the narrow mountain path—and came face to face with four Outlookers. He had never before seen any Valdani on these
high, little-known goat paths, and he simply stared at them
in stupid astonishment for a moment.

Before he knew what was happening, they had roughly
seized him. Two of them began interrogating him, while
the other two searched his donkeys. Realizing he was
caught, he now worried mainly about warning his cousin.
Unable to think of anything subtle under the circumstances, he simply shouted, "Outlookers!"

The Outlookers realized he was warning an accomplice,
and two of them rode off to search for Josarian's companion. He shouted another warning, and the two Outlookers
still holding him started to beat him. He resisted, and they
unsheathed their swords. The struggle suddenly turned into
a fight to the death.

He would never forget the moment when all his fear
vanished completely; it was the moment when he faced
them as a man, refusing to bow down to the Valdani as a
lowly *shallah*, refusing to die easily for them. One of them
wounded him, and it only made him fight all the more

ferociously. He had never killed a man before, even though bloodshed was commonplace among the *shallaheen*. He was repulsed by the sensation of flesh giving way beneath his blows, horrified by the amount of blood which splattered his face and clothing, shocked at how still and grotesque his enemies looked in death.

But deeper than his shock, stronger than his revulsion, more enduring than his horror was a new sensation. Beneath the twin moons which glowed above the snow-covered peak of Mount Darshon, Josarian looked down at the lifeless bodies of his enemies and knew a fierce exultation which was like the birth of a new spirit within him. He, an ordinary *shallah,* had said *no* to the Valdani. He looked down at these Outlookers, the occupying force of the most powerful empire the world had ever known, and all he saw were mere men—men who could be defied and defeated by *him.*

He knew in that moment that he would never say *yes* to them again. He would never again stand by as they took crops and livestock for themselves while leaving Silerians to starve. He would never again shake his head and hope for better days while the Valdani raped Sileria's rich mines, abused her people, and violated her ancient culture and customs. And until the day the Outlookers caught and killed him, he would tell every Silerian he met—whether *shallah,* city-dweller, or sea-born folk, whether Guardian, *zanar,* or Sister, whether merchant, aristocrat, or Society assassin—to say *no* to them, too.

Zimran had escaped, thanks Josarian's warning, but the two remaining Outlookers had pursued Josarian for half the night. By the time he finally crawled into an isolated Sanctuary of the Sisterhood at dawn, he was half-dead. Guessing where he had gone, Zimran joined him as soon as he was able to elude the Outlookers who now constantly watched Josarian's friends and family. Zimran stayed by Josarian's side throughout the ordeal of his healing and then kept him supplied with food, medicine, and news after he left the Sanctuary. It wasn't safe for Josarian to stay anywhere for more than a day, but he and Zim had grown up together and knew a dozen secret places where they could meet safely and regularly.

Zim wasn't with Josarian now, however; he ascended alone through the gossamer forest of Nimran. Josarian's cousin was skeptical of Guardian magic and sneered at his faith. True, neither of them had even seen a Guardian in years, and that one had possessed feeble powers, but Josarian was not one to forsake his faith just because the Valdani wanted him to. Besides, he couldn't give up his hope; not now, not tonight of all nights. The Guardians were the gateway to the Otherworld—and to Calidar.

Before he saw the clearing he sought, he heard the voices. A woman was screaming as if she were in terrible pain, and others were apparently trying to soothe her. He hadn't heard such agonized screams since the night Calidar had died. Although he had not flinched at the many dangers he had faced since the night he had killed those two Outlookers, he flinched now and was not ashamed; few things would ever trouble him like the reminder of Calidar's grim and painful death. The anguished cries unmanned him, and he could not bring himself to leave the forest until they died down to mournful whimpers. Hoping that the worst of it was over, he finally emerged from the forest and stepped into the clearing.

He had explored the caves up here many times, intrigued by their mysteries. Ancient paintings of eerie beauty decorated their interior walls, scenes from another era, an age lost in the mists of time. The paintings were said to have been made by the Beyah-Olvari, the half-human race who had been the original inhabitants of Sileria. Driven to extinction long ago, they had left behind a portait of their existence. Gazing at the evocative, graceful cave paintings eons after they had been painted, Josarian had often wondered about the fragile, blue-skinned beings they depicted.

There seemed to be more than a dozen people living here now: men, women, and a couple of children. Each of them wore a brooch fashioned into the ancient symbol of the Guardians: a single flame within a circle of fire. Once made only of gold, the brooches were usually made of copper or bronze these days; silver, perhaps, if the Guardian had served a wealthy patron. The temporary settlement was a poor place, as Josarian had expected, but no one would ever mistake these people for ordinary peasants; the fire blazing in the center of their camp burned without wood. Guardian fire magic. He had come to the right place.

No one paid any attention to him, however. They were all gathered around a young woman who lay writhing on the ground, whimpering and mumbling half-formed phrases.

"Shackles . . . he will break . . . We must come for . . . ward . . ." She gasped hard several times, then continued, "Enemies . . . terrible enemies who must . . . We must . . . We and the Society must . . ."

"No!" cried a man crouching near her feet. He stood up, glared directly at an old woman, and said harshly, "She's insane, I tell you! Did you *hear* that? *We* and the *Society?* Never!"

"At least wait until she's coherent before you simply reject what she has to tell us," the old woman argued.

"No! If this is her vision, then it's an evil one, and I want no part of it!"

"Derlen, you don't . . ." The old woman gave up as the man stalked away. She was about to turn her attention back to the young woman when something alerted her to Josarian's presence, and she whirled to face him. A cloud of fire formed to shimmer protectively around her. Seeing it, Josarian quickly stepped into the light. Recognizing him as a *shallah,* she hesitated before drawing upon more of her power.

"Who are you?" she demanded.

"Josarian mar Gershon shah Emeldari," he answered formally: Josarian, child of Gershon, born to the Emeldari clan. "I've come to ask—"

"Josarian?" she repeated. "I've heard of you."

Some of the other Guardians turned away from the

young woman on the ground, whose cries and gasps continued unabated.

"The Outlookers are searching for you everywhere," the old woman said, her fireglow fading slowly. "You're the *shallah* who killed two of them and who has been rampaging throughout the district ever since."

"I wouldn't say *rampaging*. I'm recovering from a wound, after all," he said innocently.

"You tell everyone to resist the Valdani," she persisted. "You tell them that Outlookers can be killed by ordinary *shallaheen*, and if they don't believe you, they should try it themselves."

He nodded, then added quietly, "I also tell them not to let their children starve so that Valdani children may grow even fatter."

"So I've heard." The old woman studied him for a moment, then reached out to him. He saw that she was missing several fingers, a common sign of Valdani torture. "I am Tashinar. Honor my home, Josarian, eat at my table, sleep beneath my roof." She smiled wryly at her own traditional welcome, for she had neither table nor roof.

"With pleasure, *sirana*," he said respectfully, crossing his fists over his chest. He lowered the heavy load strapped to his back and said, "I bring a gift for the Guardians of the Otherworld."

"We—" Another cry from the young woman stopped Tashinar in midsentence. She went to tend the girl, crouching over her prostrate form.

Josarian followed her. When he got his first good look at the girl, he recoiled in shock. He had heard stories of such demons—every child in Sileria had—but he had long since stopped believing that there really were such fire-haired, fire-eyed creatures lurking in these mountains. At least this one wasn't breathing fire. Not at the moment, anyhow. She was sobbing softly, tears streaming down her face as she mumbled something about a warrior.

"He comes," she muttered, "he comes. Welcome him!" Once he had recovered from his initial shock, Josarian studied her more closely. Except for the appalling color of her hair and eyes, she looked human. Moreover, her fawn-colored tunic bore the insignia of the Guardians; her brooch was made of copper.

"She's one of you?" he asked Tashinar in puzzlement. When the old woman nodded, he asked quietly, "*Is she insane?*"

With a troubled expression, Tashinar admitted, "We don't know. She is visited by strange visions which no one else can see or hear. They tell her unbelievable things. Things I can't bring myself to repeat even to you, my young friend." Tashinar took a shaky breath and concluded, "Either she is insane, or she is gifted beyond my understanding. And if it's the latter . . ." Her face dissolved into a hundred worried wrinkles. "Then everything we know will change forever."

Seeing her fear and sensing that it was not typical of her, Josarian covered her three-fingered hand gently and said, "Then surely that's a good thing, *sirana,* for we know only hunger, poverty, injustice, shame, and abuse."

The demon screamed abruptly, then moaned, "The *blood* . . ."

Tashinar turned a troubled gaze to Josarian. "Does *that* sound like a good thing to you?"

Ignoring the question, Josarian suggested, "Perhaps we should get her off the hard ground and put her somewhere more comfortable. Does she have a bed?"

"A pallet. In my cave. But the others won't touch her when she's like this, and I can't lift her myself."

"I'll do it, *sirana.*"

"Are you sure?"

"She's only a tiny thing, and my wound no longer—"

"I meant . . . aren't *you* afraid to touch her?"

"*You're* not, are you?" he countered.

"No . . ."

He grinned. "Then I'll count on you to protect me, *sirana.* Now show me where to put her."

Without waiting for a response, he scooped the red-haired woman into his arms. She was heavier than she looked; muscular and sturdy, like a good mountain girl. He realized with a sudden ache that he hadn't held a woman in his arms since Calidar's death. He swallowed the memory and followed Tashinar into one of the caves, marvelling at the way she simply blew a flame into life upon the stone wall to light the chamber where the demon-girl's pallet lay.

The young woman started to struggle, making the task of depositing her on her pallet rather awkward. His wound stretched at the last moment, and he abruptly dropped her head.

"Ow! Be careful, you idiot!" she snapped, sounding quite different all of a sudden.

He glanced at her in surprise and found that her eyes were now open, alert, and glaring at him. They gleamed a feral yellow color that awoke old superstitions, but when she snapped at him again, he couldn't help grinning.

"You don't sound like a mystic when you're awake," he observed.

Still glaring, she sat up and rubbed her head.

"Can you talk now?" Tashinar asked her hesitantly.

"Who is this man?"

"He's our guest, Mirabar." The old woman sounded slightly embarrassed by her companion's discourtesy.

"My name is Josarian. I've come to—"

"Josarian!" The girl gripped his shoulder with a hand which was surprisingly strong for its size. "I've *heard* . . ." The glowing eyes searched his face eagerly. "Could it be you?" she whispered.

"Could *what* be me?" At the moment, she *did* look a little insane.

She said nothing, only continued to study him as if seeking the answer to all her questions. Whatever the test was, he apparently failed it, for her face crumpled in pain. She tore at her hair and ground out between clenched teeth, "I don't know. I can't *tell*. You must send me a sign! How will I know him, *sirani?*"

Tashinar knelt upon the pallet and tried to calm the girl—Mirabar—who was becoming agitated again. Sensing that his presence only added to Mirabar's anguish, Josarian excused himself and went outside to find the load he had carried up the mountain. A few minutes later, moving wearily, Tashinar joined him around the woodless fire at the center of the Guardians' camp.

"She needs time alone," the old woman said pensively. "Time to think over what she has . . . been shown. She'll be better tomorrow. This mood . . . passes."

"I've never seen . . . You know. One like her."

"Ah. No. It's very rare, her look. And, of course, they're usually killed at birth."

"Why wasn't she?" he asked, knowing that had Calidar's baby been red-haired and orange-eyed, he still couldn't have helped loving it. "Did her parents protect her?"

Tashinar shrugged. "Perhaps. She doesn't know who they were."

"Was she given to you as a baby then?"

"No. Someone obviously took care of her as a baby, but she remembers no one. Somehow, as a child, she survived on her own for years. She lived as an outcast, scavenging for food. Then I found her and . . . trapped her. Tamed her. Taught her."

"Why?" he asked curiously. "She must have been very difficult to—"

Tashinar almost laughed. "Oh, she was! But I knew that the coloring that the *shallaheen* fear so much is a sign of great gifts."

"Gifts? People say it's the sign of a terrible curse."

She looked at him thoughtfully for a moment. "Once, long ago, before the Conquest," she said at last, "such coloring was revered as the mark of great power. In those days, there were many more like Mirabar. But, fearing their power, the Conquerors sought to destroy them. More important, so did the waterlords; but the waterlords were more cunning, and they destroyed them by teaching people to fear them. And so the very people they once served now stone them, drown them, burn them, or—at the very least—reject them."

Josarian considered the old woman's words carefully before finally saying, "Are you sure that isn't just another story? Like the tales that are told about them being demons? Perhaps they're really just . . . ordinary."

"No, it's true. I, after all, have special sources," she reminded him.

He smiled. "Excuse me, *sirana.* I forgot myself."

"Now why don't you tell me why you have taken time out from harrassing the Outlookers to pay us a visit?" she suggested.

He gestured to his gift. "I have brought food, *sirana.*" He'd hauled a heavy wheel of cheese—stolen from an Outlooker supply post—up the mountain tonight.

"Food is always appreciated here." She nodded her acceptance of his offering. "Now how may I serve you?"

He took a breath and looked up at the stars. Now that the moment was finally upon him, hope made him afraid. "My wife . . . she died in childbirth one year ago tonight."

"Ah," she said softly, "I see. Have you brought something of hers?"

She meant to do it! His hand trembled as he reached inside his pouch and pulled out a delicately painted silk scarf. It had been his wedding gift to Calidar, and she had treasured it. He was convinced it still smelled of her. He was reluctant to let another touch it, even Tashinar, but he knew that a Guardian needed something which had belonged to the deceased in order to summon her from the Otherworld.

"Will this do, *sirana?*" he asked, his heart pounding as he proffered the scarf.

She took it from him and said, "We shall see, Josarian."

"Can you . . . Will she . . ." He stopped before his voice humiliated him.

"I can Call her," Tashinar said. "That is all I can promise."

"Then do, *sirana.* Please. Call her to me."

Tashinar nodded, then inhaled deeply, closed her eyes, and clasped the scarf between her palms. Josarian bowed his head respectfully when she began to chant, but he sprang to his feet in panic when she tossed the scarf into the fire.

"No!" he cried.

"You must risk it," Tashinar said calmly, her gaze locked on the scarf. "You must . . . be . . ." Her voice trailed off, her strength absorbed by the ritual.

Josarian was about to rescue the scarf from the fire when he suddenly realized it wasn't burning. It danced in the flames with a life of its own, its fragile silk weave and delicate colors vivid and unharmed. Staring in wonder, he asked hoarsely, "Does this mean . . . she will come?"

After a long, quiet moment, Tashinar whispered, "She will come."

"Her name—"

"Shhh . . ." Flushed from her efforts, the old woman smiled slightly. "Her name is Calidar, and she is coming."

DISORIENTED AND SICK with frustration, Mirabar finally emerged from the cave, knowing that the longer she waited, the harder it would be to face everyone. Tonight was the first time she'd had one of these visions in front of the others; if they had doubted her sanity before, they were now probably convinced that she was quite mad. It might improve her position if she could present a coherent explanation of what she saw, but the visions were always so cataclysmically bewildering, the messages so strange and Otherworldly, that even *she* thought she sounded half-mad when she tried to relate them to Tashinar and the other Guardians.

A great warrior of terrible courage, bitter yearning, and stained honor.

Who was he? How would she know him? How should she welcome him? What must she do to prepare the way?

And even if she found him, what could one man do to free Sileria from the Valdani?

The camp seemed deserted when she emerged from her cave, as if everyone had suddenly vanished. Momentarily frightened, she then saw the reason for their absence. Josarian stood by the fire at the center of the encampment, his body taut, his attention riveted on the shade of a *shallah* woman which rose from the flames. Even from where she stood, Mirabar could see the yearning which flooded his being, which had made him long to bridge the abyss between this world and the Other one. Even from here, she could see how he had loved this woman.

A bitter yearning? Instinct told Mirabar otherwise as she crept closer, staying in the shadows. The Otherworld was a mysterious place and the dead were very different from the living, but Mirabar thought she saw Josarian's love reciprocated in the shimmering, translucent figure which wavered and flickered as the fire did.

"Calidar." Josarian's voice was harsh and choked with emotion. As the feminine shade extended her arms toward him, he fell to his knees, murmuring her name again.

The shade shimmered with the speech of the dead, a song which only Tashinar could hear, since it was she who had brought it forth. Like Josarian, Mirabar waited to hear Calidar's words. He, however, flinched when they came from Tashinar's mouth.

"Josarian," she said on a long sigh. *"Kadriah."*

Mirabar realized she had been right. The endearment meant "my destiny," which was how a *shallah* addressed a dearly loved partner in life.

"Kadriah," Josarian replied, recovering his surprise at hearing Tashinar's voice. "I have missed you more than I would miss my own heart."

"And I, *kadriah,*" murmured Tashinar as the shade of Calidar shimmered again. "I await you as night awaits the dawn."

Josarian laughed suddenly. "It may be sooner than you think, wife."

Ah, so the woman had been his wife. Mirabar listened as he told Calidar about killing the Outlookers, living in hiding, and inciting the local *shallaheen* to resist the oppression of the Valdani. Mirabar knew that Tashinar would lecture her sharply if she learned Mirabar had intruded upon this private ceremony. Unless otherwise specified, only the Guardian actually performing the Calling for a petitioner should be present. All the other Guardians in camp were now tactfully absent and undoubtedly had been since the moment Tashinar had begun the Calling.

Besides the Guardians, only the client requesting a Calling could see the shade, though no one really knew why. Even many Guardians could only see the shades they themselves Called, though courtesy still made them absent themselves from another's ceremony. The Guardians' work was a mysterious art, and Mirabar knew that many Callings failed. Indeed, some Guardians never even performed a successful Calling on their own, only succeeding as part of the group when they performed their regular rituals, seeking guidance and strengthening the bond with the Otherworld. Mirabar's gifts, however, were such that she had seen shades her whole life, long before being initiated into the secrets of the Guardians. During her savage childhood, she had taken these ghostly visions as proof that she really was a demon.

If any other *shallah* were the petitioner tonight, then Mirabar, like the others in camp, would respect his privacy. But she couldn't return to her cave, not now. She had to know more about Josarian, had to know if he was the warrior she sought. Having heard of his exploits, she had thought he might be. Now that she'd met him, though, she had changed her mind. Courage, special ability, unbearable yearning—he unquestionably possessed all of these. Yet the longer Mirabar hid in the shadows and intruded upon this Calling, the more certain she became that Josarian was not the man whose spirit and soul haunted her visions. There was no angry torment in Josarian's yearning, no apparent shame in the naked heart he offered to the shade of his wife. His spirit was made of light; Mirabar sought one darkened by shadows.

How will I know him, sirani?

"Calidar," Josarian said, his voice quickening with urgency as Tashinar grew fatigued and the shade began to disperse. *"Wait.* You must tell me—our child . . . Is it with you?"

What little Mirabar could still see of Calidar's face melted with sorrow.

"No," Tashinar said, her voice growing weak as her strength ebbed. "No, the child . . . could not make the journey."

Josarian's shoulders slumped. He murmured something so softly that Mirabar couldn't hear it. She guessed then how Calidar had died. Hard as her heart was, it ached for Josarian as he watched his wife fade into thin air, then lowered his head to weep for the child who had known neither this world nor the one beyond it. He was a big man, taller than most, with broad shoulders and strong arms, but he looked as helpless as a child right now. She felt an uncharacteristic desire to comfort him, but she went to Tashinar instead, who was now slumped over and breathing hard.

"Come," Mirabar said, "come. You must lie down." Tashinar wasn't as strong as she pretended to be, and the Calling had taken its toll. It was never a thing to be undertaken lightly, and the burden of Tashinar's gift now weighed very heavily upon her as she allowed Mirabar to help her into the cave. Once she was prostrate upon her pallet, she insisted Mirabar go back outside to be with Josarian.

"He shouldn't be alone," the old woman rasped. "Not now. He's never Called her before, and . . . You watched, didn't you?"

"You knew?" Mirabar asked cautiously.

A faint smile cracked Tashinar's lips. "You want to know if he's the one. Considering the . . . the force of your visions, I would be surprised if you didn't try to find out more about him."

Alarmed by her mentor's pallor, Mirabar simply said, "Sleep now. We can talk tomorrow."

"Go to him."

"Yes, Tashinar."

She found him still sitting before the fire, brooding in silence. She had to speak twice before he even noticed her presence, and then he refused the tisane she offered him. He held a painted silk scarf in one hand—undoubtedly the token Tashinar had used for the Calling—absently rubbing it between his fingers as he gazed into the fire.

After a few more minutes, Josarian held the scarf up to his face, inhaled deeply, and then sighed. Whatever demon chased him, he finally seemed to have escaped it. His expression lightened to a kind of melancholy peace. He looked at Mirabar with clear eyes and even gave her a slight smile. His face was open and warm, a strong, handsome face that would age well. His dark brown hair fell in thick waves past his shoulders, part of it tied back from his face. He was a man who could easily find a new wife if he wanted one; but Mirabar had seen enough to guess that his heart was still a prisoner of the Otherworld.

"I'm glad you're feeling better, *sirana*," he said gently.

She met his gaze, noting that he didn't flinch from her eyes as so many *shallaheen* did. "You needn't call me *sirana*. I'm just an initiate."

His smile was more heartfelt now. "If your gifts are as great as Tashinar says, then I want you to remember how respectful I am the next time you lose your temper with me."

She remembered snapping at him when he'd desposited her on her pallet. "What do you expect when you drop a woman on her head?" she retorted.

He grinned at that. Then, noticing how she studied his face, he asked, "What is it, *sirana?*"

No. He was not the one. She was sure of it.

"Nothing," she said at last. "You can't go back down the mountain now. Let me show you where you can sleep tonight."

3

"ONE *SHALLAH* AGAINST four Outlookers," Tansen mused, rolling his left shoulder to test his wound. "How did he do it?"

Having agreed to Koroll's deal, he had been moved to a relatively comfortable—though locked, barred, and heavily guarded—bedchamber in the fortress. He had stayed there for several days while the Outlookers, in an ironic twist of fate, did everything they could to help him recover from the wound they had inflicted. They fed him nourishing meals, cleaned, mended, and returned his clothes, and removed his shackles. They permitted him light exercise in the courtyard, treated his wound twice daily, and politely knocked before entering his chamber. He had even quietly endured the presence of a chanting Valdani priest every day. Although he would have greatly preferred the healing magic of his own kind, he would not ask for a Sister to be brought to the fortress to be terrified and humiliated by uncouth Valdani.

"The Outlookers separated to search for his accomplice in the dark," Koroll told him. "Two remained with Josarian; they were dead when the other two returned."

"And Josarian was gone," Tansen guessed.

Koroll nodded. "He knows those mountains the way a man knows his wife's body. Otherwise we'd have caught him by now."

Sitting once again at the table in Koroll's command

chamber, Tansen watched with dry amusement as Koroll blessed a cup of wine and then handed it to him. Ever since Tansen had promised to kill their rebel, the Valdani had extended all manner of ritual courtesy to him. His wound protested as he reached for the cup, but he could tell it was healing. By the time he found Josarian, he'd be in fighting shape again.

"But how did one *shallah* kill two armed Outlookers?" Tan persisted.

"By the look of the bodies, he used something to bludgeon them with." Koroll's eyes grew hard. "He beat them to death."

A *yahr,* Tansen realized instantly. Koroll wouldn't know, of course; the whole point of a *yahr* was that most Valdani didn't know. Upon seizing Sileria from the Kintish Kingdoms over two centuries ago, the Emperor of Valdania had issued a decree: all Silerians were forbidden to carry weapons, and violation of this decree was punishable by death. Most Silerians couldn't speak or understand Valdan in those days, let alone read it, and the idea of going anywhere without a weapon was so unthinkable to almost everyone in Sileria that most of them didn't believe the decree even after it was translated for them. Consequently, there had been a horrific number of executions during those early years of Valdani rule, as well as widespread chaos, countless murders, and more than a dozen bloody massacres as the Valdani disarmed whole villages at once.

Even worse, the disarmed Silerians were in more danger from their still-armed countrymen than the Valdani were. Once the weapons of a family, community, or religious sect had been confiscated, their blood enemies were more likely to attack *them* than to cause trouble for the Valdani. Recognizing this, the Valdani altered their plans and began disarming Silerians with strategic precision, dispassionately encouraging the internal chaos which destroyed what had been a relatively prosperous, if fragmented, society under Kintish rule. Within five years, the rich fields of Sileria's lowlands lay fallow and barren, dispossessed beg-

gars crowded the streets of Shaljir and Cavasar, and whole
shallah villages were wiped out. The people of Sileria,
devastated, humiliated, and ruined, became the Emperor's
slaves.

In the years following the Disarmament, Silerians began
developing weapons out of their daily tools, weapons
which couldn't be readily identified and therefore confiscated. Ever resourceful as they carved a new life out of
their fierce mountains, the *shallaheen* developed the *yahr*,
a deadly striking weapon. It was made of two smooth,
short, wooden sticks, sometimes metal-tipped, which were
joined by a short rope. If the Outlookers noticed a *yahr*,
they saw only a small bundle of sticks, or a distinctive
shallah grain flail, the tool which had inspired the weapon.

Tansen had not touched a *yahr* since the night, nine
years ago, he had used one to kill a man. *One who trusted
you*, a voice from the Otherworld reminded him; he silenced it.

Shallaheen usually used the *yahr* on their own kind;
Tansen had never before heard of an Outlooker being
killed with one. It was a good weapon, true, but even so,
Josarian must be a very good fighter to have killed two
armed Outlookers with it.

"Was he wounded?" Tansen asked Koroll.

"According to rumors, yes."

Tansen said nothing. The rumors which people chose to
share with Outlookers were not to be credited. "But he's
definitely still alive?"

"Alive?" Koroll slammed his fist down on the table.
"Alive, you ask? The unfathered son of a whore is wreak-
ing havoc throughout my district! By the Sign of the
Three, I wish his insides would rot and consume him!"

"Do go on," Tansen urged blandly.

Koroll glared at him. "He has looted an Outlooker outpost. He *burned down* another outpost. He incited villagers
to kill two tribute collectors, urging them to see for themselves that Valdani die as easily as *shallaheen* do." Koroll
rose to pace before the window in agitation. "He defiled a

Shrine of the Three less than four leagues from Cavasar!"

"He's not Valdani," Tan pointed out reasonably, "so he doesn't worship the Three."

"Don't push me, *shatai*," Koroll snarled. "I could still have you tortured to death in the main square."

"Yes, you could," Tan agreed without interest, "but you won't. You're afraid no one but me can kill him."

"Some of the peasants are already saying he *can't* be killed." Koroll almost seemed to shudder. "Frankly, enough of my men are provincial bumpkins that this kind of rumor could be very dangerous if it starts passing among the ranks."

"You really think they could become frightened of a *shallah?*" Tansen asked, letting contempt creep into his voice.

"This one . . ." Koroll nodded and slumped back down into his chair. "This one is different. He's very dangerous. Cunning. Bold. He strikes as fast as a serpent, then disappears just as quickly. I've had patrols searching for him for almost two twin-moons, and we still haven't captured him! Neither bribes nor threats get us any useful information, but everyone knows who he is and what he's doing."

Which, of course, explained how Koroll himself had learned Josarian's name. "Does he have a family?"

"Don't they all?" Koroll said wearily. "Only a wizard could untangle the net of a *shallah*'s blood and bloodpact relations, let alone his enemies."

"Where does he live when he's not hiding in the mountains and tormenting Outlookers?" Tan persisted.

"The village of Emeldar. But he won't be there."

"Perhaps not," Tansen agreed politely, "but it may be a place to start." He suspected that Josarian could sneak home every night without the Outlookers being any the wiser. If he had eluded pursuit for this long, then the locals were loyal to him. Given that and Josarian's own apparent abilities, Tansen didn't intend to put any faith in Outlooker reports. "I need a lead, a starting place. I can't look behind every gossamer tree in the mountains, after all."

"I suggest you begin your search in the Orban Pass, just a hard day's ride from here," Koroll snapped.

"Why?"

"Because I just received word this morning that Josarian attacked four of my men there."

"Four?" Tansen repeated in surprise. "How?"

"Bow and arrow." He scowled. "This is the thanks we get for allowing hunting weapons."

"Were the arrow tips poisoned?"

"Yes. The poison was Valdani. Stolen, of course."

"And?"

"They're all dead."

Tansen gazed at him thoughtfully. "How do you know it was Josarian?"

"This is Sileria, not Kinto or the Moorlands!" Koroll thundered. "Bandits here don't attack armed Outlookers!"

"Those men were a patrol looking for Josarian?" Tansen guessed.

"He found them first." Koroll's voice was bitter.

"Four Outlookers," Tansen mused.

"We're keeping this as quiet as possible."

"Word will spread."

"I know." Koroll's fair Valdani complexion was chalk white now. "And the gods will grow thirsty."

THE FOLLOWING DAY, Koroll and four Outlookers escorted Tansen beyond the city walls. His belongings had already been returned to him, bundled up in his worn satchel and strapped to the back of the saddle he now sat in. He'd also been given enough coin to live modestly until the next dark-moon; a *shatai*, Koroll had asserted, didn't need money for bribes, since only a fool would refuse to cooperate with him. His swords, however, remained firmly strapped to Koroll's saddle as they rode away from Cavasar. Tansen would not be trusted with those until they had released him. His gold, of course, would remain in Koroll's keeping until he returned with proof of Josarian's death. He didn't necessarily have to complete the job by the next dark-moon; but that was clearly when Koroll's confidence in him would begin to wane.

"If I were to be slaughtered like a goat in Cavasar upon honorably fulfilling our contract," Tansen advised Koroll as they rode side by side, "all *shatai* everywhere would be very annoyed."

Koroll actually chuckled. "If you were to come back and cut me in half for having pressed you into service on behalf of the Emperor, His Radiance would also be very annoyed." He glanced briefly at Tansen and added, "However, I think I see before me a reasonable man, despite the *shallah* blood in your veins. If we can do business together this time . . . who knows? There may well be other contracts, eh?"

"You will find that I usually charge a higher fee than the return of my own gold," Tansen said dryly.

Koroll laughed out loud at that. "All right, here's a better bargain. Kill Josarian, and I will pay you double the gold I took from you. Fair enough, *shatai?*"

Tansen smiled slightly. "I, too, appreciate a reasonable man, Commander."

Koroll grinned at him. The military governor's spirits had been light ever since seeing Tansen train in the court-yard this morning. Deprived of his swords, Tansen ran through forms and drills empty-handed, testing his endurance, exploring the limitations of his healing wound, until the sun crept high. Concentrating as he had been taught, excluding everything that might distract him from honing his skills, he hadn't realized until he was done that a dozen Outlookers were watching him in stunned silence.

Then Koroll spoke from a balcony overhead. "We don't see many *shatai* here," he reminded Tansen, grinning broadly.

Looking up at him and seeing the exultation in his captor's expression, Tansen realized that even Koroll had started to half-fear that Josarian truly couldn't be killed.

Every man can be killed, Tansen thought as he rode

beside Koroll now. *Every man.* The burden of that memory had never grown lighter, and so he turned away from it, as always. He rolled his left shoulder against the slight throbbing of his wound and reflected with satisfaction that at least Koroll now believed he could kill Josarian. He almost smiled when he considered how scandalized his *shatai-kaj* would be to learn that Tansen's ability to kill a Silerian mountain peasant had been even briefly doubted.

Koroll pulled his mount to a halt when they reached a fork in the road. He pointed to the road on the right and told Tansen it led to the Amalidar Mountains and the Orban Pass. Somewhere beyond there lay Emeldar, Josarian's native village.

"You are, of course, absolved in advance of any violent acts you are forced to commit against Silerians in your pursuit of this villain," Koroll said. "May the Three watch over you, *shatai.*"

"I'll take the protection of any gods that care to offer it." Tansen paused and added, "Twice the amount of gold you took from me—I have your word on that?"

Koroll nodded. "Frankly, it's worth even more than that to me, but I have a budget to consider."

"Yes, of course," Tansen replied blandly. He watched Koroll release the strap which bound the Kintish swords to his saddle.

"Not that I don't trust you," Koroll said, "but it's never wise to take a man for granted." He tossed the swords into the tall grass beside the road, then turned his mount around and galloped back toward the city, with four Outlookers hot on his heels.

Pleased with the impression he had evidently made, Tansen grinned as he watched them kick up a cloud of dust.

TANSEN SPENT THE first night of his quest at a humble inn where he met a small caravan of traders who had left Cavasar shortly before he had. They were travelling through the mountains to the southern coastal city of Adalian, a city which even now was still occasionally attacked by maurauding Moorlander pirates. The Valdani only controlled the northern Moorlander tribes—and they didn't even always control those very well. The southern Moorlands were peopled by fierce, barbaric tribes of hairy, blue- and green-eyed giants who, a thousand years ago, had sailed across the Middle Sea in search of gold and slaves.

In those long-ago days, the Moorlanders were united under one Great Chief to whom all chiefs swore their allegiance. They became a mighty and powerful people, driving back the older civilizations north of their lands until their empire extended well into what was now Valdania. Other Moorlander tribes pushed south, claiming the forbidding, rocky lands all the way up to the Sirinakara River, the great river which forever divided them from the Kintish.

Still dissatisfied, they had ventured across the sea, lured by the wealth and prosperity of Sileria, the vast, mountainous island floating in the Middle Sea. Daurion, the last great Yahrdan of Sileria, chosen by the Guardians to hold this island with a fist of iron in a velvet glove, drove the invaders back, killing most of them before they could return to their ships and the open sea. Legend whispered that Daurion himself had been a Guardian, possessed of their strange gifts and dangerous powers. A great warrior, he repeatedly repelled Moorlander invasions—until he was betrayed by his own kind, slaughtered by one he trusted. After Daurion's death, internal conflict, claims, counterclaims, and the chaos resulting from a divided leadership gave the determined Moorlanders the opportunity they needed. The Conquest was achieved almost overnight as Moorlanders swarmed across the land, taking what they wanted and burning down the rest.

For two centuries, the Moorlanders carried gold, crops, livestock, and slaves out of Sileria. A once-proud and free people resisted this servitude, and Sileria became a violent, lawless land. When the Moorlanders' empire finally began dissolving into warring tribes, their power collapsed and they lost their hold on Sileria. They retreated back to the sea from which they had come, leaving behind the round stone towers and thick-walled palaces they had built throughout the southern and western regions of the island. Along those same shores, some eight centuries later, one occasionally still saw another legacy of the Moorlanders, too, in a green- or blue-eyed man, in a woman whose hair was the fair shade of a Moorlander rather than the brown or black of a Silerian, or in a youth who towered over his companions.

The city of Adalian boasted its fair share of such people, as well as a brooding stone palace overlooking the entire city. Outlookers now occupied it, of course. The traders Tansen met at the inn outside of Cavasar were on their way to Adalian's famous Temple Market—so called because the market was set up in and around five vast crumbling temples built by the Guardians centuries before the Conquest, desecrated by the Moorlanders, and abandoned long, long ago.

Before leaving the inn, Tansen sold the traders the horse that Koroll had given him. Born and raised a *shallah,* he had never particularly liked horses, although his training as a *shatai* had included combat on horseback, and he had practically *lived* atop a horse while in the Moorlands; such were the ways of Moorlanders. But this was Sileria, so the horse would be a burden where he was going. Donkeys, goats, and *shallaheen* fared well on the narrow mountain paths and rocky slopes he'd be travelling, but horses slowed down a man up there—which was why mounted Outlookers were generally so inept at preventing smuggling and black market trade in the mountains.

The Kintish word for Sileria meant "The Horseless Land." The *shallaheen* had no use for horses, and the lowlanders wanted them but could seldom afford them. The aristocrats and wealthy merchants only used them in the countryside, preferring to walk or be carried in palanquins when travelling through the crowded, narrow streets of Sileria's cities. The sea-born folk went everywhere by boat, having no interest in any portion of Sileria that was neither shore nor port city. The Guardians lived even higher up than the *shallaheen*, the Sisters adhered to a vow of poverty, and the *zanareen* almost never left the rim of Darshon's volcano.

Waterlords and Society assassins liked to appear on horseback, of course, as a mark of their superiority. However, despite the power they still wielded in Sileria, the Emperor of Valdania had sworn to destroy them and had been pursuing this goal since before Tansen's birth, so many of them were obliged to live in hiding and practice a little discretion these days. And horses weren't all that easy to hide in The Horseless Land. This last consideration, even more than speed, was what motivated Tansen to get rid of his.

The traders would be taking the broad, paved Valdani road all the way to Adalian, so Tansen's horse would serve them well. Just to make sure they really needed it, he slipped out of the inn in the middle of the night, crept into the stables, and used the wavy-bladed *shir* he carried to disable one of the traders' horses. Just touching the flat of the blade to the vulnerable frog on the bottom of the animal's hoof was all that was needed. There was no serious damage, but the horse would be lame for several days. Seeing no visible wound or swelling, the traders were bewildered; sorcery certainly had its uses. Tansen, however, hated the *shir* so much that, until the day Koroll unwrapped it, he hadn't even looked at it in longer than he could remember. Nonetheless, he wouldn't have left Cavasar without it, not even if it meant dying by slow torture in the main square; he was relieved that Koroll had returned it to him without comment, apparently assuming he might need it to do his job. The required nine years had passed, but he knew there would be no ease for him until he took the *shir* back to its source. Not after what he had done.

Dazzled by the first *shatai* they had ever met, the traders accepted Tansen's advice with relief when he told them he'd learned quite a bit about horses while sojourning in the Moorlands.

"I've seen this sort of thing before. It's more common than you suppose," he lied blithely while pretending to examine the horse's leg that morning. *Shallaheen,* after all, were taught from their cradles how to lie. "Merely a bruise. He'll be better in a few days."

"A few days?" One of the traders repeated with obvious distress. "We haven't got a few days! And what if this happens again?" He turned to one of his companions with an accusing glare. "I *told* you we should have brought spare mounts."

"No, you didn't! *You* said—"

"My friends," Tan interrupted, "I think I can help."

He sold them his horse at a reasonable price, rode with them as far as the Orban Pass, and waved them off, saying he'd walk from here. Eyes wide with awe at the young, exotically dressed swordmaster who had condescended to befriend them, the chubby, aging traders rode away. After leaving Adalian, Tansen knew, they would follow the trade route going east, and Koroll's horse would effectively disappear.

Alone now, Tansen examined the site of Josarian's latest attack on the Valdani. The bloodstains had already dried to shrunken brown blotches in the dry climate. Seeing where the men had fallen, Tansen studied the surrounding cliffs, looking for the best vantage point for an ambush, then searched for a way to get there. It took him a half-hour to reach the spot. He was winded when he got there, and one hand was scraped from a spill he'd taken when loose rocks had slid out from beneath his feet. While able to outfight, outrun, and outlast most men, he realized ruefully that he'd lost the conditioning that made a *shallah* able to climb up and down these punishing mountains from sunrise to sunset, surefooted as a goat and breathing no harder than a Kintish courtesan at work.

Cavasar lay in the extreme west of Sileria, its view of

Mount Darshon blocked by the foothills of the Amalidar Mountains until one had emerged on the other side of the Orban Pass. Now, as he stood on a clifftop overlooking the Pass, Tansen was able to see the country beyond it, and the distant snowcapped peak of Darshon, wherein dwelt Dar, the goddess he had been raised to worship.

Staring at it now, seeing it for the first time since he had gone into exile, Tansen forgot about Josarian, Koroll, Outlookers, and his work. If he'd been a spiritual man, he'd have prayed. As it was, he simply stared in awed silence, fighting the emotions which burned his blood and the memories which screamed for release. In the village of Gamalan, his boyhood home, the slopes of Darshon were so near, they had seemed to stretch from one end of the horizon to the other, filling the sky. When Dar belched or bellowed, Gamalan shook. When Dar spewed fire, the *shallaheen* in Gamalan saw the smoke of the burning villages which lay close to Her angry mouth. And when Dar erupted in fury, spilling forth lava, the Gamalani carved bloodpacts on their palms to answer Her call . . . and prudently moved their children to safer ground.

As a child, Tansen had played on the rough gray and black tumbles of ash and rock left by Dar's long-ago tantrums. He had seen his elder brother go off to join the mad *zanareen* and eventually die by throwing himself into the volcano while suffering from the delusion that he was the Firebringer. Taught by his proud and crafty grandfather to honor all the traditions of his people, Tansen had prayed to Dar every day and helped gather the annual ritual offerings to placate the goddess for another year. But he had not prayed since the first time he'd killed a man, and he did not pray now.

His stomach tightened as he wondered what Dar's revenge upon him for that day would be. Vast and forbidding even at this great distance, the mountain loomed starkly against the brilliant blue sky, its snowy peak rising through the wispy clouds. Still unable to pray after all these years, Tansen bowed his head in respect. Whatever Dar's revenge, he would face it. *If,* that is, he survived the revenge of the Society.

Forcing himself to turn away from the sight which he had alternately longed for and feared these past nine years, he now searched for signs of his quarry in the spot he suspected Josarian had used to launch his attack against the four Outlookers. Within moments, he found a couple of footprints in the dust. It looked like his intended opponent was a big man. A few wisps of feather from the fletching of the arrows confirmed that the maker of those footprints must have been the murderer of the four dead Valdani. Josarian had known the Outlookers' route, planned ahead, and waited for them. He wasn't just some hotheaded brawler; he was capable of strategy, forethought, and planning. He could hold off his attack and await the right moment. And he could kill in cold blood.

Tansen absently brushed away the footprints with the toe of one well-made Moorlander boot and pondered what he had learned so far. Who was this rabble-rouser? Why had he decided to kill two Outlookers rather than accept the smuggling charge? As far as Tansen knew, smuggling still earned the offender a flogging and a year or so in the mines of Alizar, whereas the murder of an Outlooker meant—as Tansen well knew—death by slow torture. Since the two surviving Outlookers could identify him, Josarian must have known the Valdani would search every village in the district until they found him. There was no turning back once he'd killed those men.

And, having killed them, why hadn't Josarian simply disappeared? *Shallaheen* didn't travel far from home as a rule, and they were all distrustful of strangers. Certainly going away wouldn't have been easy, especially if he was wounded, but it was an obvious option; it was what Tan himself had done nine years ago. Josarian wouldn't even have to go into exile, since the Society didn't care about the murder of a couple of Outlookers. He could simply remove or alter his *jashar,* the knotted, woven, and beaded belt which revealed a *shallah*'s name and history, then go to a distant corner of Sileria and become someone else; the Valdani would be unlikely to find him or learn the truth. Yet he had chosen not only to stay right here, but also to incite the populace, risk further attacks against the Valdani, and make himself the most hunted outlaw in Sileria.

Why? Did he enjoy the fame? Was he insane with hatred? Did he simply like killing, burning, and stealing? He was obviously no fool, but it was too soon to be sure just how shrewd he was. Could he be goaded into a fight with a *shatai*, or would he run away? If he wouldn't come to Tansen willingly, could he be tricked or trapped? Would a peasant who had lived his entire life in these mountains even know what a *shatai* was? Tansen hadn't known, after all, until he'd seen one kill three men in the streets of some strange Kintish port city nine years ago.

While Tansen considered these questions, he searched for Josarian's trail and found exactly what he expected to find: nothing. Josarian wasn't careless. He had covered his escape route and left no clues about which direction he had gone from here. Tansen would have to find him some other way. Having been born and raised in eastern Sileria, Tansen didn't know this district. No people anywhere in the three corners of the world were more secretive than the *shallaheen*, and this was Josarian's territory. Without cooperation from the locals, Tansen could well spend the rest of his life searching this district to no avail. So he'd just have to find a way to make Josarian come to him.

"HE WEARS A *jashar* and speaks the mountain tongue like he was born to it," Zimran told Josarian one night.

They sat by the cooking hearth of Josarian's younger sister, who kept urging her outlaw brother to eat more. This was Josarian's first visit home in nineteen days, and his sister Jalilar had been so certain of his death that she'd even gone to see the Guardians on Mount Niran four days ago. They didn't seem to think he was in the Otherworld yet, but Jalilar knew that was no guarantee. The Otherworld was a mysterious place, and the journey to get there was long and arduous. Many never arrived, and no one knew why. Others were believed to be there, but wouldn't answer when Called. No, there were no guarantees.

So, unconvinced by the reassurances of an old woman whose three-fingered hand seemed too small and delicate to have endured torture by the Valdani, Jalilar had left the secret Guardian encampment and returned home to wait impatiently for Josarian to sneak into Emeldar one night. The continued presence of the Outlookers in the village was her proof that, whatever else may have happened to her brother, *they* hadn't caught him yet. Outlookers were such fools, they really believed that their failure to catch Josarian here meant he hadn't been home since that fateful night he'd become an outlaw. Jalilar looked at her brother again, relief warming the chill of dread which had settled into her bones. Her husband, Emelen, would be home soon, and he'd be almost as relieved as she to see Josarian, with whom he had grown up.

"You think this stranger is a *shallah*?" Josarian asked Zimran. He refused the additional food his sister tried to coax him into eating. "Jalilar, I'll burst soon."

"He must be," Zim insisted. "He has the first two blood-pact marks on his right palm. A few on his left." As an afterthought he added, "No marriage-mark on the right palm, they say."

Josarian absently looked down at the marriage-mark Calidar had carved on his palm the day they had married. It ran from the base of his thumb diagonally up to the base of his fourth finger. She had carved no child-marks across it, and now she never would.

"And he carries *swords*?" Josarian asked at last. "You're sure of this?"

"I am sure."

"Have you seen him? With your own eyes?"

"No."

"Then how do we know it's true?"

"Josarian, who would make that up?" his sister interrupted.

"Why would the Outlookers let him carry swords?" Josarian argued.

"Because he has promised to kill you," Jalilar pointed out, her voice thick with fear.

"Zimran could walk into an Outlooker outpost tomorrow and promise to kill me. Do you think they'd let *him* carry a sword? What's so special about this *shallah,* that he may bear arms based on a promise to kill me?"

Zimran shrugged, then continued his description of the man searching for Josarian. "He wears fine foreign clothes. No one is sure, but a merchant from Malthenar thinks they're Moorlander. Someone in Britar saw the swords unsheathed and says they bear foreign writing that looks like the inscriptions carved on old Kintish temples and shrines."

Having ruled Sileria for six centuries, from the fall of the Moorlanders until the Valdani had seized it from them two hundred years ago, the Kints had left behind many temples, shrines, and palaces. Josarian had an uncle who now stabled some of his sheep in an abandoned Kintish shrine on Mount Orlenar.

"Kintish swords?" Josarian frowned in perplexity. "Moorlander clothes? A *shallah?*"

"Or part *shallah?*" Jalilar guessed.

"What does the *jashar* say?" Josarian asked Zim. Although considered illiterate by *roshaheen*—outsiders— the *shallaheen* communicated information with elaborate strands of beaded knots and weaving. Any self-respecting man displayed his identity and history wherever he went by wearing his *jashar;* a woman's history was related in the woven headdress she wore on special occasions. Since this mysterious stranger wore his *jashar,* perhaps they could learn something useful from it.

"He is Tansen mar Dustan shah Gamalani," Zimran said, "born in the Year of Red Moons."

"Younger than you," Jalilar said to Josarian.

"But not much," Zimran added.

"The Gamalani?" Josarian sat up straighter. "Gamalan..."

"Does that mean something to you?" Zimran asked.

"Something Calidar told me..." He frowned and searched his memory. "A cousin... Yes, that's it!"

"What?"

"Calidar and I had to postpone our wedding because her family went into mourning for a cousin who'd been killed by Outlookers."

"Yes, I remember," Jalilar said instantly.

"The cousin had been given in marriage to honor the end of a bloodfeud. She went to live in Gamalan, which is..." He shrugged. "Somewhere east of Darshon, anyhow."

"Calidar's clan had a bloodfeud with a clan on the other side of Sileria?" Zimran asked him. "What were they fighting about?"

"Who knows? *They* didn't seem to anymore." Such was life in Sileria. "The point is, Calidar's cousin died there when the entire village was slaughtered by Outlookers."

"I remember hearing about the slaughter, but I never knew the name of the v— Gamalan?" Zimran's dark eyes widened when Josarian nodded. "And the stranger is a Gamalani who survived the slaughter somehow." Zim shrugged and guessed, "Maybe he didn't live there."

Individuals and whole families often spread out from a clan's village of origin to make marriages, seek new pastures for their livestock, apprentice to artisans and craftsmen, take possession of inherited smallholdings, or flee Outlookers, assassins, or bloodfeuds. Josarian had no particular reason to suppose the stranger seeking him was somehow involved in the cataclysmic destruction of Gamalan and its feud-withered clan—but he suspected it, nonetheless.

"A killer carrying swords and employed by the Valdani," he mused. "Who knows, Zim? Maybe he survived because he helped slaughter the Gamalani. Or betrayed them to the Valdani. Maybe he revealed something so big—a secret cache of smuggled weapons, the murder of a tribute collector—that the Outlookers decided to kill every man, woman, and child in the entire village."

"*Sriliah,*" Jalilar said, the worst thing one *shallah* could ever say about another, worse than coward, cuckold, killer, liar, thief, or whore: *traitor.*

"Well, depending on who got killed that day," Zimran said, "it might explain one thing that no one understands."

"What's that?" Josarian asked.

"They say that while he's looking for *you . . .*"

"Yes?"

"A Society assassin is looking for *him.*"

4

TANSEN WAS ACTUALLY relieved the day the assassin finally appeared. Ever since coming home, he had been waiting for the Society to make a move, to offer a sign, to find him. As with his pursuit of Josarian, Tan knew he could spend the rest of his life trying to find the waterlord he sought; so spreading his name through these mountains had served two purposes.

There was, of course, one other way to find Kiloran, Tan acknowledged, as his gaze flashed briefly on the painted silk scarf which lay crumpled inside his battered satchel. He closed the satchel and refused to think about the woman, refused to picture her face or remember her scent. *Elelar.* Even the memory of her name brought an ache that never eased. No, he would not call on her to find Kiloran; he would make Kiloran find him.

He'd known that Kiloran, the most powerful and notorious waterlord in Sileria, would hear about his indiscreet search for Josarian. Tansen was too unusual a sight here not to attract attention wherever he went. And he knew with certainty that the old wizard had not forgotten his name—or what Tan had taken from him.

He would have preferred to meet the assassin in private, but the assassin chose to confront him in broad daylight in the main square of a tiny, impoverished village half a day's walk from Emeldar. There were no Outlookers here today; like Josarian and the assassin, Tansen made a point of avoiding them. He didn't want a repetition of the incident that had led to his arrest in Cavasar.

Tansen had slept in some cave in the hills last night. Then he had come to this miserable little village this morning to buy supplies, ask questions, and make sure people got a good look at him. He considered cleaning and oiling his swords, but he'd done that so many times lately that he thought they would slither away if he did it again today. Still, it did make an impressive spectacle, sitting in some public house or village square, powdering, wiping, and oiling his engraved Kintish blades while dozens—even hundreds—of *shallaheen* watched, some discreetly, some with open fascination. If Josarian hadn't heard about him by now, then the man must be dead or halfway across Sileria.

He was debating whether or not to unsheathe his swords for another oiling or simply shoulder his satchel and leave town when he noticed the village square emptying out in a hurry. That could only mean one of two things, and since he didn't hear the hoofbeats of mounted Outlookers, he had a feeling he might need his swords for something besides play-acting today.

He shoved his satchel aside and pushed himself off the rim of the stone fountain where he'd been sitting; apparently the villagers hadn't paid enough tribute to the Society lately, for the fountain was dry. Made to fit him perfectly, his harness needed no adjustment as he stalked into the center of the village square, one sword sheathed on his left side, the other resting in the scabbard on his back. He was no longer a frightened boy with nothing but a *yahr* to

protect him; he was a *shatai,* a member of the finest warrior caste in the world, and he had faced death too many
times to fear its beckoning at this moment. Whether there
would be vows of peace or a fight to the death now, he
had no idea, but he was ready for either. He briefly tensed
and relaxed his left shoulder, testing his wound. Then he
ignored it.

When the square was empty of everyone but Tansen,
the door of the village chief's house opened, and a man
stepped out into the brilliant Silerian sunshine. He was
well fed and strong, like all of the Society's assassins, and
dressed in red and black, the colors of the Society. His
black tunic was cut in the style some assassins favored,
wrapping across his chest without laces; only a *jashar,*
dyed red, held it closed, so it could easily be slipped off
his shoulders for a sudden fight. A *shir* was tucked into
the *jashar.* Tan's gaze flicked down to the man's boots
where he saw, as expected, a *yahr* protruding from the left
one. Most assassins had a *yahr* made of petrified wood,
imported from Kinto, which was as hard as stone.

The assassin came forward, walking with the arrogant
swagger of one who had frightened the whole town into
submission with his very presence. Three boys, undoubtedly disobeying their parents' orders, crept into the square
to watch the proceedings. They gazed at the assassin with
an awe that sent Tan's mind briefly down the path of memory again. How could he blame them for worshipping this
man? Hadn't he himself revered the Society in his boyhood? Hadn't it taken shocking events and continual prodding to make him see that they weren't heroes, rebels, or
outlaw kings? Hadn't he aged a thousand years in just a
twin-moon before he saw what they really were? So, no,
he couldn't blame the three boys for the naked worship in
their eyes as they gazed at the assassin—though it made
him long to slap their backsides with the flat of his swords.

Tan studied the assassin as he came closer. He was
young, definitely younger than Tan himself. When he
spoke, his voice revealed his excitement.

"Are you Tansen shah Gamalani?"

"I am."

"Then I've come to fulfill the bloodvow sworn against you by a waterlord of the Society."

Tan's eyes narrowed. "It's been nine years. A bloodvow may last no longer than that, even if the offender still lives. No matter what the offense."

"Even when the offender runs away?" the assassin spat with contempt.

Tansen wouldn't be baited. He was working now; the *shatai* focused on the task at hand, ruthlessly suppressing the pride and shame of the *shallah* boy within him. "Even then. The Society has stayed strong by observing this tradition. Otherwise they'd still be slaying each other like *shallaheen,* killing and being killed in bloodfeuds without even remembering what started them."

"Kiloran hasn't rescinded the bloodvow," the assassin informed him, circling off to Tansen's right.

"Then perhaps I should speak to him," Tan suggested reasonably, still facing forward, watching the assassin from the corner of his eye.

The assassin laughed. "And how do you intend to find him?"

"You could help me find him."

"Now why should I do that?"

"For your honor."

"Who are *you* to talk to me about honor?"

"I have survived the nine years of the bloodvow," Tansen persisted. "You will dishonor yourself if you challenge me now."

The assassin tugged at his *jashar* and called to someone in the chief's house. A skinny, elderly woman came running out into the square to help him take off his tunic; she scurried into the shadows with it, heeding his warning to keep it clean while he fought. Tansen watched impassively as his opponent, now stripped to the waist, faced him with *shir* in hand.

"Dishonor myself?" the assassin snarled. "I will kill you for that insult, *sriliah!*"

Tan almost sighed. This would only makes things worse, but he had known all along that it was likely to be this way. The Society's much-lauded sense of honor was largely a myth. The young assassin was tired of talking and wanted to fight. As Tansen watched the man reach for his *yahr*, he recited the ritual phrase which had begun and defined his training as a *shatai*, the words which this situation clearly called for: "I am prepared to die today. Are you?"

The assassin simply grinned and said, "That's good to hear, *sriliah*," then lunged for Tansen.

The assassin looked a little surprised to find his attack blocked by two swords which hadn't even been drawn when he'd begun his lunge. Twisting one blade to throw him back, Tansen resisted an easy kill with his left sword. His *shatai-kaj* had taught him to always find a way to use adversity to his advantage, and so he would. He was now in a fight he hadn't wanted and had tried to avoid. Since this assassin was so insistent, Tansen decided he might as well use the death of this young—and, he quickly saw, inexperienced—fighter to achieve his own aims. He and the assassin circled each other, attacking, parrying, and counterattacking. After a few minutes, Tansen figured that unless this was the most cunningly deceptive man in all of Sileria, he had already seen all the moves the eager young fighter knew. And so he began killing him slowly.

He started by taking a few openings here and there, openings which could easily mean the lad's death, but which he instead used to slice and draw blood. He had never fought against a *yahr* before, and this was a good opportunity to experiment, so he did, testing the weapon's strengths and weaknesses against his blades. The assassin wasn't skilled enough to teach him much about this new challenge, but Tan managed to make it look like he was finding it hard, for the benefit of the spectators. He even let the assassin nick him a couple of times with the *shir*,

knowing the scratches would hurt bone-deep and bitterly
for a long time, for a *shir* was no ordinary blade.

The villagers would remember how bloody and horrible
the battle had been, how the stranger and the assassin had
struggled, endured, and persisted. But Josarian's most recent exploits—which included tying a Valdani priest to a
honey tree and stealing all his tribute goats—had convinced Tan that he was a shrewd enough strategist to see
past what the villagers had seen when he finally heard the
story; Josarian would hear that it had taken the stranger
half the morning to kill one young, overconfident, inexperienced opponent. He'd know he was good enough to
beat such a fighter, especially if he used some of the surprise tactics he'd been practicing on the increasingly frantic Valdani. Unless he was as placid as a Sister, he'd be
tempted to confront the warrior who was fast becoming as
famous as he was in these mountain villages.

And the trap would be sprung.

The assassin was all emotion now. All rage, seething
frustration, sweating desperation. It made him clumsy and
predictable. While Tansen didn't regret the death of a Society assassin, especially one who was clearly only alive
because he'd never before fought anyone who could fight
back, he didn't relish the slow, messy death he was bringing upon this one. He decided it was time to end it. He
caught the wooden *yahr* with his left blade and flipped it
away, then drove his right sword through his opponent's
belly.

The assassin dropped his bloodstained *shir* and fell to
his knees, his eyes wide with surprise in his sweat-soaked
face, his mouth gaping in a scream which had no sound.
He looked terribly young suddenly, and the thought came
sharply to Tansen that he would never get any older.

Searching to fill the lad's last moment in this world, Tan
said, "You fought with courage. I honor you for that."
Then he slit the assassin's throat with his free sword.

The body keeled sideways, already a corpse when it hit
the ground, blood flowing out of the severed neck to form

a fast-spreading crimson pool in the dust. Tansen stared at nothing in particular for a moment, resisting the flood of memories. Kiloran would hear about this. He glanced briefly at the staring, lifeless eyes of the Society assassin. Yes, Kiloran would hear.

Knowing that hundreds of gazes were fixed upon him, Tansen flipped the blood off his blades, then told the old woman in the shadows to bring him the assassin's tunic. It was soft, made of imported Kintish silk, finer material than most *shallaheen* would ever wear. Tansen wiped his swords on it, then sheathed them and dropped the soiled tunic on the ground. His swords, he realized absently, would actually *need* the cleaning he'd give them in the next village he came across. He walked over to where he'd left his satchel, picked it up, and turned to leave the village without a backward glance.

"*Siran!*" a young voice cried. "Wait, *siran!*"

He glanced over his shoulder. The three boys who had idolized the dead assassin were now gathered around the body. One of them used a stick to poke the *shir* which lay on the ground. "*Siran,* you must take the *shir!*"

"Fires of Dar," Tansen muttered in a flash of irritation, "I don't need a *collection* of the damned things." He called to the boy, "Leave it there."

"But, *siran,* don't you—"

"No," he said firmly. "If the waterlord who made it wants it back, let him come and get it."

KOROLL STOOD ON the parapeted rampart of the old Moorlander fortress in Cavasar that night, looking out to sea. Somewhere across that wine-dark expanse of water lay Valda, the greatest city in the world, mother of Valdania, the most powerful empire that had ever existed. The Emperor's rule extended far to the north, west into the Moorlands, and east to encompass dozens of principalities, chieftaincies, lesser kingdoms, and chaotic provinces which had once formed part of the Kintish Kingdoms. The sprawling empire of the Kints had long ago crumbled under the onslaught of the Valdani. The various exotic and admittedly vast lands which still comprised the Kintish Kingdoms were now little more than a loose association of petty states that would turn on each other with only a little encouragement. The tribes in the free Moorlands were mere barbarians who sold each other into slavery for the promise of a little more land.

Koroll knew, as surely as he knew the sun would rise tomorrow, that someday the Emperor of Valdania would rule the entire world. The Valdani would establish law and order everywhere, build roads through the forbidding, misty hills of the southern Moorlands, regulate the bizarre customs and strange rites of the scattered Kintish allies, and teach people to live as they should. With their power consolidated in the lands of their enemies, the Valdani would then push north into the unexplored lands beyond the Great Northern Desert. With the Moorlanders and Kints subdued at last, Valdani explorers would journey down the north-flowing Sirinakara River to discover the secret of its source and conquer the little-known peoples who lived beyond the edges of the civilized world.

It was a great destiny, and Koroll fully intended to be part of it. Having already been stranded in this backwater province of the Empire for four years, he was certainly not going to let one bloodthirsty mountain peasant destroy what little reputation he'd found the opportunity to build here. He wasn't going to let his name finally be brought to the Emperor's notice only because he couldn't prevent an uprising among a people who, although violent and hard to govern, hadn't presented a serious threat to the Valdani in well over a century.

Koroll gazed up at the sky, where the first moon, Abayara, was waning to a crescent. Half of Ejara, the second moon, still glowed in the night sky. As the days passed, there would be two crescent moons up there, then one, then none—dark-moon, when the night sky was lit only by the stars. Would the *shatai* return with Josarian's head by then? Would it take him longer? Would he even succeed?

Koroll quickly made the Sign of the Three, touching his left shoulder, his forehead, and his right shoulder, to ward off any ill fortune that last unbidden thought may have summoned. He had seen the *shatai*'s performance in the courtyard that final morning before they released him. Feeling the return of his strength, the swordmaster had revealed skills, speed, and agility which had left Koroll's men gaping like stunned children and Koroll himself filled with the certainty that this man could kill *anyone*.

Koroll still didn't know who Tansen was, other than some *shallah* or part-*shallah* who'd convinced a Kintish swordmaster to train him and then worked for a time in the Moorlands. Nonetheless, Koroll thought he understood him. Whether the man had come home to visit his family or to finish some business connected to the *shir* he carried, he was a mercenary and could be counted on to act like one. If he succeeded on this first assignment, he could become a useful ally, a very valuable tool. That, and a buoyant belief that his problems with Josarian were about to end, had inspired Koroll to offer to pay Tansen out of his own coffers when he returned, in addition to returning the *shatai*'s gold. Such men were bought with money, after all, not with loyalty, promises, or threats.

"Twice the amount of gold you took from me—I have your word on that?"

Oh, yes, Koroll had caught the swordmaster's attention with that offer; he had seen the look of greed in the warrior's eyes. Yes, the *shatai* would return to Cavasar for his gold, or die trying.

MIRABAR PICKED UP a stick and traced a symbol in the dirt, then stared at it, frowning.

"What is it?" Tashinar asked.

"I saw this last night. The Beckoner called me outside while everyone slept, and *this,*" she tapped the drawing with her stick, "was written across the night sky in fire."

"What is it?" Tashinar repeated.

Two curved lines, each shaped like a sickle, flanked a

strange symbol. Mirabar shook her head. "I don't know."

"It doesn't look like a picture of anything," Tashinar ventured.

"No," Mirabar agreed.

"I don't know about those two marks, but this . . ." Tashinar traced the complex symbol. "It looks like . . . like writing."

"Writing?" Mirabar repeated.

"Writing. It's what the *roshaheen* do instead of—"

"I know what it is," Mirabar snapped. "You've told me before. But since I can't read, why would the Beckoner show me this?"

Accustomed to Mirabar's embarrassment over how ignorant and savage she had been when the Guardians first found her, Tashinar ignored her sharp tone. "Since I can't read either, we'll need to ask someone else."

"Who?"

"Derlen came from a merchant family in Shaljir. He might—"

"Not Derlen," Mirabar protested sullenly.

"He is not your enemy, Mirabar." The girl was understandably angry over Derlen's insistence that she not conduct or participate in any Callings while her mind was so obviously disordered.

"Yes, he is!" Mirabar's eyes flashed yellow with hot emotion, her red brows lowered into a scowl, and her unbrushed red curls danced in the mountain wind. She looked more demonlike than usual today. "He is also a coward and a fool."

"That's enough," Tashinar warned.

"He is trying to exclude me!" Mirabar protested. "He is trying to take away—"

"He believes you're dangerous, to yourself and others, while this thing, this Beckoner, has such a hold on you. But that does not make him a coward or a fool. I understand your anger, and I don't agree with Derlen. But I will not permit you to be unjust to him."

Reprimanded by the woman who had been teacher,

friend, and even a sort of mother to her, Mirabar flushed
and pressed her lips together. Tashinar watched her struggle to control the volatile emotions which always seethed
so fiercely inside her soul; more than ever, they needed a
direction, a focus. For a long time the girl had found that
direction in her studies, applying herself tirelessly to the
difficult, sometimes frightening, often painful work of becoming a Guardian. Her extraordinary gifts and her tremendous determination had made her the most promising
initiate Tashinar had ever seen. Having lived a rootless life
as an outcast for as long as she could remember, the girl
had seized upon this newfound purpose and belonging with
passionate intensity, undergoing every hardship without
protest or complaint.

The Beckoner had stolen the peace Mirabar had started
to find, and for that, Tashinar hated him, whoever or whatever he was. Although the Beckoner continued his strange
visitations to Mirabar, cutting into her mind and ripping
into her heart, she nonetheless struggled to maintain her
studies and continue her duties; it was a hard fight, but it
meant everything to her. So she was both crushed and
infuriated when Derlen convinced the other Guardians in
their circle that Mirabar should be excluded from all Callings until they understood what was happening to her. Derlen and the others had made the choice they believed was
best, for no madwoman should be allowed to summon the
power and wisdom of the Otherworld, lest she use it for
her own gain or even for clearly evil purposes.

There was nothing personal about the group's decision
to exclude Mirabar from Callings for the time being, and
several of the Guardians regretted it deeply. Mirabar was
one of *them,* after all, and their status as hunted outlaws
had made all Guardians everywhere unconditionally loyal
to one another. But none of them knew Mirabar as Tashinar did. None of them saw the loneliness that haunted her
heart, the secret fear that she would never belong anywhere, and the proudly hidden need to be not only accepted but also genuinely wanted. None of the others knew

how their decision to exclude Mirabar from the Callings turned her once again into a hungry, skinny, scab-covered child in filthy rags, living on the outskirts of villages, huddling just beyond the circle cast by a night fire, and fleeing when superstitious *shallaheen* threw rocks at her and called her a demon.

"Shall we ask Derlen, then?" Tashinar prodded, stifling her sorrow as she watched Mirabar struggle with her pain.

Mirabar grunted and shrugged, refusing to meet Tashinar's eyes. Knowing that this was the most gracious acceptance she could expect, the old woman went in search of Derlen.

She found him supervising the packing of the gossamer that the Guardians had recently harvested and refined. Once the wealthiest and most powerful sect in Sileria, the Guardians now survived by whatever means they could. Shrewd and efficient in such matters, Derlen had long ago set up trade between discreet merchants in Shaljir and various Guardian groups. Living so high up and in such wild places, the Guardians had daily access not only to gossamer forests, but even to some mountain springs and streams that weren't controlled by the Society. If gossamer leaves were harvested at the right stage of growth, soaked, treated, beaten, stretched, and dried, then the vast, fibrous leaves ripened and softened into the most exquisite, sought-after fabric in Sileria. Silerian aristocrats and Valdani usurpers in the lowlands and on the coasts would soon be wearing elegant garments made of swathes of refined gossamer which many Guardians had broken their backs to produce and provide illegally.

The Valdani had, of course, tried to monopolize this trade, but they'd never gained access to any freshwater sources except those controlled by the Society. Refining gossamer required enormous amounts of freshwater, and the Society demanded heavy tribute for such a privilege. When Emperor Jarell ascended to the Valdani throne several decades ago, he had declared that no more tribute would be paid to the Society. The waterlords were quick

to respond; streams and rivers in Sileria had dried up overnight, and deep lakes and ponds became so cold that men
lost their hands if they dared to immerse them. Valdani
gossamer production, by then a source of great wealth to
the Empire, came to a sudden halt.

Tens of thousands of Silerians were also deprived of
water—a side effect of the power struggle, and one which
concerned neither the Society nor the Valdani.

A huge force of Outlookers, Valdania's gray-clad occupying army in Sileria, immediately attacked the moated
stronghold of Harlon, Sileria's most notorious waterlord.
The Outlookers drowned, of course, every single one of
them. Legend had it that they'd been taken by the White
Dragon; it was a brutal, hideous death which made Tashinar shudder even to think of it. The White Dragon, a grotesque monster born of a magical union between water and
a wizard, gobbled up souls as well as bodies. While many
things about the Otherworld were unknown even to Tashinar, one thing was certain: No one taken by the White
Dragon ever saw the Otherworld or any of his loved ones
again. A victim of the White Dragon lost his soul to the
monster which had killed him, and he remained in its keeping, in torment and agony, until the death of the waterlord
who had created the beast. Even Valdani Outlookers didn't
deserve such a death, Tashinar thought.

After the mysterious death of his Outlookers, Emperor
Jarell vowed to destroy the Society. The waterlords' power
in Sileria had gone unchallenged for centuries. But now
the most powerful ruler who had ever lived was waging
war on the most dangerous wizards in the world, seeking
them out despite the huge risks and heavy cost, forcing
them underground and into hiding, and, incidentally, driving thousands of Silerians into destitution and death.

The Valdani had foolishly believed their battle was won
when, after a few years, they succeeded in destroying Harlon, the Society's most powerful wizard. However, he was
eventually succeeded by Kiloran, who became even more
notorious during the ensuing years. Indeed, after so many

years of eluding the Valdani and maintaining the Society's stranglehold over Sileria, Kiloran was now reputed to be the most powerful waterlord who had ever lived—perhaps even more powerful than Marjan himself, the very first waterlord.

And *that,* Tashinar reflected wearily, frightened most Guardians even more than the Outlookers did.

However, at least the Guardians had found some small benefit in the struggle that was crippling an already impoverished land. With the vast Valdani gossamer industry now destroyed, and with the Society occupied with fighting the Valdani, the Guardians were able to turn a decent profit by supplying refined gossamer at the best prices on the black market.

"We're nearly done here," Derlen told Tashinar. "They can finish packing the rest without me—if this is important?"

"It is." The old woman led him back to Mirabar, who glanced up briefly with hostile golden eyes, then returned to brooding over the strange drawing she had made in the dirt.

Derlen's brow puckered with interest. "What is this?"

"It's something I saw in one of my mad visions," Mirabar said in her most abrasive tone.

To his credit, Derlen didn't stomp away in a huff.

Tashinar said evenly, "We were wondering if you can identify this symbol."

He traced it with a fingertip. "It looks Kintish to me."

"Kintish." Tashinar nodded. "I thought it looked—"

"Do you know what it means?" Mirabar asked, her tone a bit less hostile.

Derlen shook his head, then stroked his gray beard. He had lost his wife in a Valdani raid five years ago and was now raising his son alone, a responsibility which Tashinar suspected accounted for his turning gray so young.

"No, I know only a few Kintish symbols," he said, "ones which were relevant to my family's trade. And that was a long time ago, too . . ." He frowned at the symbol a moment longer, then shook his head again. "No, I'm sorry. I don't know what it means, but it definitely looks Kintish to me."

After he left them alone, Tashinar asked, "Do you think your warrior could be Kintish?"

Mirabar shrugged, staring at the symbol with absorption, seeking to unlock its secret. "I don't know, but I . . ."

"What?"

"I keep asking the Beckoner how I will know this warrior." The wind toyed with her red curls. "I think this is the answer."

"Are all the Beckoner's answers this oblique?"

"*All* of them," Mirabar said with evident irritation.

"A great warrior is coming . . . from Kinto?" After a moment, Tashinar said slowly, "But he still might be Silerian."

Mirabar glanced up at her. "How could a Kintish warrior be Silerian?"

"He might not *be* Kintish. He might just be *coming* from there."

Mirabar's voice was impatient as she said, "Now why would a Silerian warrior be in Kintish lands? If there's even such a thing as a Silerian warrior."

"Armian," Tashinar said, her voice wispy as the notion occurred to her. "Could he be coming at last?"

"Who?"

"Armian."

"Who in the Fires is Armian?" Mirabar demanded.

"He was Harlon's son."

Mirabar shot to her feet. "*Harlon's son?*"

"Yes."

"Do you mean to say that I've been having visions about a *waterlord?*"

"No. He's not . . . I mean, he's *probably* not a waterlord. After all, his father died before——"

"An assassin then?"

"Maybe."

"I've been having visions about an assassin?" Mirabar

sputtered. "Derlen was right! This *is* an evil—"

"No! No, not necessarily," Tashinar said suddenly.

"How can you say that? They are our enemies! They always have been. Worse than the Conquerors! Worse than the Valdani! How can I have visions of a warrior who will *free* us, whom I must *help,* if he's Harlon's son?"

"No, they say that—"

"Who says?"

"The *shallaheen."*

"What do they say?"

"They say that Armian is the Firebringer."

Mirabar was so surprised she nearly keeled over. "The *Firebringer?"*

"Yes." Tashinar added, "Sit down. You look like you're going to be sick."

"Well, wouldn't you?" Mirabar snapped. "Harlon's *son?"* Mirabar sank gracelessly to the ground. "Do the *zanareen* believe it?"

"Only if he passes the test."

"The Firebringer . . . I thought it was just a myth," Mirabar said weakly. "Do you *really* think I'm waiting for the Firebringer?"

"I don't know. I've always thought . . ." Tashinar shrugged. "I've always thought the *zanareen* were mad."

"So does any sane person," Mirabar said scathingly. She paused and then asked in confusion, "Is Armian one of them?"

"No, he's not even in Sileria. The *shallaheen* say that he was spirited away after Harlon's death. Just a helpless child at the time, he was taken across the Middle Sea to live in hiding somewhere, to keep him safe from the Valdani.

"Taken to the Kintish Kingdoms?"

"So they say, but who knows for sure?"

"Someone in the Society must know."

"If they do, they're not likely to tell us," Tashinar pointed out.

"How did he go from being Harlon's son to being the Firebringer?" Mirabar demanded.

"You know the tales the *shallaheen* tell."

"I know how they worship the assassins," Mirabar said with disgust. "I know how they cower before the water-lords."

"Harlon was a hero to them, fighting the Valdani the way he did."

"Never mind that thousands of them died because of Harlon."

"The Valdani wanted Harlon's child, they wanted him badly. I remember it well. Many people must have risked their lives to get him safely out of Sileria and out of the Emperor's reach." Tashinar shrugged. "You know how stories spin out over the years. Armian was probably still a mere boy when people began telling tales of his great skill and courage as a warrior."

Mirabar scowled. "Even *I* could kill a man with an enchanted blade—especially an unarmed man." She had seen Society assassins at work and knew their ways.

"Still, Silerians have always preferred a homegrown killer to a foreign one," Tashinar said dryly.

"So people embroidered the story," Mirabar guessed, "and said Armian was destined to return to Sileria to fight the Valdani?"

"Yes. And with that, it was not surprising that some even began to say he was the Firebringer, the long-prophesied hero who would lead us again to the glory we once knew."

"Uh-huh. But first he has to please the *zanareen* by flinging himself into the volcano and surviving." Mirabar rolled her eyes. "In which case, we'll never be free."

"You speak of freedom so often now," Tashinar said quietly. "It's been a thousand years since we were free. Do you really think we will be again?"

Mirabar looked again at the strange symbol she had

drawn in the dirt. Was the warrior coming from Kintish lands? Would he really free them?

He will succeed, and he will fail.

"I don't know, *sirana*," she said at last. "I don't know."

5

JOSARIAN CIRCLED THE tiny, isolated Sanctuary of the Sisterhood several times before finally concluding that it wasn't being watched. The Valdani were tightening their net, and it paid to be careful. Zimran had not been at their appointed meeting place, an old lightning-struck tree which was about three hours' walk from here. Josarian had arrived there to find a woven, knotted cord hanging from one of its branches; the message advised him to come here today after dark.

His brief life as an outlaw had already taught him to take nothing at face value, and it occurred to him that this might be a trap. The mysterious stranger who was searching the mountains for him was at least part-*shallah* and knew their ways and their language. It seemed possible that he had found out where Zimran was next supposed to meet Josarian, gone there himself, and left the small *jashar* Josarian had found hanging in the tree. Nothing in the area around the tree suggested that a struggle had taken place, but that didn't necessarily mean Zimran was safe. The stranger, Tansen, could have killed Zim elsewhere, or he could be holding him hostage at this small, isolated Sanctuary. Perhaps he was even now waiting inside the hut to kill Josarian.

So, suspicious and wary, Josarian arrived before sunset, circled the area several times, then crept up to the best-protected side of the little stone building, under the cover of heavy shadows. Listening at the hut's eastern window, he heard ragged breathing inside, as if someone were in panic or in pain. Moving with caution, he peered into the building—and was immediately relieved by what he saw in the shadowed interior. His cousin was on a narrow cot in the corner of the room, naked and glistening with sweat as he ground his hips against the woman who writhed energetically beneath him. With a wry grin, Josarian crept around the hut and crouched quietly by the front door, waiting for them to finish.

Calidar had always loathed Zimran for his womanizing, referring to his many conquests as the half-witted victims of his lust. While Josarian couldn't comment on their intelligence, most of the women Zimran sported with definitely didn't seem to consider themselves victims. Indeed, judging by the impassioned moans and urgent instructions of the woman inside the Sanctuary with Zimran right now, this one—like most of the others that Josarian could recall—seemed quite pleased with the situation. True, there had once been an unmarried girl who'd begged Zimran to marry her after discovering she was pregnant, and even Josarian, loyal though he was, thought Zim's recalcitrant behavior on that occasion had been disgraceful. The girl had wound up miscarrying—intentionally, some said—and was sent to live with relatives in Adalian, where it was hoped she might still find a husband.

Only Josarian's love for his cousin had made it possible for Zimran to eat at his table or sit beneath his roof after that, since Calidar openly despised Zim from that day forward, only showing him hospitality out of respect for her husband's wishes. After that close call with the marriage knife, however, Zimran had confined his amorous activities strictly to experienced women. It was rumored that Zimran had nonetheless sired a few other men's children, but as long as he didn't seduce any wives in Emeldar itself, he was still a beloved son of his native village. Widows, of course, were another matter, and most people in Emeldar looked the other way if they chanced to see Zimran creeping into a lonesome woman's house after dark. Of course, the village might be a more peaceful place if he'd confine himself to *one* widow. Josarian—who'd never touched any woman but his own wife—still blushed when he remembered the insults that two of Zimran's lovers had shouted at each other in the main square of the village one day a couple of years ago.

Josarian had also thought Zimran was crazy to seduce the bored wife of a Valdani landowner a few months ago, but he had to admit that the information she whispered to his cousin across her pillow about Outlooker movements had come in handy since he'd become an outlaw. Nonetheless, if Josarian had walked three extra hours today just so Zimran could enjoy a woman as well as meet with him, then he was going to punch his cousin as hard as he could when he finally came up for air.

"Yes, *yes* . . ." the woman in the hut wailed.

Zimran grunted harder and faster, and the cot started thudding against the wall.

Sudden desire coiled inside Josarian's belly, languidly unfurling and flowing down to pool in his loins as the couple inside the Sanctuary panted, moaned, and rode their way to ecstasy. He took a deep breath, welcoming thoughts of Calidar even as he fought them. Remembering the joys of his marriage bed only made him ache—and in a way that could be quite embarrassing if he was to meet with his cousin in just a few minutes. But sometimes the ache was as sweet as it was painful, and so he let his mind dwell on remembered pleasures that had no name and depths that had no bottom, even as his body dwelled on needs that now had no outlet—except a solitary one that was a sorry substitute for what he'd known with his wife.

Fortunately, the rhythmic noises inside the hut peaked and died before his body broke free of the shackles of his will. He heard the Sister inside the Sanctury sigh with deep satisfaction and his cousin laugh exultantly. Some of the Sisters were virgins who had felt a calling and joined the Sisterhood at an early age. Most, though, were widows who'd lost their men to bloodfeuds, disease, assassins, accidents, the mines, or the Outlookers. They had sought a new purpose in a land where there were few spare men and where the chances of remarriage were slim for a *shallah* woman. Josarian suspected that such women were pleased to have the occasional company of a handsome young lover such as his cousin.

He gave the couple a few minutes for pillow talk. Then he called through the woven, knotted, and beaded ropes which covered the doorway, "Good evening, Cousin! I hope I come at a good time."

The woman inside gasped and started whispering frantically. Josarian grinned as he heard them both scramble for their clothing, though his cousin's voice sounded calm and satisfied.

"You're early," Zimran called back.

"Stay where you are!" the woman added worriedly.

"Good evening, Sister Basimar," Josarian said politely, still speaking past the door at which the *jashar*, among other things, identified the Sister who lived here. "Are you well? A moment ago you sounded like you might be in pain."

The woman stuttered out a nonsensical response, her voice rich with embarrassment.

"Ignore him," Zim advised. "He's just envious."

"Mostly, I'm tired," Josarian corrected. "Is there a good reason—a *very* good reason—why you made me meet you here?"

A sun-darkened hand shoved aside the door *jashar,* and Zimran appeared, face and bare chest shining with perspiration. "A *very* good reason," he said with a broad grin.

"Come outside where I can hit you," Josarian said.

The woman gasped again and cried, "Don't hurt him!"

Zimran's grin broadened: "She likes my pretty face."

"Don't they all?" Josarian said wearily. "She can clean it for you when I'm done."

The woman thrust her head through several strands of the door *jashar.* She looked from one man to the other for a moment, then said, "You're teasing, aren't you?"

"Almost," Josarian said, eyeing his cousin with some disfavor.

"Basimar." Zimran tilted his head. "My cousin, Josarian."

Having made the introductions, Zimran sauntered away from the door and retrieved his gossamer tunic from the floor. Sister Basimar backed into the stone hut, and Josarian followed her. She was perhaps ten years older than he, plump, and still pretty. She wore the long, simple gown of a Sister. She hadn't laced up the front yet, and he could see that her throat and the slope of her breasts were as pleasure-flushed as her face. *No, Calidar,* he thought, *no victim.*

Basimar nervously tried to tidy her hair as she mumbled something about how pleased she was to meet Josarian. She glanced doubtfully at the cot, then apparently decided that tidying that, too, would merely call more attention to what had just happened there. Instead, she offered wine to both men. Josarian accepted and sat down at the simple wooden table in the middle of the room.

"Well?" Josarian prodded Zimran, who seemed more interested in stroking various rounded portions of the Sister's anatomy than in talking to his cousin.

Basimar blushed rosily, seeming as pleased as she was embarrassed. Nonetheless, she pushed Zim's hand away from her bottom and sat down at some distance from him.

"More news about this stranger, this Tansen," Zim said, growing serious at last.

"He killed an assassin. I know," Josarian said.

"My brother-in-law," Basimar said.

"The assassin?" Josarian asked.

She nodded. "My late husband's youngest brother."

Josarian caught his cousin's eye, realizing that there *was* a good reason for them to meet here. "Tell me more."

"Tell him what you told me last time," Zimran added.

She was a long-winded woman, but Josarian recognized the salient factors of the story pretty quickly. The stranger

was sought by Kiloran—*Kiloran!*—for some long-ago offense. Related to the slaughter in Gamalan? Apparently no
one knew. Basimar's brother-in-law had tried to claim the
bloodvow as a means of gaining recognition. He was
young and inexperienced, yet it had taken Tansen a long
time to kill him. Moreover, Tansen had not come away
unscathed; he was now reported to be carrying wounds
delivered by the boy's *shir;* those would not heal soon,
Josarian knew. They would be painful; perhaps they would
slow him down.

The woman talked at length and answered all of Josarian's questions, some in detail, some with general speculation. By the time Zimran walked him to the top of the
ridge to say farewell in private, he had made up his mind.

"Go after him?" Zimran repeated in astonishment. "You
mean to fight him?"

"Why not? We won't get rid of him any other way."

"Why *not?* Because he's got swords, and you've got a
yahr."

"I killed two armed Outlookers with a *yahr,* and Tansen
barely managed to kill an incompetent young assassin with
his swords." Josarian nodded confidently. "I can take him."

Zimran's gaze scanned the heavens as he thought it
over. Two crescent moons hung low in the evening sky.
"He'll be easy enough to find, at least."

"He's about as discreet as a marauding Moorlander,"
Josarian said contemptuously.

"All right," Zim agreed at last. "Let's take him."

"And let's make sure the Valdani think twice before
sending another one like him after me."

"I wonder . . ."

"What?"

"I wonder why Kiloran wants his blood?"

TANSEN DECIDED IT was time to increase the pressure
on Josarian, so he finally took his performance to Emeldar
itself. He'd spent days bragging loudly and boldly
wherever he went, letting his tongue run wild with incred-

ible tales after a mere cup or two in every public house, or *tirshah*, he entered—and he entered quite a few. The stories were so blatantly improbable that surely any man of sense would suspect him of being a drunken braggart of little skill and less intelligence, especially after the incompetent show he'd made of killing the assassin. He sweetened the bait, too, with increasingly insulting allusions to Josarian's cowardice.

"Why doesn't he face me?" Tansen demanded of the men in the vine-covered courtyard of a *tirshah* in Emeldar that day.

It was a warm afternoon, and the men of the village were resting after the midday meal, waiting for the sun to move a bit farther across the sky before returning to their fields, pastures, and other backbreaking work. It was a glorious Silerian day, the kind Tan had remembered with hungry longing during his long years in exile. The sky was a brilliant cerulean blue, a heat haze made the harsh mountains shimmer like gold, and the scents of spring perfumed the air. It was an afternoon to spend lying in the shade and enjoying the fragrance of the Silerian hills, or perhaps creeping into an empty shed or some isolated Kintish ruin to enjoy the sighs and softness of a woman. Instead, he was swallowing mediocre wine, inhaling *shallah* tobacco, and swaggering more than the slain assassin had ever dreamed of doing.

"I'll *tell* you why he won't face me," Tansen continued, warming to his subject. "He's *afraid*, that's why!"

All the men glared. Many argued. One or two mumbled vague threats. A few were silently attentive, apparently suspecting the stranger was right about Josarian. Things were going exactly the way he'd expected.

"He's heard about all the men I've killed," Tansen sneered. "He's heard how I fought twenty Moorlanders by myself, and defeated them all."

"We've *all* heard that one," said an old man.

"Three or four times, at least," someone else muttered.

Tansen pretended not to hear. "He's heard how I killed

a Society assassin without even breaking a sweat!"

"Quiet, friend," another man said uneasily.

Some things in Sileria were still the same, Tansen reflected. People still didn't like to hear the Society mentioned out loud in public places. Even his own *shir* wounds seemed to throb a little more when he spoke the word aloud, but he knew that was just a boy's superstition.

The conversation, such as it was, continued in this vein for a few more minutes, with Tansen finally concluding that Josarian had no balls and couldn't perform even for a Kintish courtesan possessing the finest erotic sorcery known to her kind.

As a boy, he'd seen a man killed over such an insult. Not surprisingly, someone here jumped to his feet, a *yahr* in his hand and battle in his eyes. A relative of Josarian's, Tansen guessed, or at least a friend. The man was about Tan's age. His face was so handsome it was almost as pretty as a girl's, and the gossamer tunic he wore, which couldn't have been cheap, accentuated his good looks. He was a little on the small side, but wiry and quick.

"Easy Zimran," someone said, stepping between the two men.

Zimran tried to shove past his friend. "You heard what this *sriliah* said! Let me—"

"No, you idiot!" The man shoved Zimran down onto a stool and snapped, "Are you going to challenge him here, with Outlookers swarming all over the village? Use your head!"

The warning apparently brought the pretty fellow to his senses. Fuming with impotent rage, he turned his back on Tansen and swallowed a huge gulp of wine.

Judging that he'd hit his target, Tansen studied the expressions of the men around him. Yes, no doubt about it; Josarian would hear about this, even if he was already a sojourner in the Otherworld.

"Tell Josarian I'll keep looking," Tansen warned the men, slamming down his cup. "Tell him I'll find him. He can't hide forever."

Actually, he *could;* and if he were smart, he would. But *shallaheen* were proud, and Tansen had flung too much humiliation at Josarian to be ignored much longer. He had set the trap and baited it well. Now instinct told him that the outlaw's move would come soon. And Tan would be ready for him.

Pretending to be slightly drunk, he made his way out of the *tirshah*. Once on the streets, he took care to stay well away from the main square, avoiding a potential confrontation with Outlookers. True, he'd been hired by their district commander, but most of them didn't know it, and he rather doubted his explanations would carry much weight with frustrated Outlookers tired of hunting for an elusive *shallah* rebel.

Apart from the main square and the market street, most of the Outlookers in Emeldar were posted around two houses clinging to a cliff at the edge of town: Josarian's and his sister's. Someone had identified the two dwellings to Tansen this morning. A widower, Josarian now shared his small stone house with a bachelor cousin who was apparently the bane of every father in the village.

Tansen strolled down a side street, letting people see him now that he was well out of sight of any Outlookers. The season was advancing, spring coming into full blossom. Soon it would be dark-moon again. Back in Cavasar, Koroll was undoubtedly growing impatient. Well, let him wait. Patience was a virtue worth cultivating. After waiting nine years to come home, Tansen had little sympathy to spare for an ambitious Valdan who couldn't wait more than a moon cycle for a man's death.

Emeldar was not as pretty as Gamalan had been, and Darshon was only a hazy vision from here, shimmering dreamily in the distance. Tansen had seen the burnt offering-ground beyond the outskirts of Emeldar, the thick scars on people's palms, and the sacred lava stone which was the first stone laid in any *shallah* village ever built. But no matter how sincere their worship of Dar was, these people were too distant from Her angry mouth to know

Her as the Gamalani had. Even now, the boy inside him felt Her hot gaze upon him, waiting, watching, judging him.

He felt other gazes upon him, too, of course. Most of them were hostile, since everyone knew he had come here to kill Emeldar's favorite son. They were proud of Josarian's exploits. They smirked at the Outlookers who couldn't catch him. They had come to understand, Tansen saw, that the Valdani were vulnerable.

A pretty girl sat outside her doorway with her face turned away from the street, letting only her profile show: the signal of a modest, respectable girl who was available for courting. Tansen saw a young man pacing slowly back and forth with his companions, talking with them but keeping his eye on the girl. She turned her head away as he walked past, just enough to let him know that she had decided she was not available to *him*. Momentarily disheartened, the young man then made a show of not caring.

Had Tansen's life been different, he, too, might have participated in these early courting rituals. But his introduction to affairs of the heart, like his introduction to everything else that had shaped his life, had been sudden, brutal, and as cruel as the cut of a *shir*.

On a day like this, with the brilliant sunlight gleaming on a young woman's dark hair, he could see her again in his mind's eye, as clearly as if she stood there herself: Elelar. The delicate complexion, the graceful hands, the midnight black of her hair, the scent of her skin which had always made his belly quiver with naive hunger . . .

He shook off the memory, surprised at its piercing sharpness. Elelar was no *shallah*, but there was a strength, almost a harshness, in the beauty of a Silerian woman that was unlike that of women anywhere else in the three corners of the world. Seeing the women of his homeland for the first time in so many years was bound to remind him of her.

The young girl finally heeded her mother's repeated call to come inside the house. The long-sleeved tunic draped

her body all the way down to her knees and, like the pantaloons she wore, was modestly loose. The material was
light and gauzy, though, accommodating Sileria's hot climate, and the afternoon breeze melded it lovingly against
her body. Tansen wasn't the only one who noticed the ripe
young charms outlined so gracefully as she stood up. Ah,
yes, that one would find a husband soon, judging by the
hungry gazes that followed her every move. Tansen turned
into another street leading away from town.

The streets of Emeldar were like those of any other *shallah* village: steep, rocky, and crowded with small houses
made of the cream, amber, and peach colored stone of
Sileria's mountains. The strange circumstances which Josarian's activities had brought upon Emeldar may have
subdued some of the exuberance of the locals, but the scent
of wild rosemary still perfumed the air, some slightly out-
of-tune bard still wailed ancient melodies which echoed
around the surrounding hills, and children still played in
the streets while their parents or grandparents sat in the
doorways and kept an eye on them.

No, Emeldar was not as pretty as Gamalan had been,
but it stirred an ever-present hunger inside him for the
home he'd never see again, a home that no longer existed.
It recalled the life of a boy who had never killed, never
lost his loved ones, and never turned his back on Dar.

Still hungry, he turned away from the memories, and
from Emeldar. He was heading east, and he had made sure
everyone knew it.

ZIMRAN LONGED TO see Josarian himself, to tell his
cousin what a swaggering, drunken, uncouth lout the
stranger was, but he couldn't wait all night by the spring
in the hills where he'd promised to leave a message. There
was a widow in need back in Emeldar, after all.

The lady's husband had gone off to join the *zanareen*
last year after watching all his sheep die of thirst due to
the feud between the Valdani and the Society; and now
she counted on Zim to soothe the sorrow of her lonely

nights. However, she was a modest woman who only let him visit her during the dark-moon, when she was convinced no one could see him sneak into her house. It wasn't quite dark-moon yet—Ejara hung low tonight, a glowing sliver of alabaster in the night's ebony ear—but the widow had missed Zimran sorely this month and was eager to begin the orgy of pleasure they would enjoy together for the next few nights. She'd managed to get close enough to him in the marketplace this morning to let him know she was ready: *Come tonight, come early, and be strong when you come.*

Zimran grinned as he hid a hastily knotted *jashar* under the usual rock near the spring. Why not let the lady keep believing that their affair was a secret and that half the village hadn't already guessed where he'd be sleeping tonight? A few whispered lies in the dark to ease her anxiety cost him nothing, after all.

And be strong when you come . . . Ah, yes, his was a good life.

If only Josarian hadn't had the misfortune to get caught smuggling, and then compounded the error by killing two Outlookers. But what was done was done. Dar had turned Her face from them for a moment; they must be men and make the best of the situation.

Of course, with all the trouble Josarian had caused since then, there was now no chance of the Outlookers forgiving and forgetting, or even of their accepting a generous bribe. Zimran would *never* understand why, having gotten them into this mess, Josarian now insisted on making it worse—looting and burning Outlooker outposts, harassing Valdani priests, murdering more Outlookers, and urging other *shallaheen* to do the same. These were not the acts of a rational man! Where had his happy, placid, fun-loving cousin gone? Everyone knew that Calidar had taken Josarian's heart to the Otherworld with her, but Zimran now suspected she'd taken all of his sense, too.

Arguing about it with Josarian made no difference, either.

"So what if Valdani can be killed as easily as *shalla-heen?*" Zimran had cried in exasperation one night not so long ago. "Let the Society do it! It's what they do best, anyhow."

"The Society doesn't kill them to defend us, they kill them to maintain their power over us!"

"It's always been this way," Zim argued. "Why do you think it should be different now, just because you've killed half a dozen Valdani?"

"Don't you see? If every one of us killed half a dozen Valdani—"

"Then the Emperor would just send twice as many to Sileria! What's the point?"

"Do you really want to spend the rest of your life watching the food we harvest, the livestock we raise, and the minerals we mine go to enrich the Valdani and pay for their wars of conquest against more people like us?"

"*I* want to spend the rest of my life getting rich from smuggling, and sleeping with grateful women who don't expect me to marry them," Zimran said with conviction.

And Josarian . . . Well, Josarian never stayed angry for long. He had merely smiled at that. "And so you shall, Zim. But I stumbled from the path one night, and I can never go back."

"But you don't have to make war on—"

"Yes, I do." Josarian nodded. "The scenery is different when you leave the path. You see things that you never dreamed of before . . ." He sighed and met the gaze of his cousin, who was growing increasingly convinced he'd lost his mind. "Even if I could go back, I wouldn't want to. I have a new destiny now."

"A *short* one, I'd say."

Incredibly, Josarian laughed. "I'd say so, too. But even a short life is a worthy one if it counts for something." He paused and added more soberly, "And after Calidar died, I thought mine would never count for anything again."

That was when Zimran had realized that Josarian no longer feared death. And as a smuggler, Zim knew that such a man was the most dangerous kind of all.

However, he did agree with Josarian about one thing: They had to kill Tansen. He'd been worried about the scheme at first. A hired assassin with two swords wasn't someone he felt sanguine about attacking. However, having seen the boasting, self-important oaf in Emeldar today, with his cuts from the assassin's *shir* still angry and sore, Zimran had no more doubts. In fact, he *longed* to taste Tansen's blood after what that *sriliah* had said about Josarian.

He descended the mountain, surefooted even in the dark, and made his way to an old goat path that would eventually take him to a pasture above Emeldar. From there he would slip through the back streets to the widow's house, where he would feast luxuriantly all night on some of the sweetest flesh he'd ever known. She'd be a little annoyed, of course, when he told her he had to leave tomorrow for a couple of days. He'd be back before Abayara rose in the east, beginning their titillating cycle of abstinence all over again; well, *her* cycle of abstinence—he, of course, kept busy between dark-moons. Anyhow, he had to go away tomorrow; he had promised to help Josarian kill the *sriliah*, and now he wouldn't miss it for all the diamonds in Alizar.

The *jashar* he'd left on the hillside had been detailed, assuring Josarian that Tansen could be killed without much risk, and suggesting they do it tomorrow night. If Tansen was heading east, as was rumored, they could follow him as he left the village of Islanar tomorrow and kill him on the far side of Mount Orlenar—where, according to this morning's news, there happened to be very few Outlookers at the moment, since Josarian was erroneously believed to be heading south.

Yes, Zimran would be back in time for a few more dark and furtive meetings with his favorite widow before he had to leave for the coast on another smuggling expedition, but she would nonetheless be angry when he broke the news tonight. Slipping through the back streets of Emeldar, Zimran smiled as he pictured her reaction, because she was always particularly bold in bed when she was angry or trying to get her own way. He certainly would have been a great fool to waste half the night in the hills just to have a little conversation with his cousin.

He was still congratulating himself on his good judgment when he arrived at the widow's door and slowly started to ease it open. As expected, she had left it unlatched, and the hinges were as well-oiled as ever. His expectations suffered a severe shock, however, when he found four Outlookers waiting inside for him.

Instinct made him try to escape even before he saw the widow weeping in the corner. Panic made him fight back as two Outlookers seized him and he was formally arrested. Fear made him struggle wildly as they searched him at swordpoint, and he didn't subside until they finally beat him unconscious while the widow screamed and begged for mercy.

6

THE NEWS WHICH reached Islanar the following afternoon was so disheartening that Tansen was tempted to go straight back to Cavasar and kill Koroll just to relieve his ire.

A young wife of Islanar had been visiting her mother in Emeldar yesterday, where she had spent the night before returning home today. During the night, the Outlookers had descended in force upon the village, flooding the main square and choking the streets with their vile horses and clattering swords. They broke down doors and dragged innocent people out into the streets, half-dressed and terrified. They seized twenty men—*twenty!*—and hauled them off to the Outlooker fortress north of Britar.

"They'll all be set free if Josarian turns himself in before Abayara rises," the young wife's father-in-law informed all the men in Islanar's only *tirshah*. "But if he doesn't . . ."

"Yes? What?" prodded an angry young man.

"They will kill one man a day until he finally *does* turn himself in."

This announcement was met with shocked silence. Tansen looked around the courtyard, then asked, "These men that were seized—who are they? Josarian's friends and family?"

"Every man in the village is a friend or relative of Josarian's."

"Was his cousin taken?" Tansen persisted. "The one who lives in his house?"

"Yes," the father-in-law answered. "They especially wanted that one, for everyone knows how fond Josarian is of him." The old man went on to explain that Zimran—the same man, Tansen realized, who had nearly challenged him in Emeldar yesterday—wasn't at home when the Outlookers came for him. "So they seized a child, a boy of no more than seven or eight, and held a sword to his throat. They promised the mother that they would kill him on the spot if she didn't tell them where Zimran was."

"And did she?" Tansen asked, too familiar with Valdani ways to be shocked by such tactics.

The old man sighed. "Yes. She did."

The men around them reacted to this, some nodding in sympathy, most hissing in disapproval. Silence was the traditional way here. You suffered tragedy and injustice, no matter how terrible it was, and then you sought vengeance—or asked the Society to seek it for you, in exchange for your eternal debt to them. But you never, never told anything to *roshaheen*. Such was *lirtahar*, the law of silence, and to break it always brought terrible shame—and sometimes terrible vengeance, too, usually from the Society, but occasionally from other *shallaheen*.

Tansen guessed the mother's fate even before the old man
finished his story.

"Of course, the villagers . . . They all turn their faces
from her now." The father-in-law sighed. "But at least the
Outlookers released the child. At least they did that."

The Outlookers had ambushed Zimran in the home of
some widow with whom he had an assignation—meaning
that she, too, was now disgraced before her village.

What an absolute mess the Outlookers had made of
things, Tansen reflected as he left Islanar that afternoon
and headed east along the road which hugged the side of
Mount Orlenar. Why had this happened? Had Koroll already lost faith in him and ordered this mass capture to
force Josarian out of hiding? Or had some local officer
decided to exercise a little initiative? Had Josarian heard
about it yet? Although it seemed likely that Zimran had
been his main source of information, Tansen didn't suppose for a moment that Josarian had been relying solely
on his pretty-faced cousin.

He needed to find Josarian right away. Time was running out. Outlookers and *shallaheen* would now all be eager to make sure that Josarian heard about the prisoners
being held near Britar. The Valdani, Tan knew, believed
Josarian was heading south, so they'd concentrate their efforts there. Word would spread quickly among the *shallaheen,* too, radiating outward in all directions from
Emeldar. Josarian's own escapades indicated that he was
well-informed of events and Outlooker movements in the
district. He'd find out about this soon, and when he did,
Tansen would become no more than a minor annoyance,
one that no longer commanded his attention.

If Tansen had guessed wrong and the Valdani had
guessed right, if Josarian really *was* heading south, then
Tan had already lost him. Josarian would either give himself up or get himself killed before the new moon rose in
the east.

If Tansen had guessed right, though . . . If he had
guessed right, then Josarian was closing in on him now,

his attention fixed, his target chosen, his resources committed.

If Tan was right, all he had to do was wait for Josarian to come kill him.

HE'D WAITED FOR his cousin as long as he could, but Zimran hadn't shown up. That only surprised him because the knots in the *jashar* indicated that Zim had taken a particular dislike to the stranger and wanted to help Josarian take him. However, it seemed that Zimran's innate sense of self-preservation had overcome his bravado at the last moment; swords were awfully intimidating against a *yahr,* after all. Or perhaps some woman had stimulated Zimran's ever-ready libido, making him lose track of time. Then again, maybe some lady's husband had come home at a most inopportune moment, altering Zim's plans for the day. Or perhaps there were so many Outlookers swarming around Emeldar today that it just wasn't possible to leave the village discreetly until after dark, by which time it would be much too late to get to the far side of Mount Orlenar in time.

Whatever the reason, Zimran hadn't shown up as promised. Josarian wasn't particularly worried about it. This wasn't the first time, and it wouldn't be the last. Moreover, he didn't think *anyone* was as easy to kill as Zim now claimed Tansen was, and he could concentrate better on the task at hand without his impatient cousin breathing down his neck. Besides, although he hadn't refused Zimran's offer to help, the truth was, he wanted to do this alone. Unlike the Outlookers, who came after Josarian in groups of two, four, eight, and twenty, this stranger had the courage to search for him alone. The man might be a braggart, a fool, and a clumsy fighter, but Josarian felt that his courage, at least, should be honored in a way that precluded outnumbering him.

Outsmarting him, now that was something else.

Hidden in the hills outside of Islanar, he had watched the stranger walk out of town, then stayed where he was and waited for Zimran until it was nearly dark. Realizing that his cousin wasn't going to arrive in time, he then began tracking Tansen—a task which the *roshah* had made laughably easy. Well, why not? He thought he was the hunter instead of the hunted.

When he realized where the *roshah* planned to spend the night, he felt sure it had to be a good omen: Tansen was bedding down in the abandoned Kintish shrine where Josarian's uncle sometimes stabled sheep for the night. Josarian couldn't have chosen more familiar territory himself.

Since there didn't seem to be much sense in attacking a hired assassin who was fully armed and wide awake, Josarian settled into the shadows and watched his quarry. Now that it was dark-moon, the only light on the hillside came from the tiny fire the stranger built. Having never before seen this man about whom he had heard so much, Josarian studied him with interest.

He didn't look like a swaggering fool now. His movements were smooth, fluid, and economical. His face as he stared into the firelight was serious and rather grim. It was a *shallah* face, no doubt about that. There may have been some Kintish blood far back in his line, as there was with many *shallaheen* born east of Darshon, but this was no part-*shallah* or Kint who had stolen the *jashar* of a true *shallah* and who happened to speak the mountain tongue. No, he was all *shallah*. The firelight left no doubt about that as it shifted across his sharp cheekbones and soaked into his wavy black hair.

The single, shiny, long braid he wore looked as strange as his foreign clothes—Moorlander clothes, Zim had said. Why would a *shallah* clothe himself so? But then, why would a *shallah* carry those swords? Here was a man of many parts, he guessed, the biggest part of which spoke of nothing but killing Josarian. The stranger held a palm over the fire, then turned it to study the scars in the firelight.

Seeing those scars sent a surge of fury through Josarian.

One *shallah* should not take money from the Valdani to kill another. It was worse than violating *lirtahar,* filthier than breaking a bloodpact, more despicable than stealing a man's wife. *Shallaheen* killed each other all the time, true; but they should never do so at the behest of the Valdani!

He had regarded this night's work as a job, a necessity, nothing more. But now a terrible anger filled him, and as he stared at this *sriliah* in the firelight, he knew that tonight, for the first time, he would *enjoy* killing. When he was done, he would fling the body off the cliffs above Islanar, right into the heart of the village, and he would make sure that everyone knew why he had done it: *So die all who betray their own kind; so die all who betray Josarian.*

EVER SINCE COMING home, Tansen had found that old thoughts were reluctant to be put away where they belonged. So he was still awake when Josarian finally made his move. Not that it mattered. The trap he had set was noisy enough to have awakened him the moment Josarian sprang it. It wasn't even a trap, actually; he'd just left his swords so precariously balanced that the slightest touch would bring them clattering down on the hard tiles of the ruined shrine. Judging by the indrawn breath and curse that had accompanied the noise, Josarian had cut himself, too.

The dark-moon had proved particularly convenient tonight. After dousing the fire, Tansen had simply set up the swords—a crude trick, but an effective one—where he'd been pretending to bed down. Then he'd curled up in a corner with his back braced against the shrine's only remaining wall. While he would normally never give an opponent such an opportunity to seize his swords, he knew that Josarian didn't know how to use them and wouldn't try. The outlaw hadn't taken swords from the bodies of any of the Outlookers he'd killed, and none of his victims had been killed with a blade. Josarian didn't yet think of a sword as a weapon that a *shallah* could use.

Considering how many days and nights Tansen made every move with the expectation of Josarian's imminent attack, he was relieved that it had finally come. Although obviously taken by surprise, Josarian realized it was a trap and regrouped quickly. Tansen heard the *yahr* making deadly sweeps through the air as Josarian moved in a continual circle, seeking his opponent on every side in the obsidian darkness. The sound, however, also let Tan know exactly where his quarry stood.

Having kept one of the shrine's broken tiles at hand for this very purpose, he tossed it lightly to the other side of the shrine. Josarian whirled in that direction, and Tan jumped him from behind, pressing the *shir* against his throat; hard enough to hurt, as even the briefest touch of a *shir* would do, but not enough to kill him. For the past ten days, Tansen had kept the *shir* tucked inside his clothing, close against his skin, day and night. Although he would have preferred sleeping with a venomous snake, the *shir* had proved convenient; the deadly sharp, double-edged, enchanted blade of a *shir* could not harm the flesh of the killer who possessed it—which, after all, could not be said of a venomous snake.

Despite the pain and the sudden fall to the broken tiles on the floor, Josarian fought back. So, with a sharp and well-placed blow, Tansen set the nerves of Josarian's arm on fire. When he was certain the arm was momentarily useless, Tansen groped for Josarian's *yahr*, now lying near a limp hand, and flung it away. Then he shifted and dug his elbow into those same nerves to keep the arm disabled. Josarian's harsh grunt of pain was followed by heavy breaths. Tansen waited, keeping the blade against his victim's throat.

"It was a trap," Josarian rasped. "It was always a trap."

"Always," Tansen confirmed.

To his astonishment, Josarian laughed. "You fooled everyone. You were very good. Only . . ."

"Only what?"

"It's not that I mind dying . . ."

Tansen had never known anyone, not even a *shatai,* who didn't really mind dying—but, strangely enough, this man sounded like he meant it.

"It's just that . . ."

"What?" Tansen prodded.

"It's just that I wish you weren't doing this for the Valdani." Then he sighed. "But I don't suppose you understand that. Zim doesn't. I don't know if anyone does."

"Oh?"

"But if only you hadn't done this for *them,* for the Valdani, well, then . . ."

"What?"

"I would honor you with my death."

"Why did you kill those two Outlookers the night you were caught smuggling?"

"They tried to kill me. I fought back."

"You must have resisted arrest."

"I did."

"Why?"

"It's hard to remember now."

"Try." Tansen let the *shir* draw a little blood.

"The *shir,"* Josarian croaked in sudden surprise. "They said you didn't take the *shir* that day."

"This is a different one."

"Fires of Dar! How many assassins have you killed?"

"More than I wanted to. How many Outlookers have you killed?"

"Not nearly enough." Josarian paused. "Go on, kill me now."

"You seem very eager to die."

"I'm not afraid right now. But if you keep waiting . . . Then I might *become* afraid." When Tansen didn't reply, he said, "Or is that what you're waiting for? Do you want me to beg for my life?"

"Not especially."

"Then what are you waiting for?"

"This is a little awkward," Tan admitted.

"You've killed men before. Plenty, according to your own boasting."

"Yes, but I haven't *spared* many." He felt Josarian stiffen with surprise and added, "I didn't realize it would take practice, like everything else."

Josarian was silent for a long time, lying as still as a corpse. Finally he said, "If you're not going to kill me . . ."

"Yes?"

"Could you stop digging your elbow into my arm? That hurts like all the Fires."

"A *SHIR?*" TASHINAR exclaimed. "Are you sure?"

"It goes with the symbol I showed you," Mirabar said. "They go together."

"They didn't before."

"They do *now.*" Mirabar tried to control her irritation. She, of all people, knew how hard it was to accept and understand the visions. "I'm not imagining it."

"I know."

"And I'm not mad. I'm *not.*"

"I believe you. Only . . . Don't tell this to the others, Mira. A *shir.*" Tashinar shook her head. "It will frighten them."

"It frightens *me.*"

"Yes, of course."

"I won't tell the others." They'd probably shun her. "It must be Armian."

"Perhaps."

"An assassin associated with a Kintish symbol? A *shir* linked to the Kints?" Mirabar looked at Tashinar. *"Armian."*

THEY BUILT A small fire—outside of the shrine this time, since it stank of sheep dung. Tansen wasn't quite ready to give Josarian's *yahr* back to him, but he did let him disappear to hunt up some firewood. While the outlaw was gone, Tansen sheathed his swords, strapped on his harness, and slipped the *shir* down the side of one of his expensive Moorlander boots. They had agreed to a truce, but trust was a different matter.

Josarian returned with the wood and made quick work of starting a fire. Once they had a tiny blaze to light the night, Josarian sat back on his heels and stared hard at Tansen. There was a strange look in his eyes, one that Tansen couldn't interpret.

So he finally asked: "What are you staring at?"

Josarian seemed to consider the question before finally answering slowly, "I've seen Dar spewing fire which filled the entire sky. I've seen precious gems stolen from the mines of Alizar, each one valued at more than a man's life by most reckoning. I've even seen the shade of my own wife greet me from the Otherworld." He paused. "But until tonight, I had never seen a *shallah* holding a sword."

Tansen watched him silently.

After a moment, Josarian smiled. "It's a sight that gives me strength. I have seen it now, and I will never be the same. Maybe someday . . ." He cleared his throat. "Someday you'll teach me how to use one?"

"Maybe someday," Tansen agreed, still watching him closely.

Seeing his expression, Josarian laughed out loud. "No, I won't ask for that *now,* with you expecting me to try to kill you again the moment your back is turned."

"Good." Tan sat down across the fire from him.

"Why didn't you kill me?" Josarian asked at last.

"Because the Valdani wanted me to."

"But you said—"

"I was trying to find you. Since I didn't think that anyone would tell me where you were, no matter how nicely I asked or how much I assured them that I didn't intend to betray you—"

"No, they wouldn't have, *roshah,*" Josarian agreed confidently; but his tone was inoffensive as he used the word.

"I thought it expedient to make *you* find *me.*"

"Ah." Josarian poked the fire with a stick. "So the Outlookers didn't actually hire you to come after me?"

"Actually, they did." Tansen grinned at the uneasy look Josarian cast him. He explained how he had found himself in custody back in Cavasar, robbed of his gold, and offered a choice between death or this contract.

"And you never intended to do this service for the Valdani?" Josarian asked, not looking quite convinced.

"Never." Tansen leaned forward, holding Josarian's gaze. "The Valdani slaughtered my entire village when I was fifteen years old. Every man, woman, and child." He kept his voice hard. Hatred was easier than sorrow. "They raped my sister before they killed her. They gutted my mother like one of their sacred goats. They gouged out my grandfather's eyes and cut off his fingers. They . . ." He stopped suddenly. After all these years, the details still made his heart bleed. "They did things that I see in my nightmares even now."

Josarian never looked away. "Where were you?"

"I was in hiding. I didn't know what had happened until I got there a day later and . . . found them like that." Tansen was the one who looked away. "But I was the one the Valdani were looking for."

"You? A boy? What had you done?"

"It wasn't really what I had done. It was what I had with me."

"I don't understand. They slaughtered an entire village because of—what? One boy's smuggling activities?"

"It doesn't matter now."

"Oh, I think it does, Tansen. You do not have the face of a man who has forgotten."

"What matters," Tansen said stonily, "what you need to know, is that I would rather be eaten slowly by a dragon-fish than do the bidding of the Valdani."

"Yes." Josarian nodded slowly. "That I believe."

"I won't kill you."

"No."

"Though if you try to kill me again," Tansen added, "I shall be very annoyed with you."

Josarian smiled, calm, at peace. "No. You gave me my

life, and you don't need to prove to me twice that you can take it whenever you want to." He touched his throat gingerly, then asked, "So this Valdani commander, he simply let you go?"

"Well, he kept my gold as ransom for my skills, but, yes, he let me go." Tansen absently touched a *shir* wound which had reopened during his struggle with Josarian. "Koroll saw what I wanted him to see: a mercenary who could be bought for the right price."

"As you showed me what you wanted me to see."

Tansen nodded. "Your first lesson, Josarian: never take anyone for granted, and *never* let pride lead you into a fight."

"You speak as if there will be more lessons."

"There may be."

"If you didn't mean to do this Valdani commander's bidding, then why did you come looking for me after you left Cavasar?"

"I've seen many things, too," Tansen said, studying the outlaw with an assessing gaze. "I've been to half of the Kintish Kingdoms, and I've travelled from one end of the Moorlands to the other. I've been to the edge of the Great Northern Desert, I've crossed the Sirinakara River, and I've even been inside the Palace of Heaven."

"What is that?"

"It's the forbidden palace of the Kintish High King." He continued, "I've killed men, and I've seen many killed. But until I reached Cavasar, I had never heard of a *shallah* fighting back and killing an Outlooker. Not since the Disarmament."

"Why should that matter to you?"

"Because I'm a *shallah,* too!" Tan said with more passion than he had meant to show. "Because the Valdani destroyed everything I ever loved, and because I've seen them doing the same thing all over the world." Uncomfortable with his companion's fascinated gaze, he rose to his feet. "We've been slaves to them for centuries. We used to be . . . A thousand years ago, this was the strongest land, the proudest people in the world, and now we bow down to the Valdani like beggars who are thankful for a lenient beating."

"You know, then," Josarian said on a whisper. "You *do* understand."

"When I was in Cavasar, I saw something I thought I would never see in my whole life. Koroll, that Valdani officer, with thousands of Outlookers under his command, with the weight of the Empire behind him . . . He's *afraid* of you. He's afraid of a single *shallah* who said *no.*"

"Who wouldn't bow down." Josarian rose to his feet, too.

"Who wouldn't run away." Their gazes locked and held in the flickering firelight.

"Or beg for mercy."

"Or go meekly to the mines."

"Who tells others to fight back, too."

"Yes. And he's so afraid," Tansen said, "that he half believes you can't be killed."

"Maybe I can't be. Not yet." Josarian grinned exultantly. "Maybe Dar Herself is tired of these Valdani and wants them gone."

"You and I can't get rid of them all," Tansen warned.

"No, but we can kill enough to count. Enough to make the Emperor pay dearly for holding Sileria."

"Yes." Tansen nodded and clasped the hand Josarian offered him, pressing their scarred palms together. "And I think I know where to start."

"Oh?"

"You haven't heard about what happened in Emeldar last night, have you?"

Fear washed across a face which had shown none until now. Josarian gripped Tansen's tunic. "My family? My friends? Tell me quickly."

And so he did.

THEY HEADED NORTH the next day by going straight up the side of Mount Orlenar, a trek that only *shallaheen* would attempt. They needed to move fast if they were to reach the fortress near Britar in good time to prevent the Outlookers from killing the men they'd taken from Emeldar.

"I'm almost sorry I got rid of Koroll's horse," Tansen admitted when they finally stopped for the night. Keeping pace with Josarian over these mountains was liable to kill him.

"A horse?" Josarian made a dismissive sound. "It couldn't survive the mountains, and I can't travel by road. I might be caught."

"I know."

"A horse is too easy to track, anyhow. If we had one now, *everyone* would know where we were." Josarian started gathering wood for the evening fire. "What did you do with it? Turn it loose? Let someone steal it?"

"I sold it to some traders who will probably take it all the way to Liron. Since Koroll thought I should take the damn thing, I saw no reason not to turn a profit from it."

Josarian grinned. "So now the Valdan will never know what happened to his horse. Or be able to find you."

"Yes, that, too." Why draw Koroll a map, after all? Sooner or later he would realize he'd been betrayed, but Tansen didn't have to make it too easy for him.

Josarian shook his head and mused, "A horse. He sent you to seek me out here on *horseback*. Ah, the *roshaheen* defy all reason, don't they?"

"Their latest scheme certainly seems to." Tansen assembled the kindling. "Why has Koroll had twenty men taken from Emeldar *now?* I still—"

"Oh, I don't think this Commander Koroll ordered it. He probably doesn't even know yet."

Tan glanced up at him. "Who, then?"

"A *toren* named Porsall."

The *toreni* were the traditional aristocrats and landowners of Sileria. Many Valdani had taken the title as well as the lands; Porsall was definitely a Valdani name.

"Oh? What did you do to him?" Tansen asked dryly.

"I stole some gold trinkets that had been in his family for two hundred years. They were very pretty, too. Pearl-studded, jewel-encrusted . . ." Seeing Tan's expression, he shrugged. "Well, why not? *His* family stole them from Silerians, after all."

"Why not, indeed?" Watching him curiously, Tansen asked, "And what did you do with this gold?"

"I gave it to the Sisterhood."

Tan blinked in surprise. "All of it?"

"Yes." Seeing Tan's expression, Josarian shrugged. "Well, who else would I give it to? They saved my life, after all, and they're less likely than anyone else to get caught melting it down and selling it off. The Valdani ignore the Sisters."

"I, uh . . . Yes. I see." Tan cleared his throat. "How did Porsall know it was you?"

"He saw me and asked who I was. I thought it would be bad manners to cast the blame on someone else."

"You robbed him *personally?*" Tansen asked in surprise. "A *toren?* There were no bodyguards with him?"

"Of course not." Josarian grinned. "He was in bed with his wife at the time."

Tansen laughed. "How in the Fires did you find your way into a *toren*'s bedroom?"

"Zimran told me how. He finds his way into the lady's bedroom every time the *toren* is away on business."

"By Dar, I wish I'd been there to see Porsall's face." The kindling blazed to life. Still grinning, Tansen started skinning and cleaning a hare that Josarian had killed that afternoon.

After several unsuccessful attempts to break a stubborn branch in two by stomping on it, Josarian turned and said, "Could you chop this in half for me?"

"I have no ax," Tansen pointed out.

"I meant with one of your swords." A moment later he laughed at the expression on Tansen's face. "When I was a boy, my mother once looked that way at a *zanar* who tried to convince me to go off to Darshon with him."

"Chop wood? With these?" Tansen's voice was rich with outrage. "These are among the finest swords in the world!" He unsheathed one suddenly, pleased to see Josarian jump back. "The steel of a *shatai*'s swords comes only from a secret source in the Stone Forest, guarded by sorcerers who are bound by holy oaths to the *shatai-kaj.*"

Josarian blinked. "Where? Who?"

"These blades were tempered in sacred fires, blessed in my name, and honored by the hands of my *shatai-kaj.* It's a sacrilege for anyone to even touch them without my permission!" He still burned at the memory of Koroll pawing them in Cavasar.

"I didn't mean—"

"When a *shatai* is killed, his swords must never be used again. Pilgrims are honor-bound to take them back to his *shatai-kaj,* who then returns them to the sorcerers of the Stone Forest."

Josarian looked at him skeptically. "You don't really believe that the Valdani honor such Kintish cus—"

"No." Tansen turned the blade so it shone in the firelight. "The Valdani keep such swords as trophies. Sometimes they display them, so that everyone will know they've killed a Kintish swordmaster. Sometimes . . ." His mouth twisted with disgust. "I've seen Valdani aristocrats fighting with a single Kintish sword. Fouling it with their hands."

"Only one sword?"

"They don't know how to use two. Only *shatai* do that." Tansen added, "I saw a Valdan try once. He cut himself to ribbons."

"I suppose it's harder than it looks," Josarian ventured politely.

Tansen's gaze flashed from his sword to his companion. He realized that Josarian's ignorant request had been made innocently enough and had certainly not called for a lecture on Kintish propriety. Embarrassed by his outburst, he sheathed his sword and said, "Here, you hold the wood, I'll jump on it."

Now that the subject had been introduced, however, Josarian was apparently determined to pursue it. "How did you become a . . . a *shatai?*" he asked, hesitating over the strange word.

Tansen waited for him to elevate the wood, then started stomping on a spot that looked vulnerable. "I saw a *shatai* for the first time in Kashala. It's a Kintish port city," he added.

"Yes, I know. I've helped Zimran smuggle goods shipped from there." Josarian put pressure on the branch, bending it as it started to give way beneath Tansen's assault.

"He . . ." Tan grunted as he drove his heel down again, and the wood gave way with a sharp crack. ". . . killed three armed men in less time than it's taken you and me to break this damn branch."

They each seized an end of the branch and started twisting it in opposite directions. The wood would make a good fire, and it was brisk atop Mount Orlenar tonight.

"Were they Valdani?" Josarian asked, dropping his half when it was free.

"The men he killed? No." Tan tossed aside the wood and brushed off his hands. "They were Kintish pirates who had raped a local girl. All of her father's relatives contributed money to hire a *shatai* to take them."

Josarian tended the fire while Tansen returned to cleaning the hare. "So *shatai* are like Society assassins, then?"

"No. We're warriors," Tansen said tersely. "We work for hire, and we do not swear allegiance to a waterlord or anyone else. My loyalty is to my *shatai-kaj,* my teacher. He's, oh . . . a kind of priest as well as a *shatai.* It was his duty not only to teach me to fight, but to teach me to use my skills with good judgment."

"But he doesn't tell you who to kill?"

"No. When the *shatai-kaj* decides he has taught you well enough, he gives you a test; some kind of mission or quest. Each *shatai-kaj* designs his own test, and each of his students must pass it with honor before he can become a *shatai.*"

"With honor?"

"Yes."

"What if a student is dishonorable?"

"It depends on what happened, what he did. Sometimes the *shatai-kaj* will kill him. Sometimes the next student will be tested by being sent to kill him. And sometimes the *shatai-kaj* will regard his student's failure as his own and kill himself."

"I take it you passed your test?" Josarian said dryly.

"Yes. I had a good teacher." Tansen handed Josarian the hare, which was ready to be spitted and roasted.

"And after a *shatai* passes his teacher's test?"

"He goes out into the world to live as a *shatai.*"

"And what else does a *shatai* do besides avenge abused women and promise to kill Silerian outlaws?"

"He encounters reality," Tansen admitted wryly. "He learns that in the real world, he has few chances to use his swords for good and many occasions where he may use them for evil—whether by mistake or through sheer greed. And believe me, Josarian, many people offer a *shatai* wealth beyond your dreams in exchange for the skills he possesses."

"Ah, no wonder we've never seen a *shatai* in these mountains before," Josarian said. "No money."

"*Shallaheen* enjoy killing each other too much to pay a *roshah* to do it," Tansen pointed out. "And as for professional killings, the Society would never tolerate the competition."

"We are a difficult people," Josarian acknowledged. "There's no denying it."

"Still, despite the expense, a *shatai* costs less than an assassin in the long run." Tansen stared into the fire. "Once you've paid a *shatai*, you owe him nothing and he goes his way. But once an assassin has done you a service, you are indebted to him forever."

Josarian balanced the hare's carcass over the fire. They

were too hungry to wait until the flames had died down to glowing embers, though the meat would have been better that way.

"The Moorlands, the Great Northern Desert . . . Why did you travel so far?" Josarian asked at last.

Tansen shrugged. "I was following the work."

"And you couldn't come home."

"No." No point in denying it. "I couldn't come home."

"Even a skilled warrior cannot escape a bloodvow from Kiloran himself. Not in Sileria."

"Nine years have passed," Tansen said stubbornly. "He must release me."

"But will he? What did you do to him?"

"Does it matter?" Tansen flashed him a quelling look, but Josarian didn't back down.

"It's been thought that perhaps you betrayed Gamalan to the Valdani," Josarian said quietly, "and that perhaps Kiloran cared about someone—or something—there."

Tansen felt as if he'd been cut with a *shir* again. This was an accusation so foul and degrading it had never even occurred to him. "Is that what Kiloran says?" he demanded harshly.

"Kiloran seems to be silent on the subject."

Hot with shame, Tansen asked, "Do you believe it?"

"No," Josarian said. "Not now."

Tan heard blood thundering in his ears. For a moment he smelled the stench of death again, remembered across the years. He again saw his mother's twisted corpse, her entrails streaming away from her belly in a river of blood. He saw his sister's eyes, staring sightlessly out of her battered face, her thighs bruised and defiled with Valdani seed. He saw his grandfather . . . Oh, Darfire, what they had done to his grandfather! Even now, not a day passed without Tan's thinking of the old man who had raised him and shaped his boyhood. Every prayer and curse he'd known, every secret and story, every skill and vice . . . all had been taught to him by that irascible old man before he died, slowly and in agony, at the hands of the Valdani.

"That anyone should think I had a hand in that . . ." Repulsed, Tansen swallowed and turned away from the fire. "Still, perhaps this is my due, considering . . ."

"What?" Josarian asked quietly.

"Considering what I *did* do."

Without another word, he left the fireside. He did not come back to eat, nor did he return to bed down near the warmth. While Josarian, a hunted outlaw, slept peacefully by the glowing embers that night, an honor-bound warrior sat alone amidst the barren, windswept rocks high atop Mount Orlenar and fought his demons in silence.

7

FIRE, THE FORCE which had given birth to Sileria, more powerful than anything in their world—except water. *Fire,* liquid rock churning in Dar's belly, streaming out of Her womb, bubbling up through a thousand orifices on the face of Darshon, flowing down its sides in slow-moving rivers of death and rebirth. *Fire,* spewing great fountains of glory and fury from the gaping maw atop the mountain, from the caldera at which the *zanareen* worshipped, from the glowing crater which was the gateway to ecstatic union with the goddess. *Fire,* becoming earth, air, river, and sky at the will of the goddess, and at the will of the Guardians, whom She had blessed with gifts beyond reckoning.

Forbidden to summon shades from the Otherworld while madness of her visions pursued her, Mirabar filled her days with the study of fire magic. Touched by Dar's favor, imbued with the very powers which had given life and death to these loved, hated, merciless mountains, she wove ribbons of fire through the air, shot daggers of flame into the night, and poured thick runnels of lava into the morning mist.

Sometimes it hurt. Sometimes the pain was unbearable, but she didn't retreat or withdraw. Honed in fire and fury, Darshon was greater, stronger, and prouder than all other mountains; and among the Guardians, Mirabar would be like Darshon—or she would die trying.

Sometimes she was frightened, terrified beyond what she should have been able to bear in sanity. She knew that Tashinar was afraid for her, too; knew that she took risks beyond all sense and reason. Guardians ruled fire, but they were not impervious to it. She herself had seen a young initiate lose control of her power and go up in flames, writhing and screaming in terrible agony as her own fire consumed her. She had seen an old sage weaken in a Calling and get pulled into the sacred fire, the gateway to the Otherworld, where his soul was lost forever to the dark oblivion that everyone feared would claim them at death.

Arms extended, fingers dripping molten lava, body burning with the strain, Mirabar flung spears of flame into the mountain stream where the Guardians had refined this year's gossamer harvest. The fire was doused. The lava sizzled and sank, tiny chunks of cold matter now. Disheartened and exhausted, Mirabar sank to her knees at the river's edge.

The Beckoner had shown her water the other day. She didn't know what it meant, other than apparently confirming her fears that her destiny was linked to the Society. *Water,* stronger than fire, as the sea-born folk claimed their god was stronger than Dar. *Water,* the medium through which the Honored Society had secretly ruled Sileria for a thousand years. *Water* . . . the element in which Mirabar could not sustain her own power.

How could she unite with the Society when any assassin or waterlord was likely to kill her the moment he saw her? The Guardians and the Society had been bitter enemies ever since the days of the Conquest, and no one had suffered more from their mutual hatred than Mirabar's kind.

She knew now from her visions how different the world had once been, how many more like her had once roamed these mountains, how very different her life might have been if the waterlords had never convinced the *shallaheen* that anyone with her coloring was an accursed demon who must be slaughtered on sight. A thousand years ago, she might have been a trusted advisor of the Yahrdan himself. Instead, she had grown up a *roshah* among her own kind, a starving, hunted orphan who was more animal than human when Tashinar had found her.

Now she was a *roshah* once again, for although the other Guardians in her group tried to be kind, she could already feel how far outside the circle of fire she was as a result of being excluded from the Callings. And the visions, yes, the visions set her apart—as they were intended to do. She knew now; she had guessed. The Beckoner was isolating her because he wanted her to leave the group, leave Tashinar. She didn't know why, and she didn't know where she was supposed to go, but she could see that the Beckoner was working to sever the strong bonds which kept her with the others.

She swallowed her terror, feeling tears mist her vision. She had never known safety in her entire life before becoming part of this circle. If she had ever known affection or the touch of one who cared before entering the circle, she couldn't remember it. For Mirabar, there was nothing but a demon's shadow life beyond the circle. How could she leave?

But she would. When the time came, she knew that if she didn't leave of her own free will, then the Beckoner would force her to. She had already seen enough to know he drew his strength from powers she could scarcely fathom.

Staring into the water, Mirabar blew a flame into her hand, then molded the fire into something thick and heavy. She turned her palm over and watched the liquid fire drizzle slowly into the river, stretching out from her palm like a fine strand of spider's silk, spiraling gracefully as it hit the water and sizzled into milky oblivion.

"Fire in water," she murmured. *Fire in water.* Why did the image haunt her so?

As she stared at the water, the fire she had dropped into it came suddenly, blazingly back into being. It snaked around, coiling, twisting, dividing, then came glowingly to life in a shape she had come to recognize, though she still didn't know its significance. As the strange Kintish symbol blazed beneath the fast-moving surface of the water, another image took shape with it, a water-born image which gleamed cool and silvery against the flames.

"The *shir* . . ." Again.

Fire in water.

Mirabar heard the Beckoner's voice. "How?" she asked. "How can fire be strong enough to—"

Fire in water. Find the shir.

"Is it his? Does it belong to the warrior?"

Find it and you find him.

"That's not what I asked," she snapped. She looked up. The Beckoner was on the other side of the river, his eyes glowing with orange fire, his skin shimmering with the light of the Otherworld.

Mirabar jumped to her feet, frightened despite herself. She still didn't know what he was, still didn't understand his nature or why he had chosen her.

"Is it Armian?" she demanded, wanting answers. "Is he the warrior I must find?"

Fire and water.

"Fire *in* water, fire *and* water . . . Which is it?" she demanded.

Fire and water. An alliance.

"I'm having a little trouble convincing the others," she pointed out sourly.

Find the Alliance.

"There *is* no—"

The world turned sideways as the river rose to engulf her, fire and water combining to sweep her into a terrifying vortex which consumed all her strength. She couldn't control her screams, couldn't defend against the pain, couldn't master the horror she felt.

Through the haze of fear, as the fire turned to ashes and the water turned to blood, she saw him again: Daurion, the Yahrdan with whom their freedom had died centuries ago. Through the mist of agony, she saw him raise his sword, a gleaming weapon that reached across the sky. And just before the icy waters of the river sucked her down into the domain of wizards and death, she saw him swing his blade . . . and smash the Sign of the Three.

TANSEN'S LONG SILENCES didn't bother Josarian overmuch, since he liked to talk and didn't mind the lack of competition. He quickly recognized, however, that the *shatai*'s silences were highly selective. When questioned, he seemed willing enough to talk about the strange lands he had been to, the incredible things he had witnessed, the wars of conquest being fought all around the Middle Sea, the erotic sorcery of Kintish courtesans, the strange and savage customs of the hairy Moorlanders, or the arduous training of a *shatai*. It was only when asked about himself, his past, his family, his connection to Kiloran, the origin of the *shir* which he now kept hidden inside his satchel, or the silk scarf in which it was wrapped that Tansen responded with a silence that could chill the air at midday in high summer.

This, of course, only had the effect of making Josarian pursue these subjects with the tenacity of a Valdani priest collecting tribute goats.

"You never mention your father," he said to Tansen as they sat down for a brief rest in the shade, less than half a day's walk from Malthenar.

"You never mention yours. Water?"

"Thanks." He drank briefly from the goatskin water-pouch Tansen handed him, then said, "My father died of fever. Four years ago. My mother died a few years before that."

"May the Otherworld welcome them," Tansen said politely.

Undeterred by the cool silence which followed, Josarian asked, "Is your father alive?"

"No."

"When did he die?"

Tansen's nostrils flared slightly. "When I was still in swaddling clothes."

"How?"

"Bloodfeud."

"With the Sirdari clan." It was not a question.

Tansen looked at him in genuine surprise. "How did you know?"

"They were my wife's clan." He glanced unconsciously at the marriage mark on his palm, remembering the sure feel of the blade slicing through his flesh, remembering how Calidar had bit her lip as she marked him, worried about hurting him.

"No widow mark," Tansen observed.

"I'm Calidar's husband," Josarian said. "Alive or dead, it makes no difference to the vows I swore at her side." He wondered if his companion would shake his head, as Zimran did; urge him to put his loss behind him and choose another woman, as Jalilar did; or scoff and jovially assume he'd eventually get over this sentiment, as men in the local *tirshah* did.

The warrior's dark eyes lost some of their chill. The forbidding expression relaxed a bit. He nodded, as if Josarian's response were perfectly reasonable. After a moment, he said, "No wonder you don't fear death."

"She waits for me there." His voice was soft, his heart flooded with a sudden loneliness.

"If you believe that—"

"It's true," Josarian said. "I've seen her." Seeing Tansen's skeptical look, he repeated, "It's true." He told him about the Guardians on Mount Niran, and the old woman who had summoned Calidar's shade from the Otherworld. "It was *her.*"

Tansen rose to his feet and resumed their trek. "A year after my brother threw himself into the volcano, my mother took me with her to a Guardian encampment where we offered them smuggled Kintish cloth in exchange for a Calling."

This was the first voluntary comment the *shatai* had made about his family since the night they'd met. Josarian prodded, "And?"

"She claimed she saw my brother in the circle of fire, but I saw nothing."

"Not everyone sees the shade in a Calling," Josarian pointed out. "Only the person who—"

"Perhaps some see exactly what they *want* to see."

"And perhaps some want to see nothing there," Josarian countered.

Tansen glanced briefly at him. "The Guardians are powerful."

"Indeed they are."

"Perhaps powerful enough to make a man believe he sees—"

"I *did* see—"

"But the *Guardian* spoke to you, not the shade. Yes?"

"Yes, but they were Calidar's words, and I *saw*—"

"Sorcerers who can blow flames from their mouths and pour fire from their hands . . . Who's to say they can't control what you think you see in the fire?"

"Tashinar never knew Calidar. She couldn't have spoken so much like her. Those were my wife's words that night."

"Then may Calidar welcome you when you journey to the Otherworld."

"She will." Josarian's eyes scanned a mountain pass far below them, keeping an eye out for Outlookers. "And then we will be together again." Satisfied that there were no riders in the pass, he glanced again at Tansen. "But you don't believe that, do you?"

Tansen shrugged. His long, gleaming, black braid hung down the middle of his back as he turned away and kept walking. If nothing else, Josarian reflected, the still-mysterious *roshah* no longer expected an attack from his companion. Tansen had returned Josarian's *yahr* the morning after they'd met; it was now tucked securely into Josarian's *jashar*. He followed Tansen along the precarious path skirting the side of the jagged mountain.

"The Guardians can't explain why not everyone goes to the Otherworld," Tansen finally responded.

"The journey is long and arduous."

"I've heard of weak, old, lecherous *sriliaheen* being Called every single year by some relative," Tansen pointed out, "while there are strong young men who died in a rockslide and have never once appeared in the circle of fire."

"Maybe the bodies weren't burned." Everyone knew that a corpse must be purified through fire. "Maybe that's why—"

"No." Tansen shook his head. "If it were that simple, that consistent, we would know."

"So do you believe everyone goes into oblivion?" Josarian asked curiously. Being a mercenary who constantly risked his life in combat must be terrifying to one who didn't believe in the Otherworld, or who at least doubted he'd get there.

Tansen slowed his pace and looked down at the scars on his right palm, the ones made by relatives when a baby was named and when a child became an adult. "I don't know," he said at last. "I hope not."

"Where do you think *you'll* go?" Josarian persisted.

"I think . . ." Tansen glanced into the distance, to where Darshon rose majestically above all other mountains. "I think Dar may want me for Herself."

It wasn't a boast, Josarian realized. "For punishment?" He would have asked what Tansen had done, but he knew the warrior wouldn't answer him.

The moment was over. Tansen shrugged again, then turned away and increased his pace until even Josarian would have been hard pressed to find breath for more conversation.

TANSEN WATCHED THE road outside of Malthenar while Josarian descended into the village's narrow, winding streets to get food and information from the home of some bloodpact relations. After four years of travelling alone, Tansen found the outlaw surprisingly easy company, despite his frequent questions about things Tansen had no intention of discussing with anyone. Josarian's comments also showed a quick mind and an intuitive understanding of human nature. He was intensely curious about the world beyond these mountains, too, and those were questions which Tansen didn't mind answering. It was useful for a *shatai* to be able to put clients and potential allies at ease with a ready supply of good stories, and although he wasn't a particularly talkative man by nature, Tansen nonetheless had a *shallah*'s natural ability to tell a tale.

Although he had learned a lot about Josarian while pursuing him, he was still surprised by the qualities of the man with whom he had now joined forces. He hadn't expected to like him so well. He'd been quite prepared to put up with an embittered, headstrong, and willfully ignorant sheepherder if necessary, as long as the man continued harrassing and terrifying the Valdani and encouraging others to do likewise. While looking for Josarian, Tansen had simply thought of him as a particularly effective outlaw in a land of hopeless slaves. He had not expected what he found: a visionary.

It was in Josarian's voice whenever he spoke of Sileria, his village, his family, the injustices he had seen, and the moment he had chosen a path of violence and rebellion. He wasn't just raiding supply posts and murdering careless Outlookers. No, he had sworn a bloodfeud against the Valdani—he'd shown Tansen the fresh scar on his left palm.

A bloodfeud could last for generations; whole clans could be wiped out. It was the sort of custom that had made Sileria so easy for the Valdani to conquer. Yet it was, conversely, also a source of immense strength. Men who had declared a bloodfeud could be fearless, merciless, committed beyond all sense and reason to slaying their enemies.

A bloodfeud against the Valdani. It was an extraordinary idea, one that went beyond anything Tansen had considered while watching a nervous Valdani commander sweat in Cavasar. Upon seeing how one lowly *shallah* had managed to strike terror into the hearts of the Valdani and encourage the citizens of Cavasar to riots, unrest, and civil disobedience, Tansen had thought only of joining the outlaw, of keeping him alive as long as possible. The Outlookers would commit their immense resources to destroying Josarian; but a man protected by a *shatai* was hard to kill. The longer Josarian stayed alive and active, the more damage he would do to the Valdani in this district.

However, Tansen had mostly been thinking in terms of finding a role for himself now that he had finally returned home. He couldn't fulfill the role his youth had prepared him for. He had changed too much for that; too much had happened since those days. Besides, a *shallah* was nothing without his family—a mere outcast, a *roshah*—and his people were all dead. So, after all these years, he had also seen an opportunity for revenge. No matter how much he had changed, he was *shallah* enough to still want revenge for what the Valdani had done to his family. *Shallaheen* treasured revenge.

Yet even so, until he'd met Josarian, Tansen had never glimpsed the scope of what Josarian saw. *A bloodfeud against the Valdani.* Something never-ending, something which would last for generations. Something which would survive even after their two heads decorated the spiked gate of some Outlooker fortress. A dream wherein *shallaheen* would still be shedding Valdani blood long after he and Josarian were dead.

It was a dream worth coming home for, worth living

for, and it would be worth dying for when the time came—as it surely would. They were only two men, whereas Koroll had thousands of Outlookers under his command. But at least Tansen and Josarian might be able to last a long time, do considerable damage to their oppressors, and leave a legacy for others to follow after their deaths.

A *bloodfeud.* He had never expected to swear one again, but tonight he would slice a Kintish blade across his left palm and bind himself to Josarian's cause.

JOSARIAN RETURNED WITH food, wine, clean clothes, information about Outlooker movements, and an extra *yahr* that his late father's bloodbrother had given him.

"Kintish petrified wood," Tansen noted, examining the *yahr.* "This blooduncle of yours is an assassin?"

Josarian shook his head. "His son. Killed ten years ago in a bloodvow."

A bloodvow was sworn against an individual rather than a whole family, clan, village, or sect. Bloodvows were usually the provenance of the Society and the work of its assassins.

"Kiloran offered to apprentice him—the assassin—to water magic, in exchange for betraying Baran," Josarian said. "Baran found out about his betrayal and killed him."

"Who's Baran?"

"Ten years ago he was just another waterlord. Now he's Kiloran's greatest rival." Josarian nodded toward the north and added, "They've been fighting for control of the Idalar River since before my wife died."

"That was always Kiloran's," Tansen said, surprised.

"Not anymore. Nor is it Baran's yet." Josarian led Tansen away from the village, treading more carefully now that it was nearly dark. "Last year, Baran froze the river all the way from Illan to Shaljir."

"The city must have been frantic," Tansen guessed. The large, dense population of Shaljir relied heavily upon the Idalar River for its water supply.

"The *toreni* and merchants of the city sent tribute to Kiloran, which he kept, even though he couldn't do anything about the river."

"Naturally."

"Then Kiloran flooded Baran's entire native village in retaliation." Josarian described how the floodwater had simply stopped flowing when it reached the edge of the cliff upon which the village was perched, halting as if it had run up against a wall. "Water as high as a man's waist, enough of it to cover the entire village, and it just . . . *stopped* at the cliff's edge. Stayed there for nearly a whole season before both waterlords moved on to other methods of battle."

"No wonder Kiloran wanted Baran killed," Tansen mused.

"As he wants you killed."

"He can't flood my village. It's gone."

"Have you any family left anywhere?"

"No. They were depleted pretty thoroughly by the bloodfeud that killed my father."

"Calidar's family, too," Josarian murmured. "I knew some of them. A waste of good men."

"Yes," Tansen agreed. "By the time I was born, I don't think any of them really remembered why it had started."

"And now we're starting another one," Josarian pointed out.

"It should have started centuries ago."

"Yes." After a moment, Josarian said, "I can never go back, Tansen, but you—"

"I can never go back, either."

"Then . . ."

"Together we will look forward." He looked down at his left palm. "I'm ready."

They found a place to camp. Tansen ate the food Josarian had brought back from Malthenar for him, while Josarian built a modest fire. Then Josarian pulled out his small skinning knife.

"I'll use this," Tansen said, unsheathing a sword and holding its blade over the fire.

"All right, but I'll use my own knife."

"What for?"

Josarian met his gaze. "I would like to ask you to become my brother. Will you honor me, Tansen?"

"Bloodbrothers? *Us?*" Tansen didn't even try to conceal his surprise. It was not a commitment to be undertaken by men who'd only known each other a few days, and Josarian knew it.

Josarian nodded without hesitation, despite Tansen's less-than-flattering response to his proposal. "You have no family at all. No one to trust. No one even to burn your corpse when you're dead."

"I've managed for nine years without—"

"But you're *here* now. You cannot be one of us again with no relations at all."

"You know that Kiloran is after me," Tansen warned. "How safe will any new relation of mine be?"

"About as safe as any relation of mine." Josarian added, "I do have a family, but they don't know where I am. I may die in Britar and never see them again. I would rather die with a brother at my side."

"And if we both live," Tansen said, "you'll be stuck with a bloodbrother you scarcely know."

Josarian smiled. "I know you, Tansen. I don't know what you've done, why Kiloran wants your life, or what you fear from Dar, but I know *you.* Some men's honor is in their faces, and their courage is like a banner." He nodded. "I know you well enough to swear a bloodpact with you."

A *shatai* didn't need anyone after his teacher had sent him out into the world; but a *shallah* couldn't exist without belonging to the complex web of commitments which defined who was to be trusted and who was not. A *shallah* was nothing without his kin.

Tansen looked across the fire at the man whose throat still bore the wound he'd made with the *shir* the night they'd met. Josarian was a little fairer than Tan's people had been, his build taller and heavier. His dialect, like that of everyone in these parts, sounded a little drawling to Tansen's eastern ears. Had either of their lives been normal, they would never even have met.

"If I am really to come home," Tansen said slowly, "then I will need a brother, won't I?"

"Yes."

Their eyes held until Tansen made his decision.

"Then will you honor me, Josarian?" he asked formally.

Josarian grinned broadly, but responded with equal formality, "It is I who am honored."

When both of their blades were blessed by fire and glowing with heat, Tansen drew his across his left palm in a deep, curved line following his lifeline; one cut for the two vows he would swear tonight. A *shallah* who could not do this to his own flesh without crying out was not considered a man. He held his hand over the fire, watching the blood drip down to sizzle on the hot coals and become one with the flames.

"I swear by Dar, by my honor, and by the memory of my slain kin," Tansen began, reciting the traditional words of a bloodfeud, "your enemies are now my enemies, and I will not rest or be at peace until the blood of every Valdan in Sileria flows as mine flows now."

Josarian carved a similar deep, curved line into his own left palm, then held it out to Tansen. Golden light flickered on their faces as their hands joined above the fire in a tight grip. Their blood mingled, then spilled out of their tight clasp to drip into the fire, marking them before Dar and the Otherworld as being of one blood.

Having already removed their *jashareen*, they now wrapped them around their joined hands, binding them together. Their mingled blood seeped from their handclasp to stain some of the strands of each man's *jashar*, a permanent alteration in his identity, another sign of the lifelong brotherhood he now swore.

"I swear by the souls of my dead parents and by Dar

Herself," Josarian vowed, "to trust you as a brother born of my own mother. I swear by my honor and by the memory of my wife that you may trust me and rely upon me as a brother of your own mother's womb."

Tansen swore his vows in the same steady, clear voice, promising trust and absolute loyalty. They each recited their own family lines as far back as they could, then vowed to protect each other's families, should the need ever arise.

At the end of the ceremony, Josarian prayed to Dar, asking for Her blessing. They couldn't see Darshon on such a dark night, but they knew which way to face. Unable to pray, Tansen bowed his head respectfully and listened to his brother in silence.

TANSEN APPROACHED THE fire where Josarian sat. He held out his left hand. "I don't suppose you brought anything from Malthenar I can wrap around this till it stops bleeding?"

"We'll shred your clothing and use that," Josarian said.

Tansen eyed him skeptically. "And what am I supposed to wear?"

"Something that won't stand out so much." Fumbling one-handed with the bundle he'd begun unpacking earlier, Josarian pulled out a simple tunic, oft-mended but clean. "With the weather getting warmer, you'll only be hot in those Moorlander clothes, anyhow."

"Yes, but shredding my clothes? The weather will get cold again, you know."

"Ah, but who knows if we'll live long enough for that?" Josarian grinned at him. "And if we do, I'm sure someone will give us more clothes."

"These clothes were made to last," Tansen protested. "Do you have any idea what they cost me?"

"I thought you said that money came easily to a *shatai*," Josarian reminded him, thrusting the old garment at him.

Tansen accepted the bundle with a resigned expression.

"It does, but my money was all stolen by a Valdan, if you recall."

"One who will be alert for any description of you when you fail to show up with my head."

"True enough," Tansen admitted. He eyed the traditional *shallah* clothing with some disfavor, for he had grown accustomed to finer things. The material was rough homespun and the design such that it would fit a variety of men—and fit them all rather badly. However, he knew the Josarian was right. It was no longer desirable to be so noticeable; here in the mountains, he stood out as much as Koroll's horse would have. "All right," he agreed at last, "I'll wear them." He removed his harness, unlaced his tailored, embroidered tunic, and pulled it over his head.

Josarian drew a sharp breath. "By all the Fires! Who did *that* to you?"

Seeing the direction of his bloodbrother's horrified gaze, Tansen looked down at his chest. "Kaja did it. My *shatai-kaj.*" Since Josarian still looked horrified, he added, "It's just my brand."

"Someone *branded* you?"

"It's a mark of honor, Josarian." He held up his scarred right palm. "Like these."

"What does it honor?" Josarian peered at the symbol which had been burned into Tansen's chest.

"When I had passed my test and my teacher declared me a *shatai,* he marked me as one." Tansen traced the symbol with his forefinger. "These two crescents are for the new moons. The sorcerers of the Stone Forest, who made my swords, are said to be most powerful when Abayara and Ejara are both ascending. The marks symbolize the power achieved only by the union of mind and body, spirit and flesh, heaven and earth."

"And the mark between them?"

"It's a Kintish hieroglyph."

"A what?"

Tansen smiled. "It's like a Kintish *jashar,* in a way."

"Then what does it say?"

"That I'm a *shatai*."

Josarian considered this. "The *shatai* must be very brave," he said at last, "to agree to have this burned into their flesh."

"They all have five years to get used to the idea." Tansen added blandly, "Assuming they survive the training, that is."

He removed his boots, then pulled off the finely made Moorlander leggings that fit like a second skin. With regret, he handed the garments to Josarian, who thriftily packed away the tunic for possible future use before ripping into the leggings with his skinning knife. Tansen pulled on the mended tunic Josarian had given him. He settled it over his torso, hips, and thighs, then dragged his braid through the neck of the garment.

As he did so, he realized he'd need to get rid of the braid, too, if he was to disappear into the hills as an ordinary *shallah* now. The oiled braid which fell past his waist was common enough in most of the Kintish Kingdoms, but it looked strange here. Wryly remembering how strict his *kaj* had been about personal grooming, considering him an untidy barbarian when he'd first arrived, Tan made a silent apology to the old man, then cut off the braid just past his shoulders.

Josarian watched him toss the gleaming rope of woven hair into the fire, then wrap his throbbing hand in strips of soft material from his shredded leggings.

"Now you look like a *shallah*," Josarian said with approval. "Now you've come home."

8

THE *SHALLAH* WHO walked down the long, dusty road leading to the old fortress outside of Britar that evening looked disappointingly ordinary, at least in the opinion of Myrell, the Valdani captain who'd had the initiative to imprison twenty of Josarian's friends and relatives a few days ago. The approaching stranger didn't look like someone who could kill two Outlookers with his bare hands, and he certainly didn't look like a man who couldn't be killed. If this was Josarian, then he looked like any other Silerian peasant, despite all the stories spreading about his courage and prowess.

Toren Porsall, a Valdan despite the ridiculous Silerian title, had come directly to Myrell with a complaint about the murdering, thieving villain. So Myrell—who understood these barbarians better than his thin-blooded superiors in Cavasar and Shaljir ever would—had taken immediate and brutal measures to deal with the situation.

If the Outlookers couldn't find Josarian, then they could at least turn his own people against him by making them suffer because of him. Once the Valdani started executing these prisoners because Josarian wouldn't turn himself in, the *shallaheen* wouldn't continue being so loyal to him. No, indeed. Myrell had seen the way these peasants turned on each other with only the slightest provocation. He'd seen the lust with which they pursued their bloodfeuds and the reverence they showed to assassins. Savages like these would need only a nudge to turn them against Josarian, and then they'd be so eager to kill him that the Outlookers wouldn't need to keep trying.

If Josarian didn't turn himself in, that is. Myrell now

stood on the parapet walk above the main gate, watching with immense satisfaction as a lone *shallah* approached the fortress. Surely this had to be Josarian. Time was running out for the outlaw if he wanted to die a martyr rather than be hounded by his own kind. The sun was setting, and tonight would be the last dark-moon before Abayara renewed herself and appeared again as a glowing sliver in the sky. Tomorrow night, the Outlookers would begin slaughtering their prisoners, one per day, if Josarian didn't turn himself in.

Capturing Josarian was, of course, a better course of action for Myrell than simply letting him be murdered by other *shallaheen.* Even if his commanders knew that Myrell's bold move had been the seed of Josarian's destruction, they would still take the credit themselves if he were slaughtered by his own kind. But if Myrell actually captured the outlaw, if he could bring Josarian's head to Cavasar, or even Shaljir . . . Who knew what kind of glory would be his as a result?

Myrell made the Sign of the Three and prayed that the approaching stranger was indeed Josarian, come to save his friends and relatives from certain death. It seemed an unlikely sacrifice for a *shallah* to make, but there was no denying that they could be as blindly loyal as they were bloodthirsty and vengeful.

The stranger stopped perhaps two hundred paces from the main gate. His shaggy black hair hung past his shoulders, unkempt and ungroomed. He wore the rough, homespun clothing of most *shallaheen,* and his left hand was lightly bound, as if he'd cut it—or sliced it open for one of those barbaric Silerian blood rituals. Myrell could see he was a young man, tall, slim, and straight-backed. He seemed to match the description they had of Josarian.

The stranger looked up at the ramparts where, in anticipation of his approach, some thirty archers stood at attention. He called out, in lightly accented Valdan, "Who is the commanding officer here?"

"I am: Captain Myrell. Who asks?"

"I do, obviously."

"Who *are* you?" Myrell asked pointedly, ready to signal his archers.

"Toren Porsall sends you his greetings, Captain."

Myrell hesitated. "You're one of Porsall's men?" A *shallah?* It seemed unlikely. Valdani aristocrats let *shallaheen* plant their vast fields, harvest their crops, build their roads, and tend their livestock, but they seldom let them rise to the trusted ranks of their bodyguards and personal servants.

"No," the stranger replied with a grin. "I am merely Porsall's host at the moment."

"Explain yourself, *shallah!"*

"Upon hearing that you had taken twenty *shallaheen* into custody, I thought it prudent to take a Valdani *toren* into custody before—"

"What?"

"—coming here to discuss how we might resolve this awkward situation."

"You've abducted a Valdani aristocrat?" Myrell sputtered in fury.

"Surely you know it's an old Silerian custom," the impertinent *shallah* replied. "It's how the Society keep themselves in luxury when tribute is slow in coming."

It was indeed an old custom among these wild people. Even now, with the pressure the Emperor had brought to bear upon the Society, it was still not uncommon for *toreni* and wealthy merchants—Valdani, Silerian, and foreign— to be abducted by the Society, held until a ransom was paid, and murdered if it was not. Indeed, the custom was so firmly established that many potential victims even paid a ransom upon merely receiving a message suggesting that if they simply paid *now,* then the ransom demanded would be less than if they forced the Society to go through the expensive procedure of the actual abduction. It was no bluff; anyone who refused was simply abducted anyhow. But Myrell had never heard of a mere *shallah* attempting an abduction.

"Who helped you?"

"I didn't need help. Any more than I needed help to get into his bedchamber and steal his gold."

"*Josarian,*" Myrell said with conviction.

"No one but me knows where Porsall is, Myrell. If you kill me now, he'll die where I've left him. And it will be your fault."

"*I* will not be held responsible for—"

"Won't you, when I've just explained the situation to you in front of so many witnesses?"

"I demand proof of this ridiculous claim!"

"I thought you'd say that." Advising the thirty archers aiming right at him not to be nervous, Josarian unfolded a small bundle he'd been carrying and held it up.

Myrell stared in perplexity for a moment before saying, "A bloodstained tunic? That's your proof?" His tone was scathing, but he was shaken.

"*Porsall's* tunic." Josarian lowered the shirt and examined it himself. "Too bad about the blood, but he was a little difficult to abduct, I'm afraid."

"I want to examine that tunic!"

"By all means, Captain. Would you like to come out here and join me?"

Myrell ignored the gibe and ordered a detachment of eight men to ride out of the gate to collect the tunic for examination.

TANSEN WATCHED FOUR Outlookers ride back into the fortress, carrying his once-immaculate Moorlander tunic with them. Besides being dusty and mended, it was now liberally stained with blood from the wound he'd reopened on his left palm: a little something to reinforce the fiction of Porsall's violent capture.

The other four mounted Outlookers remained with him. He had strapped his sword harness to his bare torso beneath the humble tunic he now wore. He had readjusted it so that both swords were sheathed against his back, the lump of their hilts concealed by his shaggy hair.

Now he just had to stall long enough to give Josarian the time he needed. When the fortress gate reopened to admit the four Outlookers carrying his tunic, he was encouraged by what he glimpsed within; a considerable number of men seemed to be preparing for his capture.

After examining the tunic, Myrell called down, "This is Moorlander workmanship, *shallah!* Do you take me for a fool?"

"Moorlander? Really?" Tansen asked without interest. "Does that matter?"

"Do you seriously expect me to believe it belonged to a Valdani *toren?*"

"I wouldn't know about the fashions worn by Valdani aristocrats, Captain," Tansen called back. "But since the *toren* gets all of his horses from the Moorlands, perhaps he favors their garments, too."

Myrell paused to consult with someone, then shouted down, "You'll have to do better than this, Josarian!"

"Perhaps you should send some men to Porsall's estate to confirm that he's missing," Tansen suggested.

"It's nearly dark," Myrell pointed out with open irritation. "It would take my men half the night to get there."

"That's hardly my fault."

"*All* of this is your fault!"

Tansen grinned. Counting the minutes, he judged it time to make his move. "I'll come back tomorrow, Myrell, and hope that you're prepared to be more reasonable then."

"You're not going anywhere!" Myrell screamed down to the Outlookers surrounding Tansen, "*Stop him!*"

Tansen moved to keep the mounted Outlookers between himself and the archers on the ramparts. Using the speed he'd spent years developing, he reached behind his back and inside the loose collar of his tunic to unsheath his swords. He killed one Valdan with a quick slit of the throat, then dispatched another with an upward thrust through the belly and into vital organs before the remaining two Outlookers realized what was happening. Then, enacting the part of the plan that he absolutely hated, he swung himself up onto one of the horses in full view of thirty archers, urging it into a gallop before he was more than halfway mounted. The sickening whine of arrows hummed all around him as he rode away from the fortress at top speed. The fletching of one brushed past his cheek. He lay against the horse's neck, hearing the pounding hoofbeats of the two Outlookers who followed close upon his heels. One of the archers had the wit to aim for the horse, and the beast squealed and plunged as an arrow pierced its hindquarters. Tansen shouted and ruthlessly walloped it with one of his swords, desperate to keep it running until he was out of range of the archers. If that arrow was poisoned, he had only a few moments left.

Sure enough, the horse began staggering just a few moments later. A dose of poison meant to kill or disable a man might not kill the horse—or at least not quickly—but the animal couldn't keep functioning. Hoping they were far enough away from the fortress by now, Tansen tugged on the reins, slid from the horse's back, and turned to confront the two Outlookers who were in hot pursuit. One of them cried out and fell when a stray arrow took him in the back; his horse kept running. Tansen estimated that he was now far enough from the fortress that only bad luck would make him the victim of an arrow at this range; unfortunately, he believed in bad luck.

He couldn't wound the oncoming horse of the remaining Outlooker, since he'd need it to escape from the mounted Valdani now pouring out of the fortress. He stood his ground, ducking the Outlooker's attack and letting him live to make another one, and another one after that. When he thought the horse had slowed down enough that he had a good chance of catching its reins when he killed its rider, he made his move. A deep slash across the Outlooker's sword-wielding wrist disarmed the man, and a quick thrust tumbled him from the horse. Tansen mounted the animal and, turning to make sure that the Outlookers wouldn't lose sight of him, he headed for the escape route he and Josarian had plotted out last night.

*   *   *

JOSARIAN HAD CLIMBED the far northern wall of the
fortress and crept across the roof of the barracks while
Tansen had stood talking outside the fortress gate, keeping
the attention of most of the Outlookers firmly fixed there.
He'd then managed to sneak into the garish little Shrine
of the Three where he'd forced a Valdani priest to tell him
where the *shallaheen* were being kept. Then, with the ruthlessness that had been born in him the night he'd become
an outlaw, he strangled the sobbing priest with his *yahr*
rather than risk discovery.

He looked down at the twisted body, wishing he could
return all the goats the priest had stolen from people who
needed the milk, cheese, and meat to survive.

After stealing the priest's robe and concealing the body,
he hid inside the shrine, waiting for the crowded fortress
to empty out when the Outlookers pursued Tansen through
the mountains and straight into the deadly trap he had chosen the night before: a long-forgotten Kintish quarry, abandoned centuries ago. Dozens of men galloping straight into
that after sunset were not likely to survive. Josarian just
hoped Tansen would be able to direct his own mount into
the concealed hiding place they had constructed near the
pit last night. Who was to say that a horse—maddened,
confused, unpredictable, and painfully stupid—wouldn't
ignore its rider's commands and simply plunge straight
ahead to certain death?

However, Tansen insisted that he had learned a great
deal about horsemanship from the Moorlanders and wasn't
worried about that aspect of the plan. Tan thought he was
a lot more likely to be killed by Valdani archers. If that
happened, he'd warned Josarian, the only chance to free
the hostages would be while the Outlookers were swarming all over his corpse, and it wouldn't be a particularly
good chance.

Although locals estimated that half the Outlookers
posted to this fortress were currently searching the countryside for Josarian, there were still nearly one hundred

men inside the fortress. That was far too many for Tansen and Josarian to fight; nor could the two of them sneak the prisoners past such high walls and so many men. So they'd hit upon a plan to make most of the Outlookers leave the fortress—by convincing them they were chasing Josarian, the solitary outlaw who was considered the only threat to this stronghold. Since Josarian didn't know how to ride a horse, and since the hostages were unlikely to respond with alacrity if freed and ordered to fight by the *roshah* who had come to Emeldar announcing he intended to kill Josarian, Tansen would have to pose as Josarian at the gates of the fortress.

They had studied the fortress and the surrounding area for a full day before developing their plan. If Josarian could free the twenty hostages, he estimated that the *shallaheen* would still be outnumbered by two-to-one even after Myrell ordered the majority of his men to go out in pursuit of the man he believed was Josarian; bad odds for unarmed men, but the best odds that could be offered by two men attempting to attack a Valdani fortress.

Hiding inside the shrine, he heard the sudden commotion outside: shouting, orders, panic, swords rattling. Tansen had made his move! Josarian risked peeking outside. Judging by the speed with which the Outlookers were racing frantically around, buckling on their sword belts, shouting for their horses, and galloping out of the main gate, it seemed that Tansen had successfully escaped the archers. Josarian said a brief prayer of thanks; no one wanted to lose a brother so soon after gaining him. Then he donned the hooded robe of the Valdani priest and slipped outside.

The hostages were being kept in a dungeon beneath the guarded command chambers. Never having seen the interior of the fortress, Josarian and Tansen had reluctantly concluded that once Josarian was inside, he'd simply have to rely on quick-thinking and whatever luck came his way. Now, as chaos reigned all around the command center, Josarian, dressed as the hooded priest, walked right past guards who were too confused and excited to pay any attention to him.

Once inside the building, he avoided speaking to anyone; his Valdan wasn't all that bad, but he definitely didn't sound like a native speaker, let alone an educated priest. He descended the steep, winding stone stairs described by the priest, going deep into the underground chambers carved out of solid rock. Two guards stood at the end of the passageway at the bottom of the stairs. There was a locked wooden and iron gate behind them; beyond that lay the prison cells. Even had the priest not described everything for him, Josarian would have known he was approaching the dungeon now; the stench of sweat, urine, excrement, and centuries of human misery filled the air down here.

He saw the iron keys to the heavy gate and the prison cells hanging on the wall, just as the priest had said they would be. He decided that with all the noise overhead, no one would hear what happened way down here.

He walked toward the guards. At the very moment that they realized there was something strange about him and grew alert, he pulled a *yahr* out of each voluminous sleeve of the robe and attacked. He struck the nearest guard across the face, momentarily disabling him. He used the moment to break the other Outlooker's wrist while the man was drawing his sword. He turned and quickly killed the first one with two skull-shattering blows, then tripped the second one as he attempted to run away. He picked up the Valdan's fallen sword and, handling it awkwardly, slit his throat.

Swords. Tansen had told him—had fiercely *insisted*— that since he couldn't smuggle twenty *yahr* into the fortress, he and the hostages would have to fight with any weapons they could take away from the Outlookers.

Swords. He looked down at the Valdani blade in his bloodstained hand. It felt heavy, strange, and clumsy, but . . . by Dar, he had never guessed how easy it was to kill a man with a *sword!* Silerians were only permitted to own bladed tools such as skinning knives, axes, and sickles. Neither Josarian nor any Silerian he knew—except Tansen—had ever even touched a sword, let alone wielded one to kill a man. No wonder the Valdani had disarmed Sileria after conquering it! They could never have so thoroughly subdued a people armed with such weapons.

Heart pounding, he picked up the other dead man's sword, grabbed the heavy key ring on the wall, and chose the one most likely to fit the elaborate lock on the gate. He unlocked it, hung back for a moment in case there were more guards on the other side, then rushed into the dank corridor lined by prison cells. It was lit only by two heavily smoking lanterns, one at each end of the corridor.

His brother-in-law Emelen was the first man to peer through a tiny iron grid in one of the doors to see who had entered their domain. *"Josarian!"*

"Josarian?" asked a muffled voice behind Emelen.

"Where?" came a voice through the grid on the door facing Emelen's.

"Josarian!" someone cried farther down the corridor.

"Quiet," he ordered as more familiar faces pressed up against the tiny grid of each of the dungeon's six heavy prison doors. Horror engulfed him at the thought of his friends and relatives enduring the past few days in this sunless, airless, fetid hole. He started pushing keys into the first lock, desperate to get the men out of here, even if only to die in the open air as they attempted to escape the fortress. "I don't want the Valdani to hear us. We haven't much ti— Ah!"

The lock turned, the door opened, and Emelen and two other men poured out of the cell. Josarian handed Emelen one of the swords, picked it up when his bewildered brother-in-law dropped it, and ordered him to *use* it. Then he gave his two *yahr* to the two other men and started unlocking the next door.

"Keep an eye out!" he ordered. "If any Outlookers come down those stairs, let them come all the way down, then take them by surprise. Kill them and take their weapons. *Take* their swords."

Attempting to swing the sword like a *yahr*, Emelen nodded and led the other two armed men down the dark passageway. Three more prisoners burst free from a cell as Josarian unlocked the door. They spread his instructions from cell to cell as Josarian attacked the next lock with his keys.

"Lann," he said, upon freeing a boyhood friend, "make sure everyone knows the plan. We kill everyone upstairs first, get as many weapons as we can before we go outside. That's important: *Get their weapons and use them.* Do you understand me? And the archers are still up on the ramparts and will fire when they realize we've escaped, so watch out for them!"

"Right, Josarian!"

Another door opened. Josarian moved on to the next one. "Set the supply building on fire. Set everything that can burn on fire—give them plenty to worry about besides us."

He opened another door. More men poured into the corridor. Josarian finished in a rush, "As you leave the fortress, go off in all directions, no more than two or three men at a time. Make them split up to chase us. Don't go home, it's the first place they'll look. We'll all meet tomorrow night at the Dalishar Caves." It was an ancient holy site, famous among Silerians; even hunted men who'd never been there before should be able to reach it by this time tomorrow.

He unlocked the final cell and was shocked by what he found there.

"Zim!" His cousin's pretty face was bruised and battered, his tunic was torn and covered in dried blood, and he held his left arm at an awkward angle. "Zimran . . ."

One of Zimran's eyes was swollen shut, but the other sparkled with excitement. "What took you so long, cousin? I was supposed to meet a lady two days ago."

*   *   *

TANSEN HAD NEVER liked relying on horses when his
life was at stake, but this one was holding up well. If he
lived, maybe he'd even keep it. He led the Outlookers
through a series of winding passes, some of them quite
steep with sheer drops on one side. As sunset turned to
night, he slowed his pace accordingly so that he wouldn't
lose the Valdani who followed him.

A scream in the distance made him suppose that some
Outlooker's horse had misstepped and sent him hurtling to
his death. That made one less that Tansen had to kill.

He wondered if Josarian had succeeded in freeing the
hostages—and if he were even still alive. Their plan lacked
precision. They were too uncertain of what lay beyond the
high, forbidding walls of the Valdani fortress. A better plan
would have been for Josarian, who knew these mountains
so intimately, to lead the Valdani on this chase while Tansen, who was more likely to survive close combat with so
many Outlookers, infiltrated the fortress, but the circumstances made such a plan impossible. Now he could only
carry out his part of the scheme and hope that his bloodbrother—his *friend*, he realized with surprise—survived.
He wouldn't know until he reached the Dalishar Caves.

He continued following the path Josarian had guided
him over last night, keeping an eye out for the landmarks
his friend had pointed out for him to memorize. Numerous
trails and paths intersected, crisscrossed, and parallelled
each other along this route, and choosing the wrong one
at any moment would mean he'd miss the abandoned Kintish quarry and fail to execute the plan. If the Outlookers
following him either caught him or gave up and turned
back, then they'd be free to pursue the escaped hostages
once they returned to the fortress and learned what happened. The fewer Outlookers that were searching for them,
the better chance the *shallaheen* had of disappearing and
reaching safety.

If Tansen made a mistake and missed the quarry, he
could still elude a pack of clumsy Valdani in the mountains
after dark, but he'd let down Josarian and the hostages.

These thoughts weighed heavily on his mind as he reached a three-way fork in the path that he was sure hadn't been there the night before.

Which way? he wondered, hearing the Outlookers behind him.

Stay calm. Think it through. A *shatai* was cool in combat, clearheaded in danger, free of emotions which shackled lesser men to failure and death.

The path looked wholly unfamiliar. Had he taken a wrong turn earlier? Surely Josarian wouldn't have failed to point out this three-way junction to him. Surely he himself wouldn't have overlooked it last night. What was wrong? Why didn't he know which way to go?

Which way, *dammit!*

He heard the jingling of bridles as the Outlookers came over the rise at his back. He dismounted and examined his choices on foot, hoping this more familiar perspective would help him recognize or remember something. The sound of men and horses grew louder as his pursuers drew near, and even in the dark, he knew he had only seconds before they spotted him.

Which way, Josarian? Which way?

MYRELL WAS OUTSIDE, issuing orders to another search party when he heard angry shouting from inside the command building. More annoyed than alarmed, he ordered two Outlookers to go inside and stop whatever brawl had erupted among his men when there were far more important matters to attend to.

It was only after he had issued the order that some vague alarm stirred inside him: nothing even as strong as suspicion, merely an uneasy feeling that something wasn't quite right. He finished instructing the search party, then turned to follow his men into the command building and put his mind at ease about the situation there. Faced with the excitement of pursuing Josarian, everyone had momentarily forgotten about the prisoners, who had been the focus of—

He stopped in his tracks, horrified beyond thought, as

twenty *shallaheen* poured out of the big, elaborately carved door of the command building and raced down the broad stone steps, their shaggy black hair absorbing the light cast by the newly lit lanterns. Myrell barely had time to realize they had escaped before a new and even more appalling fact struck him: *They were armed.* Swords flashed in some of their hands, striking out at the first two Outlookers the mob encountered at the bottom of the steps.

Swords! Where, by the mercy of the Three, had the prisoners gotten *swords?* And how had they escaped? Josarian was somewhere out there in the mountains, with over half of Myrell's men chasing him. Who had freed the prisoners?

He drew his sword as the swarm of barbarians split up to attack, shouting in their thick-tongued native language, baring their teeth in savagery as they launched themselves at their astonished captors. An unarmed man flew into him, striking his sword aside with . . . No, *not* unarmed! Myrell had seen a weapon like this once before, a couple of sticks joined by a piece of rope. He struck at it with his sword as it swung toward his head, then made a thrust at his opponent. He missed, but then managed to slash the man's face.

The man jumped back and stared at Myrell with fierce dark eyes, circling him and swinging his childish weapon wildly between them in a series of loops. Myrell had removed such toys from a number of detainees over the past couple of years, including some of the prisoners he now faced in combat. It had amused him to learn the *shallaheen* placed great value upon their pathetic bundled sticks and seriously believed they could defend themselves, and even kill a man, with such a device.

It didn't seem nearly as amusing now, when the thing came flying at his face. If he hadn't ducked, it might have broken his nose! How had the prisoners gotten out of their cells? What had happened to the guards? He realized with a chill of shock that the prisoners must have killed everyone inside the command building. How else could they have gotten their hands on the swords many of them carried? How else could they have seized the wooden weapons which had been confiscated and left carelessly lying around?

Only a few of Myrell's archers remained up on the ramparts. There was little they could do up there after sunset except act as sentries. Besides, in the confusion that had followed Josarian's escape, Myrell had ordered most of them to fill other posts left vacant by the men he had sent out after the outlaw. The archers who were still up there would be trying to pick off the prisoners, but they'd be reluctant to fire into the fray; the *shallaheen* and the Valdani were too closely intermingled for a safe shot. Even worse, the peculiar fighting style Myrell observed in his opponent made him a difficult target for an archer, even at this close range, for he kept circling and circling Myrell; if an archer got off an arrow, he'd risk missing the ever-moving target and perhaps even hitting one of his own men. If all the *shallaheen* were as slippery as this one, the archers wouldn't be of much help where they were. Myrell had to kill this man quickly so he could order the archers down into the combat area to fight.

He lunged hastily and missed. The swinging stick caught him on the side of the head. He was shocked at how much it *hurt*. When he looked up, another blow caught him right across the nose; he heard it break before he felt the pain. He backed away and stumbled. The *shallah* pushed him down, and the searing pain crashing down on his skull was the last thing he knew before he passed out.

JOSARIAN WAS THE last man to escape the fortress, fighting awkwardly with the sword he held in one hand and more skillfully with the *yahr* he held in the other. Somewhere during the fighting, he had taken the *yahr* from the gutted corpse of a *shallah,* then set the dead man's clothing on fire with the same torch he'd used to ignite the supply depot next to the shrine. He prayed that the *shallah* would burn, the fire purifying him for the journey to the Otherworld.

Knowing that he must escape now or die here, too, he fled through the main gate and into the darkness beyond. He kept to the shadows, eluding the Outlookers who were already regrouping from the battle to hunt down the escaping prisoners. Seeing that his wounded cousin was in no shape to fight, Josarian had ordered him to get outside the fortress walls before anyone else. Now he was startled to hear Zimran's voice in the shadows.

"Josarian! Over here!"

He found Zimran in the dark. "Damn you! I told you to get away!"

"I didn't want to go all the way to Dalishar without knowing if you'd escaped."

"And if they catch me now, they catch us *both.*"

"Then I suggest . . ."

"Let's go!"

Since Zimran's legs still worked well enough, they were able to cross the open ground around the fortress fairly quickly. They heard thundering hoofbeats behind them, but the direction kept changing, and the riders' shouts gave clear evidence of their confusion. On a twin-moon night, he and Zimran would have been easily spotted as they headed for the lemon groves east of the fortress, but no one saw them tonight. Once they reached the trees, full of shadows and hiding places, they were safe.

They didn't pause to rest, however. They needed to be well away from here by morning. They moved silently through the night, always alert for any sounds of pursuit. After they believed themselves to be well out of reach of danger, exhaustion kept them quiet, and only their will kept them going.

They had gone east upon leaving the fortress and must now circle to the south to reach the Dalishar Caves. Josarian wondered if Zimran, with his injuries, could keep up the pace. Before long, his question was answered. Zimran started losing strength rapidly, moving slowly and stumbling often as they ascended through a heavily wooded forest in the dark.

"We'll rest here," Josarian said upon finding a fallen tree trunk to lean against.

"No. I can . . ."

"No, you can't."

Josarian saw the vague shadow that was his cousin suddenly sink to the ground. Unable to see his expression, he reached out to touch his skin, checking for fever. Zimran's forehead was burning hot and drenched in sweat.

Zim slapped his hand away. "I'll be fine in a minute."

Josarian said nothing. He followed reluctantly when his cousin, breathing harshly, rose and continued their trek through the syrupy darkness of the forest. As he expected, it wasn't long before he heard Zim stumble and crash to the ground, crying out sharply and then falling silent. Moving with mountain-born instincts, Josarian found his cousin's still form in the dark. Zimran had fallen on his injured arm, and the pain had apparently combined with the exhaustion and the fever to push him over the edge into unconsciousness. While this certainly didn't make matters any easier, it at least relieved Josarian of the burden of hearing him suffer so.

Cursing the Valdani who had done this to Zimran, Josarian hauled his cousin's deadweight off the rough ground and slung him over his shoulders. His legs quivered briefly in protest as he continued his steep uphill climb, then they obeyed his will with weary resignation. Doubting that he could carry Zimran all the way to Dalishar, at least not without more rest than he had time for, Josarian started trying to figure out where he could safely deposit him between here and there. The nearest Sisters were in the other direction, and with Zimran on his back, he couldn't go there and still reach— He stopped abruptly when he heard a noise up ahead. There shouldn't be anyone up here, especially not at this time of night. Every nerve in his body tensed as he strained to hear another telltale sound. He'd been crashing through the forest noisily, convinced he was

well beyond the reach of the Outlookers. He hadn't considered the other dangers he might face tonight: bandits,
mountain cats, a lone assassin or waterlord on some secret
business . . .

He listened intently, silently cursing the darkness, praying that Zimran wouldn't suddenly groan or shift his
weight. After a moment, his patience was rewarded: He
heard tentative footsteps, moving stealthily. Whoever was
here knew that he was here, too, and was coming for him.
He was just about to deposit Zimran's body on the ground
so he'd be ready for combat when a torch appeared out of
nowhere, flaring in his face, startling and momentarily
blinding him.

"A *shallah?*" It was the voice of a man, surprised and
suspicious.

Keeping his sword between himself and the stranger,
Josarian stepped back and twisted away. He heard the
stranger gasp in surprise as the light fell on Zimran's unconscious face.

"Who's that? What's wrong with him?"

"My cousin. He's been injured."

"He's been *beaten.*" There was a pause. "Outlookers?"

"Yes."

"Of course." The voice sounded more assured now. "If
it had been an assassin or another *shallah* he'd be at home
with his wife or mother, or perhaps in a Sanctuary. But
not being hauled up the side of a mountain in the middle
of the night."

"A good guess," Josarian said cautiously, squinting
against the glowing light, unable to distinguish the dark
form beyond it.

"And you, I see, have killed an Outlooker." The voice
sounded educated, but not foreign. "Unless you're going
to claim some Outlooker simply *handed* you his sword?"

"Who are you?" Josarian stepped to one side, trying to
see past the flames.

"Not a Valdan." The voice was dry now. "Don't worry."

"Your torch is in my eyes," Josarian said tersely.

"You still haven't told me who you are, *shallah.*"

Even as the words were spoken, Josarian's vision finally adjusted enough for him to see that the light came directly from the man's palm, flames soaring up from human flesh.

"A Guardian?" he said suddenly, relieved.

"Yes. And if you've brought Outlookers upon us for some petty crime . . ."

"They haven't followed me here," he said with certainty, "and my crimes . . . aren't petty."

"What have you done?" the faceless Guardian demanded.

"I've just freed twenty prisoners from the Valdani fortress at Britar."

He heard the Guardian's sharp intake of breath. "You're *him,* aren't you?"

"Word spreads fast," he observed cautiously.

"*Josarian.*"

"Yes," he admitted, taking the risk. "Can you help me?"

The flame wavered for a moment, then the hand from which it emanated swept to one side. Josarian looked into the stranger's face. The firelight flickered and shimmered on Silerian features: about his age, intelligent, aristocratic looking. The man's dark hair was braided in the intricate style of a *toren.*

The two men gazed curiously at each other. It took Josarian a moment to realize that the flame-colored glow of the stranger's eyes was no illusion of torchlight, but the glowing fire-gold gaze of a demon.

9

REMEMBERING MIRABAR, THE half-mad but
harmless girl from the Guardian encampment on Mount
Niran, Josarian held his ground, smothering the superstitions of his kind.

"Who are you?" he asked evenly, his gaze dropping to
the silver brooch—the Guardian insignia of a single flame
within a circle of fire—that the demon wore on his cloak.
Silver. Like everything else about the man, it suggested he
had come from a wealthy family. He was no *shallah*, that
much was clear.

"I am Cheylan. My circle of companions is not far from
here."

"Why are you alone out here?"

"Messages from the Otherworld," Cheylan said vaguely,
"telling us we must be ready."

"For what?"

"We don't know, but we've been posting sentries in the
woods. We thought it might be an attack by the Society . . ." The demon flashed a smile. "But here you are."

"Then you'll help me?"

Cheylan nodded. "Of course."

"I need someone to care for my cousin until I can return
for him."

"Come with me."

"I must warn you . . ."

"Yes?"

"Outlookers will be searching for him."

"Naturally."

"They'll want him back. They'll want him very badly."

Cheylan glanced briefly at Zimran's unconscious form. "I promise you they won't find him."

There was a fierceness in the vow that made Josarian believe him. He nodded, convinced. "Then take me to your circle, Cheylan."

WATER, WATER, A house of water.

Weary and bewildered after another sleepless night, Mirabar wandered away from her circle of companions early in the morning to stare into the depths of the spring they had camped near a few days ago. Indeed, since coming to this site, she had done little *but* stare into the depths of the cool spring, transfixed by it, pulled here by the Beckoner—and desperately frustrated by the calm, unspeaking surface of the water.

Fire in water.

Fire and water.

Could the Guardians and the Society really unite? After a thousand years of enmity, was it possible?

She flinched when she heard voices approaching, then relaxed when she realized it was only Derlen and his son. She had never felt much warmth for Derlen, a fussy, perpetually worried man. She liked him even less now that he had convinced the others to exclude her from the Callings, making no secret of his fear that her visions came from an evil source. But despite disliking him, she had to admit that he was an attentive and patient father to his inquisitive son—a duty which seemed to be aging him fast.

"But why did Marjan betray Daurion?" young Turan now asked as father and son approached the other side of the spring. Mirabar sat in thick, high grass with her knees close to her chest, her head bowed, and her gaze fixed on the water, hoping they wouldn't see or bother her. "Weren't they both Guardians? Weren't they bloodbrothers?"

"Yes, that's right," Derlen said, coming to the water's edge and sitting down. He had brought a fishing pole with him, some elaborately carved thing acquired from the sea-born folk. As he spoke, he baited the hook and tossed it into the water. "Marjan and Daurion were brothers in blood and brothers in the circle of fire. They were raised together, initiated together, became men and warriors together."

"Then why did Marjan betray him?"

Today's lesson was an important one, Mirabar realized as she sat quietly in the tall grass and listened.

"The Yahrdan died, and when the Council of the Guardians met in Shaljir, they chose Daurion as the new Yahrdan."

"To hold Sileria with a fist of iron in a velvet glove."

"Yes," Derlen said, clearly pleased. "And Daurion was a great Yahrdan, a man of wisdom, courage, and conviction."

"What about Marjan?"

"He served as Daurion's right hand, as the Yahrdan's most trusted servant and advisor. They were as close as they had been all their lives. But . . ." Derlen frowned and continued, "Secretly, Marjan was discontent with his position. After all, he had served Sileria all his life, just as Daurion had. He had always fought as bravely as his bloodbrother. The Otherworld welcomed his Call as warmly as it welcomed Daurion's."

"So why had Daurion been chosen by the Council instead of him?"

"That's *exactly* what Marjan wondered." Derlen checked the fishing line, then shook his head. "When the Guardians chose a Yahrdan, they didn't chose him just by the length of his service, the strength of his arms, or the brightness of his fire. The Yahrdan was the most important, powerful man in Sileria, the ruler of all the people of this great island. He must not only be the strongest and most able of men, but also the wisest, able to rule with ruthlessness tempered by great compassion, able to judge all matters impartially regardless of his own personal needs and desires, willing to put the welfare of even the lowliest *shallah* before his own comfort and safety."

"Even a *shallah*?" Turan repeated doubtfully.

Mirabar rolled her eyes. Now *that's* the spawn of a merchant family talking, she thought derisively.

"Yes, Turan," Derlen said firmly. "The Guardians knew that in order to lead the disparate peoples of Sileria, a Yahrdan must love each one of them more than he loved himself; and Marjan loved *no one* more than himself."

"But Daurion . . ."

"But Daurion was such a man. Daurion was everything a Yahrdan should be."

"But he failed," Turan protested. "A Yahrdan should be a great warrior and powerful—"

"He *was*," Derlen pointed out. "He repelled the Moorlander invasions again and again, slaughtering those barbarians as they fled for the open sea, holding this island as he had sworn to do, slaying our enemies without mercy or fear."

"Until Marjan betrayed him."

Derlen sighed. "Yes, until then. For Daurion loved Marjan dearly, and so he didn't see the evil right in front of him. Marjan knew that he could never defeat Daurion in single combat or with fire, but there was another element even stronger than fire, one over which Daurion had no control."

"*Water.*"

Mirabar could hear the eagerness in Turan's voice. They were getting to the bloody part of the story now. Little boys were all such savages.

Derlen told his son how Marjan stumbled across the ancient mysteries of water magic, an art previously lost in the mists of time and only vaguely recalled in the ancient cave paintings and cliff carvings of the Beyah Olvari, the strange race which had peopled Sileria before passing into legend eons ago. Somehow Marjan discovered the secrets of those long-dead half-human water wizards, and he used every spare second of his time to study and secretly practice this powerful magic, forsaking fire magic entirely in favor of the new force he had discovered.

In time, when he felt strong enough, Marjan took advantage of Daurion's love and trust to destroy him. To a people who had always known fire as the most powerful substance in their land, the battle between these two giants was horrifying, signaling the end of the world, for neither Daurion's sword nor his fire could combat the voracious waves which one night suddenly rose up from the Idalar River to flood the palace in Shaljir. Though the city itself was untouched, the palace was entirely submerged. Water formed thick masks over the faces of courtiers who tried to flee, drowning them even as they stumbled away from the palace. Translucent monsters took shape out of the waves, spreading slender tenctacles to entwine and strangle all those who stood and fought. Daurion's great spears of flame and rivers of fire were dousced as easily as the ocean extinguishes a single candle. And so the last great Yahrdan of Sileria died that night in Shaljir, murdered by one he had trusted.

Chaos followed Daurion's death and the destruction of the palace. When loyalists resisted Marjan's attempt to seize power, he curled the Idalar River back upon itself and starved Shaljir of water for so long that most citizens were forced to abandon the capital. They fled in great numbers, migrating south, east, and west, abandoning one of the world's greatest cities, inciting confusion and terror as they spread their tale throughout the land.

As the Guardians united against him, Marjan recruited a mercenary force of brutal assassins, arming each man with a *shir,* the water-born weapon he had invented which was useless to an assassin's enemies—unless they killed him and took it from his corpse. Together with his assassins, Marjan seized control of whole regions. The remaining ruling families of Sileria splintered into disenfranchised factions incapable of leading their people. And then the Moorlanders came again.

This time the Moorlanders swept across Sileria in the war which came to be known as the Conquest, the war which forever turned Sileria into a vassal state of the great kingdoms surrounding the Middle Sea.

"Marjan survived the Conquest," Derlen told his son. "Not only survived, but became so powerful that the Conquerors found it easier to deal with him, cooperate with him, than to fight him. And to protect his own power, he taught the Conquerors to hate the Guardians, particularly those people who could be instantly identified as being especially blessed by Dar—"

"Like Mirâbar," Turan said.

"Yes," Derlen said slowly, "like Mirabar. Anyone whose appearance identified them as destined for the circle of fire was persecuted by the Conquerors at the urging of the so-called Honored Society. The Kintish, of course, were a more sophisticated and tolerant people. So, after they claimed Sileria as their own two centuries later, the Society changed their methods. Marjan's successors taught our own kind—our own kind, Turan—to hate and hunt anyone whose powers the Society feared. Someone like me or Tashinar, we are only dangerous after initiation, if we prove to have the gift. Someone like Mirabar, though . . . They know from the moment she's born that she will be powerful. From the time she is an infant, a gifted person like that is the Society's enemy: hated, feared, persecuted, and hunted." He held his son's gaze. "Mirabar and others like her are Dar's greatest gift to us, and we must never forget that. There are very, very few like her left, and they are all in mortal danger every day of their lives. All because of the Society."

Derlen paused. Sitting as still as a deer scenting hunters, Mirabar was startled to feel a hot tear roll down her cheek.

"This is how the waterlords became your enemies, son." Derlen's voice filled with fire. "And this is why we can never trust them, why we must oppose them every day of our lives, until we drive them out of Sileria. *Forever.*"

Mirabar was on her feet before she had even realized she intended to rise. Startled by her sudden appearance, Turan jumped up just as quickly. Derlen's face went blank with surprise as she stalked closer to them, tears streaming inexplicably down her cheeks.

"Yes, they are our enemies," Mirabar said, hearing how low and hoarse her voice sounded. "And no one—*no one* has more to fear from them than I do."

Derlen rose slowly, watching her with wary concern. "Mirabar, why are you—"

"But they are born of *us*. They are part of Sileria, too!"

"No, they are—"

"I tell you *we need them,*" she screamed, her insides churning with helpless frustration, fury, and fear.

"Don't you shout at m—"

"Do you think I *want* to unite with the Society? Do you think I *want* to go in search of a waterlord?" She gasped, startled to realize for the first time that that was precisely what the Beckoner expected of her. "Do you think I expect to live through this?"

Derlen said nothing now, gaping at her in stunned silence.

"The Valdani," Mirabar rasped. "It is the *Valdani* who don't belong here. It is the Valdani whom we must drive out of Sileria, now and forever! They are our worst enemies! They will destroy Sileria, taking everything from us to fuel their wars, to conquer the whole world!" She flung ribbons of fire into the air to punctuate her words, ignoring the way Turan flinched. *"No one* has ever been as dangerous as they have become, not even the Society!"

Derlen's city-born complexion was turning even paler than usual. "How can we trust the Society? How can we possibly—"

"I don't know! Don't you think I've asked?" she cried. "Don't you think I've *begged* for an answer?"

"You can't go in search of a waterlord. You *can't,* Mira."

Her fire collapsed in on itself, sizzling into a stream of black smoke. Her fury drained slowly as she finally stopped fighting her destiny.

"I have to." She bowed her head. "I didn't ask to be

born this way. I didn't ask to be sent visions from the Otherworld." She looked at her throbbing hand, absently noting she'd burned it in her careless rage. "But the circle of fire is the only place in this entire world for someone like me. I'm a Guardian because I can be nothing else, and I serve the Otherworld because there is no other life for my kind."

"I never thought . . . I mean, I've always envied you your gifts," Derlen said haltingly.

She had enough strength left to be surprised. That anyone in the three corners of the world should envy *her* . . . "How strange," she murmured. Her thoughts scattered like petals in a storm, and she said unthinkingly, "He was like me, you know."

"Who?"

"Daurion."

Derlen swallowed. "You've seen Daurion?"

"Seen him?" She nodded. "Yes, I've seen him. And I think it very likely that I will soon die for him." She turned away.

"Mirabar?"

She paused. "Yes?"

"Where will you go?"

"Yes, I must go, mustn't I?" she said vaguely, realizing the time had come.

"How will you find a waterlord?"

"I don't know."

"Which one will you look for?"

"The greatest one, of course. Marjan's legacy to us. Harlon's successor." She nodded. "I must find Kiloran."

IT WAS WELL after dark by the time Tansen, travelling on foot, reached the Dalishar Caves. He'd spent all of last night playing hide-and-seek with fifty Outlookers after losing his way on the path to the old Kintish quarry. Now a sentry spotted him as he approached the first cave at Dalishar, then relaxed upon seeing he was a *shallah*.

"I'm Tansen," he said, keeping his hands in sight and

coming close enough to the other man's handheld torch for his *jashar* to be easily seen.

The man nodded. "He's expecting you." He called ahead to warn another sentry, and Tansen was directed to go to the fourth chamber of the third cave.

The place was a marvel, as Josarian had promised him it would be. An ancient holy place, the caves were lit by perpetual Guardian fires, breathed into life eons ago. Many of the interior walls were covered with paintings made by the Beyah Olvari, whom most people believed had been extinct for centuries beyond reckoning. Easily guarded and blessed with good lookout points, the caves were readily defensible. Moreover, considering how thoroughly uninterested the Outlookers were in *shallah* religion and traditions, it was doubtful they even knew of the existence of this place. Yes, the escaped prisoners should be safe here.

The interior of the caves was a darker, richer shade of the honey-colored stone that made up the surrounding mountains. Fresh spring water bubbled up through several sources, neglected by the Society for centuries. His blood-brother couldn't have chosen a better spot for them to hide out in.

Another sentry stood at the entrance to the fourth chamber. He stopped Tansen with a Valdani sword. "I know your face," the man said slowly, "but I don't know you."

Tansen heard Josarian's laughter a moment before he saw him. "No, don't stab him, Emelen! It's *him:* Tansen!"

Josarian pulled Tansen into a rib-crushing bear hug, held him away to look at him, then hugged him again. Now feeling as embarrassed as he was tired, Tansen pulled away.

"I was worried," Josarian told him. "Everyone else got here hours ago. I was starting to think maybe they'd caught you. Or perhaps the horse—"

"No, I'm fine. There was just—" He winced as Josarian grinned and slapped him hard on the back. "That's *right* where my arrow wound was," he pointed out.

"Ah, as long as there are no *new* wounds!" Josarian slung an arm around his shoulders and dragged him into the next cave. "Come! I have told them all about your exploits, and they've been waiting to meet you."

"Wonderful." Josarian hadn't been present when Tansen had fouled his name with vile insults in the *tirshah* in Emeldar. Josarian hadn't seen the look in men's eyes there that day. Tansen was dubious that he was about to be welcomed as warmly as his brother suggested.

Sure enough, there was an awkward silence as he entered the midst of more than a dozen *shallaheen*. Josarian proudly introduced him to the men. The atmosphere didn't warm up appreciably. Tansen stood his ground. A *shatai* never asked for acceptance. These were Josarian's people, not his.

One of the men stepped forward. Tansen vaguely recognized him; no doubt he'd been at the *tirshah* that day. He was a big man, even bigger than Josarian. His face was bearded, an unusual trait among smooth-faced Silerians, one that usually indicated Moorlander blood somewhere in a man's ancestry.

"I'm Lann," he said in a booming voice. "My mother's brother married Zimran's mother, which makes me Josarian's cousin by marriage."

Tansen nodded, acknowledging the claim.

"I remember you, *roshah*," Lann continued. "I remember your foreign looks and your cruel words. I remember what you said about my cousin."

"And if I had said I was a friend? If I had asked you to help me find him?" Tan challenged.

Lann nodded, his expression uncompromising. "He's right. I wouldn't have helped you find him. In fact, I'd have gone to prison to stop you." Suddenly, he grinned. "So either way, I guess you'd have had to break me out of there."

He laughed and slapped Tansen hard on the back—right where Josarian had. Tansen hoped the wound was too well healed by now to reopen.

"It was my pleasure, Lann." He looked around and saw other grinning faces. Apparently everyone appreciated the joke. "It's not that I mind freeing prisoners from a Valdani fortress, but it *is* a lot of work. I suggest we all agree to stay out of prisons from now on."

The laughter surprised him, as did the wineskin another friendly soul thrust upon him. Someone had had the wits to get supplies from a Sanctuary on their way here. After taking a long swallow of some fairly good strawberry wine, he received a dozen more slaps on the back, making his previously forgotten wound throb in angry protest. Every man offered his name then, but there were too many for Tansen to keep straight in his exhausted condition. He noticed that no one wore a *jashar* and was told that the Outlookers had taken them away.

"Lest we use them to strangle our guards," Emelen, Josarian's brother-in-law, said.

"Or hang ourselves!" Lann added in disgust. "The ideas these Valdani come up with!"

Suicide was anathema among all the peoples of Sileria. Even the *zanareen* disapproved of intentionally self-inflicted death. A *zanar* who threw himself into the volcano was seeking ecstatic union with the goddess, not death; death was merely the unfortunate result of a man's failed attempt to prove he was the Firebringer, the chosen one of Dar.

At Josarian's insistence, Tansen sat down and ate the food they had set aside for him, and listened as his brother recounted the prisoners' escape from the fortress. Two men had died: Tansen had thought it likely that more than that would be killed, though he hadn't told Josarian so. Josarian's pretty-faced cousin, injured by a previous beating, had survived the escape, but then collapsed on the journey to Dalishar.

"A Guardian encampment," Josarian said, explaining where he'd left Zimran. "Southeast of Britar. They've come all the way from Liron."

"Why so far?" Tansen asked.

"They fled Liron last year because a waterlord called Verlon particularly sought one of them: Cheylan, born to a family of *toreni*."

"Oh, my heart bleeds for the *toren*," Emelen joked.

"Your heart should bleed for anyone sought by a waterlord," Lann said gruffly.

"This *toren* is a Guardian," Josarian pointed out, "and he took in Zimran."

"Then he's a better man than most *toreni*," Emelen said.

"Now tell us," Josarian said when Tansen had finished eating, "what happened last night?"

He told them the story up until the moment when he realized he'd lost his way. "I couldn't have forgotten a three-way fork in the path. I knew I must have gone the wrong way earlier." He sighed. "So I abandoned the horse and doubled back on foot."

It had been easy enough to keep out of sight in the dark until he returned to a landmark he clearly remembered, got his bearings, and determined which way to go. By then, the Outlookers had caught up with his abandoned horse and were milling around in confusion. They began searching for him, and he had to slowly draw them back to the landmark from which he was sure he could lead a headlong race through the dark and straight into the quarry. A series of sudden appearances kept them lumbering in the right direction, but it was time-consuming, and he had worried that dawn might come before he could lead them blindly into the trap. When he was finally satisfied with their position, he attacked one of them in the dark and stole his horse. The ensuing fight with several more Outlookers called enough attention to his presence to force the rest of the men to follow him. Then he set a breakneck pace all the way to the abandoned Kintish quarry.

"Everything went fine after that," he concluded, "but I couldn't keep the horse. The climb was too hard, so I left it in some almond grove."

Josarian grinned. "May it grow fat and wild there."

"Ah, the mountains are a terrible place on a dark-moon

night," Emelen said. "My father lived his whole life on Mount Garabar. He knew every rock, tree, cave, and path on that mountain. Yet he died up there on a dark-moon night, lost and wandering in confusion until he broke his neck in a fall."

"The Outlookers?" Josarian asked Tansen. "All dead, then?"

"All dead," Tansen confirmed.

"That's . . . a lot of men," Lann murmured. "A lot to die all at once. A lot to kill."

"Yes," Tan said without expression. "A lot."

"They'd have killed you," Emelen told Lann. "They intended to kill us all."

"They *still* intend it," Tansen warned. "You're not just unlucky friends and relatives of some outlaw, now. Not anymore." He looked at the solemn faces around the ancient fire, watched realization dawn in some of them for the first time. "Now you're escaped prisoners. Now you've killed Outlookers." He paused. "Now they will want you for yourselves, not just for Josarian."

They were hard words, the hard truth. He saw anger in some of the shadowed faces gazing back at him, fear and confusion in others. Now that the euphoria of escape, combat, and flight had worn off, they wanted their lives to go back to normal; but their lives could never be normal again. Lazy afternoons in the shadowed doorways of Emeldar were forever a thing of the past for these men. There was no turning back, no undoing what had been done, no escape from the path upon which destiny had set them. He remembered his youth, and for a moment he felt sorry for them.

"*You* did this," one of them said suddenly, rising to his feet and staring at Josarian with open fury.

"Falian . . ." Emelen said uneasily.

"This is *your* doing," Falian shouted. "You weren't content merely to escape arrest. You wouldn't disappear and let the rest of us live in peace!"

Josarian said nothing, just silently held Falian's gaze.

Tansen scanned the area around Falian with his eyes, wondering if the man had a weapon near him. There it was: another Valdani sword, lying on the ground near Falian's feet. None of these men had sheaths or knew how to care for a sword, he noted absently.

"No, *you* had to go out and slaughter more Outlookers, infuriating the Valdani!" Falian raged. "You had to kill and urge others to kill. We've had Outlookers swarming all over Emeldar because of you! I've been imprisoned and threatened with execution because of you! And now I'm an outlaw, now they will hunt me down until they finally catch and kill me—and it's all because of you!"

Falian scooped up his sword and lunged at Josarian, who never moved. Several of the men jumped to stop Falian, but Tansen, who'd been farthest away, got there first. Tan swiftly disarmed Falian, then cut him twice, once across the wrist and once above the eyes. As blood blinded the man, Tansen held one blade to his throat and used the other to ward off anyone who might be thinking of interfering. A quick glance around the cave, however, revealed that no one would dare consider it; they were looking at him as if he'd suddenly materialized from the Otherworld.

"Whoever threatens my bloodbrother threatens me," he said tersely, "and so pays the price of threatening a *shatai.*"

Falian dragged an arm across his blinded eyes, streaking his face with blood, and glared wrathfully at Tansen. "Do it, *roshah,*" he snarled, leaning toward the blade, "do it before the Valdani do it to both of us!"

"No!" someone shouted. "Don't!"

"He tried to kill Josarian," Emelen snapped. "Why should he be spared? So he can betray *all* of us?"

"Is this why you freed us?" another man demanded. "Is *this* what we escaped for?"

"Tan," Josarian said quietly, coming forward. "Let him go."

Tansen obeyed instantly. He knew that killing Falian was not the answer, for there were undoubtedly others who agreed with the man; but he didn't know what the answer *was*. He stepped back and let Josarian come close to the other man, though it took considerable self-control to stay still when Josarian bent down to retrieve the Valdani sword and then handed it to Falian.

"If you want to use this," Josarian said, "now is the time. I do not want to have to guard my back against my friends, against my own kind."

Falian's grip tightened on the sword, but he glanced resentfully at Tansen. "The minute you're dead, this *roshah* will slaughter me."

"Tansen," Josarian said without looking away from Falian, "promise me you won't hurt him if he kills me now."

Tansen said nothing, appalled.

"Promise me," Josarian insisted.

"I . . . promise," he muttered at last.

"He's a man of his word," Josarian told Falian. "Now this is just between you and me."

Falian stared into Josarian's eyes, his face contorted with anger and fear, his arm shaking as he raised the sword. "We played together as boys. We've worked alongside each other as men. I was bloodcousin to your wife, Josarian." Falian shook his head, still holding the sword ready. "Why? Why did you bring us all to this? *Why?*"

"Yes," Josarian said, nodding, "you have questions, good questions." With stunning disregard for his own life, he turned away from Falian and looked at the tense faces around him. "Certainly others here have the same questions." He paused. "Perhaps each of you thinks as Falian does. Even," he added, hearing Lann start to protest, "*even* if your loyalty to me prevents you from listening to the protests in your heart."

One of the smaller men came forward. "I . . . I stand with Falian," he said haltingly. "My life is ruined because of you, Josarian. What am I to do now? Tell me that, if you can."

"Ruined because of me, Amitan?" Josarian said. "Your father was killed by Outlookers while smuggling grain to

Liron where he hoped Kintish traders would offer a better price for it than the Valdani pay us—when they don't simply *take* it from us, that is."

"I have a wife now," Amitan protested. "We want ch—"

"After that," Josarian continued, "your elder brother was taken to the mines of Alizar, and you don't even know if he's still alive. When your mother went to plead for his release, she was attacked and raped by bandits on the road to Alizar. Your youngest sister is spindly and weak-boned from lack of food, because your family has been so desperately poor ever since losing your father and brother and their strong backs." To Tansen's dismay, Josarian handed Amitan a sword, too. "And you can say that *I've* ruined your life?"

"I am no assassin, to kill an unarmed man who has always been welcome under my mother's roof." Amitan tossed away the sword. "Only tell me, Josarian, how will my mother, wife, and sisters survive without me now? How am I to keep them fed, if I must live like a hunted animal with you from now on?"

"Yes, how?" Falian spat.

"Yes!" Josarian said. "Yes, that *is* the question!"

He laughed exultantly, picked up the sword Amitan had tossed aside, and waved it in the air. The men, even those most loyal to him, all looked at him as if he'd gone mad. Tansen wondered what he was up to.

"Your mother and Calidar are dead," Amitan pointed out, "and your sister has—*had*—a husband in the house. It was different for you, but—"

"The question is," Josarian boomed, grinning, "how will we feed them? How will we protect them? How, indeed, will we live now?" He looked around. "Aren't those the answers we seek?"

The men looked at each other in blank confusion. Josarian wasn't troubled by their lack of response.

"When have we ever lived as men should?" He ignored the expressions of insulted indignation this comment provoked and continued, "We haven't *fed* our women and children and parents; we've only done what we·could to keep them from starving. And we've never been very successful at it."

"That's not our fault," Lann growled. "The Valdani—"

"Exactly," Josarian interrupted. "The Valdani! Why have we borne their yoke for so long? Why have we allowed them to empty this land of all its wealth? Why have we let them take whatever they want when they sweep through our cities, villages, valleys, and farms?" He looked around, his dark eyes glowing in the firelight. "Why have *we* never taken from *them?*"

"I am no thief," Amitan said sharply.

"It isn't theft to take back what belongs to you and your kind," Josarian countered. "For two centuries, they have taken everything they could find, more than we could spare, more than they deserve. It's time to say *no.* It's time to tell them they've taken enough! It's time to start taking back what's been taken away from us!"

"This is madness," Falian said blankly. "This is not—"

"This is *reality,* the new reality of condemned men who are finally free of the yoke, the lash, the burden of saying *yes,"* Josarian insisted. "You want to feed your families? I tell you, you can feed them better than you ever have!"

"Words do not fill bellies," Amitan argued.

"No! Grain does!" Josarian answered. "Meat, milk, and cheese do! The produce of a thousand groves does!"

"But that all . . ." Lann frowned. "That all belongs to the Valdani."

"It does *not* belong to them!" Josarian said fiercely. "This is Sileria, and every crop grown, every animal butchered, and every mineral mined in Sileria belongs to Silerians!"

"You mean to take it away from them?" Falian said, sounding short of breath. "You mean to start robbing the Valdani on such a massive scale?"

"Before I die," Josarian vowed, "I mean to make them pay for every single thing they have ever taken from us. I mean to see the women and children of Emeldar grow fat upon the plenty that should always have been ours. I mean to lay the diamonds of Alizar upon every Guardian altar from here to Liron. I mean to live as a man and no longer as a slave!"

"By the Fires of Dar, we'll make our own Society!" Emelen cried, slapping Lann on the back. "We'll take what we want—"

"But *only* from the Valdani," Josarian cautioned.

"I can think of one or two *toreni* who've robbed us for centuries, too," Emelen said. He grinned at Josarian's expression and said, "We argue this another day. For now, brother-in-law, I am with you!"

"So am I!" boomed Lann. "May my sons grow strong on food taken from the Valdani! May my daughters wear wild gossamer, and may my wife grow too fat to leave the house!"

"Do you think it's possible?" Falian asked. "Can it really be done?"

Lann laughed. "Two days ago, surely the whole world would have said that it was impossible for two men to free twenty prisoners from the fortress at Britar. What is the world saying now, Falian? What is *not* possible for men who have done such a thing?"

Excited talk clamored through the cave, and Tansen realized with awe that Josarian *had* them. He had taken a group of scared mountain peasants who wanted only to go home, who had been ready to turn on him, and he had won them over! They were his now; they had been ready to break and run, but instead, they had listened to his words, been moved by his courage and his vision. They had chosen him and his way.

There was only one thing left. Amidst the shouting and laughter, Tansen held up his hand, bound with a now-ragged cloth, showing Josarian the bloodstains seeping through from his still-throbbing left palm. Josarian saw the gesture and nodded. He jumped up onto a large, smooth rock to get the men's attention, raising his own hand so that everyone could see the new mark on his own palm.

"I have sworn a bloodfeud against the Valdani," Josarian announced, "and I ask you to give your blood to our cause." He looked around and added, "You were imprisoned because of me, and you owe me nothing—*nothing*—for helping you escape. Any man who doesn't want to join me is free to go his own way tomorrow morning." He leaned over to put a hand on Amitan's shoulder, meeting his eyes with compassion. "If you want to leave, I promise to help you and your family go wherever you want, as far away from here as you need to take them for safety. I'll get some of Porsall's gold back from the Sisterhood to help you start a new life elsewhere."

Amitan gazed into Josarian's eyes for a long moment while all the men waited in silence for his answer. The small man turned away and picked up a sword. Tansen tensed briefly, then relaxed when Amitan thrust the sword into the ancient Guardian fire. When it was blessed, Amitan drew the blade across his palm and held it over the fire. A moment later, Falian did the same. One by one, the men opened their flesh and began reciting the vow as their blood sizzled in the sacred flames.

"I swear by Dar, by my honor, and by the memory of my slain kin, your enemies are now my enemies, and I will not rest or be at peace until the blood of every Valdan in Sileria flows as mine flows now."

Looking over the heads of the men as they prayed, Tansen met Josarian's gaze. Whatever the future held, he knew that nothing would ever be the same again.

10

THE SOUND OF voices gradually roused Zimran from a void of dreamless darkness. The instincts which had kept him alive in many precarious situations now governed his actions; he kept absolutely still, waiting for his senses to sharpen and his mind to clear.

He was immediately aware of the insistent pain in his left arm. It bewildered him for a moment. Then recent events started crystallizing in his mind: the terrible beating he'd endured in the widow's house in Emeldar; imprisonment in that stinking dungeon; Josarian's miraculous rescue of the prisoners; escaping in the dark with his cousin. But his memory was blank after that. What had happened next? Had they been captured again? Were they still in danger?

Realizing he must have been unconscious for a while, Zimran remained immobile, eyes closed, and tried to discern what he could about his surroundings without revealing that he was awake. He slowly recognized that he was warm and dry, resting on a thin pallet and surrounded by a woolen blanket. Moving his right hand surreptitiously beneath the blanket, he lightly examined his wounded arm and found it to be neatly splinted and bandaged.

He forced his disoriented mind to focus on the conversation taking place nearby. A man and a woman were talking. Much to Zim's relief, they were speaking common Silerian, so he knew he wasn't among Valdani. Since they weren't speaking *shallah* dialect, though, he wondered if he was still in the mountains.

"Do you really think we're safe now?" The woman's speech was slightly clipped, as if she came from the east.

"Even Verlon's power doesn't extend this far from Liron." The man's accent was smooth and educated, almost like a *toren*. "I'm safe enough."

"But Cheylan," she said, "he can ask another waterlord to destroy you for him."

"He doesn't know where we are," the man—Cheylan—replied.

"He doesn't have to," the woman insisted. "All he has to do is spread word throughout Sileria about you. You are very easy to identify, after all."

"True. But I don't think he'll tell others about me."

"Why not?"

Cheylan hesitated before answering. "It's personal."

"Personal?" When he didn't reply, she prodded, "What do you mean by personal? I thought it was simply because you're . . ."

"No, not entirely."

"What, then?"

"It's not your concern." The curt tone was clearly intended to end the conversation.

"Oh, yes, it is. I—we all—have had to flee halfway across Sileria because of Verlon's bloodvow against you, one of our own circle. That makes it my concern."

Sweet, Dar! Enemies of the Society? Zimran almost thought he'd be better off with the Valdani.

Where am I?

As Cheylan and the woman continued arguing, Zimran risked opening one eye slightly. His vision was foggy at first, but things gradually came into focus around him. He was in a small cave. Bright firelight flickered off the low ceiling. The two people on the far side of the fire were so engrossed in their conversation that they didn't even glance in his direction. The fire . . .

Zimran made a sound of surprise upon seeing that it burned with no wood, no coal, no fuel of any kind. The woman heard him and, abandoning the argument, quickly came to his side. He didn't realize he was trying to rise until he felt her gently pushing him back down.

"Shhh . . . You're among friends," she murmured.

"Guardians!" he blurted. His head throbbed when he spoke aloud, and he immediately gave into the woman's urging to lie down again.

His gaze remained locked on the woman—who was passably pretty, he noted—as Cheylan said, "Your cousin Josarian left you with us. He asked us to keep you safe until he could return for you."

"Is he safe?" Zim asked, closing his eyes again.

"We don't know," Cheylan admitted.

"May Dar shield him," the woman added.

"Dar shield us all," Zim muttered. The Outlookers would want revenge for what had happened at the fortress. He couldn't even imagine how many bribes and gifts it would take before things would finally return to normal in Emeldar. He was glad to be alive, glad Josarian had saved him from certain death at Britar; but it made him sick to think of how the Valdani would retaliate.

So he tried not to think about it. Instead he asked, "Where am I?"

"We're in the mountains. East of Britar."

"Guardians," Zimran repeated wearily. They would take care of him, but he questioned how safe he'd be here. They were hunted by the Valdani, enemies of the Society, and visited regularly by shades and spirits. He could think of company he'd rather keep.

"I'll go get you some broth," the woman offered.

She left the cave, and the man named Cheylan came forward to take her place at Zimran's side.

Zimran took one look at the man's face and tried to get up again—this time to escape. A fire-eyed demon!

"Going somewhere?" Cheylan's voice dripped with contempt.

Zimran fell back dizzily, his vision darkening for a moment. Panic warred with embarrassment. That lava-bright gaze chilled him, but the expression on Cheylan's face filled him with hot shame; the Guardian thought he was a coward.

Zim's blood thundered through his head as he stared at the man. "I . . ." He swallowed, his mind racing from one thought to the next. "Are you . . ."

"Yes?" Cheylan prodded.

No wonder the woman had said Cheylan was very easy to identify! But the woman was not afraid of him, and Zimran would not shame himself by fearing something that a woman did not. He closed his eyes and summoned his courage.

He helped Josarian. He helped me.

Zim forced himself to open his eyes again and meet that withering gaze. Still at a loss for words, he finally crossed his fists—moving his injured arm awkwardly—and bowed his head. "Thank you for your hospitality and protection," he said formally.

"Ah." A slight smile curved Cheylan's mouth. It was more arrogant than friendly, but it nonetheless helped ease the tension between them. "Now that's better."

SHAMED AND HUMILIATED, his broken nose throbbing, Myrell stood before Commander Koroll in Cavasar and recounted the hideous events of the prisoners' escape four nights ago. When he was done, Koroll's first question was not the one he was expecting.

Koroll fingered the bloody Moorlander tunic and asked, "And Josarian claimed this belonged to Porsall?"

Myrell blinked. "Yes, but he lied. I stopped at the *toren*'s estate on my way here. He's there, quite well, and was astonished at my concern for his—"

"Of *course* this tunic never belonged to Porsall, you incompetent fool!" Koroll snarled. "One lone outlaw, one filthy Silerian peasant has made a laughingstock of the Empire thanks to you!"

"He could not have been alone, sir," Myrell protested. "Someone had to have freed the prisoners. Josarian must have had an accomplice."

"By the Three, do you think it makes it better that there were *two* of them?" Koroll thundered. "Are you suggesting that *two* is a reasonable number of men to attack one of our fortresses, free our prisoners, and slaughter more than fifty of our men? *Is that what you're trying to say, you blundering idiot?*"

Myrell swallowed, swamped with shame, unable to choke out an answer. What was there to say, after all? No one in all of Valdania had ever been as disgraced as he was. There was no question that he'd be discharged from the Emperor's service; in fact, he'd consider himself very lucky not to be executed. How he hated this godsforsaken country! How he hated these barbaric people! Over fifty men led to their deaths in the mountains!

The day after the attack, as his men patched up their wounded, buried the Outlookers killed during the prisoners' surprise attack, and salvaged what they could from the burned wreckage, he'd sent patrols out after the troops which had failed to return from or report on their pursuit of Josarian. Led by a Silerian criminal who stayed out of the mines in exchange for serving Myrell as a guide and interpreter, they had tracked the troops and eventually discovered . . . Oh, Three Into One, he couldn't even bear to think of what his men had found! Over fifty men and horses were found dead out there, most lying twisted, broken, and bloody at the bottom of some vast, ancient quarry.

The first dozen Outlookers to fall over the precipice in the dark probably hadn't realized, not until the very last moment, what was happening. The rest of the men, however . . . They must have heard the screams of terrified horses and dying men even above the thunder of their own mounts' hoofbeats. There must have been a moment when they'd tried to rein in, to halt beasts born to a herd mentality and ruthlessly trained not to hesitate in the face of violence. There must have been men among them who knew they were racing straight for their deaths and could do nothing about it.

A few bodies had remained on the cliff's edge. Some were hideously trampled, maimed beyond recognition: panicked riders who had thrown themselves from their mounts, only to be killed by the horses behind them. There were several corpses, though, that hadn't been trampled. These riders had undoubtedly been at the very end of the column. Each of them had been killed by a sword. One of them, discovered later in the day, had fled the cliff's edge and been hunted down in the dark; his body was found at some distance from the carnage, his sword-arm severed and his throat cut.

The savagery of it had turned Myrell sick with hatred and made him lust for vengeance. His entire command, his men, his career, his life . . . everything destroyed by these bloodthirsty Silerian savages, a race of illiterate slaves, a people little advanced beyond the sheep they tended.

While he choked on the bile of his hatred, Koroll ordered two Outlookers to escort him to a guarded chamber, then dismissed Myrell, his voice rich with loathing.

After the former Outlooker captain had left his command chamber, Koroll picked up the bloody Moorlander tunic and examined it more closely. No, there was no doubt about it; this was the same tunic the *shatai* had worn.

Great merciful bloodstained gods! Had Josarian managed to kill even the *shatai?* Had that murdering, thieving *shallah* tangled with one of the most highly skilled warriors in the entire world and won? How was such a thing possible? Perhaps there was some other explanation.

Koroll looked at the tunic again. What other explanation could there be? How else could Josarian have gotten hold of the tunic, and where had all the blood come from? He must have carried it as a trophy until one day he'd found a use for it. He'd baited Myrell with it, using the fiction of Porsall's abduction to keep Myrell from capturing him immediately, thereby giving himself an opportunity to lead the Outlookers into the deadly trap he'd set for them in the mountains.

According to Myrell, the riders who hadn't plunged into the quarry had been killed in combat. Could Josarian have done that alone, or had someone helped him? Koroll suspected it was the latter. After all, Myrell had imprisoned twenty men from Emeldar. It didn't take much imagination to picture Josarian convincing others from the village to help him free those prisoners.

So now he had help; the outlaw was no longer alone. Indeed, all the survivors of the prison break had probably joined him now, too. He'd been troublesome enough by himself, but now he'd have a small band of men under his command.

Fear settled in Koroll's belly like a lump of ice. This *shallah* must be stopped! He'd killed armed Outlookers in ambushes and in combat, eluded capture far longer than anyone had anticipated, somehow managed to murder a *shatai*, successfully attacked a fortress and freed its prisoners, and led over fifty trained men straight to their deaths. The question was this: What would it take to kill him?

This problem plagued Koroll as he fingered the tunic. For all that Myrell was a bungling fool who'd let twenty prisoners escape to kill most of his men and burn all of his supplies, he did have one good idea: to convince other *shallaheen* to turn on Josarian. If Koroll could make them suffer enough in Josarian's name, the outlaw's own people would kill him. For two centuries the Valdani had successfully controlled Silerians by manipulating them into exercising their violent tendencies upon each other rather than upon their conquerors. It was time to bring this philosophy to a new level of efficiency.

Koroll contemplated how he could employ Myrell to further his own ends. He was one of the few living Valdani who had actually *seen* Josarian and could identify him, alive or dead. Moreover, Myrell had nothing left to lose, and Koroll had seen the hatred and fury burning inside of him. Left alone, Myrell would turn to drink, violence, and reckless pursuits in some forgotten corner of the Empire. But properly used . . . properly used, he could become as brutal, focused, and fearless as the outlaw they sought.

"BUT WHERE WILL you go?" Tashinar demanded, fear making her voice rough as she watched Mirabar bundle up her few belongings. "You can't simply walk down the mountain and assume no one will notice you!"

"I know," Mirabar said, her voice unnaturally calm under the circumstances.

"Then how do you expect to survive more than a few days?" Tashinar cried, resisting the urge to shake her initiate.

"I must . . ." Mirabar frowned absently. "I must rely upon the Beckoner to protect me."

"Protect you? All he's done is torment you ever since he first—"

"He wants me to live long enough to . . . to do whatever it is he wants me to do. So he will have to protect me from superstition and violence."

Tashinar tried another angle. "And Kiloran? How do you expect to find him? Do you think you can just go around the countryside *asking* for him?"

"I will be led to him. Somehow, I know I will be led." She sounded neither smug nor happy. But she did sound certain.

"And what about us? How will we know what happens to you? You can't expect me to simply wait and wonder—" She stopped abruptly when Mirabar burst into a peal of laughter.

"Tashinar, you of all people should be able to find out what happens to me!" Mirabar said, genuinely amused.

Tashinar blinked in astonishment. She had actually forgotten for a moment. Nearly forty years as a Guardian, and she had forgotten that she was a gateway to the Otherworld. But she was not soothed by the reminder. Her throat tightened as she said, "The next time we talk, I do not want to see you as a shade in the Otherworld."

"I don't either." Mirabar trembled briefly, and for the first time, Tashinar realized how terrified she was behind her determined demeanor.

"I'm coming with you," Tashinar said suddenly.

"You can't." Mirabar avoided her gaze and kept her

voice toneless. "You're too old to make the journey. You would slow me down."

"How dare you talk to me that way!"

"It won't work, Tashinar," Mirabar said. "You may not come."

Tashinar saw with sudden sorrow that the Beckoner was replacing her as Mirabar's mentor and guide. While Tashinar still had so much to teach Mirabar about being a Guardian of the Otherworld, the girl was right: In this matter, she was just an old woman who would interfere with Mirabar's duty.

She ruthlessly suppressed the impulse to take Mirabar in her arms and shelter her as she had during the girl's childhood, when she'd been bewildered and in need of comfort and reassurance. "You may need money down below. I have some that I've kept aside for an emergency."

"Yes, I . . ." Mirabar looked around her in confusion. "I hadn't thought about that." She had never used money, had only even seen it a few times in her life.

"Always bargain for a lower price than is initially asked," Tashinar instructed after returning to her side with the copper and silver coins she kept in a little doeskin bag. "Down below, people are less likely to feed you just because you're a Guardian. So you'll need to use this carefully." The girl could trap, hunt, and gather all manner of food, but Tashinar doubted she'd ever even been in a marketplace. Even assuming traders would deal with her, there were just so many things about ordinary life she simply didn't know. "How will you—I mean, this is very—"

"There *is* a reason." Mirabar put her hand on Tashinar's shoulder and squeezed gently. "You must believe that."

A man's voice interrupted them. "Excuse me . . ."

Mirabar whirled to face the intruder. It was only Derlen, looking unusually hesitant. "What do you want?" she asked abruptly.

"Mirabar . . ." He shifted his weight. "I know you have resented me for—"

"That's in the past now, Derlen," she said gruffly. "I'm leaving."

"Yes, I know." He took a breath and continued, "It was never personal. Anything I have done or said has been for the good of the circle."

"I know."

"I don't understand what's happening to you, where your visions come from, or where they are taking you. But I sense that your task is enormous and that the risks will be great." He handed her a portion of knotted twine; the shiny black beads of a Guardian were woven into it beside the red ones of a merchant. "My family in Shaljir are wealthy and somewhat influential. If you need help of any kind, no matter how great or small, this *jashar* will open their doors to you."

Tashinar took the message from him and studied it briefly, then handed it to Mirabar. Derlen had included a little personal news about himself and his son, but otherwise the *jashar* merely introduced Mirabar as a powerful Guardian on a sacred mission who must be aided in whatever way she required.

"Thank you, Derlen," Mirabar said, looking genuinely moved.

Unfortunately, Derlen got rather pedantic and fussy then, clearly annoying Mirabar, who snapped at him and rudely turned away. Tashinar merely sighed. After he left, Mirabar grumbled, "We will never get along."

"And I had *such* hopes," Tashinar said dryly.

Mirabar was startled into a shaky smile. "Well, perhaps when I return, we will both have mellowed."

"*Will* you return?"

"I promise."

A little while later, as she watched Mirabar, still so young, set her foot upon the path leading her away from the only safety she had ever known, Tashinar held that promise to her heart.

*   *   *

IT DIDN'T TAKE a gift of prophecy to predict that the Outlookers' first move would be to punish Josarian and the escaped prisoners by hurting their families in Emeldar. So the band of outlaws travelled quickly back toward their native village at top speed to save their loved ones from Valdani revenge. They knew they'd need supplies for their people, so along the way, they attacked and looted an Outlooker outpost by night.

At first, the people in Malthenar, the nearest village, were furious as they worried about the punishment *they* might receive as a result of this. Josarian spoke to them by firelight in the village square.

"You've broken no laws here tonight!" he reminded them. "The Valdani know who I am and what I've already done, and soon they will know just how much harm I mean them. *Tell* them who did this! Tell them who killed Outlookers and stole their supplies here tonight!" He paused, looking around at the faces in the crowd. "Tell them I have sworn a bloodfeud against them."

Standing behind Josarian's right shoulder, ready to defend him against anyone who might actually attempt what Falian had merely threatened to do in the caves of Dalishar, Tansen was heartened by the rallying effect that Josarian's announcement had on the villagers. He had well over a dozen loyal men with him now, and word was already spreading about what had happened at Britar. Josarian's legend, born on the bloody night he had killed for the first time, was growing fast.

"Yes!" a woman cried, forcing her way through the crowd to face Josarian. "Yes! A bloodfeud!"

Another woman grabbed at her, but the woman—thin and far from youth, with bitter lines carved into her face—shook her off. "They've taken everything from me, *everything*. My husband, three strong sons, my father—all killed by Outlookers or taken to the mines." She seized the small knife she wore on a frayed rope around her neck and sliced open her left palm. "I cannot use a *yahr* or raise a sword,

Josarian, but a woman can hate, a woman can help, a woman can still find a way to kill!"

Everyone watched her in shock, for a bloodfeud was not normally women's business. But Josarian held her gaze, then nodded and took her hand. He led her to the blazing torch that Lann held.

"If your vow is sincere," he said to the woman, "then this fire will serve."

She held her hand over the flames as Lann lowered the torch for her. "I don't know the exact words," she admitted, her eyes riveted on Josarian's face.

"Then repeat them after me," he said. "I swear by Dar, by my honor, and by the memory of my slain kin . . ."

Two dozen other villagers wound up joining Josarian's bloodfeud that night. Most chose to stay in Malthenar and await Josarian's instructions, but a few of the younger men—ignoring their mothers' pleas—decided to accompany Josarian and his men into the mountains. Before leaving, Josarian gave the people of Malthenar almost half of the food and supplies he had just stolen from the Outlooker outpost.

Among the supplies they now hauled with them on their way to Emeldar were more swords. Tansen realized that he'd have to teach these men how to use them properly, or they'd cut themselves to ribbons. Josarian agreed with him when they discussed it the next night, the two of them still wakeful after most of the other men had fallen asleep.

"What do you think we should do in Emeldar?" Josarian asked. "Fight, or abandon the town and scatter everyone throughout other villages?"

"Both," Tansen said promptly. "Even with your powers of persuasion, too many people will refuse to leave at first. And the Valdani believe in swift reprisal. They'll attack the village as soon as they can."

"So if we fight, this will convince the villagers of the danger they're in," Josarian concluded.

"Battles and blood are very convincing. When they see men die, when they are faced with killing men themselves,

they'll know that they can never go back." He nodded.
"They'll follow your orders then. And when they spread
news to other villages about the battle at Emeldar . . ."

"Other villages will know that they, too, can fight back."

"Perhaps," Tansen said. "It seems incredible, though."

"That we should fight the Valdani?"

"That we should fight anybody but each other."

AS MUCH AS Koroll hated to reveal these setbacks to
his commander, he knew that the death of so many Outlookers at Britar could not go unreported. Moreover, such
news was disastrous enough that he must report it in person in order to deal with the questions which would now
certainly arise about his ability to continue governing his
district in this pathetic excuse of a country. So, having
ordered one of his captains to take eighty riders and make
a lasting impression on Emeldar, Koroll set out for Shaljir
with a bodyguard of six men. He followed the ancient
coastal road, originally built by Silerians and repaired over
the centuries by successive waves of conquering peoples.

Although Myrell might now well be the best man to
lead the raid, Koroll thought it would be imprudent to release him from confinement until he had dealt with his own
superiors in Shaljir. Koroll wouldn't be able to avoid
blame completely for the mess at Britar, even though he
had known nothing of Myrell's actions or intentions at the
time; Myrell was under his command and was therefore
his responsibility. Nonetheless, he had no intention of letting Myrell's miscalculations ruin his career. Strategy suggested that he blame himself more than was necessary
when he reached Shaljir, thereby—he hoped—prompting
his superiors to be the ones to point out that he shouldn't
be demoted, disgraced, or executed for something he
couldn't possibly have prevented. It was always better to
manipulate others into speaking up for you than to speak
up for yourself, Koroll found.

If his position as military governor of Cavasar remained
secure, *then* he could release Myrell and find special work

for him. Meanwhile, Koroll had arranged for a runner to meet him in Shaljir after the attack on Emeldar. It would look good to be able to advise his superiors of quick reprisals and a show of force.

Commander Daroll was considerably younger than Koroll and, in Koroll's opinion, shouldn't have been given the highest military office in Sileria as his very first position; he was military governor of Shaljir and its district, and thus High Commander of Sileria, overseeing both Koroll and the military governor of Liron. Inexperienced and unproved, Daroll was a second son in one of Valda's oldest, most powerful families. Although Sileria was a backwater province of the empire, Daroll's current position was a prestigious one for someone who was barely a man.

Koroll was fifteen years older than Daroll and had served with distinction in the Emperor's wars before coming here, yet now he must report to Daroll, a callow youth, and treat him with the deference and obedience due a superior officer. The post in Shaljir had become vacant last year when an aging commander retired after half a lifetime here. Koroll knew the post should have been his, knew that he was more capable and deserving than the young fool who'd gotten it instead and who would remain there for several more years for seasoning. Now, with that avenue closed to him, Koroll's only hope of getting out of Cavasar and Sileria was to distinguish himself sufficiently to be promoted past Daroll and sent, at long last, to another part of the world. Such were the disadvantages of rising through the ranks, rather than being born beneath the Emperor's gaze.

Handsome, educated, and arrogant, Daroll greeted Koroll with the formal courtesy of a Valdani aristocrat when he entered the command chamber in the fortress at Shaljir. Rather than make do with oft-repaired Moorlander ruins, as Koroll did, Daroll commanded his forces from a luxurious Valdani palace which had been built right next to the old Kintish fortress. Koroll's gaze fixed momentarily on the Seal of Shaljir, the fabulous gold and jewel-encrusted symbol of Valdani power in Sileria, which hung from Daroll's neck. Envy licked at his insides like bitter flames, and he forced himself to look away from the prize which should have been his.

Since Daroll was alone, Koroll said, "I had hoped for an audience with you *and* the Imperial Advisor, sir."

It was what he had specifically requested upon arriving in Shaljir, and Daroll damn well knew it. The Imperial Advisor was the Emperor's personal representative, reporting directly to him. While Koroll didn't relish the thought of his news being reported to the Emperor, he was even less pleased with the thought of Daroll reporting it to the Advisor in Koroll's absence; who knew what this young goat-molester would say about him behind his back? Koroll dearly wanted the Advisor to hear about this from his own lips and no one else's.

"I'm afraid he's still in Liron," Daroll said dismissively. "However, if you've come all this way to tell me anything of political import, I will be sure to advise him."

I'll bet you will, you woman-faced fool, Koroll thought.

"Very well, sir," he said smoothly. "I'm sure it's best left to your judgment. I've come personally from Cavasar to report the most grievous events."

He proceeded to describe the situation, omitting his unauthorized hiring of a *shatai,* but stressing his earnest attempts to have Josarian captured or killed. He also blatantly lied, pretending that certain of Josarian's exploits had been brought to his attention only within the past few days. He concluded by taking full responsibility for Myrell's actions and the loss of so many men.

"You're damn *right* you'll take full responsibility!" Daroll thundered. "Why was I not informed of this from the very beginning?" he demanded.

"Sir, the crimes of a lone *shallah* hardly seemed worthy of bringing to your—"

"A lone *shallah* who killed two Outlookers as his very first crime, and has continued plundering and killing ever since, you blundering idiot!"

Koroll tried not to wince, remembering how he had used those very words when addressing Myrell a few days ago.

"We thought—"

"We?"

"I thought, sir, that the entire military force of Cavasar should be able to deal with one *shallah."*

"I suggest that it is not the *men* who are at fault, Koroll, but their commander."

"I have made every possible attempt to capture—"

"You have done *nothing* useful!"

"One Silcrian amidst those mountains—"

"Offer a reward, you fool! These people are hungry, like people everywhere. They'll turn him in."

"We have, sir, but the chances of a monetary reward proving successful in Sileria are quite slim, since their culture prohibits them from revealing information to outs—"

"I don't give a damn what their culture prohibits!"

"I suggest—"

"You've suggested quite enough, Commander," Daroll snapped. "Finish your report, if you please."

Koroll did so, earning an even hotter glare from his superior officer.

"Reprisals against Emeldar? *That's* your plan?" Daroll said scathingly.

"Not my whole plan, sir. Merely what I was able to set into motion before proceeding here with all due haste to—"

"Has it occurred to you that rather than imprisoning men and now butchering women and children from this obscure village, we stand a far better chance of catching this outlaw if we simply *buy* the information we need?"

"As I've tried to explain, sir—"

"Spare me your protestations about these noble savages."

"It's not nobility," Koroll insisted. "These people live and die by certain rules, sir, and one of their most rigid customs is that they never reveal anything to outsiders. Even if someone wanted the money enough to come for-

ward and betray Josarian, not only would such a man's
entire community shun him, but the Honored Society
would almost certainly assassinate him to enforce *lirtahar*—their code of silence. The Society would not let such
a violation of traditional law go unpunished among Silerians, and the *shallaheen* know it."

"The people in this country are now governed by Valdani law, Commander, not the barbaric rules of an outlawed water magic cult." Daroll silenced Koroll's reply
with a curt gesture. "I have lost patience with your excuses, Koroll. If you were an officer of lesser rank, I would
have you arrested for the mess you've created for the Emperor. However, it could adversely affect morale if the men
saw the Commander of Cavasar thrown into a cell.
Therefore, consider yourself lucky to be confined to quarters until further notice."

Daroll summoned two Outlookers and ordered them to
escort Koroll to his quarters within the palace. "He's not
to be disturbed until I send for him again."

Fuming at the insults he had endured from a mere boy,
and sick with fear as he thought of what this disaster would
do to his life, Koroll went to his quarters, a comfortable
room overlooking the inner courtyard three floors below.
Deprived of his freedom, he cooled his heels in there for
four days, alternating between fury and despair, scarcely
touching the food which was brought to his door twice a
day. By the time Daroll sent for him again, he was almost
relieved. Anything, even disgrace and punishment, would
be better than this eternal waiting.

Upon entering Daroll's command chamber, he was surprised not to find the Imperial Advisor there; he had assumed he'd been summoned because Daroll had relayed
his report to the Advisor and the two of them had decided
his fate. Daroll's only companion, however, was an
exhausted-looking Outlooker, his gray uniform coated with
red dust.

"This is one of my runners," Daroll said without preamble. "I sent two to Emeldar to find out the results of your—"

"I'm expecting my own runner," Koroll interrupted. He didn't feel much need to be respectful to a man who'd already decided to ruin him.

"Then you are destined to be disappointed." There was a coldness in Daroll's voice that Koroll had never heard before, not even during their last disastrous meeting in this very room. "None of your men—not a single one—survived the attack on Emeldar."

Koroll swayed slightly. "I . . . *What* did you say?"

"Tell him," Daroll said to the runner.

The young Outlooker looked haunted and dazed. "We two were spotted by *shallah* sentries outside of Emeldar. They killed my partner, then hauled me into the village to see . . . to see the carnage." He swallowed hard. "Bodies everywhere, dozens of them, all ours. Even more outside of the village, many more. They—the *shallaheen*—they knew the riders were coming. They set a trap in a mountain pass . . . two huge woven nets. The riders rode into one as it rose suddenly before them; then one rose behind them, too, preventing escape. The *shallaheen* on the cliffs rained rocks and boulders down upon them, then arrows. Then they descended to kill anyone who wasn't yet dead." The lad's teeth started chattering. "The riders who came from the other direction, who escaped the deathtrap in the mountain pass . . . Oh, Three have mercy! I've never seen a dead man before, and there were so *many*. I—I never— Never—"

"How do you know all this?" Koroll demanded hoarsely, his mind filled with horrifying images. "How do you know what the *shallaheen* did to—"

"He told me."

"Who?"

"*He* did. *Josarian.*"

The name was like a curse, like an evil spell that deprived Koroll of speech or strength or thought. "Josarian?" he repeated weakly.

"How did he get there before your men? You said he had no horses," Daroll snapped accusingly, glaring at Koroll.

"He doesn't." Slow-witted with shock, Koroll mumbled, "And he doesn't need them. He doesn't travel by road." Fighting through the horror clouding his mind, Koroll said, "He's travelling *over* the mountains. He's a *shallah*. But what made him go back to Emeldar? He must have known I would send . . ." Koroll's blood chilled as he realized. "Yes, he *knew*. And he came to fight them!" It had never occurred to him, not even after the attack on the fortress, that Josarian would willingly stand against eighty Outlookers at Emeldar, not when there were so many options besides deadly combat with superior forces. Yes, even after the attack on the fortress, Koroll acknowledged with heavy self-recrimination, he had severely underestimated the outlaw. "But a mere *shallah,*" he murmured to himself. "Who would have ever thought . . ."

"He raided an outpost near Mal . . . Mal . . ." The young Outlooker stopped, simply shaking his head and breathing hard.

"Malthenar?" Koroll guessed.

"Yes. Everyone's dead there. All the Valdani, I mean. That's why it hasn't been reported. There was no one left alive to . . . to . . ."

"Why did he tell you?" Koroll asked.

"He wants you to know."

"Me?"

"All the Valdani," the Outlooker corrected. "Everyone. You, me, your men, Commander Daroll, the Imperial Advisor himself. He had a message for us all." The young man's face crumbled with remembered fear. "It's why he let me live, it's the only reason. He wanted me to bring a message back to Shaljir."

"What is the message?" Koroll asked tersely.

"He says he will not stop killing Outlookers until we stop coming into the mountains." The young man was shaking by now. "He says he will not stop taking back what we have stolen from his people, not unless we give back everything that we have spent two centuries stealing."

"He's a madman," Daroll said.

"Did he seem mad to you?" Koroll asked the Outlooker, though he doubted he'd get any useful impressions from one so young and scared.

"The people there . . . they seem to love him. He . . ." The Outlooker thought for a long moment before finally saying with obvious confusion, "I know he's killed many of us, but he didn't *seem* like a killer. Do you understand?" the young man asked Koroll.

"He seemed like an ordinary *shallah*," Koroll translated.

"No," the young man said quite clearly. "Not ordinary. He was not a man you'd mistake for any other, even though those mountain peasants all look alike. There was something different about him." After a moment, the Outlooker shrugged, teeth still chattering. "I'm sorry, sir. I don't know what . . ."

"Enough." Daroll dismissed him brusquely, watched him leave the chamber, then turned to Koroll. "You've just lost another eighty men with your brilliant strategies, Commander. How long before Josarian kills every Outlooker in your entire district?"

The disaster was so total, so astonishing and overwhelming, Koroll had nothing left to say. He'd sent eighty of his men to their deaths, and he'd allowed a mountain bandit to become a famous rebel. His life was certainly ruined, and it seemed likely that it would soon be over.

"I cannot decide on your fate until the Advisor returns from Liron," Daroll said, eyeing him with distaste. "Until then, I'm placing you under arrest."

"But I'm the Commander of Cav—"

"Not anymore." Daroll seized the military insignia which was affixed to Koroll's tunic and tore it off with a sharp yank. "I am leaving for Emeldar in the morning, and I will not return until I can bring Josarian—or his head—with me. Then, Koroll, I will deal with you."

11

"YOU LEFT ME here with a demon." Zimran's first words upon being united with his cousin were spoken with an injured air.

"I left you with Guardians," Josarian corrected.

"Fire-eating mystics," Zim said dismissively. "Although there is one . . ." A reminiscent smile curved his mouth. "She pitied my wounds and nursed me back to health. A most tender woman."

"I'm so glad to know your convalescence was not entirely tedious," Josarian said. "Tell me about the demon. Does he have strange visions or sudden fits?"

Zimran looked at him curiously. "Not that I've noticed. Why?"

"I once met another who did."

"Another one?" When Josarian nodded, Zimran said, "This one is powerful, no doubt about it, but no fits or spells. I hope you at least made certain he wasn't evil before leaving my unconscious carcass in his care."

"Actually, I was in such a hurry that night . . ." Josarian grinned at his cousin's expression. Then he asked, "You've been well since then? They really have taken proper care of you?"

"I wouldn't care to stay longer, but they've been kind," Zimran admitted.

He and Josarian had been given some privacy upon Josarian's arrival at the Guardian encampment where he'd left his cousin many days ago. As Cheylan had promised, the Outlookers had not found Zimran; and as Josarian had promised, he had finally returned for him. Now as he recounted the extraordinary events which had taken place since their last meeting, he watched the emotions that crossed his cousin's face in rapid succession: skepticism, surprise, astonishment, confusion, shock.

"Eighty Outlookers?" Zimran choked at last. "You've killed *eighty men?*"

"They came to attack women and children and old men," Josarian replied. "They came to punish us by attacking our loved ones. I only wish I could kill them all twice."

"Is it *possible* to kill so many?" Zimran whispered. "Are you dreaming? Are you mad?"

"They die as easily as all the *shallaheen* they have killed."

"But what will happen to Emeldar now? The Valdani will send more men, and more after that. The village will never be at peace, never be safe from—"

"The villagers have abandoned Emeldar. Lann and the other men are helping them move to other villages, places where they have relations. Tansen is staying behind with Emelen to—"

"Tansen," Zimran repeated with distaste. "This *roshah* whom you've made your bloodbrother."

Hearing his cousin's disapproval, Josarian said, "I've told you why he—"

"Some foreign-looking mercenary appears out of nowhere and you—"

"He could have killed me at any time, and he didn't."

"The year is young!"

Josarian sighed. "I could never have freed you from the fortress without him. He made it possible."

"I'm sure that's what he tells you," Zim spat, "what he wants you to believe."

"That's what *I'm* telling *you.*" Josarian held his temper in check. "He's not with the Valdani, Zim. He killed more than fifty of them that night."

"You weren't there. You didn't see."

"I know what the Valdani are saying. I know what's going on in Britar now. I know that it happened, Zim, and *he* did it." Seeing his cousin's uncomfortable shrug—Zimran hated to lose an argument—Josarian pressed home his point. "While we trapped and killed the Outlookers invading Emeldar via the pass, Tansen led the fight in Emeldar itself. Those who were there say he fought like a sorcerer, like ten men, like nothing they had ever seen before." He paused, then concluded, "He is with us, Zim. He is with *me.*"

"If you say so," Zimran said at last, with ill grace. "But just because you trust him does not mean that I have to. Not yet."

"You will learn to," Josarian said confidently, "as I have. Now—are you ready to leave?"

"Where are we going?" Zimran asked.

"Garabar."

"Sweet Dar, why there of all places?"

Josarian grinned. "Because a Valdani caravan is carrying grain north to Cavasar, for shipment to the city of Valda. By tomorrow night, they should be camped outside of Garabar."

"And you plan to attack them?" Zimran said incredulously. "Didn't Emelen's father die by night on Mount Garabar? What makes you think *we* won't?"

"There'll be moons. Enough light to see the whites of their eyes."

"You *are* mad," Zimran said slowly.

Josarian just laughed, feeling exultant, confident. "You'll see. You'll understand soon enough. I know you will."

MIRABAR HAD VERY few worldly possessions, but she found they were growing heavy by the time she arrived at the first real village she had approached in many years. Thirsty and tired, she considered waiting until the following morning to make her first contact with the villagers. Surely tomorrow would be better . . .

No. That was just fear talking, she decided, not weariness. Though she wanted to turn around and run, she forced herself to keep walking toward the cluster of hovels clinging to the mountainside. Waiting one more night wouldn't make confronting the people in this village any easier. She had to start dealing with ordinary people sooner or later, so it might as well be here and now.

She walked past the burnt offering-ground at the edge of the village, where the sacred lava stone lay shining beneath the afternoon sun. Three small children were playing outside the nearest house. Two girls and a boy. Pretty children, with shining black hair and sunny smiles. Mirabar warmed to them as she watched them laughingly chase some toy around and around.

Maybe things would go well here, she thought. She walked closer, preparing to greet them.

One of the girls seized the toy she'd been chasing. She hoisted it over her head and whirled around in a full circle, cheering. Then she spotted Mirabar—and stopped as suddenly as if she'd turned to stone. Her dark eyes grew round. Her jaw dropped. The boy seized the toy from her and ran off laughing. She didn't seem to notice, just kept staring at Mirabar.

Mirabar smiled reassuringly. "Hello . . ."

The child screamed. The other two children scrambled around in surprise. The girl kept screaming. Now she pointed at Mirabar. Finally noticing her, the other two children started screaming, too. They ran away, howling for their mothers. The first little girl simply stood there, pointing and screeching.

"It's all right," Mirabar said, coming closer. "I won't hurt you."

Tears welled up in the girl's eyes. Her extended arm started shaking violently as she continued screaming.

"Please, don't be afraid. I promise I won't hurt you."

The girl's legs buckled and she fell down, still staring up at Mirabar with wide, watering eyes. Her screaming changed into horrified wailing.

"My name is Mirabar." She knelt beside the girl and took her hand. "I won't—"

Another piercing scream caught her attention. She looked up to see a woman running toward them, her face contorted with fear. "Don't touch her! Don't you touch her!"

Mirabar let go of the child's hand and backed away as the woman rushed forward. Scooping the wailing child into her arms, the woman kept screaming, "Don't touch her!" over and over.

"I'm sorry," Mirabar said, raising her voice, trying to be heard. "I didn't mean to frighten—"

"Over there!" It was a man's voice this time.

Mirabar looked away from the woman and child. She saw that many people were now emerging from nearby houses in response to the screams. Three men were already running toward this spot, one of them shouting, "Get away from it! Get away!"

Her stomach churning with fear, Mirabar rose to her feet and held out her hands. "The little girl is just frightened," she said clearly. "I startled her. My name is—"

"She was trying to eat my daughter!" the woman screamed.

"No!" Mirabar said. "That's not true!"

One of the three men led the woman and her daughter away. The woman kept shrieking that the demon had tried to kill her child, and the growing crowd was responding with cries of fear and rage. To Mirabar's horror, the two men closest to her now pulled out their *yahr* and started circling her.

"Don't!" She shifted on her feet as she tried to keep both men in view. "I'm a Guardian! I've come to—"

"No one wants your kind here," the taller man snarled.

"No one wants your kind anywhere," the other added.

"I don't want to hurt anyone," she insisted.

Other people were growing bolder now, twenty or more of them coming forward to confront her. She risked looking away from the two men circling her to see if she might find a possible ally among the other villagers. But every face she saw was contorted with fear and hostility. A young man started ostentatiously tossing a rock up and down while he glared at her.

"I meant no harm to anyone." She tried to keep fear out of her voice, sensing that they would descend upon her if she showed the slightest weakness. "I will go now."

Unwilling to turn her back on the crowd, she took several steps backward. No one tried to stop her yet. After a few more backward steps, she tripped on a rock and stumbled.

The young man in the crowd took advantage of her momentary distraction. His rock whizzed through the air and hit her soundly in the ribs. Mirabar gasped in pain and pressed her hand over the spot.

"Demon!" he cried. Then others began shouting it, too.

They meant to kill her. She saw it in their faces; she saw it in the *yahr* they swung as they surged toward her. Reacting instinctively, she used the only defense she had. She gritted her teeth and hissed at them, bringing forth fire to ward them off, then encircled herself with a protective glow of flame.

"Stay back!" she shouted.

They were startled enough by the sight of fire magic to stop and stare; but they didn't look any less angry or threatening.

"Go back to your homes and let me leave in peace," Mirabar ordered.

"No! Get her!" someone shouted. "Otherwise she'll return by night!"

"I wouldn't come back here for all the diamonds in Alizar," she snapped. "Now go back to your houses and leave me alone!"

Seeing that they weren't yet ready to give up, Mirabar called flame into her palms and flung bolts of fire in their general direction. That was finally enough to make them turn and run.

She did the same.

She only slowed down to a walk when the village was well behind her, and she kept travelling until it was nearly nightfall. Even so, when she finally stopped to camp deep in the woods, she was afraid to risk lighting a fire, lest someone from that village come hunting her in the night.

For the love of Dar, how was she supposed to travel across Sileria and find Kiloran—*or* the warrior—if she couldn't let ordinary people see her?

You are a Guardian.

Mirabar jumped when the Beckoner's voice came out of nowhere. She looked around the grove and nearly flinched when she saw his golden eyes peering at her from between some almond blossoms.

"Where in the Fires were *you* while I was being stoned out of that stinking village?" she snapped.

You are a Guardian. Make them remember what they have lost. Make them remember why they need you.

"Easy for you to say, but *I* can't make someone roll around on the ground, shrieking with pain and visions, whenever they don't feel like listening to me."

Make them welcome your kind again.

She drew in a sharp breath, shocked to feel her eyes sting with emotion. To be welcome? Her?

"No," she said aloud. "I will never be welcome. Surely what happened today is proof enough of that."

Make them welcome your kind again. It is the first step.

"Toward what? Finding Kiloran? Finding the warrior? Freedom?" She sighed wearily. "Or just a good night's sleep?"

When she looked up, seeking an answer, the Beckoner was gone.

TANSEN AND EMELEN hid among some rocky mountainside crevices above Emeldar, watching the activity in the village. More Outlookers had come riding into Emeldar today, no sooner than Tansen had expected. There were so many of them!

"A hundred?" Emelen breathed. "No, more, wouldn't you say?"

"A hundred and fifty," Tansen guessed.

He'd never seen so many Outlookers in one place. Having learned from their earlier mistake, this time the riders had all approached the village from the west, the route which was almost impossible for the villagers to defend; Outlooker corpses still littered the mountain pass leading into Emeldar from the east.

"It makes my belly roll to see them in our streets, our main square, our homes," Emelen murmured.

"I know." Tansen blocked out the memory of far worse things he'd seen in Gamalan.

"That one! He must be the commander."

Tansen watched as an officer rode into the main square. He was surrounded by his private bodyguards and accompanied by the full trumpet-blasting, flag-waving pomp of a Valdani commanding officer—something one seldom saw in Sileria, though it was a common enough sight in Kinto and the Moorlands.

"Who is he?" Emelen whispered.

"I don't know." Tansen squinted. "Not Koroll, anyhow."

They watched the confusion below, the sudden halt and shift of plans as the village was discovered to be completely deserted.

"Oh, Dar," Emelen prayed, "as I have been faithful and true, *please* don't let them simply leave."

"They'll think it's a trap," Tansen said. "They'll be wary."

"But will they *stay?*"

"I hope so," Tan said with feeling.

"Please Dar, let it be so," Emelen murmured.

It was nearly sunset by the time it was clear that the Valdani had decided to remain in Emeldar. Sentries were posted everywhere, every road and path into the village was blockaded, and search parties scoured the surrounding hills and cliffs. Tansen and Emelen hid in the shadowed crevices, scarcely daring to breathe as patrols passed them at regular intervals. They slept in their hiding places, cramped and uncomfortable, then renewed their vigil over Emeldar the next morning. By midday, they saw what they had been waiting for, but they couldn't safely slip away until after dark.

Cramped and stiff from spending two whole days in their hiding places, they were nonetheless elated as they stole out of Emeldar that night.

"I wonder how things went in Garabar," Emelen said quietly after they were well away from the Outlookers.

"We'll find out tomorrow night," Tansen replied.

REALIZING THAT HER red hair and burning eyes were so shocking that people either didn't notice or didn't care about the Guardian insignia she wore, Mirabar wore her cloak as she entered the village of Islanar, even though the increasingly warm weather made it a burden. She kept the hood pulled over her hair, its hem shading her eyes from view. With luck, people would take her for an old, stooped, and eccentric crone rather than a demon. She unfastened her Guardian insignia and held it in her hand, thrusting it out in front of her as she walked slowly down the main street of the village, praying that there were no Outlookers present.

Peeking out from the shadowed depths of her hood, she waited until she had the attention of what appeared to be most of the village. Then she waved her insignia around and cried, "I am hungry! I am homeless! This is the fate of the Guardians of the Otherworld under Valdani rule! Please! As you are good men and women, as you are faithful and true to Dar, I offer you my services for food!"

As she'd expected, everyone was too stunned to respond immediately. Most of them had probably never even seen a Guardian, and at least half of them probably didn't particularly believe in her talents. They *all* knew it was against Valdani law to deal with her. Hoping she could speed up events with a little show of strength, Mirabar stood upon the smooth cobbles of the main square, spread her arms in a big circle, filled her lungs, then slowly blew a circle of flame into life all around her.

It was gratifying to hear the way the crowd gasped, but

she didn't intend to use her fire to frighten anyone today.

Make them remember what they have lost, the Beckoner had advised her. *Make them remember why they need you.*

"I am the gateway to the Otherworld," she cried, keeping her head bent, wondering just how ridiculous she must look at the moment, and hoping her cloak didn't catch fire. "I will risk the fire for whosoever asks, for I come to serve."

Come on, come on, she thought. *Won't even* one *of you show a little courage?*

Finally, to her immense relief, someone stepped forward and spoke. Mirabar didn't dare risk looking up far enough to see the face, but she could plainly see the long, plain gown of a Sister as the petitioner approached her.

"*Sirana,* my husband died in the Year of Bitter Harvests," the woman said. "I . . . I *think* this is the anniversary. Near enough, anyhow, I hope. I have his knife here."

Mirabar held out her hand, subduing her flamboyant circle of flames so the Sister could come close enough to give her the knife. Swords and daggers were forbidden by law, but even the Valdani understood that no one could get through life without ordinary tools like this. Mirabar held the cold, rusted thing in her palm and groped for the gateway to the Otherworld. It had been so long since she had been permitted to participate in Callings, she knew a sudden, terrifying moment of doubt, afraid that she could no longer do it. Bluffing her way, she circled her hand in the air and made a fist, hearing the crowd gasp and chatter as her ring of flames now reshaped itself and tightened into a small circle of fire at her side.

Praying that she wasn't about to be slaughtered by the audience she had so recklessly attracted today, she began chanting. She tossed the knife into the flames and Called . . . "Goran," she said at last. "His name is Goran, and he is coming." She could have keeled over with relief, but she stood her ground and kept Calling. Naturally, no one but the Sister saw Goran, but most of the village seemed suitably impressed, nonetheless.

Someone fed her afterward, though she kept her head bowed and had to be very firm about refusing repeated suggestions that she take off her cloak before the sun got any higher. Feeling her energy return, she offered to do more Callings. By now, others were eager to accept the invitation. She performed three more Callings before her strength gave out. There were several more petitioners, and one of them suggested she remain in Islanar for another day, offering her food and shelter for the night.

That, she decided, was her cue. "You may not want me to stay, my friends, when—"

"Oh, we're not worried about Outlookers, *sirana*," an old man assured her. "They're all out searching for Josarian."

"Josarian?" she said on a choked breath. "Has he been here?"

"No, but two days ago he stole an entire shipment of grain outside of Garabar. Every Outlooker in the vicinity rode out of here yesterday in search of him."

"And Emeldar! Tell the *sirana* about Emeldar!" someone urged.

"Yes, there are many Valdani dead there, *sirana*. Hundreds!"

"It is not a thing to brag about," said the Sister; Mirabar recognized her voice by now.

"I'm sorry, Sister," someone else said, "but you're wrong."

"They were men," said the Sister, "the same as—"

"They were *Outlookers*."

"Friends, surely hospitality for the *sirana* is what we should be discussing!" a woman intervened.

Reeling from this information, Mirabar tried to pull her attention back to her own problems. "Uh, yes . . ."

"Honor my home, *sirana,* eat at my table, sleep beneath my roof."

"I appreciate your courtesy, friend," Mirabar said, "but there is something you must know about me first."

"Are you sought by the Valdani, *sirana*? They will not find you here. I promise!"

"Actually . . ."

"The Society?"

This notion provoked some distinctly uneasy murmurs, but the Sister stepped forward. "Even an assassin would not violate a Sanctuary. Please, *sirana*, honor the Sisterhood."

Sanctuary sounded like a good idea to Mirabar, since the Society would certainly be looking for her by morning. They heard everything; if they didn't already know about her misadventure the other day, they would unquestionably hear about her demonstration in Islanar today. "I will only accept your kind invitation if you repeat it after I lower my hood, Sister."

There was a long silence, then some confused whispers. Finally the Sister said, "After you lower your hood? Are you . . . disfigured, *sirana*? Surely you know that the Sisterhood—"

"I am not disfigured," Mirabar interrupted, "but some might call me a demon, accursed and damned by Dar."

Having warned them, Mirabar slowly lowered her hood, exposing flame-red hair and glowing fire orange eyes to the astonished crowd, hearing their gasps, whispers, and protestations begin even as her first curly lock appeared beneath the blazing Silerian sun.

"I am no demon," she said clearly, looking around. "But many are afraid of me. For no good reason," she added strongly. "I was born a *shallah*, the same as you. I am a Guardian and offer service to all who ask. I am blessed by Dar and sworn to uphold Her will, so long as I live."

Some people backed away. Others stared uncertainly. She saw one or two men seize their *yahr*. "The shades of the dead do not flinch from me. Your ancestors do not fear me. There *are* no demons, save those in your own hearts," she said. "But the Valdani would like nothing better than to see you kill me. If you would do their bidding, then kill me now." She watched their faces. "I will not fight you," she added for good measure. She was lying, of course, but it sounded good.

For a long, painful moment, things hung in the balance. Then, to her surprise, a child stepped forward, a scrawny, barefoot boy. Looking both confused and impatient, he said, "*Sirana,* can you Call my father? Can you? Can you? I won't let anyone hurt you. Can you Call my father?"

"Yes," she said, hoping she was telling the truth. "If I live till dawn, I will Call your father for you tomorrow."

"Live till dawn?" a young woman with three children clinging to her long tunic exclaimed. "*Sirana,* are we barbarians to believe the superstitious tales we heard as children?"

Mirabar eyed the *yahr* that an adolescent boy was slowly twirling at the edge of the crowd. "I don't know. Are you?"

To her surprise, a stoop-backed man clobbered the boy. "Save your blustering for the Valdani, as Josarian does, you fool! Would you do their bidding, as the *sirana* accuses?"

"She's a demon! Look at her!" an old woman screamed. "A demon!"

"Has she not shown us the Otherworld today?" the Sister shouted back. "Would Goran and the others so embrace the fire of a demon, you silly old woman?"

"She is well-spoken for a demon," a fat man pointed out dryly. He had very fine clothes; perhaps he was a merchant or skilled craftsman.

The barefoot little boy pressed his scrawny body against Mirabar's legs, apparently intending to protect her as he had sworn to do. "She is not a demon! Demons wear gray tunics and ride dust-blowing monsters!"

This outburst silenced the bickering crowd for a moment.

"Outlookers?" Mirabar smiled wryly. "He has a point. What could I do to you that they have not already done?"

"That's what Josarian would say," someone pointed out.

"Yes, those would be his words!"

"Josarian would tell you that she is not the enemy! They are! I have heard him say so in Malthenar!"

"Josarian's cousin was wounded at Britar and Josarian left him in the care of another so-called demon," the Sister said. That got everyone's attention, including Mirabar's.

"Another . . . like me?" Mirabar asked in astonishment.

"He was dark-haired. A *toren.* A Guardian." The Sister looked around at the crowd. "But his eyes glowed like the heart of Darshon, and he was forced to flee Liron because Verlon, an eastern waterlord, sought to kill him."

"How do *you* know this, Basimar?" someone challenged.

The Sister colored ever so faintly, faltering for a moment. Then she rallied. "After Garabar, Zimran came to my Sanctuary for healing. He said that he had learned that those like the *sirana* here are not demons, but blessed by Dar and feared by the Society, the Conquerors, and the Valdani because they are too hard to enslave!"

It was a stunning announcement, one which went against the popular misconceptions passed down for centuries in Sileria and traditionally embraced by the *shallaheen.*

"Cheylan, the fire-eyed Guardian, cared for Zimran, protected him, and kept him safe until Josarian could return for him. Are those the acts of a demon?" Sister Basimar cried.

"Cheylan," Mirabar breathed. "Another like *me.*"

"Would Guardians have taken in, sheltered, and initiated demons for centuries?" Basimar demanded of the villagers. "Would a demon stand before you now and offer her life for your trust?"

"Who knows *what* a demon would do?" someone said with open suspicion.

"*I* know," snapped the stoop-backed old man, "for I spent ten years in the mines, where demons rule the neverending night. Do not speak to *me* of demons until you have lived day after day under the lash of their whips in the caverns of hell!"

That seemed to end the discussion. While it was clear that not everyone was comfortable with her presence, Mirabar was invited to remain in the village and was shown the gracious hospitality which even the poorest of *shallaheen* traditionally offered to a welcome guest.

Make them welcome your kind again, the Beckoner had said. *It is the first step . . .*

But only the first step, Mirabar knew.

Three days later, hiding in Sanctuary, she decided it was time to give a carefully worded explanation of her quest to her small handful of new friends from Islanar. She told them that messages from the Otherworld told her she must find a great warrior who would drive out the Valdani; since half the folktales told in these mountains were about someday getting rid of the Valdani, this news didn't raise too many eyebrows.

"You've seen how difficult it is for people to trust me," she said, "so I want your help: introductions in other villages, places where you have relations."

"But this great warrior you seek, *sirana,* surely it must be Josarian?"

Mirabar shook her head. "I've met Josarian. A great man, truly, but not the one I seek."

"Then who, *sirana?* Who could it possibly be?"

"I don't know."

"Is it the Firebringer?"

"I don't know," Mirabar repeated. "I only know that . . ."

"What? Please, you are among friends. We wish to serve you as you have served us."

"To find him . . ."

"Yes?"

She took the plunge. "I must first find Kiloran."

There was a long, shocked silence. Finally Basimar said, "For that, *sirana,* you will need more than the Fires of Dar and the blessing of the Otherworld to shield you."

Mirabar nodded wearily. "I had a feeling you'd say that."

*   *   *

KOROLL ESTIMATED THAT he had been locked in his cell in Shaljir's old Kintish fortress for nineteen days when four Outlookers suddenly appeared to release and escort him—to his utter astonishment—to the Imperial Advisor's palace in Santorell Square. He had been there several times before, for Valdani religious festivities, celebrations of important victories against the Emperor's enemies abroad, or extravagant events staged to welcome dignitaries. He had never before arrived filthy, stinking, and completely ungroomed, and he was well aware of the curious stares he drew as his armed escort led him directly to the Imperial Advisor's counsel hall. A vast room of polished marble, luxuriant furniture, and imported tapestries, it seemed a place of utter chaos at the moment.

Advisor Borell, the most important man in Sileria, was bellowing at some servant when Koroll entered the crowded room, then continued sharpening his tongue on every man who crossed his path as he strode across the vast hall toward Koroll. He was an enormous man, broad enough around the girth to account for two healthy men. Yet, despite a life of luxury and a well-known taste for pleasure, he gave the impression that his enormous bulk was more muscle than fat. A mature man who still had many productive years left before him, he was shrewd, ambitious, and ruthless when it suited him.

His neatly trimmed beard, Koroll noted, was just starting to turn gray, as was his close-cropped hair. Brushing off the servant who tried to hand him a goblet of wine, Borell glared directly into Koroll's eyes, his steely blue gaze sparkling with anger, and demanded, "Why did he have you arrested?"

Bewildered, Koroll stammered, "Your Eminence? I don't quite underst—"

"It's a simple question, you fool!" Borell leaned close and repeated, as if speaking to a half-witted child with whom he had lost all patience, "Why did Daroll have you arrested?"

Treading carefully, wondering what was going on, Koroll answered, "We disagreed about the best way to handle the uprising in my district, Eminence."

"Indeed? And what were your thoughts on the matter?"

Something about Borell's manner suggested to Koroll that his very life depended upon his answer. Praying fervently to the Three that it was the right response, he said, "I felt harsher measures were needed than did Commander Daroll. I felt that his plan to solicit information with bribes would prove largely unrewarding due to traditional Silerian—"

"You warned him about this? You told him—"

"Warned him about what, Eminence?" Koroll asked, desperate for information.

Borell's face darkened with renewed rage. "Yes, you've been locked up, you wouldn't know."

"Sir?"

"Daroll is dead, as are the one hundred fifty men he took with him!"

Koroll nearly choked on his own gasp. *"Dead?* All of them?"

"Two have survived, but they're ill and will take a long time to recover."

"Wounded?"

"Poisoned."

"What?"

"We've been able to piece together what happened, based on the priests' examination of Daroll's corpse and the testimony of the two remaining men."

"Three Into One, how did—"

"This bandit . . . what's his name again?"

"Josarian, sir."

"Yes. Quite." Borell frowned. "He stole a supply of poison—meant for our arrows—from some outpost. The theft was never reported because everyone there was killed and the place was burned to the ground."

"Yes, that is his usual—"

"The filthy peasant's native village was found to have

been abandoned when Daroll arrived there with well over one hundred men. Suspecting a trap, for apparently eighty men had already been lost in an attack upon the town, he set up sentries, sent out search parties, and took all the precautions one would certainly hope he'd take after such a blunder."

Koroll held his breath, uncertain if Borell knew *who* had sent those eighty men to their deaths.

"There were no disturbances, however. Daroll then decided to use the village as his base for hunting down the outlaw, and he set up camp there." Borell ground his teeth together. "A day later, of course, the men's waterskins were all empty, so they started drawing water from the central fountain."

"And the gods grew thirsty," Koroll whispered, sinking into a chair without asking permission.

"The water was poisoned. Not enough to kill instantly. Josarian's no fool; he knew only a few would drink the water if the men who drank it suddenly died. It tooks five days for the first one to die, by which time all the men and horses . . ." Borell's shoulders slumped. "It was too late for them."

"How did two survive?"

"They were messengers sent back here on the third day after arriving in Emeldar. They fell ill in the mountains, and it took them many days to recover enough strength to continue the journey on foot—their horses were dead or stolen by then, we're not sure which. They stayed at one of those . . . Sanctuaries. The women there didn't let them die, but several *shallaheen* accepted payment from the two helpless men for messages which were, of course, never delivered to Shaljir."

"This is . . ." Koroll couldn't summon words big enough to describe such a disaster. He was already losing count of how many Valdani Josarian had killed.

"There's more," Borell said.

"More?"

"More," Borell confirmed. "You've been locked up a

long time." He went on to describe the scope of Josarian's recent crimes, which included robbing a grain shipment at Garabar which he then, incredible as it sounded, distributed to five *shallah* villages. Next, he had attacked a company of Outlookers carrying tribute for the Emperor from Adalian. No one had any idea where the gold, crops, and livestock had gone, but rumor suggested that he had distributed that, too. "Thus ensuring the loyalty of the *shallaheen*," Borell said.

"Yes, their loyalty is his shield, and he knows it," Koroll murmured, overwhelmed by what had happened during his imprisonment.

"They've started following his example, too," Borell continued. "Riots, theft, sudden attacks on our priests and on any Outlooker foolhardy enough to leave his outpost alone."

"The *shallaheen* will not betray Josarian, Eminence. We must find him without their help. We must devote all our resources to stopping him."

"I agree. So you can imagine my surprise when I returned home from Liron to learn that not only has Shaljir been deprived of its military governor, but the Commander of Cavasar is absent from his district, too—and in prison!" Borell studied him with a coldly assessing gaze. "Tell me what happened here, Koroll."

No one had been present when Koroll had reported events in Cavasar to Daroll, and now Daroll was dead. Who except he and Myrell knew the truth now? Who else could testify with absolute certainty that this mess was not of Daroll's making? Now the Three revealed his destiny to him; now Their favor was finally made apparent.

"Your pardon, Eminence. I blame myself," he said humbly. "If only I had pressed Commander Daroll harder when this disaster first began. If only I had risked his ire and been more insistent when requesting help."

"How long ago *did* this disaster begin," Borell asked sharply, "and why wasn't I informed?"

Koroll feigned surprise. "But surely, Eminence . . . I

mean, he said it was *your* ruling, after consultation with him, that we must not attribute too much importance to one lone bandit who had managed to murder a couple of Outlookers while smuggling—"

"What?" Borell sputtered.

I have him, Koroll thought triumphantly, *I* have *him!*

By the time he was done reciting a creative account of recent events, Koroll had managed to make Daroll responsible for Myrell's actions and the appalling losses at Britar, as well as the death of eighty of Koroll's men in Emeldar. He made sure that every bad decision appeared to have come from Daroll, and he subtly convinced Borell that he himself had seriously feared the ramifications of Josarian's attacks from the start but had been unable to make Daroll see this as anything more than the pranks of one impudent peasant—a view which could be attributed to the arrogant young aristocrat without much stretching.

"I am not a miltary man, Koroll," Borell said when the devastating account was complete, "and we cannot wait for a new appointee from Valda. This problem is too serious, the danger too immediate."

Borell arose and summoned an Outlooker to his side. The man brought him the Seal of Shaljir, the symbol of the highest military office in Sileria, which had been taken from Daroll's corpse. Koroll's heart pounded with elation and his mouth went dry as he gazed upon the golden, jewel-embedded seal.

"Commander Koroll," Borell said, omitting the lengthy ceremonial opening such an occasion would usually call for, "as the Emperor's eyes, ears, and right hand in Sileria, under the powers granted me by His Radiance for use in times of war, famine, and plague, I hereby name you Military Commander of Shaljir and its district, and thus High Commander of Sileria, with all of the powers, privileges, and responsibilities inherent in that office."

Borell slipped the heavy golden chain over Koroll's head, letting it slide down until the full weight of the Seal of Shaljir hung from his neck.

Mine, Koroll thought, touching the longed-for symbol of power and prosperity with trembling hands. *Mine.*

"I thank you for this profound honor, Eminence," he said, his voice rich with triumph, "and I assure you that I will not fail you, His Radiance, or the Empire."

"See that you don't." Borell's attention was diverted by a servant who entered the counsel hall in a hurry. "Yes?"

"A messenger from *Torena* Elelar, Your Eminence. Will you receive him?"

"From Elelar?" Borell's whole countenance changed, the steely eyes softening with pleasure, the dark scowl lightening with anticipation. "Yes, of course. Send him right in."

The servant bowed and hurried back out. Borell cast a dismissive glance at Koroll. "Surely you have immediate duties to attend to, Commander. I suggest we meet again after you've had time to review the current situation and formulate a military strategy for dealing with this murdering, thieving scoundrel."

"Certainly, Eminence. Considering the serious nature of the situation, I suggest that by this evening I should be able to propose—"

"No, not this evening," Borell said, smiling slightly as a Silerian servant entered the hall and bowed respectfully. "I expect to be . . . quite occupied this evening."

12

WITH A HOLLOW heart, Tansen gazed down at the body of the assassin he had just slain. This one had been more experienced than the first one: older, shrewder, and far more skilled. Tansen had killed him quickly, wanting to get it over with. This one had even hinted that he knew *why* Kiloran had once sworn a bloodvow against Tansen—knew and approved. This one had made memories come tumbling back as inexorably as water flowing downhill, memories which Tansen fought as determinedly as he had just fought the assassin.

Nonetheless, the memories came, just as pain came with the cut of a *shir,* no matter how one tried to ignore it. For the *shir* was no ordinary blade, and these were no ordinary memories.

For a moment, Tansen stood again on the southern shores of Sileria, the wind high and chill, the sea pounding violently against the rocks, the night shadowed and cruel beneath a dark-moon sky. Yes, for a moment, he stood there again, his tear-blurred eyes gazing down not upon the corpse of another nameless assassin, but upon the suddenly lifeless body of the man whose name Tansen had not spoken aloud since his boyhood—which had ended forever that very night. For just one moment, he saw again the face of the first man he had ever killed: a man who had trusted him—even loved him. And for a painful moment, Elelar's horrified screams filled the air once again: *What have you done? Sweet Dar, what have you DONE?*

Tansen drew a shallow, shaky breath and looked away, crushing the pain, silencing the memories. He flipped the blood off his blades, then wiped them carefully before sheathing them, thinking that he must clean them later. Then he turned away, avoiding the men's eyes as he brushed past them, seeking solitude.

"And what shall we tell the next one who comes looking for you, *roshah?*" Zimran snapped. "Whose liver do you suppose he'll cut out if you are not here? Josarian's? Mine? Amitan's?"

Struck by the venom in the man's voice, Tansen whirled to face him. The rest of the men watched warily, their expressions grim. More than forty of Josarian's men, those with nowhere else to go, lived up here in the Dalishar Caves now. More than a hundred others who had joined Josarian's bloodfeud still lived with their families, unknown and unsought by the Valdani so far. Ready to fight whenever called, they made up a growing network of useful informants and convenient hiding places.

Realizing that Zimran's growing hostility toward him had finally found an outlet and that it would be pointless to postpone this confrontation, Tansen stepped back into the center of the circle the men had formed around him and the assassin.

"The next one," he said, "will come only for me, as this one did. Kiloran will not be satisfied with *your* liver or anyone else's."

"Oh, and assassins never make mistakes? Or kill out of anger or frustration? The next one won't think it expedient to kill your friends and allies if you—"

"Zimran—" Josarian interrupted.

"You are blinded by him!" Zimran shouted at his cousin. "You're so impressed by his swords and his fancy fighting and his unmentionable past that you don't see that he will get us all killed!"

"I am impressed by his courage, his loyalty, and his honor," Josarian said firmly, "and so should you be. Who held off the Outlookers when they made a surprise attack at our backs while we robbed their wage shipment on the road from Cavasar? Who stole the horses at Morven so the Outlookers there couldn't pursue us after we looted—"

"And who has led an assassin straight to us?" Zimran snapped. "Do you think we can fight the Valdani *and* the Society?"

"No one can fight the Society," Falian said. "Even the Valdani cannot win against them."

Josarian whirled to face him. "There will be no—"

"Enough, Josarian," Tansen said quietly. "If Zimran and others here have something to say, let them say it."

"Then I have something to say, too," Josarian insisted. "I will not—"

"No," Tansen said. "You cannot make them trust me. Each man makes that choice for himself."

Looking unhappy about it, Josarian finally nodded his

agreement. "Then I will say only this. I trust Tansen and will continue to do so. The rest of you . . . must speak your minds and follow your hearts." He turned and strode out of the circle of men surrounding Tansen and Zimran, disappearing from view.

"I stand with Tansen," Emelen said, putting physical distance between himself and Zimran. "Regardless of who's looking for him, or why."

The days Tansen and Emelen had spent together, poisoning the precious water in Emeldar, awaiting the Valdani invasion, and travelling back to Dalishar, had forged their friendship. But Emelen, Tansen had quickly realized, had more courage and wit than most men; a fitting choice for Josarian's only sister. Others might be more apt to forget how Tansen had fought by their sides for more than a twin-moon, now that Zimran raised the specter of the Society.

It was inevitable, Tansen supposed. Most of these men had known and trusted each other all their lives, whereas they had only known him a short time; and *shallaheen* did not easily trust a stranger, especially not one whose habits were so different and whose past was largely unknown. And, of course, it was dangerous to make friends with any enemy of Kiloran's.

Although the Valdani didn't yet know where Josarian and his men were hiding, it wasn't surprising that the Society had already found out. Very little happened in Sileria that they didn't know about. The assassin who had come here today in search of Tansen was merely the first. There would be others, many others. No one would care that the nine years had passed; a warrior who had already killed two assassins would now be too big a prize to pass up unless Kiloran himself insisted he be left in peace. Before long, the assassins wouldn't be the only ones looking for Tansen, either, for killing a marked man was the very best way to gain initiation into the dark mysteries of the Honored Society.

"Why does Kiloran seek you?" Zimran demanded, his handsome features animated with anger.

"That is between me and Kiloran."

"You ask for our trust—"

"I ask for nothing. Trust can only be given freely, never demanded or—"

"—yet you give us none of yours!"

"—begged for."

Amitan stepped forward. "Zimran is right. If we are to trust you, we have a right to know why the most powerful waterlord in the world wants you dead. If you're going to bring us trouble with the Society, we deserve to know why."

There were murmurs of agreement, nodding heads, suspicious stares.

"If he says it's between him and Kiloran—" Emelen began.

"No, Emelen," Lann argued. "We deserve to know if he did something dishonorable, something—"

"I took something from Kiloran," Tansen said suddenly, surprising himself as much as the others. Seeing their expectant expressions, he added, "Something of great value to him. Something he can never get back."

"Something of great value." Amitan looked doubtfully at Tansen's humble, ill-fitting clothes, seeing no evidence that Tansen himself had this thing of value now. "Where is it?"

"Gone," Tansen said quietly. "Lost forever."

Zimran glared at him. "What was it?"

"It was . . ." Tansen hesitated. "Power."

Zim snorted with disbelief. "You had power that Kiloran wanted?"

"No. I never had it. I only said that I took it away from him."

"What power? Water magic?"

"No." Tansen looked down at the assassin's *shir* which now lay in the dust. "The power to ruin us all."

"What power was this?" When Tansen didn't answer, Zimran prodded, "How did you take it?"

"That's none of your business."

"I think it is, *roshah*. Some night an assassin may stick his *shir* between my ribs because he thinks I'm your friend."

"I *am* his friend," Lann said, his voice as loud as ever. "If he says he took something valuable from Kiloran, then I am satisfied with his answer—as long as he didn't hurt women and children." Lann raised a questioning brow as he glanced at Tansen.

"I didn't," Tansen said quietly.

Lann nodded. "Then I am ready for any killer that comes here, Valdan or assassin."

"Then you are a fool," Zimran said harshly, standing his ground when the much larger man made a threatening move toward him. "How long before Kiloran himself decides to deal with Tansen?" This had a noticeable effect on the men. "Who is to say what we might face if we keep this *roshah* among us? An *army* of assassins, when they get tired of dying at his hands one by one? Or will Kiloran send the White Dragon after us?"

Emelen scowled. "Now you try to frighten us with children's tales."

"You're a fool if you believe it's only a tale," Zimran said. He looked around at the men. "You know how waterlords kill. Everyone knows. If Kiloran can flood a whole village and make the water stop at the very edge of a cliff, if he can turn lakes so cold that Valdani lose their hands when reaching into them for a drink of water, if he can curl rivers back upon themselves and make lakes dry up overnight—"

"Yes, everyone knows that," Amitan said impatiently, "but a beast born of magical union between a wizard and water?"

"How do you think Harlon killed all those Valdani when the Society's feud with the Emperor began?" Falian prodded. "The White Dragon!"

"They drowned, you idiot," said Emelen. "Harlon pulled the lake up over their heads and—"

"And that doesn't bother you?" Zimran pounced. He

pointed inside the main cave. "It doesn't worry you that someday the spring in there may rise up to drown us all? That it will cover your face like a mask, no matter how far you run, until you suffocate? That it will freeze like ice over your body until your parts fall off one by one? And all because we shelter *him* among us!"

Everyone looked at Tansen. Now Zimran spoke of horrors that no one doubted the waterlords could inflict upon them.

"We are only outlaws," Emelen said slowly. "We are only *shallaheen* feuding with the Valdani, Kiloran's worst enemies. Why should he—"

"How do we know who Kiloran's worst enemy is, Emelen?" Zimran argued. "How do we know it isn't *him?*"

Tansen remained conspicuously silent.

"Kiloran hates Baran more than he hates the Valdani," Zimran persisted. "Baran, who's trying to take the Idalar River from him. 'Something of great value,' " he mocked. "If this *roshah* stays among us, Emelen, then you'd better pray with all your might that there really *is* no White Dragon, or you'll die in never-ending agony, tormented beyond endurance until Kiloran, too, finally dies. And *then* there'll be no Otherworld for you, only oblivion. You'll never see Jalilar again, or—"

"Enough!" Emelen said. "That's enough! I can see what you're trying to do."

"You don't know, Emelen," Amitan argued. "We don't know what Kiloran will do, we don't know how far he'll go to kill Tansen. If we get in his way—"

"Show a little courage for once in your life!" Lann snarled.

"Are you calling me a coward?"

"What would *you* call a man who turns away from a friend the first time there's trouble?"

"This is more than trouble, you fool!"

"We've all sworn a bloodfeud together!"

"I swore it with Josarian, not a stranger from Gamalan!"

"We swore the same vow Tansen did, *sriliah!*"

Amitan's eyes bulged. "Take that back! Take it back or—"

"*Stop!*" Emelen stepped between the two men before they could come to blows. "Stop it *now!* Will you kill each other so the Valdani won't have to? Will you make less work for our blood enemies?"

There was a deadly silence. Uneasy expressions, shifting weight, fingers groping unconsciously for swords and *yahr,* loyalties divided, ancient fears called up from the depths of their hearts, from the darkest corners of their minds. Tansen saw it all and knew the time had come, knew he had no choice now.

"Tansen," Emelen muttered at last. "For the love of Dar . . . *say something.*"

The *shallah* boy inside Tansen cried out for an ally, for someone to stand with him against the most powerful waterlord in the world. The *shatai* kept his expression impassive and settled coldly on the only logical decision. "I'm leaving."

"Leaving?" Emelen blurted, looking betrayed.

"Leaving!" Lann cried.

"What?" Amitan looked confused.

"Ah . . ." Zimran smiled triumphantly.

"What do you mean you're leaving?" Emelen snapped.

"Zimran is . . ." Tansen shrugged and said dryly, "Well, I never thought I'd hear myself say it, but Zimran may be right."

Someone laughed involuntarily. Zimran, who had been at odds with Tansen ever since they met, scowled. Emelen threw up his hands in disgust. Amitan still looked confused.

"I don't believe in the White Dragon," Tansen said. "I'm not even sure I believe in the Otherworld." He drew a breath. "But your fight now is with the Valdani. You cannot risk making enemies with the Society; they would finish you off like a dragonfish swallowing a guppy."

"I am not so easy to kill," Lann growled.

"When one waterlord is defied, others may well join

with him to punish the offenders," Tansen said. "In such matters, the Society have often temporarily put aside their differences; it's what has always made them stronger than the rest of us." He glanced pointedly from Lann to Amitan. Then he continued, "Kiloran's fight is with me, and only with me, but I cannot deny that he may choose to make an enemy of anyone who seems to be my friend."

"I have said that I am ready—"

"No," Tansen interrupted Lann. "You must fight the Valdani. For yourselves, for each other, for your families. *That* is your battle. I wanted it to be mine, too . . ." He shook his head. "But mine is with Kiloran, and until it's settled, I'm too dangerous an ally for you."

"Until it's settled?" Emelen repeated uneasily. "How do you propose to settle it?"

Tansen met his friend's gaze. "I must find Kiloran."

"Find Kiloran? Oh, now *that's* an excellent plan," Emelen snapped. "Why didn't *I* think of that?"

"He will kill you before you get halfway to Garabar," Zimran said, sounding rather smug.

"Shut up," Emelen ordered Zimran.

"Don't you tell me—"

"Overlooking, for the moment, that it's unquestionably the quickest way to get yourself killed, what makes you even think you can find him?" Emelen demanded of Tansen, ignoring Zimran.

"I can find him," Tansen replied. "I . . ." He sighed. "I know who to ask."

So he would ask for her help, after all. The part of him that didn't recoil in shame was sparked into blazing life at the thought of seeing her again after all these years. He would go to her because he had to, because he had no choice, because he needed her help. In truth, he would go to her because, in the end, he couldn't stay away. He was a fool, to be sure, but he would go to her again, just as a secretive, shameful part of him had always known he would.

"Even if you *can* find him," Emelen said, clearly not

believing him, "what are you going to do once you see him? What makes you think he won't kill you on the spot?"

"Nothing," Tansen admitted. "But I didn't come home after nine years to simply hide, praying that he'd just forget about me if I cowered long enough. And I won't leave Sileria again. Whether it be tomorrow or forty years from now, I will die here."

"You certainly will," Zimran said sardonically.

"I waited nine years," Tansen said. "If he kills me now, he dishonors himself."

Emelen stared at him. "You can't seriously believe he cares about that?"

"Maybe he expects you to survive for nine years *here* before he'll let you live," Zimran suggested.

"Shut up," Lann told him. "They call themselves the *Honored* Society, after all. Others have gone into exile and been permitted to come home, after nine years, to live in peace."

"Yes, but that was long ago," Amitan said. "Before we were born."

"Those were richer days, easier nights," said Emelen. "Now even waterlords must scheme and scrape and claw to survive. Even they are too bitter to honor their own customs."

"I am not so easy to kill, either," Tansen reminded him.

"No, but Kiloran can kill *anyone*, Tansen."

"I won't stay here and risk making the rest of you his enemies. I won't go into hiding. I won't go back into exile. And although I *could* kill every single assassin who comes for me, that might get a little tiring as the years go by." He met Emelen's gaze. "What else is there for me to do? I will find Kiloran. He will make peace with me, or he won't. If he won't, one of us will die."

The silence which met this calm statement indicated that they all had no doubts about *which* one would die. Inside of Tansen, a *shallah* boy screamed that he wanted to live, and a warrior prepared to face his death even as he coldly calculated how he might preserve his life. From the moment he had come home, he had known that he must face Kiloran, return the *shir,* and stake his life against the honor of a man who had none, the power of a man more powerful than any other. He had known that he would have to look full into the face of what he had done on that moonless night so long ago. He had come home to face the wrath of both Kiloran and Dar, for he could know no peace anywhere until he had done so.

"When will you leave?" Emelen asked at last, his voice thin and tired.

Tansen looked up at the sky. "Now. As soon as I gather my things. There's at least four good hours of walking left to this day."

Emelen nodded. "I'll . . . pack some food. And some money. There's plenty left from the Outlooker wages we stole."

"Pack enough for two." Josarian's voice, coming from outside of the gathered crowd of men, startled them all.

The crowd parted and Tansen looked past them to Josarian, who was seated on a rock. He'd assumed Josarian had gone off hunting—or brooding—after agreeing to withdraw from the argument. Instead, he'd been sitting right there, listening, the whole time.

"Why?" Tansen asked.

"Because I'm coming with you."

"How far?"

"All the way."

The men exploded with protests. Tansen said nothing, since they were already saying everything he would say: Josarian was needed here, to lead them; without him, their bloodfeud against the Valdani would fall apart; they couldn't plan and execute daring raids and attacks the way he could; what would they do if Kiloran killed him, too, and he never came back?

"What will happen to us?" Falian demanded.

Josarian pushed his way through the throng of panicking men and stood in the middle of the circle they formed.

"You will carry on without me." The strength of Josarian's voice refuted all argument, but men still shook their heads and muttered reproachfully. "This is a *bloodfeud,* not my private quarrel. It will live beyond my death, and I pray Dar that it will live beyond all of yours, too."

"But we've only just begun it, and no one has ever—"

"Candan mar Dishon shah Sirdari died on the first *day* of the bloodfeud he began against Tansen's clan, the Gamalani, yet it lasted for more than forty years."

"The Sirdari were not fighting the Valdani!" Amitan protested.

"And the Sirdari did not have nearly one hundred fifty men sworn to their cause," Josarian countered. "I won't live forever. I probably won't even live *long.*"

"You *definitely* won't live long if you go off with this *roshah* now." Zimran's voice was rough with mingled fury and fear.

"Zimran . . ." Josarian's expression softened slightly with affection. "Zim, the Valdani are now offering ten times the money they first offered Tansen to kill me, and the price on my head will only keep going up. Outlookers scour every village, every Sanctuary, every farm and shrine and shepherd's hut in the district searching for me. Whether I go with Tansen or stay here, you cannot count on my living long."

"Don't," Zimran begged. "Don't even say that. It's bad luck. Gods hear men who speak so carelessly of their own deaths, and they—"

"I swore a bloodfeud so the fight against the Valdani would outlive me, would outlive all of us." Josarian looked around. "Are you telling me that if a Valdani arrow finds my heart tomorrow, you'll all quit and go home?"

"We can't go home," Lann pointed out. "We poisoned the water. Only a waterlord can fix that."

"Do be sure to ask Kiloran when you see him," Zimran growled.

"If Dar wills it so, then I will return," Josarian said. "If not, then you will carry on."

"And who will lead us while you're gone?" Amitan demanded. "Someone must lead us!"

"Yes, I agree," Josarian said. "There must be someone with whom the final decisions rest."

Zimran nodded and started to step forward, then froze with shock when Josarian announced, "Emelen will take charge until I return. In my absence, he speaks for me."

"And if you don't return?" Amitan demanded.

"Then you will choose a leader from among you, whether it be Emelen or another."

Tansen saw their reluctance, but Josarian's power of command was such that they would follow his will. All except, perhaps, Zimran, whose dark eyes burned with betrayal, anger, and hurt.

"We are agreed then," Josarian said at last, seeing that no one else offered any objections.

"Not quite," Tansen said. "I won't let you come with me."

Some of the men were clearly shocked by his words. Josarian merely laughed.

"What will you do?" Josarian asked. "Kill me? No, I don't think so. Leave me behind? Hah! You can't outrun *me*, Tansen, not in these mountains. Sneak away while I'm sleeping? I'm not such a heavy sleeper."

"I'll—"

"Save your threats for someone who has something to fear from you," Josarian advised. "I'm coming with you to find Kiloran."

Tansen looked helplessly at him. *"Why?"*

Josarian shook his head. "You're in Sileria again. You're a *shallah* again. You must forget about these foreign ways you learned."

"I don't . . ."

"I'm your bloodbrother, and—thanks to the Sirdari and the Valdani—you have no other family. You can't seriously expect me to let you seek out a waterlord, one who has sworn a bloodvow against you, by yourself."

"He will kill anyone with me," Tansen said through gritted teeth.

"And the Valdani will kill anyone with *me*." Josarian shrugged. "I suggest we *both* be very careful."

13

"SIRANA . . . ARE YOU well now?"

Mirabar blinked and looked around in confusion. "Where are we?"

Sister Basimar, who had been her companion ever since she had left Islanar, said, "Beside Lake Ursan."

"A house of water . . ."

Basimar blinked. "Yes. You were taken ill suddenly while staring into the water, and you kept saying strange things: a house of water; fire in water; find the *shir* and you find him." She paused and added, "You also kept saying something about an alliance."

"The alliance . . ." Mirabar tried to sit up, then groaned and lay her throbbing head back down on the soft ground. "I'm not mad," she said, hoping she sounded convincing.

"You are troubled, though."

"*Tormented* would be a more accurate word."

"By these visions?"

"Yes. By the visions. By powerful spirits from the Otherworld. By sights and sounds I don't really understand."

"It's good you didn't have this fit until after we were well away from the village."

Although they had gained cautious acceptance in several of the villages to which Basimar had guided Mirabar, too many people still seemed to be studying her for signs of a demonic curse.

"Yes," Mirabar agreed dryly. "Rolling around on the

ground, screaming and uttering nonsense, would have created a bad impression."

"Truly, if you should have one of these fits in public—"

"I won't."

"How can you be so sure?"

"The Beckoner wouldn't want me to. He knows I'd be killed on the spot, and he wants me to live. For the time being, anyhow." She squinted up at Basimar, her eyes watering against the glare of the afternoon sun. "And I guess he knows you won't hurt me."

"I am a Sister," Basimar pointed out. "Respect for all living things is my creed. I couldn't harm you even if I were afraid of you."

"And you're not afraid?" Mirabar asked doubtfully.

Basimar shrugged. "Perhaps your life has been harsher than mine, *sirana,* and your . . . gifts are certainly unusual, but we are both women and both *shallaheen.*"

"You have a long-winded way of saying no."

Basimar laughed. "My husband used to say that, *sirana.*"

"Stop calling me that," she said irritably. "My name is Mirabar."

"Given what I have seen so far, it seems disrespectful to call you—"

"How old are you?"

"What?"

"Thirty? Thirty-five?"

"Thirty-six."

"Well, we—Tashinar and I—we *think* I'm about eighteen. So doesn't it seem silly for you to call me *sirana* all the time?"

"I . . ." Basimar sighed. "I had a daughter who would be almost your age now, had she lived, *sira* . . . Mirabar."

"There, you see?"

After a reflective silence, Basimar asked about the visions. When she felt steady enough, Mirabar sat up and drew the mysterious symbol that continued to haunt her visions in the dirt. "Have you ever seen this?"

"No, I don't think so."

"Oh, well."

"What is it?"

"I don't know." She stared at it. "But I must find it. I must find the *shir*. I think they will be together."

"Do you think they belong to Kiloran?"

"I don't *think* so." She shook her head in confusion. "I don't know. I think they belong to the warrior that I seek."

"Then . . . is Kiloran the warrior?"

"Darfire! I hope not!"

"Well, does Kiloran have the warrior, then?"

"I don't know . . . He may have the warrior with him, or perhaps he can simply point the way."

"Is the warrior his friend or ally? An assassin?" Basimar frowned. "Another waterlord?"

"I don't know."

"So . . . the warrior could even be his prisoner, couldn't he?"

Mirabar's gaze flashed up to Basimar's round face. "His prisoner?" she whispered. "Dar help us, that's one I hadn't thought of."

THE SKY-REACHING TOWERS of Shaljir loomed against the horizon when Tansen and Josarian were still far from the city. Although Josarian had once been to Cavasar, he had never before seen anything so grand and awe-inspiring as the sight he now beheld. Standing on a summit, he and Tansen overlooked the broad, paved road where traffic flowed toward the Adalian Gate, the southern entrance to the city.

Of the three hundred spires which had graced the city in Daurion's time, only a handful were left. Josarian was so impressed by the sight of these graceful spirals of stone and marble reaching toward the heavens that his dazzled mind couldn't imagine even *more* of them filling the sky.

In any event, their absence was amply compensated for by the tall round towers the Moorlanders had left behind. They were topped by enormous stone dragons and impressive horned creatures, carved centuries ago by the hairy barbarians who believed such figures frightened away the demons they feared.

The many hundreds of red-domed buildings left behind by centuries of Kintish rule pleased the eye, weaving brilliant splashes of vivid color through the stone city when viewed from this distance. And although Josarian hated the Valdani with a passion that never abated, he could not deny the beauty of the vast, ornately decorated Valdani palaces that Tansen pointed out to him from their vantage point.

"What are all of those shacks and tents outside the city walls?" he asked his friend.

"Poor people," Tansen replied, "who've come to the city looking for work."

"*Shallaheen?*"

"*Shallaheen,* lowlanders, runaways, petty thieves, prostitutes, lunatics, escaped galley slaves from ships that docked here or foundered off shore . . . The poorest of the poor." He gazed at the hovels huddling beneath Sileria's brassy sun for a moment before adding, "The Valdani clean them all out of there every so often, chasing them away and burning down their shanties. A few days later, those that survive start putting up shacks and tents near some other part of the city's walls."

"They should never have left the mountains," Josarian said, looking at the slum sorrowfully. "That is no place for a *shallah.*"

"I don't think many of them come by choice."

"And perhaps now you'll tell me why *we* are coming here. I've asked you before and gotten no answer. You've been sulking ever since we left Dalishar."

"I do *not* sulk."

Josarian grinned, pleased to see him looking offended. "Oh, I've had plenty of time these past few days to study your mood, and sulking is *precisely* what you've been doing. It got worse after I caught you trying to sneak off without me the other night."

"I told you not to come," Tansen said irritably.

"I told you not to try leaving me behind. I go wherever you go, even if you choose to be worse company than a wounded mountain cat."

"Don't force your company on me and then have the gall to complain about my mood," Tansen grumbled.

Without waiting for a reply, he started scrambling down the mountain. However, Josarian noticed that, once they reached the main road, Tansen seemed to have made some peace with his situation. He wasn't exactly affable, but at least he stopped sulking.

Knowing they would reach the city gates today, they had hidden their weapons beneath their loose *shallah* clothing. The weight of Josarian's stolen Outlooker sword and its sheath were strapped to his back beneath his long, homespun tunic, his hair discreetly covering the lump of the hilt. Since it would take him a long time to get used to that weapon, he also wore his *yahr* tucked unobtrusively in his boot.

Considering how many swords and daggers they had stolen from Outlookers recently, they hadn't been surprised to hear that everyone entering the walls of Cavasar was being subjected to a thorough search. However, they had so far confined their bloodfeud to that district, and the Valdani were nothing if not arrogant. Consequently, Tansen had said it was unlikely that Outlookers were conducting body-searches at the gates of Shaljir, which was far from the fighting.

Upon reaching the walls of Sileria's capital city, Josarian and Tansen were surrounded there by travelling merchants, foreign traders, and *toreni* coming and going through the gate in a noisy ebb and flow. Some of their retinues were amazingly large, including servants, horses, companions, household goods packed into carts, and fabulous quantities of luxuries and exotic goods which gleamed in the sunshine or spiced the air.

One foreign man mounted on a fine horse led a group of a dozen Moorlander women, who all walked behind him in single file. Josarian had only ever seen a few, and he stared in fascination at their long, fair hair and the intricate tattoos so prized by their people. Their pale skin was already growing pink under a sky more fiercely blue than their native one. They were tall, robust women in fine health, yet their exotic blue and green eyes were dull, and their strong shoulders sagged dispiritedly. Josarian realized with shock that they were tied together; a long, thick rope wove through an iron waistband worn by each woman, linking one to another, and binding all of them to the rider who led them down the road. Four well-armed guards— Valdani mainland soldiers, a rare sight here in their red-and-gray uniforms—flanked the female prisoners, their expressions tough and forbidding.

Josarian looked to Tansen for an explanation.

"Slaves," he said briefly. "The spoils of victory from some battle in the Moorlands, or perhaps just some unfortunate souls seized by a rival tribe and handed over to the Valdani in exchange for more land."

Josarian turned to watch the women as they walked down the road, away from the city. "But . . . why are they *here?* In Sileria? Where are they going?"

"Most likely, they're being taken to fill Valdani brothels in the south." He met Josarian's appalled gaze. "They're a . . . a *courtesy* the Emperor grants his men, free of charge. Like the gray uniforms the Outlookers wear or the barracks they sleep in. The Valdani believe this practice prevents their men from brawling over a scarcity of women."

"A courtesy . . ." Josarian couldn't think of what to say. "Those *women* . . ."

Tansen glanced briefly over his shoulder at the retreating captives. "When the Moorlanders conquered Sileria, they raped, pillaged, and plundered. They enslaved thousands upon thousands of our people, and they took unwilling wives from among our women. But Moorlanders seldom frequent prostitutes; it goes against their customs. Then the Kints, of course . . ." He shrugged. "Prostitution has been a specialized profession in Kinto for thousands of years. So the Kints brought their own women with them when they took Sileria from the Moorlanders."

He led Josarian toward the crowd of people awaiting entrance to the city at the Adalian Gate. "But the Valdani have always used conquered women as prostitutes. Their brothels here are filled with women from other lands because they know Silerians won't pay any attention, whereas we'd never rest if those were *our* women dying of disease and exhaustion after a year or two of lying beneath grunting Outlookers day and night."

"I never knew." Josarian shook his head, staring blankly at the ground. Like any decent man, he had been raised to respect women. Yes, everyone knew about women who had no man to provide for them and, instead of becoming Sisters, made their living with their bodies. He'd even seen one or two, and he knew they were shunned and sneered at in public by the same men who brought them money or gifts in exchange for pleasure after dark. But he had never known about the monstrosities Tansen now revealed in a steady, quiet voice devoid of all expression. It struck him as even more disgusting than what went on in the mines of Alizar, where men were treated with appalling cruelty and where so many died without ever seeing the sky again.

"Tan," he said suddenly, "how do you know about these things? Not just the Valdani brothels, but about what Kints and Moorlanders did here centuries before we were born?"

Tansen's mouth curved slightly. "It's all written down. Everything that happened here. It's in scrolls and books and—"

"Can you *read?*"

"Only in Kintish, and not very well at that," Tansen replied.

"Then how—"

"Someone who *can* read told me about it. All of this and much, much more. She taught me . . ." He seemed to fall into the memory for a moment. "And she made me want to learn more."

"She?" Josarian asked.

He could have sworn Tan's face darkened with something like embarrassment, but the moment was too fleeting to be sure. "The woman I've come to Shaljir to find. The woman who can help me find . . ." He glanced around at the crowd and concluded vaguely, "Find the one I seek."

"Really? And how does she know the one *we* seek?" Josarian asked pointedly.

"Not here," Tansen muttered, glancing around at the bustling crowd.

Josarian agreed it wasn't a good moment to discuss a delicate matter like their search for Kiloran. Instead, he contented himself with marvelling at the sights, sounds, and smells of the most exotic place he had ever seen. To his relief, as Tansen had supposed, they were admitted into the city with little more than a cursory glance at the belongings they carried and a few disinterested questions about their business here.

"Is *every* street in Shaljir paved?" Josarian asked in amazement a little later as he followed Tansen through the city.

"As far as I know."

They walked a long way, and Josarian was too enthralled to ask where they were going. They crossed vast thoroughfares four times as wide as Emeldar's main road, and they passed at least three squares which he was sure were as big as his entire village. And the *fountains!* He had never imagined there were so many fountains anywhere in the world! Some were extravagantly beautiful, some old and crumbling, some strange and foreign-looking, and some positively indecent. Did no one feel embarrassed about collecting their water from a fountain where nude women carved in marble perched day after day in highly erotic poses? He grinned, thinking how Zimran would love this place.

His astonishment deepened when Tansen advised him that many of the fine homes and ornate palaces they passed had their own private fountains, sometimes *inside* the house.

"Are they waterlords?" Josarian whispered.

Tansen laughed. "No. Just filthy rich. Valdani, *toreni,* Kints, merchants, a few pirates who've turned respectable."

Apart from the splendor of the city itself, Josarian was captivated by its inhabitants. He had never seen such an extraordinary array of human beings, had never guessed how much variety there was in the world, let alone in his own land. Aristocrats rubbed elbows with foreign mercenaries and common beggars in the crowded streets. Acrobats, actors, and musicians filled the squares. Painters displayed their art outside of wealthy villas, trying to attract patrons. Exotic strangers from faraway lands brushed past *shallaheen* who had shorn their hair for city life. Well-groomed Silerian men swaggered through the streets with the unmistakable air of assassins; but here, in the stronghold of Valdani rule, they wore ordinary clothing and concealed their *shir* rather than risk arrest by displaying their loyalty to the outlawed Society. Wild-eyed *zanareen* sought recruits amidst the populace; Sisters welcomed the sick, wounded, and frightened into ancient Sanctuaries; and the sea-born folk went about their business with open disdain for anyone who was not one of them. At one point, Josarian nearly lost sight of Tansen, so enraptured was he by his first glimpse ever of a Kintish courtesan, the exquisite lines of her body draped in gilded veils which, though they covered her head-to-toe, seemed scarcely enough for decency.

For the first time, he realized how narrow his own world was. Although he loved those merciless mountains and would never want to be away from them for long, part of him suddenly envied Tansen terribly for the strange lands he had seen, the unimaginable worlds he had known, and even the sure way he now strode through the bustling streets of Shaljir.

After some time, they came to a section of the city

where the buildings huddled together around streets barely wide enough for two broad-shouldered men to walk together. Streets began twisting into and away from each other, dividing, multiplying, doubling around and back, going over or under other streets in a series of layers which had taken centuries to evolve. The odors here reflected the density of the population in this quarter and offended a nose long accustomed to fresh air.

"When was the last time the wind got in here?" Josarian muttered, sidestepping a man he fully suspected was a thief.

"Who knows?" Tansen smiled wryly. "Eons ago, I suppose. This is the oldest part of the city. Old beyond reckoning, beyond anyone's memory, beyond any written record."

"And how does a *shallah* from Gamalan know Shaljir so well?"

"I spent some time here, after my village was destroyed."

"Why here? If you needed to go to a city, Liron would have been much closer and more familiar to you."

"The decision wasn't mine."

Josarian recognized the tone and expression. Tansen didn't want to talk about it. As usual, Josarian persisted. "Whose decision was it?"

"The one I was with."

"And who was that? The woman?"

"No. This was . . ." Tansen sighed and then said, "He was looking for the same man we're looking for."

"Does *everyone* who wants him seek out this woman?"

Tansen almost laughed. "No. That is, I doubt it very much. He and I weren't seeking *her.* We were seeking . . ."

"Who? What?"

Tansen looked around to make sure no one else was close enough to overhear. Then he answered quietly: "The Alliance."

*   *   *

"AN ALLIANCE." MIRABAR frowned as she stared into the fire she had blown into life on some hillside. "A house of water . . ."

She was aware of Basimar's gaze on her while she mumbled aloud to herself like some lunatic. Well, why not? It was a twin-moon night, two fat full moons glowing in the velvet sky; everyone knew that madness seized the weak-minded on such a night.

Basimar gestured to the basket of food they had collected after Mirabar's Callings in some village that day: it was filled with bread, cheese, fruit, pickled vegetables, salty olives, parchment-thin slices of smoked meat, wine, and the first almond milk of the season.

"You must eat," Basimar insisted. "You taxed yourself hard in the village, and then you had another fit at sundown. You must replenish your strength, Mira."

Mirabar continued muttering to herself. "An assassin linked to a Kintish symbol . . . a *shir* linked to—"

"What did you say?"

Mirabar jumped. She blinked stupidly at Basimar, who was looking at her with saucer-wide eyes.

"I . . . I don't . . ." She faltered. "A *shir* linked to the Kints."

"An assassin and a Kintish symbol and a *shir* and . . ." Basimar gripped her arm. "A Kint?"

"I don't know." She drew the symbol again in the moon-bright earth. "Another Guardian told me he believes this is a Kintish symbol." Seeing Basimar's perplexed frown, she asked, "Why? What's wrong? You told me you've never seen this before."

"I haven't, and I wouldn't know a Kintish symbol from a sea gull."

"But?" Mira prodded, hearing the confusion in the Sister's voice.

"There is a man. A warrior. From Kinto."

"What?" Mirabar sprang forward and grabbed Basimar by the shoulders. "Who? Have you seen him?"

"No. No, I haven't."

"How do you know about him?"

"He came . . . he came to kill Josarian. He was hired by the Valdani."

"No! *Kill* Josarian? No, that can't be!" Mirabar's heart pounded with excitement, her head ached with confusion. "A warrior come from Kinto! He's the one I want! I must find him!"

"He . . . he fights at Josarian's side now," Basimar breathed.

Mirabar shook her in frustration. "You just said he came to kill him! Make up your mind, dammit!"

Her harshness brought tears to Basimar's eyes. Gritting her teeth in frustration, she apologized and released her deathgrip on the woman's shoulders. She tried to moderate her voice as she asked for an explanation.

The answers came slowly, haltingly, the process sorely trying what little patience she possessed. The story unravelled rather than weaving together, for Basimar was confused and upset, and also trying to conceal her (officially forbidden) carnal relationship with Zimran, cousin of Josarian, from whom she had learned what little she knew.

Despite her creed, the Sister didn't really care that the stranger, a mysterious mercenary seeking Josarian, had killed her brother-in-law, a nasty boy who had grown up to become an assassin. Her description of the stranger's blades, which were covered with Kintish symbols, as well as the revelation that Kiloran had sworn a bloodvow against him, set Mirabar's blood on fire. She wanted to slap Basimar for her silliness! The days they had wasted wandering around these hills, all because Basimar, despite her constant chatter, had never bothered to mention that her *shir*-carrying brother-in-law had been killed by a Kintish warrior sought by Kiloran.

"But . . . the stranger . . ." Basimar protested. "He didn't take the *shir*! In fact, they say it's still lying right where my brother-in-law fell."

Mirabar rolled her eyes. Just how literal did the Sister think visions from the Otherworld *were?* "Never mind. So the stranger's search turned out to be just a trick, a trap, to get Josarian to reveal himself?"

"Yes."

Mirabar wasn't quite sure what to make of succeeding events, since the story was colored by both Zimran's and Basimar's impressions. However, it was clear that Josarian trusted the warrior, who had been fighting at his side for some time now, an integral part of the growing band of men wreaking havoc on the district and making the Valdani frantic.

"Why did you never mention this?" Mirabar snapped, abandoning her intention to treat Basimar with patience. "Why didn't you tell me—"

"He's a *roshah!*" Basimar cried defensively. "You didn't say you were looking for a *roshah! I* thought you were looking for the Firebringer! How could a *ro*—"

"Never mind." Mirabar silenced her with a dismissive gesture. "I must find him. I *must* see him."

Basimar bit her lip and looked away.

"Zimran told you so much . . ." Mirabar said slowly. "He must have told you where they're hiding."

Basimar's face quivered with uncertainty. "I swore I wouldn't tell. I—"

"They'd want you to tell me," Mirabar said firmly. "I am supposed to prepare the way for the warrior who will free Sileria." She still had no idea *how,* but this didn't seem the best moment to admit that. "Basimar—*tell* me."

The Sister swallowed, then whispered, "The Dalishar Caves. That's where they're living."

"Dalishar!" Mirabar sighed with relief.

"You know where it is?"

"Of course! It's a Guardian holy site. I was initiated there." She jumped to her feet and started gathering her few belongings.

"What are you doing?"

"We're leaving for Dalishar. *Now.*"

"We can't leave now, it's the middle of the n—"

"If smugglers and bandits can travel beneath a twin-moon, then so can I." Mirabar carelessly bundled their food into her satchel and turned to leave. She glanced once over her shoulder and said absently, "Coming, Basimar?"

14

MOST BUILDINGS HERE in Shaljir were identified by writing placed over their doorways or on plaques hanging outside. However, to Josarian's relief, a number of establishments still respected tradition enough to also hang a *jashar* from the top of the doorframe, dangling down far enough to brush the ground, and identifying an establishment, its inhabitants, and its history in an honorable manner. By day, a *jashar* kept out insects, provided privacy from passersby, and admitted visitors with informal ease. By night, everyone in Shaljir had a heavy wooden door which was closed and locked after dark, even though the climate was usually warm down here on the coast. Even on a twin-moon night, the streets of Shaljir were lined with shadows and paved with menace, and no one could be too careful.

As night descended upon the city, Josarian finished another cup of excellent ale. It was some strange, smoky concoction Tansen had recommended upon leading him into this dark, low-ceilinged *tirshah* right in the heart of the twisting, crumbling, most ancient quarter of the city.

They didn't wear their *jashareen* in the streets of Shaljir, where Josarian couldn't risk being identified; but upon entering this *tirshah*, Tansen had taken his *jashar* out of his satchel, handed it to the keeper, and said in common Silerian, "I would like to see our old friends; this will announce me." He had said almost nothing since then, had

ignored all of Josarian's questions, and had scarcely
touched the ale he had ordered while the sun was still high.
Now, as night settled in, Tansen also refused the food the
keeper brought them.

"*I* am hungry," Josarian said, accepting the food Tansen
had just rejected. Once it had been deposited on their simple wooden table by a window overlooking a narrow street,
Josarian added, "And you should eat, whether you want to
or not."

Tansen absently accepted a little of the food Josarian
pressed upon him, but mostly he sat in unmoving silence,
his expression telling Josarian more clearly than words that
he was travelling through some place in the distant past,
doing and witnessing things he never willingly spoke
about.

It was late by the time the keeper finally led them to a
room. Though it was private and clean, it was lit only by
a single sputtering candle, situated far below street level,
and so small that Josarian had to crouch to keep his head
from hitting the ceiling. The closeness of the room made
him edgy, and Tansen's watchful silence did nothing to
soothe him.

There was no bed in here, only a few mats on the floor.
Josarian eased himself down onto one to prepare for sleep.
Tansen sat on the floor with his back to the door.

"Aren't you going to sleep?" Josarian asked.

"Not yet. You go ahead."

"Tan—"

"Not yet."

Josarian sighed. Whatever demons chased his bloodbrother, they were fierce and long-fanged. If he was to help
Tansen, then he, at least, would need rest. He lay down
and settled in comfortably. He closed his eyes, thinking of
Calidar, as he so often did during the last few moments of
the day. He pulled her delicate scarf out of his tunic, where
he usually wore it pressed against his skin. Eyes closed,
he held it to his face and inhaled deeply, remembering her.
Here, in this small, oppressive room in a strange city far

from home, accompanied only by a haunted man who would not speak to him, memories of Calidar now embraced him, enfolding, comforting him, warm, scented, soft as her whispers had been . . . She awaited him in the Otherworld, and perhaps, if his mind was relaxed and his heart open, tonight she would visit him briefly, giving him a taste of the eternal joy that awaited him when his work in this world was finally done.

But the one who came to him in the dark this night, the one whose soft breath awoke him in the thick blackness of the room, was not his wife. Awakening with a start, Josarian's hands closed upon the cool flesh of a tiny stranger, someone as small and frail as a sickly child, someone whose cries of fear were chattered in a language he had never heard before.

"Josarian, no!"

More strange, high-pitched voices were crying out now, and tiny little hands scrabbled at his forearms. Their strength was negligible, but their unseen quickness was as frightening as the monsters of his childhood nightmares.

"Josarian, no, don't hurt them!" Tansen's voice pierced through his confusion.

Josarian felt Tansen's strong hands grabbing him now, warm where the little ones were cold, calming and familiar where the little ones incited him to a confused and mindless violence.

"Stop, Josarian, *stop!*" Tansen ordered.

Realizing that he was choking his unseen captive, and that Tansen knew it and objected, Josarian slowly released his grip, breathing hard with startled animalistic fear and trying to get control of himself.

"What . . . what is . . ." He couldn't think of what he wanted to ask.

"It's all right," Tansen said, his own grip easing. "The candle went out when they came in. I should have warned you, but I wasn't sure they'd come, and I knew it would sound so crazy if I tried to tell you what I w—"

"When *who* came in?" Josarian heard the soothing murmurs and relieved sighs of the little creatures who'd been battling frantically with him only moments ago. "Who are they? What in the Fires is going on?"

"Where's the candle?" Tansen muttered. "Dammit, one of you get the candle," he ordered their visitors. "I can't find it."

"You *know* them?" Josarian heard bodies scurrying and voices muttering.

"We've met before," Tansen hedged.

"Who are they?" Josarian repeated.

"They're— Ah! Good. The candle. *And* the flint box."

A moment later, the candle flickered back to life. Josarian squinted, his gaze catching glimpses of strange, improbable things as his eyes watered and adjusted to the light.

"They are the Beyah-Olvari," Tansen said. "And they see much better in the dark than you or I do."

Josarian blinked incredulously at the small, fragile blue beings who flinched away from the candle, shielding their eyes from its glare. They were quite unmistakably the same creatures whose images decorated the walls in the cave paintings of Niran, Dalishar, and countless other sites in Sileria. They were also, as far as anybody knew, extinct.

"I think," Josarian said slowly, "that you had better explain."

KOROLL, COMMANDER OF Shaljir and High Commander of Sileria, cooled his heels in the counsel hall of Santorell Palace like some lowly servant awaiting his master's pleasure. Indeed, his master's *pleasure* was the cause of the delay. Although Advisor Borell was no fool, took his position seriously, and devoted considerable energy to his office, one could not deny that the man took his pleasures equally seriously.

During their short association, Koroll had already learned that Borell loved good food, superior wine, excellent music, fine art, the best clothing, intelligent conversation, skillful performers, and brilliant poets. Borell considered these pleasures as important as his thorough knowledge of political intrigues or his surprisingly extensive understanding of military tactics. The Advisor had little respect for anyone who wasn't a discriminating connoisseur of the finest things in life, and no patience whatsoever with anyone who interfered with his own disciplined consumption of them.

It was this *discipline* which Koroll respected in the Advisor. Borell was moderate in his habits, scheduling duty and pleasure with a precision seldom seen even on military training fields. Although he put his staff through considerable trouble to import the finest wines in the Empire, he never grew drunk. Although he hosted entertainments that could last half the night, he never slept through the following morning, but was always awake and pursuing his duties at the usual time. Although he wore the finest garments available in Sileria, he never spared them when practicing his horsemanship or swordplay, but demanded tough endurance of both his body and his splendid raiment.

Indeed, despite the Advisor's reputation as the most hedonistic Valdan in Sileria, there was only one area of pleasure in which Koroll considered Borell to be completely out of control: his mistress, a Silerian aristocrat named Elelar. Although her nocturnal visits were fairly discreet, Koroll always knew when she had spent the night at the Palace, for Borell would invariably still be abed the next morning long after he should have arisen. If the *torena* visited the Advisor during the daytime, Borell would often cancel all meetings without notice or explanation and give his servants strict instructions not to disturb him under any circumstances. And the gifts Borell gave that woman! Surely even a man as rich as Borell must feel the strain of such costly gifts to his strumpet.

Yes, although he had learned to respect many things about Borell, when it came to that Silerian whore—whose husband apparently didn't care that all of Shaljir knew she was warming the Advisor's bed—Koroll considered his superior to be a besotted fool.

Today, when Borell finally showed up in the counsel hall for the meeting they had planned, he dismissed Koroll's hour-long wait with a brief, absentminded apology and listened with only halfhearted interest to Koroll's most recent reports on Josarian's known or suspected activities. Borell's pleasure-flushed face didn't surprise Koroll, nor did the scent of the Silerian woman still clinging to his skin, but it did disgust him. By the Three, it was disgraceful!

Outlookers were discouraged from sleeping with Silerians. The Emperor provided thoroughly reliable, duly inspected, conveniently housed, specially imported women to fulfill the men's needs, after all. Silerians were treacherous, dishonest, disloyal, and ungovernable, no matter how subdued two centuries of severe poverty had made them appear. Permitting the men to form liaisons with the locals in this country would be unwise, to say the least.

Koroll thought that Advisor Borell, as a government official, should set a better example for the men than taking a Silerian woman to his bed. Since coming to Shaljir, Koroll had taken a third-level Kintish courtesan as his mistress, a respectable choice worthy of the Commander of Shaljir. A man in Advisor Borell's position had a wide-ranging choice of suitable women, particularly considering his wealth. He could hire a first-level Kintish courtesan, bring a Valdani woman from the mainland to act as his official "hostess," or seek a liaison with a woman from one of the long-established Valdani families in Sileria.

There was some intermarriage between Valdani and Silerian aristocrats. Throughout history, after all, the nobility of the world had always had a way of uniting that set them apart from the common people of their own individual races. Considering such practices, Koroll grudgingly supposed that Borell, a Valdani aristocrat, might be excused for publicly taking a full-blooded Silerian as his mistress—if only Borell weren't so clearly enamoured of the woman. Koroll had met her several times by now, since she was either the hostess or a guest at virtually all of Borell's social festivities. Yes, she was lovely. Any normal man had to admit that. But she wasn't the ravishing beauty he had expected, having witnessed the evidence of her influence over Borell and having heard some of the palace gossip about her. Oh, there was unquestionably *something* about her—the way she moved, the tone of her voice, a look, a smile, a sigh—that transfixed a man's attention and turned his will to water. Yes, there was something beneath her grace and elegance which put unquenchable hunger in a man's belly. Koroll had felt it himself, to his consternation.

However, any man who let such women's weapons hold sway over his better judgment was a fool asking for grief; and Borell's normally sharp mind became as soft as overripe melon around Elelar. Perhaps the *torena* would be content with the gifts and privileges Borell showered upon her in exchange for getting between her thighs, but she didn't strike Koroll as a simple woman, and he rather suspected that she would eventually want more. Additional land and titles? Borell's official recognition of the child she was bound to bear him sooner or later, even if she couldn't prove the brat was not her own husband's get? Even, Three forbid, a divorce from her own husband and marriage to the Imperial Advisor himself?

As Koroll told Borell about the patrols currently out searching the mountains for Josarian and explained his plans for tightening security around all Valdani operations in the district of Cavasar, he idly wondered what grief would come to Borell as a result of his foolish passion for the *torena.*

"And what about soliciting information?" Borell demanded, finally focusing his full attention on the conversation.

"Ah, yes, as you know, sir, getting information out of the *shallaheen* remains our biggest challenge in tracking Josarian. I've recently put a new man onto the problem." He paused and added, "A man who, due to the disastrous consequences of following Commander Daroll's orders while in charge of the garrison at Britar, is now most eager to prove himself to you, Eminence—Captain Myrell."

"EIGHT OF THE Empire's Outlookers were murdered here, and supplies and property belonging to the Valdani were stolen or destroyed!" Myrell paused and looked around at the people of Malthenar. He had their undivided attention. "The penalty for these crimes is death by slow torture!"

He had ridden into Malthenar before dawn with two hundred Outlookers. They had dragged the villagers from their beds, hauled them out of their miserable stone hovels, and herded them into the main square. Commander Koroll, upon releasing Myrell from custody in Cavasar, had clearly explained the price of his life and freedom: secrecy and service. Since Myrell had no wish to advertise that the disaster at Britar had been his own doing, and since he burned day and night with the desire for vengeance, he had readily agreed to Koroll's conditions. He had also agreed with Koroll's assessment that they must launch a serious offensive against Josarian, taking his allies by surprise.

Malthenar had been quiet ever since Josarian had destroyed the Outlooker outpost here shortly after the battle at Britar. With his band of outlaws busy elsewhere, it seemed certain that an assault on Malthenar now would take Josarian by surprise. The village would be defenseless, and Josarian would be revealed as a very poor protector against the Empire's fury. Above all, Myrell would make his own mission clear: terrible suffering for every peasant in these mountains until Josarian was delivered into his hands.

Myrell studied the crowd, then selected a young man who looked at him with open hatred. Myrell had him hauled into the center of the square.

"What is your name?" Myrell asked.

The young man merely glared in stony silence. Myrell called Arlen to his side, the *shallah* criminal who served him in exchange for staying out of the mines. Arlen wore the shorn hair and tailored clothing of a city-dweller, but he still had the dark skin and scarred palms of a *shallah*, and the villagers instantly recognized him for what he was.

"What is this man's name?" Myrell demanded.

Arlen glanced at the villager's *jashar*. "He is Corenten mar Sarshen shah Emeldari," he answered, his voice wooden.

"Corenten," Myrell said, "you match the description we have of one of Josarian's men." So, of course, did most of the other men in the village, but this one would do for now. "I hereby arrest you in the name of the Emperor and charge you with the murder of eight Outlookers. Sentence to be carried out immediately."

Fear flashed in Corenten's eyes and he tried to break away from the Outlookers who had seized him.

"Ah," Myrell said, "then you *do* understand Valdan?"

The *shallah* said nothing, simply kept glaring.

"Just in case his Valdan is not as good as it should be," Myrell said to Arlen, "I want you to translate everything I say. Make sure the rest of the villagers hear it well."

Arlen nodded, his expression sullen. When he began translating, angry grumbles and murmurs filled the air, and the word *sriliah* was borne on the wind to swirl around Arlen, whose shoulders hunched against the shame.

"Corenten," Myrell said, "I will give you one chance to save yourself from what, I promise you, will be a truly horrible death. I want information about Josarian."

Corenten spat in his face.

Myrell pulled out his sword and slashed Corenten diagonally from shoulder to hip. The young man's knees briefly buckled as his face contorted with pain. A woman screamed. The crowd surged forward. Myrell gave the signal, and archers fired into the crowd. Screams of agony and outrage rent the air. A baby fell to the ancient cobblestones as its mother collapsed, blood pouring from her mouth as she tore weakly at the arrow piercing her chest. A brawny man broke through the crowd and flew straight at Myrell, his weapon of sticks-and-rope—his *yahr*, as Myrell had learned they called it—swinging wildly. One Outlooker tripped him, and another killed him as he fell. Milling in desperate, noisy panic, many *shallaheen* tried to break past the mounted Outlookers guarding the perimeter of the main square. They were driven back, some of them injured in the process, several killed.

It wasn't until the crowd was subdued that Myrell spoke again. "You had one chance, Corenten, and now you have lost it." He nodded to the men who held the bleeding *shallah*. "Prepare him for the executioner."

Corenten's pain-clouded eyes widened with shock, and Myrell could see that he hadn't truly expected to die. He struggled wildly, cursing in his guttural mountain tongue, until one of the Outlookers clubbed him over the head. Then, dazed and helpless, he was tied spread-eagle between two posts. As the hooded executioner approached, flanked by his two apprentices, Myrell spoke again to the horrified crowd while Arlen translated for him.

"There is one last chance to save this boy's life. If someone steps forward now with information leading to Josarian's capture, I will spare this brave young man."

People in the crowd shifted uncertainly, glances flashing uneasily back and forth, heads lowering in sorrow or in shame. Finally, a woman stepped forward. She was big-boned, strong, voluptuous, and desirable even in poverty and middle age. Her face was streaked with tears, her pale clothing smeared with dust and splotched with someone else's blood. Emotion twisted her features with pain beyond measure. Her voice, when she spoke, was low and strained.

"This woman is his mother," Arlen translated for Myrell, since the woman spoke no Valdan.

Hope surged through Myrell. "Ask her what she knows."

The woman responded to Arlen's question without ever taking her watery gaze from her son. Arlen hesitated, staring at the woman when she was done speaking.

"Well?" Myrell prodded. "What did she say?"

Arlen looked a little pale. "She says her son swore a bloodfeud against the Valdani with Josarian."

"So we've got the right man," Myrell said impatiently. "So what? Can she tell us—"

"She says that she herself will kill the first person who dishonors Corenten's bloodpact by betraying Josarian."

Myrell swayed slightly, then looked around to see if anyone in the village intended to challenge this ridiculous threat. To his disgust, heads nodded, chins came up, shoulders squared, and all gazes fixed on Corenten.

What had Koroll told him they called it? *Lirtahar* . . . Myrell sighed inwardly.

Knowing it would be a long, ugly day, he signaled the executioner to begin the torture. Corenten's screams of agony filled the air. His mother's proud features tightened with horrified grief as tears coursed down her cheeks, but she would not look away. The whole village watched, silent, stone-faced, and unflinching, as one of their own endured three hours of the most gruesome death Myrell himself had ever seen.

Three Into One, how he hated these people!

"IN THE NAME of Dar and all that is holy," Basimar said, her voice heavy with horror, "what *is* that?"

Less than a day from Dalishar now, they stumbled across possibly the most gruesome sight Mirabar had ever seen. She lowered her concealing hood, heedless of who might come upon them unexpectedly, and stared in shock.

The fresh corpse of a man was spread-eagled between two slender trees which grew alongside the road, his hands and feet securely tied to keep him in place. Carrion feeders had been feasting on the entrails hanging from his open belly; Basimar's scream had frightened them away, but the swarm of insects remained, as did the stench.

"This looks like . . ." Basimar swallowed and gagged.

Mirabar took the Sister's shoulders and turned her away from the sight. "Like who?" she choked out.

"Like Valdani torture."

Mirabar's gaze flashed to Basimar's face as the Sister fought back her nausea. "You've seen this before?"

"Once," Basimar said, her voice thick. "Years ago. A local boy who'd been sleeping with a Valdani girl. When they were caught, she claimed . . . she said . . ."

"She saved her reputation by claiming he had raped her."

"Yes."

"And the Valdani did *this* to him?"

"It's their . . . most severe punishment. Death by slow torture." Basimar was breathing in shallow gasps. "For the crimes which most offend them."

"Touching their women," Mirabar said tonelessly.

"Or killing a Valdan."

"Killing a . . ." Mirabar gasped. "We're so close to Dalishar!"

"Mira, no!" Basimar tried to grab her as she lunged forward to investigate the body.

"It might be one of . . . one of . . . Oh, Dar, it might even be *him!* It might . . ." Quivering with disgust, she picked up a stick and pushed away shredded, dangling entrails to get a good look at the dead man's *jashar*.

Trying to look at anything except at what Mirabar was doing, Basimar said, "No, it couldn't be. See how his hair is shorn, how his clothes are so immodest? Tight, almost like a Valdan's? He's a city-dweller, not a . . ."

"His palms are scarred," Mirabar argued. "He wears a *jashar*."

"There's another one!" Basimar said suddenly.

Mirabar jumped and looked around. "Where?"

"No, not a body. Another *jashar*."

Mirabar looked up and saw that a small *jashar* hung around the dead man's neck. She looked down again at the man's waist, then averted her gaze from the mess there. "He is Arlen mar—"

"So die all who betray their own kind," Basimar interrupted, interpreting the *jashar* around the man's neck. "So die all who betray Josarian."

Mirabar backed away from the corpse, gaping in horror, unable to form a coherent thought. Basimar started weeping. Appalled by the dawning realization of what her alliance with this warrior would cost them all, Mirabar fell to her knees and begged Dar for guidance.

TORENA ELELAR MAR Odilan yesh Ronall shah Hasnari emerged from her scented bath and began polishing her skin with the subtly fragrant oils that kept it sweet, soft, and reasonably fair beneath Sileria's passionate sun. No amount of cosmetics, of course, could make her as fair-skinned as the pale, bloodless women so prized by the Valdani, but at least their men did not seem to find her wanting in grace, delicacy, or beauty.

Faradar, her personal servant, began dressing her hair, twisting and weaving it into the elaborately coiled and braided style of a Silerian aristocrat. Then Faradar helped her don the clothes she had selected for the evening. She did not wear Valdani clothes, for she knew how the Valdani laughed at Silerians who aped their customs and fashions. Instead, her own clothes were so exquisite that she had instigated the new trend of Valdani women in Shaljir occasionally wearing Silerian clothes.

Now *she* laughed at *them*—but secretly. Yes, as she did everything in life: secretly.

Heavy footsteps outside her dressing room heralded the unexpected arrival of her husband a moment before he flung open the door without ceremony or apology. He stalked into the room, threw himself into a cushioned chair, glared at Faradar, and growled, "Get out."

Faradar glanced briefly at her mistress.

Elelar nodded. "That will be all. You may go."

The girl bowed and made a dignified exit. Having entered Elelar's service seven years ago, two years before her mistress's marriage, Faradar was too accustomed to

Ronall's tantrums to scurry away from him or cower beneath his angry scowl.

"I want to talk to you," Ronall began. His words were clear, but his eyes were glazed and unfocused. So it was Kintish dreamweed tonight, Elelar surmised, rather than Valdani liquor or Moorlander opiates.

"You're not dressed yet," she interrupted. "We'll be late."

"Then we can damn well *be* late!" He blinked, lost his train of thought, and asked, "Where are we going?"

"Your father's birthday celebration. Don't tell me you've forgotten?" She gazed innocently at him.

He flung himself gracelessly out of his chair and snarled, "It slipped my mind after I learned what you've been up to."

She waited, unwilling to encourage him, suppressing the flickering fear that he might have learned the truth at last. She kept her face impassive while her mind raced, wondering what Ronall could have discovered after all this time.

"You had her sent away," Ronall growled. "I warned you not to interfere . . ."

"What?" Elelar blinked, trying to follow her husband's obscure train of thought.

"The girl . . . the one with the yellow hair . . ."

She frowned, wondering what in the world he was babbling about. "What girl? What are you—Oh!" Relief flooded her mind, the sensation so strong that she briefly wondered how she managed to live with the tension of her daily existence. "That Moorlander acrobat that you so admired at the Palace?"

"The one I wanted for myself!"

"I believe you *had* her for yourself, my dear. The Imperial Stables right in Santorell Square is hardly a discreet place for such activ—"

"Where is she?"

"On the mainland by now, I assume," Elelar said. "The troop was scheduled to play in—"

"She said she would stay with *me*."

"And she's gone?" Elelar was getting bored. "Why do you suppose that *I* had something to do with it? You warned me early in our marriage not to interfere in your—"

"Damn right, I did," he snapped.

"And I have never disobeyed you since then," she reminded him.

About one year after their marriage, Elelar had helped a frightened new kitchen girl escape Ronall's persistent attentions by finding the girl a position in another household. Ronall had learned about it and been furious enough to cause a hideous scene in front of all the servants. Since that bitter quarrel, Elelar had simply avoided similar problems by always trying to ensure that none of their servants were women likely to appeal to Ronall's tastes. And, fortunately, he'd always hated Faradar too much to touch her.

"I went looking for the girl," Ronall said, apparently still convinced it was Elelar's fault that he'd lost the Moorlander acrobat. "They said a *torena* paid her to leave Sileria with the rest of the troop."

"Really?" Elelar paused in the act of rouging her lips. "A *torena*? I don't suppose you got a description of her?"

"No." He frowned in confusion. "Why should I?"

"Far be it from me to suggest that the girl was anything less than a pearl of faithful devotion to you . . ."

"But?" he prodded, glaring at her.

"Don't you think it possible that someone else became interested in her, too, and that perhaps *that* man's wife was less willing to share than I am?"

Not surprisingly, his attention was diverted away from his loss, which Elelar fully expected him to forget entirely by this time tomorrow, and shifted to a new grievance. "Share? As if you even notice my absence. When was the last time *we* shared a bed, my *dear?*"

Despite her revulsion for him, she never once backed down or shied away when he asserted his conjugal rights. She looked him right in the eye and said, "I am available, sir, whenever you feel capable of getting an heir."

He paled. Her arrow had struck home. "You can't blame that on me, you faithless bitch!" he raged. "How many others have been between your legs and not gotten a brat on you?"

"No one but Borell," she lied.

"And he can't fill your barren womb, either!"

"He takes precautions against bastards."

"You think it's *my* fault!"

"Did I say that?"

"You don't have to. It's written all over your smirking, superior, whoring face!"

She shrugged and turned away. "We've had this conversation before. I see no point in—"

"I do!" He struck the rouge pot out of her hand and seized her by the shoulders. "You want an heir," Ronall snarled, his hot breath fanning her face as he pushed her up against the wall, "then I'll *give* you an heir, damn you!"

She felt his body grinding against hers and realized with a brief flash of panic that he meant to do it. Unfortunately, no matter how Ronall abused his body and senses, he seldom lost the ability to service a woman—with about as much skill and sensitivity as the word implied.

Elelar turned her face away from her husband and endured his assault with as much dignity as she could; she had learned the hard way that fighting him when he was in this mood only produced injuries which took days to heal.

This happened seldom enough, after all, she told herself; it wasn't as if he demanded her body often anymore.

It would be over soon enough, she promised herself; he never took long.

It was her wedding night all over again. Now, as then, she gritted her teeth against the pain of his biting kisses, squeezing hands, and rough, plunging invasion. Now, as then, she begged Dar to make her womb barren, for she did not want to bear a child by the half-Valdan drunkard she had married. Now, as then, she washed thoroughly the moment he left the room, scrubbing away all trace of him until her flesh felt raw.

Now, as then, she did not permit herself to weep, for she knew her duty, and the Alliance needed her courage.

15

EONS AGO, IN an age lost beyond memory, beyond reckoning, the Beyah-Olvari had peopled Sileria in a life of peace and simplicity. Then fired-eyed, dark-skinned warriors crossed the Middle Sea to invade this vast, mountainous island. No one knew whence they came, though many believed they had come from the little known lands far to the south, from the dense jungles where great, unknown sources of water fed the vast and torrential Sirinakara River. It was said that they had braved the deadly rapids and terrifying waterfalls of the north-flowing river to come in search of a land floating in the middle of the sea, a nation promised to them in prophecy.

These warriors were a new race of beings: taller, broader, heavier, stronger, faster, and far more violent than the fragile little blue-skinned people they drove inland from Sileria's southern coasts. They brought fire into a land where water had been the source and center of all power and prosperity. They saw the island's great snow-capped volcano erupt in flaming fury, and they worshipped her, developing extraordinary abilities during their centuries of communion with her. They brought war to a land where there had never even been weapons. They brought violence, fear, and turmoil to a world which had known only peace.

"And these," Josarian said heavily, "were my ancestors."

The old Olvar nodded, his movements delicate, slow, graceful, almost as if he floated in water. Josarian looked around at the underground cavern to which Tansen and the little blue people had led him via a very well concealed trapdoor in the floor of the bedchamber at the *tirshah*. The tunnels and chambers down here were small and low-ceilinged, as befitted their diminutive inhabitants. The feeble light in these caverns came from strange plants and little quivering creatures which glowed with phosphorescent brilliance—cool, flameless, soft sources of light covering the damp walls and ceilings.

Josarian was only sure he was awake because he knew he could never have dreamed anything so fantastic.

So far, he had been treated with more courtesy than he would have expected, considering that he had begun his acquaintance with the Beyah-Olvari—the Followers of the Olvar—by trying to strangle one of them. However, after some initial confusion in the room back at the *tirshah,* they seemed satisfied when Tansen assured them that Josarian had merely been very surprised to see them—thus demonstrating a heretofore unsuspected gift for understatement. Then, after some ceremonial greetings which had seemed to Josarian to take rather a long time under the circumstances, the Beyah-Olvari had led him and Tansen into the bowels of the earth.

"Where are we going?" Josarian had asked, ready to slug Tansen if he was as unresponsive as usual.

"They're taking us to see the Olvar."

Their four tiny companions uttered something that sounded like a blessing.

"The what?" Josarian asked.

"The Olvar," Tansen repeated. He paused while the Beyah-Olvari uttered the blessing again, then continued, "He's their chief, their hereditary leader. He's sort of a sage, prophet, king, and wizard all rolled into one."

"A wizard?" Josarian repeated uneasily.

"Water magic."

"A waterlord?"

The Beyah-Olvari muttered something that sounded a little frantic.

"They do that whenever you say something evil. It's a banishing prayer," Tansen explained.

"Oh." Josarian peered at their companions in the dark. "I'm sorry."

Now they said something that sounded like a prayer with his name in it.

"A blessing," Tansen said blandly. "They like you."

"So the Olvar . . ." Josarian paused for the blessing ". . . isn't a . . . you-know-what?"

"No. But the Beyah-Olvari invented water magic. Discovered it. Whatever. And the first waterlord, Marjan . . ." Tansen paused while the tunnels around them echoed with another banishing prayer ". . . discovered their secrets long after they had disappeared. He found ancient holy sites, cave paintings, magic sources. He learned to interpret the secret symbols and sacred signs they had started adding to their cave paintings toward the end. They did it to leave a record, a memory of who they were and what they had known, when . . ."

"When . . ." Josarian prodded, hearing Tansen's voice trail off.

"When they realized they were dying off. That soon there would be nothing left to show that they had ever been here."

"Tan . . ." Josarian paused as the Beyah-Olvari began a strange, wailing chant.

"It's a mourning prayer," Tansen said, so quietly that Josarian almost didn't hear him.

"But what happened? Why——"

"The Olvar will explain it to you," Tansen said, his voice rising slightly above the echoing noise of the blessing being uttered at the mention of the Olvar. "He'll tell you who they are and how they wound up here."

And so the Olvar did, recounting the tragic history of his race in a lilting voice as his wrinkled blue hands dipped and stirred in the glimmering pool of water in which he sat hunched over. His aged features were darkly shadowed and weary whenever he looked up at Josarian; but when he peered down into the Sacred Pool, the phosphorescent light emanating from it seemed to make his face glow with youthful enthusiasm and energy.

"Yes," the Olvar said in response to Josarian's comment, his dialect strange and his accent thick as he spoke archaic High Silerian which, fortunately, was similar to the mountain dialect. "They were your ancestors. The New Race, that is *your* race."

"Then . . ." Josarian felt shame for things which had happened thousands of years before his birth. "Surely you must hate us."

"Hate . . . requires hotter blood than ours," the Olvar said. "And some of us survived."

"How?"

The Beyah-Olvari had retreated over the span of time, withdrawing first into the highest, most inhospitable mountains, then later into the dankest coastal caves. Never a prolific race, they began dying faster than they gave birth.

"Sometimes slaughtered by the New Race," the Olvar said, "but most often the Beyah-Olvari, blessings be upon the people of this name, died of disease and hunger. Diseases which your forefathers brought here with them, or new ones which they alone were strong enough to survive; hunger, as we were driven further and further from the gathering-gardens which had fed us since the dawn of time."

The small, scattered tribes sought different ways of enduring these cataclysmic events. Some moved to increasingly remote mountaintops, and no one really knew what had happened to them. Some tried to ignore the changes in their world; in the end, their bones scattered across the lowlands like feathers carried on the wind. Some tried to cross the Middle Sea, believing that if Sileria had been promised to the New Race, then surely a land for the Beyah-Olvari lay just beyond the horizon.

The mourning chant of the Beyah-Olvari who were

gathered around them now echoed sorrowfully through the cavern, sending chills down Josarian's spine. He looked around at them, then quickly looked back at the Olvar. The Beyah-Olvari wore nothing that could be called clothing, just brief leafy coverings over their loins. The *shallaheen* were a modest people, and Josarian's blood raced with embarrassed interest whenever he looked directly at any of the females here: tiny, graceful, strange beyond description, virtually naked ... and unmistakably women.

"And we who are here," continued the Olvar, "we left your world, the world claimed by the New Race, and came underground. Here, where we found the Sacred Pool. Here, where we found a gathering-garden in the tunnels."

"Food?" Josarian asked. "Down here?"

The Olvar reached out and plucked a glowing plant from the wall. He bit into it, chewed and swallowed, then handed the rest of it to Josarian. "Yes. Down here."

Josarian thanked him and ate the rest of the squishy thing, trying to ignore the foul sensations it created inside his mouth.

"Good, yes?" prompted the Olvar.

"Very good." Josarian resolutely willed himself not to gag or bring it straight back up. He glanced at Tansen, who was looking innocently at the ceiling. Then he asked the Olvar, "So are you ... are you the only ones left?"

"I believe so. But who can say for sure?" The Olvar dipped his hands into the Sacred Pool again. "But if we are the end of our race, then perhaps we are the beginning of it, too."

"The beginning?" Josarian repeated.

"The world is changing, and a new one is at hand," the Olvar said. "The portents are unmistakable. Now the Beyah-Olvari, blessings be upon the people of this name, are no longer alone. Now we have friends."

"What friends?" Josarian asked.

The Olvar stirred the waters of the Sacred Pool. "When I became Olvar, I pledged my people to the Alliance."

* * *

THE OTHERWORLD VIBRATED like a quivering arrow as Mirabar approached the Dalishar Caves. The fires up here were very ancient, and the barrier between this world and the Other one seemed gossamer-thin in the presence of so much power. Souls poured through the night, groping for the gateway to the Otherworld, brushing past Mirabar as they sought eternity and the embrace of loved ones lost long ago.

"Corenten. . . . Soladan . . . Romolar . . ." Mirabar's eyes watered as the travellers reached out to her in confusion. Some, she knew, would never complete the journey; eventually, they would wander into oblivion, frightened and alone. "Belar . . . Nevon . . . Siradar, just a baby . . ." A tear slid down her face. A baby had little chance, she acknowledged sadly.

"What?" Basimar said, shaking her. "Is it another vision?"

"No." Mirabar sniffed and jerked away. "Sojourners to the Otherworld."

"Right here? Right now?" Basimar asked uneasily.

"So many," Mirabar said in confusion. "So many, so suddenly." She reached out with her mind, trying to touch the wanderers. "Many people died at once. Quite suddenly."

"How do you know?"

"I know. This is Dalishar. The caves are very near. The gateway to the Otherworld is yawning before us . . ." She ignored Basimar's gasp. "Violent deaths . . . Terrible sorrow . . . Recently . . ."

"Yes. Recently," said a male voice behind them.

Basimar whirled to face the man. Mirabar kept her hood pulled up and her face hidden.

"I'm Sister Basimar," Basimar said quickly. "This is Mirabar, a Guardian."

There was a pause. Then the man said, "What are you doing up here? A pilgrimage?"

Mirabar decided to be direct. "We're looking for Josarian and the warrior who now fights at his side."

The *shallah* snorted. "So is everyone else in the district."

"Take me to Zimran," Basimar said. "He knows me."

"Corenten . . ." Mirabar said again, trying to separate the voices in the Otherworld from the voices in this one. "He died terribly, didn't he?"

"Yes," the man said. "Death by slow torture in the square at Malthenar. How did you know?"

"How many others died that day?"

"Twenty-seven. Killed in the riot that began when Corenten was seized for execution because he wouldn't betray Josarian."

"I must . . ."

"What, Mirabar?" Basimar asked, taking her arm.

"This man must take me to one of the ancient fires in the caves. I must petition . . ." She drew a sharp breath as more voiceless cries assailed her. "I must try to help."

The man hesitated for a moment, then said quietly, "I'll show you where to go, *sirana.*"

"Then tell Zimran we're here," Basimar said.

"I'm sorry, he's not here, Sister."

"Where is he?"

"He went to kill the *sriliah* who helped the Valdani kill Corenten and the others in—"

"Arlen," Mirabar said suddenly.

"Yes! How did you know?"

"We found his corpse by the road this morning," Basimar said wearily. "How could Zimran have done that, even to a—"

"You did not see the blood that Arlen helped the Valdani spill in Malthenar's main square."

"Even if I had, I could never approve—"

"We do not ask for approval, Sister," he interrupted bitterly. "Only *lirtahar.*"

"Only *lirtahar,*" Basimar repeated, her voice thick with sorrow. She cleared her throat and asked, "If Zimran is gone, then can we see Josarian himself? He and I have met—"

"He's not here, either, Sister."

"Is he off killing with Zimran?" she demanded.

"No, Sister." The man sounded impatient. "We don't know where he is. Or when he'll be back."

Mirabar's head reeled with the combined sensations of two worlds. She groped through her confusion and tried to focus on one thing at a time.

"And the *roshah?*" Basimar asked.

"Josarian went off with him."

"And they didn't tell you where they were going?" Basimar asked with growing frustration.

"Isn't it obvious?" Mirabar said, her vision swimming. "They've gone to find Kiloran."

"Sirana!" The *shallah* stepped closer. "How did you know? Have you seen them? Is Josarian all right?"

"How in the Fires should I know?" she said wearily. "I don't suppose the *roshah* gave you a hint about where he expected to find Kiloran?"

"Tansen? No, he didn't seem to know. He only said he knew who to ask."

"Tansen," Mirabar repeated. "That's the warrior's name?"

"Yes, *sirana.*"

"Not . . . Armian?" She could feel disappointment pierce her like a thorn.

"Armian?" Basimar repeated. "You never said—"

"Armian?" the *shallah* said. "No, *sirana,* he calls himself Tansen. Why? Are you . . ." He caught his breath and leaned close to whisper, "Are you looking for the Firebringer?"

Mirabar rubbed her aching forehead with a grimy hand. "I wish I knew." She couldn't make sense of any of this while the souls of the dead screamed all around her. *One thing at a time.* "Take me to a circle of fire," she instructed. "And when I'm done . . ."

"Yes?"

Mirabar stumbled, lost in the silent cacophony which surrounded her. The man caught her elbow. Despite the chaos in her mind, she heard him gasp when a flame-red lock of her hair tumbled out of her hood. She saw him reach for his sword. A *sword!* Only in her visions had she ever seen a Silerian holding a sword! "It has begun." She looked up into the man's face.

"Dar shield me . . ." he said, stepping backwards.

"But then . . ." She blinked and wondered, "Why am *I* needed?"

IT WAS LATE when Elelar returned home from the gathering at Santorell Palace. Ronall had left for one of their country estates this morning, planning a few days of hunting, drinking, and—Elelar supposed—whoring in rustic surroundings. Not only did Elelar enjoy being in the house when he wasn't here, it was also valuable time which couldn't be wasted.

She had excused herself from Borell's bed tonight, even though she knew that an Imperial courier had arrived from the mainland that very afternoon. It would be easiest to learn what was in those dispatches tonight, while Borell slept off the effects of passion and wine, for he tended to leave fresh dispatches lying open on the table near his bed. However, if the dispatches contained important news or orders, she could probably get Borell to tell her about it the next time she slept with him. He was shrewd and intelligent, but he trusted her. A woman spread her legs for a man, let him spill his seed inside the secret recesses of her body, lavished him with compliments about his virility, courage, and intelligence, feigned fascination whenever he spoke, and . . . A hungry puppy taking food from someone's hand was not so easy to beguile as a man convinced that a woman was in love with him. Tonight, however, with Ronall safely absent and the rest of Shaljir asleep for the night, there was business to conduct here at home which might well take until dawn: two separate meetings with secret associates, their comings and goings concealed by loyal servants; confidential letters to be sealed and entrusted to brave couriers; contraband supplies to be smuggled into the house and hidden in the underground tunnels.

There was even a body buried in her wine cellar: an Imperial courier the Alliance had prevented from returning to the mainland last year.

Ronall's absence provided one additional small pleasure, too. When he was gone and Elelar had the vast house to herself, she could recall happier days here, the years before her marriage, when her grandfather was still alive. The old man had taught her all he knew so that she could carry on the great work of the Alliance, the secret organization which, during his youth, he had founded with close friends. Her father, who had died in her infancy, had given his life for the Alliance. As far as the Valdani knew, though, her father had been a gutless *toren* who meekly obeyed all their laws. Her mother, who had died when Elelar was sixteen, had taught her how a woman's weapons could be even more effective than a man's in the secret war the Alliance waged against the Valdani.

She had inherited this grand, elegant house in the heart of Shaljir from them, and she knew secrets about it which, to her relief, her husband still didn't even begin to suspect: secret passages, hidden storage compartments, a concealed room . . . and a core of longtime servants utterly loyal to the Alliance. And beneath it all lay the secret, ancient tunnels that her grandfather had discovered more than fifty years ago, inhabited by the strange, lost race of beings whom he was the first to ever regard as Silerians, with as much right to this land as the rest of them.

. Her grandfather, Gaborian, eventually brought the Beyah-Olvari into the secret network of rebels that he and several of his closest friends were establishing in those days. Through the friends Gaborian had made abroad, the Alliance eventually joined with secret societies in other lands ruled or threatened by the Valdani. He had also been responsible for bringing certain factions of the Honored Society into the Alliance, despite the violent protests he encountered upon doing so. As he had told Elelar time and time again, the Valdani were the only enemies that counted.

"The rest of us," he would say, "are Silerians, and we must fight the Valdani together."

Elelar had been born for this work, raised in this cause, tutored day and night in this struggle. She had never once wavered in her duty. After her grandfather's death, all of Shaljir had believed that Elelar must marry soon, for a young woman with no male protector had only two respectable choices in Sileria: marriage or the Sisterhood. Some now thought that, perhaps due to grief over the loss of her grandfather, she had made an impulsive and disastrous choice in marrying Ronall; he was still rather handsome and, when he chose, even possessed a certain reckless charm, but he had proved to be a terrible husband by any standards. Others believed that she had married him for his money. Though only a second son, he was nonetheless heir to two rich country estates, an oceangoing ship, and considerable sums of wealth.

Ronall was the son of a Valdani aristocrat, got on the man's second wife, a *torena* he had married after his Valdani wife had died trying to bear him another child. Ronall was deemed—quite correctly—to be too steeped in his vices and too interested in his pleasures to pay much attention to the way Elelar slowly began acquiring control of his land and wealth after marrying him. Her own family, the Hasnari, were hardly poor, but the activities of the Alliance ate up wealth faster than it could be acquired, so getting her hands on Ronall's money had been a distinct benefit of the marriage.

Even more important, Ronall's Valdani relatives and friends had opened up many doors to Elelar. The information she had been able to gather from these unwitting sources over the past five years had strengthened the Alliance beyond all expectation. The greatest opportunity had come three years ago, when the Imperial Advisor had extended an invitation to Ronall and his Silerian wife to some vulgar Valdani religious festival at Santorell Palace. From the moment they first met, Elelar had recognized Advisor Borell's interest in her. Well-educated by her mother in the ways of winning men, Elelar made Borell wait for months before she finally pretended to succumb to passion and entered his bed.

She had been discreet at first, visiting him infrequently and staying only briefly, keeping him hungry for her. Even after becoming his mistress, she had cautiously continued occasionally seeing her other two lovers in secret: one, a half-Moorlander Valdan, the other a high-ranking official in the Imperial Treasury. She was unwilling to give up those valuable sources of information until she was absolutely sure she had Borell where she wanted him. After a year, Borell had given up other women and even stopped exchanging letters with his longtime mistress in Valda. Elelar ended her relationships with the two other men, about whom Borell had never learned, and finally gave into his pressure to make their liaison public by acting as his hostess on numerous occasions and visiting him openly by day when he requested it.

This blatant display of her intimacy with the Imperial Advisor soon caused problems with her husband. It was the only time that Ronall ever actually beat her. Borell found out and had him dragged to Santorell Palace for a confrontation, then thrown into prison for several days. Then Ronall's father took him home and talked to him. Unlike Silerians, Valdani aristocrats regarded a woman's infidelity with considerable tolerance if she slept with a man of superior rank who could somehow benefit the family she had married into. Ronall's father explained to him that Borell was a reasonable man who had promised he would ensure that the family reaped the rewards of his public liaison with Ronall's wife. Ronall never learned to like this, but with his father's stern lectures filling his ears and the memory of a prison cell haunting his dreams, he learned to tolerate it.

Meanwhile, since Borell had proved to be extremely possessive, Elelar took great pains to ensure he didn't find out that, for the past year, she occasionally spread her legs for the Kintish High King's ambassador to Sileria. When that man had first issued her an invitation to his bed, in the discreet and circumspect manner typical of his kind, she had considered it too important an opportunity to pass up. She could learn things from him that Borell simply didn't know, which made the affair worth the risk.

Though she never admitted it to Ronall, Elelar thought it very likely that the fault was hers and not his that they had no heir. There had been so many men over the years, and none had sired a child upon her. True, some of the men, especially the well-born ones, wore sheaths; on other occasions, she often took the preventive measures provided—in defiance of both Valdani and traditional Silerian law—by the Sisterhood. Nonetheless, there had been many opportunities for a child to find its way into her womb, but none ever had. It was a relief to her, since she had never lain with a man whose child she wished to bear . . . except, perhaps, for the very first one. Indeed, in her whole life, she had only ever taken one man for pleasure: the very first one. All the others were for duty.

The very first one . . . He had come across the Middle Sea, from one of the Kintish Kingdoms far inland. He was the son of one of her grandfather's foreign allies, and he had stayed here for nearly a twin-moon conducting business with the Alliance. He was twice her age, worldly, educated, and soft-spoken, with skin as dark as freshly plowed earth in the lowlands after a good rain. Elelar had never felt anything like the hot rush of longing that flooded her whenever she looked at him. He saw it, recognized it, smelled it on her skin when she brushed past him in the sunlit hallways or offered him wine at dinner. He had only been their guest for five days when he came to her room late one night, uninvited and unexpected, and taught her ignorant body exactly what it longed for. Then, with a patience she had never known in any man since, he taught her a hundred ways of pleasing a man—which she now fully suspected *he* had learned from some Kintish courtesan.

The lessons continued in secret night after night, a delirium of pleasure followed by long, whispered talks when she opened her heart and soul to him. By day, she was giddy with happiness, but so tired and absentminded that her grandfather became convinced she must be growing ill. The servants knew better. They never bothered administering any of the treatments he suggested for her recuperation, but merely turned a blind eye to the young *torena*'s shameless behavior with the *roshah* in their midst.

She cried herself to sleep many nights in a row after her lover's departure, devastated that he had never once expressed a desire to marry her, let alone spoken to her grandfather about it. Lost in her misery, she convinced herself—with the blind optimism of first love—that he would soon grow to miss her as much as she missed him. Surely he would return to marry her, or at least write a letter sending for her.

A letter from him finally arrived, addressed to Gaborian and carried through dangerous territories by trusted couriers. Elelar knew, with a joyous certainty that admitted no doubts, that it must contain a formal request for her hand. She insisted upon reading it over her indulgent grandfather's shoulder, too eager to wait for him to relay its contents to her.

The letter began by thanking Gaborian for his hospitality and expressing a hope that he and his granddaughter were both in good health. Then it went on at length about business matters connected to their secret work. There was no further mention of Elelar, not the slightest hint that he'd even thought of her since leaving Sileria. Her heart was already breaking when she read the final few lines of the letter with disbelieving horror: her lover added that he was pleased to report that his wife had just safely delivered their third child, the happily anticipated event for which he had hurried home from Sileria. With his family growing so large and his wife so increasingly inconvenienced by his long absences, one of his associates would have to take his place for any future journeys abroad which were deemed necessary for their great work.

Elelar went to her room and refused to come out for three days. Her grandfather finally recognized her youthful infatuation with their foreign guest and, his voice rich with compassion, questioned her about it through her locked door. Had the news hurt her very badly? Had she not known their friend was a married man and a father? Had she felt a special affection for him?

After a while, the questions revealed that her grandfather now began to suspect the full truth, for Elelar had never before behaved so irrationally. Had the man dishonored her? Was there anything she wished to tell her grandfather, who promised to understand no matter what she revealed? How could he help her? Wouldn't she please *talk* to him?

After three days, Elelar emerged from her bedchamber, having answered none of her grandfather's questions. She told him once, and only once, that she would not tolerate any mention of the man's name in her presence ever again. And so they never again spoke of him or the incident. She could see that her grandfather's heart was heavy with sorrow for her, but she felt too humiliated to acknowledge his compassion for her. At seventeen, she had learned a valuable lesson about men, one which she would never forget. From that day forward, the dance between man and woman was something she did only for the Alliance, never for herself.

Elelar supposed it was sheer exhaustion that permitted her mind to dwell on such maudlin memories, for this night's work had been demanding. The sky east of Shaljir was just starting to grow pale, subtle shades of pink and peach painting fantastic patterns on the vast celestial canvas as Elelar concluded the last of her business and wearily ascended to her bedchamber. She was halfway up the grand staircase when Faradar, gasping for air, came running into the main hall and stopped her with an excited shout.

Surprised, Elelar turned and met her servant, who was already running up the stairs to thrust something into her

hand. "They left something for you, *torena*. I was so
shocked! It's been *months* since—"

"Who?"

Faradar paused to get control of herself, then whispered
more calmly, "Our old friends."

Elelar drew in a quick, surprised breath. "Our old
friends" was how the Alliance referred to the Beyah-
Olvari. For their own protection, their existence remained
a closely guarded secret, so any contact was always made
discreetly. When the Beyah-Olvari wanted to see Elelar,
they usually left a message of some kind for her in a subterranean cubby hole between the house and the underground tunnels. Tonight, instead of a message, they had
left—it seemed—a silky piece of cloth.

"Hold this," she instructed, giving her lantern to Faradar
so she could more easily examine what the woman had
handed to her on the shadowy staircase.

Elelar held the material—a hand-painted silk scarf, she
now saw—up to the light. After a moment of blank confusion, she recognized it with a hot rush of mingled shock
and panic—for it had once belonged to her.

"Dar have mercy!" She swayed slightly, feeling faint for
the first time in years.

"What, *torena?*" The lantern light wavered as Faradar
caught her arm. "What's wrong? Has something happened?"

"By all the gods above and below," Elelar gasped out,
slumping down onto a stair as her knees gave way, "I
never thought it possible . . ."

"What *is* it?" Faradar demanded.

Elelar shook her head, unable to speak of what had happened so long ago, unable to form any coherent thought
except the one which now pounded inside her skull over
and over.

He's back, he's back, Dar shield me, he's back . . .

16

MIRABAR AWOKE TO find herself lying in a heap near a sacred fire. It had been a long night's work, petitioning the Otherworld for help, trying to guide shades of the dead toward the gateway, begging Dar for mercy and consideration on their behalf. She now realized she must have passed out from the strain. She looked around and discovered that someone had put food near her. Famished, she threw off a blanket—which someone had used to cover her while she slept—and attacked the meal. When she was nearly done eating, she heard a man's voice from the mouth of the cave.

"Ah, you're awake."

She jumped and turned around. He was not the same *shallah* who had led her here last night, but he had obviously been warned about her, for he didn't gasp, utter prayers and curses, or reach for his sword. Darfire—this one had a sword, too!

There was an awkward pause. She decided to break it by saying formally, "I am Mirabar, no father, no clan, a Guardian of the Otherworld."

"Sirana." He crossed his fists and bowed his head respectfully. "I am Amitan mar Kiman shah Islanari."

"Basimar's clan," she noted.

"She says that you are a Guardian of great gifts, favored with special visions from the Otherworld."

It sounded good, so Mirabar didn't contradict the description. "She says that one of you has seen another like me."

"Well . . ." A wry smile touched Amitan's mouth. "That was Zimran, and since he is given to telling tales . . ." He made a dismissive gesture, then added, "But Josarian saw him, too, so I suppose it must be true."

She asked him to repeat what both men had said. She was disappointed that the description he offered was no more detailed or satisfying than what she had made Basimar tell her a dozen times already—fire-gold eyes, dark hair, very powerful, apparently a *toren* by birth—but she listened intently nonetheless, like a child who never tired of hearing a favorite tale.

"Another like me . . ." Her mind drifted as she dwelled upon this extraordinary notion once again.

Amitan came forward, approaching her as if she were a deer who might run away. "You fought hard last night, *sirana,* to help those slaughtered in Malthenar."

"Their voices are still loud," she replied, shying away from the din. "Or perhaps they are other voices." She glanced at him. "That's why Guardians only come here for special occasions and only stay briefly. We could go mad so easily up here, where the Otherworld is so close to this one."

"I knew Corenten," Amitan said quietly. "He was a good lad. He might have married my sister."

"I'm sorry."

"Is he . . ." Amitan cleared his throat. "I know little about these things. Is he in the Otherworld now?"

She shook her head. "I don't know. I'm sorry. If you can bring me something that belonged to him, I can try Calling him. But, you must understand, he died very recently, so it may be too soon for—"

"She's awake!"

Mirabar looked up to see Basimar, at the mouth of the cave, reporting this news to someone who waited outside. At Basimar's urging, she left the cave and went out into the sunshine. There were five men with Basimar, all of them obviously curious about Mirabar but evidently prepared for her appearance. Along with Amitan, they were the only ones in residence at Dalishar.

"I thought there were supposed to be many more of you," Mirabar said.

"There are, *sirana,* but we don't just sit around Dalishar filling our bellies," said the man from last night. "We spend most of our time attacking the Valdani and distributing the supplies we've stolen from them."

"So why are *you* here, then?"

"Someone has to keep Dalishar safe," a young man said, clearly annoyed that the duty was his at the moment.

"We can't have the Valdani finding out about it and setting a trap for us here while we're all away," Amitan explained.

"So Josarian is gone. The warrior—Tansen—is gone. Zimran is gone." Mirabar frowned. "Who's in charge now?"

"Emelen."

She looked around. "Which one of you—"

"He's gone, too, *sirana.*"

"Wonderful." She sat down on a rock.

What was she supposed to do now? She had sought Kiloran ever since leaving Tashinar's side, and she was no closer to finding him than she had been then. When Basimar had revealed to her that the warrior might be found at Dalishar, she had abandoned her quest for Kiloran in favor of finding the warrior. Had she been wrong? Now that she knew the warrior had gone in search of Kiloran, she had a terrible feeling that she'd made a mistake in coming here; she should have kept looking for Kiloran, too. The warrior would be with him.

"Find the *shir* and you find him." What *shir*? If not the *shir* of Basimar's brother-in-law, then whose? "Fire and water. Fire *in* water. A house of water. An alliance."

"What's she saying?" one of the men asked, starting to back away from her.

"She does this all the time," Basimar said dismissively. "Don't let it bother you."

"I must find Kiloran," Mirabar said at last.

"We've already tried that," Basimar pointed out.

"There must be a way . . ." Mirabar looked around at the men. "Who would know where he is?"

"An assassin, I suppose," said Amitan. "One of *his* assassins."

She thought it over. "All right, how do I find one of his assassins?"

Basimar jumped as if she'd been stung. Amitan shook his head. Another of the men laughed at her.

"Sirana, you can't possibly—"

"Mira, that is the worst idea I've ever—"

"An assassin! Surely *avoiding* them is the only—"

"Haven't we had enough trouble with Kiloran?"

"What trouble?" Mirabar asked. "Surely Kiloran doesn't care if you keep attacking the Valdani?"

"I mean the assassin who came here. Tansen killed him, which puts us in an awkward position with Kil—"

"An assassin came here?" Mirabar jumped to her feet. "In search of Tansen?"

"Yes. The *shir* is still lying over there, where it fell."

"Sweet Dar, he's leaving a *trail* of them," Mirabar muttered. "Tell me, how many people know that Tansen has disappeared and may not return?"

Amitan blinked. "Well . . . no one, really. We didn't think it wise to reveal that Josarian is missing, so—"

"So not even Kiloran knows that we don't have Tansen with us right here?" she pounced.

"Yes, I suppose that's true."

Mirabar laughed. "That's it! That's how I'll find Kiloran!"

"Sirana?"

"We'll lure an assassin up here. I'll capture him and make him lead me to Kiloran!"

If she had told them she intended to march into Valda and spit in the Emperor's face, they could not have been more horrified. Mirabar waited for them to calm down, then offered to do a Calling.

*   *   *

"SOMEONE IS LOOKING for you," the Olvar said, stirring the Sacred Pool with a wrinkled hand.

"Kiloran?" Tansen guessed.

"No. An ally."

"Elelar? Is she coming?"

He kept his voice level, concealing the emotions churning inside him. It was hard to mark the passage of time down here, but he thought it must be more than a day since he had sent the scarf to Elelar via the Olvar's messenger, revealing his presence down here, alerting her to his return.

She would come. Surely, she would come. She couldn't risk *not* coming, nor had she ever been one to back away from a challenge. But part of him was still afraid that she wouldn't come.

"The *torena* is coming," the Olvar assured him. "She is in the tunnels even now, coming to meet you."

It felt as if someone had suddenly grabbed his insides and squeezed hard. He didn't risk looking at Josarian, though he could feel his friend's gaze hard upon him.

"Someone is looking for you," the Olvar repeated. "Seeks you far and wide. Takes great risks to find you."

Tansen thought for a moment. "It couldn't be Koroll, the Valdani commander, could it? He thinks we're allies, and he doesn't know what happened to me."

The Beyah-Olvari who were gathered around them uttered a banishing prayer. The Emperor's engineers had already destroyed a vast section of this underground world when expanding the port of Shaljir several years ago. Now the Valdani spoke of using Shaljir's vast network of tunnels to channel water into the city from a new source so they would no longer be so dependent upon the Idalar River; that source always required costly tribute to the Society, and it had lately become catastrophically unreliable thanks to Kiloran's power struggle with Baran. The very existence of the Beyah-Olvari was threatened by such plans.

"No," said the Olvar. "Not a Valdan. An ally. One who will be the shield, as you will be the sword."

"The shield and sword for what?" Tansen asked.

The Olvar looked straight at Josarian. "For him."

KOROLL READ MYRELL'S latest dispatch without much surprise. He had known that this brutal show of force Myrell was making in several villages in the western district was unlikely to produce immediate results, for every *shallah* was—quite rightly—afraid to betray Josarian. The Society would almost certainly take swift action against anyone who violated *lirtahar*. Moreover, the murder of Arlen, Myrell's Silerian informant, proved that Josarian would be just as quick as the Society to punish betrayal.

For the moment, the *shallaheen* built their sacred fires to send their dead to Paradise, or some such place, and made up songs about the martyrs who had died rather than give up Josarian. For the moment, they remained loyal to him.

Sooner or later, though, someone would betray him. Sooner or later, people would grow tired of suffering on behalf of this outlaw, no matter how much of his booty he gave away. Eventually, old rivalries and grievances would surface to combat this uncharacteristic solidarity. Undoubtedly, Josarian would have to kill one of his own kind again; if Koroll was lucky, next time it would be a *shallah* that some local family loved, instead of a despised stranger who had abandoned his family long ago.

The *shallaheen* were—and always had been—a violent, quarrelsome, irrational people. Whether they finally enabled Koroll to kill Josarian or whether they simply killed him themselves, surely this embarrassing rebellion couldn't last much longer.

THE ARRIVAL IN the Chamber of the Sacred Pool of *Torena* Elelar mar Olidan yesh Ronall shah Hasnari occasioned much chanting and blessing, both before and after the interminable formal greetings the Beyah-Olvari invariably bestowed upon a guest.

Tansen was glad. It gave him time to strangle a thousand

unwanted memories and emotions before he actually had
to speak to her. She was even more poised than she'd been
at eighteen; except for a brief glance in his direction when
she first entered the chamber, she managed not to look at
him again until she had finally finished exchanging lengthy
greetings with the Olvar, his family, the respected elders
of the tribe, and their families.

Graceful and elegant, she had ripened to fulfill all the
promise she had shown nine years ago. She wore a costly
confection of painted gossamer, the traditional long tunic
and pantaloons of a Silerian woman modified for the more
permissive standards of the *toreni*. The slim pantaloons
tapered down to hug her slender ankles, the grace of which
were probably lost on the Valdani clod she had married.

Yesh Ronall: spouse of Ronall. Those words had hit
Tansen hard when the Olvar's praise singer had announced
Elelar's arrival. Tan had known she would probably be
married; except for a Sister, what woman did not marry?
He had expected it, but it clawed at him, even so. She
belonged to another man—and to a Valdan! Tansen's mind
reeled. Knowing how she had hated the Valdani nine years
ago, he wondered whether she had changed beyond all
recognition, or whether this marriage was another strand
in the Alliance's tangled web of scheming and deception.

Physically, at least, she had certainly not changed beyond recognition. He would have known her anywhere.
Her smooth, arrogant face with its wide-set watchful eyes
and full mouth was just as he remembered it, though it
was the face of a woman now, rather than a girl. Her costly
clothing was designed to artfully reveal the graceful curves
and slender waist he had never forgotten. The short sleeves
of her shimmering tunic bared the smooth flesh of her
arms, exquisitely fair by Silerian standards—though the
pale Valdani probably considered her too dark for true
beauty.

However, beauty, though she had it, was not what set
Elelar apart from other women. The elaborate coils and
braids her glossy black hair was woven into, the oils and

cosmetics which she used with such obvious skill, and the exquisite garments she wore all pleased the eye as much as her face and figure, but Tansen had seen more beautiful women. There was something about Elelar which far exceeded mere beauty; it had been there nine years ago, and it had now blossomed into its full power. Was it the grace and sensuality of her movements? The mingled warm challenge and cool intelligence of her gaze? The courage which, as Josarian would have put it, was like a banner? Or was it merely the arrogant pride, so evident in every gesture, that made a man want to feel her tremble beneath him?

When he was fifteen, he had fallen instantly, irrevocably under her spell. She had ignored him, mocked him, embarrassed him, angered him. She had also taught him, guided him, and opened his eyes, ensuring that they could never close again. She had shaped his destiny more than she realized. And, in the end, she had betrayed him.

He had tried to hate her, to despise her, to cultivate his resentment against her. Sometimes he had even succeeded, but he had always found it impossible to *forget* her. And now, after all these years, he was ashamed to discover, as he gazed at her, that hatred and resentment were weak, pale things which withered beneath the onslaught of his longing.

The last time he had seen her, she had raged at him with a violence that knew no relief, with a passion that craved vengeance. Now, as she turned to acknowledge and greet him, he saw that she, too, had given long and hard study to the art of concealing her emotions. Her voice was cool and her expression betrayed no more interest than she would show in any other unexpected visitor to the tunnels. Her apparent indifference tore at his insides, even as he kept his own expression equally impersonal.

Acknowledging her greeting, he crossed his fists over his chest and bowed his head, dignifying her rank. "*Torena*, I am pleased to see you looking so well," he said formally.

"May Dar welcome home Her wandering son," she recited, not bothering to try to sound sincere. "I see you bring a friend."

"*Torena,*" he replied, "I beg the honor of presenting to you my bloodbrother, Josarian mar Gershon shah Emeldari."

Even Elelar couldn't conceal her surprise. Her dark eyes flashed to Josarian's face and she stared with open astonishment. "*Josarian?*"

Josarian looked briefly at Tansen, then crossed his fists and bowed his head. "I am honored, *torena.*"

"You shouldn't be in Shaljir," she said instantly. "If the Valdani find out you're here, you'll never escape. The city is walled and there are Outlookers everywh—"

"They won't find out," Tansen interrupted.

Elelar looked back at him, all formality forgotten. "You did right to notify us, but bringing him into the heart of Shaljir was not—"

"I didn't bring him. I have business here, and he insisted on coming."

"That was unwise. You're not safe here," she told Josarian, "and your first responsibility is to—"

"*I* choose my responsibilities, *torena,*" Josarian said, frowning at her. "But I am curious: What interest do you have in my safety and responsibilities?"

Elelar looked back at Tansen. "You haven't told him?"

"I didn't know if you would come," he said quietly. "I didn't even know if you were still . . ." He shrugged.

"I see." She paused, studying him with the curiosity she had refused to reveal before. "I was sure you must be dead by now."

"You're bearing up well under the disappointment."

She ignored that. "When did you come back?"

"Earlier this year."

"And him?" She nodded to Josarian. "How do you know him? Are you responsible for—"

"No. Coincidence. The Valdani captured me in Cavasar, upon my return, because of these." He gestured to his swords, which he now wore unconcealed. "Commander Koroll hired me to find Josarian and kill him, because the Valdani were already so afraid of him."

"So you found him and helped him kill more Valdani?" she guessed.

"Yes." He tensed as she glided forward and, without asking permission, touched the hilt of the sword sheathed at his side. Her scent wafted around him, subtle, luxuriant, intoxicating in the dank air of the caverns. The warmth of her skin reached out to him, turning him again into a boy who longed for her touch but was too proud to risk her rebuff.

"Where did you get these?" she asked. "This is Kintish workmanship, isn't it?"

"I left the Adalian coast on a ship bound for Kashala," he replied, looking down into her upturned face. He realized with absent surprise that he was now taller than she was.

She held his gaze for a moment, then suddenly turned away. "Kashala . . . I did sometimes wonder where you had gone. If you were alive. What had happened to you."

"Whether the Society had found me?" He heard the edge in his voice and clenched his teeth, reminding himself to keep his head.

"I would have heard," she reminded him.

"You know about Kiloran's bloodvow, *torena?*" Josarian asked, watching them both closely, his face dark with concentration as he tried to understand the tension between them.

Tansen's breath came out on a soft puff of laughter. "You might say the *torena* urged him to swear it."

"What?" Josarian's voice was shocked.

Elelar's eyes flashed, the aristocratic coolness of her manner melting away as anger bubbled to the surface. "What did you expect, after what you did?"

"What did you expect me to do, after all the things you said?" he challenged.

"I *never* said anything to make you do something so

reckless, so destructive, so abysmally *stupid*!" she shot back.

"You were the one who showed me the way, who taught me my duty, who taught me what *they* really are." Nine years of anger, of burning resentment, flooded his veins. He heard it throbbing in his voice, exposing him, but suddenly he didn't care. How could she have done this to him?

"You can't blame it on *me!*" she shouted. "You could have gotten us all killed! You nearly did! As it was, you ruined everything! If not for you, we could have won!"

"Won *what?*" he snarled. "Another thousand years of slavery? Another ruthless conquest?"

"The Valdani are the only enemies that matter!" she cried.

"You're wrong." He had told her so then, too, and he saw that she still didn't understand. "And you were wrong to betray me, Elelar." He shook his head and added, "I thought you had more courage than that."

Elelar stepped back as if he had slapped her. Her face was pale with the shock of his insult. The mingled blessings, banishing prayers, and mourning chants of the Beyah-Olvari were reaching deafening proportions. Such hostile, emotional outbursts were deeply distressing to them. Tansen looked around at his wailing, swaying companions and cursed himself for having lost control. He knew better. He was a *shatai*. He must focus on the task at hand.

"I did what I did to save the Alliance," Elelar said, her voice quiet but shaking with anger. "In one stupid, irrational act, you destroyed Sileria's future. You nearly destroyed the Alliance, too." She glared at him, her gaze scorching. "I couldn't change what you'd done, but I wasn't going to let you destroy the work of years, the work to which my parents, my grandfather, and so many others devoted their lives."

"The work of years?" Tansen's voice was scathing. "In a few short months, Josarian has hurt the Valdani more than the entire fifty years of the Alliance's scheming and double-dealing and—"

"And without us, he'd continue wasting his efforts on minor targets," she snapped. "Violence without intelligence is nothing! Or haven't you learned that yet? Have you totally wasted these nine years?"

"He's a *shatai*," Josarian interrupted, his voice harsh with anger, "and no one may speak to him so, *torena*. He has used his time well, and you owe him more respect than—"

"A *shatai?*" She glanced from Tansen's swords to his face, her expression confused. "I have seen *shatai*, and you don't look—"

"I, uh . . ." Tansen looked wryly at Josarian. "I underwent a slight transformation after I joined Josarian. A *shatai* would be too easy to spot in the mountains." Seeing her dubious expression, he sighed and unlaced the front of his shabby tunic enough to expose the brand on his chest. Her astonished gasp pleased him.

She came forward and stared at the elaborate scar which he had earned with sweat, pain, and skill, and which he bore with pride. "You . . . became a *shatai*." Her voice was the barest of whispers.

"I know, you're disappointed." He closed his tunic. "For nine years, I've no doubt you've been picturing me as dragonfish bait."

She rolled her eyes. "For nine years I've been busy w . . ." She stopped and stared. "*Nine years*. The bloodvow! So that's why you came back."

"Yes."

She turned her palms up. "Then . . . it's over?"

"That's what I need to discuss with Kiloran," he said. "He seems to have forgotten to rescind the bloodvow, and the Society knows I'm back."

"They'll send assassins after you."

"Two have already found me."

She blinked. "And?"

"And if this keeps up, I'll soon have more *shir* than the Society."

She looked stunned. "But . . . they're *assassins*. How in the Fires did you—"

"I'm a *shatai*." He enjoyed the opportunity to show her a little condescension. "I am not so easy to kill."

Her gaze was intent, assessing. "You're not afraid of them."

"I can kill as many as Kiloran can send," Tansen said dismissively. "That's not the problem."

"The problem," Josarian said, "is that our fight with Kiloran interferes with our bloodfeud against the Valdani."

"*Our* fight with Kiloran?" Elelar's brows went up.

"Tansen is my bloodbrother now," Josarian told her. "His clan is gone. There is no one but me to fight at his side."

Elelar looked back at Tansen, her irritation evident. "Now that's just wonderful."

"I thought you would be interested," he said with satisfaction.

"You're needed in the mountains," she explained to Josarian. "More than you're needed at Tansen's side."

He clearly didn't appreciate being spoken to as if he were a child. "Tansen cannot go back to the mountains until this business with Kiloran is settled, so neither can I."

"There are more important considerations than—"

"If you betrayed him, *torena*, then you can hardly expect me to listen to your advice." Josarian's expression revealed contempt, and Tansen suspected that it was a novel experience for Elelar to be addressed this way by a *shallah*.

"Dar grant me patience," she muttered. She glanced at Tansen. "I can guess why you've come. You want me to help you find Kiloran."

"Yes."

"You can't truly believe he'll rescind the bloodvow?"

"It has been nine years," Tansen said, knowing the words were hollow. "Honor dictates—"

"Don't waste my time pretending that Kiloran cares about honor."

"I'm bringing back the *shir.*"

"You've still got it?"

He nodded. "It's an honorable peace offering."

"Not after what *you* did." Her voice trembled with the emotions she was trying to keep from erupting once again. "He will never forgive you for what you did."

"Will you help me find him?"

"Tansen . . ." She put a hand on his arm, the first time she had touched him since entering the Chamber of the Sacred Pool. It was disgraceful, he thought, how much her touch could make him want to forgive her everything. "He's a waterlord. *The* waterlord. Even a *shatai* cannot survive a direct attack from Kiloran."

"Will you help me?" he repeated.

"Tansen, please . . ." She shook her head. "It wasn't your death I sought. It was the survival of the Alliance. And now that I see you again, I . . ." She looked away. "Let me help you get out of Sileria before he finds out that you've come to see me. Let me help you get away."

"I only want you to help me find Kiloran." His heart pounded at her nearness, ached at her softening.

"He'll kill you," she whispered. "He *will* kill you. You must know that."

"I will see him, with or without your help, Elelar," he said above the wailing of the Beyah-Olvari. "We will make peace, or one of us will die."

"Please—"

"That's how it will be." A woman's pleas, he discovered, were harder to resist than his own fear. "There is no other way." Now was the time to bait the trap. "If you help me . . ."

"What?" She didn't even bother to look up.

He glanced at Josarian. "Then my bloodbrother might show his appreciation, even after my death, by joining the Alliance."

That got her to look up. Her eyes narrowed, for she

knew the answer to her next question: "And if I don't?"

"You'll never see Josarian again."

Josarian recognized his cue. "If you help us now, *torena,* I'll swear a bloodpact with you."

Elelar held up a smooth, flawless palm. "If you come anywhere near me with a knife, I'll have you arrested."

Josarian's mouth quirked. "Forgive me, *torena,* I forgot that only *shallah* women can bear the knife with dignity."

Tansen wanted to laugh at the look Elelar flashed Josarian, for he had no doubt that she still prided herself on being able to bear *anything.*

"The point is, Elelar," Tan said, "if the Alliance wants Josarian, his men, and the *shallaheen* to join them, whether I survive or not, then—"

"Then I must take you to Kiloran," she concluded bitterly.

"Those are our terms," Josarian confirmed. He met Tansen's gaze, his look clearly expressing that he'd require a *lot* of explanations about this scene.

"Do you *want* to die?" Elelar asked Tansen.

Instead of answering, he reminded her, "You traded my life for the Alliance once before. Why hesitate now?"

She lowered her head and sighed. After a long moment, with the wailing of the Beyah-Olvari echoing all around them, she finally nodded. "Very well. I will take you to Kiloran."

17

HIS NAME WAS Najdan, and he had been born to such bitter poverty that hunger was his earliest memory. His father had been taken to the mines soon after the birth of Najdan's youngest sister, where he died without ever seeing the sky again. At fourteen, Najdan had committed his first murder, slaying a *sriliah* sought by Kiloran. It had been risky, for assassins resented ordinary men who tried to reap the glory of fulfilling a bloodvow; they often killed such a man before he could petition a waterlord to initiate him into the Society. Of course, if he survived, as Najdan had, then he became one of them and was thereafter protected by their code. An assassin could kill almost any ordinary man with impunity, but only a waterlord could order the death of another member of the Honored Society. If one assassin killed another without such authorization, then his life was forfeit. Indeed, the punishment was even worse than death: it was said that the White Dragon came after an assassin who had dishonored the Society. The rights and privileges granted by the Society were great, but so were the penalties for violating its laws.

Najdan had never regretted that first assassination, or the many he had committed since then. His mother and sisters, although he seldom saw them anymore, had full bellies and comfortable homes. He could never have accomplished that by breaking his back in lawful pursuits twelve or more hours per day, every day; hard work never changed the poverty of a *shallah*'s existence under Valdani rule. *His* belly was full, too. He wore fine clothes, replacing them regularly with new ones, and his boots were specially made for him in Adalian. His mistress kept a comfortable house for him deep in the mountains, not far from Kiloran's lair. Now, twenty years after making that first kill and surviving long enough to be initiated into the Society, Najdan feared only two things in life: hunger and Kiloran.

True, an assassin was always in danger from the Outlookers. If they caught him, they would slaughter him, send him to the mines, or throw him into some prison cell to die slowly. But the Outlookers, after all, were merely Valdani—stupid, clumsy, and easily evaded. Besides, a man armed with a *shir* was no easy victim, not even when set upon by sword-wielding Outlookers. Najdan had killed three Outlookers over the years and knew that they were not invincible; there were just so *many* of them. Even Kiloran couldn't figure out how to kill them all.

The old wizard had expressed some interest in the young *shallah* who had managed to kill so many lately. Indeed, there were many things about Josarian that intrigued Kiloran, not the least of which was how, when, and why he had joined forces with Tansen, the mysterious mercenary who had appeared out of nowhere when the year was still young.

The waterlords of the Honored Society had already agreed that they didn't mind this unexpected mountain rebellion. It made their enemies, the Valdani, suffer—and even look incredibly foolish, on occasion. It drew attention away from some of the Society's activities, thus increasing profits and power. Above all, Josarian offered no offense to the Society and did not challenge their supremacy.

It was unfortunate, however, that a man now reputed to be among Josarian's most trusted companions just happened to be an enemy of Kiloran's. Moreover, Tansen, the only surviving son of an extinct clan, had already somehow managed to kill two assassins sent to fulfill the blood-vow, thus adding to the insult of his continued existence in this world. This had given everyone cause to pause and seriously consider the situation; no one could remember the last time a mere *shallah* had killed an assassin.

Kiloran was absolutely furious. He had recalled Najdan from business on the western coast and ordered him to find and kill Tansen, quickly and efficiently. Najdan prided himself on being one of Kiloran's best and most trusted assassins. He had never possessed the qualities which might have enabled him to study the mysterious art of water magic, the secret sorcery upon which the might and power of the Society had been built, but he was exceptionally good at carrying out the Society's more practical business. True, he was not as clever as Searlon, the assassin whom Kiloran valued most of all; but Searlon came from a wealthy merchant family and was educated. However, although Najdan lacked Searlon's imagination and sophistication, he was very good at killing people, and this made him valuable to Kiloran. He acknowledged this without particular pride or regret; it simply meant that, as a mere boy of fourteen, he had chosen the right path in life. It was more than most men could say.

There was some talk about the *shallah* he sought. Strange talk about foreign swords, extraordinary abilities, a private bloodpact with Josarian—whose head he had once sought—and a past full of violence and mystery. Many members of the Society were curious about why Kiloran wanted the *roshah* dead, for no one really seemed to know who the man was or what he had done to earn the waterlord's enmity. Kiloran himself had only told Najdan, "He destroyed something very valuable that should have been mine; something that can never be replaced."

Najdan didn't actually care what Tansen had done. He'd always considered curiosity an unhealthy vice. It was enough to know that Kiloran wanted the *sriliah* dead, and that he was apparently rather hard to kill. At least he shouldn't be too hard to find, though; careful questioning in various villages revealed that Josarian's men were based up in the Dalishar Caves. A good choice for outlaws trying to avoid the Outlookers, Najdan supposed. Even Kiloran's lair was not as remote as those haunted, echoing, eerily painted caves with their eternal fires. Najdan had never been there, but every Silerian had heard them described. Although the Society had long ago surpassed the might and influence of the Guardians, Dalishar was one of the rare places where Guardian magic still reigned supreme; centuries ago, the waterlords had quietly abandoned their attempts to control the site.

Najdan didn't relish going there, but he wasn't afraid. He had killed men in worse places.

As he tracked his quarry, he discovered that Tansen's reputation was spreading through the mountains as fast as Josarian's. Village *tirshaheen* echoed with extravagant tales of the many men the stranger had killed here and abroad. He reputedly carried two Kintish swords which were said to be so powerfully enchanted that they leapt out of their sheathes by themselves and slaughtered his enemies before they had time to blink. People respected, feared, and even admired him; it was Josarian, however, whom they loved.

As Najdan ascended Mount Dalishar through rugged terrain, he supposed it was a lucky thing that Kiloran hadn't sent him here to kill Josarian. Passing through these western mountain villages, Najdan couldn't recall having ever seen anything unite the *shallaheen* like their love for Josarian. Some of it, of course, was gratitude; many bellies were fuller this season, thanks to Josarian's peculiar habit of giving away virtually everything he stole from the Valdani. But there was something else at work here, too, something which evidently gave the *shallaheen* courage in the face of violence, and strength in the shadow of grief. The Outlookers had recently staged a hideous massacre at Malthenar after the villagers refused to betray Josarian, and last night there had been rumors of another massacre at Morven, though reports were still vague.

Najdan knew these people; he had been born among them, he had once been one of them. He knew that, by now, all but Josarian's own clan should be turning against him because of the suffering his activities were bringing down upon them. Yet the destruction the Valdani were now bringing to the *shallaheen* seemed to be having exactly the opposite effect of what Najdan—and probably the Valdani themselves—would have expected. The villagers Najdan spoke to in this district praised Josarian all the more reverently for the suffering they had endured—or knew they might soon endure—in his name. Every shepherd in these mountains seemed to redouble his loyalty to Josarian now that the bloodfeud was truly a matter of life and death. Mothers from here to Islanar were saying that Corenten's mother had done the right thing and that they, too, would defend their sons' right to die honorably in the face of Valdani barbarity. Some girl who hadn't even been officially betrothed to Corenten went into Sanctuary the day after his death, reportedly determined to become a Sister and honor his memory for the rest of her life.

"Josarian is *right,*" people whispered in the markets.

"Josarian speaks the truth!" drunks proclaimed in the *tirshaheen.*

"He will not stop killing the Valdani until they stop coming into the mountains," Najdan was vehemently assured. "We will be rid of them at last!"

Not surprisingly, some *shallaheen* had even started saying that Josarian was the Firebringer.

Well, why not let them wallow in their fantasies? Najdan had seen enough of Valdani power and strength to know that a few rebellious *shallaheen* couldn't change the world. The Society, with all its power, wealth, and experience, had been fighting the Valdani for years without getting rid of them. No matter how many victories the waterlords enjoyed, there were always more Valdani sent to replace the ones they killed. It made Najdan wonder how vast the homeland of the Valdani must be, that they could keep sending men to Sileria while simultaneously conquering the rest of the world. Didn't they ever run out of people? How fast could their women possibly breed?

Surely it would take more than the Firebringer to kill so many men and make sure that no more crossed the Middle Sea to maintain the Emperor's power here. Not that Najdan believed in the Firebringer, anyhow. The *zanareen* were merely the lost, pathetic, half-mad remnants of what had once been men, so beaten by life that they retreated from the world to huddle around the lips of Darshon and pray for someone to solve all their problems for them. The *shallaheen,* too weak to seize their own destiny as the Society did, clung to the shallow hope and superstitious rubbish spread by the *zanareen.* Najdan believed a man solved his own problems, or died of them; there was no third way, and certainly no heroic savior coming to change Sileria's destiny.

It was, of course, primarily a mountain superstition, since legend said the Firebringer would be mountain-born. Nonetheless, you could find men and women at almost every level of Silerian society who half-believed in the Firebringer—the way they half-believed in the Otherworld or the White Dragon or the Beyah-Olvari or fire-eyed demons who were cursed by Dar.

The White Dragon . . . now that was one thing that Najdan *did* believe in, no matter how other men—even some assassins—scoffed at the ancient tales. Najdan was only a boy of fourteen when he first met Kiloran, and from that day, he had believed every dark legend ever whispered about the waterlords. He had never seen such power, and he didn't doubt that it extended into abilities beyond his imagination.

He wondered what legends Josarian believed—and if he would eventually start to believe what the *shallaheen* whispered about him. In order to prove himself, the Firebringer would have to throw himself into the Fires of Dar and survive. It would be too bad if Josarian took the leap, since his death would undoubtedly end the little rebellion that was making the Valdani so frantic. However, if he died in the volcano soon, at least he wouldn't have long to mourn the friend that Najdan would kill today.

The rumors in Chandar, the village closest to Dalishar, were encouraging. Josarian, whose reputed loyalty to Tansen might foolishly motivate him to interfere in Society business, hadn't been seen in many days. His men said nothing of his whereabouts to anyone, but he was believed to be pursuing Myrell, the Outlooker ordering the massacres. A couple of quick, much-talked-about reprisals against Myrell's men seemed to confirm this. Everyone seemed to think that Josarian, wherever he was at the moment, was nowhere near Dalishar.

Tansen, on the other hand, was not only there, but sick. He was said to be suffering from some kind of strange, recurring fever. This surprised no one, since he was known to have travelled widely in foreign lands, where Dar-only-knew what kind of horrible illnesses preyed upon a decent *shallah* with no woman to care for him. According to rumor, Tansen was currently lying ill in one of Dalishar's sacred caves.

Najdan thought it likely he could challenge Tansen without interference—and perhaps even come upon him by stealth and attack him without warning. Many young assassins would never consider such a course of action; traditional honor demanded that a bloodvow be fulfilled with proper formality. You'd have to go far and look hard, however, to find an assassin of Najdan's age and experience who still believed that crap. Besides, Tansen had already killed two assassins who'd approached him the "honorable" way, and Najdan hadn't survived twenty years in the Society by being a heedless fool.

Josarian's men would undoubtedly be guarding Dalishar, so he circled to the far side of the mountain, approaching the caves from above rather than below. He saw no sentries posted anywhere, not even at what was evidently the famous entrance to the six main caves up here. A faint trace of ancient paintings could still be seen on the weathered rockface. An enormous woodless fire, taller than he was, burned furiously outside the cave—Guardian fire magic.

If there was some sort of trap here, he doubted it was meant for him. Josarian's men were enemies of the Valdani, not the Society. He took a cautious step forward. To his surprise, his *shir* started shaking wildly against his side. Made by Kiloran himself, the blade was only supposed to do this when threatened by other sorcery. Najdan had heard that the Guardian fires up here were ancient and very powerful, and the one directly before him was blazing so wildly it almost seemed to be alive. Was it merely this ancient power which made his *shir* quiver like a live thing, or was there real danger for him here?

His thoughts went no further, for a sight unfolded before his eyes which drove away thought, skill, and courage as brutally as it turned his bowels to water and made his throat close up with fear.

She appeared in the fire, her arms whirling like the sails of a windmill. The flames did her bidding, moving as her hands directed, swirling around her face and form, born of her body as blood was born of men. No one should be able to survive in the nest of angry flames that surrounded her like a cocoon; but Najdan saw instantly that she was not human. Her eyes blazed the same color as the fire, and the floating curls of her hair were so red they made his eyes water.

Najdan's *shir* shuddered wildly as the demon looked straight at him and smiled—a terrible, sinister smile that burned with evil. He seized his *shir,* his hands clumsy for the first time since childhood. The demon laughed. Trying to control his shaking, he held the blade up: the enchanted blade of a waterlord's trusted servant, the deadliest weapon in the world.

The demon flung out a hand. Lava shot from her fingertips, slender threads of liquid fire that reached out to wrap around Najdan's wrist. Screaming at the pain of the burn, he dropped the *shir.* Horrified, he turned to run. A wall of fire arose in his path, halting him. He turned again. The wall of flame spread faster than he could move, surrounding him, caging him. Capturing him. Terror weakened him for the first time in twenty years. Nothing in his life had prepared him for this. He sank to his knees, trapped, disarmed, and helpless.

The roaring all around him gradually faded, eventually dying away. When he opened his eyes, he saw that he was still imprisoned, though no longer by flames. The walls of fire had changed to streams of lava which surrounded him in a gruesome parody of a birdcage. And he could see his captors now.

There were five *shallaheen,* a Sister . . . and the demon woman. Except for the demon, they all looked terrified. Were they her slaves? Other captives? Swallowing convulsively, he tried to rise to his feet. His first attempt failed, humiliating him. Trembling, he finally succeeded in standing. He was an assassin; despite his shameful lapse, he wanted to die like a man.

There was a long silence while the demon studied him and the *shallaheen* all watched the two of them. Finally, one *shallah* looked down and said, in a strained voice, "Another *shir.*"

"Bury it," said the demon.

"Bury it?" the *shallah* repeated in surprise.

"If he escapes, what do you think will be the first thing he'll try to get his hands on?" the Sister said. "Let's not make it too easy for him."

"Uh . . . *might* he escape?" another *shallah* asked.

The demon smiled, another awful, evil smile. "Not before I'm done with him."

Fear ran through him, the water-cold chill of imminent death. He tried to speak, but his voice didn't work. The demon came forward, closing in on him. When she stood only inches from the molten bars of his cage, he realized with shock that she was small. Small and young. But then, perhaps demons were ageless. He had never believed in demons, not until now. *Now* it took all his strength to meet her eyes as she stared at him.

She leaned forward and wrapped her fingers around the lava-hot bars of his tiny prison. "Tell me your name or I'll kill you," she said simply, as if commenting on the weather.

"Then kill me." He had shamed himself enough already. He only hoped his death would be quick.

"Do you really want to die?" she whispered.

He didn't answer her.

"Ah. Stubborn." Her lips curved. "Before we're through here, you *will* want to die. I promise you."

A stream of lava curled away from the others which formed his prison. It glided through the air, seeking him. Najdan's breath quickened, but he stayed silent.

"You're an assassin, aren't you?"

He flinched involuntarily as the finger of lava came so close it scorched his cheek.

"Kiloran's assassin, yes?" she prodded.

He nodded. "My master is very powerful." His voice sounded thin. Speaking more forcefully, he added, "He will punish y—"

"As if he could." Her voice dripped with contempt.

Feeling his resolve weaken as the thread of lava continued tormenting him, Najdan looked away, trying to avoid the fire-hot glitter of the woman's dreadful eyes. His gaze fell upon the small hands resting so casually on molten bars of his cage, and he started trembling again.

"He is . . ." He struggled for air. ". . . the most powerful . . ."

"Really?" She was mocking him.

"He will destroy—"

"Prove it."

"W— What?"

The lava thread circled his head, nearly setting his hair on fire. Trying to avoid it, he backed into the bars of his cage. He jumped away with a cry of pain.

"Prove Kiloran is more powerful than me," she said. "If you dare."

His blood was roaring in his ears. His eyes watered with pain, shaming him anew. "How?"

"Take me to him."

His eyes widened as he stared at her in disbelief. She had lured him here with cleverly planted tales about Tansen's weakness and isolation, then trapped him in this fiery prison . . . because she wanted to find Kiloran?

"You want me to lead you to my master?"

"Unless you're afraid I will become *his* master."

Najdan had feared only two things in the world: hunger and Kiloran. Now he had found a third thing, and whatever this creature was, she was more dangerous than anything he had ever imagined. But could she possibly be even more dangerous than Kiloran himself? Could she attack him and survive?

She leaned even closer to him, her face filling the space between two of the glowing bars. "Deny me, assassin, and you will burn like the belly of Darshon for all eternity."

What would she do to Kiloran? Was she really powerful enough to triumph over him? Najdan had never supposed anyone could be . . . but he hadn't known about this deadly female.

The wand of lava glided back and forth in front of his face. The pain of his burns clouded his mind.

"If you don't help me, I can make you *beg* me for death before I finally kill you," she promised. "Or maybe I'll choose not to kill you. Maybe your weeping will amuse me."

What should he do?

He'd like to think that her torture wouldn't break him, but he wasn't sure. He carried thirteen scars, all gotten in combat, all borne with courage; but he had never been tortured by a sorceress. His long years of association with a waterlord had taught him how powerless ordinary men were against such wizardry.

"Make up your mind," the demon advised.

If he didn't lead her to Kiloran, he had no doubt that she'd eventually capture someone else who would. His burns throbbed and sweat poured down his face as he tried to form a plan. If he promised to take her to Kiloran, she wouldn't harm him much more than she already had; she'd need him to be well enough for the journey. And if he was well enough for the journey, then he'd be well enough to attempt escape and warn Kiloran about her. If nothing else, he could lead her around in circles for several days near Kiloran's lair, so that Kiloran would at least hear about her and be ready for her.

If Najdan couldn't escape her, perhaps several days in her company would at least reveal a weakness he could exploit, and he'd kill her before they reached Kiloran. If he died in the attempt, then so be it. He had already lived longer than most assassins, and he had always known he would someday give his life to serve his master.

Even if he failed and she killed him, Searlon would still stand between her and Kiloran. Even if Searlon failed . . . Surely, he thought, *surely* she couldn't really destroy Kiloran?

"Very well," Najdan said at last. "I will take you to Kiloran."

"YOU'RE NOT PUTTING me on one of those things, and that's final," Josarian said, folding his arms across his chest and glaring belligerently at his bloodbrother.

"It's not as hard as it looks," Tansen assured him, lying.

"I won't do it."

"You haven't even tried it," Tansen argued. "Just tr—"

"No," Josarian said, turning away from the horse Tansen had been trying, for the past ten minutes, to convince him to mount.

Tansen suppressed an irritated sigh. "The *torena*'s party travels on horseback, Josarian. If you don't . . ."

Josarian scowled at him. "What part of *no* didn't you understand?"

They were arguing in the stableyard behind Elelar's palatial home. It had not taken her long to sort out her affairs in Shaljir and organize their journey into the interior to find Kiloran. The official story was that Elelar was travelling inland to inspect an estate which a bankrupt *toren* had put up for sale. While Silerians could still inherit ancestral lands under Valdani law, only someone who was at least half-Valdan could purchase land. With more and more old Silerian families becoming impoverished by heavy taxes and discriminatory laws, more and more of their lands were ending up in Valdani hands. Elelar's marriage gave her the legal right to acquire such lands in her husband's name.

Tansen briefly wondered where Elelar's husband was, for she had yet to mention him, and he made no appearance among them as servants bustled around the stableyard preparing for Elelar's journey. Tansen and Josarian were supposed to be part of the *torena*'s four-man escort. The other two men, who eyed them with open suspicion, were city-dwellers, natives of Shaljir. He had already ascertained that they, like more than half the members of Elelar's household, were part of the Alliance. That slippery bunch of schemers, planners, and plotters drew their support from among many of Sileria's disparate peoples, but they had never gained the support of the *shallaheen*, the wild, violent race who distrusted anyone who was not of the mountains—and usually anyone who wasn't a blood or bloodpact relation, too.

"*Shallaheen* do not ride horses," Josarian said firmly. "I'll walk."

"Everyone else will ride," Tansen warned him.

"Are you suggesting I can't keep up?" Josarian looked insulted.

"We're not in the mountains now."

"We're going back into the mou—"

"You don't know that, and neither do I." Elelar had told them virtually nothing about their destination. "Nor do I imagine the *torena* will choose a route which will require her to abandon six expensive mounts and climb like a *shallah*."

"I can keep up with these dumb beasts."

"Not on a paved road or good path, you can't."

"They smell bad," Josarian muttered.

Elelar's pretty maid servant laughed as she bustled past them. "Some would say that *shallaheen* do, too," she pointed out.

Josarian glared at her before saying to Tansen, "They are unreliable and easily frightened. They are dangerous beasts used only by lazy men."

"Fine," Tansen snapped. "Have it your way."

Why was he urging Josarian to ride the horse, anyhow? Kiloran, in his rage, might well kill Josarian when he killed Tansen. After Elelar had left them in the tunnels, the two men had argued fiercely about Josarian's coming with Tansen, causing the Beyah-Olvari such renewed distress that the underground chambers had practically vibrated with their wailing. Josarian would not leave him to face Kiloran alone, with no one to accompany him except a woman who had somehow betrayed him once before. Nothing Tansen said to him—about the bloodfeud with the Valdani, the other outlaws, or pointless death—could shake Josarian's stubborn resolve.

"I swore a bloodfeud so the fight would survive beyond my death," Josarian had reminded him. "I have known since the night I killed my first Outlooker that I could not live very long. If my time is at hand, then so be it."

"Fires of Dar, will you *listen* to me?"

"If he kills you," Josarian had said more quietly, "who will honor your death? Who will burn your body? Who will ask the Guardians to guide you to the Otherworld and Call you forth on the anniversary of your death? Who will take your swords back to your *shatai-kaj* so they can be returned to the Stone Forest?" Josarian nodded. "It is my place to do these things."

"Josarian . . ."

But his brother slapped him on the back and grinned. "And who's to say we both won't live? You never can tell."

Now, as he turned away to adjust the saddle on his own mount, Tansen realized that Josarian was unwittingly giving him the opportunity he needed to leave him behind. Tansen knew Elelar would cooperate—especially since she and Josarian didn't seem to like each other any better today than they had at their first meeting. When they reached a place where Tansen knew Josarian could safely find his way back into familiar territory, he'd urge the riders to disappear down the road at a gallop, leaving Josarian in the dust. If Tansen survived his meeting with Kiloran, then he'd apologize for the ruse when he returned to Dalishar.

Elelar glided into the yard, giving last-minute orders to her steward as she pulled on a pair of riding gloves. As befitted her station, she wore an elaborate headdress of knotted, woven silk cords threaded with shiny acquamarine beads—the *jashar* of a *torena*—announcing her rank, family, and lineage. The cords of the headdress modestly covered her face, protecting it from both the sun and the staring eyes of strangers. Though he couldn't really see her eyes, Tansen could tell when her gaze fell upon him. They had talked briefly in private today. She had advised him that Koroll was now Commander of Shaljir due to Daroll's death at Emeldar. She seemed to know a great deal about what the Valdani knew (or thought they knew) about Josarian—as well as the fact that Koroll and the Imperial Advisor were concealing from the Emperor just how much damage Josarian had done so far. But then, Tansen had learned long ago that the Alliance's web of informants was widespread and far-reaching.

"Josarian's life is extremely important to Sileria right now," Elelar had told Tansen, as if this fact might somehow have escaped his notice.

"I agree." Knowing what she intended to ask, he explained Josarian's unassailable determination to stay by his side and assured her that he had already tried to make Josarian return to the mountains without him. "But he won't."

"Because he's your bloodbrother. Because he thinks it's his duty." She sighed. "I hate idealists."

"It's a little matter of loyalty." Tansen had let the commment stand between them like a wall, and Elelar, for once, seemed unable to make a stinging reply.

Now he felt her gaze upon him and was relieved that, this time, he could ride a horse with skill and handle himself like a man. How humiliating he had found it, years ago, to struggle ineptly as he mounted a horse for the first time and then to sit atop the great beast like a gawky, frightened girl.

She tilted her head after a moment. When she spoke, he realized her attention had shifted to Josarian. "You're meant to *ride* the horse, Josarian, not *lead* it across Sileria."

"I will not sit on this smelly, snorting creature."

She snorted, too, though daintily. "Oh, for the love of

Dar! It won't hurt you. Good heavens, if you're that afraid, I'd be happy to get you a child's pony—I'm just not sure we can find one strong enough to carry you."

Josarian's face darkened with embarrassment, and Tansen realized that Elelar's taunts had pushed him where no amount of nagging could. So much for leaving him behind in safety, Tansen thought sourly.

Josarian said in the chilliest voice Tansen had ever heard him use, "That won't be necessary, *torena*."

As Josarian turned to mount his much-reviled horse, who stood patiently munching on its bit, Tansen quickly said, "I'll give you a leg up."

"A what?"

"Bend your knee. I'll help you get up on his back."

"I don't need—"

"Just do it," Tansen muttered, remembering how his own first-time efforts had once caused great amusement in this very yard.

"That woman has the tongue of a horned viper," Josarian muttered back.

That made Tansen grin. "Ahhh, just wait until you do something that really annoys her."

Josarian rolled his eyes, then catapulted himself onto the horse's back. Once mounted, with his feet in the stirrups and his hands on the reins, he leaned over and tried to catch the animal's gaze. "I have a sword hidden under this shirt, and I know how to use it," he warned.

Tansen turned to Elelar. "I don't suppose you'd care to finally tell us where we're going?"

"A *tirshah* near Zilar."

Zilar was reputedly one of the most beautiful villages in all of Sileria. It was famous for its lush foliage, for the vast, ancient trees that shaded it all year round, and, above all, for the fabulous gold-tiled Kintish temple built there nearly five centuries ago.

"He's in Zilar?" he asked discreetly.

"No. I go there when I need to contact his son." She

stared at him in silence for a moment, then added, "He's a man now, too."

"But probably no more likeable than he ever was."

Her laughter was soft. "No, no more likeable."

She suggested they depart without further delay. She and her pretty maid, Faradar, mounted their horses with the assistance of a groom. The party rode out of the courtyard, the two male servants in front of the women, the two *shallaheen* behind. They proceeded directly to the Lion's Gate, only a short ride away. Leaving the city in the company of a *torena* proved to be even easier than entering the city had been, and they were soon out on the open road beyond the city.

Josarian sat tensely atop his mount while Tansen quietly tried to give him some equestrian instruction. Keeping his seat required enough of Josarian's concentration that he scarcely spoke all day. Riding was a skill that used muscles which even a toughened mountain peasant had never before known existed. Josarian was stiff and limp-limbed when he finally dismounted that evening. They arrived at a rather pleasant *tirshah* near Zilar and settled in just before sunset. Elelar and her maid took the inn's best bedchamber. One male servant slept outside their door to guard them; the other slept in the barn to guard the horses. Appalled at the thought of sleeping near those beasts, Josarian insisted upon sleeping outside. With their bellies full from a good dinner, he and Tansen stretched out under the stars.

"It's good to be beneath the open sky after being in those tunnels," Josarian said. "And it's especially good to eat some decent food again. I thought I'd starve to death down there."

"Their food is not easy to get used to," Tansen conceded.

Between the Beyah-Olvari and their current companions, they had not been alone together since long before Elelar's arrival in the tunnels. Tansen knew that Josarian had many questions to ask him. There were things he had not spoken of in many years, things which shamed and humbled him, which might even lose him the friendship of a man whom he realized he had, despite his creed, grown to rely upon. But Josarian trusted him, as another had once trusted him, and this time he wanted to be worthy of that trust.

"Perhaps . . ." Josarian began.

"Yes?"

"Perhaps it's time you told me how an ordinary *shallah* boy became so familiar with a *torena* from Shaljir and earned a bloodvow from Kiloran himself."

"Yes," he conceded. "Yes. I should." Only where to begin?

"Well?" Josarian prodded after a long silence.

At the beginning, he decided. The dark shore where it had all begun. The dark-moon night when the rage of the Valdani, the hunger of a dragonfish, and the blood of a stranger had changed his life forever.

"I was fifteen," he said slowly, sitting with his back against a tree and his face turned toward the stars. "My grandfather and I . . . we fed our family by smuggling contraband goods from Kinto and the Moorlands, hauling them from the eastern shores to inland buyers. We'd made a bloodpact with the pirate who supplied us." He smiled briefly as he recalled, "He was half-Kintish and half-Moorlander, and he agreed before he understood what a bloodpact meant. I thought he'd faint when we cut his palm."

Josarian laughed. Tansen flexed the hand he had cut the night he'd sworn his bloodpact with Josarian. It had only finally healed a few days ago, having opened and reopened many times due to constant use in combat and in the daily work of a man living off the land. That was how it was supposed to be. A bloodpact was a very serious matter; the pain should remind you for a long time afterward of the vows you had taken. The scar should remind you forever.

He traced the familiar scar from his bloodpact with that

pirate as he continued, "My grandfather was growing old, though he denied it. In winter, when the long rains came, his knees hurt so badly that walking was painful, and a long trek down the mountains to the shore was impossible."

"So you went alone?"

"Yes. And one night . . . *that* night . . ." He shook his head. "The pirate didn't come. Then, after waiting for hours, I discovered the body of a man washed up along the shore. He'd been attacked by a dragonfish and was half dead, but he was able to tell me that the pirate's ship had been boarded at sea by Outlookers. They burned the ship. It seemed likely that everyone on board was dead by now."

"They burned a smuggling ship? Why? They usually just—"

"They didn't care about the smuggled goods. Not that night. They were looking for him."

"Who?"

"The man who escaped, who jumped overboard and risked death in the night sea rather than be captured by the Valdani. The man I found dying on the shore."

"I don't understand," Josarian said. "What made him so important? Who was he?"

Tansen took a deep breath, then said the name he had not spoken aloud since his boyhood: "Armian."

18

"ARMIAN?" JOSARIAN REPEATED incredulously. "He really came home?"

"He came back," Tansen confirmed, continuing his story.

A mere boy who viewed the Society with the mingled

fear and fascination of most *shallaheen,* Tansen instantly idolized the man he had found lying half-dead beneath the dark-moon sky that night. This was not just *any* Society member, either; this was *Armian,* son of Harlon, the waterlord who had fought so valiantly against the Valdani before they murdered him: Armian, who was spirited away from Sileria as a child because the Outlookers sought him so vengefully; Armian, who grew to become a warrior of great courage and prowess, who had vowed to return to his homeland someday to drive the Valdani from Sileria forever. This was the man many even believed was the Firebringer!

"Do you believe in the Firebringer?" Josarian interrupted.

"I did then." Dar would be the judge, in the end.

Armian had lost a lot of blood and needed immediate care. By dawn, the Outlookers would be scouring the coast in search of him. Tansen took him to a secret cave in the hills, not far from shore, where he kept his donkeys hidden. Armian was so weak Tansen had to half-drag, half-carry him most of the way. It was hard work, for a *shallah* boy from impoverished Gamalan didn't have the height and bulk of a grown man raised to be an assassin—and perhaps, someday, a waterlord. Realizing that Armian would soon die without skilled care, Tansen found a Sanctuary and brought a Sister back to the hidden cave. After three days of her healing magic, Armian climbed out of the depths of his weakness and started to recover.

"And did he tell you why he had come home?" Josarian asked.

"The stories were true," Tansen said quietly. "He had come to drive out the Valdani. He came from the Moorlands w—"

"The Moorlands? But everyone says he was sent into hiding in Kintish lands."

Tansen nodded. "That's what the Society wanted everyone to think. They let the Valdani believe he was in one place, while they really sent him to the other side of the world. No one looked for him in the Moorlands. He was raised by a wealthy family there, people who were somehow connected to Harlon through the Alliance."

Armian had come to Sileria as a special envoy; the Moorlanders had sent him here to contact Kiloran and the Honored Society in the hope of launching a successful attack against the Valdani.

"They knew that destroying Valdani power here, in the center of the Middle Sea, was the key to regaining control of the western sea and their own coastal lands. If their plan was successful, they thought they could even drive an attack up the coast, clear into Valda itself," Tansen said.

"So they proposed to assist us in a rebellion?" Josarian asked in amazement.

"Yes. They were ready to pledge men, ships, weapons . . ." He smiled wryly and added, "Horses."

"Horses," Josarian repeated without enthusiasm.

"It would have been the greatest military force fighting on our side since Daurion's time."

"And after the war was over, we'd be ruled by the Moorlanders again," said Josarian.

"They said not. They were prepared to offer written treaties guaranteeing full withdrawal of all their forces as soon as the Valdani were driven from Sileria." Tansen shrugged. "The Alliance believed it. The Moorlanders didn't want foreign territories this time; they just wanted the Moorlands back. They knew that while Valdania holds Sileria, she holds the entire Middle Sea."

"And this is what Armian came to do."

"Yes. To find Kiloran, without whose support the plan could never succeed, and to enlist the entire Society as a sort of army. They were the only armed Silerians, the only trained killers among us."

"The rest of us just do it as a hobby." Josarian's voice was dry with acknowledgment.

"And they do have the waterlords, whom even the Valdani fear."

"True."

The pirate who was Tansen's smuggling partner was part of the Alliance, Armian explained; it was the first time Tansen had ever heard of it. The pirate was supposed to take Armian to Adalian after unloading Tansen's cargo north of Liron. However, there'd been a *sriliah* aboard who'd given them away to the Valdani, and Armian had taken a desperate risk to escape capture. Although he had miraculously survived, the plan, the rebellion, and the freedom of Sileria were all still in jeopardy.

"So he really did come home to . . . free Sileria?" Josarian said slowly.

"He came home to destroy the Valdani," Tansen corrected. "He had little information to go on. He knew only that, if something went wrong, the alternative plan was for him to somehow get to Shaljir and contact a *toren* named Gaborian: Elelar's grandfather."

"Ahhh."

Never having been west of Darshon, Tansen took Armian back to his village to consult with his own grandfather. Upon arriving in Gamalan, they discovered that the Outlookers had tortured the pirate, and he had talked.

"*Sriliah,*" Josarian spat.

"He just wasn't one of us." Tansen shook his head. "He never could take pain. He squealed like a pig when I carved the bloodpact into his palm."

"So when you reached Gamalan . . ."

"My family was dead." His throat closed, remembering the horror of that morning. After a time, his voice hoarse with memories that had never softened or grown dim, he continued, "They had tortured my grandfather. And my mother. Raped my sister before they killed her. They did unspeakab—" He stopped again. "Well. Everyone in the village was dead. No one had been spared. Not even children." He cleared his throat, struggling to banish the images. "In the end, they apparently decided we must have already gone on to Adalian. But they left four men behind to watch the village, just in case."

"They set a trap for you?"

"No, they underestimated Armian. They thought they could simply take him in a direct attack." He looked at the waning curves of the moons and recalled, "He had a *shir* and a *yahr*. Someone had taught him well; I never asked who. Although the Outlookers were armed, he killed two of them and wounded a third. The fourth was so terrified he let us escape."

"You admired him."

"I *worshipped* him," Tansen said. "If Kiloran had another assassin like that to send against me now, I could not kill him so easily as I killed the other two. And I would regret doing it, too, for the kind of courage and skill Armian had in a fight is rare. Very rare."

"So this assassin took you with him to Shaljir?"

"He couldn't leave me in Gamalan and..." He shrugged. "You know. The last of the Gamalani died there. There had already been so few of us left, anyhow, thanks to the bloodfeud with the Sirdari." He shrugged. "I had nowhere to go."

The journey to far-off Shaljir was long. They avoided the main roads and travelled mostly by night. Armian never joined in Tansen's daily prayers to Dar as they circled the vast mountain wherein she dwelled. The assassin had no use for the goddess; when the war for Sileria was over, he would apprentice to Kiloran, who had made his *shir,* and learn water magic. Nor did Armian have much use for most of the *shallaheen* they encountered on their journey; he found them ignorant and superstitious. He even seemed to blame them for their own poverty.

"How did he treat *you?*" Josarian asked.

Tansen hesitated. "For whatever reason . . . he grew to love me like a son."

Josarian nodded slowly. "And did you love him like a father?"

Josarian waited a long time for an answer. "Yes," Tan finally admitted. "I hung on his every word. Mimicked his actions, dogged his footsteps day and night." He nodded, remembering. "I looked up to him and . . . I suppose I loved him."

Shaljir should have turned the head and fired the heart of a mountain boy seeing it for the first time, but Tansen was mourning his family. Since Armian was a man who knew how to get things done, they located *Toren* Gaborian's household quickly. To their astonishment, it was being run by an eighteen-year-old girl.

"Elelar," Josarian guessed.

Tan nodded. "Gaborian was old and very ill. Elelar tells me he grew steadily worse and died two years later."

"So you had found the Alliance."

The fabulous wealth of Gaborian's household and the strange intrigues going on there might have enthralled Tansen had he not become instantly and hopelessly enamoured of Elelar. He had never seen a woman like her, had never known the painful, tongue-tied yearning which overwhelmed him in her presence. He didn't know how to control the lust that swept through him when she brushed past him or stood so close he could feel the heat of her skin.

He had also never before experienced the acute embarrassment he felt over her amusement at his rustic habits or clumsy infatuation. He was so much less than she was in every way. For the first time in his life, he was embarrassed that he was ignorant and uneducated; her pity humiliated him and her impatience shamed him.

He was a *shallah* and she was a *torena*. Even worse, he was still just a boy, and she was already a woman.

She sent him and Armian to the same *tirshah,* in the oldest section of the city, where he would lead Josarian nine years later; the keeper was not only in the Alliance, he was also privy to an astonishing secret hidden beneath the streets of the city: the survival of the Beyah-Olvari.

"How did you find out about them?" Josarian asked.

"Armian killed a beggar. The Valdani don't approve of Silerians committing murder in broad daylight in the streets of Shaljir. They sealed off the gates and started searching the city for us, not even realizing who Armian really was. So Elelar hid us underground."

"Why in the Fires did he kill a beggar?"

Tansen sought his face in the dark. "Because Armian was an assassin, and the beggar annoyed him."

Gaborian was too ill to travel and Armian's mission had already been jeopardized once by betrayal, so Elelar decided to personally escort the assassin and the mountain boy to Kiloran. She didn't know where the waterlord was, but then, as now, she had ways of finding him.

"Are you telling me that *Kiloran* is part of this Alliance?"

"Yes."

It took them many days to find Kiloran, for Emperor Jarell was devoting considerable energy that year to his war on the Society, and the waterlord was constantly on the move. During that time, Tansen discovered that Armian's method of extracting information from people was not dissimilar to the Valdani's. Tansen watched his idol enact scenes of ruthless brutality unlike anything he'd ever seen, and though he diligently applied himself to the fighting techniques Armian had decided to teach him, something inside of him started boiling over with revulsion.

"Above all, I started to see the Society through her eyes," he said.

"Elelar?"

"Yes."

Educated, articulate, and shrewd beyond her years, Elelar knew the Alliance needed to continue cultivating the Society, for they were the strongest faction in Sileria; but she considered them almost as bad as the Valdani. Who starved the cities of water when tribute didn't arrive on time or wasn't deemed generous enough? Who ruled the mountains through terror and violence? Who controlled the *toreni* with abduction, ransom demands, and murder? Who had destroyed Sileria's last Yahrdan? Who had already killed more *shallaheen* than the Valdani ever would?

"Then why was she allied to them?" Josarian asked.

"For the same reason you will be," Tansen said, "having promised to join the Alliance."

"You didn't tell me—"

"We cannot fight the Valdani without the Society. She knew it then, I know it now. You must understand it." He leaned forward. "When I first sought you, I thought only of keeping you alive to torment the Valdani. When I swore a bloodfeud with you, I thought only of making the torment last beyond our deaths. But now I have seen how men follow you, believe in you, risk everything to join your fight."

"All men want what I want, Tan: to live freely, in peace, and be able to feed their families. That's all. It's not so much, but the Valdani have denied it to us for too long."

"I don't think any man picks up a weapon just because he wants food and peace," said Tansen. "He does it because something or someone has inspired him to risk killing and dying. Something as simple as fear or hatred, something as complex as a dream or a great man's leadership."

"I am no great man," Josarian said quietly. "I'm an uneducated mountain peasant who misses his wife and who can never go home again."

"You've changed lives all over the district of Cavasar. You've convinced frightened men to follow you, and clannish villagers to put aside their differences for a common cause. You've begun a rebellion in an utterly defeated nation by challenging the most powerful empire the world has ever known." He smiled wryly. "Like it or not, you're a great man."

"A heavy responsibility," Josarian said without enthusiasm. "I think I preferred being an outlaw."

"Before this thing is through, the Valdani will wish you had stayed a mere outlaw."

Returning to the point, Josarian said, "If he kills you, I will not be Kiloran's ally."

"I know," Tansen said. "But Elelar doesn't know that, and I need her help to find him."

"You think he *will* kill you, don't you?" Josarian prodded.

He smothered his fear. "I think he wants very much to kill me."

"Then why—"

"We've been all through this before. I'm not going back into exile. I'm not going into hiding. And I don't feel like spending the rest of my life battling assassins—who might very well start killing my friends and companions when they find it too hard to kill me." His gaze rested briefly on the swords lying beside him. "I will face him as a man, and one way or another, this thing between us will finally be finished."

Josarian sighed, nodding. "Then you'd better tell me why he wants you dead."

"Yes."

After nearly a twin-moon of searching, Armian, Tansen, and Elelar finally found Kiloran—or rather, he found them, responding to Elelar's signals.

"He was . . ." Tansen made a vague gesture. "Power radiated from him the way heat radiates from a fire. His eyes were cold and lifeless, like a snake's. The Moorlanders had chosen the right envoy, for Kiloran would have trusted no other. He treated Armian with affection; but there was no warmth in him. Me . . . I was treated courteously because Armian required it."

"And Elelar?"

He smiled. "Oh, I would have pitied the man who failed to show her proper respect, even then."

"Did Kiloran approve of the Moorlanders' proposal?"

"He was suspicious at first, as was his nature. In time, though, he grew very enthusiastic about it." Tansen's hands curled into fists as he recalled, "He saw what Armian saw, what I had failed to understand. The Moorlanders would give their support to the Society, not to Sileria, to fight the Valdani. After the Emperor was beaten here and the Moorlanders withdrew to finish the war on the mainland, all power in Sileria would be left in the hands of the Society."

"With Kiloran in charge of the whole country," Josarian guessed, watching Tansen intently.

"And Armian as his successor. They . . . were very pleased at the prospect."

"Elelar had no objections?"

"Elelar and the Alliance believed the Valdani were the only enemies that mattered; all other problems and enmities could wait until the day the Valdani were finally gone."

"So the Alliance and the Honored Society both supported the plan and intended to make a pact with the Moorlanders?"

"Yes. When it was approved, Armian was to travel to the southern coast to meet a Moorlander ship and give the Society's answer. Elelar accompanied him, to speak for the Alliance. I went with him, too, for . . ." The shame of it burned him like fire, but he finally forced himself to confess, "It was my duty. I was his bloodpact son."

"Darfire! You're Armian's *bloodson?*"

"Yes. We swore the bloodpact before leaving Shaljir." He opened his left hand and traced another familiar scar.

Clearly stunned, Josarian said slowly, "The *torena* said . . . you ruined everything, you destroyed Sileria's future." He leaned forward, undoubtedly already knowing the answer as he asked, "How?"

"I murdered Armian."

Tansen tried to look away from the intensity of his friend's gaze, apparent even in the dark, but he couldn't. Josarian said nothing, made no movement or gesture; just stared. Tansen's lungs strained for air in the cool mountain night.

"I killed my own bloodfather, Josarian. You know that there are few worse crimes." His voice was so tight he had to force it out of his throat. "And I killed the man who . . . I think he may really have been the Firebringer."

"Why did you do it?" Josarian whispered at last.

"I saw . . . I saw another thousand years of slavery for us, under the heaviest yoke of all. This pact excluded all the other peoples of Sileria. The war wouldn't free Sileria for Silerian rule once the Valdani were driven out." Shame flooded his veins as he tried to explain his unspeakable act of betrayal. "The Society, led by Kiloran and Armian, would rule Sileria—more harshly than the Valdani or any other conqueror ever has."

"We would . . ." Josarian cleared his throat and sat back. "We would never be free."

"By now, we would be looking back on Valdani rule with affection." He released his breath in an uncontrolled rush. "Who starves the cities of water? Who rules the mountains through terror and violence?" Anger sparked inside of him even now as he recalled, "She was the one who said to me, 'Who has already killed more *shallaheen* than the Valdani ever will?' She was the one who taught me the history of our people and made me understand what *they* really are. I was an ignorant boy from a violent clan which was unquestioningly loyal to a Lironi waterlord. Even when I feared Armian, even when I turned away in horror from things he did, I still . . ." He shook his head. "Well, who can say what might have been? But until I knew Elelar, it never occurred to me that there could be another way."

"And once you knew, there was no turning back. I know. I've been there, too," Josarian said. "The night I first said *no* to the Valdani . . . I could never go back, after that. I suddenly knew, for the first time, that everything could be different, and *should* be different, and *I* had to try to make it so."

"I was the one who found him and saved his life," Tansen said. "He'd reached Kiloran because of me. Sileria would be enslaved forever by the Society because of me, because I had saved Armian to accomplish this thing." He closed his eyes. "So it was up to me to stop him. I had to destroy the only link between the Society and the Moorlanders, the only person completely trusted by both sides."

"How did you do it, though? A boy against a man? A *shallah* against an assassin?"

"I knew I couldn't succeed in a direct challenge. So I took him by surprise. He . . ." His blood roared in his ears. "It was easy to catch him off guard. He trusted me completely."

They were on the cliffs east of Adalian, Tansen explained, walking rather than riding, since it was a darkmoon night and the landscape was too treacherous for horses. It was raining and the wind was high. Tired and unused to such exertion, Elelar was lagging behind. Sick in his heart over what he had decided he must do, Tansen awaited his opportunity.

"It was very dark, hard to see anything in the distance. He stood upon a cliff, with his back to me, looking down into a cove." Tansen's voice was dull and distant now, recalling each breath, each movement, each gust of wind. "He had recently given me a new *yahr,* one he'd gotten from Kiloran, made of petrified Kintish wood. I stood behind him and struck him with it."

Armian had fallen to his knees, stunned by the blow but not knocked unconscious. A great fighter, he instinctively rolled away from the second blow while simultaneously reaching for his *shir*.

"But he froze, like a statue, when he saw me standing above him swinging the *yahr.*"

If Tansen lived for all eternity, he would never be able to forget the sound of his bloodfather's voice as he said, "Tansen?" He had heard it in a thousand nightmares since then and, if he lived, he would hear it in a thousand more.

Having learned well from Armian, he took advantage of the moment of surprise, his opponent's brief hesitation, and struck him in the face with another blow of the *yahr.* The *shir* fell from Armian's hand with Tansen's third blow. By the fifth, he was dead.

"I pushed the body off the cliff, so it landed on the shore of the cove where the Moorlanders were to meet him."

"So they'd find it there . . . and consider their proposal refused," Josarian deduced.

"Well, everyone knows what a violent, irrational, quarrelsome people we are." Tan's voice was bitter.

"And also how dangerous, secretive, and unpredictable the Society is." Josarian paused before asking, "What did Elelar do?"

"Ah, Elelar . . ."

The young *torena*'s screams added to the horror as Tansen stared down at Armian's corpse. At first, the terror and shock of the sudden murder numbed her wits, and she could do little but scream or weep. Then they fought bitterly, shouting at each other on that windy cliff, for she thought he had, at the very least, lost his mind and destroyed their entire future.

"Then we saw the Moorlander ship enter the cove," Tansen said. "She became determined to go down and try to speak with them herself, to see if she could somehow salvage the proposed alliance, despite what they would find down there."

"Did you stop her?"

His mouth quirked, "Yes, and she hates me for that most of all."

He tore off the pretty scarf covering her hair in the damp, windy night, bore her to the ground, planted his knee in her back, and used the silken cloth to bind her wrists together. Then he carried her away from the site of the meeting, hauling her on his shoulders like a sack of grain. He didn't release her until dawn, when he knew there'd be no chance of her contacting the Moorlander ship.

"I planned to escort her back to Shaljir." He laughed briefly and without humor. "I had just murdered my own bloodfather, but I didn't think it right to let a *torena* travel alone." He shrugged. "She had other plans, however."

"She decided to go straight to Kiloran and tell him what you'd done, so that he wouldn't withdraw from the Alliance."

"Exactly. She felt she had to . . . prove the Alliance's loyalty to him and their mutual cause by condemning me." He gazed up at the indifferent stars. "She said that Kiloran would swear a bloodvow against me and that she would celebrate on the day she learned of my death."

"So at fifteen, with no home, no family, no clan, and with powerful enemies who would soon be searching every crevice in the mountains for you, you decided to leave Sileria."

"I still wanted to live," Tansen admitted, "despite what I had done. So I boarded a ship bound for Kashala and worked for my passage."

"And now you are a man and a great warrior. Now you have friends and a brother who will not abandon you."

"I've killed a bloodpact relative, Josarian. You should—"

"Fortunately, it's up to Dar, and not me, to judge you for that. Especially if he really was the Firebringer."

"Do *you* believe in the Firebringer?"

"I believe men must solve their own problems, rather than dreaming of someone who will come to solve them for them."

Tansen drew a fast, sharp breath.

"What's wrong?"

"That's what *he* said to me once."

"I imagine he was not altogether bad," Josarian conceded.

"No. I wish he had been. Then it would be easier to bear what I've done."

"Tansen, even the Outlookers I've killed were not, I believe, altogether bad men. Each one of them must have . . . I don't know—loved a woman well, or been kind to children, or treated his mother with respect, or even just died bravely . . .

"You're a *shatai*. You've said that you're different from an assassin, that your teacher wanted you to use good judgment when you fight and before you kill. Yet you must know that you could never kill if you required that an opponent prove his complete unworthiness to live, for how many men could oblige you? Very few, I think."

"But I killed one who trusted me, one with whom I'd sworn a bloodpact."

"Yes." Josarian nodded. "It's a terrible burden to carry, and I see that you will suffer beneath it forever. Who knows? Perhaps Dar may even decide that's punishment enough."

"Kiloran won't."

"I doubt Kiloran believes in remorse," Josarian pointed out. "But you told Elelar you will return the *shir* to him."

"The one he made. The one I picked up off the ground after throwing Armian's body off the cliff."

"You kept the woman's scarf after you untied her . . ."

"Yes."

"You returned it to her in Shaljir, and she no longer wishes for your death." Josarian put a hand on Tansen's shoulder and squeezed. "Perhaps once he has the *shir,* Kiloran's hatred will finally be quenched, too."

19

SOME MEN WERE controlled by admittance to a woman's bed; others were best controlled by their desire to get there.

Kiloran's son Srijan was a difficult man: ruthless, arrogant, violent, and selfish. Fortunately, he wasn't as intelligent as his father and he was still young enough to be ruled by his passions—particularly his sexual ones. That was why the Alliance had chosen Elelar as his chief contact with their organization in Shaljir. She knew that several of her associates within the Alliance assumed that she slept with Srijan. However, she was a better judge of men than they were.

As a child, Elelar had loved almond milk. Then one year, at the start of the season, she had gorged herself on it until she got sick; after that, even the smell of it revolted her, and still did to this very day.

Srijan had only been a boy of twelve when Elelar first met him nine years ago. Even then, she had observed his tendency to indulge in a surfeit of whatever pleased him, then quickly grow to hate it for not satisfying the deep well of his endless, nameless hunger. Elelar secretly suspected it was, in fact, a soul that he lacked; no amount of sensual indulgence or personal power could satisfy the craving caused by such a void.

Kiloran had officially made Srijan an assassin several years ago and now granted him the power and duties of a high-ranking Society member. When Elelar became Srijan's contact with the Alliance in Shaljir, he was blunt about his intention of using her as he pleased. She refused his sexual advances just as bluntly, punctuating her refusal with a well-aimed knee to his groin, and thereafter ensured that he never again found an opportunity to be alone with her; even Srijan wouldn't assault her in front of her own servants.

Quite apart from the extreme distaste she felt for his language and behavior, she knew that he was a man who, after sating himself with a woman for a while, developed an irrational revulsion for that same woman. He had ruined many a *shallah* girl this way; Elelar had hired two of Srijan's hapless ex-mistresses to work as servants at one of her country estates, far from their homes and the rumors of their ruination. She had no doubt that if she made the mistake of sleeping with Srijan, he'd soon grow tired of her, too; this would make him useless to her thereafter.

However, *wanting* Elelar seemed to give Srijan enormous satisfaction, as if he fed on his own hungers. The unspoken (and thoroughly insincere) promise she dangled before him season after season, that she would give him her body if he worked hard enough for it, had inspired his cooperation with most of her plans, proposals, and requests. It was a delicate balance, but worth the risk.

Srijan remembered Tansen, bloodson of Armian, and he wasn't particularly receptive to Elelar's insistence that Tansen must be taken to Kiloran; not even when she explained that if he fulfilled this request, then Josarian shah Emeldari and all of his followers would join the Alliance.

They held their meeting in a private room of the *tirshah*. The finest wine, freshest almond milk, sweetest fruit, richest cheeses, best vegetables, freshest bread, and most delicately seasoned oils had been laid out for Srijan's pleasure. He sat on the best cushions in the room, neglecting to offer one to the *torena*. Nor did he so much as acknowledge the servant who did everything but hang upside down to ensure his comfort. Since Srijan's presence always destroyed Elelar's appetite, she simply watched him gorge himself on food and drink while he considered her request.

By Dar, there were times when she wished she were a man! Though she was generally contemptuous of the entire sex and was baffled by what long-ago mistake had put them in charge of her world, there were nonetheless times when she wished for the size and strength to resort to mindless physical force as they so often did. Oh, for the pleasure of beating Srijan until he *begged* for the privilege of cooperating with her plans!

Suppressing her impatience and anger, she smiled warmly and leaned forward, feeling her skin crawl as Srijan's gaze went straight to her cleavage. She inhaled slowly, glad for the presence of her two manservants and Faradar, though they stood at a discreet distance from the low-voiced conversation. It was time, she realized, to stop talking about the Alliance and to convince Srijan that he would benefit personally from granting her request.

"Kiloran's assassins have sought Tansen for nine years," she pointed out, "and now the *shallah* has returned and killed two of them."

"I know," Srijan said.

He gulped down some wine, then stuffed more cheese into his mouth. He should be fat. Any woman who ate like that would be bigger than Darshon. But, being a man, he was only a bit stocky as a result of his gluttony.

She murmured, "Kiloran wants him very badly."

"And he wants Kiloran," Srijan replied. "He's already killed Armian and two assassins. Do you really think I'm going to lead him straight to my father?"

Men are beaten by their own pride, she reminded herself, *and ruled by their conceit.* "Why not?" She blinked and gasped. "Surely you don't think . . ."

He stared at her. "What?"

She smiled as if to cover a foolish mistake and shook her head. "I'm sorry. I didn't realize."

"What?" he snapped.

"That Kiloran was afraid of him."

He was offended enough to actually stop eating. "Kiloran afraid of that filthy little *sriliah*? You've lost your wits, woman!"

"Oh? Perhaps I misunderstood, then. You are afraid for him. I see."

He flung aside a piece of bread and pointed at her with his knife. "My father is the greatest waterlord in Sileria! The greatest waterlord who has ever lived! He fears no one."

"Then he's not afraid Tansen can kill him?"

"No!" He scowled and added, "And neither am I."

"Are you afraid Kiloran can't kill Tansen, then?"

"Kiloran can kill anyone."

What a thing to boast about, she thought. "Then why not lead Tansen to his own slaughter?" she suggested sweetly. "Surely Kiloran will revere the son who brings him the prize no other has been able to secure."

His eyes glittered. His face smoothed out. He shrugged and said something dismissive, then resumed eating. It would take another half-hour of coaxing and flattery, she saw, but she had him.

The victory tasted sour, for although she, the Alliance,

and Sileria had paid bitterly for what Tansen had done nine years ago, she realized that he had, too. After all these years, she didn't relish being the one to now lead him straight to his death.

She would never agree with what he had done, for the chance of freedom from the Valdani had been too precious to throw away; but she also knew that the plan had been flawed and might well have failed. Sileria might have fought a war merely to trade one conqueror for another.

For one thousand years, this land had toiled under the yoke of foreign conquerors: Moorlanders, Kints, Valdani—all strangers who did not belong in Elelar's native land. She had dedicated her life to a dream that the rest of the world mocked and that even most Silerians considered impossibly foolish. She was no fool, though; someday, somehow, Sileria would be free again. She believed it with the fierce, passionate intensity of a visionary. She longed to see it happen in her lifetime, to pledge her loyalty to a Silerian ruler, to watch her people lift their heads from the dust and walk proudly away from the centuries of humiliation they had endured.

She dreamed of destroying Valdani rule in Sileria, of defeating that race of land-eating, luxury-loving barbarians who thought that stealing culture from the Kints and wealth from the Moorlanders made them a great people. How she longed to see the gaudy Imperial Sign of the Three smashed and turned to rubble in the middle of Santorell Square. How she longed to see the gray-clad Outlookers and goat-slaughtering priests of the Empire board mainland-bound ships by the thousands and leave Sileria forever. How she longed to see her husband's family dispossessed of the houses, land, and wealth they had stolen from her own kind!

Killing Tansen would accomplish none of that, and no one could say for sure that, despite what he had done, it was truly his fault that Sileria was not free today. Perhaps she was simply practical enough to let go of her thirst for vengeance after all this time. Perhaps she even felt an uncharacteristic tug of sentiment, for she and Tansen had spent the last days of their youth together and lost it at the very same moment. For whatever reason, she was not happy to send Faradar out into the gardens to bid Tansen and Josarian to come join them now that Srijan had agreed to take them all to Kiloran.

When the two *shallaheen* entered the room, Elelar looked at Tansen and, for the first time really, saw him merely as he was now, with no remembered shadow of the boy he once had been. She could tell that Srijan was stunned by his appearance, having lacked the wit to realize that he would have changed over the course of nine years. Still, even a man with enough imagination to picture the skinny, hollow-eyed, boy as a grown man would nonetheless be surprised by the reality of seeing Tansen now.

Elelar recognized things now which had escaped her notice in the turmoil of their first meeting and the bustling activity of their preparations in Shaljir and their journey to Zilar. Tansen held himself apart from others, even in the midst of conversation, watching, waiting, judging, assessing . . . and concealing. Quite unlike the passionate, ingenuous man who now called him brother and stood at his side. Tansen had been quick and surefooted as a boy, like anyone who had survived a hard youth in the mountains; now he moved with a fluid, economic precision which spoke of absolute control and relentless discipline. A *shatai*. It seemed incredible. She had only seen three in her whole life, all full-blooded Kints. The *shatai* were the greatest, deadliest warriors in the three corners of the world.

She couldn't even imagine the pain he had endured in receiving that brand on his chest. She knew that a *shatai* was expected to stand still and unflinching while his master carved it into his torso with a red-hot poker, pausing often to pray and chant, and taking an interminable amount of time over the ritual.

Shallaheen were contemptuous of physical pain, of course. The scars which marked every important occasion or binding promise of their lives were also a symbol of their ability to endure suffering. For many days, sometimes even months, after cutting a palm, a *shallah* wasn't supposed to favor the throbbing hand during the long, hard labor of his or her daily life, no matter how much it hurt or how many times the wound reopened.

Still, not even the hard life of a *shallah* or the proud indifference to pain they learned from early childhood could prepare a man to stand still while someone leisurely carved up his chest with a red hot poker. Worldly as she was, Elelar couldn't imagine what could possibly have prepared Tansen for that, or how he had endured it. She only knew that the brand made a man respected throughout the known world, for a *shatai* carned it in ways that destroyed lesser men.

However, Elelar didn't think that even a *shatai* could survive an encounter with Kiloran unless Kiloran wanted him to. A man of great skill and quick wits might survive combat with a lesser waterlord, perhaps, but not with Kiloran. The old wizard did not manage to rule the Honored Society, and therefore much of Sileria, through the love of his people or the force of his personality; he controlled men, rivers, lakes, wealth, cities, estates, *toreni, shallaheen,* and even—sometimes—the Valdani through water, the greatest power in Sileria. Even the Emperor feared it— and that was why the Alliance needed Kiloran and the Society.

It suddenly occurred to her that if Tansen was lying about his intentions, or if he was somehow miraculously equal to Kiloran . . . well, she wouldn't be very happy about *that,* either. The last thing she wanted was Kiloran's death. He controlled and united the Society, making it a somewhat rational and relatively reliable conspirator of great power. With no clear successor—for Srijan still showed no aptitude for water magic *or* intelligent thought—the Society would descend into chaos and internal warfare if Kiloran should suddenly die. Though his predecessor, Harlon, had died years before she was born,

Elelar knew the history of those days from Gaborian's teachings. Harlon had left no successor, only a young son who was quickly removed from Sileria for his own safety. Vying for predominance, the waterlords had unleashed a torrent of violence so destructive that it ultimately weakened the Society even more than the Emperor's war against them. And the Valdani had gained power in Sileria precisely commensurate with the Society's loss of it.

Elelar had no love for the Society, but the Valdani were the only enemies that mattered. They were not Silerian; the waterlords and their assassins *were*.

"The Society's power is *our* power, too," Gaborian had taught her, "for they are of our blood and born of this land. But Valdani power, even when we marry them, is always *theirs.*"

So while she would try to convince Kiloran not to kill Tansen, she was willing to give her life to prevent Tansen from killing Kiloran. What a mess Tansen was making. She wished desperately he would have given into her urging to simply leave Sileria again.

Tansen studied Srijan for a moment, refused Elelar's suggestion that he sit down and dine with them, and asked her, "He'll do it, then?"

"The woman does not speak for me, *sriliah,*" Srijan growled.

Tansen's brow rose. His swords were not concealed now. They were sheathed in the leather harness he wore over his shabby *shallah* clothing. Elelar wished Srijan would refrain from insulting him, since it suddenly struck her as extremely stupid and rather risky.

"When do we leave?" Tansen asked smoothly.

Srijan smirked. "When I say so."

Josarian sighed and folded his arms across his chest.

"Today? Tonight? Tomorrow? Make up your mind," Tansen advised.

"In the morning."

"We'll be ready." Tansen turned to leave.

Srijan suddenly leapt from his chair, *shir* in hand, and

launched himself at Tansen's back. Before Elelar had time
to draw breath for a scream, Tansen whirled around, his
swords suddenly flashing through the air as they wove
around his attacker. Srijan cried out and fell to the floor,
clutching his forearm. Elelar rose to her feet, her scream
dying in her throat. It happened so fast, she didn't have
time to form a thought or follow the flurry of action.

She took three faltering steps forward, halting when the
toe of her slipper touched something deadly cold. Shivering, she looked down and saw Srijan's *shir* lying on the
floor. She jerked her foot away and looked at the assassin
again. His arm was bleeding profusely, staining his fine
clothes and spilling onto the floor around him. A slender
Kintish blade, gleaming beautifully and engraved with the
elegant writing of the Kints, was poised at his throat.

"Don't kill him," she choked out. This was Kiloran's
son. Kiloran would *never* forgive this death.

"If I killed him," Tansen said regretfully, "then I suppose we'd just have to find some other sheep-molesting,
dung-smelling, half-witted assassin who knows where
Kiloran is." He shook his head. "What a pity."

Srijan's reply was couched in mountain dialect so vulgar
and obscure that Elelar understood little more than the general implication, which was disgusting enough.

"Act like a man," Tansen chided. "I could have cut off
your arm, sliced your nose in half, or . . ." He drew a line
down Srijan's body with the tip of one sword, pausing
significantly at his crotch. ". . . ensured that you never mo-
lested another woman or fathered another bastard. So count
yourself lucky."

Srijan's servant, wide-eyed with fear, stumbled forward
to help his master, suggesting that the bedchamber Srijan
had claimed for the night would be the best place to clean
and bandage the wound. Before leaving the room, Srijan
tried to reclaim his *shir,* earning another cut of Tansen's
sword as he reached for it.

"It's useless to you unless you kill me, *sriliah,*" Srijan
snarled, "so give it back!"

"You're making it very *tempting* to kill you," Tansen said in a bored voice.

"You have no right—"

Elelar interrupted, "You said you would take him to Kiloran, not attack him while his back was turned. How could you do something so dishonorable?"

"You weren't expecting this?" Tansen eyed her as if reassessing her intelligence.

Then it struck her. "You were, weren't you?"

His mouth quirked. "Even more than I expect the sun to rise tomorrow, *torena.*"

TANSEN HAD FINALLY resigned himself to Josarian's accompanying him on this journey, aware that nothing short of physical force (and being securely tied to a tree) would keep his bloodbrother from his side when he faced Kiloran. He was very annoyed, however, that Elelar wouldn't leave him, either. He hadn't counted on having to protect her, too, while trying to deal with the old waterlord.

"I haven't observed a noticeable improvement in your tact and diplomacy since your youth," she had snapped when he tried to convince her to stay behind in Zilar, or even return to Shaljir. "Who do you think is going to talk Kiloran out of killing you?"

"I don't need *you* to do it." She seemed to be forgetting who had convinced Kiloran to kill him in the first place, he thought irritably.

"And after he kills you, who do you think will convince him that Josarian is more valuable to all of us alive than dead?"

That was the argument that had made him give in and let her accompany him as he set off for Kiloran's lair, wherever it was. Josarian must be left alive to fight for Sileria and the *shallaheen.* Besides . . . apart from his *shatai-kaj,* whom he hadn't seen in four years, Josarian was the only living person he loved, and he didn't intend to be the instrument of his death.

As for Elelar . . . This wasn't love, this sickness that ate away at his soul, that weakened his manhood and clouded his judgment. This mingled anger and desire, this bitter yearning, this shameful passion . . . If this was love, no one would ever sing sweet songs about it.

As a boy, burgeoning with instincts beyond his control and naively imagining how he could win her love, he had always been two steps behind, leaving Elelar in control of every moment between them. As a man, he knew better, for he had seen wild Widow Beasts in the strange lands far to the east of Kinto, and he had seen deadly shape-shifters in the misty hills of the Moorlands . . . and he recognized Elelar in them all. However, as a man, he also knew things he had only vaguely imagined as a boy, and the sure, certain, experienced knowledge of what he wanted from this woman tormented him when he was in her presence.

He kept himself in check by recalling the dripping jaws of the Widow Beast, who devoured a mate once satisfied with his virility.

He was finally wise enough to recognize what he hadn't been able to understand or accept as a boy: If Elelar opened her arms to him, she would invariably have an ulterior motive. When Elelar came to a man, he might not know why she had come, but he'd be a fool to believe passion alone had driven her into his arms.

Last night, as they camped in the hills, Elelar had sought a moment alone with Tansen to make one last attempt to convince him to give up, turn back, and go into hiding or leave Sileria. Almond blossoms had sweetened the night, and the pale glow of the waning-moons had highlighted the embroidered silks she wore. She had been all soft woman last night, wooing him with her flattery, seducing him with her concern, weaving a spell of unspoken erotic promises around him as she tried to win him over.

The word *no,* which he repeated a few times, had finally sent her stalking off in frustrated silence. Never had the self-control of his arduous training been so essential as it was when she took her warm hand from his arm and turned away from him. Never in his life had he felt such a hunger. Standing still for his branding ceremony hadn't been as difficult as standing still and watching her walk away last night.

Darfire, sometimes he wished he'd thrown her off the cliff right after Armian.

They had left Elelar's servants back at Zilar for their own safety, so Tansen, Josarian, and Elelar now travelled only with Srijan and his thoroughly submissive servant. Srijan favored his wounded arm and sulked about the loss of his *shir*. Tansen figured he was afraid of what his father would say about it. Elelar plotted, schemed, and stared into the distance most of the time. Only Josarian was good company, and most of Tansen's amusement was derived from watching him irritate the *torena*. After two days of travelling west on horseback at a reasonable pace, they made a late camp near the shores of Lake Kandahar. Srijan estimated they'd reach their destination tomorrow.

"The attack may come tonight," Tansen warned Josarian when the two of them went down to Lake Kandahar to collect water for everyone.

Josarian's glance flickered to the glowing twilight sky. "You're that sure Kiloran knows we're here?"

"Not much happens within a day's ride of Kiloran that he *doesn't* know about." He stooped to fill a goatskin with water. "I don't think he'd hide out this close to a good road, since the Outlookers would have access to such a place, but I think we must not be very far from his—"

"*Tan!*"

He saw shock on Josarian's face and instinctively reached for his swords as his friend lunged at something behind him. He had barely touched the hilt of his left sword when something thick, wet, and viciously cold wrapped tightly around his throat and cut off all his air. He struggled to withdraw at least one blade, but another icy tentacle wrapped around his body with lightning speed, trapping him. Strangling, freezing, and astonished beyond thought, he heard Josarian's screams—and Elelar's in the distance—as the tentacles dragged him away from the shore, into the center of the lake, and beneath its surface into its chilly depths.

SWINGING HIS SWORD and screaming, Josarian ran through the water, ignoring its deadly chill, following Tansen as he struggled in the arms of some obscene thing, then disappeared into the murky depths of the lake. Sword raised over his head, blood roaring in his ears, Josarian started swimming, paddling frantically when his feet could no longer touch the ground. Stunned and horrified, he treaded water in the middle of the lake, unable to find any trace of his brother or the thing that had seized him.

Torena Elelar stood at the shore now, knee deep in water, with Srijan laughing behind her. "Get out!" she screamed. *"Get out!"*

He ignored her, took a deep breath, and dived down, giving into the weight of his sword and his boots, resisting the numbness creeping into his limbs.

A geyser of water suddenly forced him back up, throwing him high into the air. When he landed, expecting to sink back beneath the water's surface, he found that its consistency had changed in the blink of an eye. It was as hard as rock now, and landing on it hurt like all the Fires. Bewildered, he hit it several times with the hilt of his sword.

Water magic, he finally realized through the chaos of his confusion and fear. "Kiloran," he said aloud.

"Josarian!"

He looked up to see Elelar now running toward him, her dainty feet skittering across the crystal surface of Lake Kandahar. Srijan approached at a more leisurely pace. Josarian flipped his sword over and started chopping fruitlessly at the diamond-hardness of the water, screaming his bloodbrother's name over and over.

Elelar fell to her knees when she reached his side, gasping for air, trembling and babbling questions. He had never handled a woman roughly in his life, but now he grabbed her by the hair and demanded, "Is Tansen dead? You know Kiloran's tricks! What's happened to Tan?"

"I don't know!" she cried, gritting her teeth against the pain and trying to pull away.

He pushed her aside and jumped to his feet, lunging for Srijan. The assassin flinched with surprise, apparently not having expected an attack from Josarian. Faster, smarter, stronger, and unhampered by a wound, Josarian drove him down to the cold, hard surface beneath their feet and held his sword to Srijan's throat.

"Kiloran!" he shouted. "If you truly know everything that happens here, then know this: I will kill your only son *now* if you don't release Tansen alive!"

Elelar scrambled forward on her hands and knees. *"No! He'll kill you, too! No!"*

She flung herself at Josarian and tried to wrestle his sword away. His kicked her away and stilled Srijan's struggles by slicing open his cheek. Srijan screamed in pain. Elelar cursed and begged and flung herself at Josarian again.

"Kiloran!" Josarian dug the blade into Srijan's throat, ready to cut.

The surface beneath him moved, knocking him off balance. The sound of rushing water filled his ears, even louder than Srijan's moans of pain. He stared in bewilderment as a small whirlpool of water churned in a frantic circle nearby. His heart thudded as it widened and deepened into a tunnel. He pressed his blade even harder against Srijan's throat to keep him still, watching as the swirl of water and magic glittered in the dying light as he prayed to Dar to bring Tansen through that tunnel.

When the water stopped moving, he found himself staring at a familiar, coiling structure, but his mind could form no coherent thought. It was Elelar who crept forward, studied it, and finally identified it: "It's a staircase."

"A *staircase?*" he repeated, gazing in confusion at the

gleaming, crystalline steps leading into the depths of the lake. "I don't . . . understand."

"It means . . ." Srijan croaked, ". . . my father is inviting you into his home."

20

MIRABAR WAS GROWING weary, for keeping the assassin prisoner was proving to be hard work. His first escape attempt had nearly succeeded. She'd been more vigilant since then, but it hadn't stopped him from trying again. The third time had been only last night, and it was terrifying; he had tried to kill her.

They were travelling over the mountains, avoiding contact with other people. Sister Basimar, Amitan, and another of Josarian's men, young Kynan, accompanied Mirabar and the assassin. Mirabar didn't want to lead so many people into Kiloran's clutches, but she couldn't control the assassin day and night by herself. Indeed, he had attacked her while she slept last night, and she knew she might well be dead now if not for Kynan's and Amitan's help.

She wondered if all assassins were as tough as this one. He now bore bruises and minor wounds inflicted by the two *shallah* men, as well as the burns Mirabar had inflicted when she captured him. Remembering that confrontation still nauseated her, and she knew Tashinar would be appalled by what she had done. Yet despite the pain and exhaustion he must be suffering, Mirabar's captive didn't look like a defeated man.

Perhaps she should have listened when Basimar and the others had tried to discourage her from capturing an assassin.

She was very tired and knew she must save strength for

her imminent encounter with Kiloran, so she insisted they make camp early that day. She blew a campfire into life so that Basimar could start cooking their evening meal. Then she approached the assassin, whom Amitan had tied securely to a tree. His dark eyes were watchful and wary.

"Assassin . . ." She paused, then said, "You might as well tell me your name." When he didn't respond, she added irritably, "Just so I know what to call you."

His gaze held hers for a long moment before he finally replied, "Najdan."

"Well, Najdan, how much farther to Kiloran?"

He shrugged.

"Tell me. Or I will *make* you tell me." She was aware that her threats were growing thin.

"He is near now," Najdan said stonily.

"How near?"

"Near enough to know that you are here." There was confidence in his voice.

"I see." She studied him for a moment. "Then I look forward to meeting him."

Najdan's confidence worried her. Realizing that Kiloran might attack them, rather than cordially await her visit, Mirabar decided to set a ring of protective fire around the camp that night. Even if it didn't keep Kiloran out, it would deflect any ordinary assassins and alert her to danger.

Blowing life into the ring of fire was an utterly exhausting task, and keeping it going all night would tax her strength. Consequently, she was anything but pleased to hear the Beckoner calling her when she was done igniting the blaze.

"Go away," she snapped. "I'm tired."

Come . . . You must come . . .

She resisted. "In the morning!"

"Who's she talking to?" Najdan asked warily.

"I don't know," Amitan said. "*Sirana*, who are you talking to?"

Now is the time.

"You'd better tell me what I'm supposed to do when I find Kiloran," she warned the Beckoner.

"Who, me?" Najdan asked.

"I think it's a vision," Basimar said. "She'll go into fits and screams in a minute. Don't let it bother you."

"Thanks for the advice," Kynan said dryly.

Come to me. You must come.

"Oh, all right!" Without looking at the others, she got up and followed the Beckoner, knowing how he would torment her if she continued resisting.

He led her through the woods, to the other side of Mount Kandahar, and down into the valley beyond. It was a long walk, and she was very tired by the time the sky grew dark.

"Couldn't I have visions closer to my bedroll?" she asked irritably, hating the Beckoner with all her heart.

The force of his will pushed her hard, carrying her on a wave of insistence, tumbling her through the air. She landed on the shore of the lake. Stars glittered on its surface. The waning crest of Ejara gleamed and undulated as she stared at the water.

Water. A house of water.

"Kandahar." Mirabar shook her head. "Surely it's not possible . . ."

A house of water.

"So . . . *this* is where he hides from the Valdani?"

A blaze of fire appeared above the surface of the water, sketching the foreign symbol of the warrior she sought.

"Is he here?" she asked.

Only you can save him now. The others have tried and failed.

"What others?" Her throat was dry.

Without him, the shackles remain.

"What must I do?" Her heart ached with fear.

The burning symbol sank slowly into the water, its light blazing gloriously even as it sank deep, deep into the black depths of Kandahar.

Fire in water.

"No . . ." She shook her head, feeling her feet take steps backwards as she spoke. "I can't."

Fire in water . . .

The symbol kept blazing.

"I *can't.* No one could!"

Find the shir, *and you find him.*

"Please . . ."

The alliance lives or dies tonight. Find the shir . . .

"Oh, Dar shield me!" she begged, falling to her knees. Knowing she had no other choice, she finally asked, "How? How do I do this?"

She looked up and saw the Beckoner out in the center of the lake, hovering above the water's surface, surrounded by the glow of the Otherworld; the only good thing in an evil place. Terror clouded her vision as she rose to her feet again, consigning her life to his care, knowing that he wanted her to live to fulfill the dreams of dead rulers in living flame.

He opened his arms, reaching out to her across the span of centuries, across the barrier of death, through the void of destruction and despair, past the sorrow of a humiliated people and a culture condemned to servitude. He reached out and she went to him, offering her life and her power to the Fires beyond.

TANSEN SHIVERED WITH cold, annoyed that he couldn't control this instinctive reaction. There wasn't much point in his body's life-seeking efforts to generate heat, since he'd be dead in a few minutes anyhow.

Nine years ago, he had only seen the luxuriant camp Kiloran lived in while travelling through his territories, something a waterlord had to do regularly to keep his power secure. He had never known where Kiloran lived permanently, what sort of a place the wizard called home. Judging by the expression of shocked awe on Elelar's face, she had never known, either, not until tonight. And Josarian looked like he was so far past shock that not even a personal appearance by Dar would surprise him now. Srijan merely gloated, making Tan sorry he hadn't killed him the other day.

They were in a shifting palace of air far beneath the surface of Lake Kandahar—so far that Tansen had nearly drowned before being unceremoniously dumped here by the twisting coils of water which moved in response to Kiloran's will. It was as grand as any *toren*'s house, with its high ceilings, luxuriant furnishings, sweet-smelling candles, and vast rooms. The ceilings, floors, and walls of a *toren*'s home, however, didn't pulse and fluctuate—at least not unless an earthquake was taking place.

This palace, though, responded to its master's will as easily as a *shatai*'s limbs answered his demands. Any portion of it could open or close like a mouth, to admit or exclude visitors; expand to comfortably encompass more people or constrict to drown them; become as hard as crystal, as soft as a feather tick, or as wet as . . . water. The blazing torches which lit the dark depth of this night were rooted into the shifting walls the way trees rooted into the soil. The floor beneath Tansen was as smooth as glass, and almost as chilly as the touch of another man's *shir*.

Soaking wet and chained to this cold, smooth floor by coils of icy water more unyielding than any bonds of iron, Tansen shivered and waited to die. Two of Kiloran's trusted assassins had disarmed him earlier while he lay helplessly gasping and strangling in the grip of the monstrous tentacles that had brought him here. Upon examining Tansen's swords—swords that no man should touch without permission—Kiloran had recognized the workmanship and instantly suspected the truth. He'd ordered his man to rip open Tansen's threadbare tunic, exposing the brand he wore on his chest.

"A *shatai* . . ." Sitting upon a throne of shells which were joined together by exquisitely worked gold to form an enormous chair of astonishing beauty, the old waterlord had glared hard at Tansen. "You trained long and hard to come home and kill your master, boy."

They'd heard Josarian's shouted threats echoing deaf-

eningly through the watery caverns of Kiloran's lair; some
sorcery by which Kiloran knew everything that happened
overhead. His expression frosty with fury, the old wizard
had permitted the others entry to his domain by way of a
glimmering staircase of water—which disappeared a bare
moment after their arrival.

Josarian held his sword across Srijan's throat and demanded Tansen's release. Kiloran kept Tansen lashed to
the floor and promised his instant and very painful death
if Josarian didn't release Srijan. Elelar pleaded with everyone to exercise some restraint and intelligence—to no effect.

Kiloran had grown older and bulkier, but he was as impressive and imposing as ever. His once-dark skin had
grown sallow over the years, probably from hiding so long
in a sunless, Dar-forsaken place like this. His hair had gone
from gray to white, and his face betrayed what the years
had cost him. His cold, lifeless eyes still glowed with dark,
watchful intelligence, though, and Tansen had only to consider his frankly hopeless situation to realize that Kiloran's
power had, if anything, continued to grow over the past
nine years.

"Enough, *torena*," Kiloran said, silencing Elelar with a
voice full of authority and deadly warning. "You know
this *sriliah*'s crime. If you continue to plead for his life, I
will have to question your loyalty."

His speech was as cultured and educated as Elelar's,
giving credence to the legend that his mother had been a
torena who fell in love with an assassin and abandoned
her family, rank, and home for him. Legend had it that,
upon the violent death of Kiloran's father, the woman had
taken the boy to apprentice to a waterlord so that he might
become powerful enough to avenge his father's murder.

It had given Tansen some pleasure to see Elelar beg,
and to hear her plead for *him*, but he knew it was useless.
Kiloran had taken him by surprise, revealing powers none
of them had suspected, and now had the upper hand.
Stripped of his swords and staked out like a sacrificial

offering, Tansen was helpless and would soon die. He thanked all the gods above and below that pride and rage, at least, were stronger than fear, for he didn't want to die cowering, quivering, and begging for mercy. He was embarrassed by his present situation, for this was no way for a warrior to die, but even *shatai* were not invulnerable to sorcery such as this.

For himself, he would hope for nothing more than a quick death. For his companions, however . . . Well, Elelar had nine lives and would somehow manage to get out of this alive, he believed. But Josarian looked determined to free Tansen or die trying, and Tan wasn't optimistic about finding a solution to this problem in the few remaining moments of his life.

"He has survived the nine years of a bloodvow," Josarian said, his sword pressed so tightly against Srijan's throat that the assassin had trouble breathing. If Josarian lessened his grip for even a second, if Kiloran saw a single opportunity to attack Josarian without getting his son killed, it would be all over. "The time has come to call off your assassins and let him live in peace, Kiloran."

Kiloran rose from his throne, radiating fury. "Does a *shallah* think to tell me my business?"

"When you dishonor yourself this way, I do." Josarian's grip was ruthless, his concentration fierce.

"Do you know what this *sriliah* did?" Kiloran demanded. "He killed his own bloodfather!"

"After nine years, it's now Dar's place to punish him for that. Not yours."

"How quaint," Kiloran spat.

"You don't care that he betrayed a bloodpact," Josarian said. "You think you could have been Yahrdan, and a mere boy took it away from you. You can never have it back, and *that's* why you want him dead, old man."

Elelar swallowed her breath, and even Tansen tensed. It wasn't a good idea to insult Kiloran in front of his men— and in his domain—with such open contempt. The wizard's sallow complexion warmed up slightly as anger red-dened his face.

Josarian continued, "It was business, this thing between you two, nothing more. You lost. That's all." Pressing his advantage, he tightened his grip and made Srijan bleat like a lamb. "Now take back the bloodvow before you lose something much more personal."

Picking up the thread of Josarian's argument, Elelar said, *"Siran,* the *shallah* has come in good faith to make peace with you. I swear it upon my life. He has brought the *shir* back to you."

Damn! He wished she hadn't told them that. After strip-ping him of his swords and shredding his tunic, they hadn't bothered to search him for another weapon. The *shir* was tucked inside his boot. Far from being a peace offering, it was now the only thing he had in his favor if something broke Kiloran's concentration long enough for him to es-cape these bonds. He didn't intend to meekly give it up so they could slaughter him in perfect safety.

Kiloran's attention shifted back to Tansen. "The *shir* . . ."

The wizard's dark eyes glittered with interest. Oh, yes, he would want the *shir* back. It was too powerful a weapon to leave in the hands of an enemy. A waterlord made such weapons only for his trusted servants, for a *shir* was too effective against even himself to be trusted in the hands of anyone whose loyalty was questionable. An enemy's possession of a *shir* was a serious threat to the waterlord who'd made it, which was why returning the *shir* of a slain assassin to its maker was regarded as an honorable peace offering. Tansen had brought the thing here with every intention of making an honorable peace offering. Now he wanted nothing more than the chance to slit that fat old man's throat with it before he died. Even Kiloran's own water magic couldn't protect him from a *shir,* especially not from one he himself had made.

Hoping, but not really expecting, that he could delay the

inevitable, Tansen said, "It's hidden in our baggage. I didn't expect to see you tonight, Kiloran."

"He keeps it wrapped in a silken scarf he got from the *torena,*" Josarian added, lying very smoothly. He knew perfectly well that Tansen had kept the thing on his person ever since leaving Shaljir.

"If you promise to let me go once you have it," Tansen added, searching for a way to get Josarian safely out of here, "Josarian will show your men where it is."

"Then perhaps he would release my son now, in good faith?"

"Don't do it," Tansen said quickly. As long as he was within Kiloran's reach, Josarian would only survive while Srijan was his shield.

Kiloran whirled on him. "Do you take me for a fool, boy? Do you think I really need either of you to find it?"

Water suddenly tunneled straight down from the wavering ceiling overhead, splashing onto Tansen's face, then forming a mask that smothered him. Fighting it, chest burning as he struggled for air, body jerking convulsively against his bonds, he could hear Elelar's screams, Josarian's shouted threats, and Srijan shrieking, *"Father! Father!"*

Something vibrated frantically against his calf while water filled his mouth, nose, and throat. The weight of death pressed on his chest, the icy grip of Kiloran's wrath claiming his life at last. There was more shouting now, but the noise was barely noticeable through the roar of blood filling his ears and the blackness descending upon his senses.

I am prepared to die today . . . He tried to recite his creed silently, to find dignity at the last moment as his body struggled for life and his soul railed against death.

I am prepared to die . . . No! No, I'm not!

Like any living creature, he fought it blindly, mindlessly, furiously.

Suddenly the clinging mask of water melted away from his face. The smothering weight was lifted from his chest. His body convulsed in a wave of coughing and sputtering.

He thought briefly that Kiloran must have been bluffing. His lungs heaved, sucking air into his half-dead body. His head pounded and his eyes throbbed. He heard Kiloran's assassins shouting frantically. He weakly turned his head to see who was dead.

He was vaguely surprised to see that everyone looked fine. He was even more surprised to see that Kiloran's attention was no longer on him or Josarian, who still held Srijan in a death grip. Taking advantage of the confusion, Elelar rushed to his side, kneeling on the cold floor and stroking hanks of wet hair off his face.

"Wh . . ." He struggled to force even a single word out. "What . . ."

"I don't know," she whispered, surreptitiously testing his bonds. "Something's frightening them. Can you move at all?"

"Fright . . ." He was wracked by another spasm of coughing. Ignoring the burning in his chest and the pounding of his head, he focused on the unfamiliar sensation he had noticed at the moment the world started going black. "The *shir*," he choked out.

It was shuddering wildly inside his boot, like a live thing trying to escape. It was only supposed to do that when threatened by other sorcery.

Something else had come to Kandahar tonight. Whatever it was, it held Kiloran transfixed. He stood staring up at the domed ceiling while his assassins babbled with fear. Exultation filled Tansen as he felt his bonds start to dissolve, turning once again into mere water. Whatever was out there, it was providing him with the chance he needed. With his arms and legs freed a moment later, he rolled over and rose silently to his feet. Crouched and ready to make his move, he reached into his boot and withdrew the *shir*. No matter how it quivered, it was still a blade and could still do the job. Moving before Elelar guessed his intentions, he stalked Kiloran. Now was his chance!

An enormous ball of fire, like the roaring heart of a falling star, blazing with sound and fury, suddenly broke through the watery ceiling, plunged into their midst, and landed directly between him and Kiloran. Steam instantly arose around it, as if it were melting the interior of the sorceror's palace.

Tansen fell back against Elelar, squinting against the brilliant light, one arm held up to shield his face. For a moment, the thing gave off so much heat he thought it would devour them all. Then it seemed to collapse in on itself, drowning in the shower of water that followed its descent.

He stared in shock, his mind blank, his muscles slack, scarcely hearing the screams around him. What in the Fires was this thing? Had it fallen from the sky? Had it come from . . .

"Dar?" he whispered, finally finishing the thought.

The flames continued to sizzle away beneath the falling water. As the heat, brilliance, and fury faded, Elelar crept around him and stood at his side, staring with equal shock and amazement.

"What is it?" she breathed.

He looked across the weakly blazing ruin in the center of the hall and sought Kiloran. At least the waterlord looked as stunned as they were. Whatever this was, Kiloran had never seen its like, either.

The flames continued to sizzle away, finally revealing quite possibly the last thing Tansen would have predicted.

"A girl . . ." he whispered.

She was lying curled up on the floor, struggling feebly to gather her strength and get up. She was drenched and gasping for air. She wore ordinary *shallah* clothing, which seemed incongruous with such a grand entrance. It was only when she shifted and the dying firelight flickered over strands of her wet hair that he realized . . . it was *red*. The red of child-eating demons, the red of lava-eyed monsters cursed by Dar.

Old superstitions, yes, but powerful ones. He stood his ground like a man, but he wanted to hide like a child from this strange female.

Saying nothing, asking no one for help, she slowly pushed herself off the ground, breathing hard, her body tensing against exhaustion or pain—or both. When she rose to her full height to face Kiloran, Tansen saw that she was rather small. He also saw the waterlord's face twist with emotion. Shock? Fear? Disbelief?

The girl looked around, as if searching for someone. As she turned this way, the wet, clinging cloth of her thin summer tunic revealed that, although small, she was indeed a woman full grown, with all of a woman's attributes. Dark-skinned, like any *shallah,* she wore a roughly made copper brooch fastened at her shoulder: the insignia of the outlawed Guardians.

Then she turned her face to him, turned her gaze upon him, and he saw what had made the others flinch, one by one, as she confronted them in silence. He heard Josarian murmur *"sirana"* in a voice which sounded both pleased and bewildered, but he paid no attention. He heard Elelar say something, but the words made no sense to him. He stared back at the woman who had entered their midst in a violent blaze of glory, and he saw only the fire-golden eyes of the creatures of his boyhood nightmares.

Her gaze dropped to his chest, and he felt the burn of the branding ceremony again. Her expression grew exultant, her horrible eyes shining like the lava-churning belly of Darshon. With a smile that made his bones turn to water, she reached out and came for him.

MIRABAR STOPPED ABRUPTLY when the warrior stumbled backwards, away from her outstretched hands. His revulsion was plain in his face. She had searched so long and hard for him. Stung by his rejection, she swallowed and stared stupidly at him.

He was the one. There was no doubt. The strange symbol which had burned in her visions for so long was carved into his chest, a big, fierce scar which he must have earned with great pain. Yet he was a *shallah,* not some *roshah* from a strange land. Like her, he was soaking wet. His tunic was torn open, and he looked like he'd been through an ordeal—one of Kiloran's making, no doubt.

"Tansen?" she said, recalling his name.

He reached for the woman at his side and pushed her protectively behind him. A *torena,* Mirabar observed. Poised for combat, dark eyes glittering with silent threat, he demanded, "Who are you?"

"Her name is Mirabar. I met her on Mount Niran."

She jumped with surprise, noticing Josarian for the first time. A wounded man crouched at his feet, his face cut and bloody, his arm wrapped in stained bandages. He wore the clothes of an assassin. The man's eyes practically bulged as he gaped at her.

Josarian, at least, was smiling now. "I'm pleased to see you again, *sirana,* but this is hardly a place for a Guardian."

"Josarian." She was relieved to find an ally in this strange domain, among these hostile, staring people.

"Josarian, you know this—this—her?" Tansen said at last, his voice sharp, his gaze suspicious.

"She is a gifted woman." Josarian added more quietly, "And she is no danger to us, Tan."

He was like a blade, this man. Lean, hard, quick, sharp. She sensed that no one present feared her more than he did; yet he would be the first to risk death and confront her if he sensed a threat. The others gaped in fear, but he stood ready and watchful. *A man of terrible courage* . . . He was the one who had killed two assassins, who would have killed Najdan, too. He was the one who had sought this confrontation with Kiloran, a wizard so dangerous that everyone who was not of the Society avoided him at all costs. Yes . . . he was the one she sought, the one she had been sent to help. But *how?*

"Find the *shir,* and you find him," she muttered, finally noticing the weapon in his hand.

Suddenly a tower of water poured down from the ceiling, crashing down upon her. Choking and gasping, she scrambled away from it, aching as if she'd been beaten by human fists. Knowing the source of this pain, she flung a bolt of fire at Kiloran. A wall of water sprang up around him, and her fire hissed like an angry snake, battering repeatedly against it to no effect, then dying.

"This is his son, *sirana*!"

She whirled in response to Josarian's voice and, before Kiloran had time to react, wrapped a ring of fire around the shabby-looking assassin. Josarian barely jumped out of the way in time to avoid being burned.

She turned back to Kiloran and forestalled another attack by saying, "Now can we talk?"

"You want to talk?" Kiloran's voice was chilling, and she knew that her fears of dying here tonight might well be realized. "You've forced your way into my home, wrecked my hall, attacked me, and now threaten Srijan . . . and you say you want to *talk*?"

She saw the attack coming just before Kiloran did. The waterlord flinched at the last moment, just as the warrior leapt for him, taking them all by surprise.

"*No!*" she screamed, knowing that this wasn't what the Otherworld intended to take place here tonight, though she still didn't know quite what *was* supposed to happen next. "No!"

Tansen held the wavy blade of the dagger against Kiloran's throat. Even from here, she could see how wildly it quivered in his hand; a response to her presence, her power. The sight gave her courage. She was a Guardian, gifted by Dar and the Otherworld, sent here by the Beckoner and Daurion himself! She could do whatever had to be done.

"You want me, old man?" the warrior growled into Kiloran's ear. Kiloran gasped for air as the blade drew blood. The cut was not fatal, but it was undoubtedly painful, for a *shir* wounded as no other weapon did. "Let my friends leave."

"Kill me now . . . and you all drown here," Kiloran rasped.

"Let them go, and you may get another chance to kill

me," the warrior replied coldly. "If not, you've got six seconds to live."

The *torena* screamed, "Tansen, no!"

The assassins started circling nervously, afraid to die, looking for an opening to take Tansen without getting their master killed. Srijan was cursing in a fear-maddened voice.

"What do I do now?" Mirabar asked Dar, Daurion, and all the lesser the gods.

Find the shir, *and you find* him.

"I've found him, so what?"

Find him.

"What do you mean, find *h* . . ." She gasped, a long gurgling sound. "You're not an assassin!" she cried in sudden realization.

"Three seconds," he warned Kiloran, meaning it.

"The *shir*!" He had left behind the *shir* of the two assassins he had killed. "You shouldn't be able to touch it!"

"Two seconds."

"No, you mustn't, Tansen!" the *torena* cried. "We need him!"

"Whose *shir* is this one? Who did you take it from?" Mirabar demanded. "Who did you kill to get it?"

Find him!

Mirabar hauled air into her lungs and blew it out as fire—right where Tansen held Kiloran in a deathgrip. The shuddering blade leapt from his hand as the flames startled him into jumping back. He and Kiloran scrambled away. Josarian and the assassins lunged for them at the same time. Torn between preventing them from killing each other and keeping Kiloran from dousing her fire, Mirabar circled the flames, shouting at them, threatening the waterlord's son, partaking of the chaos instead of preventing it.

And then she heard the Calling, a voice unlike any other, roaring through the barriers separating this world from the Other one, craving her attention. She fell to her knees as an explosion expanded the fire and rocked the entire palace. Water from the damaged ceiling showered the fire now, for Kiloran's strength was being pulled in too many directions at once. The clear drops of water glowed with magic and turned to lava as they entered the flames. Bellowing with rage, Kiloran called tentacles of water out of the walls to wrap around the fire and strangle it. They, too, turned to lava as they touched it.

"An alliance," Mirabar choked. "Fire and water." She met the waterlord's appalled gaze. "The Guardians and the Society." Tears of fear, exhaustion, and exultation streaked down her face. "Now is the time."

The men stopped fighting. The *torena* stopped shouting. Even Srijan stopped bleating. The hall was silent but for the crackling of the fire and the voice coming from the Otherworld in response to the *shir*'s dance in the sacred flames.

"He is coming . . ." Mirabar breathed. "And his name is . . ." She gasped and turned to Tansen, feeling utterly betrayed. *"Armian?"*

21

TANSEN'S FACE FLUSHED with shame as this creature, this woman, this *demon* turned her fiery gaze back upon him and repeated, in a voice thick with betrayal: *"Armian?"*

Painfully aware of everyone's attention, he nodded. "Armian. It's his *shir.*"

An awful expression crossed her face. "You *killed* him. You killed Armian."

He let no expression show on his. "I killed him."

"Can you . . . Are you bringing forth a dead man?" Elelar asked, staggering forward without her usual grace.

The red-thatched head bobbed. "Yes."

Her demon eyes closed with concentration, her body tensing with some unseen effort.

No! he cried silently. *Not Armian. Not this . . .*

"I can crush you," Kiloran warned the girl.

She didn't even bother to open her eyes. "You won't. You want to see Armian. He wants to speak to you." She gasped and her head rolled back. A sheen of sweat broke out along her cheekbones and her breath came harshly, like a woman caught in the throes of passion. Or deadly terror. "A windy night . . . wet and windy . . . The *pain* of the blows, the pain of the betrayal . . ."

No, I came to face Kiloran, but not this! Not this.

He had lived life on the fine edge of fear, taking risks, pledging his life to combat, offering his blood to Josarian's cause. He was no coward and had never run away from anything in fear, but he wanted to run now. He could willingly swim toward the gaping, sharp-toothed jaws of a dragonfish before he could face the bloodfather he had murdered. He had faced death alone many times, and he had chosen to face the wrath of the greatest waterlord in the world. But he had never expected to face Armian again, and he knew he couldn't do it.

The fire grew in size and intensity, the *shir* glowing in their midst, the water of Kiloran's strange world marrying the flames wherever the two elements met and touched. Heart tugging at his lungs and twisting his belly, Tansen inwardly retreated as the Guardian told them that Armian was very close now.

He *could not do this.* He would run. He would walk through those watery walls and drown before he would do this!

A hand took his arm in a firm grip and held him steady. He whipped his head around to see who dared . . . His gaze collided with Josarian's. He wanted condemnation, accusation; he saw only understanding. He wanted disgust, revulsion, hatred; he saw only a brother's love.

Dar have mercy, why hadn't Josarian stayed behind? Tansen could have turned and run away if not for the firm support of that hand, the childlike trust in that face. But how could a man do the wrong thing in front of one who never doubted he would do the right thing? How could a man betray himself if it meant betraying another's blind belief in his courage and strength?

Gritting his teeth and wishing Josarian on the far side of Ejara, Tansen stood his ground and awaited Armian.

MIRABAR IGNORED KILORAN'S grousing about the feeble tricks of Guardians. She ignored the *torena*'s perplexed questions. She even ignored the shame which practically radiated from the warrior now that she had exposed his secret. *A man of stained honor* . . . Now Armian would come, and she would learn why Tansen had killed the man rumored to be the Firebringer, the one who might have set them all free. Now she would learn why she had been sent to confront these strangers and enemies in this watery underworld to which no Guardian had ever been admitted until tonight.

He arose in the flames, and she saw instantly that he was different from any other shade she had ever Called forth from the Otherworld. He reached out and seized his *shir,* something he should not have been able to do. He looked at them *all;* something he should not have been able to do. He *addressed* them all directly, instead of speaking through her.

Wary of what kind of power she had just unleashed with her Calling, Mirabar held the flames steady as Armian floated in the fire and linked this world to the Other one.

"Kiloran . . ." His voice was rich with power, strength, intelligence. *"Siran . . .* Now is the time. We were wrong. *Now* is the time."

Kiloran's breath rasped sharply. His aged lungs wheezed against the shock of the first Calling he had ever seen, for a man who pursued water magic gave up any claim to communion with the Otherworld.

"Sileria . . ." Armian seemed to sigh. "Oh, to breathe her scent again. To see her peaks and valleys again. You never

knew, *siran*, I never told you. You would have laughed
. . . but I loved her as if she were a woman . . ."

"She could have been ours." Kiloran's voice was heavy
with hatred. "I could have ruled all of Sileria! *We* could
have, if not for *him.*"

Armian swayed like a willow in the wind. "Tan . . ."

So . . . Armian had somehow promised Sileria to Kiloran, and Tansen had stopped him. By killing him? Mirabar felt dizzy with the implications. Confusion swamped
her. And even through the humming of her senses and the
music of death, she could feel the warrior's tension and
shame as Armian repeated his name.

"I am here," Tansen answered at last. "I . . ." His breath
was harsh, choking off his words.

"You . . ." Armian's shade wavered with sorrow. "You
were the only thing I ever loved unselfishly, asking nothing
in return . . ."

"I . . . I know . . ." Tansen stumbled forward and stood
so close she could feel his trembling.

"My son . . ."

His *son?* Mirabar was so startled she nearly lost control
of the fire. Armian's shade wavered as she wrapped her
will around it again, concentrating fiercely.

Armian's shadowy gaze burned into the man who stood
at her side. "I trusted you . . . See what you've done to
me . . ."

Tansen fell to his knees at Mirabar's side. Unable to
speak, he crossed his fists over his chest and bowed his
head respectfully, swallowing hard, shoulders shaking.

"Let me kill him for you now," Kiloran urged. "Let
me—"

"You need him." Armian's floating voice drowned out
the waterlord's hatred.

"Why?"

"Because Josarian needs him, and Sileria needs Josarian . . ."

"For *what?*"

"To drive out the Valdani . . ."

"Now?" Kiloran's voice was hoarse with surprise.

The *shir* twisted and turned gracefully. "Sileria will be Silerian again, free of invaders for the first time in a thousand years . . ."

Now it was the *torena* who spoke, her voice high-pitched and full of desperate hope. "Truly? How? Will I live to see it?"

"Elelar . . ." Armian's arms moved subtly, as if drawing her nearer. "If you had been only a little older . . . Ah, but I could never take the woman Tan wanted so desperately . . ."

Bitter yearning.

"And then you betrayed my bloodson for killing me . . . You paved the way for all that he became . . ."

A bloodpact son. Armian had taken Tansen, a *shallah* boy, as a bloodpact son! Mirabar started to recognize the tangled connections, the strands of life and death, of enmity and alliances, of love and betrayal which had led her here.

"You spoke of freedom," Elelar said rather pointedly, addressing Armian.

"I spoke of defeating the Valdani . . ."

"Well?" she prodded, not sounding as respectful as she had at first. A very arrogant woman, this one.

"We were wrong then . . . The Moorlanders . . ."

"Meant to betray us?" Kiloran asked.

"Were too weak . . ."

"Too weak to fight a war on two fronts?" Elelar guessed.

"Yes . . . The war here . . . Must be *our* war and no one else's . . ."

"But it can be done?" Elelar asked.

"Not by the Society alone. Not by the *shallaheen* alone. Not by the Guardians, the Alliance, or the sea-born folk . . . alone . . ."

"An alliance," Mirabar breathed, finally understanding. "All of us together. All the peoples of Sileria, fighting together against the Valdani."

"The Society and the Guardians?" Kiloran blurted. "Never!"

"Don't you think the Alliance has tried?" Elelar said, sounding exasperated. "The *shallaheen* trust no one. The sea-born folk care about no one but themselves. The Society and the Guardians are blood enemies. The lowlanders hate the *toreni*, and the city-dwellers fear the *shallaheen*. The Sisters and the *zanareen* will fight no one, not even the Valdani. The *toreni* and the merchants are unwilling to risk their wealth in an all-out rebellion. How can we possibly—"

"I didn't risk my life to come here and listen to you whine about how difficult it will be!" Mirabar snapped.

"You know nothing about this," Elelar shot back. "I have spent years—"

"I have seen visions of our future," Mirabar insisted hotly. "I have seen *his* swords breaking the shackles that enslave us!" She pointed at Tansen. "I have seen fire and water together, neither destroying the other. An alliance of our power!" She risked a glance at Kiloran and then returned her attention to the fire she kept blazing for Armian, at great cost to her strength. "I have seen Daurion's sword smash the Sign of the Three, a great structure made of marble and gold which sits in a place of—"

"In the the middle of Santorell Square," Elelar said breathlessly, "in Shaljir."

"I don't know where. I only know that we can smash it together. All of us, fighting as one, for the first time."

"With Josarian leading the *shallaheen*," Elelar murmured.

"The Society and the Guardians joining together?" Kiloran said with obvious distaste.

"Yes . . ." Armian's voice echoed around the palace.

"And this Alliance of yours . . ." Mirabar said.

"This Alliance of ours," Elelar said, "bringing all the people together into one. Against them."

"Against the Valdani."

"The sea-born folk, the Sisters, the *zanareen*, the lowlanders . . ." Josarian's voice trailed off. "Will they join us?"

"If you prepare the way . . ." Armian promised. "Not at first, but you must believe . . . They will come if you pre-pare the way . . ."

"How? When?" Elelar demanded.

"The city-dwellers, the Guardians, the Society . . ." Armian continued, ignoring her. "The *toreni,* the merchants, the *shallaheen* . . . Not all at once, but you can convince them . . . Not all with the same strength, but they will come . . ."

"If we prepare the way," Mirabar said.

"Then Sileria will be ours?" Kiloran asked.

"Then Sileria will be free of the Valdani . . ." Armian vowed. "They will leave . . ."

"What must we do?" Josarian asked.

"Enemies must become allies. Bloodvows must be re-scinded, bloodfeuds between the mountain clans must be ended," Mirabar said, finally understanding the substance of her visions.

"Yes . . ." Armian gestured to her. "She is guided by the will of the Otherworld. You must respect her . . ."

"She's a demon!" Srijan cried.

"She will be the shield," Armian said, "as my son will be the sword . . ."

"The Olvar." Tansen suddenly said, coming to life at last. "That's what *he* said."

"You five . . ." Armian's voice grew thinner. "You can change the world if you make peace tonight . . ." Mirabar was growing weaker, letting Armian fall back through the barrier. She pursued him, using the last of her energy to pull him closer to this world. "If you fail . . ."

"What's wrong?" Elelar asked suddenly.

"I'm losing him," Mirabar muttered, her spirit following his into the fire, depleting her strength. She felt the pull of the Otherworld as she drew closer. She ignored it, clinging to Armian.

"The chance won't come again . . ." They could barely

hear his voice now. ". . . for another thousand . . ."

"Armian!" Kiloran's voice was urgent, willing him back.

"A thousand years . . . You must . . ."

Mirabar lost Armian and stumbled too far while trying to reclaim him. Her strength crumbled suddenly, leaving her stranded in the void between this world and the Other one. The fires roared around her as she lost her way, the world of the living growing black and distant as oblivion reached out to gather her to its bosom for all eternity. Lost in the void of the gateway, searching for the path back to her body, she cried out in silent terror. She had seen others die this way and had always feared it. Now there was not even another Guardian present to help her find her way. Screaming for the Beckoner, she groped blindly, resisting the pull of death and oblivion.

The shock of freezing cold water snapped her back into place with the force of an explosion. Sputtering and blinking, she shook her hair out of her eyes and looked around in dazed confusion. Kiloran, she realized vaguely, had saved her by destroying her own fire; water was still rushing in from a collapsing wall of the palace, pushing her across the floor and flooding the room.

"Stop it!" she finally shouted, afraid of drowning.

Arms folded across his chest, he gazed at her with a cold, unfriendly expression as the wall closed itself up and stopped pouring water into the room.

Trudging through knee-deep water, the assassins went to Kiloran's side, standing protectively around their leader. Tansen hauled Elelar to her feet, swept her into his arms as she sputtered and coughed, and set her down on Kiloran's throne, ignoring the wizard's angry objection. Srijan climbed atop a shell-encrusted chest and watched them all warily. Josarian helped Mirabar to her feet and, apologizing for the familiarity, checked her for injuries.

"You saved my life," she said to Kiloran, aware that her tone lacked the gratitude one should normally express for such an act. "Does that mean . . ." She stopped uncertainly.

"It would seem that, after a thousand years of enmity, the Guardians and the Society must become partners," Kiloran said. He added, in a voice that dripped with sarcasm, *"Sirana."*

"And the *shallaheen* will join the Alliance," Josarian said. Then he shook himself like a dog.

"The waterlords and the assassins . . ." Kiloran's face twisted with displeasure. "We will call a truce on our internal disputes until . . ."

"Until after the war," Elelar said, shivering. "Until after Sileria is free of the Valdani."

Kiloran nodded. "And we will pledge ourselves to this . . . bloodfeud sworn by the *shallaheen.*"

"So will the Guardians," Mirabar vowed. She hoped she was right. She was only an initiate, after all, but she didn't think this the best moment to mention that.

"Now is the time," Elelar said, dwelling on the words. "We will win. We will live to see the Valdani withdraw from Sileria."

Without asking Kiloran's permission, Tansen sloshed across the hall and retrieved his swords. Arming himself, he said, "There is one minor point I'd like to clear up before the rest of you start planning the victory celebration." He turned to face Kiloran and said, "Call off the bloodvow."

"We seem to be right back where we started," Kiloran muttered.

"Cheer up," Tansen advised him. "If I'm to fight a war against the Valdani, you can count on my dying soon, anyhow."

"He will be the sword," Mirabar said, her teeth chattering. "We cannot do this without him."

"I *won't* do it without him," Josarian added. "Call off the bloodvow, or the *shallaheen* will join no one."

Looking like he'd just swallowed seawater, Kiloran said, "Bring me the *shir.*"

Tansen sloshed over to the spot they'd last seen it and groped around in the water. Finally finding it, he knelt before Kiloran and formally offered the dagger to its maker: "Lord of water and all its power, you who made the *shir* and who can unmake our thirst at your will, I have no wish to quarrel with you, and so I beg your forgiveness for killing Armian mar Harlon shah Idalari. I return his *shir* to you as a sign of my good faith and my earnest desire to make peace with you."

Kiloran accepted the *shir* and held its blade against Tansen's forehead. "Tansen mar Dustan shah Gamalani, I accept your peace offering. Before these witnesses, I hereby forgive you the death of Armian and now rescind the bloodvow I swore against you. Whosoever your other enemies may be, you will no longer be pursued by me, my friends, ôr the friends of my friends, so long as you offer me no further offense."

Tansen rose to his feet, met Kiloran's gaze, and nodded. Then he looked long and hard at the assassins, as if to make sure they didn't have any doubts about the ritual.

"Now we can be allies," Josarian said with satisfaction. "Now we can fight the Valdani together."

Shivering, Mirabar said to Kiloran, "Can't you do anything about all this water, dammit? I'm freezing!"

Elelar sighed. The assassins looked shocked. Tansen actually laughed.

Kiloran glowered at his guests. "Since you weren't invited, perhaps you could all *leave* now?"

"We still have things to discuss, plans to make," Elelar objected.

"Later," Kiloran said.

"Up there, *torena*," Josarian suggested, pointing overhead. "Where we might be more comfortable."

"Go!" Kiloran snapped.

Josarian caught Mirabar's eye and grinned. "Well, *sirana*, this shade from the Otherworld never said we all had to learn to like each other."

Part Two

"I CAN TAKE CARE OF MY ENEMIES,
BUT DAR SHIELD ME FROM MY FRIENDS."

22

KOROLL HAD NEVER before been in Shaljir during the summer. Now, as Commander of Sileria's exotic capital, he couldn't abandon the city and retreat to the countryside as every other person of means did during these mad days of relentless heat, dust, and sun. A tolerable, if crowded, place during the rest of the year, Shaljir became a virtual cauldron in midsummer, a prison of seething heat and stench which simmered slowly beneath Sileria's fiercely blue sky. The torment ended only when the city was finally soothed by the first northern winds which came at the end of the season, bringing relief and—everyone prayed—rain.

Violent crime rose sharply within the city walls during the brain-baking days of high summer. Tempers flared, passions erupted, and patience withered as helplessly as the lush blossoms of spring in this maddening heat. The Valdani followed the customs of previous conquerors and pronounced more lenient sentences for violent crimes committed by Silerians—against *other* Silerians—during the height of summer. Any crime committed against a Valdan, of course, was still punished by a sentence of death or a term of hard labor in the mines of Alizar.

Theft, always a worry in Shaljir, became an even worse problem during summer. The wealthy and privileged abandoned their homes and palaces here every summer, leaving only a handful of servants behind to guard them. So now, when Shaljir's many criminals weren't busy assaulting each other, they were breaking into the city homes of Valdani aristocrats, *toreni*, wealthy merchants, foreign traders, and important government officials to steal whatever they could. The Emperor encouraged Sileria's richest inhabitants and most important foreign visitors to maintain property and wealth in Shaljir, the most heavily taxed city in Sileria, by faithfully promising to protect it. Now it was up to Koroll to ensure that the arrangement continued to work well. Consequently, at a time when he most needed his men stationed in the mountains to fight Josarian, he'd had to bring an extra five hundred Outlookers to Shaljir to keep the "peace."

Fortunately, and contrary to all expectations this year, there was enough water to satisfy the needs of Shaljir's vast population. Summer would be a grim time of many deaths if water was withheld from the city. However, Kiloran seemed to have finally solved his problems with Baran, for water flowed plentifully into Shaljir from the Idalar River now. As usual, Kiloran doubled his tribute demands to keep the city supplied at the height of the season. Although the Valdani were making plans to use ancient tunnels located beneath the city to bring water to Shaljir from a new source, they were still vulnerable to Kiloran's power for the time being. The Emperor's official instructions were to refuse to pay tribute to that bandit; the Silerians might give into this kind of extortionate barbarism, but the Empire would not. However, Advisor Borell was a realistic man who looked the other way when Koroll siphoned off enough gold from various sources to complete the Outlookers' share of the city's contributions to the Honored Society for yet another season.

Advisor Borell was also a lucky whoreson who was spending the summer in a fabulous cliffside villa on Sileria's eastern shores, cooled by ocean breezes and untroubled by the growing rebellion in the west. The new Commander of Cavasar, an appointee from the Emperor's court, had already arrived from the mainland; not surprisingly, he turned out to be a nephew of Borell's. Koroll had by now realized that Borell was no more anxious than he to reveal the scale of their problems in Sileria. It didn't look good to be the first provincial government in some two hundred years that couldn't keep these people under control. It became clear within a few minutes of meeting Commander Cyrill that he was loyal to Borell and would do what his uncle told him to.

So we're still safe. For now.

Naturally, they hadn't been able to conceal the deaths of so many Outlookers. The families had to be notified, as did Emperor Jarell, and new recruits had to be requested. Moreover, the death of Commander Daroll, a son of one of Valda's most powerful families, had created an unwelcome stir back home. Daroll wasn't the sort of officer who was expected to die in service, especially not in a backwater like Sileria. He was just supposed to give orders and await an inevitable political appointment. The official story now, agreed upon at Santorell Palace, was that Daroll had bravely risked—and lost—his life while trying to negotiate with the mountain bandits and prevent further bloodshed.

It's half-true, after all. Why mention what a fool he was?

A military man rather than a diplomat, Koroll had let Borell do much of the talking when an Imperial Councilor came to Shaljir to demand a detailed explanation of the events described in their dispatches. After three days of verbal dancing and lavish entertaining, Borell managed to convince the man that, while there was undeniably a problem in Sileria, they had the situation well in hand and would soon crush these bandits. *Torena* Elelar had served a useful purpose for once, showing commendable loyalty to Borell. She had assured the Councilor, who was thoroughly charmed by her anyhow, that the other peoples of this splintered society thoroughly disapproved of the *shallah* outlaws, who had by now gained all the support they were ever going to gain. Yes, the *torena* had been very helpful, Koroll conceded privately; perhaps he had misjudged her.

The Councilor had returned to Valda with optimistic reports. The Imperial Council had sent more money to pay for destroying these provincial bandits, and two thousand Outlookers were about to be relocated to Sileria from a

Kintish province which had been in the Empire's possession for over three hundred years. No men from the Moorlands could be spared. The Emperor was pushing his armies south to expand the Empire's territory in the Moorlands, leaving only Outlookers to hold the northern tribes.

In truth, even getting men transferred from a Kintish province conquered long ago, no matter how peaceful, hadn't been easy. The Kintish High King was now so old it was a wonder he was still alive, and his only heir was a mad princess who apparently could not be convinced to marry and get sons. Although the Empire was already straining under the burden of its huge size, the difficulty of policing so many subjugated races, and the immense cost of the Emperor's continuing wars of conquest, the Imperial Council had just decided that now was the time to move against the Kints. The Kintish Kingdoms, a loose association of petty states with a history going back more than three thousand years, had sacrificed many outlying territories over the centuries to avoid an all-out war with Valdania. However, since enmity for the Valdani was the one thing that united the remaining Kintish nations, Emperor Jarell had chosen long ago to devote his reign and resources to more likely conquests: nothing, after all, seemed capable of uniting the tribes of the Moorlands.

Suddenly, however, the Emperor and the Council had changed the policies of the past fifty years, perhaps because Jarell, too, was now very old and longed to complete the conquest of the Kintish Kingdoms before he died. Ah, to enter the Palace of Heaven as its new ruler after three thousand years of Kintish supremacy, to sit in the Throne of Heaven, the most coveted seat in the three corners of the world . . . It was an ambition worthy of even the most powerful leader in the world, and Koroll could not blame Jarell for seizing the chance now that he saw it. With no one to occupy the Throne of Heaven except a dying old man or a mad girl, this time the Kintish union would crumble completely under the Empire's onslaught. This time, the remaining Kintish Kingdoms would fall.

This time, Kinto will be ours.

It was a thrilling moment in history, a magnificent time to be a Valdan, and Koroll would give anything to partake of the glory. He had no hope of receiving a promotion and a transfer to the mainland, however, while mountain bandits wreaked havoc on this provincial backwater. Consequently, destroying Josarian now became even more important than ever before.

He was therefore less than pleased when Captain Myrell arrived in Shaljir, covered in dust and sweat, to inform him that Josarian was not only still on the loose, but growing stronger and more popular than ever. It was estimated that the number of Josarian's followers had increased tenfold just since the beginning of summer, and that dozens of men were now flocking to his cause every day. His raids against Outlooker targets were growing increasingly bold and costly. His disruption of regular trade routes was starting to seriously damage the local Valdani economy. And now, Myrell reported, Josarian had discovered a new way of earning enough money to feed his vast band of rebels and to buy the continued silence of the mountains.

"Abduction?" Koroll said in astonishment. "He's taken to *abduction* now?"

"Yes, sir," Myrell confirmed. "He recently returned *Toren* Porsall's wife after receiving a ransom of two hundred thousand in gold. The *torena* says she was treated well, but she was so frightened she has been unable to give us any useful information about the identity of her captors or where they held her for twenty-seven days."

"What can you expect of a woman?" Koroll said dismissively.

"Toren Emmeran was not only safely returned after his family paid the ransom," Myrell continued, "but he evidently became so fond of Josarian during the seventeen days he spent as his captive that he will give no evidence against him."

"What?"

"He *is* a Silerian, after all, and they are an irrational—"

"What do you mean he won't give evidence—"

"Emmeran now claims that he was merely meditating in Sanctuary for seventeen days, has never met Josarian, and had no idea that the outlaw was making ransom demands during his absence."

"A *toren* is protecting a *shallah?*" Koroll stared at Myrell.

"I'm afraid it gets worse, sir."

"Go on," Koroll said woodenly.

"I decided to have Emmeran arrested, thinking that would make him see reason. The eight men I sent for him were killed on their way to his estate."

"Then send fifty men, you fool! We can't allow this!"

"I'm short of men, sir. They're busy combing the hills in search of two Valdani aristocrats who were abducted four days ago. The ransom demand is one million, in gold."

"Josarian's mad. The Society will never tolerate this."

"Apparently, Commander . . ."

"Yes?"

"The Society is cooperating with Josarian."

"They'd *never* cooperate with Jo . . ." His voice trailed off as he stared at Myrell. "How do you know this?"

"That's the good news, sir. I finally have an informant."

"An informant? Three be thanked! What can he tell us? Does he know where Josarian's men are based?"

"Some place in the mountains called Dalishar. I gather it's a holy site or something."

"At last!"

"Frankly, it doesn't sound like we can attack him there, sir. It's very deep in the mountains, inaccessible to riders, approachable only by a couple of narrow mountain paths, and . . ."

"Well?"

"There is talk of . . . Silerian fire magic up there."

Koroll frowned. "The—what do they call them—Guardians?"

"I believe so." Myrell shrugged. "Just superstitious talk, of course, but many of my men are . . ."

"Susceptible to such talk," Koroll concluded.

"Exactly." Myrell hesitated, then said, "You've been here longer than I have, Commander. Is there any truth to it?"

"I've never seen any of these fire sorcerers the Silerians whisper about. They've been outlawed for centuries, you know."

"The waterlords are outlawed, too, but they . . . maintain a strong presence in this land."

Koroll nodded. "I imagine that, as with the waterlords, some of what these people say about the Guardians is true, but most of it is wildly exaggerated."

"My informant claims that Josarian has the support of the Guardians now, too."

Koroll glanced sharply at him. "The Society *and* the Guardians? You're sure?"

"Absolutely. He was quite clear about it."

Koroll frowned. "Then I suspect he may be hand-feeding you lies that Josarian would like us to believe. If you would bother to learn something about these people—"

Myrell stiffened. "I believe you're going to tell me that the Guardians and the Society have been enemies for centuries."

Koroll nodded. "Exactly. Since long before the Empire conquered these people."

"According to my informant, they have put aside their differences to help Josarian."

"The Society and the Guardians?"

"Yes, sir."

Koroll leaned back in his massive wooden chair. A chill took hold of him. He knew little about Sileria's secretive, outlawed fire magic cult, but even he knew that once, centuries ago, they had ruled this island in its wealthy heyday. Over a thousand years ago, three hundred spires had graced the skyline of Shaljir when Valda had been little more than a collection of thatched huts squatting in the mud. Ancient history, of course, but the Guardians . . They had somehow survived the centuries, outlawed and hunted, enemies of both the Honored Society and the Valdani. And now, if this informant of Myrell's was to be believed, they had joined forces not only with Josarian, but also with their ancient enemies, the waterlords.

The Society, the Guardians, and the *shallaheen* . . . The three factions of Silerian society which had the least to lose: two because they were outlawed, and the third because they were so crushingly poor. The Society, whose power even the Emperor feared; the Guardians, whose whispered sorcery was a mystery in modern times and whose strength could only be guessed; and the *shallaheen,* the most numerous of Sileria's diverse peoples—violent, vengeful, and increasingly committed to the bloodfeud that Koroll had learned Josarian had sworn against the Valdani.

"We'll need more men," Koroll muttered at last, dread settling into his bones.

"I agree, Commander." Myrell cleared his throat. "There have been reprisals . . ."

"Reprisals?"

"Every time we raid a village to try to force someone to give us information about Josarian . . . he hits us back twice as hard as we hit his people." Myrell's jaw worked silently for a moment. "You know that I've lost many men this summer, Commander. Too many. More than even our worst estimates."

"We'll need more men," Koroll repeated, his mouth dry. How had it come to this? One lone smuggler whom they'd clumsily let escape; just one mountain peasant seeking vengeance. How had his outlawry become a widespread rebellion costing the lives of hundreds of Outlookers?

After a heavy silence, Myrell continued, "My informant does not know Josarian's movements, but he has been able to give me the names of some of Josarian's most trusted men."

"We'll add their names to the wanted list and the reward offers." Koroll reached for the list of names Myrell handed him and skimmed it briefly. He stopped suddenly on one name that leapt into at him like a striking snake. "Tansen shah Gamalani?" He looked up at Myrell. No, surely it couldn't be the same Tansen; it must be another of the same name.

"An easterner." Myrell nodded. "From the district of Liron."

"What else do you know about him?"

"It's interesting that you should single him out, sir. He is apparently much talked about in the mountains." Myrell shook his head. "Exaggerated tales, of course. They say he's a Kintish swordmaster, a . . ."

"Shatai." Koroll's throat ached as he said the word.

"Yes, that's it. Can you credit that? A *shallah* claiming to be a *shatai!*" Myrell allowed himself a brief moment of genuine amusement. "Apparently he does carry two Kintish swords, but I . . . Commander? Are you unwell?"

"No . . . it's just . . . this damned heat." He swallowed, fighting an attack of nausea. "Go on, Captain."

"Hot as all the Fires today, as the Silerians say," Myrell agreed morosely. "Anyhow, this Tansen, he must be a good fighter, even so. Who knows? Maybe he actually managed to kill a real *shatai* and take away his swords."

"They say he's a good fighter?"

Myrell shifted uncomfortably and lowered his voice. "They say he helped Josarian attack the fortress at Britar. It seems that he's the man I took for Josarian." His face reddened as he admitted, "They tricked me. The whole incident has become a popular folktale already."

Koroll shot out of his chair. "Why didn't you tell me he used two swords, damn you?"

Myrell's eyes grew round and stupid. "I . . . I didn't *see*, Commander! It all happened so fast. He . . . stood out there in front of the fortress, and . . . The next thing I knew, two men were dead and he was on a stolen horse, halfway to the forest. Two men pursued him closely. One was killed by a stray arrow. The *shallah* killed the other rider, but it was too far away to see what was happening. Besides, he was on foot again, since his horse—"

"Good God!" Koroll wiped a linen sleeve across his mouth. He felt beads of sweat trickling down his face, his back, his chest. "The *shatai* is out there with Josarian!"

"Commander?"

"Get out!" He waved an arm at the door and shouted, "Get out! Get yourself cleaned up! Get whatever you need! Then . . ." He tried to control himself, tried to *think*. "Return here this evening," he said more calmly. "We have a lot of plans to make."

He sank down into his chair and buried his head in his arms, whispering over and over to himself, "What happened? What happened out there?"

Had Josarian turned the *shatai?* Was he that convincing, that compelling, that he could win the loyalty of a mercenary? Or was the *shatai* more of a *shallah* than Koroll had realized? He'd looked so un-Silerian. He had spoken so contemptuously of the *shallaheen*. He had seemed so reasonable.

"Three have mercy," Koroll whispered against the sticky dampness of his own flesh.

Had the *shatai* merely bided his time, playing Koroll for a fool until he was free? Or had Josarian woven some wizardry around him? If they'd fought together to free the prisoners at Britar, then the *shatai* must have become Josarian's ally soon after leaving Cavasar. The two men had been together all this time, and now the *shatai* was known to be one of Josarian's most trusted men.

Three Into One! It was a disaster! In turning loose a *shatai*-trained *shallah,* Koroll himself had helped arrange the slaughter at Britar—as well as Three-only-knew how many Valdani deaths since then! He had sent one of the finest warriors in the world into the mountains to join the most dangerous *shallah* who had ever lived!

He prayed fervently that none of the Outlookers back in Cavasar ever made a connection between the *shatai* Koroll had housed in the fortress there for several days and the *shatai* now roaming the mountains with Josarian. He calmed down slightly only upon realizing that Myrell had mistaken Tansen for Josarian. Even a fool like Myrell wouldn't have mistaken a *shatai*'s distinctive appearance for an ordinary *shallah.*

The conclusion was obvious: Tansen had altered his appearance after entering the mountains. So it seemed probable that only a Valdan who had spoken with him, actually spent time with him—only Koroll—was likely now to recognize him as the same man who had been groomed as a Kint and dressed as a Moorlander months ago in Cavasar. If Tansen was dressed now as just another grubby Silerian mountain peasant . . . May the Three make it so! Perhaps Koroll's secret would yet be safe.

He soaked a gossamer cloth in scented water and ran it over his face. Tansen's *shir* . . . The Society. What was the link? Had *he* convinced the Society to support Josarian?

Koroll felt ill. The Society, the Guardians, the *shalla-heen*, Josarian, and the *shatai*.

How much bigger would this thing get? How much worse? Who would join them next?

ACCOMPANIED BY FARADAR and two trusted men, Elelar was weary by the time she arrived at the summer home of the Kintish High King's ambassador to Sileria. After ten days in Borell's luxurious cliffside villa north of here, she had made excuses and left. She was a landowner and another man's wife, so getting away from Borell was seldom problematic. He might not appreciate the other apparent demands on her time, but he understood them.

Ambassador Shiraj's summer villa was set amidst some of Sileria's most dramatic and heart-stoppingly beautiful scenery. Sitting on the mountainous coast north of Liron, the villa's eastern rooms provided splendid clifftop views of the sea. The western rooms looked out at Darshon, whose vast slopes filled the sky and whose snow-crusted peak looked almost close enough to touch from here.

Tansen had originally come from this part of the country, she knew, from an impoverished village destroyed by the Valdani during their search for Armian nine years ago. Now, after all the years in exile, he was spending a good part of the summer roaming these eastern mountains again, seeking support for Josarian from among the mountain clans around Liron and Darshon. Josarian's brother-in-law was with him, and so was a Guardian named Cheylan. One of Baran's assassins rounded out their party.

Cheylan was not only a Guardian, Elelar had been told, he was also a *toren* from this district, though his family had kept him hidden away for years before eventually turning him over to the Guardians. While his appearance wasn't supposed to be quite as startling as Mirabar's, he was nonetheless rumored to be unmistakably demonic-looking.

Demons. Such fears were common among the lower classes, Elelar knew, but it appalled her that even many members of her own class, with all their access to education and culture, still harbored such barbaric superstitions. She knew relatively little about the Guardians, who had retreated to Sileria's most remote mountains centuries ago, but she *did* know that they had ruled this land wisely through centuries of prosperity before the Conquest. If the Guardians said that so-called demons like Mirabar and Cheylan were specially gifted by Dar and sent to serve Her people, then Elelar was willing to believe them.

And the Guardians *did* say so; most emphatically. Derlen, who was now the link between the Guardians in the west and the Alliance in Shaljir, was most insistent on this point—despite his apparent personal dislike of Mirabar.

Well, Elelar couldn't say that she blamed him. She hadn't spent much time with the girl, but she was developing a hearty dislike for her, too. No one could deny Mirabar's courage or commitment; abducting an assassin and going to Kiloran's lair to serve the Otherworld represented a suicidal level of bravery. But the girl had all the charm, tact, and patience of a hungry mountain cat. On the other hand, Elelar supposed magnanimously, being regularly tormented by prophetic visions was bound to make anyone a bit difficult.

They had all camped at Kandahar for another day after that cataclysmic night in Kiloran's watery palace. As once before, Armian had proved to be the one messenger Kiloran would trust, and so even the crafty old waterlord had joined in their planning and cooperated with their ideas. From Kandahar, they had set out to alert their allies and make peace with their various enemies.

Elelar had so far spent most of the summer establishing a reliable network among old enemies, picking and choosing the right emissaries to go from one faction to another. Mirabar linked the Society to the Guardians, since she was probably the only one brave and crazy enough to willingly venture into the shadowy world of the waterlords; she also had the ability to Call forth Armian, which helped to favorably impress those members of the Honored Society who cherished their private feuds more than they treasured any dream of freedom. Tansen had gone east with Emelen and Cheylan; among other things, they were meeting with the Alliance's leaders in Liron. The assassin travelling with them must not only get the support of Verlon, Liron's powerful waterlord, for the rebellion, but he must also convince him to call off his bloodvow against Cheylan. No one seemed to know precisely why Verlon wanted Cheylan dead, but Elelar had learned from Derlen that the Society feared anyone marked with power the way Cheylan and Mirabar were.

With the thousand-year-old feud between the Society and the Guardians now in a state of truce, the Guardians were braving death at the hands of the Valdani to descend from their remote hiding places and spread the word among the *shallaheen*. As Elelar herself had seen, sometimes a message from the Otherworld convinced people in a way that no amount of rational argument could. Meanwhile, the Society was helping Josarian's men finance and feed the growing rebel movement by teaching them the fine art of abduction. The Alliance, with its many connections, was able to provide them with reliable information on the location, habits, and finances of dozens of wealthy Valdani aristocrats, unpatriotic Silerian merchants, and *toreni*.

There were problems, of course. Unlike Josarian, the Society did nothing without considering the profit involved. They wanted to keep a substantial percentage of every ransom they helped Josarian collect. The new partnership had nearly fallen apart several times over this. Moreover, as the rebellion spread from Josarian's native ground and expanded into less familiar territory, they encountered more risk of betrayal and a greater need to buy silence. Elelar had tried to explain to Josarian that loyalty could be expensive; it was another fruitless conversation, and she gave up before long.

However, the summer had not been without its amusements. *Toren* Porsall had paid the ransom for his wife within a few days of her capture, yet at least twenty more days went by with still no sign of her. Sneaking into Zilar for a meeting, Tansen had wryly explained to Elelar that they'd chosen an easy target for their first abduction: the woman was lovers with Josarian's cousin and had readily agreed when Zimran asked if she would help him get a ransom payment out of her husband. Zimran took her to some assassin's comfortable home in the mountains, and the woman was enjoying her abduction with him so much that the rebels were having considerable trouble convincing her to go back home.

Now *Toren* Emmeran, one of Ronall's shiftless, aimless friends, had apparently become a patriot after seventeen days of Josarian's companionship. He had defied Outlookers during interrogation and had even recently notified Josarian about the arrival of a Valdani tribute collector at his estate.

Best of all, Josarian had dealt a crippling blow to Valdani morale in Adalian by attacking the Outlooker brothel there! Upon receiving the news two days ago, Borell had sputtered as if he might have a seizure. It had taken all of Elelar's self-control not to burst out laughing when he reported the news to her, his face red with outrage. She might dislike Josarian, but she had to admit he was a brilliant rebel leader. The brothel had been an easy target, yet its loss had thrown the Outlookers into an uproar. Moreover, Josarian was sending the enslaved women of the brothel back to the Moorlands on a ship secretly provided by the Alliance. A realistic woman, Elelar sadly wondered if anything better than disgrace and poverty awaited them at home. However, it was a gesture which would be generally appreciated by the Moorlanders, and that was important. For even if this improbable alliance of all Sileria's peoples now came to pass, Sileria would need allies who could coordinate their movements with hers: hence, Elelar's unexpected visit to Ambassador Shiraj today. Borell had unwittingly told her how Sileria's interests could best be served in Kinto now. Destiny had taken a hand. Now all the months she had discreetly cultivated Shiraj's acquaintance might pay off beyond her wildest dreams.

The sun was lowering over Darshon as she dismounted before Shiraj's villa. Even when uninvited, a *torena* was never kept waiting outside; a servant showed Elelar into an airy, breeze-cooled room furnished with exotic Kintish finery, then went to fetch the Ambassador. Shiraj's wife had never come to Sileria, preferring to stay at the Palace of Heaven and guard her husband's back there. His mistress, a first-level Kintish courtesan, was undoubtedly here with him, but the woman was a professional who would know better than to make a scene because Shiraj's occasional Silerian bedmate had just walked boldly into the house.

As expected, Shiraj appeared almost immediately to greet her. A Kintish aristocrat who had survived twenty years of scheming and plotting around the Throne of Heaven did not readily show his emotions, but Elelar didn't doubt he was very surprised to see her. Sneaking into his house in Shaljir occasionally was one thing, but leaving Borell's side to come to Shiraj's summer home was rather risky; it would be much harder for her to come up with an innocent explanation should news of *this* meeting ever reach Borell's ears. Of course, what Shiraj didn't yet realize was that infidelity would be the convenient excuse Elelar used to conceal her real reason for coming here today, should excuses ever become necessary.

"*Torena,*" Shiraj said. "What an unexpected pleasure."

He smiled and came forward to greet her. His dark almond eyes glinted with pleasure and curiosity when she rose to kiss him. His olive skin was dark from the summer sun, glowing with good health. He hadn't covered his blue-black hair with a turban today, so she caressed it lightly with her fingers. She couldn't claim to be fond of him; she didn't know him that well. But he was intelligent, considerate, and even handsome. She supposed that if she gave it much thought, she would like him.

He returned her kiss delicately. A very different man from Borell, who usually greeted her with voracious hunger after only a few days' absence. And *very* different from Tansen, who probably wanted her more than either man, but who had rejected her overtures before Kandahar. But then, these men had been shaped by wealth, privilege, and power, whereas Tansen had been shaped by bitter poverty, grief, shame, pride, vengeance, and courage; the same forces which had shaped Sileria. Like the land itself, his life had made him hard, fierce, and resilient in ways Shiraj and Borell could never understand, let alone emulate.

Shiraj took one of her hands in his and said tactfully, "I am honored by your visit, *torena,* but I'm afraid that I am not alone here." Meaning his Kintish mistress was here with him, as she had supposed.

"I understand." She smiled and sat back down, urging him to join her. "However, I came for another reason today."

His brows lifted with interest, for there had never been

anything but sex between them before. "Oh?"

"The time has come to tell you a little more about myself than I had originally intended," she began. Without risking anyone else's safety, she told him about the Alliance and her part in it; coolly explaining the reasons for her marriage to Ronall and her liaison with Borell.

Shiraj studied her with a carefully masked expression which revealed nothing of his thoughts or reactions. It suddenly reminded her of Tansen; a very un-Silerian habit he had learned during his years in Kinto, apparently.

Shiraj finally said, "I'm flattered by your trust, *torena,* and intrigued by this information. Naturally, as the High King's Ambassador, I was aware of the existence of some underground anti-Valdani activities in Sileria, though . . ." He shrugged gracefully, too polite to say that the Palace of Heaven did not concern itself with the activities of a few Silerian malcontents. "Since you have been so forthright with me, I will say plainly that we have watched this growing mountain rebellion with interest." He paused. "However, my dear, if you've come here to solicit our support—"

"I haven't," she said smoothly. "I've come to offer our friendship."

Suspicion glinted subtly in his eyes. "In exchange for what?"

She smiled. "In exchange for *your* friendship."

"Is that all?"

"As proof of our friendship, I bring you information which has come to Advisor Borell directly from the Imperial Council in Valda."

He didn't bother to conceal his surprise. "Go on."

She gave him the weapon, praying that she was acting wisely. "The Emperor and the Imperial Council have decided that the time has finally come for Valdania to move against the Palace of Heaven and destroy the remaining Kintish Kingdoms, incorporating them into the Empire at last. To this end, they are committing the entire might of their armies east of the Moorlands."

He shook his head. "They can't do that. They have territories to hold, conquered lands to secure, borders to—"

"They are doing it," she said steadily. "The Empire's Outlookers will hold the conquered territories and patrol the Empire's borders while the imperial armies march into the Kintish Kingdoms."

"Outlookers?" he said contemptuously. "They can't even hold Sileria anymore."

"The Imperial Council doesn't know that. Borell and Commander Koroll have minimized the scope of the rebellion here in all their dispatches to Valda. The Emperor thinks the situation here is under control."

He leaned forward. "Why are you telling me all this? What do *you* gain?"

How refreshing it was to deal with a man who assumed she wanted more than just the privilege of serving him. She met his gaze squarely. "If Kinto falls, we all go down. The free Moorlands won't last another decade. The rebellion in Sileria will die with Josarian. The Palace of Heaven and all its ancient power will be used by the Valdani to subjugate the entire world." Seeing his hesitation, she added, "Borell has bragged to me about it! He and the High Commander of Sileria have talked about it right in *front* of me, Shiraj."

"But this is still Sileria. How can *you* know so much before our own spies in Valda?" he argued, but she could see that she nearly had him.

"Borell has no secrets from me, not even those that he tries to keep. He is advised of every decision in Valda which could possibly affect Sileria. Dispatches have come this summer explaining why there are delays in sending more men here to fight the mountain bandits, why Borell must increase taxes, why Koroll must be more efficient in collecting them."

"To help pay for the coming war against Kinto." Shiraj's voice was barely a whisper.

"The Valdani believe the Kingdoms will crumble under the pressure because the High King is old and ill, and even if the Kints would accept a woman as his heir—"

"The princess is . . ." He cleared his throat.

"They say she's mad." Elelar studied him. "You must have known, you must have *all* known how precarious the union of the Kingdoms is, with the future of the Throne of Heaven so uncertain."

"Valdania's armies are overextended in the Moorlands, sustaining heavy losses there. We thought we were safe as long as the Moorlands held out."

"The Valdani are a race who feed on their own hungers. There will never be enough land, enough people, enough wealth, enough wars to satisfy them," Elelar said fiercely. "They have seen your weakness and are coming to devour you."

Shiraj looked older suddenly, the weight of responsibility resting heavily on him. "War," he said pensively. "With Valdania." He sighed and admitted, as if he had forgotten her presence, "I don't think we'll survive."

She fought to keep her voice from betraying her eagerness. "But you will fight?"

"Oh, yes. The one thing that unites the Kingdoms like nothing else is the threat of Valdani conquest. We will fight." He nodded slowly. "The one thing we have always known is that someday we would have to fight Valdania. We just . . ."

"What?"

He smiled sadly. "We just all hoped to die of old age long before it finally came to pass."

23

TANSEN HAD GROWN used to Cheylan's demon eyes as the sun-stunned days of summer passed, but he didn't think he'd ever be at ease with the man. Not because of those fire-hot eyes, though they could be unsettling, but because of Cheylan himself. He was a man whose moods and actions were as unpredictable as they were inexplicable. His power was extraordinary, his position among the Guardians was one of trust and respect, and his courage in facing Verlon to get the bloodvow rescinded was undeniable . . . but Tansen didn't like him. Too many of Cheylan's comments seemed vaguely double-edged, as if he laughed at his own allies even as he assisted them. His fine-featured face seemed to express contempt or private amusement on too many occasions. There was something about him that didn't seem entirely trustworthy, despite the risks he took for the rebellion, despite the fire and strength he pledged to their cause.

No one knew why Verlon wanted Cheylan dead, and Cheylan refused to discuss it. Since this so closely mirrored Tansen's own situation with Kiloran, he could appreciate Cheylan's desire for privacy. Nonetheless, Tansen couldn't help wondering about the past that Cheylan and Verlon shared. When Verlon had met with the rebels and rescinded the bloodvow, Tansen—though he couldn't say exactly why—had come away with a feeling that Cheylan and Verlon knew each other much better than anyone realized.

Tansen was reluctant to express his uneasiness to anyone else, however. He was well aware that old prejudices might be clouding his judgment. Cheylan was a *toren,* after all, and they were different. Elelar always had two meanings for every sentence, three plans for every situation, and five reasons for every action. Perhaps it was just bred into the *toreni* to be subtle and slippery, as well as arrogant.

Childhood superstitions lingered in Tansen's heart, too, more powerful than they should be. Sometimes, if he caught a flash of those flame-gold eyes in the dark, if his mind was wandering or if he awoke suddenly, his hands reached for his swords before he realized what he was doing. Cheylan had noticed, and Tan had a feeling that the Guardian despised him for it. Tansen had once tried apologizing for the instinctive reaction, but the apology had only made things worse. Cheylan also seemed to despise anyone who acknowledged a mistake.

They had spent the summer travelling through the eastern mountains, gathering support for the rebellion, strengthening old alliances, forming new ones, and ending old enmities. The combined strength and conviction of the Society, the Guardians, and the *shallaheen,* along with Josarian's growing legend, served their cause well. A blood-feud begun by one lone peasant had now become a true rebellion, with a scattered army whose strength numbered in the thousands. Several successful attacks on Outlooker targets in the district of Liron had drawn even more *shallaheen,* waterlords, assassins, and Guardians into their ranks. Leaving Emelen, Cheylan, and a high-ranking assassin of Baran's behind to continue the good work, Tansen now travelled back to Dalishar to report to Josarian.

He had met with Elelar two days ago, prior to heading west into the mountains. She had passed most of the summer living openly with Advisor Borell, the most important Valdan in Sileria. Tansen didn't ask, but he couldn't help wondering what manner of man her husband was, that he tolerated such behavior in his wife. Tansen knew by now why she slept with Borell, of course. As a result of spreading her legs for the Imperial Advisor, there seemed to be nothing Borell knew which Elelar could not find out. Now she had news which confirmed the visions the demon girl had spoken of at Kandahar, the prophecy that Armian's shade served: Valdania and Kinto were about to fight an all-out war, the Kintish Kingdoms resisting the Empire's attempt to crush them at last after centuries of awaiting the right opportunity.

"Valdania's armies will be fully committed to the wars in Kinto and the Moorlands, with Outlookers left to hold the rest of the Empire." Elelar's voice had been rich with promise. "The Valdani won't have enough weapons, men, and money available to suppress a full-scale rebellion in Sileria."

She had gripped his forearm in her excitement, the soft unscarred palm of a *torena* pressing against his skin. She had whispered to him like a lover, "There will never be a better time."

So now, at summer's end, he returned to Josarian's side to share the information and make new plans. Elelar had been ordered to return unfashionably early to Shaljir, before the northern winds had finished cooling the summer-baked city. She was urgently needed to act as a link between Josarian and the Alliance as they gathered support and information for the rebellion's boldest move yet. Tansen approved the Alliance's new plan, and he believed that Josarian, the Society, and even the Guardians would, too. After the Empire entered into its first violent engagement with the Kintish Kingdoms and became irrevocably committed to the war there, then the Silerian rebels would strike a blow that would be felt in Valda itself.

CAMPED DEEP IN the mountains south of Britar, Zimran relieved Lann in the empty hours of the night, taking over the sentry duty as the others slept. Clumsy as the Outlookers were, they had nonetheless raided a rebel camp four days ago, killing nine people—including two Guardians. *So much for the Otherworld,* Zim thought; he didn't see much point in communing with shades of the dead if they didn't bother to mention that you were about to *become* one of them.

Mirabar had wanted to put a ring of protective fire around the camp's perimeter tonight. Zimran thought few things were more likely to attract Outlookers than a vast circle of magic fire blazing away in the middle of the night, but it was actually Najdan who had talked her out of it, convincing her that good vigilance would suffice. Zimran tried to picture Amitan's description of how the assassin and the demon girl had met, but he couldn't really; by the time Zimran had joined up with them, Najdan had become—at Kiloran's order—Mirabar's constant shadow.

Mirabar . . . well, she wasn't a bad girl, really, not once you got used to her. Zimran could think of women he'd rather be spending his days and nights with—a brief memory of the "abduction" of Porsall's wife made him smile— but he didn't really mind Mirabar. Recuperating in Cheylan's camp after escaping from the fortress at Britar months ago had taught him that superstitions about demons, like all other superstitions, were just children's nonsense. Admittedly, Mirabar was even stranger looking than Cheylan. That *hair* . . . Lann had practically fallen to his knees and started praying when Josarian had first brought her back to Dalishar to meet them.

Josarian had told them all incredible tales about journeying to Shaljir, meeting with a *torena* who had introduced him to something called the Alliance, going to Zilar to meet Kiloran's son Srijan, and finally finding Kiloran himself. The story of that night strained Zimran's credulity: a palace of water beneath the surface of Lake Kandahar, a ball of fire plunging through the water and turning into a girl, the shade of Armian greeting them from the Otherworld, prophecies of destiny and freedom . . . The other men at Dalishar had swallowed it whole, though, letting this wild tale slide down as smoothly as ripe summer melon.

Remembering it now, Zimran shrugged. Exaggerated though it probably was, it was the most amazing story he'd ever heard, and it brought men to Josarian's cause by the hundreds. That was just as well, because as the Outlookers stepped up their efforts to suppress the rebellion, men were dying faster, too.

When will it end? When will Josarian be satisfied?

Driving out the Valdani was a nice dream, but Zimran was highly skeptical that it could be accomplished. The Valdani ruled the world. They had ruled Sileria for two centuries. That was how it was. Could the fierce Moorland tribes drive them out of the Moorlands? No; and there were more Moorlanders than Silerians. Could the conquered Kintish states make them leave? No; and the Kintish were wealthier than the Silerians.

Zimran hated the Valdani, too; of course he did! He'd been out risking his life and smuggling goods past the Outlookers for years while Josarian sat at home with his wife and urged his neighbors to keep the "peace." They'd caught Zimran twice, too. The first time, he'd beggared himself paying bribes to stay out of the mines. The second time . . . Josarian had killed two of them.

One impulsive act of madness, and Josarian had run amuck. Now Zimran could never go home—even if the Outlookers would let him, Emeldar's water was poisoned. So he and the others all lived like bandits in the mountains now, risking their lives every day, fighting the Valdani, killing, looting, burning, stealing . . . and then giving away whatever they stole.

All spring, even into summer, Zimran had prayed for peace. Even after Britar, he had continued to hope. The Valdani undoubtedly wanted this costly insanity to end. The mountain clans would soon grow tired of suffering in Josarian's name. The merchants and *toreni* would finally weary of the inconvenience of a rebellion in their backyard. The Society would eventually object to the increased numbers of Outlookers patrolling the mountains. *Someone* would surely have sense enough to insist on a truce, and Josarian would come to his senses and agree. Bloodfeuds were started in anger and ended in the cold light of reason. Josarian himself bemoaned the way the Sirdari had destroyed themselves with their endless bloodfeuds! He knew

that the season for violence must be a short one. Zimran
had clung to this belief and, loyal to the cousin he loved,
had fought by his side in the meantime.

Josarian had abandoned them at summer's birth to honor
his bloodpact with Tansen; much as Zimran loathed the
roshah, he had to admit that his cousin had done what a
man should. Humiliated by Josarian's betrayal—leaving
Emelen in charge—he had nonetheless remained loyal in
his cousin's absence. He and Emelen had made vicious
reprisals against the Outlookers for the massacres at Malthenar, Morven, and Garabar. They stood by those who
stood by Josarian and brutally punished anyone who
didn't. Zim still felt nauseated when he remembered the
way he and Emelen had killed Arlen; but they had to make
sure no one would be tempted enough by Valdani gold to
follow in Arlen's footsteps.

Zimran blamed Josarian for killing those first two Outlookers on the smuggling trail; but Josarian had saved *him*
from capture that night. Zimran blamed Josarian for getting
him and twenty other men thrown into prison; but Josarian
had risked death to free him from the fortress at Britar.
Zimran was a smuggler who didn't like being a rebel any
better than he had liked being an outlaw. But he would
stand by Josarian as Josarian had stood by him, for that
was how a man lived.

The new moon lay on her back in the lush sky, ending
the nights of total darkness. Zimran briefly recalled the
widow he used to visit during the dark-moon. She was
displaced, like everyone else now, her home abandoned,
her life shattered. The first northern breezes crept through
the mountains tonight to soothe the heat-cracked earth. The
nights were becoming cooler, the days softer. The season
was advancing, and Zimran knew they were running out
of time to make peace. The Outlookers, who had no flesh
for Sileria's summer sun, would find the days more bear-
able now. They would not tire so quickly now as they did
in the heat of summer. They would not give up as easily

now. The northern winds would give them heart, and the fighting would grow even worse.

Zimran hadn't been particularly surprised that the Guardians had joined Josarian, for his cousin was a persuasive man, and who could expect sense from a bunch of ghost-talking, fire-breathing sorcerers anyhow? But the Society . . . Zimran had never expected that. And now this thing called the Alliance, made up of merchants and city-dwellers and *toreni!*

Now men spoke of war instead of a bloodfeud. Now men spoke of making the Valdani leave Sileria forever, instead of just leaving the mountains alone. Now they spoke of freedom and glory and . . . *now* there was no end in sight for any of them. Would this mad dream of Josarian's go on until they were all dead, slaughtered by Valdani swords?

Zimran, who had loved his life, wanted to weep for its loss.

A CRAZED *ZANAR* stumbled into Dalishar sometime after dawn. Sentries had already warned Josarian of his approach, as they had warned him of Outlookers patrolling all access routes to this site. As was bound to happen, someone had finally told the Valdani where Josarian was based. He'd had his men trying to find out *who* for nearly a twin-moon.

Wondering what had brought a *zanar* here, Josarian invited him to enter one of the sacred caves. His sister Jalilar, who had come to live here this summer after growing tired of sleeping without her husband, offered the man food and drink. Even a *zanar* probably wanted some refreshment after the long climb to Dalishar.

Skinny, unkempt, and shaking with fatigue, the *zanar* drank deeply but refused the food. Then he stared long and hard at Josarian. Finally he asked, "Are you the Fire-bringer?"

Jalilar burst out laughing. Josarian cleared his throat. The *zanar* looked like he had expected no better.

"You know that they're saying you are," the *zanar* said.

"They also say that I'm dead, that I'm a disinherited Valdani prince trying to get revenge, that I'm the ghost of Daurion . . ." Josarian shook his head. "They say a lot of things."

"What do you intend to do about it?"

Josarian shrugged. "Nothing."

"Nothing?" The *zanar* rose to his feet, sputtering. "You may be the Chosen One! The Awaited One! You may be the one destined to lead us out of bondage, to drive out the Conquerors—"

"The Kints drove out the Conquerors," Josarian pointed out as kindly as possible. The legend was very old.

"And he will lead the people to glory, making of them a warrior race once again; and drive out the foreigner, drive away the roshaheen . . . Surely you know the scriptures!"

"I can't read."

"Then I will recite them for you!"

Jalilar hopped to her feet. "If you'll excuse me, there is much work to be done in camp."

Josarian glared at her retreating back as she escaped from the cave. Before the *zanar* could do as threatened, he quickly asked, "What is your name?"

"Jalan."

"Jalan, I have never claimed to be the Firebringer, and—"

"He will not claim his glory himself! That is for Dar to do! He will plunge into ecstatic union with the goddess and—"

"Yes, I understand. But I'm not the one."

"But you *are* . . . I look at you and I see the favor of the goddess."

What did Tansen always say? Men saw what they wanted to see. Josarian changed tactics, "Then I am honored to be favored of the goddess, for I have been faithful and true all my life, b—"

"You must come back to Darshon with me."

"I can't," he said firmly. "We're fighting a rebellion."

"Yes!" Jalan cried. "Yes! And if you are the Firebringer come at last—at *last!*—all Sileria will flock to your banner, and our liberation shall come to pass!"

"And if I'm not the Firebringer, I'll die in the volcano," Josarian pointed out reasonably. "Wouldn't it be better if I just stayed here and *fought* until—"

"Your light cannot be mistaken! Has no one before ever asked you to come forth and embrace Dar?"

"Well, yes, but . . ." The *zanareen* were *always* seeking recruits.

"I knew it! Why did you not go?"

He almost laughed. "My mother wouldn't let me. I was only thirteen, and—"

"Yes! It would have shown by then! The light of Her favor! Yes, you were young, *young,* but already a man by then . . . Your destiny has always been to embrace Her. You should have gone!"

Perhaps another argument would be more effective. "But surely Armian is the Firebringer?"

"He's dead! The story of his shade bringing prophecy to you is all over the mountains."

In spreading the story, they had kept Tansen's relationship to Armian, as well as the murder, a secret, and had revealed only certain aspects of the extraordinary events at Kandahar. Even Kiloran honored their silence on certain subjects, for he was not eager to tell the world he had been defied and defeated by a boy nine years ago.

"Then you know," Josarian said, "that Armian convinced the Society and the Guardians to join the *shallaheen.* Our union was born of Armian's—"

"The Firebringer can't be *dead* before the battle is even begun, you fool! The Firebringer will *lead* us against the foreign invaders! Not spew prophecy from the Otherworld!"

The *zanareen* could be *so* single-minded. "Nonetheless, he—"

"And he was an assassin! Do you really think the goddess would embrace an *assassin?*"

Josarian held up his hands. "I claim no knowledge of what the goddess—" He stopped abruptly when Jalan seized his right hand.

"A marriage-mark." Jalan studied the scar made by Calidar years ago. "You have a wife?"

"I did. She died."

"Ahhh." Jalan's eyes gleamed with satisfaction. "Of course. The goddess took her."

Josarian prickled. He did not like casual talk of Calidar's death. "*Childbirth* took her."

"The goddess freed you from her—"

"No."

"—that you might be free to embrace Her at Darshon, to serve Her will, to follow your destiny!"

"*No.*"

"Don't you see?"

"Many men lose wives, Jalan, and mine—"

"Yours was *destined* to die, to free you for a higher purpose."

"There *was* no higher purpose than loving Calidar," he snapped, smarting with anger, recoiling from this madman's suggestions.

"You see?" Jalan pounced. "Dar knew you would not leave your wife willingly, not as others have. Dar knew you must lose her before you would consecrate your life to the Fires!"

Disgusted, Josarian pulled hard to get his hand away from Jalan. "You're wrong."

"You know I speak the truth! You *feel* it in your heart. You hear the call of the goddess!"

"*I* hear a madman gloating about my wife's death!"

"In time, you will go to Her. Even *I* feel Her pull in your presence."

"Then *you* go to Her."

"She calls you, not me, to the Fires."

"How convenient."

"You will feel Her call, too. In time, you will go to Her, as is your destiny."

"In time, I will die on the point of a Valdani sword," Josarian said, rising to escape, eager to get away from this man. "Now, if you will excuse me . . ."

"And he will join with Her in ecstatic union, offering his flesh to the Fires as a man offers his flesh to a woman . . ."

Josarian escaped into the sunshine and kept walking until he was well away from the sound of that voice, the offense of that quavering, insistent proselytizing.

Falian, whose face was now scarred from Tansen's blade and the events of that first night at Dalishar, was outside. He paused in the practice of his swordplay, looked over his shoulder, and smiled sympathetically. "No one likes *zanareen*."

Josarian nodded and forced an answering smile, not wanting Falian and the other men present to see how disturbed he was by the encounter. Dar knew he had blamed himself often enough for Calidar's death. If he had not gotten her with child . . . He wanted her back, wanted her here now more than he wanted to fight the Valdani or be free. Without thinking, he drew her scarf out of his tunic and pressed it against his face. Sorrow and loss pricked him sharply, because he realized, for the first time, that the silky material no longer bore her scent. It smelled like *him* now, from the many months it had spent pressed against his heart.

Calidar . . . A small thing, in its way, the loss of her scent on a scarf which, he knew, probably hadn't *really* smelled of her for months and months. But it crushed his heart, all the same. Longing for her, he called up a hundred aching memories, rekindling her life in his mind.

She'd had a temper, his wife, as well as a deep, wicked laugh. Her waist was tiny, though the rest of her was generous; she hadn't minded losing that tiny waist to bear a child. And *strong*, ah, that woman had been strong. Not as strong as him, but she could lift anything that Zimran could. She used to go barefoot all year, until the weather got too cold, disdaining the fine shoes he'd once brought her from Cavasar. She usually stood with her right hand on her hip, gesturing with her left, and her unruly dark hair was always tumbling down her back by the day's end. The marriage-mark on her right palm had grown inflamed after their wedding, making a fat, irregular scar when it finally healed. A sign of bad luck, some said, but she had loved her husband fiercely and merely laughed at such superstitions . . .

Calidar . . . Josarian turned away from his men so they wouldn't see the mist in his eyes.

By all the Fires, if he believed he had condemned her to death by marrying her, then he would gladly throw himself into Darshon—or off a cliff. But it was an insane suggestion, one he'd have to be more than half mad to listen to.

Calidar . . .

Sick with longing, with a grief that hadn't been this sharp in months, he deserted camp to find solace in the lonely wildness of the mountains. Some memories a man ran from, such as Tansen's; some memories, such as Josarian's, a man held dear and clung to. Some memories should never be profaned by the ravings of a wild-eyed fanatic.

Summer was dying now, the brutal heat of the days softening into glowing warmth. The land was stunned, withered, and brown from the blazing sun and dry skies of the cruelest season. Even up here at Dalishar, distant from the world, he could often smell brush fires on the wind.

Tansen was due back any day now to report on his progress in the east. Josarian was merely waiting for his bloodbrother before going out on another raid, another campaign to gain support, more meetings with Guardians, assassins, waterlords, and the Alliance. Mirabar was busy farther south. Giants like Kiloran and Baran understood what was at stake and had called a truce, but some of the lesser waterlords were a little harder to convince. Some simply did as they were told, but others, it had quickly become apparent, needed the sort of convincing spectacle that only Mirabar could provide. To the amazement of the other Guardians, she had developed such a strong bond with Armian that she could Call him even without the *shir*. That was just as well, too, since Kiloran had no intention of letting her have it.

Hoping Jalan had finally gone away, Josarian returned to camp that afternoon with a stag slung over his shoulders, slain for his sister. Jalilar had come to Dalishar to be with Emelen who, to her consternation, wasn't even here. After clobbering her brother for turning her into a widow while her husband still lived, she had decided to stay here anyhow—and Jalilar really knew how to dress meat and feed a man. He'd miss her when she left, as she surely would before long; tired of sleeping alone, she intended to go east with the next runner he sent from Dalishar to Emelen. Meanwhile, he and his men enjoyed her cooking.

He recognized a familiar figure when he approached the caves. Tansen was there, lean, quick, and sharp as a blade, instructing half a dozen men in the use of their swords. Josarian grinned, glad to see him. As always, Tansen was more reserved than he, but plainly glad to see him, too.

They went into Josarian's cave and sat down together over a bottle of smuggled Kintish spirits that Tan had brought back from Liron, exchanging news and information. The rebellion was already spreading in the east, and they had struck the Outlookers hard several times over the summer. Josarian had heard about some, but not all, of the raids.

"The Outlookers weren't expecting trouble in the east," Tansen said, taking off his harness and relaxing into cushions stolen from some Valdani estate. "They thought the rebellion would stay confined to the west."

"It's the same in the district of Shaljir. They were unprepared for attack. Their losses were heavy at first."

"I know. People talked of little else as I came through

there on my way here." He eyed Josarian and added, "There is *one* other thing they talk of, though."

"What's that?"

"The Firebringer."

Josarian rolled his eyes. "Don't *you* start."

"I met Jalan when I got here." Tansen's mouth quirked. "His conversation is limited, but very interesting."

"I thought *you* thought the Firebringer was dead."

"Well . . . the Valdani are still here, so I guess I was wrong."

Josarian sighed. "This will be a long night, if you're going to start siding with Jalan."

Tansen looked at him in surprise. "I didn't think it would bother you so much."

"Then he hasn't told you *all* his theories."

Tansen stripped off his tunic. "You can tell me while I wash. I'm carrying half of Sileria's dirt around with me."

So he told him. Tansen had shared far more horrifying things with him, after all, than the insulting ravings of a madman.

Soaking wet and shivering a little from the cold water, Tansen wrapped himself in a blanket and sat by the woodless fire. He was silent for a long time, which made Josarian uneasy; he was accustomed to Tan's skepticism and didn't like the thoughtful expression on his face.

"You don't think it's true, do you?" Josarian challenged at last.

"Actually . . . no." Tansen stared into the flames. "But I know what it is to feel you've caused the death of someone you love." He met Josarian's gaze at last. "Did everyone in Gamalan die because I found and sheltered Armian? Would they have died even if I had not helped him? Would I have died, too, if I had been there, instead of on the coast that night? Even if I had never seen him? What part did I play in what happened to my mother, my sister, my grandfather . . ."

"Tan . . ."

"I'll never know." He leaned forward. "And neither will you."

"I . . ." Josarian looked away. "Jalan was right about one thing. I wouldn't be here if Calidar were still alive. I wouldn't have started smuggling with Zim. I would never . . ." He shifted restlessly. "And if I hadn't . . . would any of this be happening?"

Tansen shrugged, frowning in thought. "The demon girl's visions were of me, not you."

"Mirabar?" When Tansen nodded, he asked, "Then would you have led the *shallah* rebellion?"

"I don't know what I would be doing if you were safely tucked in bed in Emeldar right now," Tansen admitted. "I wanted vengeance when I came home. I wanted Valdani blood. But . . . I had no plan, no purpose, no goal. And I didn't have your vision." He put his hand on Josarian's shoulder, doing the comforting for a change. "You looked into the future and saw rebellion, war, maybe even freedom. You saw something that would outlive both of us, something much bigger than personal vengeance or private hatred. I never saw any of that until *you* showed it to me. I can't be sure that I *ever* would have seen it, without you."

Josarian stared into the flames. "Then if I must be here for all of this to happen . . ." He sighed, wishing the ache would ease. "I would have rather died a hundred times than be the cause of Calidar's death, but . . ."

"But?"

"*She* would have rather died for something than nothing. For a reason, rather than sheer chance."

Tansen inhaled deeply and leaned back, staring into the sacred flames. "To see *shallaheen* drive Valdani tribute collectors out of their villages," he said slowly, "rather than cower and let them take whatever they want. To see Silerians put aside their bloodfeuds to pick up swords, standing side by side against the Outlookers. To see the dust of mounted riders fleeing from us in fear, and to dream of them someday fleeing Sileria and leaving it forever. To claim our land, our cities, our *pride* after a thousand years of serving foreign rulers ..." He nodded, his voice warming well beyond its usual measure of laconism. "Josarian, I want to live more than you do, and *I* think it's worth dying for. Maybe she would have, too."

"Maybe she would have, too," he echoed softly. "I just wish I could have asked her."

24

NAJDAN HAD FEARED only two things in life: hunger and Kiloran. Then *she* had appeared, overwhelming those fears with the fury of her fire. Young and small, fine-boned and tireless, blessed by Dar and cursed with visions, unprotected by rank, family, clan, or companions, Mirabar had gone alone into Kiloran's lair, faced the most powerful waterlord in the world, and somehow conquered him. Alone beneath the surface of Kandahar with a merciless wizard, his deadly assassins, those dangerous mountain rebels, and an arrogant *torena*, she had bent them all to her will, and now they served the shades she Called forth and the visions which haunted her.

Now, as ordered by Kiloran, Najdan served Mirabar, too. For his master's sake, he tried to learn all he could about her. For her sake, he protected her from danger. Now that they were no longer enemies, he honored her courage and her power; and he respected her as he had previously respected no one but Kiloran.

Najdan no longer feared Mirabar as he had in the beginning. He knew now that, whatever else she was, she was no demon; she wasn't even a killer. She had captured and caged him, could have killed him at any time, and probably should have; but she hadn't, not even when he'd tried to kill her.

He had finally recognized her true greatness at Kandahar. The others there all did as she told them. Even Kiloran, though he clearly did not like it, bowed to her judgment, and the assassins at Kandahar were afraid of her. Searlon had not been there, but Najdan suspected that even Searlon himself would have to acknowledge that forces beyond his reckoning guided Mirabar, just as powers beyond Najdan's dreams acted through her.

And so Najdan served her, with the courage and loyalty he had offered Kiloran for twenty years. Najdan was not a great man, but he was ideally suited to serve great men—or a great woman. He had pulled himself out of the most hopeless poverty a man could be born to and made a success of his life by knowing what he could do better than other men and who could best reward him for it. For twenty years, Kiloran had made him one of the wealthiest assassins in Sileria. Whatever this girl could offer him in exchange for his service, Najdan knew it wouldn't be wealth; she was poor even for a Guardian. He only knew that when a man saw a prophet, a visionary, a sorceress feared even by Kiloran, then he'd be a fool to count pieces of silver and gold to weigh her worth.

He escorted Mirabar north from Britar now, her mission there successfully completed, a recalcitrant waterlord brought into the rebellion in accordance with the will of the Society *and* the Otherworld. Now their small party of four argued about which way to go. As usual, the two rebels, Lann and Zimran, were not showing Mirabar the respect which Najdan increasingly felt was her due. And as usual, Mirabar used her tongue the way an assassin used a *shir*.

"Dalishar," Zimran insisted. "We're suppposed to return to Dalishar, and I don't care *what* kind of cryptic messages come to you in your visions, I'm—"

"And I don't care who is waiting back at Dalishar to spread her legs for you," Mirabar snapped. It took only the briefest acquaintance to understand what most motivated Zimran. "We can't go there!"

"Sirana," Lann said, "perhaps if you explained why we can't go . . ."

Najdan decided he did not need explanations. If Mirabar said they must not return to Dalishar now, that was good enough for him. She was a powerful sorceress, while the other two were mere *shallaheen.* He said so, glaring coldly at Lann and Zimran.

"Some of us have been used to doing our *own* bidding all these years," Zimran said contemptuously, "rather than following the dictates of a waterlord and—"

"Shallaheen follow the will of the Society, too," Najdan snapped. "Not to mention the dictates of the Valdani, the *toreni,* the merchants, and the Guardians. The lowest of creatures always do the bidding of all the others in the forest."

Lann's face darkened as he reached for his sword. Seeing his movement, Mirabar slapped a small hand against his chest—hard—and physically jumped into the center of the argument, her eyes blazing as she whirled to glare at them all.

"Enough," she said fiercely. "Will we kill each other so that the Outlookers don't have to bother doing it?"

"No woman waits for me at Dalishar." Zimran sounded sulky. "My cousin is there. May I respectfully remind the *sirana* who leads the *shallah* rebellion?"

"And who leads Josarian?" Najdan countered. "He listens to the *sirana* better than you do, you woman-faced—"

"All right, let's leave insults out of the discussion, shall we?" Mirabar eyed the way Zimran's hand twitched toward his *yahr.* "I'm telling you we will not live to reach Dalishar if we attempt to go there right now."

Zimran looked sharply at her. "So the Otherworld *does* warn some of you?"

She said only, "The Sign of the Three blocks the path to Dalishar in my visions. We must go to Zilar."

"Zilar?" Lann's hairy jaw dropped. "Sweet Dar, *sirana,* why so far away?"

Mirabar sighed. "I don't know. The Beckoner wants us

there." She shrugged. "We are needed in Zilar."

"That's a long way," Najdan said slowly. They had nearly run out of money. "We'll need to rob a Valdan again."

To his surprise, Lann laughed. "I never thought that robbing Valdani would become such a humdrum matter!"

Zimran thought it over for a moment, then smiled slowly. "I believe that the Imperial Advisor owns an estate between here and Zilar."

The argument settled, Najdan smiled, too. "Ahhh."

"IT'S A FILTHY business, this." Josarian's voice was subdued, his expression tight as he walked through the streets of Zilar, followed by a silent, grim-faced crowd.

"Something an assassin would do," Tansen agreed, walking at his side.

Srijan, who accompanied them, glared at them both. "Would you rather we had not discovered him?"

The *sriliah* they had been seeking for over a twin-moon had given enough information to the Outlookers to cost the *shallah* rebels money, lives, safety, and time. The names of nearly thirty of Josarian's men were now known, with substantial rewards offered for all of them. Josarian, of course, headed the list; the Valdani were now willing to pay enough for his head to turn a *shallah* into a minor *toren*. The next-highest reward was offered for Tansen shah Gamalani, an "escaped felon" who had stolen the valuable swords of a *shatai* who had briefly been a guest of the Commander of Cavasar earlier in the year.

So, Tansen reflected, Koroll had not only finally figured out what had happened, he had even come up with a creative story to conceal his own part in Tansen's release from captivity, all those months ago, fully armed and secretly eager to help Josarian kill more Outlookers. Well, such ingenuity had undoubtedly helped Koroll wind up where he was today: High Commander of all Sileria.

Far worse than the minor—and inevitable—inconvenience of many of the *shallah* rebel leaders now being known to the Valdani were the additional problems caused by the *sriliah*'s violation of *lirtahar*. The countryside around Dalishar was now so heavily infested with Outlookers that coming and going had become virtually impossible without entering into battle, usually with the distinct disadvantage of being the attacked rather than the attackers. Leaving behind enough men to defend the caves (and his sister), Josarian had recently spread word through the mountains that no one was to go near Dalishar until the territory could be fully secured by the rebels. So many Outlookers were now permanently based at Chandar, the nearest village to the Dalishar caves, that it was tempting to poison the water there, as they had done at Emeldar. However, in fear of such a plan, the Outlookers now routinely forced a *shallah* prisoner to drink before they did every single time they drew water from a Silerian fountain, well, stream, or lake.

In addition, a rebel camp had recently been attacked, and nine people were killed, including two Guardians. An attack on a huge tax shipment had failed a few days ago because the Outlookers had clearly been expecting it; someone had obviously told them about the rebels massing in the area the previous day.

The Society had finally discovered the *sriliah* in Zilar, though they had revealed the information only to Josarian. The man, still unaware that he'd been identified, had been clever and careful—but not quite enough, in the end.

Two days ago, Josarian had instructed his men to spread a false rumor in Zilar, indicating that he was about to abduct *Toren* Ronall—Elelar's husband. Yesterday, a tailor named Harjan, who enjoyed a more comfortable life than most *shallaheen*, had discreetly disappeared from town for the day while his wife claimed he was in bed with fever. Josarian and Tansen had followed him to a meeting with an Outlooker whom Tan had instantly recognized: Myrell. It had been tempting to kill that putrid, baby-murdering Valdan on the spot, but there were only two of them against twenty Outlookers, and they had more urgent business at hand. They'd followed Myrell's runner last night, making sure that there was no mistake, that he was definitely heading for Ronall's nearby estate to warn him. At dawn, they'd watched Outlookers riding to the estate to prepare for an attack.

So now, positive that they'd finally found the man who'd betrayed them to the Valdani, Tansen and Josarian made their way through Zilar to Harjan's comfortable house.

"What are you going to do?" Srijan asked eagerly, keeping his voice low to avoid being overheard by the villagers who followed them.

The people here knew that something deadly was about to happen, almost as if this were a Society assassination. Josarian and Tansen would not simply enter a town unannounced and walk boldly through it, grim-faced and subdued, because they had nothing better to do today. Everyone knew that they had been searching for the traitor in their midst. Tansen had witnessed many scenes similar to this in his boyhood. Oh, yes, people knew why he and Josarian were here today, and why Srijan was there to display the Society's support for them. People here had already guessed why they had come to Zilar. Now hundreds of dark eyes watched them, round with apprehension, shadowed with suffering. For no one yet knew whom they had come to punish, and everyone feared it might be a loved one, a friend, or a relative.

"What will you do?" Srijan repeated.

Tansen glanced at Josarian's tense face, then gave Srijan a quelling look. The assassin had retrieved his *shir* from the *tirshah* where Tansen had left it lying at summer's beginning, but Tan could easily take it from him again if need be. However, Elelar had lectured him firmly on the foolishness of angering Kiloran—as if he might have already forgotten what it could lead to—and he had promised to try to tolerate Srijan for the sake of the rebellion.

"We'll do what's necessary," Tan said briefly.

Josarian's breath was uneven, his face slightly pale.

"I've killed many men," he said softly. "Far too many already, really, though I know there will be many more. But . . . I've never killed a Silerian. Another *shallah*. One of us."

"Oh, they die as easily as Valdani, you'll find." Srijan smirked.

Josarian ignored him. "I wish . . ." He sighed. "Oh, well. It cannot be helped. I will make enemies here today. Everyone honors *lirtahar,* everyone understands assassination. Everyone knows why I will kill the *sriliah* . . . But surely someone here cares about him, and so I will make enemies."

It was true, Tansen realized. Now that they were here, now that they had found the traitor, they were caught in the paradox of Silerian culture. If Josarian did *not* kill Harjan today, he would lose respect and influence overnight. Women would doubt him, men would despise him. There would be more betrayals, too, because not only would the risk of betrayal suddenly seem negligible, but betraying such a weak man wouldn't be considered nearly as great a sin as betraying a respected one. And the Valdani were offering so much gold for any break in the silence . . . However, if Josarian *did* kill Harjan today, then, yes, he would make enemies. Everyone disapproved of a *sriliah,* but even among those who reviled Harjan's betrayal and understood Josarian's actions today, there would nonetheless be those who, probably because of a bloodtie to Harjan, must become Josarian's enemies after this. From there, discontent would spread. Not seriously, perhaps, but the rebel alliance was too young to shrug off *any* threat to the unity of the *shallaheen.* Just as they couldn't afford any appearance of weakness in Josarian, they also couldn't afford a single *shallah* resenting his sword or claiming personal vengeance against him.

Tansen knew what he must do.

I did not come home to kill shallaheen . . .

Was this Dar's vengeance, that he must do this hideous thing today, that he must become like the assassin—the bloodfather—he had murdered in silence on that dark, windy cliff nine years ago?

Please, there must be another way, another answer. I do not want to slaughter my own kind!

Even as he silently cried out for escape from his duty, the *shatai* in him focused on the task at hand.

"You will make no enemies here today," he said to his bloodbrother. "You must . . . stand as the injured party. I will do the rest."

Srijan jerked with surprise. Josarian shook his head.

"No, Tan. It is my office."

Tansen kept his voice low. "You can't perform it," he said tersely. "You can't afford enemies, and you know that we cannot walk away from this."

"I am the one—"

"Who must lead the rest."

"A man faces his own—"

"I told you once before: never let pride lead you into a fight."

"What about honor?"

"Yours must be served in a different way." Keeping his voice low, he stopped and looked hard into Josarian's troubled eyes. "Think like a leader instead of a *shallah*, and you'll see that I'm right. If this were Arlen and the aftermath of Malthenar, you could do no wrong, for no one knew or cared about him and everyone craved vengeance then. But this . . ." He shook his head. "This is a native son of a comfortable village on a quiet day. No one here has seen the bloodshed Harjan has caused. No one here has suffered because of him."

Josarian looked down, looked away, looked everywhere but at Tansen. "This is not how it should be."

"I agree. But this is the way it is."

Srijan sneered at them both. "Tansen is a hired killer, anyhow, Josarian. What's the problem?"

They ignored him. Face crumpling with emotion, Josarian finally nodded. "Yes, Tan," he said at last, his voice borne on a note of sorrow. "You're right."

Tansen turned and continued walking to Harjan's house. "Stay silent. You stand only as the injured party." It was a position usually reserved for one who had petitioned an assassin to seek justice on his or her behalf. By custom, the injured party could seek the death of an offender without, in most cases, instigating a bloodfeud.

"You are *not* an assassin," Srijan muttered contemptuously.

"No," Tansen agreed. "I'm a *shatai,* a son of the greatest warrior caste in the world, honed in stone and steel, honored by the gods of Kinto and the sorcerers of the Stone Forest, respected by all men and feared by most. *You,*" he concluded with bitter satisfaction, "are merely a murderer with an enchanted blade." He strode up to Harjan's house and left Srijan sputtering behind him in outrage.

Josarian took his place, in plain view behind Tansen, and stood by silently while Tansen called Harjan out of his house. Straightening his gossamer tunic, Harjan came outside and gave Tansen a smile which was nervous and quizzical. His wife stood in the doorway of their home, a plump woman with a wrinkled forehead and thick fingers. Tansen didn't allow himself to wonder if she loved her husband, if there were children inside the house, or if the man's brother was somewhere behind him in the crowd. He focused on what he must do.

"Harjan. Here stands Josarian mar Gershon," Tansen began, "whom you have injured with betrayal to the Valdani."

Though they were undoubtedly expecting the accusation, the crowd gasped collectively and began arguing excitedly. Harjan's wife brought her hands up to her mouth, her face contorting with fear. Harjan shook his head and immediately starting babbling denials.

Unperturbed, Tansen recited the events of the previous day, recounting how he had witnessed the supposedly bedridden Harjan's meeting with Myrell, the butcher of Malthenar, Morven, and Garabar. When he was done, the

villagers watched Harjan with hard expressions, waiting
for an explanation.

"The Outlooker captain had—had placed *orders* with
me, *siran*!" Harjan insisted. "It was a . . . a *business* meeting! Yes, yes, I know the Valdani are supposed to be our
enemies now, but—please, *siran*! A man must be practical! I have a wife and children to feed! I have—"

"Zilar was the only village to receive news of the
planned abduction of the *toren* named Ronall," Tansen interrupted. "You are the only man from Zilar to have seen
Myrell yesterday. Myrell sent a runner to warn Ronall last
night. This morning, Myrell's men rode to Ronall's estate
to await Josarian."

"That—that has nothing to *do* with me!" Harjan cried,
sweating profusely now.

"How else did Myrell learn—?"

"How should *I* know how the Outlookers get their information?"

"Why did Myrell give you gold yesterday?"

Harjan was breathing heavily, almost panting. "What
gold?"

"We saw you accept it from him, Harjan. We saw you
count it."

"He was paying me for . . . for the work I'd done for
him!"

"What work?"

"I'm a tailor. He admired my work in . . . when the Outlookers were here in the spring, and he ordered—"

"You brought him no clothing," Tansen said. "You only
talked with him."

"He paid me for garments already delivered!"

"When?"

"I—I—"

"Srijan," Tansen said, enlisting the support of the Society in front of the villagers, "the last time Harjan met
with the Outlooker captain, did he deliver garments to
him?"

"No," Srijan said. "He spoke to him, and he received

gold, which I watched him count. The next day, sixteen *shallaheen* and four assassins died while attacking a tax shipment in the Amalidar Mountains. It was obvious that the attack was expected."

"You've been attacking lots of shipments," Harjan said frantically. "Of course the Outlookers—"

"How many times is Myrell paying you for those garments?" Tansen snapped. "You must have worked nonstop day and night since the day I was born to earn so much gold that you can't carry it all home in one trip."

A woman in the crowd pushed her son forward, surprising them all. As was proper, Tansen showed the mother respect and allowed her to speak.

"My son is Harjan's apprentice, *siran,*" she told Tansen.

"Ah." He looked at the boy. "Speak up, then. Has your master indeed filled an order for the Outlooker captain?"

"No, *siran,*" the boy said, wide-eyed and shaking. "There has never been such an order. We have never had a client from among the *roshaheen.*"

Harjan made one last attempt to deny his betrayal. "An ignorant boy, *siran*! He doesn't know who my clients are!"

Disgusted by the performance, tired of prolonging the inevitable, Tansen struck him hard across the face. The wife in the doorway screamed. Harjan fell to his knees and started weeping.

"Answer the charge against your honor, *sriliah,*" Tansen said quietly. "Get up and fight."

Harjan spoke with difficulty, forcing the words out between huge gulps of air. "I . . . can't . . . You are Tansen. You slaughtered twenty Moorlanders in a single night. You slayed an entire ship of Kintish pirates."

Tansen recognized the ridiculous boasts he had spread through the mountains while seeking Josarian. Now that he had survived the bloodvow made by Kiloran, now that he fought at Josarian's side, people actually believed and repeated those absurd stories.

Harjan looked up at him with fear-glazed eyes. "If I answer your challenge, you will slay me before my hand is halfway to my *yahr*. And what use will a *yahr* be against your swords, anyhow?"

"Then I will kill you quickly," Tansen promised quietly, "and tomorrow we will purify your body with fire for your journey to the Otherworld." Today they would leave the corpse where everyone could see it and recognize the price of taking Valdani gold in exchange for betraying Josarian.

Harjan convulsed with sobs as Tansen's right sword hissed out of its sheath and flashed brilliantly in the sunlight.

"Dar have mercy on my soul!" Harjan wailed. "They offered so much money. So much! And you must all die soon, anyhow! How much longer can it last? How much longer can mountain peasants defy the most powerful Empire in the world?"

"Bid your wife farewell," Tansen ordered, raising his sword, "and make your peace with Dar."

Harjan's wife leaned weakly against the doorway, weeping silently, tears streaming from her eyes as she kept a plump hand clamped over her mouth.

"Go to Liron," Harjan advised her with his last moments of life. "There is no rebellion there."

"Yes, there is," Tansen said. "You're a poor informant, Harjan. Seventeen clans in the east are already sworn to Josarian's cause, including the Lironi themselves. Soon they'll convince their cousins in the city itself to join them."

Shock washed across Harjan's face. "You're lying," he whispered.

"You chose the wrong side when you betrayed your own kind," Tansen told him, speaking loud enough for everyone to hear. "We will win. And anyone who isn't with us is against us, and will pray the price!"

His blade flashed as he brought his arms down, its sharp edge cutting through flesh and muscle, dividing small bones, releasing a torrent of blood as it separated Harjan's head from his shoulders. The body fell sideways and lay upon the cobblestones in a fast-spreading crimson pool.

The head rolled once, then came to rest with blank, open eyes staring up at a sky more fiercely blue than any other.

Tansen gazed down at it for a moment, heart pounding, face expressionless. He flipped the blood off his sword, then wiped it quickly on Harjan's gossamer tunic, willfully shutting out the screams of the man's wife.

He had never told anyone this—not his *kaj,* not Josarian, not anyone—for it would have seemed a strange thing for a *shatai* to say; but the truth was . . . killing always sickened him.

THE BODY OF the *sriliah* still lay where it had fallen when Mirabar and her three-man escort entered Zilar toward sundown. The people here had heard of her by now, for the demon girl who had convinced the Society and the Guardians to join Josarian and Tansen was already famous—and infamous—throughout the mountains. Of course, even though they'd heard of her, people still had a tendency to recoil in shock when they first saw her. However, with Najdan at her side, fingering his *shir* and silencing any disrespect with the cold glare of an assassin, Mirabar scarcely noticed the Zilari as she watched Zimran bend down to examine the corpse lying on the cobblestones.

She immediately recognized the twists of woven rope Zimran held up for her to see, the strands dotted with the rough clay beads of a *shallah: So die all who betray their own kind. So die all who betray Josarian.*

Mirabar looked up at the villagers and asked the first one she singled out, "Who did this?"

Caught by her gaze, the man backed away in fear, saying nothing. Najdan stalked over, slapped him, and snapped, "Answer the *sirana!*"

"T . . . Tansen, *sirana.*" The villager swallowed. "It was Tansen. Only today."

"He was here today?" she repeated.

"Y— Yes."

"Alone?" Lann asked.

"No." The man's face brightened. "Josarian himself was with him! And, uh, Srijan the assassin. After . . . after it was done, Josarian gave the widow money and said he would ensure that her children do not starve, now that their father is—"

Zimran rose to his feet. "Where did Josarian and the others go afterward?"

The villagers looked at each other nervously. Najdan shook one of them impatiently. "We're with them, you idiot! Now tell us where we can find them."

"The *tirshah* at the edge of town. The one with the beautiful gardens."

Najdan's eyes narrowed. "The one that *toreni* use?"

His informant nodded and whispered breathily, "A *torena* is there right now, *siran.*"

"Ah." Najdan glanced over his shoulder at Mirabar. "It seems you were right, *sirana*. We're needed in Zilar today."

Zimran grinned. "Now isn't a good thing that I convinced you all to come here when the *sirana* suggested it?"

Mirabar rolled her eyes and proposed that Najdan lead the way, since he seemed to know which *tirshah* they were looking for.

Even the discovery of the *sriliah*'s corpse and the news of her allies' presence here was not startling enough to distract Mirabar from the beauty of Zilar itself as she passed through the rest of the town. She had heard about Zilar's wealth, its beautiful views, its lovely foliage, and, of course, its vast gold-tiled temple. As she followed Najdan past the enormous Kintish structure now, she found it far and away the most impressive building she had ever seen. Though its size alone would have been extraordinary enough, the exquisite workmanship of long-dead Kintish craftsmen pleased the eye and stunned the senses even after centuries of decay. Nothing, not the repairs which were obviously needed, or even the garish Sign of the Three the Valdani had erected in front of the temple more than a century ago, could mar its beauty.

The *tirshah* at the edge of town seemed too grand for the name, far more elegant than the few buildings Mirabar had ever set foot in before. Worried about the reaction her appearance would cause here, she started to pull a long, gauzy scarf over her flaming hair, but Najdan forestalled her.

"Kiloran owns the *tirshah*," he told her, too quietly for Lann and Zimran to overhear, "and the keeper is loyal to us."

"Kiloran?" she whispered.

"No one knows." He added, "Probably not even the *torena*."

"It's Elelar, isn't it?"

"Probably. She comes here to alert Srijan when she wants a meeting. She has done so for . . ." He shrugged. "Several years, anyhow."

"And they're here, too . . ." Eager to find out why they had all been gathered together again, except for Kiloran, she preceded the men into the *tirshah*.

Her appearance in the entrance hall caused considerable consternation, but Najdan's orders were obeyed quickly and unquestioningly. The party of four was shown into a reception room where Tansen, Josarian, Srijan, and Elelar were absorbed in conversation.

Josarian greeted them with surprised pleasure and affection, particularly his smooth-talking cousin. Tansen was mildly friendly to Lann, distantly polite to the rest of them. Srijan nodded briefly to Najdan and ignored the rest of them. Despite the circumstances, Elelar nonetheless displayed some of the ritual courtesy of a *torena*. Zimran, who had never seen Elelar before, was instantly transfixed by her. Having spent considerable time around Zimran, Mirabar found his intense reaction to the beautiful *torena* no more surprising than heat in summer. Mirabar cut short the greetings by asking Elelar what she was doing here.

"The Valdani have attacked a fortress on the northern

border of the Kintish Kingdoms," Elelar answered. "They met with surprisingly strong resistance. The Kints, it seems, expected the attack and were fully prepared to repel it." Elelar smiled with satisfaction. "The Palace of Heaven has acknowledged the attack as an act of war and is withdrawing all its ambassadors from Valdania and the Empire's provinces."

"War," Josarian said. "And a harder one than the Valdani expected."

"Yes. Meanwhile, the Empire's western armies are still fully engaged in the Moorlands," Elelar added.

"The Valdani are overextended," Najdan guessed.

Josarian nodded. "There will be a shortage of men available to come fight in Sileria."

Mirabar nodded slowly, staring at Elelar. "You wanted a meeting."

"I won't bother to ask how you knew," Elelar replied dryly.

"You have a plan."

"The *Alliance* has a plan."

"Well?" Mirabar prodded.

Josarian grinned, clearly relishing what he was about to tell her. "Ah, *sirana,* what's the one target in Sileria that would cripple the Valdani here overnight? A blow that even the Emperor himself would feel? The victory that would encourage *all* Silerians to join us now?"

"*I* don't know." Mirabar shrugged. "I'm a Guardian, not a . . ."

She gasped, suddenly realizing what he was suggesting. Her jaw dropped as she looked from Josarian, to Elelar, to Srijan. She looked finally at Tansen, trying to interpret what little his expression gave away. If *he* believed it could be done, then *she* would believe it, too.

"By all the Fires," she whispered. "You're going to attack the mines of Alizar!"

25

IT WAS A cool evening in Shaljir, the northern winds blowing with unseasonable force. Rain would follow the wind, and if Elelar couldn't get out of the city ahead of it, she would be stuck here until the roads dried. She stifled her impatience as she lay beside Borell in his vast bed. It was *his* fault she was still here when she had so much to do elsewhere, so many plans to make in preparation for the attack on Alizar.

However, tomorrow was some important Valdani holy day, and Borell wanted her here in Santorell Palace with him for the festivities. He had been most insistent about it. She gritted her teeth and silently reminded herself that in exchange for everything Borell unwittingly contributed to the Alliance's goals, he was occasionally entitled to demand that Elelar act like a mistress.

Sensing her restless mood, Borell rolled toward her, gathering her to him. "What are you thinking about, my love?"

She didn't feel like talking to him, so she replied, "Ronall." That would shut him up. He disliked any mention of her husband.

Unfortunately, Borell was in an unusual mood tonight. "What about him?"

She had little enough to say about her husband, actually, to whom she usually gave less thought and attention than she gave to the cats in her stables. She searched for a comment.

"He's been so edgy ever since learning that the bandit Josarian was planning to abduct him," she offered.

The official story in Shaljir was still that the mountain

uprising was nothing more than a bunch of bandits who'd grown too bold, too numerous, and too strong. Koroll and Borell knew better, of course, but they were trying to save face and preserve their reputations.

And that will be our weapon, she thought with satisfaction. *They are beaten by their own pride and ruled by their conceit.*

"Ronall is *still* whining about that?" Borell frowned. "That was at summer's end! He should act like a man."

She controlled her impatience. Borell *still* complained about the minor robbery several of Josarian's men (Najdan, Lann, and Zimran, actually) had committed at his country estate around the same time that Ronall had heard the rumors of his own planned abduction. She briefly wondered what Ronall or Borell would do if they knew how closely she worked with the men who had so offended them.

"The Outlookers still haven't caught Josarian," she pointed out, rubbing a little salt into her lover's open wounds. "So Ronall's afraid to leave Shaljir. He hasn't been away from the city since then, when he fled here in terror."

Borell went absolutely still. She thought he was thinking about Josarian, so his next comment surprised her. "Ronall's been here since then? The whole time?"

"Yes."

"I didn't realize." After a tense pause, he asked, "Has he had you since coming back to Shaljir?"

Had me. As if she were a piece of meat. She loathed the expression. She loathed the idea. Sometimes, she truly loathed men.

Borell's grip on her tightened. *"Tell me."*

"I'm his wife," she pointed out. A possession, she acknowledged bitterly, one that both men deeply resented sharing.

"How many times?"

Not: *Has he hurt you?* Not: *Does your flesh crawl when he touches you as a husband?* Not: *Do you want to talk about it?*

Only: *How many times has he enjoyed my plaything?*

She wasn't feigning her reluctance when she said, "Borell, I don't want to t—"

"How many times has he had you, dammit?"

She sighed. "I don't know. Often."

"How often?"

"I don't *know*." She didn't like this conversation. Mistress or not, her conjugal relations were none of Borell's business. "Every five or six days since his return."

To her surprise, Ronall had been sober and rather polite about it the first time, coming to her room, calmly asking Faradar to leave, and then reasonably suggesting they attempt to get an heir. There was far too much bitterness between them for her to enjoy the coupling, but at least it hadn't hurt or been humiliating. In fact, she was painfully aware that he had tried rather hard to *make* it enjoyable for her several times since then, occasionally even staying all night and holding her while they slept. She didn't resist him, but her body remained passively unresponsive under his touch, her mind busy elsewhere. It surprised her, though, that she had briefly considered pretending pleasure for his sake on one or two recent occasions. Since his return to Shaljir, there was something subdued and, well, rather sad about Ronall. He had admitted to her one night that learning of Josarian's plan to abduct him had made him confront his own mortality. The incident seemed to be having a sobering effect on him; but Elelar knew it wouldn't last.

"Every five or six days?" Borell sounded angry. He lifted his head and scowled. "He's trying to get an heir, isn't he?"

"I imagine so," she replied, knowing a more affirmative response would only anger him.

"He thinks I'll give you up if he plants his seed in you."

"Won't you?"

The sudden grip on her arms surprised her as he hauled her off the soft sheets and said fiercely, "I'll *never* give you up!"

"A mistress eight months pregnant with her husband's child would be a distinctly inconvenient woman," she pointed out. Since she doubted there was much chance of her conceiving *any* man's child, she wasn't particularly worried.

"But *my* wife bearing *my* child?" he suggested. "Now that would be different, indeed."

Her wits were unusually slow tonight. "Are you planning to marry again?" she asked in some confusion. She knew his first wife had died before he ever came to Sileria. He hadn't mentioned plans for a new one, though, she was sure of it.

"Perhaps." His foreign blue gaze held her. "Marry me, Elelar."

She couldn't have been more shocked if he'd thrown a bucket of cold water on her. *"Marry? You?"*

He laughed at her shrill voice and stunned expression. "Yes! Why not?"

"Why *not?*" He must be going mad. "Because I already *have* a husband."

Borell dismissed Ronall with a shrug. "Divorce him."

"I . . ." Her jaw worked, her mind reeling. "I can't."

He grinned, unperturbed. "Why not?"

"We . . . Divorce is not our custom here," she said weakly. She had never ever foreseen this danger when weaving her spell around Borell. *Marriage!*

His grin broadened. *"Our* custom?" he teased. "Sileria is part of Valdania now. *Our* customs are *your* customs now." Elelar controlled her shudder of disgust as he continued, "You live under Valdani law, not some barbaric Silerian tradition."

"My husband is half-Silerian," she protested, groping at straws.

"His family is Valdani."

"But *my* family—"

"Elelar, trust me. I'll make it worth Ronall's while to let you go. He may resist at first, but his father will make him see reason, as before. As for your family . . ." He shrugged. "You've always said you have only a few distant relatives anyhow, so what do they matter? Besides, if they object too much, you can just abandon your inheritance. Let them have it, and that will shut them up."

"But I don't want to aban—"

"I don't want your lands and estates. I want *you.*" He kissed her fiercely. "And I'm a very rich man, my love. You'll want for nothing."

"But . . . it—it's not right for a *torena* to rely solely upon her husband for wealth. My . . . family honor demands that I—"

"Do you think I would ever deny you anything you wanted? Do you think I could?" His hands were tender on her body, molding her, easing her into his plan. "If necessary, if nothing less will satisfy you, I will sign over some of my property and money to you, making it all your own."

"Oh, Borell . . ." She tried to swallow her panic, afraid she might be suddenly sick. *How could this be happening?*

"My love . . ." He took her speechlessness as a sign that she was deeply moved, and he embraced her.

She tried one last time. "Ronall will never agree." She prayed that it was true. "No matter what his father says, he will never suffer the humiliation of—"

"Shhh." He kissed her gently. "Leave that to me, sweetheart. I'll take care of him. I'll take care of everything."

"But he won't—"

"Shhh, don't worry. One way or another, I promise you'll be rid of him by the end of the year."

Sweet Dar, would he murder *Ronall to have her all to himself?*

"I'm the Imperial Advisor," he reminded her. "I can do whatever I want."

Josarian, help! The arrogance of their Valdani overlord united her with the mountain rebel as closely as if they were brother and sister. She didn't like Josarian, but in this moment, as Borell bore her into the pillows with passionate fervor, her mind reached out to Josarian in kinship. He and she were one with this land, in their ambitions, and in their separate hells. He slept alone, missing his dead wife, living on the run, in constant danger. She spread her legs for the questing hand of the Valdan who murmured endearments in her ear, and she knew all the loneliness tonight that the *shallah* did, all the fervent longing for freedom, all the willingness to risk everything in the fight for Sileria.

Borell's mouth was damp against her breast. "Let's start now."

"Hmmm?" She pulled her thoughts back from those wild mountains, from the ally who liked her no better than she liked him, but who she hoped would understand and respect the strength of will she needed to smile into Borell's languid eyes and tighten her legs around his thick waist.

"Let's start tonight." His hand moved over her belly, flattening out, warm and caressing. "I want you to give me a son."

Not a daughter. Not a child. A son.

Not a Silerian. Not a *toren*. A Valdan.

She hid her revulsion behind a slow, wet kiss.

"A son . . ." She wrapped her fingers around his engorged penis. He would not use a sheath, she realized; not now, not ever again with her. "Yes. Your son, Borell. Tonight."

Lifting her hips to meet him, she silently begged Dar to make her womb as barren as the rocky rainbow cliffs of Liron.

HEAT AND ECSTASY melded together in his dreams. Fire engulfed him, melting his flesh, incinerating his soul, turning his bones into molten liquid. Agonizing pleasure. Glorious pain. Exquisite torment. The erotic churn and bubble of lava called out to him, luring him into its depths. The embrace of the explosive flames made him cry out, made him scream, his terror and his passion fusing into one single glorious sunburst of emotion. Exaltation. Rapture. Delirium. A joy beyond bearing.

Fire flooded him, pooling in his loins, roaring through his veins, spilling out of his mouth and ears and eyes.

Fire was in him, of him, one with him, and he would bring it to them. He would bring them the Fire. Firebringer.

"Josarian!"

Water, the icy chill of another power, another domain, quenched his mad passion, destroyed the glory of this holy union . . . and woke him up.

Sputtering and coughing, he blinked rapidly, shoving hair out of his eyes, shaking his head. He looked up in confusion. Tansen stood over him, his lean silhouette unmistakable against the light of the moons.

"Are you all *right?*" Tansen's voice was tense, worried, taut. He held the waterskin in his hands like a weapon, clearly prepared to throw more water over his brother if he thought it necessary.

"What do you think you're doing?" Josarian demanded.

"You've been screaming in your sleep."

"And you thought throwing *water* on me in the middle of the night was a reasonable response?"

Hearing how normal Josarian sounded, Tansen dropped the bucket and sat down quite suddenly, without his usual grace. Josarian was shocked to see that Tan's hand trembled as it raked through tangles of black hair.

"When you started screaming . . ." Tansen's voice was disturbed, a little breathless. "I spoke to you. Grabbed your shoulder. I shook you. I *hit* you . . ."

"You hit me?" And he'd slept through that?

"Five or six times, Josarian." He shook his head. "I . . . I thought you might even be dying. *Terrible* screams. I thought some kind of brain fever was upon you. Or you were being attacked."

"Attacked?"

"In other lands, there are wizards who can reach into

the mind and . . ." Tansen shrugged. "I don't know quite *what* I thought."

"I was dreaming . . ." Frowning in thought, Josarian rose slowly. He grabbed the now-drenched tunic which had been lying beneath his head and hung it up on a tree to dry. Sensations started returning to him, memories as strange as they were stirring. "Fire, lava, heat, flames . . ."

"A volcano?"

He nodded. "I was *in* it."

"You've been . . . thinking about what people are saying about you?" Jalan wasn't the only *zanar* now demanding that Josarian prove himself by jumping into Darshon. And the *shallaheen* were listening. Listening and talking.

"It was . . . pain like you can't imagine, not even with that brand you bear. Pain such as I have no words for."

"Yes, I suppose it would be."

"But it was ecstasy, too."

"Josarian . . ."

"Ecstasy like . . . like a woman can give you. Only greater, much greater."

"It was a dream!"

He heard the snap in Tansen's voice and looked at him in surprise. He came down from the heights of memory and realized with astonishment that Tansen was . . . *afraid*. For him.

"I'm not losing my mind yet," Josarian assured him dryly. Perhaps he should keep his dreams to himself in the future.

"Have you . . ." Tansen cleared his throat. "Have you had this dream before?"

"I'm not sure." He shrugged. "Probably not. You would have noticed, eh?"

"Maybe you don't always scream." Tansen's voice was so soft Josarian had trouble hearing him.

"And maybe I just shouldn't have drunk so much almond wine tonight." Before going to sleep, they had consumed a bottle of the stuff given to them by a villager yesterday. As usual, Tansen had drunk very little, which meant that Josarian undoubtedly had drunk too much. He slapped Tansen on the back. "Let's get some sleep. It will be a long day of hard walking tomorrow, if we're to reach Baran before sundown." He added ruefully, "Do you know, there are some days I almost miss the *torena*'s horse?"

TANSEN SAT QUIETLY in the late afternoon sunlight, waiting and watching, his mind troubled by these recurring dreams of Josarian's. They had come four times now, by his count, since that first night he'd doused Josarian with cold water. Mercifully, nothing unusual had happened during the night they'd spent in Baran's lair, a crumbling old castle surrounded by a deadly, enchanted moat which could only be crossed with the waterlord's blessing. Baran had agreed to their plans for attacking Alizar, pledging his full support and assuring them he could carry out his part of the scheme.

However, the dreams had come again after they had left Baran's palace, tormenting Josarian once every few days, ripping the nights open with fear. Normally the most cheerful and earthy of men, Josarian looked haunted and distracted in recent days, as if he saw visions similar to the demons girl's. Tansen kept an eye on him, worried and perplexed. Was this some sorcery? Some madness? Was it truly destiny?

The Firebringer.

If Tansen believed at all in the Firebringer, then he also believed he had murdered him. He awaited Dar's vengeance for this, as he awaited Her punishment for killing his own bloodfather. He doubted that any man since Marjan had so offended the goddess. He had already faced Armian's shade, though, and he could face Dar when She came for him. He could face anything after what he had faced in Mirabar's prophetic fire.

Could he have been wrong about Armian, though? It had been easy enough for an ignorant boy to believe that the godlike figure of the celebrated assassin was the Firebringer. It was much harder for a worldly warrior to believe the mad ravings of the *zanareen* and the fervent whispers of hopeful *shallaheen* when they spoke of Josarian.

Oh, there was no question that Josarian was a great man, whereas Armian had merely been a privileged one, or that Josarian was a courageous man, whereas Armian had primarily been a violent one. Josarian was worthy to be chosen by Dar to lead Sileria to freedom; whereas Tansen had willingly committed a heinous crime against Dar and all decency, so convinced was he that Armian would lead Sileria straight into the cruelest slavery it had ever known.

Yes, if there was a Firebringer, then Dar would do well to choose Josarian rather than Armian. But mystical heroes of legend like the Firebringer were harder for an experienced man to believe in than they had been for a mere boy. Conversely, Tansen's heart couldn't easily relinquish any portion of the shame it had harbored for years, believing he had already slaughtered the Firebringer—though murdering one's own bloodfather would be shame enough to satisfy most men.

Ah, but a shatai, he thought ruefully, *is not most men.* If his glory was greater, then so must be his burdens, to maintain balance and harmony . . . Not that Tan had known much of either.

Could a man really fling himself into Darshon and survive? Men had been jumping into the volcano for centuries, and they died one after another. The legend of the Firebringer was man-made, mountain-born. Some said it was goddess-inspired . . . but then, people said a lot of things. Who could possibly sort out the real from the imaginary among the peoples of Sileria, the greatest storytellers, liars, and mythmakers in the three corners of the world?

After all, Tansen knew that people in these mountains already told the most extravagant, extraordinary tales about him. Who was to say that the legend of the Firebringer hadn't been born, as had Tan's own lesser legend, from the ridiculous boasts of an afternoon? Who was to say that the precious scriptures of the *zanareen* were founded on anything more than drunken, credulous gossip from a *tir-shah* which had crumbled into dust centuries ago? Who was to say that there was a single word of truth in the improbable prophecies with which wild-eyed fanatics and superstitious peasants now badgered Josarian? And these dreams which were taking hold of Josarian's mind . . . Couldn't they simply be the product of weariness, guilt over Calidar, and Josarian's own private fears?

Tansen wished he knew. He wished *someone* knew. He wished there was someone he could ask.

He was on sentry duty now, awaiting Elelar's arrival at the Sanctuary of Sister Basimar. They were closing in on their most ambitious target ever, and this meeting would confirm their final plans for the attack on Alizar. It was a terrible risk. Failure could cost them everything, destroying their rebellion in its infancy. Victory, however . . . He pushed away the temptation to dwell on such thoughts, focusing instead on the moment at hand.

It was late afternoon, the sun casting long shadows amidst the cliffs overlooking the road down which the *torena* and her escort would come. The fragrance of wild fennel sweetened the air, something he'd forgotten about during his years in exile, he realized. And the sound of a woman's soft misery floated to him on the southern breeze.

Perplexed, he turned to study the forest behind him, try-ing to pinpoint the sound. Choosing a direction, he stalked silently through the woods, searching for the intruder. Bas-imar's Sanctuary was isolated. That's why they had chosen it for this meeting. There shouldn't be anyone around here today who was not one of them. If the weeping he heard was coming from some jilted girl crying over a broken heart, he'd have to warn the others to be careful. This spot was only twenty minutes' walk from the humble hut where some of the most-hunted rebels in Sileria were waiting to meet with a *torena* whose loyalty to them, if discovered and exposed, would cost her her life.

If the weeping were coming from a woman who was

injured, ill, or abused and far from safety . . . He repressed
a sigh. His *shatai-kaj* had taught him well. He would have
no choice but to assist her, whoever she was. But it would
complicate things.

He brushed past a gossamer tree, the leaves of which
were still wrinkled and withered from the brutal summer;
they wouldn't be soft and lush again until the long rains
had soaked the soil. The weeping was coming from just
up ahead now. Broken-hearted, desolate, steeped in sorrow. He paused, worried that he might be intruding on a
mourner. There was always so much death in Sileria.

He needed to be sure. He crept around an enormous
tree—and found the demon girl sitting on the ground,
weeping as if her heart would break. He gaped foolishly
at her. He had seen her angry, tormented, annoyed,
amused, frightened, and pensive, but he had never imagined her crippled with sorrow and sobbing like a child.

Her head was bent, her face turned away from him.
Even here in the late afternoon shadows of the forest, her
hair glowed like fire. It was curly and, as usual, unkempt.
He had noticed that the wind liked to toy with it, almost
as if pulling at the girl, seeking her attention. It was the
fanciful sort of thought that struck him in her presence.
She seemed more elemental than other people, closer to
the earth—or to the Otherworld, he supposed. Nature
seemed to flow through her, even though the Guardians
were not a nature cult; yet although the Sisters *were,* he
had never met a Sister who seemed as close to the earth's
heartbeat as Mirabar.

She was wearing the ordinary *shallah* clothing she always wore, though she had apparently left her cloak back
at the Sanctuary. She wouldn't need it until darkness fell,
perhaps not even then, not with southern winds this evening. The air ought to be soft and balmy all night, carrying
the faint scent of distant jungles from across the Middle
Sea.

She was only a little thing, he noticed once again,
smaller than Elelar or Basimar, and much smaller than Jal-

ilar. But muscular and sturdy—and brave. Yes, he had seen that. They had all seen that. Indeed, he had seen few men with such courage. Really, it was too bad she was so strange looking, for she was a rare young woman, one that the best of men might have competed for had she been even passably pretty. Sad, too, that but for that hair and those eyes, she *would* have been pretty. Who knew? Perhaps some sophisticated city-dweller whose childhood had not been filled with fear of such creatures might want her someday, if she should ever leave the mountains and meet such a man.

Or perhaps Cheylan will want her, he realized suddenly. Cheylan had asked Tansen about Mirabar several times during the summer, curious, interested, intrigued by the notion of another like him. A little jealous, too, Tansen thought, of her power, her growing stature.

Ah, well. He almost smiled, considering how he had once felt upon hearing about a Moorlander woman who was now one of the most famous fighters in the world, a captured slave who entertained the Valdani in combat arenas throughout the Empire. She had even beaten a *shatai* or two, it was said, and none of them liked the sound of that rumor. A woman! So Tan supposed that Cheylan could be excused a little jealousy over the *shallah* girl whom even Kiloran bowed to at times.

He wondered if he should just leave now without disturbing her. Almost as if she had heard his thoughts or the whisper of his breath, she suddenly stiffened, sat up, and looked around. She choked on a gasp when she saw him.

"What are you doing, sneaking up on me?" she snapped.

"I heard you crying." He kept his voice even.

She looked away again. "Oh."

She scrubbed angrily at her face. He realized he had embarrassed her.

"Do you need help?" he asked.

"N . . . N . . ." She shook her head quickly. Her shoulders trembled with a fresh sob which she struggled to contain.

Unlike many men, he was not made helpless by a woman's tears. A *shatai*'s work often brought him into the realm of tears, always so close to the realm of bloodshed. He would leave if Mirabar wanted him to, but he could stay if she needed company. He was not some boy afraid to be alone in the woods with a demon as the sun slowly set.

"*Sirana* . . ."

"Ohhhh, stop calling me that!"

"Mirabar." He crouched down, trying to see her face. "What's wrong?"

She put her head in her hands and rocked back and forth. "No, it's foolish."

He doubted that. He wished Josarian were here; his brother seemed to have a rapport with this girl. However, Tansen would do what he could.

"Is it something from the Otherworld?" he probed. "Visions? Proph—"

"No, no."

She shook her head, face still covered by her dark, fine-boned hands. He saw a healing scar, like a burn mark. Evidently she was not always impervious to fire. He didn't try to touch her, sensing that she would bolt. Besides, he privately admitted to a certain reluctance to touch her; superstitious, yes, but genuine.

"Are you hurt?" he asked.

She made a terrible sound in her throat.

"Injured?"

She lowered her hands. Her eyes were closed. She tilted her head back and took a huge breath, trying to smother her sobs.

"No," she said at last, sounding unbearably weary. "I am not injured."

She turned suddenly and looked at him, her eyes flashing brightly. He remained impassive, but their gazes locked. He suddenly recalled the first time he had ever seen her: his backward step, his unconcealed revulsion. The memory was in her eyes, too, and also in the breath she released on a watery sigh.

"I let . . . Srijan . . ." She shook her head. "I let him upset me."

"Srijan?"

She laughed shakily at his contemptuous tone. "You see? I told you it was foolish."

He frowned. "Did he attack you, *sir* . . . Mira?" Srijan was about as subtle as an earthquake when he approached a woman, and he was growing restless and impatient as they all awaited Elelar in this isolated spot.

"No. I am in no danger of that from him." She looked away, her complexion darkening. "He said that . . . it was too bad I am so strange looking, because I am not so ugly otherwise, and some man might have wanted me if not for the curse Dar laid upon me in the womb."

Tansen drew breath through his teeth, disgusted by Srijan's casual cruelty, sorry for Mirabar, and, above all, ashamed that he and Srijan could have similar thoughts about something.

Mirabar looked down at her hands. "You get used to people shying away. You get used to them . . . not wanting to meet your gaze. Not wanting to touch you. Being afraid of you. You get used to the looks and the stares and the whispers . . . You never get used to them stoning you and chasing you and wanting to *kill* you, of course . . ." She sighed. "I did not choose to be what I am. I am, however, used to it. I understand it as the price I pay for the power I was given. In another time, in a long-ago era . . ." She made an impatient sound and scrubbed again at her face. "I only weep when I think of what might have been."

"Everyone does that, Mirabar." He, too, could cry like a woman if he let himself dwell upon what might have been.

She ground her teeth together. "And I . . . I am a fool to do so. I might have been born like other women, paying for my food and shelter by spreading my legs for a husband, rather than by Calling shades of the dead. I might have had the privilege of dying in a river of blood and pain, trying to bear him a child . . ." Her eyes shimmered with tears as she added more truthfully, "I might have been loved by my mother, my father, by . . . some man, some-day . . . somewhere . . ."

"You're still young," he pointed out. "And prejudice, like enmity, can change into acceptance. With time."

She looked at him knowingly. "Enough for that? When even the warrior I am destined to serve backs away from me in disgust?"

He shrugged, a casual denial. "I was startled." He lifted one brow. "Anyone would have been startled. That was quite an entrance you made that night."

"It was me, not my *entrance*, that you protected the *torena* from. I saw you."

It was true. He nodded. He would not insult her again with false denials. "I was born to a violent, superstitious people. Some things are reflexes, even though I know better."

Her eyes narrowed. "You are still backing away, Tansen."

He avoided her gaze, but he would not lie to her. "I'm sorry, Mirabar."

"Reflex." After a moment, she added in a voice that sounded bitterly amused, "Well. At least I shall never have the *torena*'s problems."

He felt his face flush with embarrassment, a reaction that few people could evoke in him. Judging it time to change the subject, he said, "I must go back to the clearing and watch for her arrival. She doesn't know how to find the Sanctuary."

She rose to her feet. "While you wait . . ."

"Yes?" he asked uneasily.

"I know that you were in the east with Cheylan. I was wondering . . ."

He smiled, relieved. "He asks about you, too."

26

TANSEN HAD ALREADY noticed the way Zimran watched Elelar, and he didn't like it. He also noticed that Basimar didn't like it. Zimran shared the Sister's bed while they were all camped here at the Sanctuary, but Tansen suspected that he dreamed about the *torena*. Srijan watched Elelar, too, of course, but there was something so uncouth about him that Tansen paid him no heed. Zimran, though . . . He was a man who knew what women wanted, what they liked; he knew how to please them. He knew far better than any other man present—or any other man Tansen could recall—how to offer a woman a subtle compliment, a thoughtful gesture, a private smile. He exercised his skills on every woman, young or old, plain or pretty, available or not.

Like most things, Tansen thought wryly, *it takes practice.*

Basimar was unmistakably enamoured of Zimran. Mirabar tolerated him without much interest, but even she clearly appreciated the gestures of man-to-woman courtesy he showed her. Elelar had undoubtedly known enough artful seducers to easily recognize this one, but there was enough invitation in the smiles she shared with Zimran to make Tansen's belly clench with unwanted jealousy.

With their plans now firmly established, their resources committed, and their duties assigned, the allies would break camp the following morning to set in motion the ambitious scheme they had agreed upon in Zilar. Tansen was glad. The season for planning had come to a close; the season for action was upon them. Although it had noth-

ing to do with the task at hand, Tansen privately admitted
that he would also be glad to see distance come between
Zimran and Elelar now. He didn't like the way he felt
when they were near each other. Nor did he like suspecting
that Mirabar somehow knew how he felt.

"You're even quieter than usual tonight," Josarian
chided, coming to sit beside him at some distance from
the fire.

"I'm thinking." He avoided Josarian's gaze, expertly
running one of his cherished honing stones along the blade
of one of his swords.

"Thinking?"

"Focusing. Preparing." The stone whispered over the
blade. "Soon we will face our enemies. We must be
ready."

"Our enemies?" Josarian laughed softly and gestured to
some of the people who had gathered here for this meeting.
Speaking only loud enough for Tansen to hear, he said,
"Look at our allies, Tan. *Torena* Elelar, who dislikes me
and who betrayed you. Najdan the assassin, who went to
Dalishar to kill you. Mirabar, a Guardian whom most people take for a demon. Srijan, who dreams of murdering us
both, but who may be respectful enough to let his waterlord father do it instead. Falian, who perhaps still secretly
hates me for ruining his life. And the others . . ."

"No, Tan, I'm not worried about the Valdani." Josarian
looked back at his bloodbrother. Even in the dark, Tansen
could see something fierce glittering in his eyes as he concluded, "I can take care of my enemies, but Dar shield me
from my friends."

Tansen nodded. "I suppose it *is* a little like mating with
a wild Widow Beast."

"A what?"

"Never mind. I'll be watching your back."

"Ah, but then who will watch yours?"

"Luckily, *shatai* are trained to watch their own backs.
I'd have died during training if I hadn't learned how."

*   *   *

TANSEN ESCORTED ELELAR and her servants part of the way the following day. This was bandit country. Of course, all the bandits in Sileria were now part of Josarian's army, but they didn't know that Elelar was, in her way, one of them. Even if they knew, they still might not care, not enough to forgo robbing her if she weren't well-protected. Kiloran had brought Sileria's many bandits (who routinely paid him a percentage of their booty, as tradition demanded) into the rebellion, but he hadn't exactly tamed them. However, they knew Tansen by now—who had slain twenty Moorlanders with a single blow, after all—and so would grant the *torena* immunity while the *shatai* rode with her.

"The Imperial Advisor has asked me to marry him," she announced suddenly as they rode side by side through the morning sunshine.

He didn't bother to conceal his surprise. "Surely you told me you already *have* a husband?"

"A minor impediment that he intends to eliminate."

"Divorce?" It was anathema in a clannish society where bloodties and loyalty mattered more than wealth, but he supposed that the Imperial Advisor didn't concern himself overmuch with Silerian tradition—especially not if it interfered with his plans.

Elelar cleared her throat. "Divorce is the possibility he specifically mentioned."

He noticed how strained she looked. "You're afraid your husband might refuse, and Borell will resort to more brutal measures?" When she nodded, he asked, "But why? Surely a Valdan will divorce you. They have no—"

"He's half-Silerian, Tan." She briefly explained her husband's lineage and background.

"So," he surmised, "you married him for his money and his Valdani connections."

"And because he was unlikely to find out about my work in the Alliance."

"Why?"

"Because he's a drunkard and a fool."

He almost winced at the open contempt in her voice. He rather pitied her husband, married without love or respect, and now openly cuckolded. Indeed, Tan didn't doubt that there'd been other men besides Borell, and it was possible that *Toren* Ronall, though a "fool," suspected it, too.

"Was he a drunkard before he married you?" he asked rudely. There were times when, desire notwithstanding, he knew that living with her could be worse than living without her.

She glared at him but didn't respond to the insult. "I do not seek his death."

"Why not? You sought mine." He could feel his temper starting to fray.

She kept hers in check. "Nor do I seek marriage to the Advisor."

That surprised him. "Why not? I would have thought—"

"Do men ever think?" she asked bitterly. "As the wife of a half-Silerian drunkard, I go where I please and do what I want. My house is a haven for our allies and for fugitive rebels. I can conduct much of the Alliance's business there."

He was starting to understand. "But the Advisor's wife would live at Santorell Palace, meaning you'd need an excuse every time you went to your house, a property which he'd probably pressure you to give up anyhow."

She nodded. "The wife of the Imperial Advisor would be under constant supervision. My time would be completely taken up by ceremonial duties and assisting my husband in politics. My privacy would be compromised by my husband's servants, all my activities and behavior subjected to the continual scrutiny of courtiers . . . It would be a nightmare for any intelligent woman, but a disaster for one connected to the Alliance. Besides . . ."

"There's more?"

She made a sound of immense impatience. "He's from Valda, not here. This is a political posting, not his home. He would like to be sent to a more prestigious post or even given a seat in the Imperial Council."

"And he would take his wife with him when he left Sileria."

"Forever," she acknowledged bleakly.

"What are you going to do?"

She shook her head. The knotted cords of her headdress, which she had tucked away from her face, fell over her eyes. She brushed them away. "I don't know. I've been racking my brain trying to come up with a plan. He's made it quite clear that he doesn't need Ronall's cooperation in order to marry me."

"I don't suppose you can just refuse his proposal?" Tansen ventured.

"I'm the one who made him fall in love with me," she said impatiently. "I made him trust me, rely upon me, believe in my love."

Tansen shrugged. "You could reject him. Give him up. Break it off. I know he's been valuable to the Alliance, to us all, but if you've got to—"

"He thinks I'm in love with him, too." Another impatient sound. "I've given him ample cause to think so."

"You're a woman. Surely no reasonably intelligent man pretends to truly understand women. He'll be bewildered at first, but then . . ." He shrugged.

"That's it?" she asked doubtfully.

"Well . . . Angry, hurt, broken-hearted, confused, enraged . . . But he will know he's not the first man ever abandoned by the woman he loved, or the first to wonder why."

"I don't know. He might still try to eliminate Ronall, thinking my husband has threatened me or forced me to give him up. He might attack me, out of vengeance. His power is absolute in Shaljir. No one could help or defend me if I . . . If he . . ." She made a vague gesture.

"Stall him until after Alizar, then," Tansen suggested. "If we succeed there, then there will be war. He *is* the Advisor, after all, and he'll have a disaster on his hands. He may well forget, at least for a while, his personal concerns."

"Stall him . . ." She let out a long, shaky breath. "Stall him . . ." She straightened up suddenly. "I know! I'll tell him I won't feel worthy to be his wife until we know for sure I can conceive his child. He's positively *fixated* on impregnating me."

He didn't want to hear this, didn't want to see the visions that her comment brought vividly to life. "That's a good plan," he said briefly. "Stick to it." He kicked his horse and rode ahead to check for an ambush in the pass they were approaching.

HARJAN'S DEATH WAS a loss that Myrell felt strongly, for the tailor had been a good source of information, saving the Empire lives and money on more than one occasion, and leading to the death or capture of more than a few rebels. It was Harjan who had first advised Myrell that a *torena* often stopped at the *tirshah* on the edge of Zilar when travelling between Shaljir and her estates. There was nothing remarkable about this, of course, since the *tirshah* was a very fine one and many of Sileria's wealthier citizens broke their journeys there for a night.

Harjan had grown bold and greedy enough to break a silence which no other informant was willing to violate: he whispered to Myrell about the Society, a subject that most *shallaheen* never discussed with outsiders, no matter what inducements were offered or what punishment was threatened. *Lirtahar,* and the brutal methods by which the assassins enforced it, ruled the mountains. Employing his own viciously brutal measures, Myrell had been unsuccessful in convincing anyone to talk about the Society, even in those rare instances where they *would* talk about Josarian.

Harjan, alas, had been the one man greedy enough for gold and confident enough of his own cleverness to risk the Society's wrath by speaking about its business to a Valdan. Not that a tailor from Zilar knew anything important about their business—he did, however, observe various details and events which eventually proved to be the threads of a much larger tapestry. Although he was dead, he had given Myrell the tools with which to start unravelling the fabric.

Harjan had always aspired to more than the miserable poverty of a *shallah,* and so he had patronized the fine *tirshah* at the edge of town, despite the high prices the keeper charged for food and wine there. A man of mediocre talents, he had nonetheless harbored the hope that he might acquire a few wealthy or aristocratic clients if he haunted the luxurious *tirshah*'s public rooms. This explained how he knew that twice during the past year, the *torena* in question had stayed at the *tirshah* on the very same night as an assassin.

It was surprising enough that a lone *torena* would risk a second visit to an establishment frequented by an assassin. It was even more surprising that, on that second occasion, one of the public rooms was closed because—as Harjan had learned after creating a scene—the *torena* was dining privately in there with the assassin!

Since Myrell paid him for any news whatsoever about the Society, Harjan had related this startling news to the Valdan at one of their meetings. It was a surprising announcement in any event, for the *toreni* were well aware of the risk of abduction and usually took pains to avoid the assassins. However, a man and woman might well meet for many reasons. Apart from the possibility that the assassin was the *torena*'s lover, Myrell could conceive of a variety of possible explanations for the discreet assignation: the assassin might be blackmailing the woman; she might have petitioned him about a bloodvow, something that was beneath no one in Sileria, despite the airs the *toreni* gave themselves; or, yes, they might even be resolving an abduction or threatened abduction, that barbaric custom that Silerians treated like ordinary business.

Indeed, with so much work and so many worries to occupy him, Myrell might have completely disregarded Harjan's brief tale, except for one thing—the identity of the woman: *Torena* Elelar. He knew that Koroll had some

contact with the Imperial Advisor's mistress by virtue of
his position as Commander of Shaljir, so he had brought
the news directly to his attention. Koroll would have the
means to determine if there was anything in this information which concerned them. Such a possibility seemed
so improbable that Myrell had almost felt embarrassed to
report the incident, but Koroll had pounced like a mountain
cat and congratulated him for uncovering it. The Society
was now allied to Josarian, and the Advisor's mistress was
meeting with a Society assassin. Whether the Outlookers
discovered a link between Elelar and Josarian, or merely
collected enough information to personally discredit the
torena, Koroll found this news worthy of considerable attention.

Harjan had been publicly executed by the rebels only a
day after reporting to Myrell that Josarian was planning to
abduct a *toren*—Elelar's own husband, in fact. The abduction had never taken place. Had it been a ruse? Or had
Josarian called off the plan upon realizing he'd been betrayed?

Myrell had argued with Koroll afterward, pointing out
that the *torena* was unlikely to ally herself to a *shallah*
planning to abduct her own husband. Even if she loathed
Toren Ronall, surely not even a woman would be foolish
enough to beggar herself paying ransom to her own accomplice. Even if Josarian returned the money to her,
which she'd be a fool to expect, what would be the point
of such a laborious exercise?

Koroll, however, suspected that getting rid of Ronall
was probably precisely why Elelar had sought an assassin
and, through him, perhaps Josarian. He had no doubt that
the Advisor's whore thought Borell would marry her if she
became a widow. Josarian's men had already killed one
Valdani abductee and were quite capable of killing another.

"Three have mercy," Koroll had added, "I think the
woman may be right, too. I think Borell has become besotted enough to marry her."

Koroll had assigned his best spies to the task of discovering the *torena*'s secrets while Myrell returned to the fighting in the mountains. Now that he had returned to Shaljir for another meeting, Myrell was astonished by what Koroll's spies had learned in his absence—and by what Koroll planned to do with the information.

Torena Elelar, it seemed, was far more than a woman who had broken the law by contacting those in league with the bandit Josarian, and her scheming went far beyond getting rid of an inconvenient husband.

The woman was clever, secretive, and discreet. At first, in fact, the spies had reported that they believed Koroll had been mistaken in his suspicions. They had persevered at his insistence, but every unusual action or unexpected visitor to the house in Shaljir had a plausible explanation. Koroll, however, remained unconvinced. Midnight couriers; unusually large expenditures; servants who could read and write; one or two *shallaheen* showing up every six or seven days to solicit employment, then leaving Shaljir immediately after being privately interviewed and apparently found unsatisfactory . . . Koroll had perceived explanations which were not as innocent as the most apparent ones, but which he considered just as plausible.

Then a servant hired at summer's end had left the *torena*'s employ in disgrace. Caught stealing in Elelar's private chambers, the young woman should have been grateful that she was only dismissed. Silerian aristocrats still had considerable power over the lower classes, after all, and the Imperial Advisor's own mistress could have even had the girl executed for the offense, had she been vindictive enough. However, like most thieves, the girl wasn't sorry she'd committed a crime, only sorry that she'd been caught. One of Koroll's men, dressed as a civilian, showed her a good time one evening and offered her a sympathetic shoulder to cry on. She had taken full advantage of his generosity on all counts, eager to complain about the strange household with its clannish longtime servants and unyielding rules.

And that was how they learned that a seemingly insignificant merchant—a man with graying hair and a precocious young son—who visited the *torena* fairly often was, in fact, a Guardian.

The Guardians and the Society. A woman connected to both; both connected to Josarian.

"She has Borell's trust," Koroll said. "She undoubtedly has had access to information which could benefit the rebels, since we had no idea that she was *one* of them. Who knows how much this damned woman has hurt the Empire while spreading her legs for Borell?"

"But how will we prove it, Commander?" Myrell asked as he sat with Koroll on a fragrant morning in Shaljir.

"I'm having her house searched today. I'm sure you'd like to join me in supervising the operation."

Myrell almost choked on his shock. "Borell's mistress? He'll have you sent to the farthest reaches of the Moorlands! To the land that swallows the sun!"

"Are you suggesting that wouldn't be preferable to being in Sileria?" Koroll muttered.

"Commander, I respectfully submit that the *torena* will run straight to Borell the moment you reveal your intentions, and he will—"

"The *torena* is still wandering the countryside somewhere. Unfortunately, my men lost her in the mountains, so we've no idea where she is or how long she intends to stay there." His face twisted with mingled skepticism and distaste as he added, "The official story is that she's gone into Sanctuary, as is her annual custom, to commune with the spirit of her dead grandfather."

So many Valdani were appalled by the extensive death cult in this country that the Guardians, the most mystic sect, the ones that claimed they could actually *talk* to the dead, had been outlawed—that and fire magic, of course. Even assuming that Silerians exaggerated the power of their fire wizards as much as they exaggerated most things, the Empire could not condone such dangerous sorcery among its subjugated peoples.

"Commune with . . . She admits to such things?" Myrell asked. "Why does Borell tolerate such disgusting practices and su—"

"Because he thinks with an organ very distant from his brain when dealing with Elelar." Koroll sighed. "Besides, she's a woman and she's of another race. The Advisor is a worldly man. I imagine he makes allowances for the strange rites and superstitions of a Silerian female, no matter how high-born—as long as she continues to please him."

"Her husband is gone from home, too?" Myrell asked.

Koroll shook his head. "He's here in town. But, as Commander of Shaljir, I happen to know that a contingent of eight Outlookers is about to escort him from his home to Santorell Palace, by force if necessary, for a personal meeting with the Advisor."

"Why?" Myrell was startled.

"I was not informed why." Koroll's voice was rich with contempt as he explained, "I assume it is in relation to the Advisor's personal life. I have heard that Ronall was dragged to the Palace to face Borell once before over matters regarding the woman who is wife to one and mistress to the other. Apparently neither man is . . . very good at sharing."

Myrell studied his superior officer, admiring him. "So there will be no one at home except servants when we arrive today. They will have just seen their master dragged off by Outlookers, and they'll be so frightened, so convinced of total disaster that they will not resist when your men start searching the house. It will not even occur to them to protest or stall you."

Koroll nodded. "The less we say, the better. If there are those among them who know Elelar's secrets, let's encourage them to assume that we know what we're looking for, that we're merely collecting material to validate an arrest which cannot be escaped or avoided."

Yes, Myrell admired this man. Koroll had wrestled glory out of the disaster at Britar, rising to the post of High

Commander of Sileria, now second in importance only to Borell himself. He had achieved this feat by mastering many situations such as this one, calculating every plan down to the finest details, predicting and accounting for every contingency. Oh, yes, there were few men who could have turned the tide as Koroll had done, creating a brilliant career out of defeat and certain disgrace. And he had given Myrell another chance, too, for which Myrell would always be loyal to him.

Yes, Myrell's commanding officer was a genius, a visionary who was also a practical man. Together, they would rise to incredible heights, just as soon as they'd finished off Josarian and his mountain rabble. Together, they would someday march back to Valda in triumph: heralded, fêted, honored, and admired. All they had to do was kill a lot of Silerian peasants first.

ELELAR APPROACHED THE Lion's Gate late in the day, just before sundown. Faradar and her two most trusted manservants rode with her. They were all tired, for she had pushed hard to reach Shaljir today. Borell expected her at Santorell Palace tonight and, weary as she was, she would go. It was her duty, after all.

She looked down at the Outlookers guarding the gate and prepared to announce herself and her business in Shaljir. *A bath,* she thought wryly. No words ever escaped her lips, however, for four new Outlookers suddenly burst through the door of the guardhouse and, to her astonished horror, pulled her off her horse, handling her like some brothel-slave, and dragged her toward the building.

She heard fighting behind her as she was hauled away; her servants were trying to defend her. Terrified and desperately hoping this was some bizarre mistake, she prayed that Faradar kept her wits and remembered what to do. They had talked about it often.

You are "only" a woman, Elelar had told her many times. *If I am taken, it is unlikely that anyone will pay attention to you. Not at first, anyhow. You must use that time to slip away. Whatever happens to me, you must escape. Warn the others. Warn Josarian. Tell Tansen; he knows who to contact in the Alliance if I die.*

Yes, she hoped this was a mistake, but deep down, she *knew:* her time was at hand. Nonetheless, she fought as she had been trained to fight, as an aristocrat.

"*Take* your filthy hands off me, you ham-fisted, fatherless clods!" she snarled at the Outlookers trying to force her through the doorway of the guardhouse. "Let go, you fools! Advisor Borell himself will geld you for this! Do you know who I am? I am *Torena* Elelar yesh Ronall mar—"

They bodily threw her through the door and slammed it behind her. Her head hit hard wood as she fell to the floor in a heap, where she lay dazed and winded.

The voice which addressed her next was one she recognized all too well, one she had heard in anger and in passion, in public and in private, in fury and in tenderness. It chilled her blood and proved that this was no mistake.

"Yes, they know who you are," Borell said. He sounded unutterably weary. "And you have lost the right to invoke my name or my support, *torena.*"

She would brazen it out. What else could she do? She lifted her throbbing head and weakly murmured, "Borell? By the Three, what's going on here?"

"You're under arrest." Indeed, he sounded positively ill. "The charges are extensive. In fact, we don't even know them all yet."

"What?" She slowly pushed herself into a sitting position, removed the traditional headdress which had already fallen off most of the way anyhow, and rubbed her aching head. She gazed at her lover with wide, limpid, confused eyes. "You're . . . arresting me? I don't understand!"

Commander Koroll was there, too. So was a gloating Outlooker officer whom she had never seen before; the fellow had a stupid face and a nose which had been badly set after being broken. Her mind worked furiously, wondering what she could do. How much did they know? A lot, she assumed, if they had convinced Borell to arrest her. Darfire, the damned man had lately talked of nothing but wanting to marry her!

Borell looked older to her, as if he'd aged ten years since her departure from the city. His eyes were red-rimmed, evidence of sleepless nights. They were also . . . glassy, bleak, unfocused. Like a man in shock, a man who'd just suffered a loss so sudden and devastating that his mind couldn't yet cope with the grief.

She knew him, however. She knew this man well. However much he thought he loved her, he loved himself more. Her betrayal would destroy his career, and he would punish her for it—especially if he thought exposing and punishing her might somehow yet salvage his reputation in the Imperial Council. This man had been easy enough to beguile, despite his intelligence. Elelar's apparent adoration of him had only echoed his opinion of himself. No, he had not been the challenge for her that another man might have been, but she had always known how dangerous he would become if she ever hurt him. And what, after all, could hurt a proud man more than this—the discovery that the woman he loved had used him and betrayed him over and over, coldly, rationally, and ruthlessly, from the very beginning?

Elelar met her lover's gaze and she saw the knowledge burning in his foreign eyes, etched in his Valdani face, turning his fair skin as white as chalk. *He knew.*

It was the very worst thing that could have happened. No matter how much proof Koroll had against her, she knew she would have been safe as long as Borell chose to believe in her innocence. Without Borell's support, however, the slightest offense, even the vaguest suspicion, was enough for them to arrest, imprison, punish, even execute her. She was only a Silerian, after all; the Emperor's laws did not protect subjugated races from the Valdani. As a Silerian in Sileria, she had fewer rights than a goat.

"We've observed your movements for well over a twin-moon, *torena,*" Koroll said, breaking the loud silence be-

tween her and Borell. "We conducted a thorough search
of your house two days ago. We have found considerable
evidence of your traitorous activities against the Empire,
the Outlookers, and the Advisor himself."

She kept her expression under control, radiating innocent confusion and ignorant fear, concealing how much
this news shocked her. She wanted to ask exactly what
they had found, but she was half-afraid that her own questions might reveal too much, might ultimately lead them
to something they hadn't already found. There was so
much to hide: the Alliance, the rebels, the dispatches from
Kintish contacts, the path to Kiloran's lair, their Moorlander associates, Derlen and Mirabar, the secret chamber in
her house, Ambassador Shiraj, the loyal servants who
knew too much for their own safety, the body buried in
her wine cellar . . . the *Beyah-Olvari*.

Her chest hurt so much she wondered if she was having
an attack. Blood roared in her ears. She struggled to make
sense out of the chaos of her thoughts, knowing that panic
would guarantee failure.

Ronall, she suddenly thought distractedly. Where in the
Fires was Ronall while the Outlookers were searching the
house? Had he discovered her secrets? Or was he merely
a liquor-fogged bystander, as usual? Was he under arrest,
too? Dead? Cleared of all suspicion?

She struggled to pull her mind back to important matters. Ronall was not her problem, not her responsibility.
Many lives rested on her silence now, many plans. The
rebellion, the attack on Alizar, the war . . . She had dedicated her entire life to the events which were about to
come to pass. She would not fail now.

"Borell . . ." She let a pleading note creep into her voice.
"I don't understand. What *traitorous activities?* I would
never betr—"

"I could believe you." Borell's voice was hoarse. He
nodded, gazing at her, his expression hard with misery.
"Yes. You sound convincing, you look . . . like the woman
I loved. The woman who told me how much she feared

the mountain bandits, how little she knew about the Society, *how much she loved me . . .*"

Without warning, he burst into motion, flinging a stool across the room, and came after her. "Now I know why your husband beat you!" he roared. His hands seized her by the throat, his pale face suddenly red with murderous rage. *"Now I know what you can drive a man to, you lying, whoring, traitorous BITCH!"*

He shook her, and she flopped around like a rag doll, scrabbling frantically at his hands, struggling for air as her vision darkened and her lungs burned, barely able to hear his bellows of rage above the pounding of her own desperate heart. She saw flashes of the faces of the other two men, heard fragments of their shouts. They didn't want him to kill her, not yet. They wanted to know what she knew, what secrets she had shared with whom. They wanted her to talk. Knowing Valdani methods of persuasion—*Malthenar, Morven, Garabar*—she suddenly gave herself over to Borell's hatred. This would be a quicker and kinder death than the one they had planned for her. Let him choke her, let him break her neck. It would be over in a moment. She only hoped someone would burn her body. The Valdani custom of putting their dead in the ground sickened her. How could a spirit reach the Otherworld when it was covered by dirt and worms? How could it be purified while rotting in a hole in the ground?

She was so close to unconsciousness that she didn't realize Borell had let her go until she became aware of the cold, hard wood of the floor beneath her cheek. Cheated of her chance to die quickly, she hauled air into her aching lungs and rubbed her watering eyes. If she had to face him again, now, she would face him as a *torena,* as a Hasnari, as she had promised herself a thousand times she would face this hour when it finally came. She heard him shouting at Koroll and at the other man to get out, *get out* and leave the two of them alone.

The door slammed, and then she felt Borell's hands on her. She briefly thought he had sent the two men away so he could kill her, after all, but then she felt him tugging at her tunic, brutally ripping off her pantaloons, and she knew why he had wanted to be alone with her one last time. She had lain with him a thousand times, but now she was flooded with even more disgust than she'd felt the time Srijan had tried to bed her. Borell had arrested her and tried to strangle her, and he thought he could bed her one last time? He surely intended to have her executed, but he wanted her to pleasure him first? He knew that she had never loved him, had only slept with him to serve Sileria, and he thought she would still spread her legs for him?

She fought him. She sank her teeth into the lips that sought hers, relishing the taste of this fat Valdan's blood. She clawed and scratched at the hands that ripped away her clothes, that moved roughly, insultingly, over her flesh. She fought for her life, fought to kill him rather than let him abase her this way.

An enormous hand slapped her, making her head snap to the side, making her vision swim. Then a big-boned, heavily muscled forearm pressed down on her throat and shoulders, pinning her to the floor, restricting her air supply. She fought the weight of his heavy, dense body as it pressed her into the unyielding wood. She struggled to breathe, trying to defeat him with the sheer force of her hatred.

"No!" she screamed furiously, feeling him probing between her legs. She tried to twist away, tried to evade the plunging, tearing, painful invasion, the humiliating violation, the grotesque profanity of his body forcing its way into hers.

"Nooooooo!" she screamed again as he heaved frantically on top of her, groaning, panting, sweating, eyes rolling as he gritted his teeth and grunted again and again.

"No!"

She felt the hot torrent of his release, the sickening sensation of his seed flooding her womb, the ecstatic shudders of his body as his hips jerked convulsively. She wanted to vomit on him. She wished she could. She wanted to kill him, and she would look for an opportunity to do so every single minute between now and the moment she died. She wanted to geld him.

He lay panting on top of her, his lungs heaving, his flesh damp, his muscles limp.

She wanted to geld him, and that, at least, she could do.

"It was no different from all the other times," she said, staring at the ceiling, blinking back tears as her body throbbed with vicious pain. "I wanted to vomit every time you ever touched me. My skin crawled every time you put your hands on me."

He stiffened, his spine going rigid. He tried to control his breathing.

"You're so proud of that pathetic thing between your legs," she said bitterly. Her voice could have chilled even Kiloran. "You don't know how the Palace servants laugh about it. Such a little weapon on such a large man."

"Stop." She felt his hand in her hair, pulling, trying to force her to look at him. "Stop, Elelar."

"Do you really think I ever felt a single moment's pleasure with it flopping around inside me?"

"Enough, woman. You've had your say."

"Not that it was ever in me for long. I've seen fish that last longer than you."

"I will stop your mouth!" he warned, hauling back his hand.

"Will you hit me again?" she asked venomously. "Does hitting a woman make a man of a Valdan? Is that how it works?"

He stared at her with horror-clouded eyes, his jaw slack, his expression stupid.

"You never even guessed how many other men I spread my legs for, did you, Borell?" she taunted him. "Did you really think a woman would be satisfied with you?"

"Your insults don't change wh—"

"Ambassador Shiraj knew how to please a woman. *He* was not some fumbling, thick-waisted oaf."

"Shiraj?" Now Borell looked as if *he* might vomit.

"Who do you think told him about the Imperial Council's plans to attack the Kintish Kingdoms? Who do you think—"

"You told him?" Borell bleated.

"How do you think the Kints knew the Empire's plans? Why do you think the Kintish armies were expecting—"

"Three Into One! You?"

"Everything I ever learned from you, I told to your enemies."

A sickly pallor was fast replacing the sexual flush on his skin. He dragged one arm across his shiny forehead. His hand was shaking. "Three have mercy . . ." His voice was thick and slow. "Do you have any idea how many deaths you've caused, woman? Three thousand men died in the first battle against Kinto."

"Deaths *I've* caused?" She gathered her torn clothes around her torso and sat up, glaring at him, letting him see just how much she hated him. "The Council sent tens of thousands of men to fight in Kinto, intending to carve a path straight to the Palace of Heaven, killing everyone who got in their way. You *bousted* to me that the Empire would destroy the Kintish Kingdoms at last. You *gloated* about how the Valdani would seize the Throne of Heaven and vanquish a three-thousand-year-old dynasty. And you can accuse *me* of causing deaths?"

She pulled her pantaloons up over her hips, wincing with pain, filled with revulsion at the sticky fluid between her legs. "You've starved my people, sanctioned torture to get information, seized land and crops and livestock at your whim, and raped my country's mines. You sign papers authorizing the importation of captured women for your brothels and complain about *supply problems* when they die within a year or two. You have never once prosecuted a Valdan for rape, murder, assault, or theft when the crime was committed against a Silerian."

Her hands shook as she tried to find a way to keep her torn tunic fastened. She wanted to weep with humiliation, with pain, with rage, with fear. But she would not let a Valdan see her do that, so she kept her expression hard and hate-filled as she looked again at Borell.

"And you thought I could love you?" Now that her life was over, she wanted him to know. She wanted him to feel his disgrace until his dying day. "I betrayed you with other men. I betrayed your secrets to Kints, Moorlanders, and Silerian rebels. I read your dispatches after you slept. I spied on your private meetings. I did it because it was my duty, because I would do anything to free Sileria." She nodded slowly. "And the only part of my work that I truly hated was letting you touch me."

A horrible expression crossed his face, a mingling of nausea, fear, and hatred. He looked like he might try to kill her again. Then he surged awkwardly to his feet. For a moment she thought he intended to kick her, but then he strode to the door, yanked it open, and bellowed for some Outlookers.

"You may take the *torena* now," he said, his voice rough with emotion. Then, without looking at her again, he left— still dishevelled from their struggle and forgetting his light cloak.

She assumed the guards were taking her to the old Kintish prison across from the Outlooker headquarters. As she rose to her feet, she could tell that they had heard her screams while Borell raped her. Upon seeing her now, battered and abused, the youngest of the four men looked shocked. Another smirked and stared insultingly at the flesh exposed by the rents in her clothing. The other two kept their faces impassive, their gazes impersonal.

Outside, she saw the bodies of her two manservants, who must have died trying to save her. She furiously blinked back tears. She would never let the Valdani see her cry. There was no sign of Faradar. She longed to know if the maid had escaped, but she couldn't risk inciting pursuit by asking about her.

She thought of her mother and Gaborian, of the journey to the Otherworld, and she realized how afraid she was.

She tried very hard not to think about actually dying; death by slow torture now seemed a certainty.

Most of all, she thought about the mines of Alizar.

Oh, Dar, as I have been faithful and true—in my way—I beg you to help Josarian take Alizar.

27

THERE WAS NO day or night in the mines, no sun or moons, no dawning sky or twilight glow. There was only the obsidian maw of the earth's belly and the sickly glare of smoking lanterns. Once upon a time, employment in the mines had been an honorable trade, a hard and dangerous profession which attracted men because of the rewards they could reap. In another era, many young men came here for a few years to earn enough to pay a bride price, buy land, or establish a business. In that distant time, hope had flowered almost daily at Alizar and dreams had filled the air.

Or so they said. Najdan was always skeptical about the stories people told. If you listened to the whisperings of the mountains these days, after all, you'd learn that Tansen had slain an entire shipload of Kintish pirates in a single night, Mirabar was an immortal spirit, and Josarian was the Firebringer. There was nothing the *shallaheen* loved better than a good story.

Anyhow, whatever life at Alizar had once been like, it was now a never-ending nightmare of hellish misery. While the *shallaheen* kept their children under control by threatening to feed them to the fire-eyed and flame-haired demons that roamed the mountains, the Valdani menaced Silerians with the threat of a sentence in the mines of Alizar. The other mines in Sileria—minerals, gems, and pre-

cious metals—were small, private operations. A few were
still Silerian-owned, but the vast majority of them belonged to wealthy Valdani, whether taken from Kints two
centuries ago or stolen more recently from overtaxed and
disenfranchised Silerians. When people referred to "the
mines," however, they invariably meant Alizar: the vast,
enormously rich mines owned and run by the Emperors of
Valdania for over two hundred years.

Alizar was where Silerians served criminal sentences for
most major and minor crimes. Yes, some crimes so enraged the Valdani that they sentenced the offender to
death; but most of the time, they found it more profitable
to send a man to the mines, where he worked until his
sentence was served or he died—whichever came first.
Yes, some criminals were simply imprisoned; but they
were not safe from the mines, for they were usually just
being held in reserve in case the mines suffered a shortage
of workers after a cave-in or major accident. Almost anyone caught breaking Valdani law in Sileria could count on
being condemned to servitude in the mines of Alizar. Brib-
ery was the only way out, and most couldn't afford it.

Of course, even a law-abiding man wasn't necessarily
safe. Despite harsh laws and a disobedient populace, the
Valdani didn't always have enough prisoners to keep the
mines operating at their full capacity. When this happened,
the Outlookers would simply raid villages, rounding up
men, chaining them like slaves, and taking them to work
in the mines. That was how Najdan had lost his father.
Many of these men were eventually released. Sometimes,
though, they died in the mines, as many convicts did. It
was worst of all, of course, when a family could never
even find out what had happened to a man. The Valdani
seldom deigned to answer questions about their prisoners
at Alizar. So the men who survived the mines and returned
home were often questioned endlessly by people trying to
discover if a loved one still lived. People willingly walked
for days to reach a village where a man was rumored to
have recently returned from the mines, just to ask: *Have*

you seen my father? My husband? My brother? My son?

No one had ever been able to reveal the fate of Najdan's father. Najdan was a practical man and therefore did not torment himself with foolish hope. Petty criminals often drew sentences of only a year or two, and so survived the mines. But Najdan's father, who had committed no crime, had been gone for over twenty years; no man had ever survived that long in the mines. Some people, however, held on to hope even longer than that. A man would have to have a heart of stone not to pity them.

Those who did manage to survive long terms in the mines seldom lived long upon returning home. Though they must have been very strong men to have survived a decade in Alizar, the struggle always took its toll. A thirty-year-old man coming home from Alizar always looked at least fifty and usually died within a few years, living out his days tormented by illness and weakness.

Now Najdan was here in the black pits of hell, where whip-cracking devils ruled the never-ending night. The rebel plan of attack required men on the inside. When the fighting began, men down here would need to lead the prisoners in an underground fight, too. Najdan was one of forty rebels who, posing as ordinary men, had willingly been caught in some petty crime during recent days. Unfortunately, some were still awaiting sentencing tonight, but most of them had already been transported to the mines and sent deep into the elaborate earthworks of Alizar.

It had taken courage to give himself up to the Outlookers and the mines. Najdan had wanted to do it, to prove to himself that despite what had happened that day at Dalishar, he was still a brave man who could coldly face death. Now that he was down here, he saw courage in a new light, encountered bravery such as he had never seen among the assassins. In this shadowy world of pain, hunger, exhaustion, loneliness, and total slavery, men still somehow found the courage to survive. In this underground world of darkness and hopelessness, men still recited the names of their children, recalled the women they loved, and spoke of going home when they'd served their sentences. When the Outlookers weren't looking, *shalla-heen* cut open their palms with their mining tools to swear bloodpacts with each other. When one drink of water could mean the difference between life and death, a *shallah* might still give up his ration to save the life of a blood-brother.

Then again, there was also depravity down here unlike anything that even a Society assassin had ever seen. While most Outlookers were merely indifferent to the suffering of their prisoners, Najdan had already encountered one who positively enjoyed it, and he'd heard stories about several others. Nor were the prisoners all men he looked forward to freeing. There was one he'd already decided to assassinate when the fighting began; the *sriliah* routinely betrayed his fellow prisoners for extra rations, and Najdan didn't doubt he would side with the Outlookers when the attack on Alizar commenced—at least until the battle clearly favored the Silerians. Then there were others who had been made petty, vicious, and cowardly by their lives down here; but perhaps some of them had always been that way. Finally, there were those who had gone mad. Anyone too deranged to work was often executed; but, over the years, Najdan had seen a few madmen wandering the mountains, released early from the mines due to the insanity which made them useless workers. Some long-term prisoners therefore risked pretending madness, gambling that they'd be released instead of killed. Najdan would make no move against any of the madmen here, real or feigned, unless they jeopardized the battle.

He was a strong, healthy man, so although the poor rations left him hungry, he was still well able to do the backbreaking work down here. His wrists and ankles were already chafed and sore from the iron finery of an Emperor's miner, but he was an assassin and contemptuous of pain. For this reason, he could also withstand the lash without much trouble. He ignored the human stench and misery all around him, since he considered himself apart from it. He had come here to do a job, and when the rebels attacked, he would either die or go free. There was no possibility in his mind of spending more than a few days down here.

The one aspect of his term down here that troubled him, however, was the feeling of being *closed in.* He felt the earth pressing down upon him, around him, suffocating him. Sometimes his chest constricted, as if he were smothering, and it took all his self-discipline not to lash out like a madman, battering at the rock-solid walls, floors, and ceilings that engulfed him. Some men who returned home from the mines were never able to sleep inside again, didn't even like to *go* indoors; now he knew why. When he got out of Alizar, he'd be much more amenable to Mirabar's preference for sleeping under the stars when they travelled.

Mirabar. He thought of her up on the heights surrounding Alizar, gathering strength with the other Guardians. He had already lost track of time down here. It was impossible to mark the hours in a place where there was no day or night. Now he had no way of knowing when the attack would begin. He *thought* it would be soon. Hoping he was right, he slowly, carefully began to spread the word, making sure that no one he deemed untrustworthy found out what the rest of them needed to know.

TASHINAR'S KNEES ACHED from the long journey to Dalishar, but she didn't tell the others. *I'm getting old,* she thought. Her youth seemed to have been in full bloom only yesterday. Now she was already an old woman, an elder of her sect, someone whose aged presence was needed to hold the Guardians together in this unprecedented moment. The mystic sorcerers who conjured fire from their own breath and flesh, who communed with shades of the dead, and who hid like children from Outlookers, waterlords, and assassins . . . the *Guardians* were about to enter into battle.

Naturally, Tashinar knew the history of the Guardians. She knew that they had once governed Sileria, that there had been many thousands of them, and that there had even been many like Mirabar. She knew that there had been warriors among them—including Daurion himself. Yet the thought of Guardians entering into battle against the Outlookers . . . Well, it was almost as extraordinary as the thought of them working together with the Society.

She knew from the moment Mirabar first returned to their circle of companions—*with an assassin in tow*—that something extraordinary had happened. The Guardians had already learned from their own communion with the Otherworld that a new age was at hand, that their entire world was about to change. Fire, water, and the blood of thousands would mingle to herald a new beginning in Sileria. Then Mirabar had found them again, had come home, bringing peace offerings from Kiloran himself on behalf of the Society. Two of Josarian's men came with her, too, and they spoke of something called the Alliance, a secret society now pledged to Josarian. Confident, impatient, and driven, Mirabar had become the leader of her former mentors. At her instructions, they had spread through the mountains, alerting other Guardian circles, forging links with the Society and the *shallaheen*, cooperating with emissaries from the Alliance, and sending their own companions into the heart of danger when necessary.

Derlen, Tashinar thought suddenly. He was supposed to be here tonight. He had not come, and no one knew why. Shaljir was such a treacherous place, the very heart of Valdani power in Sileria . . . Tashinar sent up a silent prayer to Dar that Derlen was all right.

When Mirabar had first told her of this plan, Tashinar thought it would be difficult to convince the Guardians to assault what was the most heavily guarded site in Sileria outside of Shaljir. The diamonds of Alizar were the Emperor's single most important source of income in Sileria, and he now protected the vast mines with a force of over one thousand well-armed Outlookers. Almost every Guardian, however, knew someone who had been sent to the mines; many knew someone who had never come out.

There were also those who had seen the roundups, when the Outlookers would seize innocent men and force them into service because there was a shortage of prisoners at Alizar. With their confidence bolstered by Josarian's many victories against smaller targets, and their fear of the Society temporarily appeased, most of the Guardians had proved readily willing to contribute their special talents to the battle at Alizar.

Kiloran was here, too, tonight. *Kiloran himself.* She didn't know precisely where he was, and she'd be just as happy not to encounter him—tonight or any other night—but she could *feel* him. Oh, yes, she knew he was here, and she suspected he *wanted* her to know it, wanted them *all* to know it. He honored the truce between them, but there could never truly be *peace* between the servants of fire and the masters of water. Eternal enmity was in their flesh, their blood, their bones, and Kiloran let the Guardians preparing for battle at Alizar know that he had not forgotten. A subtle vibration of power chilled the air and warned them: *We are allies, not friends.*

Emerging from the darkness, hugging the shadows and moving stealthily, Mirabar joined Tashinar on a summit overlooking Alizar. They exchanged a brief, silent greeting, then Mirabar noticed her nervous twitch as Kiloran again stung the night with his cold venom.

"Ignore it," Mirabar said sourly. "He's just showing off."

"He's not to be underestimated," Tashinar murmured. They both kept their voices low, wary of any remaining Outlookers patrolling the area. "Or trusted."

"No, but he knows there are assassins down there tonight. Some are imprisoned in the mines. Many will be fighting beside Josarian. Kiloran is unconscionably evil, but he doesn't waste his own men."

Tashinar nodded. Why worry about what would happen after tonight, when no one yet knew who would live or die here?

"Who would have thought we would come to this?" she

said, grateful she had at least lived long enough to see this moment. "I never imagined a moment such as this, a dream such as the one you and Josarian share."

"It's everyone's dream, Tashinar. When the Outlookers cut off your fingers as a young woman, didn't you dream of—"

"Not really. Until this . . . you, Josarian, Tansen, the Beckoner, the Alliance, Kiloran . . ." Tashinar shook her head. "Freedom was a tale told by wild-eyed *zanareen* and superstitious mountain peasants."

"*Zanareen.*" Mirabar rolled her eyes. "How they pester Josarian!"

"You've told me that Armian definitely wasn't the Firebringer."

"No. Of course he wasn't."

"Then couldn't it be Jo—"

"Tashinar, you're not seriously suggesting Josarian throw himself into Darshon to—"

She stopped speaking the moment they heard feet shuffling against dust and gravel. They both tensed as the soft footsteps came closer. Mirabar had already warned her that if an Outlooker found them here, they must be ruthless. Tashinar didn't know precisely what that meant, but she had seen the changes in Mirabar since the beginning of the year, and she realized that the girl not only knew what it meant, but had, of necessity, learned how to be more ruthless than most. Josarian's men had begun the first part of the plan soon after nightfall: killing all the sentries and patrols around Alizar. Tashinar tried not to think about her allies stalking men in the dark and strangling them or cutting their throats. She tried not to think about the quiet warrior called Tansen, the man Mirabar had sought for so long. She could tell that he knew far too much about killing other men.

Her heart pounded as she marked the quiet approach of someone coming through the surrounding brush and scrub. She relaxed a moment later when she heard the soft flutterbird call that was the agreed-upon signal. Mirabar returned it, and their ally appeared a moment later: a handsome young man named Zimran.

"Ah, ladies! Right where you're supposed to be *and* on time. Could a man ask for more?" He grinned and, even in the dark, Tashinar could feel the measure of his charm. Many girls must have lost their heart to this one, she surmised.

"Well?" Mirabar prodded.

"Kiloran is ready. Josarian is ready. Tansen is ready."

"The Guardians are ready, too," Mirabar confirmed.

Zimran's breath came out in a rush. "And I guess I'm as ready as I'll ever be. So if you can begin . . ."

"We'll give you enough time to get out of the way," Mirabar said. "Go."

"As always, *sirana*, it's been a pleasure."

After he'd departed, Mirabar grumbled, "He irritates me."

"So I observed," Tashinar responded dryly.

"Are you ready?"

"As the young man said . . . As ready as I'll ever be."

TANSEN HAD RECEIVED word from Zimran that the first part of the plan—eliminating the sentries and patrols around Alizar—was completed. Now Tansen crouched in the dark, waiting to signal the men at his back. Josarian was in the hills on the other side of Alizar, with more men. They had close to forty rebels in the mines tonight, and they also expected some help from the prisoners, once the battle began. There were hundreds of Silerians here tonight, far more than Josarian had ever before committed to a single plan. If Alizar fell tonight, then thousands of Silerians would join the rebellion while the Outlookers tried to recover from the disaster. The Emperor would be furious, as well as financially wounded. The Imperial Council would want to send every military man in the Empire to Sileria; but almost every man in the Emperor's forces was already committed elsewhere. Oh, the Empire's resources were vast, and they'd unquestionably be able to send men, probably more men than the rebels had killed all year; but they wouldn't be able to send as many men as they wanted to. They wouldn't be able to send enough to sweep clear across Sileria and destroy the rebellion overnight.

If Alizar fell tonight, then the Empire would have a war on its hands in Sileria. The long-conquered nation, the imperial province least likely to unite in rebellion, the most thoroughly humbled people in the three corners of the world would astonish men and women from one end of the Empire to the other. Born in shame and servitude, they would carve out a new destiny on the map of Valdani conquests. They would claim their freedom in the rubble of the Empire's humiliation. They would smash the Sign of the Three in Santorell Square and live to see their own Yahrdan take his rightful place in Shaljir.

Nothing will ever be the same.

If Alizar fell.

The alternative was not one Tansen cared to dwell on. If they failed tonight, then he, Josarian, and anyone else who could be identified would be sentenced to death by slow torture. And the rest of the rebels would have merely saved the Valdani the trouble of actually transporting them to the mines for lifelong imprisonment. Not that a life lasted long in Alizar. Barring an accident, most men survived a sentence of a couple of years. Some even survived ten years. No one survived more than that, though. And no one would want to, based on what Tan had learned from the ex-prisoners the rebels had consulted while planning the attack. Indeed, he thought he had never known a braver man than the former prisoner who had volunteered to be one of the forty men positioned inside the mines tonight. The years the man had spent there were carved on his face, but he had gone back, insisting that he'd be most useful to the cause down there.

Tansen had wanted to volunteer himself, for he didn't like asking other men to do something he did not do. However, he couldn't possibly have smuggled his swords into the mines, and—just as someone who knew those tunnels was most useful down there—a *shatai* was most useful in combat when he had his weapons. Killing Outlookers was the task at hand, not bolstering his own pride. Besides, he had needed to set a good example for Josarian, who all too often wanted to act like an ordinary rebel instead of the leader of the rebellion. Josarian could say what he wanted to about how the fight would go on without him, but Tansen knew the truth: men followed *Josarian* more than they followed a dream of freedom. They wouldn't be glowing with courage and anticipation tonight if Josarian were imprisoned in the earth's belly rather than leading them into battle.

It seemed a long time since Tansen had given the signal confirming that his men were ready. He chained his impatience to his will, knowing that every part of the attack depended on every other part. When everyone was ready, then they would move. And all of it would begin with an old woman and a demon girl up on the summit . . .

CAPTAIN FORIDALL WAS working very late tonight, examining the most recent production records. The Emperor's war against the Kintish Kingdoms had gotten off to a bad start, so now there was pressure on Alizar to cut costs and increase profits. The Emperor's demands, coupled with the strain of poring over these barely legible documents well into the empty hours, had given Foridall a headache tonight.

The production records were written in aggravatingly tiny handwriting, since parchment was so costly in Sileria. *Everything* worth having cost extra here. Foridall had spent a fortune acquiring a fifth-level Kintish courtesan last year; she could charge outrageous prices since there simply weren't enough like her to go around, not in this godsforsaken land. Then she'd grown bored at Alizar and deserted him within a season! Foridall was feeling distinctly frustrated these days, true, but he still had no intention of standing in line along with his men to get five minutes on top of some miserable, diseased Moorlander woman. Besides, the bandit Josarian had already sacked two brothels, and a man didn't want to be worrying about some Silerian peasant cutting him in half at precisely the moment when his attention was rather firmly fixed on matters of the flesh.

Those mountain outlaws—well, rebels, if truth be known, despite the official story—were generally making every aspect of Foridall's life a terrible trial these days. Traditional supply lines were frequently disrupted, the roads were no longer safe, costs had soared, and you practically needed to stage a riot of your own to get the attention of Advisor Borell or Commander Koroll lately. While no one seriously supposed that the bandits would be foolish enough to attack Alizar, Foridall had convinced his superiors that there was no point in trying to predict what those bloodthirsty rebels would do. They would be wise, Foridall had insisted, to assign extra men to protect Alizar.

Well, wouldn't you know it? Foridall had gotten his extra men, but not the funds to supply them with food, housing, extra uniforms, and their pay. Many of the men who' had been reluctant to be posted here in the first place became openly resentful when Foridall couldn't magically make these problems disappear overnight.

If it wasn't one thing, it was another. As soon as Foridall's term of service was over, he was going back home for good. Meanwhile, the mountain rebellion had made it impossible to convince another woman to join him at Alizar, even when he offered double the going price. He was getting so desperate he'd even consider a discreet liaison with a *Silerian* woman, by the Three, except that he didn't relish the thought of what would happen if they were discovered. Silerians were very touchy about their women. He'd heard such stories of gelding and other atrocities that it made him consider the whole prospect quite unworthy of the risks involved. These people were barbarians! No wonder so many of them wound up in the mines!

With his head aching and his mind unable to absorb another series of numbers, Foridall quit for the night, doused his lantern, and went outside. Alizar was a vast place aboveground, easily as large as an important village. It was even bigger underground, which was one reason so many Outlookers were needed here. Silerian prisoners made terrible miners and had to be supervised even more closely than a man had to watch a Priest of the Three around his daughters.

Or sons, as the case may be.

Walking toward his private quarters, Foridall morosely supposed that, in the absence of a woman, he could indulge in some of the Kintish dreamweed he'd brought back from his last trip to the coast. It had cost him a fortune and was only mediocre in quality, but at least—

His thoughts ground to a halt as fire suddenly arose from a hilltop directly north of Alizar. One instant, there was nothing, then suddenly . . . there was a blaze that looked as tall as one man standing on another's shoulders. Even as he stared in confusion, it started spreading across the hill. Three Into One, had one of the sentries been smoking a little dreamweed of his *own* and set the brush on fire?

"Captain!"

He looked in the direction a nightguard was pointing and saw that another fire had started. And another! And yet another . . .

"The bandits," Foridall choked, his heart constricting with fear. "It's Josarian!"

"Captain, look, it's . . ."

The fires were spreading like trails across the mountains, stretching out to greet each other. Surrounding Alizar. Surrounding *them*.

"Captain, he's brought his fire sorcerers with him! They—"

"Sound the alarm, you fool!" Foridall shouted. "Wake everyone!"

He had known this was a possibility, and he was not unprepared. Hah! Josarian was a fool to attack the best-guarded spot in Sileria outside of Shaljir! Even now, in the middle of the night, there were never less than two hundred Outlookers on duty aboveground, patrolling the area, guarding the storehouses, watching the tunnels. Within moments, those two hundred men would be joined by all the others; Josarian would suddenly find himself facing a force of over one thousand men! Moreover, Foridall would send runners to two nearby Outlooker strongholds; even *more* men would be here by dawn to clean up what was left of the rebels!

He ran back to his headquarters and immediately started giving orders, galvanizing his men, rallying them to action.

"Captain, sir . . ."

"What?"

"We're surrounded, sir. How will runners get through *that?*"

The Outlooker pointed up to the solid wall of fire now surrounding Alizar. It was slowly moving downhill, Foridall suddenly realized, constricting as evenly as a noose.

"It can't be real," he said, breathing a little harder. "It's a petty sorcerer's trick." But the way some of the men stood gaping belied his effort to diminish the extraordinary spectacle bearing down upon them. He wondered if the Silerians meant to attempt to burn them out. *"Water,"* he exclaimed. "We'll put out their fire."

Following his orders, men ran to the central well, the main source of Alizar's water supply. They started hauling up buckets and passing them along a line, preparing to meet the fire. It was always good to focus frightened minds on a productive task. Foridall congratulated himself.

Without warning, water geysered up from the well, erupting like an angry volcano, spewing moutain-high. Men screamed and retreated from the well, swords drawn, faces distorted with terror. Foridall stared in blank shock, wondering what was happening. Then he realized: *the waterlords.* He'd heard the rumors, of course, that Sileria's mysterious Honored Society was in league with Josarian, but he'd assumed it was just another tale. He'd also assumed that the stories of the waterlords' great and terrible sorcery were wildly exaggerated.

As if responding to his doubts, the water took on a new shape and fury. Foridall watched in horror as the tower of water developed *tentacles* which writhed and reached out in search of victims.

One of the Outlookers bellowed wildly and attacked an outstretched tentacle with his sword, trying to sever it like an arm. It evaded his blade with a quick flash of movement and then wrapped around his throat. Another man tried to help him; a shower of water poured down upon him, and he screamed as if being consumed alive.

"Get back, get back!" Foridall ordered, sickened and appalled. "Get *away* from it."

Ordering his men to retreat did nothing to quench the fury of the water shooting straight up from the well. It splashed onto another Outlooker's face and *clung* there, molding over his mouth and nose like a mask, suffocating him.

Foridall's mind reeled, unable to comprehend what he was seeing. He was incapable of coherent thought, frightened of the fire closing in on Alizar, terrified by the water magic slaughtering his men . . . And then he heard the war-cry in the hills. He looked up and saw the encircling wall of fire turn to slim columns of flame, swaying and parting like young saplings to permit men to pass through: hundreds and *hundreds* of men.

With the firelight behind them, he could only see their silhouettes as they descended from the hills and entered Alizar. Ghostly dark shapes, they waved their stolen swords and crude native weapons as they whooped and hollered like all the demons of the underworld. Their shaggy hair flew wildly as they ran, long wisps of black against the glowing background. Behind them, the forest of fire-pillars exploded with new life and became a wall once again, permitting no further passage, allowing no more men to join or escape this battle.

We're hemmed in, Foridall realized. They had undoubtedly already killed all his sentries and patrols. So many men could not have gotten this close without warning unless they had slaughtered every Outlooker out there.

No, there would be no runners, Foridall knew. No relief from other outposts. And no escape for him or anyone else.

His men here should be in battle formation, ready to smoothly repel this disorganized rebel rabble descending upon them. But dragging most of them out of a sound sleep had taken precious minutes, and the fire and water magic had unhinged their minds and destroyed the value of their training. They were already mindless with fear, and then the fire-backed sight of those howling, hairy barbarians swooping down upon them . . .

"Fight!" Foridall screamed, urging himself as much as his men. *"Fight, damn you!"*

Rebels poured into Alizar from every direction while water continued shooting skyward from the central well. The two opposing forces came together. Bodies clashed, metal rang. Screams of rage and pain promised that blood would soon mingle with the dust. Chaos and terror ruled the flame-lit night.

"Get the guards out of the mines!" Foridall ordered. "Get every man up here to *fight!*"

The Outlookers, though, never came out of the mines. The signal for the guards' evacuation was also a signal for a battle to begin in the belly of the earth. The guards down there were hopelessly outnumbered by the prisoners. Security had always been strict in the mines, but until now, until this very moment, rebellion had never been feasible inside the mines, because hundreds of Outlookers were also out *here,* awaiting anyone who fought to escape the tunnels. Somehow the men in the mines knew what was happening tonight, knew that this was their chance. Someone had told them; someone had *organized* them.

The battle was over well before dawn. Foridall couldn't understand how this had happened. He had more men, better weapons, better training, more money . . . Yet it was over. He had lost. He had recognized his defeat the moment prisoners starting swarming out of the mines. Now all of Alizar ran red with the blood of more than a thousand men. Almost all of the Outlookers were dead. At least the rebels had not won without sacrifice; there were Silerian bodies littering Alizar, too, as the sky turned pink.

The fire in the hills had faded. The central well was ... merely a well again. Foridall had never even seen the sorcerers who had changed the shape of his life forever. He was less than a man now, and far less than a leader: the rebels found him hiding in one of the outlying storage houses. His only consolation in the midst of this catastrophe was that almost none of his men were still alive to see him hauled before his own headquarters, ridiculed, spat upon, reviled, kicked, and frequently knocked down. At least only these foreign peasants were here to witness his humiliation.

They presented him to a lean, hawk-faced man whose simple peasant clothes were covered in blood. Foridall saw the two swords the man wore and suddenly blurted, "You're the one Koroll wants almost as much as he wants Josarian! The one who stole those swords from his Kintish guest."

The man's mouth quirked. "Yes, that's me," he said in good Valdan. "And who are you?"

"I am Captain Foridall, commanding officer of Alizar."

"Ah. So *you're* in charge here." The man looked over his shoulder. He spoke in that guttural mountain dialect this time, but Foridall distinctly heard what he called the man who looked up in response to his comment: *Josarian.*

The most-hunted outlaw in Sileria—in the entire history of Valdani rule in Sileria—fixed him with a hard stare. He and the two-sworded man exchanged a few more sentences, then he—*Josarian*—limped over to where Foridall stood waiting to confront him.

"CAN YOU BELIEVE this skinny, pale thing ran the mines?" Lann said, shoving the Outlooker captain forward for Josarian's inspection.

Someone had stabbed Josarian in the left thigh, and it hurt like all the Fires. He was glad the Sisters had finally arrived to tend the wounded, though some of their faces were set with grim disapproval. They abhorred all violence, whatever the cause or provocation.

"Hurts, doesn't it?" Tansen said blandly, glancing down at Josarian's leg. Without waiting for a reply, he added, "I told you—how many times have I told you?—you've got to stop leaving your left side blind. The way you cock your head to the right—"

"Tan, only women can get away with saying, 'I told you so,'" Josarian interrupted. "Go talk to Kiloran. Take Mira with you. We need to finish the job here."

Tansen nodded and left. Josarian studied their captive.

"Er, I don't suppose anyone else here speaks Valdan?" the man asked nervously.

"I do," Josarian replied. "So you were in charge of the mines? What's your name?"

"Foridall. I, uh, I'm sure you understand why I hid to escape capture. It's my duty to try to . . . report to my superiors what has happened here. But I will take my place as your prisoner now."

Despite everything, Josarian almost pitied him. "Foridall, we're rebels in our own conquered land. We don't take prisoners."

It took a moment for his meaning to sink in. Then panic flashed in those foreign eyes. "But . . . but you've won! You've got Alizar now, the Emperor's greatest source of wealth in Sileria! The mines are yours. You don't need to k—"

"Actually, in another hour, I hope the mines won't be anyone's."

"What do you mean?"

"We're going to try to flood them."

"Flood them? *Flood* the richest mines in Sileria? Perhaps the richest in the world! Are you mad?"

"Not yet, but I do worry sometimes," Josarian said wearily, thinking of his dreams.

They had decided that, after conquering Alizar, they couldn't spare the men to defend it. However, if they simply abandoned it, there was nothing to stop the Valdani from recommencing operations here before long, recruiting new slave labor and new Outlookers. Their best choice seemed to be to ensure that no one could mine Alizar again, at least not for a while. They would carry away all the considerable wealth in the storehouses which had been awaiting transport to the coast. Then they'd burn the buildings. Letting Kiloran use water magic to flood the mines created the risk that he would someday be the only one with access to them, but Josarian had been unable to come up with a better plan and had reluctantly agreed with Elelar's insistence that they must concentrate solely on fighting the Valdani for now.

"Why did you attack the mines," Foridall demanded, "if not to take over production and reap the benefits?"

"The *roshaheen* are really something," Zimran muttered in disgust. His Valdan was better than Josarian's, and he had no trouble following the conversation.

Foridall clearly didn't understand. "What are *rosh . . .*"

"Admittedly, we wanted to wound the Emperor where he'll feel it most," Josarian said. "In his treasury." He leaned forward, despite the way his leg throbbed, and explained to the man he was about to kill, "But we have no wish to emulate him, no wish to enslave men to fill our purses or pay for our war. No wish to rob men of their freedom and dignity. No wish to slowly kill men, day after day, until the years wear away their flesh and their will to live."

"But . . . But they are . . . were *prisoners!*" Foridall protested. "You yourselves punish anyone who breaks your rules. We have a government to support, laws to uphold! They were *criminals.*"

"They were our brothers and our fathers," Josarian said coldly, "and you ran the deathtrap that enslaved and killed thousands of them." He unsheathed his sword. "Make your peace with your gods, Foridall."

"I was only doing my duty, damn you! My *duty!* You can't kill me! You can't! I'm—"

His wailing speech ended on a gurgle as Josarian slit his throat. Watching the wide-eyed corpse bleed a crimson river into the dust, Josarian instructed his men: "Cut off his head. Kill all the remaining Outlookers but one. Give him Foridall's head and send him back to Shaljir on a fast horse. Then gather your wounded and get ready to leave. Spread out, according to your instructions. Everyone must be gone from here by midmorning. Understood?" He tore his gaze from Foridall's body and added, "Tansen and I will stay behind long enough to torch the bodies of our dead."

The losses had not been heavy, considering the target. Josarian felt every single one of them, though. Men had died following him, trusting in him, believing in him. Not one hundred paces from here, young Kynan lay faceup, his long hair spread around his lifeless face, a Valdani sword sticking out of his chest. Many other *shallaheen* lay dead among the slain Outlookers, too. Meanwhile, the thousands of prisoners they had liberated from the mines now rejoiced at their freedom and called for blades that they might open their palms and pledge their lives to Josarian's cause.

He knew he needed them to continue the fight. He knew that all the rebels had entered last night's battle knowing they might die. He knew he would go on with the war, actively recruiting more men. No, he didn't doubt the path he had chosen.

This morning, however, weary, bloodstained, and dizzy from the pain of his wound, Josarian wanted no more lives pledged in his name. This morning, he wanted no more Silerian deaths to his credit. This morning, he felt the unbearably heavy weight of being a man whom others followed.

28

FOR ELEVEN DAYS and nights, Elelar waited in her cell at the old Kintish prison. Waited to die. Waited to be tortured. Waited for something to end the agony of waiting.

To her surprise, an Outlooker had brought her clothing and toiletries from her own house on the third day of her imprisonment. On that same day, the Outlookers had stopped serving her their nauseatingly inedible prison food and started serving her cold but palatable meals prepared by her own chef and brought to the fortress in elegant baskets. The food, like the other items sent from home, was always thoroughly examined before being given to her.

Despite these comforts, however, she was not allowed visitors. That didn't surprise her, for Koroll undoubtedly feared she still had information to share and would try to find a way to communicate with her allies, however obliquely. She would not, in any event, have risked the safety of anyone important by trying to get messages to the Alliance now that she was exposed and condemned. Indeed, she prayed that no one had been foolish enough to ask to see her; such a request would undoubtedly condemn the petitioner to death, too.

It was the lack of news or action that she found most difficult to endure. After the painful and humiliating debacle at the Lion's Gate, she had been dragged here and thrown into this cell. Koroll had come here the following day. Not bothering to conceal his pleasure at her battered condition and humbled situation, he had questioned and threatened her for an entire morning, promising her that it would be "better" for her if she simply cooperated and told them what they wanted to know.

Better for me, she thought with a sneer. Yes, it was positively touching how concerned the Valdani were for the welfare of a condemned woman. They were just terrified of how much she probably knew and desperate to find out what she had shared with whom before they killed her. Once she was dead, there'd be no way to unlock the secrets which would die with her.

Hurry, hurry, hurry, she prayed to Death. She had already determined that escape was impossible. Now dying with silence and dignity was her only goal. She focused on it as determinedly as she had focused on every other goal in her life.

Myrell, the one with the crooked nose, had come here on her second day in prison, sent by Koroll. The butcher of Malthenar, Morven, and Garabar lived up to his reputation for brutality. She had welcomed his blows, fighting back, taunting him, trying to manipulate him into drawing his sword and killing her in a blaze of fury. Her death would come quickly that way—and she would take one more Valdan down with her upon dying, for Myrell would surely be punished for murdering such a valuable prisoner without authorization.

She had nearly tricked him into doing it, too, but then he had hesitated and drawn back. Although the man was both a brute and a fool, even *he* apparently wasn't stupid enough to kill her without orders. What a pity.

If only her cook would poison her food, she thought morosely. If only someone would *tell* the woman to do it. She wondered what was happening at her house now. She worried about the safety of the servants who were loyal to the Alliance, about the secrets the house contained, wondering which—if any—had escaped discovery, and about the Beyah-Olvari. She also wondered why, ever since her third day in this dank hole, she was given the courtesy of food and clothing from home. Why hadn't Koroll and Myrell questioned her since then? She didn't like to think about it, but she knew perfectly well that they had barely scratched the surface in terms of their attempts to make her talk. If they were going to give up so quickly, then why hadn't they already executed her? Why hadn't she even been sentenced yet? Why wouldn't the guards answer any of her questions? Why was there no news? Did Borell mean to simply leave her alone in this cell until she went mad from boredom and inactivity?

She had too little to do or think about in here. Her mind was normally prone to planning, not introspection. She was a doer, not a dreamer. She knew what she wanted and concentrated only on how to get it, letting others trouble themselves with more ponderous questions of right and wrong, good and evil, cruelty and kindness. As a *torena,* she knew her duty to the people who lived under her care, and she never shirked it. As a rebel, she knew her duty to Sileria and committed herself and her resources to it completely, without hesitation or reservation. As a woman, she used the tools Dar had given her to successfully accomplish every duty placed upon her shoulders by her dual identities.

Dar had blessed (or cursed) Mirabar with gifts of fire and prophecy, gifts so rare that they set her apart from all others. Josarian had been born to lead men in battle, to be respected and admired by them. Kiloran had grasped the cold power of water magic in an apprenticeship granted only to men. Tansen had shaped his destiny out of the bitter ashes of his boyhood, carving a new destiny in stone and steel—with skills which were taught only to men.

And I, born a woman, smarter and braver than most men . . . Bitterness flooded her, for what man did not look upon her and see only what Koroll had seen, desire only what Borell had desired? The same attributes which were respected in a man—courage and intelligence—were ornaments, or even handicaps in a mere woman: a mere vessel of men's pleasure; a mere breeder of more men. Elelar was not the right sex to be a warrior, statesman, assassin, or waterlord, and she had no gifts such as Mirabar's. She had a woman's gifts, though; some taught to her by her mother, some simply born into her flesh. So she had coupled those gifts with a cold mind and a brave heart to pursue a dream she would now never live to see; and men, who freely slept with as many women as they chose and who broke their marriage vows with impunity, would call her a whore for this when she died.

She prayed now only for a death that would honor her, such as any man might pray. Even more than she feared death by slow torture, she feared the humiliation of a *woman's* death, the sort of sentence the Valdani inflicted on the female Moorlanders they imprisoned in their brothels. If the Outlookers slowly disemboweled her before vast crowds in Shaljir, she would bear it with more courage than any mere *man* would show, despite her fear and her pain. Only, please, Dar, don't let Borell simply give her to a hundred Outlookers who would rape her until she was dead and then leave her lying facedown in the mud until she rotted.

Please, Dar, as I have been faithful and true—in my way—let my death honor me.

She was astonished to suddenly hear someone unlocking the door to her private cell. No one came here anymore unless it was mealtime, and she had been served a meal not long ago. Her heart pounded with mingled anticipation and fear, wondering who had come to see her and what news—or torment—he brought. She brushed back a stray wisp of hair and composed herself as the door opened.

"Ronall?" she blurted.

She didn't bother to hide her astonishment as her husband was admitted to her cell. She hadn't thought about him since the day the Outlookers had brought her here. Two Outlookers stood in the open doorway now, witnesses to the meeting. Elelar was used to them after eleven days, and Ronall had obviously drunk just enough not to care that they were there.

He came forward, took her hand, then held it uncertainly for a moment, trying to decide whether to kiss her mouth, kiss her hand, or just forget the whole thing. After an awkward moment, he simply dropped her hand and shifted on his feet.

"You are well?" he asked, his gaze searching her face.

Leave it to Ronall to be banal at a moment like this. "As well as can be expected under the circumstances."

The ice in her tone made his cheeks darken. He whirled away from her in an explosive move, only coming to rest when he reached the barred window. He gripped the ancient ironwork there, as if *he* were the prisoner, and looked down into the courtyard far below. Some prisoners were exercised in that yard, but not Elelar. Her captors were afraid to risk her making contact with anyone at all, even another prisoner or an Outlooker who hadn't been personally selected by Koroll for the task of guarding her.

"What are you doing here?" Elelar asked at last, realizing that Ronall wasn't going to say anything without prompting.

"I *am* still your husband." His voice was bitter.

"Not for long," she said dryly. "Presumably they've told you they intend to—"

"They've told me a remarkable number of things." He didn't look at her, just kept clinging to the prison bars and staring out the tiny window. "Before you returned to Shaljir, I was imprisoned and questioned for two solid days. Allowed no sleep or food during that time. Beaten unconscious at some point." He inhaled deeply. "I didn't know why. I didn't understand their questions."

"Ronall . . ." She made a helpless gesture. "I'm sorry. I didn't know. No one told me."

"At first I thought it was because I had refused to give you a divorce. I thought Borell must have ordered the Outlookers to convince me to agree to it."

"Borell asked you to divorce me, then?" It didn't matter now.

"*Asked* isn't quite how I would phrase it."

He looked at her briefly. His wounded expression startled her. *Male pride,* she thought derisively. In a moment like this, as I await death in prison, he resents a blow to his pride.

He looked away again. "When they showed me things they'd found in the house, I was sure at first that there'd been some mistake, that they must have found them in someone else's house. The Outlookers are such fools, it seemed like a mistake they could make."

"It was my house," she said wearily.

"Yes. So I learned."

"Since they've allowed you to see me, I assume they know you were never involved."

"I don't think Koroll ever really thought I was. But he wanted to be sure."

She nodded, wishing he would leave. She shouldn't have to put up with Ronall anymore. "No, why would they truly suspect you? You're half-Valdan, after all."

His brief laugh was quite humorless. "To you, I'm half-Valdan. To them, I'm half-Silerian. A half-caste man belongs to no one in this country, Elelar."

"You'll forgive me if your self-pity doesn't move me to tears at this particular point in my life."

He winced. Closed his eyes. Leaned his head against the bars. "Of course. I've forgiven you far worse, haven't I?"

She folded her arms across her chest. "I recall resentment, anger, accusations, blame, bitterness, and quarrels. I recall a beating. A few rapes." His head seemed to lower with each word she uttered. "But I don't recall a single word of forgiveness from you, not once in over five years of marriage."

"Marriage?"

His shoulders started shaking. She heard him gasp unevenly a few times. To her astonishment, she realized he was laughing. After a few moments, he tilted his head back and gazed sightlessly at the ceiling. She saw tears gleaming in his dark eyes.

"Marriage?" he repeated. "We weren't married, Elelar. We were locked in combat, like two caged mountain cats, neither able to escape."

"Then why did you refuse to divorce me when Borell ordered you to?" she said impatiently.

He laughed again. It unsettled her that laughter could sound so unhappy. "Because I still loyed you."

Her shocked expression made him laugh even harder. She gaped speechlessly at him for a moment, watching him laugh while tears slipped from his eyes. "You're going mad," she guessed.

"Oh, Elelar . . ." He gasped for air, wiping at his eyes. "Surely I've been doing that for years."

"I wouldn't dispute that."

"Ah, my dear wife, your contempt seems to be the one constant in my life, even when everything else has been turned upside down."

"You've earned it," she snapped. "And I am free of the need to pretend to be your wife any longer."

"You *are* my wife," he pointed out. The vehemence in his tone and the possessive expression on his face were more familiar to her than the sad, strangely giddy man he'd been a moment ago. "And I might add that it's the only reason you're still alive."

She frowned in confusion. "What do you mean?"

"As the wife of a Valdan—*half*-Valdan, that is—you are entitled to certain rights not granted to Silerians, no matter how high-born."

"I doubt that Borell and Koroll care."

"My father, who is not without influence, made them care. After I was released, I insisted that no matter what you had done, you were my wife and therefore entitled to courteous treatment after your arrest. Considering the charges of high treason, you are also entitled to a trial before three members of the Imperial Council."

"Your father agreed to this?"

"I . . . convinced him that Borell had arrested you and made these claims because you wouldn't divorce me."

"And your father believed you," she breathed, stunned that Ronall would lie to protect her.

"Since I had been dragged before Borell, ordered to divorce you, and then imprisoned after refusing, it was a rather convincing story," he said dryly.

"And Borell agreed to your father's demands?" Elelar asked incredulously. Borell, who had everything to lose if she had a chance to publicly reveal how arrogantly careless he had been around his Silerian mistress.

"Not at first. But his accusations against you were so . . . slanderous that my father became doubly convinced of his treachery. Borell did not seem to be in control of himself." Ronall nodded and smiled bitterly before continuing, "So Father sent his own messenger to Valda two days after you were arrested, then warned Borell that he had done so. It will look very bad for Borell if anything happens to you before the Council decides whether or not to grant my father's request that you be tried as the wife of a Valdani aristocrat."

Elelar sat down on her cot. "So after your father sent a messenger to Valda, Borell agreed to let you send me some of my things and some decent food."

"Yes." He studied her sadly. "I assume that Borell's accusations were, in fact, all true?"

"Probably," she admitted, seeing the knowledge in his face.

After a long pause, he asked quietly, "Were there really that many other men?"

"Oh, is that all you can think about?" she snapped.

"Well, it—"

"You, who've had so many other women these past five years?"

"I, who was never welcome in my wife's bed," he shot back.

"Did you really think I would ever welcome you again, after our wedding night?" she hissed.

He stepped back as if she had hit him. He closed his eyes as if in pain, then reached blindly for the cold iron bars and rested his cheek against one. "No," he whispered, eyes closed. "I really never thought so."

Fury bubbled up in her now, because she might have

even bothered to be a good wife to this sot, if he had made any effort at all to be a decent husband. "Coming to my bedchamber stinking drunk, grabbing at me, tearing at my clothes . . ."

"I . . . don't remember that very well . . ." His voice was the barest of whispers. His eyes were squeezed shut.

"Do you remember how you hurt me?" she snarled. "How I begged you to stop, to wait, to be gentle?"

Another tear crept out of the corner of his eye. She was only sorry it wasn't blood. "I think I remember," he whispered. "But was it that time or another time?"

"You were *always* drunk." Her voice vibrated with disgust. "Once in a red-moon you'd claim the rights of a husband, and you were always drunk."

He opened his eyes. He met her gaze once, then quickly looked away. "I don't remember those times very well. I remember drinking a lot before coming to you." His breath came out on a soft puff of derisive laughter. "For courage." He sighed deeply. "I remember being afraid beforehand, and afterward feeling . . ." He shook his head. "I don't know. I only know that enough time had to pass for me to forget the feeling, and then I had to empty enough liquor bottles to risk coming to you again."

"*Risk?*" She practically spat the word. "You can speak of risk when *I* was the one who got hurt?"

"Yes, I hurt you." He nodded and repeated, "I hurt you. I wanted to make you love me, but . . ." He shook his head. His mouth turned down at the corners. "The part of me that rules my life and makes me what I am . . ." He drew his breath between his teeth. "That part wanted to hurt you. That part always wanted to hurt you back."

"Hurt me *back?*" she repeated, outraged.

"For never loving me. For despising me. For making me feel small and pathetic and foolish. For making me afraid of my own wife's bed."

"I did nothing—"

"Didn't you?" He smiled sadly and looked out the window again. "I'm no scholar, like your grandfather was. I'm no poet, no warrior, no statesman, no . . . I'm nothing." He pressed his forehead against the bars. "And you always let me know it. From the moment we met."

"You were drunk the moment we met," she reminded him. "You were a drunkard long before we met. You're drunk *now*."

"Not drunk exactly . . . I had just enough to get me here. Get me through that door. Get me to face my wife." The self-disgust in his tone surprised her.

"If facing me is always such a trial, why on earth did you marry me?" she asked irritably.

To her surprise, he laughed again. "At least I no longer have to wonder why you married *me*. What an awful lot of my money is missing, Elelar." He sounded more weary than angry. "Koroll's men discovered that. I never would have, of course. And you counted on that."

"I gambled on it," she corrected.

"Then there were all those people you met through me, people who probably wouldn't have associated with a Silerian *torena* unless she were allied to a Valdani family." He gave her a hard look. "Advisor Borell, for example."

She returned his gaze, her own expression equally hard. "I was a woman alone, after Gaborian died. I needed a husband. You had money, Valdani connections, and you were too interested in liquor and dreamweed and wenching to pay much attention to my activities."

His mouth worked for a moment. Then his sigh was like a surrender. "So. In my own way, I was the perfect husband."

"I would have preferred one who never hit me."

"I know." He was quiet for a long time before asking, "Did you mean to marry him?"

"Borell? No. It was his idea. I tried to talk him out of it, but he wouldn't listen. No man cares what a woman wants, when he wants her."

"You never . . . cared for him, either, did you?"

"A Valdan?" The loathing in her voice was answer enough.

Ronall idly rubbed the back of his neck. "Well, I daresay this has all been harder on him than on me, in a way, even though I'm the one who got locked up and beaten."

"I've been locked up and beaten, too," she pointed out impatiently.

His heavy-lidded eyes flashed wide open at that. "What? When? Who beat you?"

"What do you care? You've beat—"

"I'm your husband, damn you! Of course I care if someone has beaten my wife!"

"Myrell," she said, surprised to hear herself confide *anything* to Ronall. "My second day here. Trying to make me talk. And . . ."

"Yes?" he prodded.

"Borell." Ah, it felt good to tell someone, even if only Ronall. "He assaulted me when he arrested me."

"Borell." He seemed less surprised than she would have supposed. "Did he—"

"He hurt me badly." She didn't want to go into details. The expression on Ronall's face made it plain that he needed none.

"He, uh . . ." Ronall nodded slowly. "As I said, this is harder for him than for me. He believed that you loved him. I always knew that you despised me."

She stared. "Are you making excuses for Borell?"

"No." His smile was wry. "I'm not even making excuses for myself today, though I'm sure this state of mind won't last long." He came closer to her, studying her face intently. "I'm not even making excuses for you, Elelar." He sighed, looking at her as if trying to memorize her. "We are what we are, I suppose."

She felt uncomfortable under that sad, hungry scrutiny. For the first time, *she* wanted to make excuses. "I would have been a good wife to you if you'd have—"

"No, you wouldn't have." He didn't even sound angry. Just terribly weary. "Even if I'd been . . ." He gestured vaguely. "A man. Sober. Tender on our wedding night." His face crumpled vaguely. "Even if I had been brave enough to be your husband, to stare down the contempt that was in your eyes from the moment we met . . ." He laughed briefly and said, "Even if I had been someone *else*, you wouldn't have been a good wife, Elelar."

She was angry again. "You are hardly in a position to lecture me about being a good—"

"No, I'm not," he agreed. "And perhaps I deserved you."

She choked on her outrage. "You deserved one of your serving wenches or farm girls or foreign acrobats, not—"

"And it was a relief to you when I went to them."

"Yes." She arched one brow and reminded him, "And you warned me never to interfere."

"It was bad enough that you thought I wasn't good enough for *you*," he said, grimacing over the memories, "but more than I could stand when you thought I wasn't even good enough for a kitchen girl."

"One who wanted to be left alone!"

That silenced him. He looked away again, his skin flushing again. "Well," he said at last. "You're quite right. I'd have been a bad husband to any woman. And you'd have slept with the Imperial Advisor and the Kintish High King's Ambassador no matter who your husband was."

She couldn't deny that, so she said, "I had a duty to perform, and . . ." She clenched her hands in helpless frustration. "I may not carry a sword! I may not enter government service or run a fleet of trading ships! I could never be recognized as a scholar! I had to marry or join the Sisterhood!" She shook her fists, pouring out her anger on Ronall. "I am allowed only a woman's weapons to fight the Valdani. Borell took another's man wife to his bed and revealed hundreds of imperial secrets to her, but who is in prison now?"

His expression softened as she raged at him. To her astonishment, he reached out to lightly stroke her hair, as if trying to soothe her. He had been gentle enough in bed recently, but there had never been any simple gestures of affection between them before.

"I always thought it was just me that you hated," he said. "I never realized it was *all* men."

Feeling sheepish, she said, "I don't hate all men." Seeing his doubtful expression in the wake of her outburst, she added more honestly, "Well, not *always,* anyhow."

He grinned. For a moment, the years of dissipation faded away, and he looked young again. He was a handsome man. Elelar was so used to despising him, she often forgot that he was rather fine-looking when he wasn't bloated and pale, or greenish and withered, from the abuse he heaped on his body. Her personal revulsion had made her often overlook the most obvious reason so many women opened their arms to him.

He sat down next to her on the cot. She stiffened. He felt it. The Outlookers in the door suddenly seemed less like furniture and more like an audience. She and Ronall had been speaking common Silerian, so the Outlookers were unlikely to have understood a word they said. Still, she realized that the dramatics between her and her husband must have been keeping them entertained.

"So I'm to be held here without being harmed until the Imperial Council announces a decision?" she asked politely, discouraging any further emotional moments with her spouse.

"Yes. Father and I will speak to Borell again, warn him that we know you've been . . . handled roughly by both him and Myrell, and that we fully intend to report this. It should discourage them from attempting anything else. They would be suspects in your murder should you happen to fall off the roof of the prison one night." He tried to match her cool tone, but she was still much better at it than he was.

"Borell wants me dead. He *needs* me dead to protect himself."

"I've grasped that," Ronall assured her dryly.

"If the Council refuses your petition, I will be dead within an hour of Borell's learning about it."

"They won't refuse. They *can't* refuse." His voice was fierce.

She looked at him, curious and baffled. "Ronall, even if . . . politics don't interest you, I've betrayed you in every way possible and dragged you and your family into public humiliation. Why don't you want me dead just as much as Borell does? How can you possibly care what happens to me?"

He shrugged. "Caring about you is my curse to bear, I suppose. Perhaps it will never leave me until I learn to bear it like a man." He leaned over and held his head in his hands. "Dar and the Three know I've borne nothing else like a man."

THE REBELS SEPARATED into smaller, more efficient groups and moved fast after Alizar, sweeping through the countryside, sacking Outlooker outposts, burning down Valdani estates, seizing hostages for ransom, and flooding major Valdani roads. Kiloran had succeeded in making the mines of Alizar completely inaccessible to the Valdani— or anyone else. Now the Society held the rebellion's valuable hostages in watery prisons until ransoms were paid, and urged lowlanders and city-dwellers to join the cause. The *shallaheen* provided Guardians with safe escort into the lowlands to bring Sileria's ancient religion back to her people—and to use the influence of the Otherworld to draw them into the fold.

The Outlookers retaliated by razing whole villages without warning. The price on Josarian's head went up again. Myrell the Butcher swept through the Amalidar Mountains on a brutal rampage of torture and destruction, trying to force information out of the *shallaheen*. One woman gave in and told Myrell what little she knew in order to save her son. In this harsh land where betrayal was regarded as a worse crime than murder, she was thereafter shunned by the other villagers and had to leave the mountains. Another man broke down and talked when the Outlookers started torturing him. Someone slaughtered him that very night, leaving behind the message that left no doubts about why: *So die all who betray Josarian.* Tansen and Josarian heard about it, but never knew who had done it. The assassination was attributed to Tansen, though he had been halfway across Sileria at the time.

After Alizar, Josarian decided it was time to take control of the territory around Dalishar. He'd left men and his sister up there, not to mention Jalan the mad *zanar.* It was a good base, one he didn't intend to give up. The country around it was rough, hard country for Outlookers and *roshaheen.* He had so many thousands of men under his command now, he didn't even know quite how many there were. The rebellion was starting to spread out of the mountains now, infecting the lowlands, inciting the city-dwellers. News of the victory at Alizar made people understand that things *could* be different. The Valdani were numerous and powerful, but not invincible!

They die just as easily as we do, Josarian thought once again, remembering the moment he had first realized it, remembering how hard it had been, at first, to convince others.

Now Cavasar, the first city to hear of his exploits and strain against the harsh reins of Valdani rule, was in a state of constant turmoil. Five hundred more Outlookers had just been shipped in from northern Valdania to keep the "peace" in Sileria's westernmost city. Emelen had sent a runner to Josarian from the east saying that there'd been riots in Liron, too. The runner had had trouble finding Josarian because he was moving so fast; the news, which was nine days old, had only reached him this morning.

Armian had been right. Bit by bit, piece by piece, the tapestry of a new Sileria was starting to weave together, and the resultant canvas would be far stronger than any of its individual strands.

The rebels destroyed Valdani supply lines around Dalishar, then destroyed their supplies. They attacked Chandar and took it from the Outlookers in their bloodiest encounter since Alizar. Afterward, Josarian paid a small fortune

to some Moorlander horse traders to get them to haul fifty
Outlooker bodies to Adalian and abandon them right out-
side the city's main gate one night. Let the Valdani in
Adalian think about *that* for a while.

Josarian was limping when he finally climbed up to Dalishar again, for he hadn't given his wound from Alizar any
time to heal. He greeted his sister and let her fuss over
him while Jalan ranted about prophecy and portents and
the fiery mating between Dar and the Firebringer. Sitting
on a rock overlooking the surrounding region, Josarian
reveled in the knowledge that, astonishingly, all the land
he could see was now controlled by rebel forces.

It was a realization that took him far beyond his original
dream. Yet it was still a long way, he acknowledged, from
the dream instilled in him by a red-haired Guardian one
night in Kiloran's underwater palace.

Zimran arrived the next day bearing messages from various allies and news about events west of here.

"There are three Valdani estates that have been abandoned right here in our territory," Josarian told Zim as they
relaxed together that evening and drank some chestnut
wine. "We got this, among many other selections, out of
their wine cellars."

Zimran wrinkled his nose. "A bit sweet for my taste."
He sighed. "Ah, but the Kints like this stuff. I could have
gotten such a good price for this, before the war."

"It *is* a war, isn't it?" Josarian mused.

"It was a war for us even before Alizar." Zimran added
with a sneer, "But I hear that the Commander of Cavasar
still refers to it as 'the mountain uprising' in his dispatches."

"I wonder what's happening in Shaljir?"

"Still no word from the *torena?*"

"No. Has there been any word from Derlen yet?"

Zimran shook his head. "Not that I know of. But ever
since Alizar, Shaljir has been locked up more securely than
a houseful of virgin daughters after dark. We haven't been
able to risk sending anyone in, and it seems that the Al-

liance hasn't been able to risk sending anyone out."

Josarian considered this. "I suppose all the violence in the countryside would make it hard for Elelar to reasonably explain more trips out of the city, especially at this season. The harvest festivals will begin soon . . . Perhaps she'll be able to leave then." The festivals would be fewer and leaner this year, due to the war, but Silerians wouldn't entirely forgo their social pleasures and banned religious observances.

"You think something's happened, don't you?" Zimran guessed.

Josarian frowned. "I don't know. Dalishar was inaccessible until yesterday. Zilar has too many Outlookers stationed there now for a meeting to be safe. Elelar probably doesn't know how to reach the caves on Niran, and we've been covering a lot of ground almost every day. If she has somehow managed to get out of Shaljir when no one else can, she could be trying to reach us and just doesn't known where to look." He met his cousin's eyes and added, "But the long silence bothers me. No word at all from Shaljir. Not from her or anyone else." He nodded. "It bothers me."

Turning his attention to something more within their immediate control, Zimran said, "I told Sister Basimar about your wound. She sent some salve back with me."

Josarian rolled his eyes. "Jalilar has fussed with it enough already today."

Zimran grinned. "And nagged you the whole time about how you've neglected it, I'm sure."

"*And* nagged me about giving her an escort to go to her husband. I must have told her twenty times today, I'm not sending her *anywhere* now until I'm sure it's safe for my sister to travel that distance." He sighed. "Dar alone knows how Emelen puts up with her."

Zimran nodded his agreement, but replied, "He must be missing her, though. That's a long time for a man to be without a woman. And while he may have been tempted in the east, he values his parts too much to risk them should Jalilar find out he'd used them on another woman."

Josarian laughed but insisted, "Ah, he loves her. You wouldn't know about this, not yet, but when the right woman comes into a man's life, he still enjoys looking at others, but he needs no more than the one he's got."

"Plenty of men want more than the one woman they've g—"

"Plenty of men live their whole lives without finding the *right* woman."

"Or finding the right woman twice?" Zimran guessed, his expression softening.

Josarian lost his smile. "I still miss her."

"I know."

"Everything is so different now, too. It's been so long since I've seen the village we lived in, the house we shared, the bed we slept in together. All I have left of her is her scarf," he said, briefly touching the place where he kept it folded against his skin, "and my memories."

"For a woman like that, memories should serve a man well enough."

It was good to talk to someone who had known her, even though Calidar and Zimran hadn't gotten along well. Tansen listened with sympathy, with empathy, for he had lost loved ones, too, but he hadn't *known* Calidar. And no words could sufficiently conjure up the living vibrancy of the woman who had been Josarian's wife.

"Do you remember the cow she bought the year after you were married?" Zimran said suddenly.

Josarian chuckled. "Ah, the meanest cow in all of Sileria."

"Even its milk was sour."

"And *how* many people did it attack?"

Zimran laughed. "I could never keep count. Calidar's legendary attack cow, meaner than any mountain cat!"

"And Calidar, the only creature in Sileria more stubborn than that beast. Sweet Dar, how I begged that woman to give up her vicious cow!"

"Begged her? I remember the time you gave Lann money to try to buy the damn thing from her. And she wouldn't sell. She was so determined to make it a good, docile milk cow, no matter how long it took."

"Oh, and the *cost* of a cow." Josarian rubbed his forehead, smiling wryly as he remembered their fights about it. "It took everything we had to buy that worthless animal."

"Even so, you tried to set it free one night while Calidar was visiting her mother."

"And nearly got gored for my efforts," Josarian recalled.

"Which was nothing compared to what your wife would have done to you for driving away her precious cow."

"Thank Dar, the tribute collectors finally took it."

"Ahhhh, so the Valdani did have their uses, eh?"

"Only that once."

They grinned at each other and fell into reminiscing about earlier, happier days. It felt good to spend this time with Zimran, to feel close to him again. They had grown up almost as brothers together, had been loyal to each other throughout their lives, from their first boyhood fibs all the way through the dangerous days of Josarian's outlawry. But a rift had grown between them ever since the start of the rebellion, ever since Josarian had chosen a different path in life. Ever since other men had chosen to join him.

He knew that Zim didn't like Tansen and positively *hated* Josarian's friendship with the *shatai*. Josarian had chosen to make Tan his closest male relative when he swore the bloodpact with him, and he knew that Zimran felt betrayed. Nonetheless, if he could go back, he would do it again without hesitation. Not only was he proud to call a man like Tansen his bloodbrother, but he now needed Tansen in a way that . . . he would never need Zimran again. Tansen had been the first man to join Josarian's bloodfeud against the Valdani, and he had never wavered. He was a man of courage, intelligence, commitment, and extensive experience. No other man could support Josarian's leadership as Tansen could. He was invaluable to Josarian. Without him, there couldn't have been a rebellion. In fact, without Tansen, Josarian would have died

with twenty other *shallaheen* at Britar, long ago, and life
in Sileria would have soon erased even the memory of his
bloodfeud against the Valdani.

He trusted no one the way he trusted Tansen, the man
who guarded his back, the man whom he consulted on
every move, every plan, every idea. Of course, Josarian
still loved Zimran, his lifelong friend and companion. He
would go back into the fortress at Britar all over again to
free him. But Zimran, he knew, was only a rebel because
he had no choice. Josarian and the Valdani had forced him
into a life he hadn't wanted and didn't believe in; and his
lack of commitment meant he couldn't lead men in this
cause. Josarian knew that Zimran also felt betrayed when
he made leaders of Emelen and others while Zim simply
protected Mirabar or Tashinar, intercepted Valdani couriers, carried messages between Josarian and the Guardians,
and took orders during major attacks.

Zimran was a brave fighter and a loyal cousin, but even
now, he still didn't truly believe in their cause. Even now,
he would like nothing better than to make peace with the
Valdani so that he could go back to his lucrative smuggling
trade and his easy seductions.

*Sometimes, if he weren't my cousin, I even wonder if he
would . . .*

Josarian chose not to complete the thought, for it was
far too ugly and dishonorable a thing to consider, even in
the silence of his mind. Especially tonight, when he and
Zimran felt close again, as they had throughout the long
years before Josarian had killed those two Outlookers on
a moonlit smuggling trail. Tonight, for a while, the rebellion was out *there,* a thing to be escaped for a few hours.
Here, in the glowing light of ancient Guardian fires, he
and Zimran laughed and talked, once again—if only
briefly—as close as brothers.

When morning dawned over Dalishar, Josarian awoke
from fiery dreams of agony and ecstasy. Sweating with
mingled desire and terror, gasping for air like a drowning
man, he looked across the cave at Zimran. His cousin slept

peacefully. Josarian sighed and closed his eyes, grateful that he hadn't shouted and howled in his sleep. So far only Tansen had seen him in that state. And considering how much it disturbed Tansen, he dreaded the thought of Zimran, Jalilar, Jalan, and the others finding out about it. About the dreams. About the madness and mystery claiming his mind.

He rose silently to his feet, pulled on his tunic, and went out into the fresh air, trying to calm his shattered nerves and reeling senses. Dalishar was high enough to afford him an excellent view of Darshon. The volcano was peaceful, as it had been all year. Only a slender wisp of smoke arose from the belly of Darshon today. The mountain stood vast and majestic against the pink-and-peach-streaked sky, her snowcapped summit piercing a thin, fragile cloud.

She called him, as insistently as the Beckoner called Mirabar.

"Dar," he whispered, as he used to whisper Calidar's name.

Was he mad? Or insanely egotistic? Or doomed by the superstitions of his people? He knew what they said about him: *Josarian, the Firebringer.* He'd have to be deaf, dumb, and blind not to know. He didn't even believe in the Firebringer! And Tansen believed he himself had *killed* the Firebringer. Mirabar, blessed by Dar Herself and gifted with visions of prophecy, said nothing about his being the Firebringer, and almost seemed to sneer at anyone who *did.*

Dar, are You really calling to me? Or am I drunk on power and victory?

No answer came. He concentrated so fiercely that he didn't hear the footsteps approaching him until they were practically right behind him. He jumped as if he'd been stung and whirled round, swinging the *yahr* he had seized instinctively. He stopped when confronted by a shrieking young woman.

"Don't *do* that!" she snapped in common Silerian.

She was pretty and nicely dressed, but dirty and very unkempt. He finally recognized her.

"Faradar?"

"They've taken the *torena*! Days and days ago!" she cried. "I've been looking everywhere for you!"

29

KOROLL SWUNG AN arm and violently knocked drinking cups, lumpy candle stubs, an empty lantern, the remains of three meals, and an inkwell off his desk. *"Damn the Emperor and his wars!"*

He glared hotly at the Outlookers surrounding him, his gaze warning them that his words had better never leave this room. *He* had scarcely had a chance to leave it in more days than he could count.

Damn the Emperor. Damn the Moorlanders and the Kints. Damn Borell. And DAMN Josarian!

The rebel conquest of Alizar had been announced in Shaljir by the arrival of Captain Foridall's head in a sack. Koroll himself had led troops into Alizar, hoping to encounter Josarian but knowing full well the bandit would be long gone. What he found there was an unparallelled disaster. The richest mines in the Empire had been flooded. Koroll immediately assumed this was water magic. If he'd had any doubts, they'd have been dispelled when one of his men, ignoring orders, touched the stuff. Though liquid, it was cold enough to destroy a man's hand on contact, freezing it so deeply it killed the flesh. Koroll had heard such wild tales of the waterlords' power but found them hard to believe. Now the sight of it sickened him to the bone. No wonder the Emperor had tried so hard to destroy the Society!

· So Alizar was lost to them, at least for now. His engineers had no idea how to drain the mines of enchanted water that no one could even risk touching.

The Emperor's single richest source of income in Sileria, probably in the whole Empire—lost. Destroyed overnight. It was a catastrophe that might well have unhinged a lesser man.

If things were running smoothly in Valda these days, Koroll would certainly lose his position, and quite possibly his life, for allowing this to happen. However, the Imperial Council was somewhat preoccupied with the currently unsuccessful war against the Kints, the increasingly costly war in the Moorlands, the riots in Valda due to food shortages resulting from a minor revolt in the north . . . Indeed, the Emperor's ·current problems almost made Koroll's seem manageable. *Almost.*

Three Into One! He'd had over *one thousand* men guarding the mines. The greatest single concentration of Outlookers in Sileria outside of Shaljir! He'd granted extra men to Foridall as a precaution, knowing it to be a wise move, but reasonably supposing that Josarian, who had confined his attacks—after Britar—to modest targets, would never attack the second-best protected site in all of Sileria! Now the bodies of those Outlookers were nothing but a hill of charred bones and of ashes being slowly carried away on the winds. The rebels had burned their corpses, presumably along with the Silerians killed in the battle. Koroll shuddered at the thought, for burning bodies was anathema to the Valdani. These Silerian barbarians didn't know that a corpse should be left intact after death for resurrection·by the Three.

The description given by the battle's sole survivor, an Outlooker who sounded as if he'd never be quite sane again, created bloodcurdling visions of fire magic, water magic, and a prisoner uprising all coinciding with an attack by a rebel force far, far larger than any Josarian had ever before·committed to a single operation. This alliance between the *shallaheen,* the Society, and the Guardians was

no casual thing, no mere matter of the Society's permitting
the rebels to commit abduction and the Guardians' letting
them use a holy site as their base camp. They were fighting
side by side. They had cooperated in a huge—a devastating and astonishing—military assault that must have required long and arduous planning.

And the torena *helped them*, Koroll fumed.

He didn't doubt it for a moment. The evidence they'd
discovered in her house revealed an extensive network of
contacts and informants—none of whom, unfortunately,
were careless enough to identify themselves in their cor-
respondence. Nor had he or Myrell been able to convince
the *torena* to identify her many accomplices in the brief
period they'd been allowed to question her. He acknowledged with considerable frustration that his men had also
blundered their opportunity to catch the few identifiable
people he suspected were involved in her secret business.
The Outlookers had killed the *torena*'s two manservants
at the Lion's Gate and could answer no questions about
what had happened to her maid, having paid her no heed:
She was only a woman, after all, Commander. Although
spies believed that several suspect servants—as well as the
Guardian who was posing as a Shaljir merchant—were in
Elelar's house when the Outlookers arrived to search it,
they were never found inside and had not been seen since.
Obviously, they'd escaped the house somehow, though
Koroll had ordered his men to watch every exit. Now
every possible exit from the city was being carefully
watched. Descriptions of the hunted individuals were cir-
culated, and the few people even allowed to leave the city
were thoroughly searched and questioned.

Meanwhile, the family of Elelar's idiot husband was
protecting her, preventing further interrogation and demanding she be treated as a Valdani aristocrat and even
given the privilege of a trial before three Imperial Councilors! Three have mercy, next they'd be insisting Koroll
release the little trollop!

He had loathed having to permit her cuckold of a husband to visit her once, but Ronall's family had brought pressure to bear on Borell, who had in turn pressured Koroll. No, Elelar's drunken sot of a spouse wasn't connected to her traitorous activities. Koroll had never really suspected the idiot, there was no evidence whatsoever against him, and two days of relentless interrogation had proved to Koroll's satisfaction that Ronall was as ignorant as he was stupid. One of the Outlookers assigned to witness the meeting between Elelar and her husband understood common Silerian; an unusual and very useful trait. The meeting had been maudlin and emotional, revealing little of interest besides evidence that their marriage was every bit as dreadful as Koroll had always supposed. Nonetheless, Koroll didn't like letting that woman have contact with anyone except his hand-picked men. She had fooled all of Shaljir for years; he couldn't even begin to guess for how long, actually. She had bewitched and betrayed Borell, hoodwinked her husband and his entire family, and even eventually convinced Koroll and an Imperial Councilor of her loyalty. There was no telling what that woman was capable of, how far her treachery would go, or what kind of damage could arise from permitting her even the most seemingly innocent meeting.

Borell was frantic now that an imperial trial had been requested. Ronall might only be a half-caste drunkard, but his family was powerful enough that it was possible their request would be granted by the Council. Koroll assumed Elelar would try to proclaim her innocence, despite the evidence against her. Borell feared she would instead choose to ruin as many of them as possible—starting with Borell himself—while admitting her guilt. Borell had the most to lose, of course; besotted with Elelar, he'd apparently been routinely less discreet about state secrets than a Moorlander was about his sexual conquests while indulging in his favorite opiates. Well, Borell deserved to go down for that, and Koroll had no intention of stretching out a hand to try to save him. Nor did he intend to let Borell have the woman killed until Koroll had had a chance to find out precisely what secrets she had shared and with whom. Most important, the woman probably knew more about Josarian than anyone he'd ever encountered; he wanted whatever she knew, and he didn't care what he had to do to get it from her.

First, however, they must await news from the Council, for her family could destroy Koroll if he damaged Elelar in any way now. This was most inconvenient, because although Borell had the most to lose by Elelar's staying alive, Koroll wasn't entirely immune to damage from her. If that woman did descend in flames at her trial, he had no doubt that she would take down as many men as she could. He had been careless around her more than once, openly discussing the Emperor's planned attack on the Kintish Kingdoms in her presence, revealing his plans to combat Josarian while she sat at Borell's side . . . Yes, he could blame Borell, claiming that the Advisor had ordered him to speak freely in front of the woman; but it wouldn't look good to the Councilors, even so.

Damn Elelar. Damn Ronall and his family!

If only Koroll could have tortured her, gotten what he wanted, and killed her. Everyone would be much better off that way. Instead, the Outlookers were forced to treat an adulteress and traitress like visiting royalty who just happened to be staying in their prison!

Apart from that, Koroll didn't see how things could possibly get any worse in Sileria . . . but he suspected with dread that they would.

Josarian had cleared out the storehouses at Alizar before burning them down. Every officer at Alizar was dead. All the production records were destroyed, too, when the rebels had torched the interior of Foridall's headquarters. Consequently, no one knew, or could even reasonably guess, how much wealth Josarian had taken away from Alizar. A lot, presumably, since he had timed his attack only days before the next heavily guarded shipment from the mines was due to leave for the coast, where it would be loaded into a ship bound for Valda.

Josarian would divide up the spoils, of course. The Society would insist upon claiming a share, and he'd be a fool to refuse. He'd probably also keep some hidden away somewhere, selling it in small, unremarkable quantities to Sileria's merchants and gem cutters, conducting the sales via routine and innocuous means. Koroll didn't doubt he could do it. The lion's share of the haul, of course, he'd sell to foreign smugglers at prices below market value. There were plenty of smugglers among the *shallaheen* and Josarian would have ready access to their contacts. Even with a reduced profit on the gems' true value, the rebellion would now be incredibly rich. They could buy silence, smuggled weapons, supplies, loyalty . . . They could ultimately threaten Shaljir itself.

They had been busy, too, since their assault on the mines. They did so much damage in the days following Alizar, from Cavasar all the way to Liron, that Koroll had been forced to send dispatches to Valda admitting that the mountain uprising had become a full-scale rebellion capable of threatening Valdani rule in Sileria. He requested thirty thousand men, hoping he'd get fifteen. He was given only five thousand and no estimate of when more would be sent, let alone how many. He requested additional money to reinforce defenses around Liron, Shaljir, Adalian, and Cavasar; he was given barely enough to repair the damage already done by civilian riots in every city except Shaljir.

He was tersely informed that this was not a convenient time for trouble in Sileria, since the imperial armies were encountering unexpected resistance in the Kintish Kingdoms. Meanwhile, the war in the Moorlands dragged on, growing increasingly costly as the Emperor's forces plunged deeper and deeper into that lush, green land, extending their supply lines ever farther from Valdania. Now, when the Empire was so close to achieving its greatest day of glory—conquest of the free Moorlands and the remaining Kintish Kingdoms!—the Emperor counted on his provincial Advisors and military governors to keep his subjugated peoples under control. Particularly, one dispatch had added scathingly, an impoverished province of feuding factions, a backwater which had been someone *else's* conquest when the Valdani had seized it two centuries ago! The Imperial Council sincerely hoped they didn't have to remind Koroll that control of Sileria was essential for control of the Middle Sea, without which the Empire could not easily control the rest of its possessions.

If it's so damn important, then why won't they send me men, money, and supplies?

Attempting to phrase this question in more diplomatic language, he drafted yet another dispatch to the Council. The mountain uprising was no longer a "problem," it was now a *war*. Although he knew there was no chance he'd get any of the Emperor's prime men, he nonetheless requested imperial fighting forces. Outlookers had less training than the armies. Their pay was lower, and their weapons were older. They were a less combative force than the armies, for their duty was to occupy, hold, and police lands conquered by the imperial armies after the treaties had been signed and the fighting had stopped. Older Outlookers were often ex–army men who'd decided they were too old to continue that arduous life. Young Outlookers were often men who had either failed to get into the armies or who had specifically chosen this branch of service to their Emperor because they believed they were less likely to get killed this way. Koroll himself had become an Outlooker because he believed that advancement through its ranks would be easier for a man of his high intelligence and low birth than it would be in the armies.

In less chaotic times, the Imperial Council would have sent a wartime army to Sileria in view of what was happening here now. With the armies now fully occupied elsewhere, they *should* send Koroll every Outlooker in the Empire who could still walk and hold a sword. But the Outlookers were now overextended, too, on the mainland, trying to hold every single region of the Empire that wasn't in a state of open warfare.

In calmer times, the Imperial Council would also send a wartime commander to take over military rule of Sileria. Even if Koroll were not terminated because of Alizar, he would certainly be forced to take orders in his own province from such a man. Like the armies, however, army leaders were now all fully committed to the wars on the mainland. Consequently, while facing the greatest disaster of his career, Koroll knew that he still had a chance to turn this into the triumph which could propel him to fame and honor in Valda itself. Short of men, money, and support, facing a rebel army strong enough to take Alizar in a single night, burdened with a war sweeping across Sileria from the port of Cavasar all the way to the cliffs of Liron, saddled with an Advisor who was about to lose everything because of a woman . . . If Koroll could wrest victory out of this situation now, then the Emperor would exalt him, would honor him at court, would promote him to a position of power and prestige such as he had not dreamed of before now.

He could still do it. He could still create victory out of catastrophe. But, Three help him, he could not do it without more men! He had bent over backwards for so long to minimize the threat and significance of Josarian's rebellion whenever communicating with the Council that it was now extremely difficult to convince them of how serious things had become here. The lack of men already meant that, according to today's reports, he had just lost control of the region around Dalishar. The rebels had taken it over. *Rebels actually held a portion of Sileria now.*

The loss of Alizar currently concerned the Emperor and his Council far more than sacked brothels, razed outposts, disrupted supply lines, minor battles, abductions, riots, and violent chaos in a faraway province. They wanted Alizar rebuilt and operating again, just as soon as possible, and they were most insistent on this point. They had already sent Koroll several engineers—who had accomplished

nothing. Now they announced that they were sending him
northern wizards, Valda's High Priest of the Three, and
almost anyone else they could think of who might have a
chance of vanquishing Silerian water magic.

How soon, Koroll wondered, before the Society withheld water from Shaljir? Knowing this was an obvious
plan, one that would cripple the Valdani, who based their
power here, Koroll had already given orders to start storing
water within the city walls. If their supply dried up, they
must be ready to hold out until they could end the rebellion. The city reservoir was always brimming now, and
every official building and private Valdani home was filling up with barrels of water. Coopers were earning a fortune, raising prices as the demand for barrels increased.
They took on extra apprentices, and their workshops were
busy even in the middle of the night lately. Koroll encouraged Shaljir's vast Silerian population to store water,
too; he could confiscate it from them when the time came.
He'd keep Shaljir's Valdani population safe for that much
longer, and the rebel alliance would be killing their own
kind as they starved the city of water. It would therefore
be an effective scheme in several ways.

He had nearly finished composing the dispatches he intended to send back to Valda when yet another of his men
entered his chamber in a state of near-hysteria. This was
becoming so common he didn't let it affect him anymore.
The man's outburst, however, *did* surprise him.

"Commander, please, you must come to Santorell Palace! Something terrible has happened there!"

AMITAN WAS LYING wounded in one of the caves on
Mount Niran, a Sister tending him and Tansen at his side,
when Mirabar arrived with her two *shallah* guards and
Najdan. There were over a hundred men living up here
now, and they had obviously recently returned from battle.
Several were wounded, and she noticed fresh offerings on
the altar that her own circle of companions had constructed

here last spring. The offerings were a sure sign that men had been lost in the recent fighting.

She'd already heard the news that the rebels had taken back Dalishar, as well as the surrounding region. While most rebels were still living in scattered groups no bigger than this one, over five thousands rebel fighters were now based in and around Dalishar. Refugees from farms and villages sacked by the Outlookers were streaming into the rebel-held territory now, setting up camps, harvesting the crops from abandoned Valdani estates, cooperating in the tasks of daily life under the direction of rebel leaders.

Part of Sileria is already ours.

It seemed incredible to her, now that she was returning to Niran, where her visions had begun, where her journey into destiny had commenced. Now there was more than talk in the lowlands, more than speculation in the cities. Some were ready to join Josarian. Some were still waiting to see which way the wind would blow before committing themselves. And some, she knew, were still awaiting proof that Josarian was the Firebringer.

Destroying Alizar and seizing territory from the Valdani isn't enough for them. No, they won't be happy until Josarian jumps into Darshon!

She could tell the men up here were surprised to see her. Many greeted her with respect now, though she fully suspected some would scream like frightened children if they happened upon her in the dark without warning. It wasn't her appearance that surprised them now, though, for they all knew about her and most of them had seen her before. She just wasn't expected here. This was an unplanned visit. She hadn't needed a message from the Beckoner to understand that she must tell Tansen what she had just learned. She just feared what he would do about the news she brought. She had a feeling she knew; she also knew she must try to talk him out of it.

This was not the moment to share the news, though. She found him tightly gripping Amitan's hand as the man lay dying on the floor of a cave. Men hovered around the cave entrance, silently watching, waiting for a verdict on Amitan's life. Pushing her way through the crowd, Mirabar joined Tansen, accepting his brief nod as greeting enough, then glancing questioningly at the Sister. Pale with fatigue, the Sister slowly shook her head. Nonetheless, she sprinkled the wound with some soothing balm and started chanting. She had been at it a long time, Mirabar realized, hearing how hoarse her voice sounded.

The wound in Amitan's belly was narrow and fairly clean, but the fever and pain, the trembling and grimacing, and the *smell* . . . His innards had been pierced and were poisoning him. It was a gruesome way to die. It was *wrong*, for Amitan, who wasn't much bigger than a woman and who always had a thoughtful argument ready, was a brave man loved by the wife, mother, and sisters who depended on him. Mirabar remembered his courtesy upon meeting her, despite his fear; his assistance with her plan to capture an assassin, despite his horror over such a wild notion; his willingness to accompany her to Kandahar, despite his terror of Kiloran.

She remembered how he had hoped to find his brother, taken long ago, among the prisoners freed from Alizar, and how subdued he had been afterward, not having found him. Najdan had never expected to find his father; if he had felt any disappointment upon not finding him, then he hid it well. But Amitan had taken it hard.

Now young Kynan, who, like Amitan, had been among Mirabar's first rebel companions, was dead at Alizar; and Amitan, she could see, would be dead within a day or two. Her throat filled with sorrow and guilt, for she had brought him to this moment, as surely as Tansen and Josarian had. She was as much a cause of men's violent deaths as she was part of their pursuit of freedom.

"Tan . . ." Amitan's voice was thin, his breath harsh with pain. His teeth chattered while he sweated.

"I'm here."

"My women . . ."

"We'll take care of them. You know that," Tansen said quickly, his voice subdued but even.

"P . . . Prom . . ."

"I promise."

"L . . . Lann . . ."

"Here!" The big man stumbled forward from the mouth of the cave and collapsed at Amitan's side.

Amitan said nothing. Just smiled weakly at him. Lann, a mountain of a man with a hairy face and a smuggled Moorlander sword that Mirabar doubted she could even lift, started weeping. Amitan looked away—and his gaze fell on her.

"Sirana."

"Amitan . . ." She tightened her face against the tears she felt gathering. "I will miss you."

"You will see me again . . . I hope. Take my . . . knife. Give it to my . . . wife when you . . . see her."

"I will. And when the time comes, I will Call you myself."

"Prettier . . . than I used to . . . think, *sirana.*"

She smiled, almost embarrassed. "As handsome as I always thought, Amitan."

He tried to smile but was wracked by another wave of pain. His eyes sought Tansen's. "I . . . ready."

Lann, whom Mirabar had seen fight Outlookers with vengeful fury and laugh with exultation when most men were weak-kneed with fear, now convulsed with sobs. She felt a tear slide down her face and wiped it away.

"Ready for what?" she asked.

Tansen met her gaze. His was dark and blank. "Take the Sister outside now," he told her. "Lann?"

"I'll stay," Lann insisted between watery gasps.

The Sister looked uncertainly from Amitan to Tansen. "You're not really going to do it?"

Mirabar frowned. "Do what?"

"Take the Sister outside," he repeated quietly, his grip tight on Amitan's hand.

"But w—"

She stopped in midsentence, realizing. Understanding. Amitan didn't want to linger in terrible agony for another day or two. Her gaze flashed briefly to the now-familiar soft-leather harness lying on the cave floor nearby, to the two sheathed swords the warrior tended as attentively as mothers tended their children. Killing enemies was his talent, whether he liked it or not. But killing a friend . . . He would do it because he knew someone should, and no one else would be willing. He would show no emotion afterward, and some men here might even say they'd expected no better of a mercenary. And Tansen . . . he would carry this moment in his heart, another private scar.

Mirabar nodded in acknowledgment of his order, laid a hand briefly upon Amitan's shoulder in farewell, then dragged a reluctant Sister out of the cave. She used the sharp edge of her tongue to make the men stand back, giving the three rebels inside the cave a little privacy as one of them began his journey to the Otherworld.

Hovering at the mouth of the cave after ordering the others away, she heard the faint hiss of a steel sword leaving its sheath. Voices murmured low. There was a rustling sound and some groaning. She imagined Lann shifting Amitan's body to expose his neck for the quickest, cleanest kill. Then the silence stretched out, straining her nerves. Just as she was wondering if it had already happened, if it could have ended so silently, she heard the muffled sound of Tan's blow, followed by the mourning note of Lann's wail.

While Lann sobbed inside the cave, Tansen stalked past Mirabar. He held a bloodied sword in one hand. His harness was clutched in the other, its sheathed sword dragging through the dust as he walked past the silently staring men and disappeared into the gossamer forest.

HE DIDN'T RETURN to camp until long after dark. Until after Amitan's body had been burned and the ashes scattered on the wind. He had no intention of tolerating compassionate comments or wounded gazes. He didn't want to endure another moment of Lann's weeping for his boyhood friend. He didn't want to think about the same thing he knew Josarian would dwell upon when the news reached him: Amitan had wanted to live in peace. He'd joined Josarian's bloodfeud because he'd had no choice, and he had initially resisted joining it. True, he had ultimately embraced the dream and committed himself unreservedly to the rebellion. But if not for Tansen and Josarian, Amitan would be home in bed with his wife tonight, poor but alive, in Emeldar. It was the image which would not be banished as Tansen had killed him.

He came back to camp long after everyone but the sentries had gone to sleep. *She* was waiting for him, however, and he supposed he should have counted on that. She hadn't been expected at Niran and wouldn't have come unless it was important. And Mirabar was not one to be distracted from something important.

Knowing she was capable of setting fire to his bedroll if he tried to get into it without talking to her, he joined her around the small, woodless fire she had made in the center of camp, far out of earshot of the sentries. She glanced briefly at him, then returned her pensive gaze to the flames. He studied her warily. At such moments, it was difficult to tell if she was communing with the Otherworld, a practice he had stopped doubting after Kandahar, or merely thinking.

The dark night and the glow of the fire made her look particularly demonic tonight, especially since weariness had sharpened her features. Those golden eyes seemed to almost absorb the flames, dancing as they did, hot and magical. With her expression intent and mysterious, he was startled to realize there was sometimes almost something . . . erotic about her: the passion, the power, the secrets, the courage. He'd been without a woman for a long time, fixated on only one woman since returning to Sileria; a woman he couldn't have. He was surprised to realize that, if not for the boyhood superstitions burned into his heart, there were things about this woman that might have drawn him to her like a moth attracted to her flames.

Strangely embarrassed by his thoughts, he shifted uncomfortably.

She noticed. Her smile was brief and slight. "Don't worry. He's not coming."

He shrugged. "I didn't think he would. You've said it takes time for the dead to reach the Oth—"

"No, I didn't mean Amitan." She held his gaze. "I meant Armian."

His belly tightened. He didn't know what to say for a moment. Then he heard himself blurt, "You've never asked why I killed him. My own bloodfather."

"I know why you killed him," she said simply.

"How could you know that?"

"Because *he* knows, and I know what he knows."

"He knows?"

"I didn't say he understands," she pointed out, "only that he knows. You didn't want Kiloran, Armian, and the Society to rule Sileria. He knows, but he doesn't understand."

"And you?"

She looked surprised. "I understand. Of course I understand."

"You haven't . . ." He fished awkwardly for the right phrase. "You haven't explained it to him?" It sounded foolish when he said it aloud. Armian was *dead,* after all.

Mirabar shook her head. "The dead are . . . Well. Very different from us."

"Dead, for one thing," he said dryly.

She gave him a look, one that made him grin despite the topic of their conversation. "They are merely *shades,*" she said. "A shade is a kind of . . . essence. They are not really who or what they once were, though when this world revolves in harmony with the Other one, sometimes we can Call them forth in the form of a shadow of what they once were." She sighed and added, "People Call forth a loved one and tell him . . . how the children are growing, what's happening in their lives, whether or not the harvest was good . . . We—the Guardians—don't stop them. It makes them feel better, and there's no harm in it. But these things are meaningless in the Otherworld, just as the Otherworld is a mystery to us."

"Then the only point in Calling these shades is to make the living feel a little better?"

"No." She tried to make him understand, her face animated as she spoke. "Shades can guide us, if we listen well, for they have a wisdom free of earthly fears and desires."

He returned to the subject which most interested him. "But Armian wouldn't be able to understand if I tried to explain . . . I mean . . . If, uh, you—"

"No." She seemed to feel sorry for him, which humiliated him. "He's not really Armian anymore, you see. No longer someone you can argue with and convince of something. Not someone who can change and . . . adapt. He's . . ." She shrugged, looking a little frustrated. "He's a shade of Armian."

"Who knows everything that Armian knows."

"Everything that Armian knew when he died."

"More than that," Tansen reminded her. "He knows the Moorlanders would have failed us nine years ago. He knows we can win now. He has urged—"

"He is guided by powerful forces, the same forces which sent me to Kiloran's palace in search of you. He is their tool, their instrument, nothing more. The Beckoner is no mere shade, and Daurion and the others I have seen . . ." She slid a fine-boned hand into her hair and tugged on it. He could see how much her own ignorance about these forces still frustrated her. "I think they are gods, but I'm not sure."

"So Armian knows why I killed him," Tansen said slowly, "but he doesn't understand. I assume that means he also doesn't forgive me?"

"I don't . . . We are taught that vengeance is an earthly matter, not a concern in the Otherworld."

"I didn't ask if he wants vengeance, I asked—"

"He loved you," she said. "That remains within his shade."

He was silent, frustrated by her answer but unwilling to plead for a better one.

She seemed to know this. "I'm sorry, Tan. Forgiveness was evidently not in his nature, and it's not in his shade. So I just don't know."

"Can you ask him?" He was ashamed, couldn't imagine why he was doing this, but he had to know. "Next time you—"

"I don't think there'll be a next time."

That stopped him. "What do you mean?"

"I mean he's not needed anymore, and so the link between us seems to have been dissolved. He has accomplished what he was sent to achieve. The Society, the Guardians, you, me, the *shallaheen,* the Alliance . . . We are together now. We've started a war. More people will join us, or not, for their own reasons, but not because of Armian."

"So that's it?"

"I think so."

I'll never see him again.

Darfire, he hadn't even wanted to see him in the first place! But he had loved Armian as much as he had hated him, he supposed, and some foolish, weak part of him had privately seized upon the notion that he might even see him again—and perhaps be forgiven.

"I'll never see him again." He was appalled to hear himself say it aloud. And to a woman. But this woman, he acknowledged, had already known what he was thinking. This woman knew what Armian knew.

"Not," she said, "unless you can get his *shir* back from Kiloran and bring it to me close to the anniversary of his death."

"Of course. I'll just ask Kiloran for it when we meet in Idalar," he said dryly.

Her smile was wry. "*He* hasn't forgiven you, of course."

"He hasn't forgiven the Sister who spanked him when he was born."

She laughed at that. He wasn't sure, but he thought it was the first time he'd ever heard her laugh.

Realizing that she must be very tired and eager to retire, he thought he'd better find out why she had come here. So he asked.

She sobered instantly. "There's finally news from Shaljir. It's very bad."

Elelar is dead.

He couldn't even breathe. "Go on." His voice was tight and hard.

"The *torena* is in prison. The house has been ransacked. It's not certain how much the Outlookers know, but they've obviously learned enough to arrest the wife of a Valdan."

"Half-Valdan," he said absently, hearing the relieved pounding of his own heart. Would Elelar freeze with horror if news of *his* death were brought to *her?* Hah! He'd be a fool to even hope so. "How did you learn this?"

"Derlen. He, his young son, and the servants who worked with Elelar were in the house when the Outlookers began searching it. They escaped." She fixed him with an interested stare. "They fled into underground tunnels that you apparently know all about."

"Did Derlen tell you what they found down there?" he asked carefully.

"Beyah-Olvari." Seeing the confirmation in his expression, she breathed, "So it's true."

"You doubted him?"

She shrugged. "Well, no one could be less given to flights of imagination than Derlen, but it sounded so incredible."

"Josarian knows, too, but no one else. We must protect them for now."

She nodded, understanding. "They stayed in the tunnels for many days. The *torena* was arrested and imprisoned upon entering Shaljir, before anyone could warn her. Then

the Alliance in Shaljir ceased all activity while they tried
to determine who else was being watched. The Outlookers
searched the city high and low for Derlen and the others,
and no one could leave by the city gates or the port without
a thorough search and interrogation." She smiled as she
added, "They finally disguised Derlen—and his boy—as
sea-born, so he could escape Shaljir on a fishing boat."

"They've tattooed him?" It was a custom the sea-born
folk had adopted from the Moorlanders a thousand years
ago.

"No, just painted him. He found it humiliating, nonetheless. Derlen's dignity is *very* important to him." She
clearly enjoyed the image of Derlen covered in fake tattoos. "Anyhow, he sought me as soon as he was free and
back on land."

"Elelar was definitely still alive when Derlen left Shaljir?" Mirabar would have told him if Derlen had said otherwise, but he had to be *sure*.

"Yes."

"Why?" he asked. "Surely—"

"Her husband's family have requested a trial. Appar-
ently this means exchanging dispatches with the Imperial
Council and, if the request is granted, sending Elelar to
Valda."

"Her *husband's* family?"

"Perhaps she convinced her husband she was innocent,"
Mirabar suggested. "I have observed that men's brains often go numb in the *torena*'s presence."

"True enough." He decided not to wonder—let alone
ask—if she included him in that observation. "But surely
this would only increase Borell's interest in killing her. He
can't afford a trial. It would expose him, too."

"The husband's family knows it. They're evidently prepared to charge Borell with Elelar's murder should anything happen to her before her trial—if she's granted one."

"And if not . . ."

"She probably won't live to see the sun set on the day
that Borell and Koroll find out she's been refused a trial."

"Where is she being held?"

"The old Kintish prison in Shaljir, across from Out-looker headquarters." She paused, then said, "The rebels can't attack Shaljir, Tansen. We're not ready."

"I know."

An expression of dread spread slowly across her face. "You can't free her. You must know that. No man could—"

"I'm a *shatai,*" he snapped. "I can do what other men can't."

"*Your* brain is useless, too, where she's concerned," Mirabar snapped back. As he rose to his feet, she said, "Come back here!" She jumped up and followed him as he walked away. "This isn't settled!"

"Yes, it is."

"What are you going to do?"

"Leave."

"Right now?"

He met her gaze. "You didn't really think I'd simply go to sleep and hope for the best, did you?"

"You're going to Shaljir?"

"By way of Idalar. Josarian will be there, meeting with Kiloran. He expects me there, too. I think he wants me to go east again."

"Tansen . . . You should know better than to risk everything for a personal—"

"It isn't only personal," he lied. "She's too valuable to leave rotting in a Valdani prison. Josarian wouldn't leave his friends to die in prison at Britar, and I won't leave one of the most important assets to the rebellion in prison in Shaljir until Borell and Koroll finally feel free to slaughter her."

"You have responsibilities that—"

"*I* decide my responsibilities, *sirana.*" He suddenly recalled Josarian once saying something similar to Elelar.

He left Mirabar cursing under the stars as he stalked into a cave to gather his things. When Lann awoke, he simply told him he was restless and would leave tonight for Idalar. His tone prohibited argument.

Back outside, Mirabar stood waiting for him, her own satchel slung over her shoulder.

"Where do you think *you're* going?" he demanded.

"With you."

"I don't need a nagging woman on my back from here to Idalar."

She gritted her teeth. "I am a Guardian of the Otherworld, gifted by Dar herself, blessed with visions of prophecy, and *you* should be a little more respectful."

"You won't be able to talk me out of this. You and Josarian *together* won't be able to talk me out of this."

"Then I'm apparently doomed to help you."

"I don't want your—"

"I risked my life searching half of Sileria for you. I don't give a damn what you want. I'm not about to hand you over to the Otherworld until you've finished your work in this one!"

"Najdan won't like this."

"Najdan will catch up with me later."

He made one last effort to get rid of her. "Descending Niran in the dark is very dangerous. And I won't help you or hold your hand," he lied.

She glared at him. "Haven't you heard? Demons can see in the dark."

30

"YOU KNEW?" TANSEN snarled at Josarian. "You *knew,* and you didn't send a runner to Mount Niran?"

Josarian made a helpless gesture, his expression softened by a pity that infuriated Tan. "Faradar says Elelar was seized just before the twin-moon. The Valdani surely killed her long before Faradar finally found us at Dalish—"

"Derlen has recently escaped from Shaljir with news that Elelar is still alive."

Josarian's face revealed his astonishment. "Why?"

Tansen briefly explained what Mirabar had related to him. They were staying in Kiloran's camp near Idalar. The country around here was swarming with Outlookers, but the camp was well protected by *shallaheen*, assassins, and water magic. The information they'd leaked to the Outlookers suggested that Tansen was somewhere in the west, that Josarian was still at Dalishar, and that Kiloran was near Alizar, since it behooved the rebel leaders to keep their meetings secret.

"Alive," Josarian said at last. "Tan . . . we cannot attack Shaljir. Not yet."

"Have I asked you to?"

"You're going anyhow, aren't you?"

"Yes." And he'd knock Josarian unconscious if he tried to stop him.

He should have known better.

"I'll come with you," Josarian said.

Damn. "No."

"You came with me to Britar."

"This is different."

"Not that different."

"Times have changed."

"You mustn't go al—"

Someone said, "I'll go with him."

They both whirled to confront the man who had intruded upon their conversation. Josarian relaxed when he saw it was his cousin. Tansen eyed Zimran without trust or favor.

"No, I'll go," Josarian said. "It is a brother's du—"

"You've got to work on the lowlanders," Tansen reminded him. "We need them, and they're stalling."

"When we get back," Josarian assured him.

"You're not coming with me. You're too important to risk in a jailbreak in Shaljir."

"So are you, but you're going."

He knew that Josarian knew it wasn't a decision based entirely on loyalty to an ally. Unlike Mirabar, though, Josarian didn't criticize him for letting his head be ruled by . . . something else. Darfire, that girl had a tongue like a *shir!* And she had cut him with it all the way from Niran to Idalar. She thought she was coming to Shaljir with him, too, but he'd slit his own throat before he'd put up with her *and* Elelar at the same time. Besides, this was going to be tricky enough without trying to sneak the most easily identified rebel in Sileria through the city gates; the Valdani had a description of Mirabar, and there was no denying how much she stood out in Sileria.

Cooling his temper, Tansen said to Josarian, "You and I can't both go, and you know it."

Josarian started to argue, but Zimran interrupted him. "Tansen is right," he said. "So I will go in your place, Josarian, as is my duty, since we are blood, too. By birth."

Tansen ignored the less-than-subtle posturing. He was Josarian's closest living male relative now, and Zimran knew it. He wasn't going to lower himself by jousting with Zim about it.

Moved by the gesture and wholly unsuspicious of its motives, Josarian swallowed hard, agreed to the plan, and embraced his cousin. Tansen merely tried not to roll his eyes. However, he realized he was hardly in a position to question or ridicule Zimran's motives for accompanying him to Shaljir. He didn't want Zim's company, but he supposed that he might need some help for this reckless scheme. At least this way, he wouldn't have to waste any more precious time arguing with Josarian.

"I'll need a woman with me, too," he said, "but not Mirabar."

"Faradar will want to go," Josarian said.

"Then she'll need to get ready right now. I'm not staying."

"Zim," Josarian said, "will you go tell her?"

After Zimran had left them alone, Tan realized there was something else he needed to tell Josarian. Something that he was ashamed he had scarcely thought about since learning of Elelar's capture: Amitan.

"Josarian . . ." he began uncertainly. Josarian had grown up with Amitan, had been fond of him, and had used the full powers of his persuasion to bring his boyhood friend into the bloodfeud. He would take this news hard. "There's something I must tell you. I bring you sad news . . ."

MIRABAR FUMED FOR more than a day about Tansen's having left her behind at Idalar. Josarian had delivered the stern and unyielding orders that she remain with him until given new instructions, but she knew that the *shatai* had made him do it. And it infuriated her. She had risked everything, left her circle of companions, and braved Kiloran's wrath alone to find Tansen and unravel the mystery of his—and Sileria's—destiny. She knew he wasn't supposed to die yet, but now he was risking everything for that woman.

There was no denying that the *torena* was fully devoted to the cause, but Mirabar detested her all the same: so smug, so superior, so arrogant. So manipulative. Some men simply couldn't see past her allure and so fell completely under her spell. It might be helpful to the rebellion when Elelar used her talents to entrap the *roshaheen,* but it was nauseating when she did it to her own kind. Tansen, Mirabar had realized, knew precisely what that woman was, yet even he gave in to her wiles. He was worse than the other fools! He knew better, yet he couldn't stay free of the *torena*'s web, even so.

Now it seemed that the *torena* had lost control of one of her spells. According to Derlen, Borell's rage was reported to be more personal than political, for he had believed that Elelar was in love with him. He had even intended to marry her! Mirabar might be a stranger to the dance between man and woman, but she nonetheless knew just how much a man hated to be made a fool of by a woman. *Especially* the woman who slept in his bed. By the time the Alliance had found an escape route for Derlen, the rumor was apparently all over Shaljir that Borell had raped and beaten the *torena* upon arresting her. It was so widely known because he'd been indiscreet enough to assault her in the guardhouse of one of the city's busiest gates! Mirabar shuddered with revulsion, part of her full of pity for the *torena* and an empathetic rage at the Advisor. This was how men dealt with their female enemies. It was as humiliating and debasing as it was painful. Mirabar might loathe the *torena*, but she nonetheless wished she could incinerate Borell's parts for what he had done to the woman. In the mountains, bloodvows were sworn for such an offense, and bloodfeuds began over such an outrage. However, Mirabar doubted that Elelar's Valdani relations-by-marriage would slay Borell as he deserved. What a pity.

Naturally, she hadn't told Tansen about this. She'd already known how much she risked even in telling him about Elelar's imprisonment. She had wanted to be the one to inform him of the *torena*'s capture so that she'd also have a chance to try to stop the insane thing she fully suspected he'd decide to do upon hearing the news. If she'd told him about Borell, too . . . There was no telling what he would do. Borell deserved to suffer for what he had done to Elelar after arresting her—as if imprisoning, torturing, and planning to execute her weren't punishment enough!—but Mirabar didn't intend to lose a prophesied warrior by encouraging him to break into Santorell Palace to fulfill a bloodvow.

If Tansen actually succeeded in getting the *torena* out of prison, Mirabar only hoped that Elelar had the wit to keep her mouth shut about Borell, at least until they were safely away from Shaljir and it was too late for Tansen to turn back.

Here at Idalar, there were important matters to occupy Mirabar while she worried about what would happen in

Shaljir. To her surprise, Kiloran had convinced representatives from the major clans among the lowlanders of the western and central districts of Sileria to meet with Josarian. They'd been brought here by assassins, who had blindfolded them while escorting them to Kiloran's camp, lest any of them consider betraying rather than joining the rebellion. Even more surprising—astonishing, in truth—was the arrival of ten leaders of the sea-born folk.

Having never been to the coast, Mirabar had never before seen the sea-born, for they seldom ventured inland. Indeed, many of them never even left their boats. Sea-born folk might go their whole lives without ever once setting foot on dry land. Mirabar repressed a shudder; her experiences at Lake Kandahar had given her a general distaste for large bodies of water. However, the sea-born were, for Silerians, relatively free of the influence of Kiloran and the Society. The waterlords had no power over the sea, a domain ruled solely by the powerful gods worshipped by the sea-born folk.

Fascinated by their exotic appearance, Mirabar studied them with unconcealed curiosity. The sea-born studied her in turn, for they, too, had heard about her. Unlike the *shallaheen,* however, they hadn't been raised to fear someone like her, so their gazes merely revealed interest.

The lowlanders and the sea-born folk were enthused about the destruction of Alizar, where many of their own kind, too, had been imprisoned over the centuries. They were impressed by the rebellion's control of the territory all around Dalishar and properly respectful of the rebels' daily attacks on Valdani targets. Yes, they knew that the imperial military forces were overextended on the mainland and therefore couldn't send the amount of men, money, and supplies they would have sent to Sileria only a year ago, had the rebellion begun then. *However . . .* They were also well aware that that which the greatest empire in history might consider a poor supply of men, weapons, and money might nonetheless be a far greater force than the rebels of one long-impoverished imperial province could ultimately vanquish.

True, they admitted, all of Sileria was in turmoil now. There had been major riots in every city except Shaljir, and additional Outlookers were arriving only slowly. *However* . . . The Empire would fight hard to keep Sileria, for possession of the vast island-nation was essential for control of the Middle Sea and thus essential for the security of the other imperial provinces bordering the sea. The Valdani may have grown careless and overconfident, but they knew how important Sileria was to the Empire and would strive to keep it once they began to truly fear losing it.

"So why are you *here*?" Mirabar asked irritably, bored after listening to more than an hour of this sort of thing and tired of struggling with common Silerian, a language she seldom needed in the mountains.

Oh, the lowlanders and the sea-born folk were interested in the rebellion, they assured the rebel leaders. They just had more to lose than hunted Guardians, outlawed waterlords and assassins, and impoverished *shallaheen,* so they were more cautious.

Kiloran, who was gowing impatient, too, suggested they go home now and perhaps come back after the long rains—if they were feeling less cautious by then. He had no need of allies who evidently weren't willing to enter a war without guarantees.

"We don't want guarantees, *siran*," said the primary spokesman for the lowlanders. "Just assurances."

"Just one assurance, actually," said an elder of the sea-born folk.

Josarian shook his head. "The only assurance we can give you is that we will fight until the Valdani are gone or every rebel in Sileria is dead. There is nothing else we can offer you."

The sea-born elder and the lowlander exchanged a glance. It was subtle, but Mirabar caught it. Suddenly she knew why they had decided to come here now. She knew what they were going to say next. She knew—yet she couldn't believe it.

"There is only one assurance required," the tattooed old man said to Josarian, "and you are the only one who can provide it."

Josarian looked puzzled for a moment, and then Mira saw that he knew, too. A series of conflicting emotions washed across his face as the lowlander explained.

"We know what they say in the mountains about you. They've started saying it in the lowlands, too, and along the shores. They're starting to say it in the heart of the cities. Perhaps they're even saying it in Shaljir itself."

Kiloran started muttering. His words were indistinguishable, but his glower would have silenced men whose mission was any less imperative than this one was. The waterlord's disapproval cast a physical chill on the proceedings, but his guests did not back down or hesitate.

"If you are the Firebringer," the old fisherman said, "then the sea-born folk will join the rebellion. We will fight in your name, and we will not stop, either, until the Valdani are gone or we are all dead."

"So will we. We will serve prophecy and the destiny of Sileria," said the lowlander. "If you are the Firebringer."

"If you prove it," said the old man.

"According to the prophecy," said the lowlander.

The old man fixed Josarian with a hard, uncompromising gaze. "If you enter the volcano and survive, we will join you. And the rest of Sileria will soon join us, too."

"And if not?" Josarian asked hoarsely.

The old man shrugged, his face shrewd and calculating. "If not . . . Can the rebellion grow fast enough to repel the tens of thousands of Outlookers the Valdani are undoubtedly trying to free from duty on the mainland and ship to Sileria even as we speak?"

"If Josarian dies at Darshon," Mirabar snapped at the old man, "then what happens to the rebellion?"

"Ah, *sirana,* but if he refuses to go to Darshon now,"

the old man replied, "what, indeed, happens to the rebellion?"

WEARING CLOTHING BORROWED from Kiloran's obsequious but elegant mistress, Faradar followed Tansen's instructions and posed as a *torena* when they entered Shaljir through the old Kintish Gate. During interrogation by the Outlookers guarding the gate, she identified herself as *Toren* Porsall's half-Valdani wife and claimed that the two scruffy *shallaheen* with her were loyal lifelong servants from her country estate whom her husband had ordered to accompany her to Shaljir. She hated city life, she informed the Outlookers, but her husband insisted that the countryside had grown too dangerous for her. After all, she'd already been kidnapped by Josarian and his rebel bandits! Who knew when they would return to slaughter her in her own bed?

It was a plausible story, since more than a few people who feared the rebels were fleeing to Shaljir these days. Faradar was well-spoken and elegant enough to pass for a rural half-Silerian aristocrat, and Zimran had provided her with a wealth of details about the private life of the woman she was impersonating, which she chattered about to the Outlookers in a convincingly empty-headed manner. Zimran and Tansen were unarmed and properly subservient.

Their weapons were wrapped in silk and tightly strapped to the insides of Faradar's legs beneath her baggy pantaloons; this was the purpose for which Tansen had wanted a woman to accompany him to Shaljir. He couldn't feasibly rescue Elelar without his swords, and he knew he would be searched, like all other men, upon entering Shaljir. It was, however, hard to imagine even the Outlookers sticking their hands between the legs of a respectable half-Valdani *torena* whose reasons for coming to Shaljir were similar to those of many hundreds of other people in these violent times. They'd taken a horse from Kiloran's camp, too, since no *torena* was likely to walk to Shaljir. However, Faradar couldn't mount and dismount with steel swords strapped to her legs, especially not in front of the Outlookers. So they arrived on foot, leading the horse and claiming it had grown footsore just before their arrival at the Kintish gate.

Tansen expected the plan to work, but he was nonetheless immensely relieved when the Outlookers let them go and turned their attention to the next new arrivals.

They stabled the horse at a discreet establishment close to the city walls. They didn't expect to need it again, but it was hard to turn such a large animal loose in the middle of a city without attracting considerable attention. Then Tansen led his companions to the same *tirshah* where he had once taken Josarian. After asking the keeper to contact the Beyah-Olvari for him, he and Faradar privately explained to an alternately stunned and skeptical Zimran precisely whose realm they were all about to enter. Tansen also warned him what he would do to him if he ever betrayed the Beyah-Olvari. Faradar was shocked by his threat, but Zimran looked as if he'd expected no better of Tansen.

They were taken to the Olvar that very night. The Beyah-Olvari were as loyal to Elelar as they had been to Gaborian. They had shielded Elelar's trusted servants until the Alliance could arrange for their escape from Shaljir, and they were ready and willing to help Tansen free the *torena*.

The Olvar confirmed that the vast network of ancient tunnels under Shaljir led, among other places, to subterranean caves near the Kintish prison.

"Then we'll find a way in," Tansen said with determination.

"*Is* there one?" Zimran asked the Olvar.

The Olvar swayed with uncertainty. "We have never tried to find one . . ."

"There's water going into the prison and sewage flowing out," Tansen said. "We'll find a way in from the tunnels."

"Sewage," Zimran repeated with distaste.

"We'll need a guide to take us to the right part of the tunnels."

"Yes. We will assist you in entering the prison," the Olvar vowed.

"But your people must stay below," Tansen advised.

"No," the Olvar said, sounding almost argumentative. "The time has come—"

"Not yet." Tansen shook his head. "There will be violence and killing in the prison, *siran*. That's not the work of the Beyah-Olvari."

The Olvar sagged, his body trembling with sorrow as he stirred his hands in the Sacred Pool. "It is always so with your people, isn't it?"

"Always," Tan agreed without expression.

ELELAR WAS SURPRISED to hear a noise at the door of her cell so late at night. She'd been about to undress for bed. When the heavy door opened to admit Myrell, she was even more surprised. She hadn't seen him since he'd beaten her soon after her incarceration.

"What do *you* want?" she demanded.

He stared hard at her, his face distorted by some powerful emotion. She didn't know what was going on in that twisted mind, but there was an intensity about him that was very unsettling. He looked . . . pleased, she realized. Excited. Smug.

I've been denied a trial.

Her insides quivered with fear. Her mind rebelled with mingled fury and despair. She had tried to be disciplined after Ronall's visit and his astonishing news about her possible reprieve. She had tried not to let herself hope. She had fought against the temptation of believing she might live a while longer, perhaps even yet find some way out of this disaster. She had tried so hard, but she knew now that she had failed. She *had* hoped. She *had* clung to a renewed desire to survive; she could feel it in the terror that seized her now as she stared at Myrell.

Will they just kill me, or will they torture me first? Will

*they do it tomorrow in public, or tonight with no wit-
nesses?*

She tried to control the panic racing through her mind.
She would not reveal her fear to the Valdani—and most
especially not to *this* Valdan.

"What are you doing here?" she repeated in the hardest
voice she could muster.

Without answering her, Myrell summoned two Outlookers. They entered her cell and seized her.

Elelar struggled against them, forcing fury into her voice
as she demanded, "What's going on?"

"We're taking you to the cellar, *torena.*"

Bile rose in her throat. The cellar was where they tortured prisoners. They'd threatened her with it during her
two "interrogations" here.

"You can't!" she snarled, struggling against the two
strong men who were trying to drag her out of her cell. "I
am the wife of a Valdani aristocrat! I am awaiting trial by
three Imperial Counc—"

"Denied." Myrell's voice was rich with triumph.

She froze. "Denied?"

"Denied," he repeated. "Imperial Councilors have far
more important things to do than waste time listening to a
traitorous whore try to save her own life by telling lies at
a trial. Especially the faithless wife of some half-Silerian
drunkard."

She should have known, she realized. She'd been a fool
to hope it might be otherwise, despite the influence of Ronall's family. She wondered vaguely if the Council had
come to these conclusions on their own, or if Borell's influence had swayed them. It didn't really matter either
way. It was over.

"So now I'm to be taken to the cellar for . . . questioning."

She forced hatred into her voice, contempt into her expression. She'd been a fool not to prepare herself better
for this, not to be ready for this moment day and night.
She'd been a fool to let Ronall's optimism and hope affect

her. He was weak, and she had known she must be strong. She clenched her teeth to keep her mouth from trembling.

Myrell was gloating. "I suppose this cell has been less than you're used to, *torena,* but at least I can promise you you'll never have to see it again."

"So you're going to kill me now, I take it?" She hoped that he couldn't see the fear bubbling up inside her, prayed that he didn't know how her stomach heaved.

"My orders are to kill you after you talk," Myrell replied, "and not before. And by then, I promise you . . ." He leaned close and whispered, "You'll be begging me to kill you."

She believed him, though she didn't want to. She fought to banish the images flooding her mind. "Are these Borell's instructions?"

His smirk was oily. "Ah, you haven't heard, of course."

"Heard what?"

"Borell is dead."

"Dead?"

"Suicide."

"He killed himself? Why?"

He shook his head. "Ah-ah, Elelar. I ask all the questions from now on." Smiling viciously, he added, "Before we begin, let me just remind you that how long you take to die is entirely up to you. If you tell me everything right away, it will be better for you."

She would later be tempted to believe him, she knew. She must remember, must keep repeating to herself that he would torture her a long time anyhow, no matter when she talked or how much she told him. He wouldn't be convinced she was telling the truth until he'd made her repeat her words again and again, until he'd put her in enough pain—for a long enough period—to be sure she was telling the truth because she was no longer capable of fabricating lies. She must remember that every promise he made was a lie, and every lure he offered was merely a trap.

Dar, please give me strength. Please give me courage!

She did not resist again when the Outlookers obeyed Myrell's renewed order to haul her out of her cell. There was nowhere she could go, no way she could escape this. She thought of Corenten of Malthenar, as well as the other martyrs of the mountain resistance. She prayed her death would honor her as theirs had honored them. She prayed for the courage they had shown.

They descended to the ground floor of the prison, then crossed the vast, stone-paved hall of the old prison to reach the cellar door. Elelar looked toward a window, observing the moon glow for the last time. She inhaled deeply, knowing she'd never smell fresh air again. She tried to master the nausea forcing its way up into her throat, tried to conceal the weakness in her rubbery legs as she approached a death more agonizing than most men's worst nightmares.

Suddenly they heard fighting on the other side of the heavy wooden door that concealed the steps to the cellar: frantic shouts, the clang of metal against metal, a scream. The men holding her froze and looked questioningly at Myrell. He instinctively reached for his sword. She had only a moment to wonder if another prisoner was attempting to escape, and then the cellar door burst open.

"Tan!" She could not have been more surprised to see Dar Herself emerge from the shadowed staircase behind that heavy door. He was soaking wet, his skin gleaming with moisture in the torchlight, his clothes clinging limply to his body. His swords were red. There were splashes of red on his clothes and his face, too.

Blood, she realized.

He never paused, never hesitated, didn't even seem to know she was there. He killed two Outlookers before the second had even finished drawing his sword, then moved on to two more. Another *shallah*—Zimran, she saw— emerged from the bowels of the prison and plunged into the hall, bloodied sword drawn, *yahr* swinging in his other hand.

"Take her back to her cell!" Myrell shouted, launching himself into the fray. "Lock her in!"

They had come to free her!

She struggled wildly, resisting the two Outlookers trying to haul her back to the staircase she had just descended. They were big, strong men, though. They simply picked her up and carried her to the stairs while she fought them. When she felt one of them lift his foot to find the first stair, she poked him in the eye as hard as she could. He howled and stumbled backwards—right into more men running down the stairs. They tumbled and fell, some right on top of Elelar. She lay there winded and dazed as the fight continued all around her.

She heard the screech of metal-on-metal, the screams of dying men, the panicked shouts of Outlookers in the stairwell overhead and in the courtyard outside.

There are too many! We'll never escape.

How could she help? What could she do?

She felt an Outlooker's hands upon her, grabbing, scrabbling, trying to seize her again. She rolled over and slid her hand down his belly and over his groin. Before he realized her intention, she squeezed as hard as she possibly could, driving her nails into the yielding fabric of his gray uniform. She yanked with all her might, picturing herself tearing his genitals off his body, then let go and leapt to her feet as he lay there screaming.

Fire, she thought suddenly, remembering how Mirabar had held the assassins at bay in Kiloran's lair. The fallen men struggled to get to their feet. Several brushed past her, racing for Tansen, whose flashing double blades and whirling motion left bodies littering the floor around him. Elelar seized a lantern from the wall and, not allowing herself to think about this horrible act, swung her arm around and threw it against the stone wall at the bottom of the steps. Oil and fire spread everywhere. Men who had been descending the steps fell back, shouting. Men lying dazed at the bottom of the stairs screamed in agony as the flames and lantern oil swept across them, burning them, incinerating their clothes.

Tansen swung his arm and cut the throat of a staggering

man who shrieked wildly as his clothes burned.

"Go! Go!" Tansen shouted at Elelar as four more men poured in from the courtyard, entering the hall through the main entrance, alerted by the noise and flames.

Elelar ran to the entrance as soon as it was clear of Outlookers. Behind her, she heard Tansen shout, *"Not that way!"* She ignored him. She pushed the enormous wooden door closed, then smashed another lantern against it, setting it on fire and effectively blocking it for the time being.

"Kill her!" Myrell screamed. "Don't let them take her! Kill her now!"

"Zim!" Tansen shouted.

Realizing that she had just become the center of attention again, Elelar ran along the wall trying to reach Zimran. Tansen moved to block Outlookers lunging for her. Someone lost an arm right in front of her. Her hands came up to her mouth in horror as blood flew into her face.

"MOVE!" Tansen shouted at her, very close suddenly.

"Elelar!" Zimran's shout gave her confidence. She seized another lantern from the wall, flung it into the center of the hall, and used the explosion to cover her flight to Zimran's side.

"Behind me," he ordered, fighting off another Outlooker, using the *yahr* far better than he used the sword.

She crouched behind him, keeping an eye out as they slowly backed toward the cellar door, Zimran fighting a shouting Valdan the whole time. A torch, rather than a lantern, blazed at the top of the winding cellar stairs. Elelar seized it and stuck it in the man's face. When he flinched and turned his head away, Zimran grabbed his chance and killed him.

"Into the cellar," he told her. "There's no one left alive down there. *Go!* I'm right behind you."

"Tansen!" she cried. He was surrounded by four men, including Myrell. Two more were coming down the stairs now that the flames were subsiding.

"GO!" he shouted, felling one of the Outlookers.

"Go," Zimran repeated, trying to push her down the stairs.

"No! We can't leave him!"

An Outlooker screamed as Tansen slashed him across the face.

Zimran grinned. "Ah, I guess you haven't seen him fight before, *torena*. Go!" This time, his shove nearly sent her flying headlong down the stairs. "He'll catch up."

Zimran was right behind her when she reached the cellar, the foundation of whatever castle or fortress had existed on this site even before this six-hundred-year-old Kintish structure. She tried not to look at the four gray-clad bodies down here, even though she knew they'd been awaiting her, prepared to help Myrell slowly murder her. She tried even harder not to look at the tools Myrell would have used on her to make her talk.

"Where are we going?" she asked, hearing how breathless and scared she sounded.

"To our old friends," Zimran replied with a sly glance.

She gasped. "The tunnels!"

"We found a way into this place from the tunnels by going through old—*really* old—sewage conduits."

"That's why you're all wet," she suddenly realized.

"You probably haven't noticed the smell, in all the excitement," he said, leading her through a dark passage and into a small, stinking cell. "But in a few minutes, I guarantee it'll be all you'll think about."

There was a hole in the floor in the corner of this tiny, low-ceilinged room. There'd been a rust-encrusted grate over the hole; now it lay on the floor next to the hole, ready to be replaced when they escaped. The edges of the hole, like the floor around it, were coated with ancient, hardened substances and faint stains that Elelar didn't even want to *think* about, let alone touch. The smell rising from the hole was truly indescribable.

"We're going down *there?*" she choked.

"We have only two choices," he pointed out, "and I

want to go back upstairs even less than I want to go down there."

"Oh, Dar shield me," she muttered. Knowing he was right, she pulled her delicately embroidered sleeve over her hand, then used it to cover her nose and mouth. She glanced at Zimran and said, "After you."

TANSEN FOUGHT IN eight directions and on three levels, as he had been taught. He caught a few cuts on his forearms but ignored them, as he had been trained. He saw the way his opponents' shoulders moved, the way their weight shifted, and so he knew where their blades would go as soon as *they* knew; even sooner in the case of the inexperienced ones. He moved economically, never wasting motion or breath. A *shatai* divorced his emotions from his work, never let the combat become personal, never let rage or hatred cloud his judgment or diminish his skill. Never, that is, unless he was facing a man such as Myrell the Butcher.

He saved Myrell for last. As the commanding officer here, Myrell should have been Tansen's first target, for Outlookers often lost courage and momentum when their officers fell. Myrell was also slightly more skilled in combat than his men, meaning he was a greater threat and should be eliminated first. However, among all the men Tansen had ever fought as a *shatai*, this was the first one whom he truly, personally, passionately hated, and so he ignored the tenets of his arduous training. He relinquished his own ruthless self-discipline and intentionally let Myrell live until the others were dead and the *torena* was gone.

He knew he had only seconds left in which to make his own escape. More Outlookers would flood the hall in just moments. Even in the middle of the night, Shaljir never lacked for Outlookers who were wide awake and ready to kill Silerians. But before he killed Myrell and escaped, he wanted the butcher of Malthenar, Morven, and Garabar to suffer at least a little, as payment for all the suffering he had caused Tansen's kind.

Tan plunged one sword into Myrell's guts, an excruciatingly painful thrust. Pale, wide-eyed, sweating with exertion and agony, Myrell dropped his sword from a limp arm and fell to his knees. His mouth opened, but no sound came out.

"Is that where you made the first cut on Corenten, you baby-killing maggot?" Tansen asked, speaking Valdan through gritted teeth.

He twisted the blade and jerked it up. A horrible sound came out of Myrell's throat. Blood dribbled through his lips.

"Did the women you slaughtered feel like this when they died?" Tansen whispered into his ear, suddenly remembering Gamalan, too, and the long-ago deaths of loved ones there. "What about the children?"

He ripped his blade out of Myrell's torso, widening the terrible wound even further. He looked down at Myrell's blood-drenched body as it collapsed on the floor. He would have preferred to leave Myrell like this, dying slowly in terrible agony. Dying the way Amitan had lain dying. But he couldn't leave a survivor, not even one as close to death as this. He couldn't risk that Myrell would find a way to tell his would-be rescuers that the attackers had escaped through the cellar. And so, wishing it could be otherwise, he killed Myrell quickly, then ran to the cellar door, closing it firmly behind him and finding his way down the long, winding stairs in the dark.

31

"GREAT MERCIFUL BLOODSTAINED gods!"
Having reviewed the mess at the ancient prison, Commander Koroll was running out of words to express his absolute fury over this unparalleled disaster.

In the middle of the night, his men had roused him from a heavy slumber induced by the ministrations of his third-level Kintish courtesan whose loyalties, in this time of warfare, were based on purely professional considerations. The men's hysterical, garbled explanations had been so vague and incredible, he hadn't really believed there'd been a prison break until he himself saw the wreckage of what had once been the main hall of the prison. There were seventeen dead men in the hall. Four more were reported dead in the cellar. None of the survivors had seen the rebels enter or leave. A fire in the stairwell and another incinerating the main door had prevented entry soon after the fighting had begun. Two men who'd been stuck outside said they'd seen no one except a Silerian *torena*. One of them resolutely believed she had somehow escaped alone—until he saw the carnage inside. Another man who'd been knocked unconscious in the stairwell also remembered seeing no one besides the *torena*. One man claimed there'd been two *shallaheen;* only two, and he had no idea where they came from. Someone else said he was sure the attackers must have been disguised as Outlookers. Several other men claimed there'd been numerous attackers, but no one agreed on how many, and Koroll had no doubt they were exaggerating to save their own necks. The survivors were all basically confused and uncertain, and all trying to decide whether they'd look worse if they admitted that the prison had fallen to only a couple of attackers, or if they confessed that many attackers had somehow gotten inside unnoticed.

Surveying the disaster, Koroll could scarcely believe his own eyes. Seventeen men—including Myrell!—lay dead. Right inside the Outlookers' own prison in the heart of Shaljir! By the mercy of the Three, how could this have happened? How had rebels gotten past the city gates? How had they gotten weapons into the city? How, by all the gods above and below, had they gotten into the prison to free the *torena?*

Had they been disguised as Outlookers? Three Into One,

had they had the audacity to enter Shaljir posing as Out-lookers? Or had Koroll's men been so incompetent, so unforgivably negligent, that a rebel rescue party had entered the city and stormed the prison without being seen or caught?

An even worse notion occurred to Koroll as he returned to his command chamber at the Outlooker headquarters across from the prison: What if the rebels and their weapons had already been in Shaljir when the *torena* was arrested? What if they had been here for many months? What if there were far more armed rebels within the walls of Shaljir than he had ever guessed or suspected?

He felt ill as he thought of it. He felt even worse when he acknowledged the ramifications of his having lost *Torena* Elelar.

Three pity me, that woman has caused nothing but misery!

This was going to be *very* hard to explain to the Imperial Council. It would have to be done, though; they were expecting Elelar to be brought to Valda for her trial. Koröll sat at his desk and buried his head in his hands, wishing it would stop pounding.

The last imperial courier had brought a dispatch to Advisor Borell informing him that the request of Ronall's family had been granted: Elelar would be tried before three Imperial Councilors as the wife of a Valdani aristocrat. Showing all the courage of a spring lamb, Borell had promptly climbed into a hot bath and slit his wrists. Fortunately, the servant who found him summoned an Outlooker immediately. The Outlooker, in turn, immediately summoned Koroll to Santorell Palace.

Koroll was admitted to Borell's chamber alone. Thus it was that Koroll was the first man to examine the scene of Borell's death, read his sealed suicide letter, and see the imperial dispatch granting Elelar's trial.

Knowing that the trial would utterly ruin him, Borell had tried to avoid public humiliation in the traditional way of the Valdani upper classes: death. He left behind a rather maudlin, self-pitying note requesting that his body be buried back in his homeland.

Koroll's initial irritation had slowly warmed into exultation as he began to recognize the opportunities inherent in this new turn of events. He burned the imperial dispatch and Borell's letter. He then wrote a new suicide letter, using a shaky hand and liberally smearing the ink. If the letter was ever examined by anyone who knew Borell's own hand, then Koroll hoped the unrecognizable writing would be attributed to Borell's devastated emotional state.

The new letter, Koroll's own creation, explained that the Imperial Council had just denied *Torena* Elelar a trial. She was now condemned to death by slow torture, sentence to be carried out immediately by the Outlookers. Because he had loved her, Borell could not live with the shame of her betrayal and the pain of her terrible death, and so he intended to take his own life immediately after sealing this letter.

After sealing the letter with Borell's ring (a thoroughly distasteful process), Koroll summoned Outlookers and servants into the chamber, ostensibly to begin cleaning up the mess and preparing Borell's body for its funeral rites and transport back to Valda. He really wanted them there, of course, to witness his "finding" the suicide note. He broke the seal and read it aloud in front of witnesses, none of whom appeared to have the slightest doubt of its veracity. Everyone had seen how besotted Borell was with the *torena* and how devastated he was by her betrayal.

However, Koroll privately mused, few things fed hatred like a love betrayed. Borell had furiously denied the charges against Elelar at first. Then the quantity and quality of the evidence seized from her house had mounted until the woman's overwhelming guilt was indisputable, and Borell had grown stupid with shame, grief, and boiling rage. Koroll was the only person who knew how eager Borell had eventually become to see Elelar quietly murdered before she could reveal his disgrace to anyone.

It was a perfect plan. Koroll would get what he had

wanted all along. Myrell would take Elelar to the cellar, torture her until she told them everything she knew, then kill her; it was the sort of work for which Myrell had shown an undeniable flair. Not only would they get the information they needed now, but the *torena* would then never have a chance to tell the Imperial Councilors that, though he'd never been the fool that Borell was, Koroll had nonetheless grown careless around her, too. Besides, if she knew Josarian and the rebels, she undoubtedly knew who had originally turned Tansen loose on the countryside, and Koroll had no wish for the Council to find out about that!

And, of course, when Ronall's family protested and the Council demanded an explanation, Koroll could simply show them Borell's letter. The *torena*'s unlawful murder would be blamed on the vengeful and emotionally distressed Advisor, who had unwittingly given the rebels hundreds of state secrets before slitting his own wrists. There was no longer an imperial dispatch in existence in Sileria to contradict the orders which everyone here would insist had come straight from Borell in his final moments of life.

Yes, it was a perfect plan . . . *Until those murdering scoundrels attacked the prison, freed Elelar, and killed my men!*

Now all he had was a sacked prison, a pile of corpses, and the ominous loss of the most valuable prisoner he'd ever arrested. He thought he would be sick. Myrell was a great loss, for he had excelled at tasks that repelled many men. Koroll had never liked the oaf, but there was no denying the value of a man so feared and hated by the enemy.

As dawn rose over Shaljir, Koroll knew that last night's events were not only a serious blow to his career, but they would also give a tremendous boost to the rebels' morale.

There were two obvious tasks to concentrate on now. He must find out how the prison rescue was launched and ensure that it could never happen again. And he must get the *torena* back. The daring rescue proved to Koroll that she was every bit as valuable to the rebels as he had suspected. He wanted her back because *they* wanted her so very badly. He *needed* her back, too, because the Imperial Council would eat his parts for breakfast if he couldn't turn this disaster around somehow.

He assigned one of his senior officers to supervise the examination of the prison wreckage in an attempt to discover exactly what had happened there last night. He ordered another officer to tighten security everywhere in Shaljir.

"I don't want any more rebels getting in. Even more importantly, if *Torena* Elelar and last night's rescuers are still in Shaljir, I don't want them getting out," he ordered. "Understood?"

He had a feeling that the *torena* wouldn't have lingered here, however. Wondering how to get her back, he could devise only two plans. The first was to have her husband arrested and imprisoned. They would charge him as an accomplice and hold him in custody in her place. It was a perfectly legal maneuver under the circumstances, one that even Ronall's powerful family couldn't counter. Koroll doubted that Elelar would be sentimental enough to return for her husband's sake, but there was no predicting what a woman would do, after all. Perhaps he could eventually exchange Ronall for her.

The other plan was the old-fashioned kind: pursuit. It seemed likely that the rescue party would take Elelar back to the rebel-held territory around Dalishar, the only place they could keep her safe now. It would be their best move, since Koroll couldn't reach her there, not until he got enough men to take the territory back from the rebels. If he could catch her before she reached rebel territory, though . . .

"I want two hundred combat-ready riders on fast mounts," he ordered one of his men. "We leave within the hour!"

*   *   *

"WHERE *ARE* YOU, damn you?" Mirabar cried.

She had left the safety of Kiloran's camp and entered the woods, begging the Beckoner to come to her. The expression on Josarian's face ever since the departure of the lowlanders and the sea-born folk terrified her. *He was really thinking of doing it!*

He had sought her alone several times since then. Questioning her, probing her understanding of the Otherworld, seeking guidance. And she couldn't give it to him! She had no answers, no hints, no visions about this. She knew only the panic of any ordinary person when confronted with the extraordinary. Josarian was thinking of throwing himself into Darshon to prove once and for all whether or not he was the Firebringer.

"What can I tell him?" she begged the empty, unanswering void. "Answer me! I know you hear me!"

But the Beckoner always Called her, she had never Called him. He came only when it suited him, never when it suited her. He came for his purposes, not hers.

"I *must* know what to tell Josarian . . ."

Tears stung her eyes. She felt helpless, frightened, frustrated. Josarian had confided his dreams to her, cataclysmic and mysterious dreams about painful yet ecstatic union with fire and lava. It could mean anything, though. He said that Tansen—the only other person who knew about the dreams—thought his mind was just reflecting the thoughts, fears, and feelings naturally inspired by the constant rumors and Jalan's mad ravings. Mirabar knew the dreams could even mean that Josarian was destined to become a Guardian; such dreams and visions often afflicted someone being called to serve Dar and the Otherworld.

She supposed it could even be some evil form of Valdani sorcery. She knew little about their wizards and their magic, for the cult of the Three had risen to eclipse more ancient Valdani religions in recent centuries, and the Valdani now placed their trust in the might of their arms and the wealth of their treasury, rather than in mysterious and unpredictable arts. But who could say for sure that these dreams were not being fed to Josarian by some powerful enemy? Mirabar had heard of such things, and she had seen enough strange wizardry in her own short life to know better than to simply ignore the possibilities of things she hadn't yet seen.

She had never believed in the Firebringer, mostly because the *zanareen* who awaited him were so patently mad. What if she had been wrong, though? If the Firebringer was real, then surely there had never been a more likely candidate than Josarian.

So many choices. So many possibilities . . . If only she knew what to do! Josarian sought guidance from her, and she sought guidance from the Beckoner—and, so far, they were both disappointed by the lack of answers.

Burning with helpless fear and rage, she shouted into the empty woods, "Damn you! I have done everything you have asked of me! *Everything.* Now I want an answer!"

She rent the night with fire and fury, flinging her will against the locked doors of the Otherworld, trying to force her way through the barriers between this world and the Other one.

Her failure was as sharp as physical pain. Exhausted and despairing, she slumped onto the rain-softened ground and lay there weeping, lost in her misery, oblivious to the world.

There was a chill in the air, due to the season as much as to Kiloran's nearby presence. The harvest would soon begin in full measure, and then the long rains would come. The earth would sleep and renew itself, preparing for another long year under Sileria's merciless sun. The *shallaheen* would know no rest, though; they would keep on fighting until every Valdan was gone or every rebel was dead. Would the lowlanders and sea-born folk join them? Mirabar sighed wearily, having no answers . . .

She felt his presence long before she heard his footsteps, long before she heard his voice for the first time ever. There was a faint touch, almost like a caress, along senses sharply attuned to visions no one else saw, voices no one else heard. There was a melding, a warmth, a subtle vibration. It was so unfamiliar that it should have frightened her, especially out here alone and unprotected. There was nothing threatening about it, however; on the contrary, she was drawn to it the way she had always been drawn to fire, even before she had understood who and what she was. Like fire, she sensed that this, whatever it was, was something extremely powerful which could be terribly dangerous, but she felt a communion with it which overruled any sense of caution. She sensed, too, that it had found her by following her violent Call to the Beckoner.

He approached quietly and was very close before she heard his footsteps. She had no doubt it was a man's step, no matter how soft and subtle. She had grown up wild in these mountains and knew the sound of every creature that roamed them. She stood up and looked through the trees, waiting for his shape to separate itself from the thick shadows. It was nearly dark out. She had stayed away from camp a long time.

When she saw him approaching, she knew who he was even before he spoke. She had heard him described so many times; had *demanded* his description so often from Josarian, Zimran, and Tansen. He was taller than Tansen. Not so broad as Josarian. Better dressed than any of them, with a silver brooch as his Guardian insignia. A series of elaborate braids kept his dark hair off his face; seven long, gleaming curls fell from the knot at the nape of his neck. He was . . . rather handsome, really.

And his eyes . . . His eyes glowed like the Fires of Dar.

"Cheylan," she breathed.

He stared back, taking in the glowing red of her hair and her flame-hot eyes. No one in her life had ever looked at her this way, before. Hungry, eager . . . pleased. Warmth fluttered in her stomach, spread through her limbs, heated her cheeks.

"I thought . . ." He smiled slowly, almost self-deprecatingly. "Ah, but they did say you were young."

He was perhaps Josarian's age. "I just didn't . . ." He shrugged.

He spoke common Silerian. Hers was not particularly good. She had never cared until now. Now she did not want this man to think her some ignorant peasant girl— even though she was.

"I . . . I don't know how old I am," she said haltingly.

He smiled again and, to her surprise, gently pushed her hair off her face. "I'm sorry, I don't speak *shallah* very well."

She flushed. "My Silerian is not *so* bad," she said defensively.

"No, it's not," he agreed. "And it will improve as we talk, Mirabar."

"What are you doing here?" she asked. "You're supposed to be in—"

"I came to tell Josarian that there's been an uprising in Liron."

"Really? Have you seen him? He's down—"

"Yes, he and I have already talked."

"Has Liron fallen?" she asked eagerly.

"Not yet." He took her hand and suggested they find some place to sit down. They settled themselves on a couple of boulders, and Cheylan blew a small fire into life to light the night. Then, at her insistence, he recounted events in the east to her.

"The Outlookers have killed many people and regained control of the city, for *now,* but they're short of men and money, and their overland supply routes have been destroyed, leaving them only those supplies which arrive by sea. And Kintish pirates are now taking about one out of every three Valdani supply ships bound for Liron—with the blessing of the Palace of Heaven, now that Kinto and Valdania are at war." He stopped, at her request, to repeat something she had not understood. Recognizing her embarrassment, he spoke more slowly as he continued, "The Outlooker commander in Liron has written to Koroll twice to request more men, but we've intercepted his couriers.

He doesn't yet know that his reinforcements will never arrive."

"Liron will fall," she murmured.

"Does the Beckoner tell you that?" he probed.

"Common sense tells me that." When his brows rose, she said, "The *torena* is right about one thing: the arrogance of the Valdani will be their undoing."

"*Torena* Elelar?"

"Yes."

"I hear she's been captured."

Mirabar nodded and, in response to his questions, told him what she knew about Elelar's capture and Tansen's intentions to rescue her.

"A brave man," Cheylan surmised, his voice smooth, rich, and cultured.

"He's very fond of the *torena*," Mirabar replied with all the tact she could muster.

"You are not," he gathered.

"Fortunately, I don't need to be."

He grinned at that. Then he asked her about herself. Following the path set by his questions, Mirabar told Cheylan how little she knew about her birth, and recounted some of her childhood. Embarrassed about her youthful savagery, her responses were halting at first. She would have found pity as appalling as contempt. Cheylan, however, *understood,* and the simple, unfamiliar beauty of that loosened her tongue until she was speaking freely, with scarcely any prompting from him. She told him about her loneliness and ignorant fear, cast out from society and hunted as a demon, haunted by visions, dreams, and powers which convinced her she was as evil as people claimed. She told him about being found at last by Tashinar, who captured her, tamed her, and taught her what she truly was; told him about her initiation and her training as a Guardian.

Born into an ancient family of *toreni,* Cheylan's life, as he described it to her, had been very different from hers. His family was wealthy, ensuring that he was well-fed, elegantly clothed, thoroughly educated, and sufficiently protected. Yet his loneliness had been identical to hers, his sense of isolation remarkably similar. Like Mirabar, he had been an object of scorn, superstition, and ignorant fear.

"I was kept inside during most of my childhood," he said, speaking more fluidly as her ears grew more accustomed to his speech. "Either in our house in Liron, or else at my family's country estate in the district. I'd stay with my tutor at one house for a while, usually without my parents, who didn't like to look at me. Sooner or later, there would always be trouble: a frightened servant, a superstitious merchant, a bad harvest in the country, a terrible accident in the city . . . Then there would be talk and threats. And so, keeping me concealed, my family would move me to the other house."

Mirabar understood, too. She didn't suppose the luxuries of his life had made up for his being an outcast. Even as a rag-clad starving child, she had longed for affection and acceptance far more than she had ever longed for wealth or comfort. She had cherished private fantasies wherein people loved her and begged her forgiveness, not fantasies wherein she became richer than the rest of them.

"In the end, though," he said, "I found my path in life with the Guardians."

"Have you ever . . . seen another like us?" she asked.

"Two," he answered promptly. "The Guardian who initiated me was very much like you. I never got to know him well. The Society had him assassinated."

"I'm sorry."

He nodded in acknowledgment. "And there is a boy somewhere near Liron. Guardians keep him hidden, of course."

They talked easily about the mystery of who and what they were, about the dangers and difficulties, about whether or not there were more and how they came to be.

"There were once many," she told him. "I've seen it, in my visions."

He took her hand, surprising her, making her blood

move a little faster. "Tell me about the visions. The Beck-oner."

"I, uh . . ."

His gaze held hers in the firelight. His hand was very warm; hard, like a *shallah*'s hand, despite his birth and the lack of scars. Guardians led hard lives, after all, as did rebels. Something unfamiliar danced in her belly, a min-gling of danger and excitement. He was a man, one of the few who had ever looked at her with no hint of fear or revulsion, without even surprise. He was sophisticated like Elelar, worldly like Tansen, kind like Josarian. He was the first person she had ever met who could truly understand her life. And he was appealing enough to incite feelings she recognized but didn't know how to act upon.

So she wasn't quite sure why something warned her not to discuss the Beckoner with him now. She didn't under-stand the reluctance she felt, but she had stayed alive this long by obeying her instincts.

"Kiloran is here," she said at last, feeling the chill in the air. *That must be why.* "I do not want to tell you about the Beckoner near him."

He accepted her response easily. "Of course." He'd had plenty of trouble with the Society, too, after all. "Another time?"

"You have seen Kiloran?" she asked.

"Not yet. But he makes his presence known, doesn't he?"

She smiled at his dry tone. "Oh, yes. Very much so."

"You're shivering," he said suddenly, standing up and drawing her to her feet. "And you have no cloak. Here, take mine."

She nestled into the cloak's body-warmed folds as Cheylan wrapped it around her shoulders. It was finer than anything she had ever worn, though not so fine as Elelar's things.

Cheylan's arms stayed around her, his body close and strangely tense. His gaze was hooded, the bright glitter of his eyes shielded by dark lashes. He smelled of the wind and the woods. He was so close, she could even smell the wine he had recently drunk; Josarian must have offered him some. She could feel his breath on her face, slower than her own—which was all at once coming inexplicably fast.

He was staring at her mouth, she realized suddenly. She had seen men look at Elelar like this, but never at her. Her heart banged hard against her chest, beating out a rhythm that thundered through her head. She suddenly felt small and weak. Even in Kiloran's watery palace at Kandahar, she had not felt as vulnerable as she felt now. She'd been more sure of herself when facing the waterlord and his assassins that she was now, facing one man who looked at her . . . the way a man sometimes looked at a woman.

She suddenly remembered how Tansen had looked at her at Kandahar, the sudden flash of revulsion after all she had gone through to find him. She remembered how wounded she had felt. Now, remembering that moment, rebelling against all the moments like it, something inside her unfurled and unfolded, responding to the expression on Cheylan's face, quivering in answer to the tension in his body. She wanted to be wanted; she suddenly wanted that more than anything.

More experienced than she, he sensed the change in her, the sensation of surprise and uncertainty yielding to need and desire. He leaned down to her, his head slowly descending toward hers, giving her one more moment to think it over. She started shaking in earnest, her mind blank and her emotions whirling. She hoped he had already guessed how little she knew, how totally inexperienced she was. She had never been kissed before and didn't want the first time to be a humiliation of disappointment and embarrassed apologies.

He was very sure, though, despite her hesitancy and awkwardness. His arms tightened around her as his mouth touched hers, pulling her against his chest, making her feel weightless. Darkness swallowed her as their lips melded, rubbing, caressing, exploring. Her mind reeled, astounded that so simple a contact could make the world whirl around her, could create the sensations of an earthquake. She sighed when he lifted his head slightly, then opened her eyes and gazed at him, dazed.

His eyes were as hot as flames. It excited her. She wondered if hers were the same, wondered if it excited him, too. If so, she knew it would repulse any other man, and so she burrowed into this one, determined to enjoy what other women enjoyed, what she had resolutely pretended not to need or want until this moment.

She kissed him again, more sure of herself this time, giving as well as taking now. His hands moved demandingly over her back, shaping her, molding her, pulling her even closer so that every curve and crevice of their bodies flowed together in harmony and hunger. His kisses were hot on her face, his breath now almost as fast as her own. She sighed again, enraptured, lost in him . . .

"Sirana!"

The sound of Najdan's shocked voice was like a bucket of cold water. They both froze. Too disoriented to respond to the intrusion with dignity, Mirabar stumbled out of Cheylan's embrace and faced Najdan. She was breathing as if she'd just run all the way to Dalishar and back. She could only guess what she looked like. Najdan's gaze was fixed on Cheylan, rather than her; he looked suspicious and disapproving.

It infuriated her. He had a mistress near Kandahar, one he visited whenever they passed that way. Was she entitled to less just because of an accident of birth? Just because other men couldn't stand the sight of her?

"What do you want?" she snapped.

Najdan blinked in surprise at her tone. He had followed her to Idalar and was angry that she had run off without him like that, leaving Niran in the middle of the night without warning. She'd been very nice to him ever since his arrival here, trying to make up for it.

"Well?" she prodded, furious with him.

"Josarian's asking for you. You've been gone since well

before sundown." Najdan's voice was cold, smarting with
insult that she should speak to him this way in front of a
virtual stranger. They had come a long way since their first
meeting at Dalishar, and he had grown to expect a certain
consideration from her. "I was worried and thought I'd
better find you. I saw the fire, and . . ." He shrugged.

She tried to control her temper, something she seldom
bothered doing. Najdan's surprise was natural, since no
man had ever before touched Mirabar and this one was a
stranger. Najdan had perfectly good reasons for seeking
her out. She had duties to perform. She had been gone too
long from camp and had caused concern. She took the
biggest breath of her life and let it out very slowly. Then
she met Najdan's gaze in the firelight.

"I'm . . . sorry." Dar, how she hated saying those words!

Najdan knew it, too. Having won an apology from her,
his look was smug as he replied magnanimously, "I startled you, *sirana.*"

"Yes," she agreed, "you startled me."

Cheylan said nothing. Too embarrassed to look at him
again right now, Mirabar asked, "What does Josarian
want?"

Najdan shifted uneasily. "I believe he wants you to Call
his wife, *sirana.*"

32

ZIMRAN WAS NOT surprised when Tansen
caught up to them in Shaljir's ancient, underground tunnels. He'd seen the *roshah* fight often enough to know how
hard it was to kill him. It would take more than a few
Outlookers to get rid of the *shatai.* So, no, Zimran was not
surprised—only a little disappointed. After all, Tansen had

long ago replaced Zim in Josarian's favor. There was also something—though Zim wasn't sure what—between Tan and the woman that Zimran now secretly wanted more than he'd ever wanted any other. So there were few men whose deaths would have caused Zimran less sorrow than Tansen's.

To Zim's relief, they escaped the tunnels the same night they freed the *torena* from prison. Carved out of underground lava flows thousands of years ago, probably by the now-extinct volcano of Mount Shaljir which filled the skyline beyond the Lion's Gate, the tunnels were a wonderland of strange blue beings, exotic plant life, and little glowing creatures. However, a brief visit was more than enough to satisfy Zimran, who hated enclosed spaces and felt as if he couldn't breathe properly until they were once again in the open air. Unfortunately, they fled by sea, and like most *shallaheen,* Zimran had no sea legs.

Tansen believed that their only chance of escape from the city was to leave Shaljir while the Outlookers were still stumbling over themselves trying to figure out what had happened. The following night would be too late. And so, collecting Faradar from the Beyah-Olvari, they escaped via the same route Derlen had used, covering themselves in blue designs and symbols to disguise themselves as sea-born folk. They exited the tunnels at the port, where they joined a boatload of sea-born folk ostensibly setting out for their fishing grounds many hours before dawn.

Afraid of disgracing himself, Zimran just concentrated on trying not to throw up everything he'd ever eaten while the boat heaved and swayed. Meanwhile, Elelar and Tansen consulted with their hosts. The sea-born folk and lowlanders had recently sent representatives to meet with Josarian, though no one knew where. This clan Zim was sailing with, already part of the Alliance, believed that their people were nearly ready to join the rebellion. There was just one small problem.

"They want Josarian to prove he's the Firebringer?" Elelar repeated incredulously. "You can't be serious!"

Even wearing sea-born clothes and covered in strange indigo designs, she looked beautiful in the faint, shifting lantern light. Zimran had never before seen such a beautiful woman. Every gesture and glance tugged at his loins, drew him further into her web, made him long all the more for her. He was no fool; he had known that he had no chance of winning her while she was a *torena* living in a palace in Shaljir, sleeping with her aristocratic husband and also with the Imperial Advisor. He had flirted with her because he couldn't resist, but he had known she was beyond his reach— even though the *shatai* didn't seem to know that she was also beyond *his*.

Upon learning from Faradar that the *torena* had been captured, Zimran had believed, as Josarian had, that she couldn't possibly still be alive. Knowing that Josarian would seek privacy with Tansen at Idalar to break the news to him, Zimran had followed his cousin into the woods and eavesdropped. He wanted to see the pain on Tansen's face when he learned Elelar was undoubtedly dead. It wouldn't be as satisfying as seeing the *shatai*'s corpse lying in the mud after some battle, but it would be enough.

Naturally, upon learning that Elelar was, in fact, alive, Zimran had known instantly he must go to Shaljir with Tansen. Since the *torena* couldn't go back to her palace in the city or to her grand country estates, she would have to live with them, become one of them. Suddenly she was within Zimran's reach, and he would not let Tansen get to her first. He would not sit idly by while that *roshah* won her by rescuing her single-handedly from Shaljir. He knew that the *shatai*'s plan was an insanely dangerous one, but he also knew that if anyone could make it succeed, it was Tansen. Zimran decided it would be better to die like a man in Shaljir rather than stay in the mountains and wish he himself could have been the *torena*'s hero. So he went, praying that he would survive and hoping—but not expecting—that Tansen would get himself killed.

Having exhausted the improbable topic of Josarian's flinging himself into Darshon, Zimran's companions turned to a new subject while the boat rocked the way his bed once had during an earthquake in Emeldar.

"Dalishar?" Tansen repeated in response to the captain's question. "No, we can't go back there. The Valdani will expect it, so they'll be watching every road and raiding every village on the way." He sighed. "They'll want the *torena* back very badly, and they'll do a lot of damage trying to get her."

"You sound as if you think you should have left me where I was," Elelar said sourly.

"Don't you?" Tansen replied without heat.

She hesitated, then admitted, "Perhaps."

Wishing the deck would stop heaving beneath him, Zimran protested, "Your death could only be counted as a terrible loss, *torena*. Your life is worth whatever it costs us."

Tansen rose to his feet. "Oh, for the love of Dar."

He stalked away—though it wasn't possible to go very *far* away on this boat. Darfire, Zimran couldn't wait to get back on dry land!

At least Elelar smiled at him. Warm. Sweet. Welcoming. At least there was that.

CALIDAR'S SILKEN SCARF danced in the circle of fire. Josarian watched it, absently rubbing the dull ache in his wounded thigh while Mirabar chanted. She had tried to talk him out of attempting this.

"It's the wrong season," she'd argued, "the wrong time of year. Your wife died in the spring. This world and the Other one revolve together, one moving as the other does. She will be out of reach right n—"

"You can do what others can't," he had argued right back, "and I *must* see her."

She had continued protesting until Cheylan delicately offered to perform the Calling in her place. That changed her mind fast enough. Tansen had once privately mentioned to Josarian that Cheylan seemed a little jealous of Mirabar's power and reputation. Now Mirabar clearly felt that Cheylan's offer to help Josarian trespassed on her territory. Guardians, Josarian wryly observed, were not so different from ordinary people, after all. Realizing that Josarian would indeed turn to Cheylan if she continued denying him, Mirabar agreed to Call Calidar. Cheylan had tactfully disappeared after that.

Now, alone with Mirabar and her fire, Josarian waited and prayed. The dreams, the visions, the prophecy . . . Jalan's ravings, the whispered rumors, the outright challenge from the lowlanders and the sea-born folk . . . He could face death, even such a painful one as jumping into Darshon. He had been facing death for a long time now, and he would embrace it when it came, carrying him all the way to the Otherworld and Calidar. But he didn't want to leave the rebellion in disarray by dying at the behest of his own overblown pride. He wanted to die fighting for Sileria, not stupidly seeking vainglory and legend. He wanted to die for a reason.

Perhaps the answer to his dilemma lay in finding out if Calidar had died for a reason, as Jalan had suggested.

She came at last, answering the Calling despite Mirabar's doubts and warnings, despite the natural and supernatural forces which should have kept her away. She came to him to answer his prayers and his questions, and that in itself was almost answer enough. He basked in the presence of the woman—the shade of the woman—he had loved more than life itself, the woman he had never stopped missing and longing for.

"*Kadriah,*" he murmured, "I swore I would mourn you forever."

"Now another waits for you," Mirabar said, her gaze glassy and unfocused, her voice soft and breathless.

"Did you . . . leave . . . to free me for Her?" he asked at last.

Calidar's shade didn't deny it or correct him. "Go to Her now . . . She awaits you . . ."

"And you?" He heard the pleading in his voice and didn't care. "I don't want to forget you."

"I await you in the Otherworld," Mirabar said on a sigh,

her voice eerily like that of his dead wife. "I will wait for you forever."

"Calidar . . ." He inhaled, wishing he could smell her familiar scent, wishing he could touch her warm flesh one last time. *"Kadriah."*

"Now is the time . . ."

He heard Armian's words, and he knew his destiny. Sorrow, rather than glory, filled his heart. Acceptance, rather than fear, flooded his veins. He would go to Darshon. He would give himself to the goddess. He would offer himself to She who would never, as his dreams had made clear, share him with the memory of Calidar.

Lost in his thoughts as Calidar faded from his vision for the last time, he was startled into awareness by Mirabar's cry of dismay. He saw her thrust her hand into the heart of the fire, then withdraw it with a scream, nursing burned flesh as Calidar's scarf went up in flames.

"Josarian!" Mirabar looked up at him, tears of regret filling her flame-hot eyes. "The scarf! I'm sorry. I tried . . . I'm so sorry . . ."

He wanted to grieve, but he knew he could not mourn his wife any longer. It would not be tolerated; Dar was a jealous goddess. He knelt and cradled Mirabar in his arms.

"Shhh . . . It's all right," he crooned. "Don't, Mira. It's all right. I won't need it again."

"You're going to Darshon, aren't you?" Her voice was weak and despairing.

"Yes."

"Then I'm coming with you."

He smiled. "I know."

She was supposed to leave here with Kiloran, but she'd never go now. He'd send Cheylan in her place, he decided. Nothing would keep Mirabar away from Darshon now, and Josarian knew he might need her there.

He rose to his feet and summoned one of his men. "Send a runner to Dalishar. Tell Jalan I'm ready. I'll meet him at Darshon."

*   *   *

HIS FAILURE TO recapture the *torena* meant that Koroll would have to inform the Imperial Council that she was irretrievably gone. Several days of combing the countryside and slaughtering peasants had produced no results whatsoever. Koroll even began to suspect that people might actually be telling the truth; the rescue party might not have brought Elelar back to rebel-held territory after all. He also had to stop the search sooner than he wanted to, for he couldn't risk going much closer to the region around Dalishar with only two hundred men. Even assuming that informants were exaggerating, Koroll knew that there were thousands of armed Silerians living in rebel territory now, and hundreds more were joining them every day: refugees from sacked villages, more *shallah* clans pledging their blood to Josarian's cause, escaped convicts, more assassins, bandits and smugglers, ambitious fools and naive idealists . . . It made Koroll shudder to think of social life within rebel circles. He derived some small satisfaction in picturing *Torena* Elelar now stranded amidst such company.

However, the satisfaction was very small, indeed, when he considered how to phrase his dispatch to the Imperial Council. There were only so many ways to explain that the prison in Shaljir had been ransacked by rebels who had liberated his most valuable prisoner—and none of the ways made Koroll look good. He decided not to even mention Borell's "final orders" *or* the trial Elelar wouldn't have lived to see. Koroll's previous plans on that score were irrelevant now that the *torena* was gone; her death would have been *so* much easier to explain away than her escape would be.

On the road back to Shaljir, his company came across a small rebel group returning from a raid. Vastly outnumbered, the rebels tried to flee rather than fight. More than half of them got away, but Koroll's men were able to run down a few. Galloping up to where four Outlookers had seized a big, well-fed, surprisingly well-dressed rebel, Koroll stopped his men from killing the man. He'd had trouble impressing upon the new recruits that they needed to keep some rebels alive for information. Silerian rebels were not usually talkers, not even under torture, but one must try, after all, even if success was rare.

This attempt was failing. Even when the Outlookers tied this rebel like a trussed chicken and began beating him, he struggled, spat, cursed them, and generally disappointed any hopes that he might talk in exchange for his life—or for a quick death.

However, Koroll at least discovered why this man was such a healthy, wealthy specimen: he was an assassin. One Outlooker, favoring a hand which seemed to have been burned, showed Koroll the wavy-edged dagger the man had been armed with. It now lay on the ground nearby. The Outlookers had disarmed the rebel but found they could not touch his dagger, which burned with a bitter cold worse than fire.

A *shir!* And a captive assassin. Unlike the ignorant men he commanded, Koroll knew what this meant. He had taken the trouble to learn about Silerians and their ways. He knew how powerful a *shir* was, and he knew what a man had to do to get one. This assassin might not give Koroll any information, but he would give him something almost as valuable.

Without another word, without warning, Koroll unsheathed his sword and slit the assassin's throat. Silent with surprise, his men watched him turn and pick up the *shir.*

It came into his hand almost as if answering his summons, and it felt more sure and powerful in his grip than any sword ever had. It was a lovely thing, easily as beautiful as the only other *shir* he'd ever seen, the one owned by Tansen. The wavy, water-made blade shimmered almost like the finest-cut diamonds from Alizar; it practically seemed to ripple and move of its own volition, as if still connected to the currents of the spring or river which gave it birth. Even the hilt was very fine, made of petrified Kintish wood with silver and jade inlays. It was as exquisite

as it was deadly. Koroll wondered who had made it. The
waterlord who had fashioned this thing would fear it, too.
To make his loyal servants powerful, effective, and feared,
he had imbued this weapon with enough power to threaten
him, too. Whoever he was, no matter how mighty, he was
vulnerable to this thing.

*Kiloran himself? Ah, perhaps that's too much to hope
for.*

Koroll ran the blade along his thumb and discovered that
the legends were true. Although the *shir* was sharp enough
to cut through cloth as if it were thin air, it could not harm
him. It could not drink his blood now that he possessed it.

He slipped it inside his tunic. It would live from now
on against the soft flesh of his belly, where no Valdan
would ever dream of keeping an unsheathed blade. Perhaps
he would kill more rebels with it. Someday, he hoped, he
would even use it on the waterlord who had made it.

ELELAR WAS EXHAUSTED by the time they finally
reached the mountains. They had travelled from the coast
on foot, something she wasn't used to. Nor was she used
to hauling her pampered body over rough ground, nego-
tiating uneven trails narrower than her hips, or climbing
straight up the side of rocky mountain faces to "save time."
She would like to complain sometimes, just to relieve her
ire, but it would only cause more trouble between her two
companions, and she didn't need that.

Men.

Besides, she knew that Faradar was just as tired, and
the maid said nothing. A *torena* should show no less courage.

Fully aware of the danger they were in, knowing how
desperately the Outlookers would be searching for her,
Elelar allowed Tansen to push her to the very edge of her
endurance—and sometimes beyond. She knew he didn't
do it lightly or without careful consideration, for she often
caught him studying her, as well as Faradar, trying to assess her strength, trying to determine how much farther

she could go. He insisted on brief but regular rest stops, even in the mornings when the two women felt fresh; it would make them last longer, he said, and help build their endurance. He pushed Elelar hard, though, so hard she was furious at him more than once. She understood why he did it, but she needed somewhere to direct her feelings of fear, exhaustion, helplessness, futile rage. He knew; sometimes he even purposely inspired this rage to fuel her strength.

He's playing me like a harp.

Having exercised similar skills on many men, she recognized the tactics. Since she knew he was doing it to ensure her survival, she permitted it.

Zimran, on the other hand, offered her all the courtesy and solicitude of a *toren* courting a virgin. He found shady places and smooth boulders for her and Faradar during their brief rests. He offered them water at regular intervals. He gave Elelar a hand over rough portions of ground, scavenged wild harvest fruits and fresh honey for her, and scouted ahead to warn her when the going was about to become rough or reassure her when it was about to become easier.

Zimran and Tansen, both *shallaheen,* didn't even seem to breathe a little harder during what Elelar considered a punishing, life-draining uphill hike. Unfortunately, this left them plenty of breath to argue.

Zimran thought Tansen should be more considerate of Elelar; Tansen thought Zimran should stop coddling her. Zimran thought Tansen's pace would kill the *torena;* Tansen thought Zimran's dawdling would get her killed. Zimran thought a particular place was a good spot to stop for the night; Tansen thought they shouldn't stop for another hour. And so on. At times, Elelar felt like a juicy bone being fought over by two hungry dogs.

Zimran was a handsome man, and quite charming when he chose to be. Elelar found it a pleasure to return his simple gestures of flirtation with easy smiles and uncomplicated appreciation. After her recent experiences in Shaljir, she enjoyed such gentle and undemanding consideration.

Tansen was, of course, more challenging company. Elelar was actually somewhat fond of Tansen, perhaps because of their long history together, or perhaps because he had grown into an extraordinary—if difficult—man.

She just wished, she thought wearily, that he and Zimran would stop bickering so much.

Suddenly exposed by the Valdani and condemned after all these years, this was the first time in Elelar's memory that subterfuge, evasions, misdirection, and false promises weren't part of her daily life. There was little that Tansen didn't know about her, and neither of them liked to allude to the events of which Zimran and Faradar knew nothing. So, for the first time in her memory, she wasn't living in a nest of tangled lies.

She had expected to die in Shaljir, or to be taken to Valda where she'd stand trial—and probably die anyhow. Now finding herself unexpectedly free in a way she had never foreseen—for who would have thought even Tansen would do something so daring and mad as break into Shaljir's prison?—she found herself thinking only day-to-day, sometimes only moment-to-moment, for the first time in her life. For the very first time, she had no hidden agenda, no secret purpose, no false friendships or pretended enmities. Suddenly she was just a rebel escaping through the mountains, hoping to survive, attempting nothing more complex than reaching safety.

She had never felt so free. It surprised her that she could walk all day without thinking about much besides putting one foot in front of the other and trying not to break her neck by falling down a steep slope or slipping off a sheer drop. She was amazed by how quickly and deeply she fell asleep at night in the cool mountain air, for she had always been prone to lying awake long into the night, planning and scheming, waking often from a shallow sleep. For once, she didn't feel compelled to make two plans for every possibility and three counterplans for every contingency. For once, she simply lived the moments as they came, light-headed with her own freedom.

No Borell. No Shiraj. No Ronall. For the time being, no Alliance. No orders or duties.

It was a revelation to her to see the unconcealed desire in Zimran's gaze and realize that only one factor influenced her response: whether or not she *wanted* him as a lover.

She had taken only one man, the very first man, out of desire. All the others—and there had been so many—had been for duty. The bitter heartbreak of that first man's betrayal was only a memory now, lost in the elaborate maze of her secretive life; but choosing or rejecting every lover for a purpose, to serve a concealed goal, had become second nature to her in the succeeding years. She had forgotten what simple desire was, and she had certainly never expected to accept or reject another lover based solely on what she wanted as a woman.

The freedom to do so now was so unfamiliar, she was almost giddy with it. Had her life been different, had she been a different sort of woman, she might have thrown her arms open to Zimran now, gleefully eager to defy her aristocratic upbringing by taking a *shallah* lover. However, so many men from so many walks of life had groped for their pleasure between Elelar's thighs that her true freedom now lay in the ability to say no.

No. She rolled the word around in her mind, enjoying the echoing silence of it.

No, I just want to sleep *at night.*

What a luxury! How restful, that suddenly no man could call her to his bed upon a whim, or invade her bed just because he felt like it. What a privilege, to reserve her body for what would please her. For so long, her body had been merely a tool, a vessel, a means by which she secretly bargained with unwitting men to get what she needed— what Sileria and the Alliance needed.

What an extraordinary feeling it was now, this freedom to give or withhold herself without such considerations!

Poor Zimran. He would be disappointed. He would undoubtedly think it was because she was a *torena* and he was a *shallah*. Being a man, he probably wouldn't understand even if she tried to explain it to him. Ah, well. She would enjoy his charm and courtesy, and she would return it in kind—when she had the strength—but she was in no mood to admit another man to her bed now.

She wondered if Tansen would be disappointed, too. His desire had been transparent when he was a boy, but now he seldom let his feelings show, and she found them confusing when he did. Oh, he still wanted her, she didn't doubt that; there were some things a woman could smell on a man's skin, no matter how stern he kept his face. There were just so many conflicting and fleeting responses mingled with his desire: mistrust, amusement, resignation, wariness. There were moments when he was silent and secretive, but also moments when he spoke to her almost as he spoke to Josarian—honestly, directly, letting his thoughts come uncensored to his lips. There were times when he seemed to respect her, but also times when he fairly radiated contempt and exasperation.

She couldn't think of another man who had such complex reactions to her. Josarian tolerated her. Zimran longed for her. Borell had wanted to possess her. Koroll had dismissed and overlooked her. Shiraj had enjoyed her. Ronall . . . She decided not to think about Ronall. Not now. This was not the time or place to dwell upon thoughts of the half-Valdan husband who had made such startling revelations in her prison cell in Shaljir.

Tansen was enough to fill her thoughts for now. He pushed and prodded, coaxed and goaded, keeping Elelar moving, making her go just a little farther than she thought she could each day as they approached Mount Niran. She would stay there until the Valdani stopped looking for her and it was safe for her to travel to rebel-held territory around Dalishar.

They stopped at a Sanctuary this evening, earlier than Tansen wanted to. Zimran had convinced him of the advantages. Besides giving the women a chance to wash, rest, and eat hot food, it would give Zim a chance to make contact with men in a nearby village, gathering news of the war. So Tansen had agreed to the plan. Immediately after washing and eating, however, he'd left the simple comfort of the Sanctuary to prowl the surrounding area. The Valdani were barbarians who did not respect the inviolability of the Sisterhood. They routinely captured Sisters and regularly raided Sanctuaries searching for outlaws and rebels. So Tansen was watching for Outlookers.

Faradar was exhausted and so, after combing and dressing Elelar's newly washed hair, excused herself and went to bed early. As the sun set over the mountains, Elelar found herself bored by the Sisters' conversation and too alert for sleep. Knowing it would annoy him, she nonetheless went outside to search for Tansen.

He came up silently behind her, after she'd been calling for him for several minutes, and snapped, "Yes, I can hear you. The people in *Adalian* can probably hear you."

She jumped and whirled to face him. "There you are!"

He sighed. "What do you want?"

Her brows arched at his tone. "Are there hordes of bloodthirsty Outlookers in the hills?"

"No. Is that all, *torena?*" He turned to leave.

"Wait." She put a hand on his arm. He froze. Very slowly, he turned back to her.

"Well?" he prodded after an awkward silence between them.

"I would like to thank you for saving my life." Suddenly feeling uncharacteristically self-conscious, she pulled her hand back and continued, "I was denied a trial. Myrell was taking me to the cellar for . . . death by torture. He promised he wouldn't let me die until I told him everything he wanted to know."

"He won't be torturing anyone else." Tan's voice was quiet. "Ever again."

"So I . . . owe you my life."

"I hardly recognize you when you're being humble."

"You don't make humility easy," she countered.

He smiled. "Ah, forgive me. Very well, *torena:* I pray you, don't mention it, I'd do the same for anyone."

"Would you?" she whispered.

He went absolutely still for a moment, then looked away, as if ashamed. She could hardly hear him when he replied, "No. And Mirabar knew it."

The sudden shift in topic unsettled her. *"Mirabar?"*

"She's the one who told me you were still alive. She brought the news from Derlen."

"He escaped?" When Tansen nodded, she asked, "And my other servants?"

"As far as I know, they're all safe. Probably all trying to reach Dalishar."

She wanted to collapse with relief. "Thank Dar! I was so worried. I wanted to know, wanted to ask. But, of course, I couldn't. I couldn't risk letting the Valdani know whose safety I cared about."

"It must . . ." His voice softened. "It must have been very hard for you in there."

She nodded. "Now I know why men—warriors—say it's better to die quickly. Waiting, struggling against hope, trying to keep your worst fears at bay . . . It weakens you, drains you. Sometimes I wondered if Borell was doing it on purpose, even though he surely wanted me killed quickly before I could disgrace him even more."

"Was he vengeful?"

She knew what he meant. "Yes," she replied, remembering. She had been vengeful, too, then.

He took her hand and asked formally, "Shall I swear a bloodvow, *torena?*"

"He's dead," she said briefly. "Suicide."

"Suicide?"

"Yes. Because of the disgrace, no doubt."

He released her hand. She suddenly realized how seldom he had ever touched her. She idly wondered what he was like as a lover. Yes, now that she was free to choose, based solely on whom she wanted, Elelar knew she would think

of him more often. There was no trace in him of the
skinny, ignorant, awkward boy brimming with painful infatuation. He was all man now, experienced, confident, and
ruthlessly disciplined. He was a man of grace and courage,
intelligence and honor. What a rare lover for *her,* she
thought wryly. He was special, but the complexity of their
lives had forced her to look beyond his qualities as a
man—until now. Now she was free to think of him as any
other woman might, and she was vaguely surprised by how
pleasing the sensation was. Besides, it would also be a
practical liaison; there was no one Josarian trusted more
than Tansen, and she . . . Elelar almost laughed at herself,
suddenly aware of what she was doing. Even now, she
couldn't help considering how it would serve the Alliance
if she took another lover.

Old habits die hard.

She decided to let the matter rest for a while. This was
one man, she was surprised to realize, to whom she might
hope to open her arms someday with no hidden purpose.
It would be the first time since her girlhood. But she wasn't
ready for such a relationship, not yet, not so soon after her
complicated life and near-death in Shaljir. If Tansen still
wanted her after all these years, then she supposed he'd
probably still want her even if she made him wait a little
longer. Perhaps she'd even wait until after the long rains,
until the New Year. Perhaps she would just *rest* for now.

She was tired, soul-deep *tired,* she realized. As tired as
Gaborian had been when he died. The thought of rest was
so immensely appealing, it pushed other thoughts from her
mind.

"Would he . . . have mourned you, do you think?" Tansen asked.

She didn't know what he meant. "Who?"

"Borell." Sensing her bewilderment, he added, "You
said he wanted to marry you."

"That was before he found out about me."

Tansen shrugged. "He felt betrayed. He was vengeful.

He would have ordered your death, no doubt, if not for the maneuvers of your husband's family."

"Exactly." She couldn't understand the expression on his face, which she could still see clearly in the twilight.

"It doesn't mean he wasn't still in love with you."

"Still in love with me?" She rolled her eyes. "If he was, then he was a bigger fool than I took him for."

"True, but . . ."

"But what?" she said impatiently.

He shook his head, then looked at her in that way he sometimes had, that way that—infuriatingly—suggested he was so much wiser than she. "Have you never loved someone you also hated?"

"Never." She folded her arms against the descending evening chill. "I loved one man who . . . betrayed me. From that moment on, I hated him. There can be no mingling of two such feelings."

"Can't there?"

She sighed with irritation. "Have you ever loved and hated someone at the same time?"

He stared at her for a long moment before answering simply, "Yes." He looked away and added, "More than once, *torena.*"

"If you—"

His hand over her mouth suddenly silenced her. She went still and pliant, for he had moved suddenly and now stood alert, listening to something she could not hear.

"Someone's coming," he whispered. "Go behind those trees and don't come out until I tell you to."

She nodded and hid. The scared pounding of her heart slowed with relief a few moments later when she recognized Zimran's voice. He was very excited. Elelar spoke and understood the mountain dialect, having learned it in childhood from her *shallah* nurse. However, she had trouble following such fast, breathless, choppy dialogue as this, and the two men were standing so far away she couldn't hear all of their words. They were discussing something to do with Josarian, but that was all she was sure of. Wondering what was wrong, she remained obediently hidden until Tansen finally remembered she was there and called to her.

"I'm leaving," he said abruptly.

"Now?"

"Now," he confirmed. "There's no time to waste."

"You can't travel these mountains in the dark!" she protested.

He ignored her comment. "In the morning, you and Faradar will continue on to the rebel camp on Mount Niran with Zimran. You'll be safe there for now."

His voice was harsh with strained emotion, his gestures uncharacteristically stiff and jerky as she and Zimran accompanied him back to the Sanctuary.

"What's happened? What's wrong?" she demanded, struggling to keep up with him.

He stopped abruptly and turned to face her. A curt gesture silenced whatever Zimran was about to say. "You deserve to know," Tansen said. "You should be prepared."

"For what?"

"The rebellion may be over. We may lose everything."

She grasped his arms. "Why? *What's happened?"*

"Someone has finally convinced Josarian that he's the Firebringer. He's on his way to Darshon to prove it by flinging himself into the volcano."

"No!" The rebellion was still too new and scattered. If the leader of the *shallaheen* died now, the whole thing could collapse. "You've got to stop him!"

Tansen shook her off. "Darfire, do you think I'm going there to give him a push? Of course I've got to stop him!"

"He's gone mad," Zimran said. "What other explanation could there be?"

"You heard this in the village?" Elelar asked.

"Yes," Zimran confirmed. "He announced his intentions in Kiloran's camp and sent a runner to Dalishar. Word is spreading already." Zimran looked at Tansen. "You'll have trouble catching up."

"Nonetheless," Elelar said, "he's got to try. It's our only chance."

"He's a few days ahead of me and his starting place was closer to Darshon, but I know the *zanareen*," Tansen said. "My brother was one. He died in the volcano. The *zanareen* aren't likely to let Josarian simply walk up and jump. There are days of rituals and ceremonies they'll want to put him through. It might take up enough time for me to reach him before he . . . before he can do it."

"Will he listen to you?" she asked desperately.

"I'll make him listen," Tansen promised.

Elelar rubbed her forehead. "What could have happened? What is Josarian thinking of?"

"I don't know, *torena*." Zimran shook his head. "He is not the man I knew. He is no longer the cousin I grew up with."

"We're wasting time," Tansen said. "I'll go get my things. Zimran, get me a travelling lantern and plenty of fuel." He almost smiled. "There are times I actually miss Mirabar. Guardians come in handy in the dark."

"If she's so handy, why didn't she stop him?" Elelar snapped.

He sighed. "Who knows?"

"I'll have the Sisters pack some food and water for you," she offered.

Tansen nodded and went to get his satchel. Hurrying into the Sanctuary to get food for him, Elelar mourned what she might have had, what was already out of her reach again. There would be no rest now, no time for living simply as a mountain rebel. This changed everything.

33

JOSARIAN IGNORED THE crowd of *shalla-heen* following him as he trekked up the slopes of Mount Darshon. He and Mirabar had met Jalan at a Sanctuary at the base of Darshon, where the *zanar* had immediately started preaching to the local *shallaheen*. No one ever paid much attention when yet another *zanar* flung himself into the volcano, but hundreds of mountain peasants who heard Jalan's ravings evidently felt they couldn't miss seeing Sileria's most famous rebel do such an insane thing.

Josarian also ignored Mirabar, who had been pleading with him, ever since leaving Idalar, to wait until she could consult the Beckoner about this "madness." But her elusive Beckoner remained silent on the subject, frustrating Mirabar and confirming Josarian's conviction that only one thing could resolve his dilemma: He must jump.

They were close to the snowy summit of Darshon when Mirabar interrupted his silent musings once again. "We must stop. I need . . . I need to rest."

He would not be stalled or delayed. "You stop, then." He didn't even glance at her to soften his brusque tone. "I can't."

"Josarian, please."

He ignored her. Her voice was thin and weak, a puny human sound he could barely hear amidst the passionate roaring that filled his mind as they approached the mouth of the volcano: Dar was welcoming him. She knew he was here. She awaited him as eagerly as Calidar had awaited him on their wedding night.

Pain rippled through his head, and he knew it was Dar

reaching out to punish him for betraying Her now with even the briefest memory of his wife.

He was resolved. There could be no turning back.

Calidar, Calidar . . .

One hot tear trickled down his wind-chilled face as he banished the last memory of her from his heart. Until they met again in the Otherworld, until then . . . he would belong to Dar and no other.

I am coming, Dar.

"Josarian comes! He comes!" Jalan cried as they approached Darshon's summit. "Welcome him!"

Welcome me. Welcome me, for I have given up my heart for You.

"Josarian!" Mirabar called as he quickened his pace to meet the crowd of *zanareen* coming down the slope to greet him. "Wait!"

"Stay here," he ordered.

"No!" She sounded breathless and scared. "I'm coming . . . with you . . . damn you."

He would have smiled under other circumstances, accustomed by now to her sharp tongue. Now he thought only of what was to come.

More *zanareen* appeared up ahead. He could hear them shouting his name, cheering, ecstatic with religious fervor. There were, however, also dissenters.

"Go back!" one *zanar* screamed, startling him. "You are not one of us!"

"He is the Firebringer!" Jalan cried. "Stand back!"

"No, he is just some lawless peasant!"

"I stand with Jalan!" someone else proclaimed.

"I will jump and prove that Josarian is nothing but a pretender!"

"No one may jump before Josarian does!"

"He has no right!"

"He has more right than—"

"Oh, for the . . . love of Dar," Mirabar said. "Is there someone . . . in authority here?" She was breathing hard. The air was so thin this high up.

"Who is this woman?" a dirty gray-haired *zanar* demanded.

"She is a demon!"

"She is beloved of Dar," another *zanar* insisted, studying Mirabar. "Just look at her and you can see that, you fool!"

"She is my trusted advisor," Josarian said sharply. They all stopped bickering and stared, as if astonished he could speak. Taking advantage of their momentary silence, he continued, "I come here with all due respect. I bring reverence and devotion to Dar. I offer Her my life in exchange for Her favor."

"You are not one of us!"

"Nowhere does it say that the Firebringer must be one of us!"

"He is Josarian! If he is not the Chosen One, then who is?"

"Yes, let him jump! Then we will know!"

"It is sacrilege!"

"*Must* you all shout?" Mirabar said testily. "My head is pounding."

"He will not profane this sacred site!" A furious young man leapt forward and swung his *yahr* at Josarian's head with deadly accuracy.

"No!" Mirabar cried.

Josarian ducked, rolled to the ground, kicked the man's legs out from under him, and disarmed him. He tossed the weapon aside as he rose to his feet, leaving the humiliated attacker lying in the snow.

"*That* was sacrilege," said the gray-haired *zanar,* glaring down at the young man on the ground.

"No fire," Mirabar gasped, her hands stretched out in front of her. She looked strangely pale. "I have . . . no fire."

"This is Darshon," said Jalan, "where we all stand helpless and humbled before the goddess."

Mirabar hugged herself, shivering in the cold wind that swept across the mountaintop.

"Enough of this," Josarian said. "It is Dar, and not the *zanareen*, who will determine who the Firebringer is."

"Yes! That is true."

"Let him jump!"

"No! I will jump! I will jump now, and you will know him for the liar and pretender that he is!"

"Stop," Josarian said as a *zanar* turned to go to his death. "If I die in the volcano, then you'll know; then you can jump. Don't throw your life away now."

The *zanar* cursed him, then turned and started ascending the slope as fast as he could.

"I guess you said . . . the wrong thing," Mirabar surmised.

"Stop! You are not purified!" the gray-haired *zanar* called after the young man. "I will not condone . . ." He gave up shouting after the retreating figure and returned his attention to Josarian. "You are correct. Only Dar can decide."

"Then take me to Her."

"Josarian . . ." Mirabar's voice was pleading.

"Let him go." Jalan stepped between her and Josarian, separating them. "You must. Surely you know that by now?"

She stopped and stared at Jalan, her hot eyes glowing in a face gone sallow with cold and fatigue.

Jalan turned to address the growing crowd of *zanareen*. "All of Sileria awaits the answer now. The war, the future of our people, our freedom . . . All of it now depends upon what happens here."

"It's true," Josarian said, raising his voice to be heard above the wind. "It's why I have come. Sileria will have the answer, even if it means my death. I ask for your blessing, but I will enter the Fires without it if I must."

"No," said the gray-haired one. "You must be purified first. It would not be fitting to offer yourself to the goddess without proper preparation."

"I am ready," Josarian replied. He had expected this and he would cooperate. Dar and the *zanareen* had waited centuries, and he would not dishonor them by rejecting the rites and rituals of Darshon.

"Let us waste no more time," Jalan said, taking his arm and leading him away. "Come."

"Josarian?"

He heard a catch of panic in Mirabar's voice and looked back at her. Four men were blocking her path as she tried to follow him. "She goes where I go," he told them.

"No woman goes where you are going now." Seeing his hesitation, Jalan added, "No one will harm her. But she may not come with us."

He met her worried gaze. She had run out of words and pleaded only with her eyes now, those eyes which glowed like the heart of Darshon.

"Go back to the Sanctuary down below," he ordered her. "Wait there."

"Wait for what? News of your death?" she protested. "Josarian! Come back! Josarian!"

He turned his back on her, steeling himself against her pleas as he went in pursuit of his destiny.

KOROLL WAS ADMIRING his newly acquired *shir* when one of his men admitted Shaljir's new prison chief to his command chamber. The former prison chief was on his way back to Valda, under armed escort, to face formal charges. He was accompanied by a courier carrying a carefully worded dispatch from Koroll explaining that this incompetent fool had permitted rebels to break into the prison and steal *Torena* Elelar. Unable to mitigate the disaster, Koroll did the next best thing and cast blame elsewhere.

The new prison chief, mindful of how precarious his position would be if anything went wrong, had come to make a full report to Koroll. It was possible, he advised the commander, that the rebels had entered the prison through the sewage system, though how they got into the system in the first place, or how they knew which outlet led into the prison, was anybody's guess. The chief discussed several other possibilities, but Koroll rather favored the image of the *torena* wading through waist-deep sewage as she made her escape.

Koroll ordered all water and sewage conduits to be secured with heavy new equipment and double locks. There was no point in trying to track the *torena*'s escape route, though. There were too many possible directions for her to have gone, and it wasn't as if she would have left footprints in the subterranean rivers of sewage. The Outlookers were still conducting a house-to-house search of Shaljir for her, but Koroll had no doubt that she was far from the city by now.

Meanwhile, her worthless husband was in a small cell on the top floor of the prison. He was guarded day and night by no less than four men at all times. He was forbidden visitors and never allowed outside of his cell.

Ronall's family was powerless to help him now. They had championed Elelar, and she had escaped and fled—after being granted the honor of a trial. Not only was Ronall's family disgraced, they were even in danger of having their property and assets seized by the Emperor in retaliation. Consequently, their protests on Ronall's behalf, after he was imprisoned, began mildly and soon faded into silence. Elelar's husband was alone now, completely at Koroll's mercy. Koroll knew that the *torena* hadn't been fond of Ronall, but the drunkard was the only leverage Koroll currently had, and he intended to find a way to use him.

Consequently, Koroll had given the new prison chief strict instructions to watch Ronall and report anything of interest.

"What do you mean he's sick?" Koroll demanded, upon receiving the prison chief's full report. "I told you to take care that nothing happened to him! He's half-Valdan, you fool, and a hostage for his rebel wife!"

"Sir, we *have* taken care," the chief insisted, "but he's vomiting, sweating, feverish, shaking. He seems to be having visions and delusions and . . ." The man made a helpless gesture. "It's not our fault. It's the liquor and the

Kintish dreamweed and the Moorlander cloud-syrup."

"You've been giving a *prisoner* liquor and dreamweed and—"

"No! No, sir." The chief flushed and quickly explained, "I mean, it's the lack of those things that's making him ill."

Koroll stared at him. "That's ridiculous. A man gets sick from too much of those things, and a man like Ronall undoubtedy misses them when he's deprived of them, but—"

"According to the priest whom I asked to examine him, deprivation is the problem, sir. *Toren* Ronall's body is so accustomed to regular and large quantities of these things that the lack of them is making him ill."

Koroll shook his head. "And Elelar is married to *that*," he mused.

"Sir, he's been asking for . . . begging for something— anything."

Koroll frowned. "Does the priest say he'll die without it?"

"He's still young and relatively strong, so the priest doubts it, but—"

"Then the answer is no."

"But," the chief continued stubbornly, "there's no guarantee, sir. He *could* die."

"If we give him something to soothe him now, what about tomorrow?" Koroll demanded. "I've barely got enough money in my treasury right now to feed my men, and we're trying to fight a war! Do you really think I can spare you the money to acquire imported dreamweed and cloud-syrup for one useless half-Silerian prisoner?"

"Then perhaps some liquor, sir, at least some—"

"No!" Koroll thundered. "Tell that sot to be a man and pull himself together!"

"Commander, you warned me not to let him die. If he—"

"The warning still stands," Koroll snapped. "I suggest you tell that priest to get to work keeping him alive." As an afterthought, he suggested, "And get a Sister to treat him, too. He's half-Silerian, after all, and they put great faith in the Sisters' healing powers. You shouldn't have any trouble finding one," he added. "We've probably got more Sisters in Shaljir than there are whores in Valda."

His face pink with anger, the prison chief said, "Yes, sir."

THE CHANTING OF the *zanareen* rolled through Mirabar's aching head, echoing, thundering, growing faint, then growing strong. They had been at it nonstop for days, and she'd finally reached the point where it took all her self-control not to throw some of them into the volcano while they all waited for Josarian to take the fiery leap.

She hadn't known much about the *zanareen* before coming to Darshon with Josarian. She'd known they were all crazy, and spending the past few days among them had only served to thoroughly confirm that impression. As a Guardian living in remote mountain hideouts, she'd had little contact with the madmen who seldom left the snow-capped peak of Darshon. Any *zanareen* that did leave here were usually searching for new recruits, which they knew they wouldn't find among the Guardians. Now that she was here, she wished she could have remained ignorant of their ways.

She had hoped that after she and Josarian ascended to the volcano's rim, he'd take one look at the churning lava lake, change his mind, and suggest they get back to the war with all due haste. Yes, she had hoped—but she hadn't counted on it. From the moment he'd announced he was setting out for Darshon, she had seen the resolution in his face.

Mirabar didn't know how to talk him out of it, either. She had tried repeatedly on the way here, but without as much conviction as such arguments needed. After all, she had been right there when his wife, speaking through *her* from the Otherworld, had urged him to go to Dar's embrace.

The Otherworld was a strange place, of course, and the dead could be so infuriatingly vague, their messages laced with symbols every bit as incomprehensible as those offered by the Beckoner. There were many possible explanations for Calidar's message to Josarian that night at Idalar, as Mirabar had tried to tell him several times since then. However, she didn't really believe it herself, so she hadn't been convincing enough when arguing with Josarian.

Like Armian, Calidar had answered the Calling when she shouldn't have been able to. She came to answer Josarian's questions; surely she would have given some indication, if she were urging Josarian to go to someone beside Dar Herself.

The dreams, the visions, the prophecy, the Calling . . .

Josarian had followed his destiny all the way to Darshon, as Mirabar had once followed hers to the icy waters of Kandahar. If only she could be sure now! If only the Otherworld or the Beckoner would answer her questions, give her a sign! Josarian was about to fling himself into the volcano, and ever since arriving at Darshon, Mirabar had been as useless and powerless as any ordinary peasant girl. She couldn't even read the scriptures which the *zanareen* were probably thrusting under Josarian's equally illiterate gaze.

The roar of Dar's power was so loud and strong up here, there was no room for anything else. Waterlords, one of the *zanareen* had told Mirabar, were just as powerless at Darshon as she now was. She couldn't even conjure a small fire to keep herself warm up here at the icy, windblown, snowcapped summit of the mountain. She had never been so out of touch with her power in her whole life, not even as a savage child.

Where was the Beckoner? Why had he abandoned her? Who was he and what did he expect of her now? Why didn't he *come?* She had never felt so helpless or frustrated.

She had also never expected to spend such a long time

up here. She had thought that Josarian could simply arrive at Darshon, look down into the bubbling womb of the goddess, and jump. She'd been wrong.

The *zanareen* had been awaiting the Firebringer for centuries, since long before the Kints had seized Sileria from the Moorlanders. During that time, they had developed many rituals around the testing of the Firebringer. Josarian's claim to the title evidently required even more purification ceremonies than usual, since he wasn't even a *zanar*—in fact, he was the first outsider to ever claim the right to jump, a controversy over which the *zanareen* were bitterly divided. Some believed that Josarian was unquestionably the Firebringer and were already preparing for his predicted triumph, but others violently rejected his claim. With her powers stripped from her in Dar's presence, Mirabar knew she couldn't protect Josarian from another physical attack, and she was afraid for him.

Where in the Fires is Tansen when we need him? Off rescuing his damned torena *from a fate she probably deserves.*

At Mirabar's insistence, Najdan awaited them in a Sanctuary at the base of Darshon. The gateway to Dar's womb was no place for an assassin, and Mirabar would not commit sacrilege by bringing him here, no matter how reluctant he was to let her go without him.

He had startled her after leaving Idalar by asking her about Cheylan's intentions toward her. As if he were her father and she an ordinary *shallah* girl! Head reeling and chest aching, she almost smiled even now. At least the subject seemed less embarrassing here before Dar, on the brink of disaster or destiny. She'd been mortified, at the time, by Najdan's awkward attempts to question her. Particularly since she had no answer for him.

Cheylan . . . A man unlike any other. She recalled his kisses with a toe-curling shiver. She had resented his offer to Call Calidar for Josarian, but perhaps he had only suggested it because she was so obviously reluctant to do it herself. Still, she didn't want another Guardian to serve

Josarian; that was her right. She had not been jealous, however, when Josarian ordered Cheylan to leave Idalar with Kiloran. That would normally have been Mirabar's duty, but it wasn't one she regretted abdicating. Now she wondered how Cheylan was faring with the deadly waterlord. She supposed she should have warned Cheylan to guard his tongue—and his back—around Searlon, the sleek and shrewd assassin who seemed to her almost as dangerous as Kiloran himself. But she had been so distraught upon departing from Idalar with Josarian, and then when Cheylan had taken her in his arms to say good-bye . . .

After that, she fended off Najdan's questions like an errant girl lying to her father. Now, waiting for Josarian to seek the goddess, it all seemed long ago and very unimportant.

As a mere woman, Mira was kept far away from Josarian now, since he mustn't be "contaminated" by her presence before his leap into destiny. The *zanareen* insisted that every ritual, like every word of the ancient scripture, was goddess-inspired. Mirabar thought it just as likely that a few madmen had thought it all up one night, centuries ago, after too many sips of smuggled cloud-syrup.

There were hundreds and hundreds of *zanareen* at Darshon, most of them living in caves, tents, and tiny stone huts. It was bitterly cold this high up. Mirabar wore two cloaks all of the time—hers and Josarian's—but she still shivered day and night. Thick wrappings covered her feet and hands now, which were always numb with cold. Though she had lived in the mountains her whole life, she had never touched snow before, for the rest of Sileria was a warm country. She had also never before been so high up that it was hard to breathe. The air was thin and weak here, and even a brief walk left her gasping like a pudgy merchant trying to scramble up the side of a mountain. Her head ached all of the time, and she was perpetually dizzy. Her body rebelled by rejecting every mouthful she tried to eat. All in all, she'd never felt so close to death in her life.

The rim of the volcano was free of snow, since the heat melted it down to bare lava stone. Sometimes Mirabar went closer to the volcano to get warm, but the intense heat rendered her nausea and her headache even worse, so she never stayed there long. Besides, she didn't particularly like looking down into the caldera where Josarian was about to risk his life. It was vast, bigger than a village. Streams of bubbling lava, orange and spotted with leaping flames, flowed around expanses of newly hardened lava. Mirabar watched in awe as the flowing lava slowly engulfed and swallowed the black rock. How could Josarian's flesh withstand *that?* Sometimes the rock itself moved, shifted, and heaved in response to the surge of red lava beneath it. The *zanareen* were excited by this activity and said that Dar was growing impatient, that She wanted Josarian.

In the center of the caldera was the seething, bubbling, fire-spewing, red-hot lake of molten lava wherein dwelled Dar, goddess of fire, ultimate ruler of Sileria. It was said She had been born from a union of earth and sky. She had travelled the three corners of the world in search of a home before finally coming to rest at Darshon, the mightiest of mountains in the most beautiful of nations. She was a destroyer, wiping out whole villages on a whim. Her cruelty had shaped Her people, making them ruthless, unforgiving, and violent. However, it was She, too, who had made them the strongest, fiercest, bravest people in the world.

Prophecy foretold that it was the Firebringer who would make them once again the *proudest* people in the world. With the coming of the Firebringer, the people would drive out the *roshaheen.* The conquerors would leave Sileria, and the island would belong once again to Silerians.

Mirabar let her aching head drop between her knees and covered herself with her cloaks, trying to get warm. The *zanareen* had been quoting nonstop from the scriptures ever since Josarian's arrival. The prophecy was vague, self-contradictory, and open to interpretation. Josarian's supporters found material in the scriptures to support his claim; his detractors found material therein to refute it. She herself had begged Dar for an answer. Right here, at the very gateway to Dar's womb, she had been ignored.

Someone brought her water, which she accepted halfheartedly, hoping she wouldn't bring it right back up. Water was plentiful at Darshon, for the goddess lived right beneath the skin of the mountain. Hot rocks and small lava pools melted the snow, sometimes creating waterfalls and fast-moving streams. Boiling hot geysers erupted from the earth farther down the mountain, creating warm pools of water in which the *zanareen* bathed. Mirabar might consider going down to one of those pools herself to get warm, but for two things: she didn't think she could face the climb back up with no air, and no one would tell her when Josarian would jump. She didn't intend to be washing when it happened.

The water she drank went down smoothly and seemed like it intended to stay in her belly. She smiled her thanks at the man who had offered it to her, relieved that he didn't shy away from her lava-red hair and fiery gaze. He wasn't a *zanar,* but rather one of the local *shallaheen* who had come to witness the event. Hundreds upon hundreds of them were streaming to Darshon now; word was spreading fast that Josarian had come at last to embrace the goddess.

How long before the Valdani hear about his presence here and come looking for him? How long before he jumps?

Practical and spiritual fears plagued her until she worried she was becoming as demented as the *zanareen.* She alternately dreaded the event and longed to get it over with. She was utterly exhausted and didn't know how much more of this she could stand; yet she couldn't convince herself that Josarian wouldn't simply die in that life-eating lava lake as so many others had. She felt sick every time she remembered the screams of the man who had thrown himself into the volcano when she and Josarian had first arrived. She supposed it was better than death by slow torture—but not much.

There wasn't even any relief in sleep up here, for the nonstop chanting of the *zanareen* made slumber almost impossible. Day and night, night and day. The lack of air, the lack of sleep, the bone-numbing cold, the deadly heat of the volcano, the poor food, the nausea and headaches . . . No wonder the *zanareen* were all crazy. She soon would be, too, if she stayed here much longer.

Suddenly the chanting stopped. Just like that.

Mirabar fumbled her way out of the folds of her cloaks and lifted her throbbing head. They had been chanting without mercy for days, now suddenly, without warning . . . silence. There was no noise except for the sound of the brutal wind whipping across the summit of Darshon and the unsteady rumble of the volcano itself. Mirabar looked around, trying to figure out what was different, what had stilled the voices of the *zanareen*.

Then a crowd of more than one hundred chanters parted as smoothly as if separated by the hand of Dar. They fell back silently. Appearing among them, Josarian came forward. He was naked. Mirabar averted her eyes, momentarily shocked. Then practical considerations asserted themselves: he would freeze out here! She rose to her feet and started forward, intending to give him his cloak. Her path was suddenly blocked by four *zanareen*.

She swallowed, understanding. "He's ready, isn't he?" Her voice came out as a dry croak.

"He is ready."

She looked at Josarian again, but he didn't seem to see her. She wanted to call out to him, but her voice wouldn't work. She watched in helpless silence as he walked to the far side of the volcano rim. Once there, he approached a slab of smooth, glossy, black stone, a cliff overhanging the lava pit. He was too far away for Mirabar to see his face as he walked to its very edge and stood there, poised high above the rumbling lava lake which led to the very heart of the goddess.

"Josarian!" Mira tried to shout, but it came out as the barest of whispers. Even so, someone slapped her. She didn't even bother to glare at him. Her gaze was riveted on Josarian.

Josarian raised his arms overhead. The chanting began again. Mirabar's head throbbed in time to the frantic, atonal wailing. Pausing there for so long, Josarian's bare feet should be burning on that hot rock; his flesh should be protesting against the heat rising from the caldera. Yet he simply stood there.

Tears of exhaustion, fear, and helpless confusion streamed down Mirabar's rigid face as she waited for him to jump.

THE TRAIL WAS long, uneven, and rough. Tansen had come to Darshon once before, in his childhood. In the succeeding years, he had forgotten what a hard climb this was. Pink, peach, brown, and black lava flows, the remnants of Dar's many tantrums, coiled, curled, rolled, and braided into a thousand tangled shapes, and he had to pick his way through or climb over them all. He passed through what had once been a forest. The trees had been incinerated, their trunks covered by flying chunks of lava. Now they squatted beneath Darshon's snowy summit like great, lumpy trolls; as a child, he had believed every story inspired by these monstrous visions crouching on the mountainside.

There were no trees higher up. Higher still, even the shrubs and plants grew scarce. The lava took on fantastic and incredible shapes as thick clouds slid down the mountain's slopes to meet him. He passed geysers of boiling water shooting angrily into the air, warning him away from the goddess's domain. Warm pools of water where the *zanareen* liked to bathe were now completely deserted, as were all the huts, tents, and caves that he passed. The *zanareen* were all up there. With Josarian.

Fear churned in Tan's belly. Fear for his bloodbrother, who was about to jump to his death. Fear for himself, for Dar would not welcome him here. Everywhere he looked, he saw evidence of what Dar could do on an angry rampage. She was the destroyer-goddess, not some soft-hearted foreign deity who could be placated with a few generous bribes. She was a goddess of fire and fury, and he had offended Her sorely, murdering his own blood-father, slaying the man he had believed to be the Fire-bringer. And now Tansen was coming to deny Dar the one man whom many believed She wanted more than any other.

He climbed past rocks shaped like crescent moons, like loaves of bread, like dancing girls frozen in time. He climbed past lava flows which hideously suggested gigantic parts of human bodies. He passed bubbling lava pools, rocks glowing with heat, and streams created by heat-melted snow. His once-fine Moorlander boots sank ankle-deep as he climbed powdery cinder cones. He fell several times in his haste, cutting himself on sharp fragments as the ground crumbled beneath him. Blood from a cut on his forehead temporarily blinded him, but he wiped it away and kept on going. Higher up, great splits in the earth revealed gooey-looking purple and yellow innards, rich and bristly with crystals sharp enough to drive through a man's heart.

The air grew thinner as he went even higher, making his lungs ache and his head spin, slowing him down. It was cold now, so *cold.* He was nearly there, though. Just a little farther. And then he could stop Josarian.

Suddenly the ground split open before him. The crack widened into a huge rent before he could leap across it. Wisps of steam arose from the earth's wound, clotting swiftly into a column of thick yellow smoke. The poisonous miasma choked him, forcing him backwards.

"Dar!" he shouted. He had stopped praying to the goddess the night he killed Armian, but he addressed Her now: "I *will* stop him!"

The black interior of the earth melted into bright red. The lava smelled like blood and was hotter than fire. It pushed apart the crack, widening the gulf between him and Josarian. The skin-charring heat drove him farther back.

Molten rocks began spurting into the air, chunks of yellow and orange fire leaping out at him, driving him back down the slope up which he had just come.

"Dar!" he screamed. *"You'll have to kill me first if You want him!"*

But he was only a man, and She was a goddess. His swords, his training, and his skills were useless against Her. Even his courage meant nothing in the face of Her power. Yellow smoke poured out of the fresh wound in the mountain, its acrid scent stinging his nostrils. It filled his throat, choking him, strangling him.

"Josarian . . ." he rasped.

He coughed, his chest burning. The pain and lack of air drove him to his knees. He struggled against Dar, but She was stronger. He had finally found a greater opponent.

He gasped for air, unable to move, unable to breathe, eyes watering until he couldn't see. And he knew his destiny had caught up with him at last. He would fail.

He suddenly thought of *her*. He'd never see her again. The intensity of his sorrow shocked him, sweeping through him without warning.

"Mira . . ."

Mirabar, the demon girl, plunging through the waters of Kandahar in a ball of fire to face Kiloran himself . . .

He heard the rumble of the volcano overhead. Dar was gloating as She destroyed him.

"No . . ."

The bitter gall of his defeat burned his chest, sucked away his strength. *He would fail.* Dar would have Her revenge on him at last. Josarian would die. The rebellion would crumble. Dar had wanted him to die knowing this.

He tried to push himself to his feet. The ground crumbled away beneath his hand. A chunk of molten rock set his sleeve on fire and scorched his arm. Head spinning wildly, he fell backwards as he tried to get away from the clinging pain. Far above him, at the summit of the mountain, Dar rumbled victoriously, having vanquished Her foe.

*   *   *

EVERY SENSATION FADED into insignificance under the onslaught of Dar's summons. Josarian could feel the hot, smooth rock baking the soles of his feet. He could hear the ecstatic wailing of the *zanareen*. His body quivered from the exquisite heat rising from the lava lake directly below him. His naked flesh shivered against the scintillating chill sweeping across the mountaintop.

Yet all these sensations were as nothing compared to the soul-shaking power of Her ardent call. The *zanareen* had kept him isolated for days, alternately sweating beside a small lava pool then immersing himself in an icy stream. He had fasted according to their traditions, consuming nothing except the mind-spinning tisanes Jalan brought him. Hunger, cold, heat, pain . . . They meant nothing to him anymore. For days, he had felt nothing except this intense longing for Her, yet they had kept him from Her.

Day and night, he heard nothing but Her beckoning. Never asleep or fully awake, he felt nothing but the insistent pull of Her yearning. There was no hunger in him except his consuming need for Her. He could almost smell Her on his skin, almost taste Her on his tongue. Fire and brimstone, lava and heat, earth and sky . . .

Man and goddess, joining as one.

They had waited until now to let him go to Her, waited until they were sure he thought of nothing else, remembered nothing else, knew no need, desire, or ambition other than embracing Dar. As long as he remembered or cherished any portion or particle of his life, She would not have him, for She was a jealous goddess. Only now, when he knew nothing but this craving, remembered nothing of his life before coming to Her, only now was he worthy. Only now would She accept him.

He raised his arms overhead, surrendering to Her. She rumbled and roared in triumph, reaching out to him, welcoming him. Her heat rose from the lava lake to wrap around him, caressing him, coaxing him forward. Head reeling, heart pounding, he gave himself up and went to

Her. He arched his back luxuriantly, then soared forward into space, tumbling into Her embrace. He heard a distant screeching, but it was so faint, lost in the fiery thunder of Dar's welcome.

34

A SCREAM — A terrible *screech*—pierced Tansen's senses. His eyes rolled wildly for a moment, sending the world spinning as he jerked into awareness.

Pain. He clenched his teeth and squeezed his eyes shut against it. Then, taking short, heavy breaths—desperately gulping at the thin air—he glanced down at his right arm. A few charred wisps were all that was left of his sleeve. The flesh was reddened and sore but, fortunately, only the crease of his elbow was burned badly enough to have started blistering. There was blood in his eyes again; the cut on his forehead was bleeding copiously as a result of his passing out so that he lay with his head downhill.

He sat up and started coughing, his abused lungs trying to expel the deadly fumes he had inhaled.

Slowly gathering strength, he rose to his feet. He looked around, dazed, bewildered. At first, he could find no sign of the cataclysm which had nearly killed him. Shivering with cold beneath his cloak, he scrambled back up the hillside until he found the crack in the earth. It had been as wide as the Idalar River when he passed out; now it was no wider than his hand, and it was slowly oozing together, closing completely as he watched. After a few moments, only a glowing, gooey trace of red was left to mark the fissure, like the clotting blood of a minor cut.

"Dar," he whispered.

Why didn't You kill me?

The answer was obvious. She wanted him alive. She had a purpose for him. Whatever it was, She would make it known to him in Her own time. Meanwhile . . . he had a feeling he knew whose scream had awoken him, as well as what had made her scream.

Josarian has jumped.

He slowly started hauling his body up the side of the mountain, shivering with cold, feeling light-headed and thirsty. His sense of urgency was gone.

Josarian has jumped.

His lungs were heaving hard by the time he reached the crowd of spectators. Hundreds of *shallaheen* huddled together against the cold, carrying hearty provisions of food and water. They saw his swords. They saw the brand on his chest, which was exposed by the tattered rags of his tunic. They murmured his name, knowing his legend. They told him what he already knew.

Josarian has jumped. My brother is dead.

The rebellion . . . He couldn't even think about that now. *My brother is dead.*

They offered him food, water, and wine. He accepted only the water, then asked for Mirabar.

"Where is she?" His lungs ached so, he could hardly force the words out. "Where's Mirabar?"

They directed him past hundreds of resolutely chanting *zanareen,* glassy-eyed fanatics who ignored him, never taking their gazes off the Fires of Dar.

He spotted her at last. She stood at the rim of the volcano, poised as if she, too, intended to jump.

Over my dead body.

His feet felt as if someone had weighted them down. Every step took concentration. The freezing air burned his lungs. He was shaking hard with cold by the time he reached Mirabar's side.

"Mira . . ." He sounded as if someone had just tried to strangle him.

She turned slowly. Her eyes were glassy, too. Unfocused. Dazed. There was dark circles under them. Her cheeks were hollow, her neck was shadowed. Her skin was almost as pale as the snow, but two spots of hot, red color stained her cheeks. She was breathing as if she'd just plunged through the waters of Kandahar again, and shivering as hard as he was.

She didn't look surprised to see him, nor did she seem to notice his bloodied, ragged condition. She looked as if she barely recognized him, had to struggle to recall his name.

"Tan . . ." she whispered at last. "He jumped."

My brother is dead.

The next words out of his mouth were not the ones he'd intended to say. They shocked him, but she seemed to expect them: "Why didn't you stop him?"

She didn't answer. Didn't look away. Just returned his gaze, breathing hard.

He snapped. He seized her shoulders and shook her. A *woman.* A tiny little thing. He shook her with every ounce of strength he had left and snarled, "How could you have let him *do* it?"

Her head tilted back. She squeezed her eyes shut and gritted her teeth. A sound, a *terrible* sound, started deep in her chest, rose up through her throat, and burst from her mouth in a horrible, grief-stricken howl. Fine-boned hands came up to clutch her demon-red hair.

"Nooooo!" she screamed.

She yanked away from him. Afraid she would stumble into the volcano, he reached for her. She tore herself violently out of his grasp, then fell to her knees, howling, keening with misery.

It would have been a lot easier if she had just hit him. The sound of her grief, unleashed by his own cruelty, was like the cut of a *shir.* He sank to his knees beside her and tried to put his arms around her.

"Mira . . ."

"Nooo . . ."

"I'm sorry."

"The visions . . . the dreams . . ." she gasped, sobbing

and gulping air. "The Calling . . . *Calidar* . . ."

"Shhh . . . I'm sorry. I didn't mean—"

"Calidar told him . . . She sent him here. He would not listen . . . *I thought it was the will of the Otherworld!*"

"Shhh."

Her whole body convulsed, then she heaved violently, again and again. Dry choking sounds wracked her throat. Nothing came up, though, not even spittle.

Through the fog of his pain, exhaustion, and grief, he finally realized that in addition to being upset, she was very, *very* sick. Her skin was burning up, and those violent shivers were from fever as much as from the cold. He'd seen this once before. Some bodies, no matter how strong, couldn't adjust to being this high up. She would die if she stayed here much longer.

"We have to leave," he said.

"*Nooooo* . . ." She started weeping again.

He didn't try to soothe her this time. He knew she'd be irrational until he could get some water into her body and find a warm place for her to lie down. It needed to be farther down the mountain, though, because her main problem was the lack of air. She wouldn't improve until she could breathe again.

His exhausted, aching muscles screamed in protest as he stood up and lifted her into his arms. His burned arm felt like the flesh was being torn from it. Mirabar was petite and she'd lost weight up here, but she was still a solid *shallah* girl—woman—and his own weakness would make this downhill trip a gruesome expedition. They wouldn't go far. Just until they got below the snow line. He knew he could go no farther than that today.

She struggled weakly in his arms, hurting him. His trembling legs betrayed him and he stumbled. They fell to the ground together.

A fierce roar, the birthing screams of a goddess, suddenly filled the air. Mirabar lifted her head, trying to peer into the caldera. Pain forgotten in the terror of the moment, Tansen tangled his fingers in her red curls and dragged her head beneath his shoulder as the sky howled and the earth trembled. He flung his leg out and rolled on top of her, shielding her—though he didn't know from what direction the threat came.

Heaven and earth seemed to collide. The sky all around them turned orange. The clouds themselves seemed to catch fire. The ground heaved like the waves of the ocean.

"Dar!" Mirabar cried. Senses drowning in the roar of the goddess, Tansen could barely hear Mirabar's voice, so close to his ear, as she shouted, "It's *Her!* Let me go! It's Dar!"

He wouldn't let go of her, though. Dar already had Josarian. He wouldn't let Her have Mirabar, too. She'd have to take *him* first, and She had already proved that She didn't want him yet.

Lava shot straight up from the volcano, spinning high into the air, then falling back into the caldera. Tansen lifted his head and stared in wonder. He had seen Dar's explosions before, during his boyhood, but he had never seen anything like *this*. This was no series of violent eruptions spewing destruction over the mountain and across the land. Lava gushed sky-high as smoothly, regularly, and gracefully as the water in Shaljir's finest fountains. At its peak, the thick, red-hot flow blossomed into a thousand slender, glowing strands which fell gracefully back to their source. A billion tiny drops of molten lava flew in all directions, but they threatened no one, not even those cowering nearby.

"The hair and tears of Dar," Mirabar murmured, her eyes glowing yellow with religious fervor as she stared.

"Is *that* . . ." He couldn't speak for a moment. "Is that Dar?"

"I don't . . . know . . ."

A ball of fire erupted from the top of the lava fountain. It flew straight at Tansen and Mirabar. If it *was* Dar, then She had evidently just changed her mind; She wanted her revenge *now*. He folded Mirabar back beneath him, practically smothering her, and flung an arm over his head, suddenly less ready to die than he had supposed.

The ball of flame landed so close to them it nearly set Mira's cloak on fire. Tansen rolled away from it, clutching the woman protectively, ready to defend her from the goddess she was struggling to see as he pressed her face into his shoulder.

"It's *him*," she cried. "Don't you see? It's—"

Someone started screaming wildly, jumping up and down and pointing into the flames. Heart quickening with hope, Tan rose to his knees and stared into the heat of the fire.

"Josarian?"

A shape slowly solidified in the leaping flames. It *might* be a man's body, crouched down on one knee, poised as if about to rise. It wasn't Josarian, though. It glowed as if made of the hottest coals.

"It's *him,*" Mirabar breathed, gasping for air, tugging on Tansen as she tried to rise to her feet.

The flames started sizzling and smoking, slowly fading the way ordinary fire did when there was no wood left to fuel it. As the fire died, the glowing shape within it became more distinct. Tansen's heart nearly stopped when the thing *moved,* but he didn't back away. Mirabar said that creature was Josarian, and Tan would not flee from his brother, no matter *what* he had become. Moving as slowly and painfully as a very old man, the shape in the fire pushed itself off the ground and rose to its full height. It stood there glowing, radiating heat and power, as the flames all around it withered and died.

Then the figure, too, started changing. The fiery glow, so similar to Mira's eyes, was fading, *cooling,* then sliding away to reveal the body of an ordinary man. Moment by moment, familiar parts of him appeared beneath the glowing skin which had covered him: the gleaming dark hair; the sun-browned flesh; the two scars left by Valdani swords; the marks on his palms.

He was breathing hard, and his naked body was drenched in sweat. His eyes were closed, his expression unapproachable. He seemed to be focused on some inner vision. Tansen stepped forward, but Mirabar clutched his hand, stopping him. The tightness of her grip warned him not to speak or disturb Josarian.

The *zanareen* went wild, screaming, cheering, flinging themselves against each other. The *shallaheen* were shouting Josarian's name, crying out their triumph at the coming of the Firebringer.

The Firebringer.

It was true. It was Josarian. He had done it!

The volcano's furious activity subsided, until nothing was left of the fire and fury which had consumed both earth and sky only moments ago. Dar's voice was once again only an unsteady murmur in the caldera. Everything at Darshon again looked as it had always looked.

Except that the Firebringer is among us now.

"He is come!" Jalan cried, leading a swarm of wild-eyed men toward Josarian.

"Don't let them disturb him," Mirabar said quickly, her voice meant for Tansen's ears alone.

Obeying her, for these events were far more of her realm than his, Tansen unsheathed both his swords and jumped between Jalan's people and Josarian.

"He is the Awaited One!" Jalan screamed. "We are his servants! You cannot keep us from him!"

"I know. Just give him a few moments," Tansen advised, secretly fearing that Josarian might need a whole lot longer than *that*.

"Tan . . ."

Tansen whirled instantly, recognizing the voice. Only minutes ago, he had believed he would never hear it again. "I'm here."

Josarian's eyes opened at last. Tansen had feared what he would see there, but this was the same familiar gaze he knew, the same ingenuous brown eyes he had looked into more than a thousand times. Josarian's expression was exhausted and dazed, but . . . this was unquestionably still the face of his brother. Relief coursed through Tansen.

"How . . . do you feel?" Tan asked at last.

The wind whipped across Darshon. Josarian shivered, frowned, and said blankly, "I'm *cold.*"

Mirabar struggled to her feet. "Here. Take this." She tried to take off one of her cloaks, a voluminous one which Tansen suddenly recognized as Josarian's; but her arms were as weak as a baby's.

Tansen sheathed his swords, went to her, removed one of the cloaks, and forced her back down to the ground before she *fell* down. The *zanareen* and *shallaheen* watched the three of them, whispering, murmuring, but wary of interfering.

"I guess the scriptures are a little vague about what happens next," Tansen surmised. His burned arm was smarting again, howling against all the recent abuse it had endured.

Josarian blinked and looked at him more alertly now, focusing his gaze. "Tansen." A slow, tired grin stole across his features. Astonishingly, he started to laugh. "Tan!"

Josarian stumbled forward and flung his arms around him, giving him the sort of openly affectionate bear hug that Tan usually found embarrassing in front of the men. Now he blinked back tears and returned the fierce embrace.

Thank You, Dar. Thank You. Thank You for giving him back.

After a long moment, Josarian pushed him away to seize his shoulders in a hard grip. Tansen winced against the pain, but Josarian didn't notice.

"Tan! You'll never believe it!" He shook his head, his expression vivid with amazement. "It wasn't Armian! *I'm* the Firebringer!"

NAJDAN WAS WAITING for them when they finally entered the Sanctuary at the base of Darshon. He had some idea of what had happened up there, since witnesses to the miracle had descended the mountain to start spreading the word even before Josarian was recovered from his ordeal.

The Firebringer.

It made Najdan's chest tight with wonder. He had never

believed in the Firebringer, and he had certainly never imagined that he would know and serve him.

His next thought was that Kiloran would not be pleased. No man in Sileria was more feared than Kiloran; but now one would exceed him in fame and glory, and in the awe he inspired. The Firebringer would command even greater power and respect than the mightiest waterlord in the world, and Kiloran would *hate* that.

Najdan had stayed here, obeying Mirabar's instructions, awaiting her return. The day after word of Josarian's triumph came down the mountain, a runner had arrived with news from Tansen, who was up there, too, now: the *sirana* was very sick and would need care and attention when she arrived that evening. Najdan would have ignored her previous orders and climbed to the very peak of Darshon to retrieve her, except that he didn't want to upset her if she was already unwell. She believed it would be a sacrilege to bring him with her to the volcano wherein dwelled the goddess she worshipped. Respecting this without resentment, for the Honored Society did not concern itself with Dar, Najdan remained where he was, supervising preparations for the *sirana*'s arrival and impatiently watching the mountain path for her.

When Josarian, Mirabar, and Tansen finally arrived, they were accompanied by a veritable herd of *zanareen*. Loyal and obedient to the point of idiocy, Josarian's followers camped outside the Sanctuary as he ordered. They had brought Mirabar down the mountain on a pallet. Josarian lifted her limp body and carried her inside the Sanctuary, accompanied only by Tansen.

Najdan could see at once that everything had changed. Josarian, who had always been strong, now looked invincible, positively radiating power, energy, and confidence. It was Tansen, however, who looked as if he had recently faced death and barely survived. His entire right arm was swathed in dirty makeshift bandages. His humble clothes hung in tatters on his lean frame, torn, singed, and smeared with blood. An angry gash stood out boldly on his forehead. Josarian had made haste to Darshon, knowing that if Tansen survived his adventure in Shaljir, then he would try to stop his bloodbrother from embracing Dar in the volcano. Looking at the *shatai* now, Najdan could see that he had indeed tried. He had challenged the goddess, fighting Her honorably. He had failed, and Josarian had stunned them all with his divine triumph. But Tansen had survived his own ordeal, and a man who had lived through a battle with a goddess would never again be the same.

Unconscious in Josarian's arms, Mirabar seemed the most changed of all. She looked pale, weak, and half-dead. Forgetting the respect that a man owed to the Firebringer, Najdan snatched the *sirana* out of Josarian's arms and snapped, "What's happened to her? What did you let those madmen up there *do* to her?"

"It was the altitude," Tansen said wearily, ignoring Najdan's accusatory tone. "The lack of air. Some people can't adjust to it."

"But she's a *shallah!*"

Tansen shook his head. "It doesn't matter."

"How could you let this happen to her?" Najdan snarled. "How could you let her get like this?"

"I wasn't there." Tansen eased himself onto one of the wooden benches in the Sanctuary, nodding to the Sisters now hovering around them. "Let the Sisters take her, Najdan. She'll be all right now that she's here. She just needs rest, warmth, and plenty of broth."

Najdan glared briefly at Josarian, then swung around and carried Mirabar off to a chamber where the Sisters could give her whatever she needed.

LATER THAT EVENING, wearing fresh bandages and someone else's clothes, Tansen enjoyed a quiet meal with Josarian. He kept reminding himself that Josarian was the Firebringer now. But every time he looked up, he just saw. . . . Josarian. Changed, yes, undeniably changed somehow; but still the brother he had grown to love.

"You might as well ask," Josarian said at last. "I know you're dying to ask."

He smiled wryly. "All right. *How?*"

"It was like my dreams."

"Pain and ecstasy?"

"Pain that should have killed me, driven me mad, melted my flesh and pulverized my bones. Pain worse than I imagine death by torture to be."

"And ecstasy . . ."

Josarian nodded. "I have no words for it." He smiled. "My father taught me no words for what a *goddess* can do to a man, only a woman."

"But you and She . . . Dar, I mean . . ." He wasn't quite sure how to phrase it.

"Yes." Josarian looked out the window into the black night, his expression distorted by a sudden, intense longing. *"Yes."*

It was a look which spoke of Otherworldly things, the kind of look Mirabar sometimes wore. It made Tansen uneasy. "And then?" he prodded after a long silence.

With obvious effort, Josarian pulled himself back to the present moment, back to Tansen's question. "I didn't want to come back. I tried to stay. But, uh . . ."

"She sent you back to us."

"Yes, to finish the war. To get rid of the Valdani."

"And then?"

"And then . . ." He shrugged. "Perhaps I will go back to Her."

"What about Calidar?"

"Or perhaps I will go to *her.*" He met Tan's gaze. "I may not mourn her any longer, though. Not in this life. That was part of the price. I may not love another . . . woman."

Tansen felt a stab of sharp surprise. "So you think . . . So Jalan was right," he whispered.

He saw the grief and confusion in Josarian's expression before it was slowly washed away by resolution and obedience to Dar's will. She truly was a ruthless goddess.

"Yes," Josarian said at last. He shrugged and lightened his tone. "Mirabar says that in the Otherworld, I can be with them *both.*"

Tansen hated his brother's pain and so tried to help him lighten the mood. "Ah, like some Kintish potentate whose palace is full of his jealous wives."

Josarian smiled. "Somehow, I don't think that's quite what Mira meant."

"Why, by all the gods above and below, did you let her go up there with you?"

"How was I supposed to stop her?" Josarian scowled. "Have you ever tried to talk her out of doing something she was determined to do?"

Tansen laughed. "I withdraw the question."

"I didn't know she was growing ill." Josarian's eyes were soft with regret. "The moment we arrived, they separated us. I was stripped, isolated, put through rituals and ceremonies I would be too embarrassed to describe even to you, and fed nothing but potions which made my head spin. After the first day, I don't think I even remembered she existed."

"Then your memory is kinder than mine. I felt the sting of her tongue long after I left for Shaljir. Even in the tunnels beneath the prison, my ears felt hot."

Josarian grinned. "Ah, and you didn't even hear what she said after you left her at Idalar."

"I'm glad I didn't."

"I think even Kiloran was shocked."

They laughed.

Then Josarian said, "The *torena* should be safe on Mount Niran by now."

"As long as they didn't encounter any Outlookers on the way." Now that he could spare the energy to worry about Elelar, the thought troubled him. "We were pretty high up when I left her."

"And Zimran would do everything in his power to protect her the rest of the way."

"I know." He tried to keep the sour note out of his voice.

Apparently he failed, for Josarian said, "I'm flattered you left the *torena* alone with my cousin to come after me."

"The lady can fend him off without my help."

"Are you certain she'll try?" Josarian asked gently.

He wasn't, and it bothered him. "Who can be certain *what* a woman will do?"

"True enough," Josarian agreed. "I've been lucky. I've never cared for a woman who . . . whose affections were uncertain. It would be a hard thing for a man to bear."

Tansen quickly changed the subject. Josarian respected his feelings and followed his lead, discussing new plans for the war, now that they were certain the sea-born folk and the lowlanders would join them. With the age of the Firebringer now at hand, even the *toreni* and city-dwellers were bound to come round before long. Mirabar's visions, Armian's words, the ancient prophecies of the *zanareen* . . .

"It will really happen," Josarian said, his face filled with wonder. "We will make it happen."

"And we will see a new Yahrdan take his rightful place in Shaljir."

Josarian's eyes glowed. "For the first time in a thousand years."

"I never thought I would live to see that."

"Neither did I."

"Perhaps it will be you," Tansen pointed out.

"Me?"

"Who better?"

Josarian shook his head. "Not me."

"Why not? You're the Firebringer, after all."

Josarian made a vague gesture. "I'm supposed to make the Valdani leave. What happens after that . . ." He shrugged. "There's no prophecy about that. Once the Valdani leave Sileria forever, my destiny is as uncertain as everyone else's."

And, Tansen realized with surprise, Josarian didn't care. His epiphany had not changed that. Josarian dreamed only of freeing Sileria from the *roshaheen,* nothing else. The events at Darshon had given him the means by which to do it, and he had willingly paid the price. Now he returned to the war, more focused and committed than ever.

Najdan joined them as they were discussing strategy and debating tactics. He advised them that the *sirana* was much improved. She had kept down a bowl of broth and was now sleeping peacefully, free of fever and nausea. Relieved to hear it, Josarian then drew Najdan into the conversation.

The long rains would soon be upon them, the traditional season for the Society's most frequent and most profitable abductions.

"But not this year," Josarian warned Najdan. "We will abduct only Valdani. No Silerians, whether wealthy merchants or *toreni.* The rebellion needs them, and they won't join us if the Society is busy abducting them."

Tansen saw Najdan shift uneasily, his loyalties divided. Though Najdan lacked imagination, he was no fool. He knew that Josarian was right, but the habits of twenty years were hard to break.

Najdan finally said, "The Society needs money—"

"They got plenty out of Alizar," Josarian argued.

"Ah, but the war is expensive, *siran.*"

"Everyone is making sacrifices," Josarian said rather pointedly. "The Society can, too. Tell Kiloran—and tell him to tell the other waterlords: There are to be no abductions except those which I authorize."

"Kiloran won't like it," Tansen warned.

"The waterlords won't like it," Najdan added.

Josarian stood up. "I'm the Firebringer. From now on, Kiloran and the waterlords will do what *I* tell them to do."

"But, *siran—*"

"Things have changed. The Society will just have to get accustomed to it." Josarian's expression ruled out further protest from the assassin. "Driving out the Valdani is all that matters now."

Tansen watched him leave. He wasn't sure he agreed

with Josarian's decision, but his expression warned Najdan not to try to win him over to a more moderate position. His loyalty to Josarian was as unassailable as Najdan's was to Kiloran—or to Mirabar, these days. Najdan was right, however: The waterlords wouldn't like this. Fortunately, though, the rest of Sileria would be behind Josarian. Tansen didn't think the waterlords could afford to defy Josarian's orders if everyone realized that the Society was all that stood in the way of a unified and free Sileria.

"We're leaving first thing the morning," Tan told Najdan.

"I'll stay here until the *sirana* is well enough to travel."

"I know." He could leave her here with Najdan. No one would protect her more ferociously. "Then you must find Kiloran. She'll help you convince him." Kiloran didn't like Mirabar, but he did listen to her—albeit reluctantly.

"Yes." Najdan poured himself a cup of wine, then announced, "Cheylan is with him."

"Oh?"

Najdan nodded. "Since Idalar. Josarian sent him with Kiloran in the *sirana*'s place after deciding to come to Darshon."

Tansen waited. It was obvious Najdan wanted to say more.

The comment, slow in coming, couldn't have surprised him more. "I found him . . . courting the *sirana* at Idalar."

"Cheylan?"

Najdan nodded. Then, as if relieved to finally have someone to share this with, he said in a rush, "Embracing her. Alone in the dark. Very . . . passionately."

Tansen felt as if someone had just slapped him. He didn't know why. Mirabar and Cheylan . . . It shouldn't be that surprising. Each of them had worn out Tansen's voice by insisting he answer questions about the other, after all. Mirabar and Cheylan were alike in ways that ordinary people could scarcely imagine. They had undoubtedly shared similar hardships, despite the vast differences in their birthrights. In fact, it was hard to picture a man and woman more likely to seek passion and comfort in each other's arms. Tansen himself had once supposed that Cheylan might well be the man for the demon girl.

Yet the thought of Mirabar locked in a "very passionate" embrace with Cheylan now made Tansen feel physically sick. It made him want to burst into her bedchamber right now and demand what in the Fires she thought she was doing that night at Idalar. It made him want to change Josarian's orders and send her anywhere in Sileria except back to Kiloran and back into Cheylan's arms.

Finding his voice at last, he asked, "And the *sirana*. Did she seem to . . ."

"She returned the embrace." Najdan's face darkened with embarrassment. "I know that you were in the east with him. Perhaps you know what kind of man he is. Perhaps you can tell me if he is . . . worthy of the *sirana*."

If I say 'no,' you're going to slip your shir *between his ribs the next time he touches her, aren't you?*

"I, uh . . ." He knew he'd better tread carefully. He wasn't entirely in control of his own thoughts, and assassins weren't known for mastering their violent impulses. "You, uh, feel that Cheylan will . . . persist?"

"I do."

"And that Mi— the *sirana* will receive his attentions favorably?" *Darfire, I sound like my mother.*

"Yes."

"Well . . ." He was aware of an overriding desire to encourage Najdan to drown Cheylan in Lake Kandahar the first chance he got. He faltered, wondering what to say next.

"To be honest, Tansen . . ." Najdan fingered his *shir*. "I do not like him."

Aware that Mirabar wouldn't thank him for this, Tansen sighed and admitted, "To tell you the truth, Najdan, neither do I."

MIRABAR HAD FULLY recovered from her ordeal atop Mount Darshon by the time she arrived at Kandahar, accompanied by Najdan. She had no doubt that Kiloran already knew what had occurred at Darshon, since he knew everything that happened in Sileria. Her duty now, explained to her by Josarian before they had parted company, was to convince Kiloran to obey the Firebringer's orders.

From the rim of the volcano to the depths of Kiloran's underwater palace ... Such a life was enough to make even a Guardian feel a little fainthearted. She almost wished the Beckoner had chosen someone else to bring the will of the Otherworld to the people of Sileria.

Unfortunately, she was starting to fear that he *had* chosen someone else, or had at least decided to abandon her. He had not come to her since long before Darshon, and she was increasingly worried that he might never come again. Was the Beckoner's work done? Had she failed him? Had he chosen another Guardian? Why was he silent? Such questions plagued her night and day now.

When she and Najdan reached Lake Kandahar, they found Cheylan awaiting them along its shores, beneath a sky filled with storm clouds; the long rains were finally coming. Mirabar had known Cheylan was here and had looked forward to seeing him again. Perhaps she could even discuss these fears about the Beckoner with him; surely he would understand in a way that ordinary people could not. So she was disappointed to learn he was leaving Kandahar.

"I was only delaying my departure until I could greet you," he said, taking her hands in his.

Mirabar ignored the way Najdan glowered at them both. "Where are you going?"

"A runner came from Josarian two days ago, ordering me to go east again."

"Oh." She looked away, feeling awkward and unsure of herself.

"I'm sorry," he added. "I had hoped we could talk more."

"Me, too."

"*Sirana*, perhaps we should go pay our respects to my master now." Najdan's tone could have frozen water.

"You go ahead," she replied. "I'll join you in a moment."

The assassin shifted position indecisively, clearly reluctant to leave her alone with Cheylan. She was about to speak sharply to him when Cheylan intervened by saying, "I believe Searlon is taking his leave of your master even as we speak. Perhaps you would like to join them?"

"Yes," Najdan agreed.

"I doubt they'd want a Guardian to intrude," Cheylan said innocently. "I'll keep the *sirana* company here until Searlon leaves and Kiloran is ready to receive her. Agreed?"

Najdan scowled but evidently decided not to make a scene. As he curtly excused himself from their presence, a crystal-hard path started magically forming in the water, leading out to the center of the lake. Najdan followed it, then disappeared into the water's depths, going to join his own kind in Kiloran's lair.

Mirabar's chest felt tight as she turned back to Cheylan. "I wish you could stay, at least for a little while."

"So do I." He brushed a strand of hair off her cheek. "But I have been ordered to return to Verlon's side. Immediately."

"But didn't he . . . I've heard that he once swore a bloodvow against you."

"Yes, that's true."

"Then why does Josarian keep sending you to him?"

He shrugged. "Because I am useful there. I know Verlon better than anyone except his most trusted assassins."

She frowned. "But how? You're a Guardian, and he's a waterlord."

Cheylan hesitated for a moment, as if trying to decide whether or not to respond. Then he admitted in a quiet voice: "Verlon is my grandfather."

35

THE LONG RAINS brought water to a perpetually thirsty land, softening the fields for spring planting, conditioning the gossamer leaves for another harvest, and filling Sileria's rivers, lakes, streams, and wells. The rainy season was the traditional time for most abductions, since it was when the Society most needed income. The waterlords' power was at its lowest ebb during the brief season when water was so plentiful in Sileria that no one need pay them tribute or do their bidding.

If Kiloran planned to deprive Shaljir of water, Koroll knew, he would now have to wait until after the long rains had stopped. Nothing could turn back the Idalar River, not even Kiloran's power, when it was close to overflowing its own banks and rushing into Shaljir like a bridegroom coming to his bride's bed.

This was, however, the only consolation that the season offered Koroll. Otherwise, the war in Sileria had become such a disaster that even he no longer believed he could save himself with clever tactics and shrewd strategy.

Just before the harvest began, the sea-born folk and the lowlanders had joined the rebellion. The Valdani hadn't realized this for a while, of course, since the rebels didn't send them an announcement. Koroll found out about it when the port of Cavasar was sacked by sea-born folk and an arriving Valdani warship was destroyed. Commander Cyrill, young, inexperienced, and already distressed by the disgrace and death of Borell, his uncle, had yet to get the city back under control after all this time.

Now it was nearly spring, nearly the New Year. Almost one year exactly since Josarian had killed two Outlookers and commenced the most unexpected rebellion in history. No one had ever believed this could happen in Sileria. *Sileria,* a land which hadn't been free since the ancient days when Valda, now the greatest city in the three corners of the world, had been an obscure village located in a forgotten province between two great empires!

Now Valdania, the greatest empire which had ever existed, was on the verge of losing one of its humblest possessions! One which previous empires had lost only to *greater* conquerors, not to a bunch of native peasants. It was a humiliation which would destroy Koroll's life and make his name reviled for centuries after his death.

Josarian had struck out from Dalishar, conquering the surrounding region, expanding his territory day by day throughout the long rains. At the moment, Koroll estimated that fully one-third of Sileria was now under Josarian's control. Probably more, since the rebellion's influence had spread into many isolated corners of Sileria which Koroll simply did not have enough men to patrol and maintain.

Unlike Koroll, Josarian wasn't having trouble feeding his men, either. The lowlanders had already seized over one hundred of the richest Valdani estates in Sileria, attacking with such shocking brutality that many landowners were now voluntarily abandoning their land *before* it was attacked, even if this meant returning to Valda as paupers. Some of these cowards were important enough to get an audience with the Emperor upon returning home, meaning the Imperial Council was regularly sending dispatches to Koroll demanding to know why the Outlookers in Sileria were no longer able to protect some of the Empire's weathiest (or formerly wealthiest) citizens.

The rebels left Silerian landowners alone—if they declared their loyalty to the rebellion and formally severed all connection with the Valdani government in Sileria. More *toren* families were doing this than anyone would ever have expected, and not always out of fear for their lives, either. There was a rumor running through Sileria which dwarfed every other wildly improbable story Koroll had ever heard from these people. Now they were actually saying that Josarian had flung himself into the fiery heart of Mount Darshon's volcano and survived, proving that he was the Firebringer, the long-prophesied warrior who would drive out Sileria's conquerors and free his people forever from foreign domination.

The legend was an old one. Koroll didn't know much about it, since even most Silerians had never seemed to give it much credit. He had seen mad, wild-eyed *zanareen* proselytizing and seeking new converts, but what society didn't have its strange cults and crazy fanatics, after all? It had never occurred to him that Josarian would find a way to make use of the legend, or that so many Silerians— including those who should know better!—secretly half-believed the ancient prophecy and would succumb to the lies of the first charlatan who claimed to have fulfilled it.

Yet even in the heart of Shaljir, the most sophisticated city in Sileria, people seemed to believe the wild tales spread by the *zanareen*. In fact, Koroll had decided to issue a decree forbidding the *zanareen* to enter the city anymore. Meanwhile, while the mountains, the coasts, and the low-lands were now all under seige, slipping through the Empire's grasp, even the cities, which had always been the heart of Valdani power here, were no longer secure.

Liron's overland supply routes were now under rebel control. Between attacks by Kintish pirates and Silerian sea-born folk, no Valdani supply ship had managed to reach Liron's port since before the rains began. Without more support from the mainland—and soon—Liron would fall. The rebels were already starving the city; when the time was right, they would probably storm it and slaughter every Valdan they found within its walls.

Riots had begun in Adalian soon after Josarian had sent fifty Outlooker corpses to the gate of the city, and things had grown worse there in the succeeding months. The last three ships to leave Adalian had never reached Valda. It was believed they were destroyed by Moorlanders who had been alerted by the Silerians.

The Outlookers' thorough search of *Torena* Elelar's house had exposed evidence of a complex network of secret rebels, informants, and Silerian loyalists working against the Valdani. Months of investigation had revealed only a little more about this network, which apparently called itself the Alliance. Based in Shaljir, its tentacles spread across the island, organizing Sileria's disparate peoples into an effective force under Josarian's leadership. Since Elelar had apparently been an important member of this secret society, the Imperial Councilors were now very interested in it. They reasoned that if one aristocrat had been involved, then there must be others; and aristocrats, whatever their nationality, could reason with each other. Peasants, bandits, foreign wizards, and outlawed religious cults could not be expected to speak, think, or act sensibly. But an organized network of intelligent, literate aristocrats connected to Josarian? Yes, this interested the Council enormously in view of the growing disaster in Sileria. Koroll had been instructed to find out how the Council could contact the Alliance to negotiate an end to hostilities.

Negotiate an end to hostilities . . .

Koroll thought the phrase had an ominous ring to it. There could be no negotiation with *Silerians,* as he had tried to explain to the Emperor and his blasted Council in several recent dispatches. They were a violent, untrustworthy, superstitious people. Their history was nothing but a long list of betrayals, meaning they would certainly betray any accord reached with the Valdani. *Torena* Elelar had been the wife of one Valdan and the mistress of another, and yet look at what she had done to Valdania! She personified the treachery of her despicable race!

Josarian and his followers had made it very clear ever since Commander Daroll's death that they had no interest in compromise, no wish to discuss living peacefully under Valdani rule again. They weren't interested in more lenient laws or paying less tribute to the Emperor. They wanted the Valdani out of Sileria, and they would not settle for anything less. This was not the time to negotiate. This was a time for all-out war against a conquered race now rising up against their masters. This was the moment when the Empire must demonstrate before the entire civilized world what a terrible fate befell anyone who challenged Valdani supremacy!

The Imperial Council, alas, was interested in more glamorous conquests. The Councilors were convinced they could conquer the free Moorlands at last, if they could only free up more men, money, and weapons to do it. A major Valdani victory against the Moorlanders had recently strengthened their resolve and rallied a flagging populace to this cause once again. And Emperor Jarell . . . he saw the Throne of Heaven even in his *sleep,* Koroll suspected, so badly did he want it before he died. The northernmost city of the Kintish Kingdoms had just fallen, and this victory spurred the Emperor on, convincing him that his goal was within reach.

In view of such glory, the Emperor and his Council were unwilling to make the necessary sacrifices to retain one impoverished province conquered long ago, especially now that the mines of Alizar yielded them no profits. Koroll sent dispatches reminding them how important Sileria was to control of the Middle Sea, as they had once reminded him not so long ago. He sent dispatches reminding them that he *was* still trying to do something about the mines of Alizar; the only response was a scathing request that he estimate just how much more time he expected to spend trying to break the power of some Silerian water wizard who was costing the Emperor a fortune every single day. Every dispatch Koroll sent was accompanied by a request for more men, money, weapons, and supplies. He received less than he requested on every occasion, and only very slowly. Sometimes he merely received stern advice to stop "wasting" the men and supplies he'd *already* been given.

Indeed, the only news of interest these days was that Valda was finally sending a new Imperial Advisor to replace Borell. Koroll had never thought he'd be pleased to

see another smug aristocrat inhabiting Santorell Palace, but
he had found the dual duties imposed by Borell's death to
be a tremendous burden in Sileria's current state of war.

Depressed, discouraged, and exhausted, Koroll was preparing to quit work for the evening and retire to the pleasures of his Kintish courtesan. Her contract would be due
for renewal soon, and he fully suspected she intended to
raise her price; Kintish courtesans were even better busi-
nesswomen than they were lovers. He wouldn't be able to
afford her anymore if she did raise her price, so he intended to take full advantage of her remaining days in his
bed. He was just about to leave his command chamber
when a mud-stained Outlooker was admitted bearing an
urgent message from Liron.

The man closed the door and handed the message personally to Koroll, who absently dismissed him as he
opened the dispatch. It read:

If you want to live, stay silent.

He didn't even have time to inhale before he felt the icy
touch of a *shir* against his throat, singeing his flesh with
its frigid fire. *An assassin,* disguised as an Outlooker and
speaking excellent Valdan. He didn't bother to wonder
how the man had gotten into Shaljir or past his own
guards. This one was very good; Koroll had never even
seen the attack coming from halfway across the room.

Summoning all the courage he had ever possessed, he
asked very softly, "Considering the situation, why would
you want me to live?"

"Now that, Commander, is a very good question." The
assassin's Valdan really was excellent, Koroll noted. Then,
of course, Tansen's had been, too. "I can see we're going
to get along well."

"I wouldn't go *that* far," Koroll said dryly.

"Better and better." He sounded coolly amused. "Before
we proceed any further, Commander, let me just make one
thing quite clear. If you cry out for help at any point, even
after we're done talking and I'm on my way out of your

formidable headquarters, I promise you, I will kill you. Count on it."

"I do."

The *shir* pressed against him a little harder. "And if I don't, my master certainly will, for he sent me to you in good faith."

"He might have warned me, then," Koroll pointed out.

"So you could arrange a suitable welcome for me?"

Koroll didn't want to spend all evening in a verbal dance. "Are you going to tell me who sent you?"

"Kiloran."

Koroll drew in a swift, sharp breath and looked up into the face of the man who held a deadly, enchanted blade at his throat. He was a strong, fine-looking fellow, though his cheek was marred by a long scar. He was sleek, swift, and confident, and he smiled at the reaction Kiloran's name had provoked.

"Kiloran?" Koroll repeated hoarsely. "Why did he send you to me?" If Kiloran hadn't sent the assassin to kill him, then he couldn't imagine what the waterlord was planning.

"Ah, Commander. You and my master have a mutual problem."

"We do?" It was hard to imagine.

The assassin nodded. "His name is Josarian."

His heart was beating so heavily it hurt. Hope, withered by the disastrous defeats he had endured throughout the long rains, began to bloom again within his breast.

Kiloran means to betray Josarian.

He didn't ask why. He didn't *care* why. Silerians couldn't help themselves. It was in their nature, their blood, their history. They could never unite, not for more than a fleeting season.

I can still win.

The taste of victory was already in his mouth when he said, "Yes, evidently we do have a mutual problem. Have you perchance come to discuss how we can help each other?"

"That's *exactly* what I've been sent to discuss, Commander."

Koroll risked moving away from the *shir*. The assassin didn't try to stop him. "In that case, you won't need that. Please ..." He paused before asking, "What's your name?"

"Searlon."

"Please, Searlon." Koroll gestured courteously. "Take a seat, and let's talk like civilized men."

The assassin grinned. "Why, thank you, Commander."

KILORAN'S FURY KNEW no bounds. Though Elelar could not sense such things, Mirabar had commented that the air vibrated with the chill of his rage. Elelar had only to look at the old sorcerer's face, however, to know he was on the edge of abandoning the rebellion.

They were meeting, of all places, near Britar, at the same fortress Josarian and Tansen had liberated in their very first attack together. The *shallaheen* were using its burned-out interior to stable livestock which they grazed on the rich local pastures they had seized from Valdani landlords. The lowlanders were keeping stolen horses in many of the vacated fortresses and outposts that they took over; the mounts were more practical in the lowlands than in the heart of the mountains. Most *shallaheen* still preferred travelling by foot and letting surefooted donkeys carry their supplies. The sea-born folk burned and sank every ship they attacked, but soon Liron would fall, and the sea-born folk would be granted control of the city's port as their reward.

The *toreni,* merchants, and city-dwellers were finally flocking to the cause. Some believed the story of Josarian's triumphant leap into the volcano. Some merely feared what the rebels would do to them if they didn't join the rebellion. Others believed the end of Valdani rule was finally at hand and wanted to be part of their native land's victory over the foreign invaders. Many were influenced by friends, relatives, and associates within the Alliance who could, for the first time in their lives, be bold and forthright about their mission.

Elelar still couldn't return to Shaljir, of course, and the estate she had inherited from Gaborian was still in Valdani-occupied lands. When he judged it safe, Zimran had escorted her to the ever-growing territory controlled by the rebels, spreading out in all directions from Dalishar. Respected as a *torena* and a leader of the rebellion, Elelar, along with Faradar and several of her former servants who had reached safety, was housed at an abandoned Valdani estate near the village of Chandar. These were chaotic times, so she didn't have all the comforts to which she was normally accustomed, but she was far better off than she had expected to be. Besides, almost any place seemed luxurious after spending the rainy season in the caves of Mount Niran.

She had come here to discuss the assault on Shaljir now that the long rains were ending. It was nearly the New Year, nearly spring. It seemed incredible that the world had changed so much in only one year.

It seemed incredible that a *shallah* was now hailed as the Firebringer and leading Sileria to a new age of freedom from foreign rule.

· At the moment, actually, it just seemed incredible that Kiloran didn't call up the mythical White Dragon to consume Josarian on the spot.

Since Kiloran's power, though great, was finite, he couldn't control the mines of Alizar (which the Valdani were trying to reclaim with all manner of engineers, priests, and exotic wizards) *and* stop the Idalar River from flowing into Shaljir. Consequently, Josarian was ordering him to release the river to Baran's control so that *someone* could starve the city of water and help the rebels begin their siege upon the nation's capital.

Since the Idalar River represented the Society's single greatest source of power, and since whoever controlled it was traditionally the most prominent and powerful water-lord of the Society, Kiloran was—to say the least—reluctant to follow orders. He and Josarian had been fighting ever since his arrival, and they still seemed no closer to a solution. Josarian insisted Kiloran give up either the mines or the river, and Kiloran emphatically refused.

"We're getting nowhere," Elelar advised Tansen when he arrived from the east that afternoon, two full days after her own arrival. "At this rate, Commander Koroll will *retire* before the Silerian rebels attack Sileria's capital city."

She had seen Tansen only once since the events at Darshon. The story of Josarian's rebirth from Dar's womb seemed so wildly improbable, so typical of *shallah* legends and tales, that she wouldn't have believed it if Tan himself hadn't told her about it. She sensed that his description of that day did it no justice, that there was a great deal he kept to himself. There was a new scar on his forehead and a fading burn mark on his arm which he wouldn't discuss. The look in his eyes suggested that he, too, had met the goddess in his own way.

Indeed . . . Tansen, Josarian, and Mirabar were all somehow different after Darshon. Strangely, Josarian was the least altered of the three of them. He was more focused, more purposeful, more intent than he had been when she'd first met him. Unfortunately, he was also more unyielding, uncompromising, and uncooperative. He could get away with it because, despite the reservations that some people might have about the events at Darshon, the *shallaheen*, the lowlanders, the Guardians, the Sisters, the *zanareen*, and the sea-born folk now all believed wholeheartedly that he was the Firebringer and followed his orders without question or pause. A considerable number of *toreni*, merchants, and city-dwellers were convinced, too, and Najdan's manner suggested that even some assassins believed it. It gave Josarian a power which he now wielded ruthlessly against the waterlords. They didn't like it, but—so far—they bowed to his wishes.

All except Kiloran, that is.

Mirabar, the only person whose opinion ever seemed to carry much weight with Kiloran, had been unable to con-

vince him to follow Josarian's orders. She had to leave
Britar today to return to her circle of companions in time
to prepare for the Guardians' sacred rites welcoming in the
New Year. Elelar, who had neglected her religious observances for years, had only a sketchy idea of what this
entailed, but she gathered it was a long and exhausting
process for the Guardians, and one which they considered
extremely important. Consequently, after one last unsuccessful attempt to sway Kiloran, Mirabar stayed at Britar
only long enough to ask Tansen for news of Cheylan, who
was once again in the east, as was Josarian's brother-in-
law.

The changes in Mirabar since Darshon were readily apparent to Elelar. Mirabar had still been a girl the last time
Elelar had seen her; now she was a woman. To one who
had crossed that threshold herself, the differences were
unmistakable though hard to define. Confidence, maturity,
grace, self-assurance, a certain femininity in her gestures
. . . Whatever it was, it was there. Nor was Elelar the only
one who noticed the difference, she realized. Tansen's
gaze no longer dismissed or avoided Mirabar the way it
once had, and his voice, when he spoke to her, was both
more intimate and more courteous than it had been in former days.

However, Elelar couldn't pretend to like the sharp-
tongued, opinionated Guardian any more than she ever
had. After one particularly noisy encounter between Kiloran and Mirabar, Elelar had been sharply rebuffed by the
other woman when she suggested that persuasion usually
worked better than confrontation when a woman dealt with
a powerful man. No, Elelar was not sorry to see Mirabar
abandon Britar, accompanied by four guards and faithfully
followed by Najdan the assassin. If Tansen was sorry, he
kept it to himself.

The changes in Tansen were harder to discern, but Elelar
had known him longer than most people, if not necessarily
better. His gaze strayed often to where Darshon rose
through the clouds, though the expression on his face usu-

ally suggested he was somehow daring the goddess, rather than communing with her. He seemed paradoxically more serene yet more troubled than before, and his manner silenced any questions she tried to pose about what had happened to him on Darshon. He wasn't curt or rude when she broached the subject, just . . . so distant as to be unreachable.

One thing was clear: the events on Mount Darshon had drawn Tansen, Mirabar, and Josarian even closer together. Unfortunately, the coming of the Firebringer didn't have a resoundingly positive effect on all of Josarian's associates. The waterlords resented his growing power and Kiloran was now openly suspicious of him. And then there was Zimran, who felt alienated by Josarian's relationship with Tan and Mira, eclipsed by his cousin's glory, and left out of the extraordinary events sweeping across Sileria.

Elelar understood by now why Josarian assigned only menial tasks to his cousin, despite his personal affection for him: Zimran's heart was not in the rebellion, not even now. Indeed, Zimran's heart was invested in very little beside Zimran . . . though she knew he believed he was in love with her. She kept her distance these days, for she was not ready to take another lover, and when she finally was, it would not be Zimran. She could be ruthless, she had never denied that; but she wasn't wantonly cruel. She had no wish to encourage a man she didn't want, need, or intend to accept.

Unfortunately, the man she *might* accept was proving to be particularly difficult today.

"You have Josarian's ear," she said to Tansen. She sat alone with him as the sun rose over Britar the day after his arrival. "You must convince him to compromise with Kiloran."

He sat polishing his swords, tending them with more concentration than Elelar suspected the task actually required of him after all these years. He didn't even look up. "You want him to compromise, *you* talk to him."

"He won't listen to me."

His mouth quirked. "Probably because you tell him to do things like compromise with Kiloran."

"He's alienating Kiloran. You must see that."

He finally glanced up at her. His eyes were hard. "Kiloran is alienating the Firebringer. You must see *that.*"

"Even the Firebringer can't defeat the Valdani without Kiloran."

"I don't recall the prophecy saying anything about Kiloran."

"Oh, for the love of Dar!"

He lifted one brow in response to her outburst but said nothing.

She sighed and sat down close to him. Very close. "I was at Kandahar, too," she reminded him, banishing the impatience from her tone by force of will. "Now I believe in visions and prophecy, Tansen. I have seen things I never dreamed of."

"So have I." His voice was expressionless.

"You have told me what happened at Darshon, and I honor Josarian's union with Dar and his place in our destiny."

There was no mistaking the irony in his tone as he said, *"But?"*

"But even Mirabar would tell you—"

"You don't know *what* Mirabar would tell me."

"—that we cannot stand by idly. We must take part in our destiny. She moved heaven and earth to find you. Risked her own life at Kandahar. Nearly died at Darshon . . ."

"Yes." His expression revealed nothing of his thoughts, but the tension in his body surprised her.

"She brought us Armian, who told us that all of us *together* must fight the Valdani."

"Kiloran was there, too. Why should *we* compromise? Why shouldn't he?"

"Because he won't, and you and I both know it." He said nothing, but his strokes were hard and fast against the blade of a sword. She realized he was angry—and not entirely at her. "You know I'm right," she murmured.

"I know that you *believe* you're right, which is entirely different." His dismissal was not convincing, however.

"If we lose Kiloran now, we lose the entire Society."

He sheathed one blade, then pulled out the other and began cleaning it. Trying to reach him, she put one hand over his, stopping his work. She shifted so that her breasts brushed against his arm.

"Please," she whispered, pressing her thigh against his.

He went rigid. She could practically feel the sudden flush of desire which washed through him. His jaw flexed, a tiny movement that spoke volumes about the control he exerted on himself.

"We could still lose everything," she murmured. She moved her face closer to his, letting her breath caress his darkening cheek.

He turned his head slightly toward her. His eyes closed for a moment. She could sense the struggle inside of him.

"You and I . . ." she whispered. "We have risked too much, lost too much, to throw away victory now."

His eyes snapped open, dark and blazing with anger. He roughly pulled away from her and returned to polishing his sword. She thought he would lash out at her, but his anger almost seemed to be directed at himself.

"If you want to convince Josarian of your point of view, then *you* talk to him." His strokes were short and almost violent. "Don't ask me to go against my brother, Elelar." He kept his gaze fixed on his blade as he warned, "Don't *ever* ask me again."

Knowing she had lost, she escaped from his presence with as much grace as possible. She wandered alone back toward her tent, a luxurious shelter which had been abandoned along with the estate she currently inhabited. She almost believed she could feel the chill which Mirabar said Kiloran sent through the air. Surely it was just the damp of the early morning, but even so . . .

Dismay filled her when she came across Kiloran's many servants packing up his camp. He was leaving without reaching an agreement about Shaljir, Alizar, or the Idalar River.

Knowing she had little time to turn events around, she approached one of Kiloran's most trusted men, an extremely dangerous, polished assassin whose face bore a scar left by the first man he had ever killed.

"Searlon," she said, "I must speak with Kiloran."

"The time for talking is over." His voice was brusque. "We leave for Kandahar within the hour."

She regarded him with all the arrogance of her rank. "And do you speak for your master now? Would he appreciate your turning away a *torena* without consulting him?"

Searlon hesitated for a moment, then crossed his fists in front of his chest and bowed his head respectfully. "Forgive me, *torena*. We are all on edge, are we not?"

"Yes," she agreed graciously. "Please tell your master that I humbly beg an audience with him."

She was admitted to Kiloran's tent a few minutes later. Its grandeur positively shamed the luxurious one in which she slept. Kiloran dismissed his mistress with a brief glance, then turned his cold, snakelike gaze upon her. Elelar repressed a shudder, suddenly feeling a newfound respect for Mirabar, who had risked the waterlord's wrath more than once.

"*Siran.*" She crossed her fists and bowed her head. Even the *toreni* bowed before Kiloran. "I humbly beg you to stay until we have resolved this matter. I don't need to tell you how important the att—"

"When that *shallah* is prepared to discuss the matter reasonably and respectfully, I will meet with him again. Not before." His voice was as hard and unyielding as his expression, discouraging further comment.

Though she had never been timid, Elelar's stomach churned with nerves as she persisted. "Allow me to speak with him before you leave, *siran*, to attempt—"

"I have no more time to waste here," he snapped. "If

you can make him see reason, then you may contact me through my son."

"How, *siran?* Zilar is still under Valdani control, and we—"

"There is a *tirshah* at Golnar. Not as comfortable as the one at Zilar, but Srijan will tell them that you may appear."

"Siran," she said, even though his expression warned her not to annoy him, "we are allies. Is there no way we can reach an understanding here at Britar?"

"He wants to rule the waterlords." His pale complexion colored briefly with fury. "He wants to rule *me.*"

"He wants only to defeat the Valdani."

"He intends to control the Society to do so." He studied her intently. "He already controls the *shallaheen,* lowlanders, *zanareen,* sea-born folk, and Guardians. Doesn't this worry you?"

"Should it, *siran?* He is the—"

"Do you really intend to let him rule Sileria after the war is over?"

The question surprised her. "I hadn't thought—"

"Then it's time you and your people did think, *torena.*" He leaned forward, his expression intent. "For you will find that power is much harder to take away than it is to withhold."

ZIMRAN COULD HEAR raised voices as he approached the caves of Dalishar. Elelar and Josarian were arguing hotly about Kiloran, the Society, and the war. Though Zimran had not been at the meeting near Britar ten days ago, he had already heard that it hadn't gone well.

With the hour of the New Year approaching, the sacred caves were a hive of bustling activity. Here at one of Sileria's holiest sites, there were many Guardians preparing for the final religious rituals which would welcome in the New Year tomorrow at dawn. Throughout rebel-held territory, people were excitedly getting ready for the festivities which would follow tonight's religious observances. Zimran had promised Josarian that, the war notwithstanding, he would join him at Dalishar, for they had celebrated every New Year of their lives together.

Unfortunately, the mood up here was tense with anger rather than anticipation. Tansen completely ignored him as he walked past, totally absorbed in practicing with his swords. He must have been at it a long time, for he was drenched in sweat, despite the cool air of the season. Most of the rebels seemed to be going out of their way to avoid the sounds of Josarian and Elelar's argument. Lann paced alone, nervous and concerned, outside the cave where the two of them fought.

After greeting him, Zimran asked, "How long have they been at it?"

"Too long," was the gruff answer. "And they don't want to be interrupted."

So Zimran waited quietly with Lann as the angry discussion inside Josarian's cave finally lost momentum, faded, and died. When Elelar emerged from the cave, her expression made it clear that they hadn't reached an understanding. Zim's mouth went dry upon seeing her again, for it had been too long. She was dressed for the ceremonies which would begin after sundown, and she looked as elegant and beautiful as only she could. Heat rushed through him as he returned her greeting. Before he could ask after her health or think of some excuse to touch her, Josarian came out of the cave, too, his scowl melting into a big smile when he saw his cousin.

"Zim! You've come!"

"I promised, didn't I?"

Josarian swept him into an affectionate hug, then slapped him hard on the back and called Jalilar. Zimran reluctantly let his attention be dragged away from the *torena*.

"You're still here?" Zimran said to Jalilar, for she had wanted to go to Emelen's side ever since summer.

"Still here," Jalilar confirmed with an arch glance at her brother. "He has promised to send me east at last—with Tansen, when he goes back."

The *shatai* approached them at the mention of his name, his skin gleaming with exertion, his breath coming a little fast. He barely acknowledged Zimran, instead glancing from Elelar to Josarian with a wary, assessing gaze.

"The day is nearly gone," Elelar said to Josarian, her tone rigidly polite. "May I have an escort home?"

"You're not staying, after all?" Tansen asked. He didn't sound surprised.

"I think not."

Before the *shatai* could offer, Zimran said, "I'd be honored to escort you home, *torena.*"

Tansen went very still, but he didn't protest. Elelar was accepting the offer when Josarian interrupted, "But, Zimran! You'll never make it back here tonight."

"I'll come in the morning, then."

"But I thought we would . . ." Josarian glanced at the *torena*'s icy expression, then suppressed his obvious disappointment. "Naturally, I would not wish to deprive the *torena* of a safe escort."

"Thank you," she replied. Zimran had known Outlookers to sound friendlier than she did right now.

"I just . . ." Josarian shrugged, turning his gaze back to his cousin. "We've just never spent the New Year apart. That's all."

Zimran shrugged, for he saw possibilities on the horizon tonight which precluded any sorrow over yet another break with the life he had known before Josarian's war. "Well, everything is different this year, eh?"

"Everything," Jalilar agreed, glancing from Josarian to Zimran. Her expression was almost sad.

Unable to resist, Zim pointed out, "Anyhow, Tansen will be here."

Now the *shatai* spoke. "Yes. I will." There was contempt in the gaze he directed at Zimran.

Smugly aware that he had won the prize that Tansen would have liked to claim tonight, Zimran said, "We should leave immediately, *torena.* You don't want to travel in the dark, I'm sure."

Josarian's farewell was as effusive as his greeting had been. Zimran felt a brief stab of guilt as he left him. It disappeared, however, when he took one last look over his shoulder and saw Josarian deeply engrossed in conversation with the *shatai*, his gaze intent and trusting as Tan spoke.

"*We* used to be that close," Zimran said to the *torena*, upon seeing her gaze directed at the same scene.

She turned away and started down the mountain path. "He still loves you."

"Yes, but . . ." He shrugged, aware that Elelar was still furious with Josarian about matters concerning the rebellion. Why such a woman—or any woman—should worry so fiercely about men's business always puzzled him, but he used her anger at Josarian to his advantage as he confided, "He is no longer the man I knew."

She looked at him intently for a moment, then repeated softly, almost as if to herself, "He still loves you . . ."

"Before the *shatai* came, before the war . . . Things were different then . . ." A woman's compassion was a powerful force, and he had often been successful at evoking it.

"He trusts you."

Before he could respond, she turned away. A strange sadness seemed to have taken hold of her. He was perplexed, since he sensed it had little to do with him or the womanly warmth he was trying to inspire in her.

Patience, he reminded himself. He was trying to seduce a sophisticated *torena*, not another bored widow, some lonely Sister, or the neglected wife of a boorish rural Valdan. He had taken his time with this one, knowing she would have to be wooed slowly, patiently, subtly. Tonight might well fulfill his dreams, as long as he didn't push her. He must coax her, win her, make her want him the way he wanted her.

She said little as they descended Dalishar, seemingly lost in thought. He didn't speak much, either, but pursued his seduction with subtle, unyielding intent. He took her hand over many rough and not-so-rough portions of the path. He let his hands linger on her slim waist whenever he helped her down from steep tumbles of rock. Sensing that she didn't object to such familiarity, he let his hands linger a little longer each time.

He wasn't sure at first, but by the time they reached the end of the trail that day, she was unquestionably permitting—even inviting—his attentions. Her gaze held his with silent promise more than once as he let their thighs brush together while setting her down on her feet. Her hand slipped smoothly into his on several occasions when he could tell she really needed no assistance over the path.

When they finally arrived at the half-ruined villa which Josarian had allocated to the *torena* and her servants, he was not surprised by her invitation to join him for a quiet, private dinner. As twilight descended over Sileria and Elelar's servants abandoned the house to participate in the religious rites being conducted in Chandar, he knew she wouldn't suggest that he, too, should leave now.

As the last dark-moon night of the year poured the scents of spring's birth through the windows, Zimran joined Elelar on the soft, imported silks covering her bed and finally reaped the rewards of his long, patient seduction of her.

36

THE SCENT OF spring was rich and loamy as Josarian made his way to another meeting with Kiloran. Tansen was not with him; he had gone east again, taking Jalilar with him. Lann and Falian were Josarian's companions today as he proceeded to the site he had chosen in response to Kiloran's recent message suggesting that they end this stalemate and attempt to reach an agreement. They were heading for an isolated Sanctuary in the wild mountains west of Dalishar, less than a day's hike from the sacred caves.

Ever since taking to the *torena*'s bed, Zimran had been so reluctant to leave Chandar for more than a day that Josarian had decided to leave him behind on this occasion; in fact, he had not even told him about this sudden meeting, not having seen him recently. Besides, Josarian had already guessed that anything he told Zimran these days was bound to reach Elelar's ears by nightfall, and he didn't need that woman lecturing him *again* about the need to cooperate with Kiloran.

Anyhow, Kiloran finally seemed ready to capitulate. Josarian could guess why, too: Liron was about to fall. Even the Valdani knew it, and the city's Valdani citizens were leaving Liron by the thousands, boarding ships sailing out of the harbor under a white flag of truce. The Outlookers would hold out, of course, and there would be a bloody battle before the city finally came under rebel control, but it *would* happen. After Liron fell, Adalian would not hold out for long. One by one, the cities of Sileria would fall to the rebels.

Kiloran's refusal to cooperate during the meeting at Britar was already widely known. Some Silerians were starting to mutter about this, criticizing Kiloran—whose name many people had been afraid to even say aloud in former days! But now Kiloran was defying the Firebringer and delaying the siege of Shaljir. Now Kiloran wanted Josarian to attack Shaljir without him, for his hold on Alizar and the Idalar River mattered far more to him than the additional lives that would be lost if the rebels fought for Shaljir without his help. Men weren't so shy about expressing their resentment when they knew they were more likely to die at the walls of Shaljir because Kiloran refused to help take the city. Women didn't keep their opinions to themselves when they realized that they risked losing their husbands and sons while Kiloran refused to risk losing anything.

Kiloran had ears everywhere and undoubtedly knew

what people were starting to say about him. He was no fool and must surely know that even he, powerful as he was, couldn't easily withstand the growing tide of resentment against him. Sileria smelled freedom in the wind for the first time in a thousand years, and her people would not forgive anyone—not even the greatest waterlord in the world—who stood between them and their newfound dreams of liberty and glory. He would have to give in; he would have to compromise.

Josarian had been waiting for a summons from the old waterlord, and he had finally received it. Kiloran was ready to talk as a true ally. Josarian was pleased. When Liron fell, Valdani influence in the east would completely collapse. There would never be a better time to strike out at Shaljir, the very heart of Valdani power in Sileria.

If the war could end this year...

If the war could end this year, then the profits the rebellion had reaped from the sacking of Alizar wouldn't all have to be spent on the war; some of it could be used to rebuild Sileria after the Valdani left. If the war could end this year, fewer men would die. Only this year's spring planting would be disrupted; a hard enough burden, but one they could survive. But if the war dragged on another year, two years, five years ... Josarian hoped it wouldn't come to that; he could guess what it would do to his land and his people. He prayed that he was destined to wrest freedom from the Valdani quickly, forcing them to leave behind a nation which was not too devastated by war to enjoy its liberty.

While Josarian was lost in such thoughts as he approached the Sanctuary where the meeting would take place, Lann was in high spirits, still bragging about his victories in various contests of strength and endurance during the New Year's festivities. Josarian finally laughed at a boast so improbable it made Falian roll his eyes. Shaking his head, Josarian shoved Lann out of his way and stepped past him to announce their arrival to the Sisters.

He heard a hiss, a sudden *thwack,* and a groan. Such

sounds had become so familiar during the past year that he crouched and dived for cover before conscious understanding entered his mind.

He heard Falian cry, *"Lann!"*

More arrows flew at them from every direction, whining through the clear mountain air. Falian screamed when he was hit. An arrow shuddered as it sank into a tree trunk inches from Josarian's head.

Falian was hit again. Arms flailing, legs buckling, he tried to run into the Sanctuary where—Josarian realized dimly—the Sisters were screaming in horror.

Struggling to get up, Lann unsheathed his long Moorlander sword and bellowed with rage.

"Stay down!" Josarian shouted at both men, keeping his head low.

Lann heard him and dragged himself into a clump of nettles; if he lived, he'd find his hiding place more painful than all the Fires. A Sister opened the door of the Sanctuary and ran outside to help Falian. An arrow went clean through her throat. She fell to the ground, clutching at her neck, drowning in her own blood. Horrified, Josarian jumped to his feet. The fletching of an arrow brushed past his cheek, and he hit the ground again.

"Get back!" he screamed at the remaining two Sisters who hovered in the Sanctuary's doorway, wanting to help the two dying people on their doorstep but too terrified to move. "Get back!"

He realized that all his shouting had helped pinpoint his location for his attackers, so he crawled away on his belly, trying to form a plan, trying to think.

Archers were the worst opponents, the hardest to kill, because it was so hard to get close to them. Fortunately, the Valdani usually committed relatively few of them to a battle, preferring to use their talents to guard fortresses and walled cities. And this wasn't even a battle, Josarian suddenly realized; this was an ambush in the heart of rebel territory. The Outlookers couldn't have gotten a full fighting force this close to Dalishar without his knowledge.

There must be only a few of them, and someone had to have helped them get here.

Kiloran has betrayed me.

Even if rebels wanted to betray him, no one except Lann and Falian had known precisely where Josarian was going today. No one else had been present when he had given the location to Searlon, who took the news straight back to Kiloran. And Kiloran had obviously decided that the Firebringer had become too great a threat to the Society.

It was a trap.

He wondered if there werc assassins lurking here, too, or if Kiloran had fastidiously left the business of violating Sanctuary strictly to Valdani barbarians. He hoped the Out-lookers were alone out here, for killing them would be hard enough without tangling with assassins, too.

One of the few advantages of fighting Valdani archers was that if you *could* get close to them, they were seldom as good with a sword as they were with their bows. And if he had to fight them, this wasn't such a bad spot. He had the advantage of the same dense forest and thick brush which currently hid them from view, and he was a *shallah*, not some clumsy *roshah*.

Using the same skills his father had taught him for stalking shy mountain deer and deadly mountain cats, Josarian pulled his wits together and started hunting his attackers.

In the end, they made it easier than he had hoped. He quickly and quietly killed the first one he found, strangling him with his *yahr*. The man was dressed as a city-dweller, but he was clearly a foreigner and his equipment was un-questionably that of an Outlooker. By the time Josarian found and killed another one, so much time had passed that the remaining Outlookers thought he had fled, and so they grew careless. They started tromping noisily through the brush, calling out to each other; it made the next one easy to find. This one let out a warning shout before Jo-sarian slit his throat—a shout so brief and vague that one of his companions thought he was being summoned and walked straight into Josarian's trap.

That made four. Wondering how many were left, Josarian heard voices in the clearing and crawled through the dense spring shrubbery until he could see what was happening. Two more thinly disguised Outlookers had left their hiding places. They stood out in the open, looking down at the bodies of Falian and the Sister who had tried to help him. The Sister stared sightlessly up at the sky. Falian was on his belly. Four arrows had pierced his body, and a trail of blood had followed him as he crawled toward Sanctuary. A bitter bile of mingled grief and rage rose up in Josarian's throat.

"Falian," he whispered.

Falian had been bloodcousin to Calidar. He and Josarian had played together as boys, had known each other all their lives. An innocent man, Falian had been seized and imprisoned at Britar because of Josarian's outlawry. Like Amitan, he had initially opposed the bloodfeud. Like Amitan, he had eventualy been won over and had sacrificed everything to the rebellion.

Like Amitan, now he is dead.

He wanted to weep.

Dead in my name.

The guilt was unbearable, ripping into his heart, tearing him apart as he stared at the corpse of the boyhood friend who had died in agony during an attempt on his own life.

The Outlookers looked around, argued briefly, then came to a decision. Josarian could barely hear them, but their actions were clear enough. They unsheathed their swords and started beating the bushes where Lann had disappeared. Josarian crept closer, waiting for his chance.

"Over here!" one of the men said in Valdan. "I've got him." He bent over to examine his find, then said, "He's still alive."

Josarian wondered if Lann's lack of response meant he was dying or merely unconscious. Outlookers often coated their arrowheads with strange potions and poisons; it was how they had managed to seize Tansen in Cavasar.

The other Outlooker came over to examine the first

one's discovery. He cursed and jumped back, nursing a hand stung by the nettles. Then he asked, "Do you think he's Josarian?"

The first one shook his head. "Josarian is clean-shaven, they say, like most of them. This one has a beard."

"You don't see many . . ." The other Outlooker snapped his fingers. "This one is on the list. A great big *shallah* with a beard."

The first one glanced over his shoulder at Falian's body. "Maybe that one was Josarian?"

"With our luck, Josarian was probably the one that got away, and I doubt *this* one will tell us the truth either way." He heaved a sigh and looked at Falian again. "But Searlon can identify Josarian, so let's take the body with us."

The man who had found Lann bent over, gingerly poked through the nettles to seize Lann's hands, and then heaved. "Three have mercy, he's as heavy as an ox!"

The other Outlooker shouted up into the surrounding forest. "We've taken one alive! Get down here and help!" Receiving no immediate response, he scowled and added more harshly, "*Now*, dammit! We've got to get out of here. The one that got away may come back with a hundred rebels by sundown, so get y—"

He stopped speaking and whirled around to face the two angry Sisters who came bustling out of the Sanctuary, eyes blazing, tongues wagging. Now that the surprise attack and mind-withering explosion of violence seemed to be over, they were furious.

"This is a Sanctuary of the Sisterhood!" one shouted in *shallah* dialect.

The other cried in common Silerian, "How dare you profane this Sanctuary with violence and bloodshed!"

"Three Into One, what are they babbling about?"

"I didn't mean to kill the woman," the first Outlooker said. "It was an accident. She got in the way. Tell them that."

"How do you propose I tell them that?" snapped the first. "I don't suppose you speak any Silerian."

"Er, no . . ."

One Outlooker turned away to confront the Sisters bearing down upon him. The other returned to struggling with Lann's unconscious body while simultaneously trying to avoid contact with the nettles. Josarian saw his chance. He sprang out of his hiding place and swung his *yahr* into the face of the startled Outlooker confronting the Sisters. The man's nose broke; he fell to his knees, howling as he clutched his suddenly bloody face. The Sisters started screaming again. Josarian ignored them and turned to the second Outlooker. The man dropped Lann's arms and struggled to unsheathe his sword. Josarian jumped at him and slit his throat, then turned back to the other Outlooker and killed him before he had time to collect himself.

It was over very quickly. Suddenly there was no sound in the clearing except the hysterical weeping of the Sisters, which drowned out the sound of his own heavy breathing. He tensed for a moment, wondering if there were still more Outlookers hidden in the hills. Weapons ready, he looked around, waiting for the sickening whine of an arrow.

The only attack, however, came from the elder of the two Sisters. After what had just happened, though, even she didn't really have the heart to keep shouting at him for having killed two men right in front of her. Her rage subsided into heartbroken weeping within a few moments, then faded to hollow-eyed grief when Josarian asked the Sisters to help him with Lann.

A brief examination revealed that Lann was wounded badly enough to keep him from fighting for a while, but he would probably live. Josarian almost wept with relief and gratitude. Unfortunately, although there was no better place for Lann than Sanctuary right now, Josarian couldn't leave him here. If Searlon was waiting somewhere to guide the Outlookers safely back out of rebel territory, then he might well come here looking for them when they didn't show up; and Josarian doubted he would come alone. Searlon was no fool, and he wouldn't be as careless as these Outlookers had been.

Kiloran has betrayed me.

Kiloran had just dissolved the Society's alliance with the rebels, though no one but Josarian knew it yet. Indeed, he suspected that Kiloran didn't *want* anyone else to know it. Too many people would never forgive the waterlord for betraying the Firebringer, so Kiloran had planned Josarian's death very carefully. He had humbly suggested a quiet, private meeting, hinting that he had reconsidered his unpopular position. He had let Josarian choose a site for the meeting deep within rebel territory, and at a Sanctuary. No Silerians, not even the Society, had ever committed violence within the boundaries of a Sanctuary.

Having no reason to suspect trouble, Josarian had come here as vulnerable as a lamb, accompanied by only two men, both of whom were also supposed to die during the attack. Kiloran would tell his own story about today's events after Josarian was dead, and only a handful of Josarian's closest companions—those who knew he intended to meet Kiloran today—would ever even think to question it. The Sisters would verify that Outlookers had attacked the Sanctuary, and rebels would blame the Valdani for Josarian's death, leaving Kiloran's position of respect and power secure. The Valdani had probably promised the moons to Kiloran if he helped them destroy Josarian.

Fury consumed Josarian as he set a torch to Falian's mangled corpse. Rage ate him as he laboriously slung Lann's unconscious body over the back of the Sisters' strongest donkey and led it away from the Sanctuary.

Betrayal was the worst crime a Silerian could commit, and the rebels punished *sriliaheen* according to the traditions established by the Society itself. Josarian knew what Kiloran's punishment should be, but he also knew how impregnable Kandahar was. As far as he knew, only Mirabar had ever breached Kiloran's power there, and he didn't think she would willingly help him return there to slay Kiloran now.

If he couldn't kill Kiloran, then he would follow another course. Tansen had tried to protect Josarian and the others from such a fate when he'd left Dalishar to confront Kiloran and return Armian's *shir* to him. If Josarian couldn't punish Kiloran's betrayal with death—and it seemed he couldn't—then he would punish him by slaying someone close to him, someone he treasured so much that his own life would be destroyed by the loss.

This was the way of his kind, the only way he knew. Josarian had been born to a violent, unforgiving, and ruthless people. His heart had twisted with pity when Harjan the tailor had knelt in the streets of Zilar and begged for his life, but he had known that no one in Sileria would respect him for mercy.

A Sister, a *toren*, a Guardian, even a Yahrdan could be merciful. But an outlaw, a warrior, a rebel leader, the Firebringer . . . No. He must be ruthless if men were to continue following him, risking their lives at his side, pledging their blood to his cause, helping him fight his enemies.

Above all, he must be ruthless because if he wasn't, more of his *friends* would betray him.

ELELAR AWAITED SRIJAN in a private room at the *tirshah* in Golnar, still fuming over Josarian's recent behavior. Two days ago, he and six men had arrived at the half-ruined villa in which she now lived. Without even a faint show of courtesy, he had asked if she had a means of contacting Srijan. She explained that Kiloran had given her new instructions, essentially identical to the method by which she had contacted Srijan in the days when they used to meet near Zilar.

Barely allowing Faradar enough time to pack for the journey, Josarian had insisted they leave at once for Golnar, even though it was too late in the day for such a plan to be practical. He had refused to answer Elelar's questions about the reason for this sudden, unplanned meeting. Sharing her tent that first night on the road, Zimran had sulkily admitted that Josarian wouldn't discuss it with him, either. Since reaching Golnar yesterday afternoon, Josarian and his men had stayed completely out of sight, almost as if he had deserted her after bringing her here.

So, bored and bad-tempered, she had simply spent the past day awaiting Srijan. She hoped Josarian was calling this unexpected meeting because he meant to end the stalemate with Kiloran. She suspected, however, that he would instead further strain his relationship with Kiloran by flinging new demands and accusations at Srijan, harsh words for the assassin to take back to Kandahar.

She'd been worrying about this so much lately that it gave her a perpetual headache—the very excuse she had used last night when Zimran's warm hands had sought her in bed.

Charming, attentive, considerate, and a skilled lover, the *shallah* was not bad company, she supposed. Still, her days of freedom had been too short, and she resented Josarian and Kiloran for creating a situation wherein she'd felt compelled to admit Zimran to her bed.

She needed someone close to Josarian who was also close to her; someone he trusted, someone who had his ear, because—since Darshon—he no longer even made a pretense of listening to her. She had wanted Tansen to be her chosen ally, but he had made it painfully clear at Britar that she could never count on him. Then on the eve of the New Year, as he escorted her away from Dalishar, Zimran had made it equally clear that she could count on *him*, if she were willing to pay the price.

The same price I have always paid.

This time, it seemed a higher price than ever before, even though Zimran was a Silerian, not some Valdan, and she minded him less than she had minded some of the others. It was harder this time, though, because she had been foolish enough to believe everything had changed.

Such a fool.

She now realized she may have been foolish in her choice of lovers, too, for apparently Zimran no longer had Josarian's ear, either. She closed her eyes, wishing she were alone now, wishing she could weep.

"Kadriah . . ."

She opened her eyes at the sound of Zimran's voice. His fingers brushed her cheek, possessive, familiar.

"Are you unwell?" he asked.

"Just tired."

He scowled. "He should not have made you travel so far so quickly, and without any warning."

"He still won't tell you what it's about?"

He shrugged. "I haven't even seen him today."

"It's as if they've all disappeared."

"I don't understand why he—"

They heard horses outside the window. Elelar looked outside and saw four riders: Srijan, a servant, and two assassins. The four men dismounted. The assassins led the horses around the *tirshah*, taking them to the stables out back.

Elelar heard Srijan's voice in the entrance hall. The door to this chamber swung open a moment later. To her astonishment, Srijan sprang into the room with his *shir* in hand, ready to fight. Zimran stepped in front of her as she rose to her feet, his *yahr* already in hand.

"What's *he* doing here?" Srijan snarled, looking ready to attack as he glared at Zimran.

Elelar blinked in confusion. "I always bring an escort. You know that."

"Why *him?*"

"What?" she asked, bewildered by Srijan's hostility.

"The keeper said a *shallah* was in here with you. Why him? Why Josarian's cousin?"

"Srijan, what are—"

"I go where the *torena* goes." Driving the point home, Zimran added, "Day and night."

Srijan looked from Zimran to Elelar, then back again. After a long, uncertain moment, he laughed. "So," he said, "she finally let someone besides a Valdan between her legs, eh?"

Zimran moved as if to attack, furious at the insult. Elelar stopped him.

"Don't," she warned. "His words . . . mean nothing to me."

Rigid with outrage, he nonetheless obeyed her. He always obeyed her. It was his greatest virtue.

Srijan was clearly enjoying the moment. Elelar was still afraid the two men would tangle, so she suggested everyone sit down; everyone except Srijan's wide-eyed servant did.

"So, *torena,*" Srijan said, "to what do I owe the pleasure of your presence here? Not bad news, I trust."

Something was wrong. Her instincts warned her that something was *very* wrong, but she had no idea what. "Bad news?" she repeated.

Srijan didn't take the bait. He shrugged. "Good news, then?"

Elelar found his casual attitude . . . unconvincing. "Actually," she said, watching him carefully, "it was Josarian who wanted to see you. I just—"

"Josarian?"

"Yes." His disbelieving stare made her ask, "Why does that surprise you? He—"

Srijan shot out of his chair, his face distorted by mingled confusion and fear. "He's dead."

Zimran rose, too. "What?"

"He's supposed to be dead," Srijan blurted, pulling out his *shir* again. "Where is he? When did you see him?"

"What are you talking—"

The door suddenly flew open, and Josarian burst through it, armed and attacking. Srijan whirled to confront him, but Josarian was a far better fighter than the ordinary peasants Srijan had spent his youth terrorizing. The assassin screamed as Josarian disarmed him and drove him to his knees with a sword thrust through his belly.

Elelar was screaming, trying to shove past Zimran, who was blocking her way and shouting, *"What are you doing? Stop! What are you doing?"*

Srijan's obsequious servant moved, and Josarian turned and struck him unconscious with his *yahr.*

"Are you mad?" Elelar screamed.

"You will die for this," Srijan snarled between gritted teeth. "My father will hunt you to the ends of the earth."

Elelar finally slipped past Zimran and ran to kneel at Srijan's side, coming between him and Josarian. She glared up at the *shallah*. "This will *not* convince Kiloran to do your bidding."

"The time for that is past," Josarian said. "Kiloran has already betrayed me and become my enemy."

"What?"

It was a horrible story, one she could scarcely follow as her mind reeled away from the catastrophe inherent in every word. An ambush by Outlookers deep within the heart of rebel territory, at the site of a private meeting which Kiloran had requested with Josarian.

"They knew Searlon," Josarian concluded. "They were going to show him Falian's corpse to see if it might be mine."

She wanted to protest, to find another explanation for the disastrous events he'd described, but Srijan was a fool whose own words had already condemned him beyond any rescue: *He's supposed to be dead.*

She knew what Josarian intended, and she couldn't let him do it. This would be the end of the rebellion, the end of everything she had worked for her whole life. This would be the end of Sileria.

"No." She was so frightened she could hardly breathe, let alone speak. "You can't kill him."

"Get out of my way," Josarian ordered her.

"You can't!" she cried. "For the love of Dar, *think,* damn you! Kiloran will never forgive this! He will *never* make peace with you after this!"

"Zim," Josarian said, his voice harsh with warning, "get her out of my way."

She shot a desperate glance at Zimran. "Talk to him! Don't let him do this!"

"Josarian, please . . ." Zimran begged, clearly torn by conflicting loyalties and shocked confusion.

"Get her out of here!" Josarian shouted.

"There are two more assassins," Zim said desperately. "In the stables. If you do this, none of us will leave Golnar alive."

"They're dead by now," Josarian said.

Elelar gasped. "The other men you brought. This is why you haven't let anyone in Golnar see any of you." He had used her, making her an unwitting part of the mad vengeance which would destroy them all. "No!"

"Zim," Josarian repeated.

"Don't hurt her," Zimran warned. "I can't le—"

"Talian's dead. Lann's barely alive." Josarian raised his sword. "I was *supposed* to die."

"My father will destroy you all!" Srijan screamed, struggling to get out of reach. He fell away from Elelar's protective grasp. "No! *No!* N—"

Josarian's blade came down with a sickening sound, slicing through the air before it severed Srijan's throat. Blood splattered onto Elelar's face, warm, sticky, wet. She jumped back, her red-stained hands warding off the sight of Srijan's death throes. She screamed again and again in helpless horror as her whole world collapsed in a single moment of madness.

37

THE NEWS DIDN'T reach Tansen until ten days after the fall of Liron. He had expected to spend the spring consolidating rebel power in the east and sweeping across the land toward Adalian, a city already trembling before its imminent fall, but now he knew he must return to Dalishar.

When Liron fell, Tansen, like everyone else, had been

caught up in the euphoria inspired by the greatest victory since Alizar, perhaps the greatest since the beginning of the rebellion. To wander through the empty palaces of Liron and know that they would never again be inhabited by Valdani, to watch ships leave port overloaded with the city's last few fleeing Valdani civilians and disarmed Outlookers, to walk through the streets of Liron and know that no Outlooker could ever again stop him here, question him, abuse him, arrest him . . . He had once told Josarian that it was a dream worth dying for; now he discovered that, more than that, it was a dream worth *living* for, an achievement worth every sacrifice it had required.

Thank You, Dar. Thank You for letting me live to see this.

She still hadn't revealed Her intentions for him, but he felt that She had declared a private, temporary truce when She let him survive that day at Darshon. It return, he supposed it was only fitting that he offer Her an occasional prayer. Mirabar had assured him that, despite his having murdered his bloodfather and having tried to keep Josarian from Dar, it wouldn't be a sacrilege.

"No one can ever profane Dar with prayer," she had insisted.

Since such matters were Mirabar's realm and not his, he was willing to take her word for it.

Mirabar . . .

He had wondered often about her since leaving Dalishar with Jalilar. Mirabar had changed after Darshon. No longer a girl, he realized. *And no longer a demon.* Among other things, he wondered if she had returned any more of Cheylan's "very passionate" embraces since Darshon. He had seen Cheylan here in the east, of course, but he would cut out his tongue before he'd discuss such matters with him. It was a relief that Cheylan, having met Mirabar himself, no longer asked Tan about her. Tansen sometimes wondered where she was, what she was doing, if she was well.

Now he just wondered if she knew about Josarian. The

moment he and Emelen learned what had happened, Tansen had known he must return to Josarian's side.

After killing Srijan, Josarian had dragged his body out into the street and left it there as a warning to everyone, including Kiloran: *So die all who betray Josarian.* Srijan's wounded servant had been left alive to return to Kiloran with the news of his son's death. Tansen couldn't even imagine what had gone on that day at Kandahar, how Kiloran had responded, what had been said. He could hardly bear to think about what Kiloran would do now; but he knew he must.

He set out from Liron as soon as he heard the news. He would go to Josarian's side and stay there. Kiloran would never forgive Josarian for this, would never accept peace between them now. Tansen understood why Josarian had done it. After Kiloran's betrayal of Josarian, everyone must choose a side; there could be no middle ground. Josarian knew his people. Though he was the Firebringer, many Silerians would only choose him over Kiloran if he made it clear that he was as ruthless and powerful as the greatest waterlord in Sileria, unafraid of his wrath and unforgiving of his betrayal.

Josarian had never taken a bigger risk, not even when he had jumped into the Fires of Darshon. Yes, Tansen understood why Josarian had done it, but he wished he hadn't. Now Kiloran would never stop trying to kill Josarian, no matter what it cost him.

So Tansen was returning to Josarian's side now. A man protected by a *shatai* was very hard to kill. It was small consolation, but it was all Tansen had.

"DON'T TAKE IT out on *me,* Commander," Searlon snapped, fingering his *shir* in the lantern light. "It was *your* men who made a mess of what should have been a perfectly smooth—"

Koroll snapped back, "Since you weren't even there—"

"*We* cannot violate Sanctuary."

"A fine distinction, since you led the ambush party straight to—"

"The distinction is that we do not fight or kill on land claimed by the Sisterhood," Searlon said coldly. "Josarian knows this, and it's why he should have been as vulnerable as a baby when he—"

"Then what went wrong?"

"Your men bungled the attack!" Searlon sneered at him. "My master was right. All Outlookers are fools."

Koroll's face burned at the insult. He longed to have this assassin hauled off to prison right now, but he couldn't. Kiloran, though evidently enraged, had not withdrawn his cooperation. Koroll longed to have Searlon killed before his very eyes, but he still needed the assassin and his master.

"Do you have access to this thing they call the Alliance?" he asked Searlon, rigidly controlling his temper.

The assassin lifted one brow. Koroll had learned that the gesture signaled surprise in his cagey companion. "Yes." Searlon's smile was insolent as he added, "I even have access to *Torena* Elelar shah Hasnari."

Koroll's belly churned with humiliation. He knew that Searlon was laughing at him again. Though they were allies for the moment, the assassin never bothered to hide his contempt. Wanting to spit into that smiling face, Koroll merely said, "I see."

"Why do you ask, Commander?"

"The newly appointed Imperial Advisor has arrived."

Wealthy, aristocratic, arrogant, and very demanding, Advisor Kaynall was one of the Emperor's many nephews. His distinguished career in the Palace of Heaven had been interrupted by the war, but the Emperor had found a use for him at last, sending him to war-torn Sileria. Quite a disappointing assignment after ten years in the Palace of Heaven, Koroll imagined. He might feel sorry for Kaynall if he didn't dislike him so much.

"And?" Searlon prodded.

Actually, Searlon rather *reminded* Koroll of Kaynall.

"*And* he wants to hold a secret meeting with someone who can speak for the Alliance. Under flag of truce, of course."

"To discuss what?"

"I have no idea," Koroll lied, just as he was certain Searlon was lying every time he claimed ignorance of Kiloran's plans and intentions. "Can it be arranged?"

"I will ask my master."

It was the answer Koroll had expected. He suspected that Searlon had far more power and autonomy than he admitted to, but the assassin kept his own skin safe and his master's reputation intact by pretending to the Valdani that he was a mere messenger.

"Since you have access to Elelar," Koroll said, "you might tell her that her husband is in custody here."

"Indeed?"

"Yes. She might not recognize him, though. I doubt she's ever seen him quite so sober."

Searlon shrugged. "I doubt the *torena* will care. I understand that she has a new man these days."

"What a surprise," Koroll said dryly. Her husband was in prison and Borell was barely cold in his grave, but Elelar already had a new lover. "Some things never change."

"And some fools never learn." Searlon leaned forward, his expression dangerously cold as he said, "We are not pleased about the recent massacres, Commander."

"We did not do it to please you."

"If you want my master's cooperation—"

"He is still the enemy," Koroll snapped, "and I will not tolerate your trying to dictate Valdani policy in Sileria."

What little there still is of it, that is.

Hoping to crush the rising spirits of the peasants in the remaining Valdani-occupied portions of Sileria, he had ordered a wave of brutal attacks all along the borders of rebel-held territory.

Searlon's dark eyes glittered with loathing. "You are clumsy and savage."

Koroll's expression was equally cold as he pointed out, "Yet you came to me for help against Josarian."

Searlon shrugged. "As my master has so often said: allies need not be friends."

"Indeed, if they were," Koroll murmured, "then I would pity Josarian his friends."

TASHINAR WAS ILL and keeping to her cave on Mount Niran when she heard the news. Mirabar had scarcely left her side these past few days, she was so worried about her. The long rains had been a bad time for Tashinar this year, making her joints ache terribly. Her lungs had finally succumbed to the damp, too, and she couldn't seem to get rid of this liquid cough that wracked her body day and night.

I'm old. How did I become old so soon?

She was touched by Mirabar's concern and solicitude. Unfortunately, when it came to watching over a sick old woman, the girl—*woman,* Tashinar corrected herself, for Mira had changed a great deal in recent months—was about as calming and gentle as a volcanic eruption. Mirabar's fears about Tashinar's health made her tongue even sharper than usual. Just last night, she had once again caused the Sister tending Tashinar to burst into tears. Moreover, the men camped up here routinely entered the cave one after another all day long to talk to Mirabar about the rebellion, the Otherworld, Josarian, Tansen, the fall of Liron, the latest news about Adalian, and numerous other plans which overwhelmed Tashinar's mind and disturbed her rest. Najdan the assassin was never far from Mirabar's side, and Tashinar would never be able to rest anywhere near a *shir.* She didn't know how he could rest, either; his enchanted dagger often twitched and shivered in Mirabar's presence as if it were alive.

All things considered, Tashinar had been trying to think of some way to convince Mirabar to leave Niran without hurting her feelings. But this . . . No, this wasn't how she had wanted it to happen. The news had just reached them: Josarian had murdered Kiloran's son.

Dar have mercy, we are finished.

The news had brought chaos to the camp within moments. Assassins and rebels were squaring off, choosing sides, launching bitter accusations against each other. Kiloran had betrayed Josarian, some said, and this was the Firebringer's revenge. No, Josarian had gone mad, others said, drunk on power and glory.

Baran's people had suffered too much over the years to really care what happened to Kiloran or his men right now. Given a choice between the Firebringer or a waterlord who was their own master's chief rival, they preferred Josarian. The lowlanders, sea-born folk, and Guardians would remain staunchly loyal to Josarian, for they had never pledged themselves to Kiloran. However, some *shallaheen* would be torn and divided by these events. Many of them still feared Kiloran too much to oppose him, and some clans had sworn loyalty to him many years before they'd ever even *heard* of Josarian.

This will destroy the rebellion.

Tashinar felt immensely old as she listened to Mirabar and Najdan argue in hushed, desperate voices. Mira's eyes were hot and yellow with panic. Najdan seemed to have aged ten years in the past ten minutes. Tashinar didn't truly understand the loyalty between these two, but from the first moment she had seen them together after the birth of the rebel alliance at Lake Kandahar, she had seen how strong their bond was. Now it was dissolving in the disastrous tide of events beyond their control.

"This is the end of the rebel alliance," Najdan told Mirabar, his voice weary and full of regret. "It's over, *sirana.*"

"No!" Mirabar shook her head, fighting the destiny which had already overtaken her own plans and dreams. "I will go to Josarian. You will talk to Kiloran. We will convince them—"

"Kiloran will never forgive this."

"He can postpone his revenge until after the war."

"He will not, *sirana.* And Josarian knew it when he killed Srijan."

"Then I will go to Kandahar and—"

"No!" Najdan's response was sharp and forceful. "He would kill you, *sirana.*"

Mirabar's hands twisted desperately in the folds of her tattered tunic. "Then let that be the price of Srijan's death. Let Kiloran kill me in Josarian's place."

Heart pounding, Tashinar protested, "No, Mira, you can't! You—"

"*Nothing* is more important than defeating the Valdani," Mirabar insisted. "Not you, not me, not anyone. Josarian's destiny is to drive them out of Sileria, and so we must protect him from Kiloran."

"Kiloran will accept no death in place of Josarian's, *sirana,* not even yours."

"Let's ask him."

"I know. Far better than you," Najdan pointed out. "I have served him since before you were born." He shook his head. "It must be Josarian. No one else."

Mirabar leaned forward, her gaze intent. Her hand trembled as she laid it over one of Najdan's. "Then help me kill Kiloran," she whispered.

He jerked away as if she had burned him. "No."

"You and I, together, we could—"

"*No!*" He shook his head. "He is my master. I am his servant. I swore an oath to him twenty years ago. My life is his, *sirana.* I cannot betray him."

Anger washed across her expression. "I know what these oaths are worth to assassins! How many of your kind *have* betrayed their masters?"

"I don't know," he said through gritted teeth. "But *I* won't be one of them."

"He betrayed Josarian. He betrayed us all."

"We have only Josarian's word for that. A secret ambush by a handful of Outlookers—"

"At a meeting place known only to Kiloran and Searlon!"

"A Sanctuary!" Najdan shouted. "One where Josarian has had meetings before! A site *he* chose! Who's to say that another cowardly *shallah* didn't betray him? It's happened before!"

"He said that the Outlookers knew Searlon!"

"He was already locked in a quarrel with Kiloran! What better way to attack my master than by pretending—"

"Would he pretend something that would destroy the rebellion?"

"He has changed since Darshon!"

"He has not gone mad, though!"

Their argument was interrupted by Tashinar's coughing. Mirabar came to her side and tried to ease her through the spasm. Her chest ached. She could hear phlegm moving through her lungs. Her head reeled from the argument. Her nerves quivered from the explosion of emotions in this tiny space. When the spasm ended, she lay back on her pallet, gasping for air, cursing old age and its burdens.

"*Sirana* . . ." Najdan's voice was filled with regret as he held Mirabar's gaze. "I must leave. I must return to my master. You are loyal to Josarian, and I know that is as it should be. But I . . . cannot honorably continue to serve the servant of my master's enemy."

"Najdan . . ." Mirabar's eyes filled with tears.

"I would never betray you. If my master . . . planned an attack on Josarian, he never confided in me. And regardless of why Josarian killed Srijan, you and I must now be enemies." Najdan looked away so as not to see her tears. "Serving you has been the greatest honor of my life, *sirana.*" He rose and turned to leave. Speaking over his shoulder, he said quietly, "I wish you health, happiness, and a long, fruitful life."

"Najdan . . . When your time comes . . ." Mirabar's voice broke for a moment. "I pray Dar that the Otherworld will welcome you."

The assassin lowered his head to slip through the low-hanging mouth of the cave, then disappeared from their lives. Mirabar drew in huge gulps of air, struggling not to weep.

"What will you do now?" Tashinar asked her.

"I must leave, too." Mirabar nodded wearily, forming her own plans. "I must find Josarian. I must . . . protect him from Kiloran." She sighed, a soft sound full of sorrow. "I know why he did it, but . . ."

"But?" Tashinar prodded.

"Must it always be this way here?"

"Always? I don't know." Tashinar closed her eyes, unbearably weary after a lifetime in Sileria. "I only know that it always *has* been this way here."

ADALIAN FELL EVEN sooner than expected, but Zimran could not find it in his heart to celebrate when he heard the news. The *torena* had been desolate ever since Srijan's murder. At night, she allowed Zimran to comfort her in the dark privacy of their bed, but she was distant and dismissive by day. Moreover, she went away often now and didn't always take him with her. Sometimes she was gone for only a day; sometimes for three or four days. She revealed little about her activities when he questioned her, saying only that the Alliance was busy discussing how best to govern the cities coming under rebel control. Even when they were together at the villa near Chandar, she seemed to have less and less time for him lately, always writing letters or holding meetings with other high-born members of the Alliance.

It was perhaps only now that he realized how much he loved her, for he would not have cared about the long, unexplained absences of any other woman. Indeed, any other woman's inattention would merely have spurred him on to his next conquest. But Josarian had been right: Now that Zimran had found Elelar, he wanted no other woman. He wanted *this* one to pay attention to him as she had in the early days of their liaison; nothing else would make him happy again. He had briefly considered pursuing another woman as a means of making Elelar jealous, but he had quickly dismissed the idea. He knew enough about her by now to recognize that he would almost certainly lose her with such behavior.

Although Elelar's habit of excluding him from her thoughts and activities since Srijan's violent death made Zimran increasingly unhappy, he hadn't quarrelled with her about any of this until today, when she summoned Tansen to the villa for a private meeting—one which she arrogantly insisted Zimran leave when he discovered them together. Tansen and Elelar's angry voices seemed to preclude any possibility of the meeting being a mere pretense for more intimate activities, but Zimran was furious all the same. He knew how much the *shatai* had always wanted his woman, and he knew how close together anger and passion could live in a man's heart. Zimran left the two of them alone as ordered, but his heart raged with jealousy and humiliation. As soon as the *roshah* left, his lean face dark with anger, Zimran confronted Elelar.

"We argued about Josarian," Elelar informed him wearily. "What else?"

"Then why couldn't I be there? Why must I be sent from the room like some child?" he snapped.

"Because you and he do not get along," she said reasonably, "and the conversation was difficult enough without adding that kind of tension to it."

He hated it when she was reasonable, when her arguments were irrefutable and sensible. It made him sulky. "You are always having secret meetings these days. Always writing letters. Always going away."

"This is the life I led before being imprisoned in Shaljir," she said. "The life I have always lived."

"Can't you rest now? You are no longer living a secret life in Shaljir, and this war should not be women's business, anyhow."

She went very still. For a moment, he feared he had said the wrong thing. She could sometimes be rather difficult. But, then, she was a *torena,* and they were different. He must remember that.

Trying to call up her softness, the part of herself that she reserved for him alone, he slipped an arm around her waist and whispered in her ear, "I worry about you so, *kadriah.* These are dangerous times, and I can think of nothing but your safety when you go away without me."

"I'm . . . I know," she murmured, softening under his touch.

Her waist was so slim, her stomach so smooth and flat. He usually took pleasure in the exquisite beauty of her body, but now he longed to see her waist thicken and her belly swell with his child. He had always dreaded the thought of fatherhood, had once even resisted pressure from Josarian and his self-righteous wife to marry a girl in Emeldar who claimed to be carrying his child. He enjoyed women for the pleasures they could share with him, not for the hungry mouths they could burden him with. Like so many other things, though, he found that this, too, had changed now that he was in love with Elelar. He wanted to plant his seed in her belly, to create a new life within her and someday watch her nurse his son.

Such an idea would have been unthinkable before the war; even their relationship would have been unthinkable not so long ago. But everything had changed, and with the world daily turning upside down, Zimran intended to keep Elelar as his own. Forever.

He slid his palm up over her breast and gently massaged her, feeling her body quicken delightfully under his touch. Maybe a child would be just the thing, he realized. Maybe a baby would make her settle down at last, leaving the business of war to Josarian, Tansen, and their kind. Maybe if Zimran got her with child, then the two of them could settle into a quiet life together, free of all this madness. Whether or not Josarian fulfilled the destiny of the Fire-bringer, he was good as dead anyhow; Kiloran would never rest until he had avenged the loss of his son. In the meantime, with Liron and Adalian already fallen and all of Sileria now involved in the war, surely destiny could play out the rest of this game without Zimran and his woman.

He kissed the slender column of her neck, inhaling the subtle fragrance that clung to her fair skin. He pulled her closer, glad he had locked the door when he had entered this room to quarrel in private; a *torena*'s household was full of servants who were always inconveniently underfoot, bursting into her presence without warning or apology. It was so long since she had allowed him to make love to her in the middle of the day. He kissed her long and hard, intending to override any protest she might make now.

She let him unfasten the silken ties that held her tunic together. Beneath it, she was warm, delicate, fine-boned, and tender. His mind reeled away from the sudden unbidden memory of Srijan's blood covering the face he now kissed, soaking the hands which now slipped between his legs to stroke him. How could Josarian have murdered Srijan right in front of Elelar? Fury filled him as he thought of it again, fury which flooded him with protective fervor as he swept her up into his arms.

How could Josarian have endangered her so?

What if there'd been a fight and she'd been hurt? What if Kiloran, who undoubtedly knew of her presence, didn't believe she was an innocent bystander who had actually tried to save Srijan?

Zimran had despised Srijan, but he knew that Elelar was right: Killing him, no matter what the provocation, had been an insane act. A *shallah* did not cross a waterlord and survive. Josarian may be the Firebringer, as people said, but this was Kiloran he had offended. And Kiloran undoubtedly now regretted having shown mercy to Tansen, Josarian's brother, a show of mercy which had obviously made Josarian lose respect for him. Kiloran would not make the same mistake twice.

Surely Josarian was doomed. How could he live much longer? But considering how Josarian had abused and endangered Elelar that day at Golnar, Zimran could not even find it in his heart to be sorry that his cousin might die soon.

ELELAR WAS FINDING it more and more difficult to get away from Zimran. Sex always pacified him upon her return home, but he was becoming increasingly sulky, quarrelsome, and demanding before each departure. She would turn him out of her household except that her rift with Josarian had grown so wide that Zimran was now her only reliable connection to him.

Josarian might be half-mad since his leap into Darshon, but he was still no fool. He knew that Zimran told Elelar everything, so he said little to his cousin about the war, his plans, or his enmity with Kiloran. Nonetheless, careful questioning of Zimran after he saw his cousin still always revealed more than Elelar could have learned without him, so she continued to let him stay with her. Luckily, in a doomed attempt to win Zimran away from her, Josarian had recently sent him off on some innocuous mission. Zimran deeply resented the separation from Elelar, but— at her insistence—had accepted the assignment and proved his loyalty to his cousin by obeying orders. Not only did it serve to reestablish some of Josarian's waning faith in Zimran, but it freed Elelar for an extremely important assignation with Searlon, one which would take her away for more days than Zimran would have tolerated without making trouble for her.

She had met briefly with Searlon once before, at the behest of the Alliance. Her associates were deeply concerned about the rift between Josarian and Kiloran. So far, it seemed that the Valdani knew nothing about it, which was a relief; revelation of the crumbling rebel alliance would renew Valdani confidence just when they were finally losing it. Whichever side of the quarrel Silerians took, it was in everyone's best interest to ensure that the Valdani didn't find out about the unbreachable chasm of hatred which now separated the Firebringer and Sileria's most powerful waterlord.

Adalian and Liron had already fallen. Cavasar was in a state of constant turmoil and completely cut off from Valda. Moorlander warships now patrolled the waters off of Sileria's western coast, and the sea-born folk had controlled Cavasar's port ever since sacking it. One half of

Sileria's land was already under rebel control. The Silerians still living in Valdani-held lands were now openly loyal to the rebellion, preparing for their own liberation.

Indeed, at this point, the Valdani must be nervously wondering why the rebels had not yet made any move against Shaljir. At least the rebels' frustrating inability to take action at this time was having one useful effect: the delay was driving the Valdani mad with nervous anticipation.

Elelar knew from dispatches making their way through Liron and Adalian that the Emperor's two-front war was devastating the economy of Valdania. If the Imperial Council had thoughts of calling for peace with either the Kintish Kingdoms or the Moorlanders, it was too late now. They had gone too far, committed too much. Neither the free tribes of the Moorlands nor the Palace of Heaven would accept an offer of peace now. They would know it was merely a sign of weakness, an indication that they might now have an opportunity to carve up the distant reaches of the Empire for themselves.

The Silerian rebels, however, had no ambitions on the mainland. They wanted nothing from the Valdani except unconditional withdrawal from Sileria. So, after two hundred years, the Imperial Council had suddenly decided that Sileria was expendable.

The new Imperial Advisor in Sileria had been instructed to meet with the Alliance under a white flag of truce to negotiate an end to hostilities. Unable to risk proposing peace to their two mighty foes on the mainland, the Valdani were evidently ready to cut their losses in Sileria. It would relieve them of an increasingly costly problem, and they undoubtedly believed they could reclaim Sileria at some later date, after securing the victories they still anticipated in the Moorlands and in the Kintish Kingdoms.

The Valdani wouldn't believe the prophecy about the Firebringer, if they even knew it: The enemies he drove out could *never* return to Sileria. And Elelar certainly had no intention of trying to win them over to Silerian mysticism at this late date. After all, they'd be so much more likely to leave as long as they thought they could simply come back later.

Her heart almost ached with hope as, escorted by Searlon, she made her way to the negotiations she had been ordered to attend. The meeting was so secret that she had been instructed to tell no one about it. Not even Faradar knew where she was now. Would the Valdani really make an offer—and if they did, would it be sincere?

Will the war really end?

As Searlon guided her to the edge of rebel territory and beyond, Elelar saw plenty of evidence that it would be best for Sileria if the war did end soon; this year—perhaps even by summer. The rebels were prepared to fight for much longer. Now that the Firebringer had come, they would fight forever, if need be. But this impoverished land was already suffering under the burden of fighting the world's wealthiest empire. It would be so much better for Sileria if the fighting could end before her land was too war-torn and her people too devastated to reap the benefits of victory.

Above all, Elelar longed to see an end to all the killing. She had heard about the terrible massacres occurring all along the borders of rebel territory, but none of the stories had prepared her for the horrors she now witnessed as she rode beside Searlon.

Village after village had been attacked. Many had already been burned, the tragedy so great that the survivors simply torched entire towns rather than trying to resurrect their lives amidst such devastation. In some villages, where survivors remained, Elelar heard such horrific stories of brutality, murder, torture, and slaughter that she felt physically sick. Even women, children, and dying old people were not safe from the Outlookers rampaging through the lowlands in a wave of violence so vicious that it eclipsed all memories of Myrell the Butcher.

The orders came from Commander Koroll, of course, and his name was on everyone's lips. Having failed to hold

Sileria, he now sought to destroy her in his humiliation. It made Elelar think of what Borell had done to her in the guardhouse at the Lion's Gate. Now she saw that a man could try to do the same thing to a whole nation, that he could hate an entire people that bitterly.

He must be stopped.

Josarian knew it, of course. He was fighting to defend the helpless villages falling victim to Koroll's vengeful rage. However, the Outlookers had finally learned a thing or two from the rebels. These attacks on undefended, non-military targets always occurred by surprise and usually in the middle of the night. They were secret operations. Even if Elelar were still living in Shaljir, sleeping in Borell's bed, and privy to his discussions with Koroll, she'd probably be unable to learn about the planned attacks in time to save the victims.

Koroll must be stopped.

And the war must end soon, if possible. It might have been different if Josarian and Kiloran were still allies, but now that they were enemies, time was running out. The rebellion was crumbling already, splitting up into warring factions in the wake of Kiloran's betrayal and Srijan's murder. The Alliance must negotiate for the Valdani to leave *now*, before they could take advantage of Sileria's internal weaknesses again.

It's only a matter of time . . .

Of course, Elelar knew she might be riding to her death even now. Kiloran apparently knew and believed that she'd had nothing to do with Srijan's murder. She wouldn't put it past Searlon to toy with her before assassinating her, but he'd had many opportunities to kill her or lead her into a trap during these past few days, and he hadn't done so. So she believed he was indeed taking her to the Alliance's meeting with the Imperial Advisor now. On the other hand, she had even less reason to trust the Valdani than she did the Society, so she wasn't certain she would live through this.

Searlon said the invitation had initially come through an

assassin the Valdani had captured and then released in the hope that he could, as he claimed, eventually get a message to the Alliance. Elelar had resisted at first, assuming it was merely a trap laid by Koroll. The commander wanted them all, and he probably still wanted *her* more than anyone else. Indeed, Searlon himself had passed along the news that Koroll had imprisoned Ronall in the hopes of using him as some sort of bait or exchange hostage for her. Ronall! Evidently Koroll was too big a fool to realize just how unlikely Elelar was to ever again take two steps out of her way—let alone return to prison—for the sake of her husband. Anyhow, he was a Valdani aristocrat; surely keeping him in custody was the worst that Koroll would do to him.

She remained suspicious about this meeting, but the Alliance had ordered her to be one of the four representatives who would attend. She assumed it was because, among her associates in the Alliance, she was the closest to Josarian—though none of them realized how much that had changed. Even Searlon, whom no one would ever describe as a trusting sort of man, seemed to believe today's meeting was genuine rather than a trap. So Elelar went, praying that she wouldn't find herself right back in Shaljir's prison as a result.

When they arrived at the crumbling ruins of a Moorlander fortress in Valdani-ruled land, Elelar saw the white flag of truce flying over a round tower which was decorated with the remnants of the demon-slaying stone creatures so valued by the Moorlanders. As she approached the ruins, her skin prickled in anticipation of archers' arrows, and she knew that even the company of Josarian's entire army would not have made her feel safe right now.

Someone emerged from behind the tumbling stone walls. Relief flooded her when she recognized *Toren* Varian of Adalian. The old man had been an associate of Gaborian's for over forty years and was now one of the chief authorities within the Alliance. His presence gave her hope that the meeting was indeed genuine. Searlon helped her dismount, then watched her follow Varian into the ruins.

This meeting was for the Alliance only. The Imperial Council believed they could reason with aristocrats, *toreni,* and even wealthy merchants, but not with illiterate peasants, assassins, wizards, fire-eating mystics, outlaws, bandits, and warriors.

"War is the business of one kind of man," Varian advised her as he guided her into a large tent flying another white flag, "and peace the business of another."

And the business of women is to make you all do the intelligent thing and let you believe it was your own idea all along.

She had failed at Golnar when Josarian killed Srijan. She had failed the night Tansen had murdered Armian. Both failures had cost Sileria dearly. She vowed that she would not leave this meeting without securing peace for her people.

Varian introduced her to Advisor Kaynall. He had obviously heard of her, and she found his assessing gaze insultingly familiar as it travelled over her. He made some remark about envying Borell. She didn't comment, only returned his gaze coolly, hating him as she hated all Valdani. She ignored the seat he offered her, choosing another instead.

"Tell me," he said, "just out of curiosity—after all the effort your husband went to to procure your right to an imperial trial, why did you then flee Shaljir?"

She stared at him. Realizing he meant the question seriously, she said, in the tone of one addressing the village idiot, "Because I preferred escape to death by slow torture."

"But death by slow torture was by no means a certainty, particularly considering—"

"I was being dragged to the cellar for that very purpose when my compatriots broke into the prison to rescue me. How much more certain do you think I needed to be?"

The Advisor frowned. "That's impossible. You had just been granted a trial. Surely that's why Borell killed himself—to avoid the disgrace."

She shook her head, confused. "No, Captain Myrell said that I had been denied a . . ." She stopped suddenly, realizing. *"Koroll."*

Kaynall's eyes widened. She saw that he was quicker than Borell had been. "I . . . gather that your testimony could have damaged Commander Koroll as well as Advisor Borell?"

"Not as much, but it would have been damaging." She leaned forward, reconstructing the events as they must have occurred. "Borell got the dispatch granting me a trial and killed himself. Koroll somehow suppressed the news before anyone else knew about it, then worked out a scheme wherein he could get away with killing me before I could embarrass him at trial."

Following the conversation with his own quick mind, Varian guessed, "And he would have found a way to cast blame elsewhere."

"Onto Borell, probably," Elelar mused, "who couldn't defend himself once he was dead."

Varian smiled blandly at Kaynall. "Evidently life in Santorell Palace isn't all that different from that in the Palace of Heaven, which is notorious for such scheming and deception."

Kaynall was too experienced to reveal the fury he must be feeling over the High Commander's self-serving subterfuge, *or* the embarrassment he must surely feel at having it revealed to him by an enemy—and a woman.

He merely returned the bland smile, then said to Elelar, "I'm afraid your husband and his family have suffered severely due to these misunderstandings. The Council honored you by granting the right of an imperial trial to a Silerian, and His Radiance considered your violent escape from prison a personal insult. It is small reparation, but I give you my personal guarantee that your husband will be released from custody the moment I return to Shaljir."

"The Emperor, my husband, and my husband's family are all Valdani," Elelar said. "Their suffering, their sense of insult, and their freedom are of no concern to me."

"Well." Kaynall's brows rose. "How refreshingly direct."

"Would you care to be direct in return?" she invited. "Rather than spending two days leading up to it, why don't you simply tell us right now, with no prevarication: what do we have to do to secure total and unconditional Valdani withdrawal from Sileria?"

"Ah . . ." Kaynall steepled his fingers together. "I think you'll be surprised at how little we want, *torena.*"

"What?" she prodded.

"Only one thing. Just one. But it's not negotiable."

"*What?*"

"We want Josarian's head."

38

TOTAL AND UNCONDITIONAL *withdrawal.*
Elelar's mind reeled as she remembered that meeting amidst the ruins left by an earlier conquering race.

The Valdani wanted only one thing in exchange for leaving Sileria: *Josarian.*

She'd lost weight since returning home, unable to eat ever since Kaynall had made his startling announcement. Varian's bland reaction had told her that the price of freedom came as no surprise to him; she suspected he and Kaynall had already talked.

Kaynall's position was clear, and he'd been more candid than she had expected. The Valdani knew they must give up Sileria. They were going to lose it anyhow. Unless they experienced a sudden and miraculous change of fortune in their wars against the Kints and the Moorlanders, they simply couldn't send enough men and supplies to Sileria to win the war here. Oh, they could send more if they had to—but ultimately, not enough. In the end, the rebels would win. So the sooner the Valdani withdrew, the sooner they could divert the men, money, ships, weapons, and supplies being wasted here to the mainland, where they were very badly needed.

In case she hadn't fully understood the threats inherent in Kaynall's speech, he made them brutally clear. If the Alliance did not cooperate, then the Valdani *would* drag out the war. Yes, the rebels would probably win in the end, but the Valdani would make sure it was a long, bloody victory which cost the nascent nation more than it could afford—especially after years of being looted and impoverished by its conquerors. Though such a course of action would hurt the Empire, it would hurt Sileria far more.

Unfortunately, Kaynall explained, although immediate withdrawal from Sileria was a practical plan, it would not be a politically popular move back in Valda.

"We are a proud people, you understand," Kaynall had said. "A people of conquest, not peace. A people who take provinces, rather than give them back."

The Imperial Councilors therefore needed something they could show to their enemies and offer to their people in exchange for losing possession of Sileria—a backwater province that no one in the world had ever expected to see rebel and claim its freedom. The Valdani needed something to salvage their pride upon losing Sileria. The Council had decided that that *something* must be the life of Sileria's most notorious rebel: the illiterate peasant whose name was now bandied about even in the streets of Valda itself, the charlatan who had convinced his credulous race that he was a godlike being whose coming had been foretold by some obscure Silerian cult.

Josarian had started this war. He was personally responsible for the deaths of thousands of Valdani, including many civilians. He was hated and feared as much in Valda as in Santorell Square. His very name stood for all that threatened the Empire in these violent, troubled times.

The times wouldn't be so violent if the Empire would just stop attacking its neighbors.

"Peace will never be accepted by the citizens of Valdania until Josarian is dead," Kaynall had said.

"You mean peace will never be offered by the Imperial Council until they can find a way to save face." Elelar hadn't bothered to hide her sneer.

They had fought and bargained for days. *Of course* the Valdani wanted Josarian dead, Elelar had insisted; they believed the rebellion would crumble without him. Why on earth should she believe the Outlookers would withdraw from Sileria once the Alliance had helped them do what they'd never been able to do themselves—kill Josarian? Besides, what made the Valdani believe the Alliance would ever betray one of their own kind?

"I understand there is some trouble among the rebels," Kaynall had said, carefully studying the faces of his Silerian enemies. "Not everyone is as loyal to Josarian as they once were. I merely thought . . ." His shrug was too suggestive to be casual.

Kiloran betrayed Josarian to the Outlookers, and Kaynall is no fool—but how much does he know?

If Kaynall's comment had been designed to inspire panic in his Silerian companions, then it had succeeded. Nonetheless, Elelar and her associates pretended that they had managed to repair the internal strife which had led to the ambush upon Josarian, and they continued to bluff during the remaining days of negotiation.

Since Valdani promises were worth far less than the expensive parchment they were printed on, the Alliance had proceeded to develop a detailed plan for the withdrawal, each side fulfilling certain conditions to establish mutual credibility. The war would end with the final two events cited in the treaty: the Alliance would turn Josarian over to the Valdani, and the Valdani would turn Shaljir over to the rebels. Until then, if either side failed to fulfill even *one* of the conditions of the agreement, fully and completely, then the entire treaty would be declared void.

Should this occur, each side would undoubtedly try to gain the upper hand by exposing the other. The Alliance would use their contacts to reveal the Imperial Council's failed plans to their military enemies, their political opponents, and the discontented people of Valdania. The Valdani would show the rebels proof that the Alliance had intended to betray Josarian.

But he is the Firebringer.

Varian had considered her private protests and finally said, "The Firebringer's destiny is to make the foreign invaders leave Sileria. Isn't that what Josarian is doing?"

"But—"

"Elelar, you know how vague the prophecy is. It never tells us precisely *how* the Firebringer will drive out the conquerors."

In the end, she had finally agreed. Josarian would die eventually, anyhow; Kiloran would see to that. This way, Josarian would die to free Sileria. This way, he would fulfill his destiny.

SUMMONED RATHER LATE in the day to Kiloran's underwater palace at Kandahar, Najdan crossed his fists in front of his chest and bowed his head as he confronted his master. He was surprised to see Searlon here. Although Searlon was Kiloran's most trusted and valuable assassin, he was seldom at Kandahar; he was too useful in too many other capacities.

Searlon was younger than Najdan and had entered the Society at a later age, but he was a man of such talents that he had already exceeded Najdan in importance. Najdan didn't mind; he himself had come awfully far in life for a hungry, illiterate, fatherless *shallah* boy. Searlon had been born to a wealthy merchant family in Shaljir; however, he had eventually followed in the footsteps of his mother's assassin brother. Yes, Searlon had started life from a better position than Najdan, and had already achieved greater heights at a younger age. However, Searlon had worked hard for his rewards, earning them, and

Najdan begrudged nothing to a man who could honestly claim that.

They had known each other for more than ten years and had worked together on many occasions. The two assassins greeted each other now with respect.

"The Valdani," Kiloran announced to Najdan, "are about to give up Commander Koroll to a rebel ambush."

Najdan didn't bother to conceal his astonishment. He could tell that Searlon already knew about this—had perhaps even brought the news to Kandahar himself.

"Why, *siran?*" Najdan asked.

"In a recent meeting, the Imperial Advisor made a secret treaty with the Alliance," Kiloran said, his voice rich with energy for the first time since Najdan had returned to Kandahar. "Not the rebels. *Just* the Alliance."

Najdan glanced at Searlon. "You were there?"

"Not exactly. But I know what was discussed. Who said what. What threats and promises were made."

"Presumably Koroll was not there," Najdan said dryly, wondering whether it was a Valdan or a Silerian who was sharing such volatile secrets with Searlon. *Both probably.* Searlon was not a man to be underestimated.

"Ah, the Valdani choose their men poorly," Kiloran said with contempt, "and then fail to rule them."

The same could never be said of Najdan's master. A hunted and outlawed sorcerer did not control an army of ambitious assassins, an entire territory of Sileria, and the Honored Society itself without good judgment and shrewd tactics. Nor, Najdan acknowledged, did he do so without rewarding his men for their loyalty. Though devastated by Srijan's death, Kiloran had nonetheless greeted Najdan cordially upon his return to Kandahar and rewarded him generously for deserting Mirabar to return loyally to his master's side.

"The commander has fallen into disfavor with his masters," Searlon said. He explained that the secret treaty included a series of exchanges of hostages, one of whom was to be Koroll—a man whom all Silerians, whatever their loyalties, had grown to hate more than any other Valdan. "Commander Cyrill will request a meeting with him halfway between Cavasar and Shaljir."

"That's far from rebel territory," Najdan pointed out.

"A handpicked man of the Advisor's will assist a small rebel party in entering and leaving Valdani territory unmolested."

"Ah." Najdan met Searlon's gaze. Thinking of the stories surrounding the ambush on Josarian, he said, more coldly than he had meant to, "And that *can* be done, can't it?"

Searlon merely smiled, the scar on his cheek flowing into a long and incongruous dimple.

Resisting the insolent urge to question his master about his quarrel with the Firebringer, Najdan asked, "And what do the Valdani get out of such an exchange?"

"The former Commander of Liron, who is apparently the cousin of an Imperial Councilor, and is still being held hostage somewhere near Liron," Searlon said. "The Valdani want him back, and the Alliance can arrange it."

"Koroll's capture . . . a secret treaty . . ." Najdan nodded slowly. "The war is ending, isn't it?"

"The war against the Valdani, yes." Kiloran's cold, hard gaze held his. "The . . . disagreements among our own kind are now our primary concern."

After all these years, Najdan was still riveted by that gaze, awed by the shrewd and dispassionate genius behind it. "Yes, *siran.*"

"Fortunately," Searlon said, "it looks as if the Valdani and the Alliance are going to give us all the assistance we need."

TANSEN HAD SUSPECTED a trap from the very beginning, so he had insisted that Josarian have no part of the scheme proposed by Elelar. Somehow the Alliance had found an ally who was in a position to betray Koroll and arrange an ambush somewhere on the road between Shaljir and Cavasar. No matter how many times Tan questioned

Elelar or how many details she provided, something about the plan bothered him.

Politics had always bewildered him. Evidently Koroll had become such an embarrassment to his masters that they felt they'd look better if he died in combat in Sileria, rather than being transported back to Valda to face charges and execution. The Imperial Council, after all, had left a corrupt and incompetent commander in charge here through sheer ignorance and negligence, Elelar insisted. Now they were eager to conceal from their people—and especially from their political opponents—how much their own carelessness had contributed to the loss of Sileria.

"They admit they're going to lose?" Tansen had asked.

"Well, only one or two of them. And only in secret," was Elelar's response.

She made the plan sound logical and convincing. She also made it sound too easy, and *that* was what bothered him. Travelling deep into Valdani territory to ambush the one man who should be better protected than any other Valdan in Sileria except the new Imperial Advisor . . . Well, it should *not* be easy.

Yet, incredibly, it *was*. Everything went perfectly, exactly as Elelar had planned, without any of the contingencies, disasters, or betrayals Tansen himself had counted on and planned for. Disguised as Outlookers escorting rebel prisoners to a coastal fortress, Tansen's party of six men had been met by a quiet, cold-eyed Outlooker at the edge of rebel territory. He guided them safely to the site of the proposed ambush, travelling by night, hiding by day, asking no questions.

When they finally spotted Koroll, he was travelling with an escort of twenty men. Exactly as Elelar had predicted, at a prearranged signal from Tansen's Outlooker guide, sixteen of Koroll's riders simply turned around and galloped away, heading back to Shaljir and abandoning their commander to his fate. Even Jalan, confronting the newborn Firebringer at Darshon, hadn't looked as stunned as Koroll did now.

The four men who remained with him had been hand-picked by Koroll himself long ago, and so they had not been included in the plan devised by someone senior to Koroll, someone able to order sixteen Outlookers to abandon their commanding officer to certain death. The Imperial Advisor, perhaps? Someone on the Council?

And they say that we *are a treacherous people.*

The Advisor's man stayed hidden and merely watched while the rebels attacked the remaining four Outlookers guarding Koroll. The battle was brief and deadly; four men died for their loyalty to a doomed man.

Alive, alone, abandoned, and disarmed, Koroll raged furiously, hurling threats and insults at the "Outlookers" confronting him—until he saw Tansen. His eyes flew wide open with shock and he sought air in a long, noisy, horrible gasp.

"Tr . . . *trap,*" he heaved at last.

"Yes, Commander." Having posed as a rebel prisoner during the journey, rather than as an Outlooker, Tansen was wearing his own clothes. Despite the changes in his appearance since their encounter at Cavasar, he saw recognition flash in Koroll's eyes. Of course, a man who carried two Kintish swords was hard to forget in Sileria. He sheathed them now and said, "Outlookers ambushed Josarian disguised as Silerians, so *we* . . ." He shrugged. "As you see."

Koroll gazed at the mounted gray-clad men around him with glazed eyes. *"Rebels."* Making an obvious attempt to pull his wits together, he looked down the road in the direction his escort had disappeared. "And them?"

"Genuine Outlookers," Tansen said dryly. "The Emperor's finest."

Moving slowly, Koroll turned back to him. He looked around, as if reconstructing the shocking events of the past few minutes. Finally he said, "I've been . . . *betrayed.*"

"Yes."

Koroll frowned. "Did you bribe my men?"

Tansen grinned. "You flatter us, Commander. We don't have *that* much money."

"*Kaynall.*" Koroll's face crumbled with sorrow for a moment, then turned red with fury. Clenching his fists, he snarled, "The Council! Those fatherless goat-molesters! I *told* them I needed more men, more money! I *told* them I couldn't hold this godsforsaken land for them with nothing but prayers, threats, and luck! Daroll was a *fool*. Borell was a *coward*. And I—"

"And you, Commander," Tansen said without sympathy, "are a liar."

Koroll's eyes glittered with hatred. "A strange accusation for a Silerian to make. Your accursed race invented the practice."

"You give us too much credit," Tansen replied. "We merely perfected it."

"You did a good job in Cavasar, *shatai,* I'll grant you that."

"You saw what you wanted to see." He lifted one brow and added, "And then you tried to hide your mistake with another lie. Really, Commander," he chided, "telling people that I *stole* my own swords?"

"And will you use them to kill me now, *shatai?*"

"It would be easiest," Tansen admitted, "but Josarian wants to deal with you himself, so I must bring you back to him."

"So you serve him." Koroll sneered. "He's an illiterate peasant who'd never have gone beyond those savage mountains if not for you. And you, a *shatai,* do his bidding."

Tansen ignored the clumsy attempt to insult him. No one who knew Josarian would doubt his worthiness to command even a *shatai.* So he merely replied, "That's right."

"I don't understand you." Koroll frowned and shook his head. "Why? Tell me that. Before you deliver me to him, just tell me *why.*"

"Why *what,* Commander?"

Koroll came forward, holding his gaze. "Why did you do it? Three Into One, you're a *shatai!* You could have been anything you wanted to be, gone anywhere in the three corners of the world. A man like you . . . You could have been a potentate in the far reaches of the Kintish Kingdoms or become a personal servant of the High King. You could have made yourself a great chief in the Moorlands!" Ignoring the warning gesture made by one of the rebels, Koroll seized the front of Tansen's tunic. "Of all the things you could have done with your life, why—by all the gods above and below—did you join forces with a lone *shallah* outlaw and make war on the greatest empire in the world?"

"Because I'm a Silerian," Tansen said simply. "And a full-blooded *shallah,* by the way."

"I would have kept my promise." Koroll's hot breath fanned his face. "I'd have doubled your gold, given you more contracts, made you my right arm in Sileria."

"I didn't want to be your right ar—"

"I could have made you rich!"

"Ah, but you couldn't have made me free."

"You believe that tripe, too?" Koroll exclaimed, clinging to him. "Even you?"

"What tripe is that?" Tansen tried to shove him away.

Growing demented, Koroll clung like a leech. "The Firebringer! A mystic fireborn saviour! Freedom? *Here?*"

"All right, Commander, I think it's time—"

Tansen saw it coming too late. Realized his mistake too late. He had underestimated Koroll. He had been careless and arrogant with a prisoner. The rebels hadn't searched Koroll for concealed weapons, assuming the High Commander wouldn't carry any while riding under armed escort well within his own territory. *Mistake.* A cry of agony escaped Tan's lips as the wavy-edged blade of a *shir* slipped through his ribs seeking his heart.

Cold. Bitter cold. A poisonous cold that burned worse than the Fires of Dar.

"Tan!" He heard the horrified shout of one of his men.

Koroll's arm was around his neck. The commander held Tansen's sagging body between himself and the rebels. The deadly chill of the *shir* against his throat made Tan's eyes water. The pain of his wound made him dizzy and sick. Blood coursed down his side, soaking his tunic.

"All of you! Dismount now!" Koroll shouted.

"Kill him!" Tansen ordered.

"Quiet!" Koroll dug the *shir* into his flesh.

"Tansen!"

"Kill him!" Tan repeated.

"If you even move, he dies!" Koroll warned.

The wound was bad. He could tell. Very bad. He might well die even without getting his throat cut. He would certainly pass out in another moment.

A shir . . . Who did he kill to get a shir?

"Off your horses! Move over there. Now!" Koroll shouted. It was a tone that had commanded thousands of Outlookers. It was having its intended effect on rebels who were stunned by the sudden destruction of someone they had always considered invincible.

Ah, but every man can be killed. Every man.

"That's right," he heard Koroll say to the rebels. "Just do as you're told."

"Kill him . . ." Tansen's tongue felt thick. His voice sounded weak.

Armian . . . I'm coming. You'll have your vengeance at last.

His mind was wandering. He was weakening.

Focus on the task at hand.

He had just one chance. He might as well take it, since death was otherwise certain instead of just probable.

He gathered what was left of his strength and moved suddenly, throwing Koroll off balance just enough to enable Tan to slip his arm between the *shir* and his neck. Koroll recovered quickly and attempted to slit his throat; he merely made a painful cut on Tansen's forearm now, and *shatai* were trained to ignore such things.

Tansen shoved at Koroll with one arm, positioning a

foot to make him stumble. He simultaneously used his
other arm to unsheathe a sword and sweep it across Koroll's belly, all in one move. The Outlooker doubled over,
and Tansen brought the blade down on his neck, killing
him instantly.

He was not a *shatai* for nothing.

You should have known better, Commander.

Agony washed through him as he stared at the corpse
of his enemy. He was breathing much too hard for so brief
an encounter. He felt hot and cold at once. There was a
lot of blood—Koroll's or his? He didn't know.

He didn't realize he had fallen to his knees until he felt
two men trying to help him up. He tried to rise, but his
legs buckled.

A Valdan with a shir. What next?

The sky looked . . . very blue today. There would be no
rain for a while now. Dust choked him, and the ground
felt hard beneath his head.

"Tansen . . ." The voice was far away. "Can you hear
me?"

It was dark suddenly. Pitch black. A dark-moon night?
He was dizzy. And *tired*. So very tired . . .

"Nev . . . N . . ."

"What, Tansen?"

Koroll should never have tried to get the best of him.
Koroll, of all people! He had known what a *shatai* was,
after all.

And how Josarian would laugh. The great warrior who
was always correcting Josarian's form and criticizing his
technique had been slaughtered by an aging Valdani prisoner in a moment of carelessness.

Ah, how Josarian would weep . . . He was sentimental
sometimes, Josarian was.

I am prepared to die today. Are you?

39

HE IS A blade, this man.

At the moment, though, a very dull and worn one, indeed. Dissatisfied with the clumsy Sister who had been attending Tansen upon her arrival, Mirabar had sent for Basimar. The woman could be irritatingly foolish at times, but Mirabar had seen enough of her healing skills to have faith in her ability to keep Tansen alive and make him whole again. However, now that he was getting better and she was less worried about him, Mira almost regretted the decision, for Basimar kept her busy with the most menial tasks she had performed since her early days among the Guardians.

Until Basimar's arrival, Mirabar's primary role here had been to supervise the previous Sister (Lann's assertion that she had "terrorized" the woman was untrue, unfair, and outrageous) and offer prayers to Dar for Tan's recovery. Now Basimar had her washing and rolling bandages, preparing broth, emptying a wooden bucket that served as Tansen's chamber pot, and changing the linen on Tansen's pallet with monotonous regularity—a chore he certainly didn't make any easier with his bad temper and dark scowls.

"I am a Guardian of the Otherworld," Mirabar said aloud, speaking to the savage wilderness of the mountains looming in the distance. "I have better things to do with my time than boil, hang, dry, and roll rags for some warrior's wounds."

She looked hastily over her shoulder, afraid she might have spoken loud enough for Basimar to hear her. Fortunately, no critical comments emerged from the Shrine of the Three where Tansen lay recovering under the Sister's strict supervision.

It was a relief to everyone to know that Commander Koroll was dead, but the price of that monster's defeat had seemed too high during those first few days that Tansen lay hovering between life and death. A *shir* wounded worse and killed faster than other blades. Even if the victim survived, a *shir* wound was more disabling than an ordinary wound and took longer to heal. Although the rebels had had to leave Koroll's *shir* where it fell, one of them was able to identify it as Baran's distinctive workmanship. The commander had undoubtedly slain a rebel to get it. With all of the battles and chaos of the past year, the waterlords were growing increasingly nervous about how many *shir* were lost and unaccounted for these days. Now Mirabar saw what could happen when a Valdan got his hands on one, a Valdan who knew about Silerian water magic. It was lucky that the wound hadn't killed Tansen, and a virtual miracle that the journey back into rebel territory hadn't finished him off.

He hangs onto life, that one; even when this world uses all its might to push him into the Other one.

The rebels travelling with Tansen knew that the journey, and failure to get immediate help for him, might well kill him; but they thought that remaining in Valdani territory was even more likely to cause his death—as well as all of theirs. They had done their best to stop the bleeding, then they strapped him to a makeshift pallet behind a horse and returned to safe territory as fast as they possibly could. Their destination was this Valdani ruin, the first landmark on this side of the invisible border between two warring peoples.

A runner had found Josarian soon afterward. With Mirabar at his side, he came immediately to his brother's sickbed, travelling all night to reach him. A Sister was already in attendance, but it had taken Mirabar less than a full day to decide to send for Basimar. Despite the many demands placed upon him these days, Josarian had refused to leave until he was certain Tansen would recover.

The *shatai* was getting better every day now—as his increasingly bad temper confirmed. A man like that did not react well to being confined to bed and ordered around by two women. Eight men, including Lann, were staying here, too, to guard Tansen. Although she would like to leave now that Tansen was better (and now that Basimar was making her do all manner of disgusting chores), Mirabar must remain, too. If Kiloran's assassins learned where Tansen was—and how weak he still was—she would be his best protection.

When he was well, Tansen would be much harder to kill than Srijan had been, and Kiloran knew it; he'd lost assassins trying to fulfill a bloodvow against Tansen before the war. How long ago that now seemed . . . The disastrous feud between Kiloran and Josarian had cost the waterlord his son, so it seemed likely that he would relish the chance to deprive Josarian of his bloodbrother if he learned that Tansen was lying wounded and helpless in a poorly protected area at the edge of rebel territory. In a few more days, when Tan was well enough to be moved, they would take him to safer ground. Some place where Kiloran couldn't reach him.

Must it always be this way here?

So far, the war against the Valdani continued despite the internal chaos of the rebellion. Everyone still wanted the Valdani out of Sileria, even Josarian's enemies. Consequently, everyone still fought them; there was just no more mutual cooperation between the rebellion's quarreling factions. However, assassins and *shallaheen* loyal to Kiloran had recently seized four villages in the west, slaughtered hundreds of Outlookers, and sent the survivors fleeing back to Cavasar. Rumors suggested that Kiloran would move against Cavasar itself before long. Meanwhile, Josarian expanded his territory a little farther every few days. Yes, the war against the Valdani continued.

Mirabar, like many others, was increasingly worried

about how long a divided Sileria could continue to fight Valdania. She had witnessed the miraculous events at Darshon, and she believed it was the will of the goddess that Sileria should finally be free of foreign rulers. Prophecy and visions had united to bring about these events, and surely Dar and the Otherworld were more powerful than Kiloran and the Society.

Nonetheless, destiny did not simply *happen*. It required effort, commitment, sacrifice. She wished she knew what she could do to influence events now, but the Beckoner continued to ignore her cries for guidance. Unless he relented and came to her again, it must be someone else's role to ensure victory now. But who? Josarian? Tansen?

Tansen ... She had seen his swords breaking her people's shackles in her visions, time after time. Yet it was Josarian who had become their leader, who had embraced the goddess and become the Firebringer. Once, that first night at Kandahar, she thought she knew how all the pieces fit together, what all the portents and symbols meant. Now she was confused again. Had Tansen already fulfilled his role in Sileria, or was his destiny only beginning?

Well, until I'm sure of his destiny, I suppose I'd better keep him alive.

This practical attitude enabled her to endure another morning of mind-numbing boredom as she prepared bandages and boiled unappetizing broth. She didn't even snap or snarl when Basimar reminded her that it was time to change Tansen's bedding.

He didn't snap or snarl, either, when she entered the garish shrine and announced her intentions. He looked utterly defeated, like a man who'd endured all he could.

"Please, don't," he begged. "Let's just both *tell* the Sister you did."

She regarded him with wide-eyed innocence. "You mean . . . *lie?*"

"Surely it won't be the first time, *sirana.*"

"I don't see why you're whining about it. *You* just have to lie there, while *I* do all the work."

"*I* just have to put up with you poking, prodding, and shoving me all over this lumpy pallet while I simultaneously try to preserve what precious little is left of my modesty." Basimar kept him naked beneath the sheets.

She sighed. "Shall I get Lann to help you outside for some air while—"

"No, don't," he pleaded. "If I have to listen to him tell one more story about his New Year's victories, my eyes will cross."

She laughed. "All right. I will spare you. No change of linen and no boring stories."

He stopped her when she would have left. "Don't go yet. She'll know you're lying if you try to pretend you changed the bedding in only two minutes." Using his good arm, the one which wasn't bandaged and healing from a deep *shir* cut, Tansen took Mirabar's hand and gently pulled her down to sit beside him.

"You're looking better," she commented.

He had lost the ghastly pallor of those first few delirious days when they had all been certain he would die. He needed to get back into the sun, and he looked too thin, having swallowed nothing recently besides broth and Basimar's noxious tisanes, but he was indeed starting to look more like himself again.

"You're looking better, too," he said.

"Me?"

"The first time I opened my eyes, you looked like—"

"A demon?" She wanted to say it herself rather than hear it on his lips.

He squeezed her hand, surprising her. "No, a hag."

"Oh. And here I thought you were going to say something unkind."

"There were circles under your eyes, your face was dirty, you were pale, and your hair was so tangled it looked like you hadn't combed it in days."

"I hadn't. I had more important things to do."

"Like bullying that poor Sister."

"I didn't bully . . ." She pursed her lips when he grinned

knowingly at her. "Well . . . I may have been a little sharp with her."

"Only a little," he assured her with patent insincerity.

She shrugged. "It's my duty to keep you alive."

"I see."

His voice was soft, his expression . . . soft, too. The silence lengthened as their gazes held. His eyes were liquid brown and his mood wholly unfamiliar to her. Feeling suddenly self-conscious, she lowered her eyes, remembering all the times he had avoided her flame-gold stare. She was afraid of seeing him do so again even now, when he showed no inclination to look away.

The elaborate scar on his naked chest stood out boldly, only partially covered by the strips of cloth Basimar had wrapped around him to hold the fresh bandage in place over the terrible wound in his side. Mirabar had seen that exotic Kintish symbol blazing through her visions so many times before learning what it meant, before finally seeing it carved on a man's warm, living flesh.

"Here." Tansen's voice was husky. He guided her hand to his torso, tugging a little when she resisted. "Go on," he murmured. "You can touch it if you want to."

She did want to, she realized, so she let him drag her palm over his hard chest. She shivered a little when he flattened his hand over hers, letting it rest there, light as a feather, filling her with warmth. *Heat,* actually.

She swallowed and traced the ridges of flesh on his chest, the scars he had earned with hard work and pain.

"Did it hurt much?" she asked.

"Yes," he whispered.

"The fires of initiation hurt, too," she told him.

His gaze shifted to the body hidden beneath her clothes. "Did it leave scars, too?"

"Not usually." A *lot* of heat. "Not on me."

"The scar . . . honors a *shatai.*"

She nodded. She understood. She was a Guardian, after all. "The mark of your endurance," she murmured.

"Yes." His hand started sliding up her forearm.

"Your . . . courage."

"Hmmm." His fingers slid under the loose hem of her sleeve.

"Your . . ." The heat was spreading fast now. ". . . skill?"

He inhaled, his breath light and shallow, but didn't answer her. His hand slid above her elbow, to the tender flesh which was suddenly more sensitive than she had ever realized. Exerting subtle pressure there, he started urging her closer. Their eyes locked. She suddenly wanted to weep and couldn't imagine why. He saw the sorrow in her eyes and froze. His hand slid away from her arm and rose to trace a dangling curl of lava-red hair.

"Mira . . ."

"Riders!"

They both flinched when they heard the cry outside. Mirabar practically tumbled over backwards trying to get to the door. Tansen pushed himself into a sitting position, then fell halfway back down.

"My swords," he rasped, sweat breaking out on his brow at the pain caused by his sudden movement.

She picked up the leather harness and tossed it in his general direction. Basimar burst through the elaborately painted doorway, bumping into Mirabar.

"Mirabar, the sentries have—"

"Yes, we heard. Stay with him."

She ran outside, preparing to meet their enemies. By the time she reached Lann's side, though, she could see it was a false alarm. He was grinning as he peered down into the narrow road leading to the shrine.

"Who is it?" she asked.

"Zimran." He paused and added, "And the *torena.*"

"Elelar?"

"Yes. And an escort."

"What's *she* doing here?"

Lann shrugged. "I'm sure she'll tell us."

"Oh, you're sure, are you?" Mirabar said sourly. Did

anyone ever really know what Elelar was up to?

The *torena* came bearing food, fresh bandages, almond milk, dried figs, and the best of last year's strawberry wine. A little too beautifully groomed to be convincing as a fugitive in a war-torn country, she pressed Tansen for details about the ambush in which he had nearly died. Above all, she expressed concern about his safety, insisting that he should be moved sooner than Basimar thought was reasonable.

"How long do you think you can keep his presence here a secret?" Elelar argued when Mirabar supported Basimar's position—merely because it was in opposition to Elelar's position. "How well do you think you can protect him from Kiloran here with only eight men?"

"I'm well enough to travel," Tansen asserted, eyeing all three women with an uneasy expression.

Mirabar glared at him. "So you were merely pretending when you nearly fainted a few minutes ago?"

"Is he that bad still?" Elelar asked.

"Yes," Basimar said, "and I think it's too soon to move him."

"But what if he—"

"Would you all stop talking about me as if I wasn't—"

"Isn't it rather late in life for *you* to worry about what Kiloran might do to him, *torena?*" Mirabar snapped.

Elelar treated Mirabar to a chilling stare. Tansen sighed. Basimar suggested they all discuss this later.

"No, I can't stay," Elelar said.

Tansen looked up quickly. *Too* quickly. "You can't?"

"I only came to see how you were and to—"

"Kadriah?"

They all turned at the sound of Zimran's voice when he came through the doorway. He greeted them all briefly, then relayed some information to Elelar about a horse that had gone lame, suggesting she exchange it with one of the horses here if no one was going anywhere for a few more days.

"Ah. First you urge us to leave, now you want to strand us," Mirabar said to Elelar.

"Mira." Tansen's voice held a warning note that she didn't like. He had no business trying to govern how she talked to Elelar—or anyone else.

She took a deep breath, trying to cool her temper. "If you're well enough to travel," she told him, "then we will leave at first light. Therefore," she added to Zimran, "we'll need all our horses." She loathed the creatures, but they were useful here in the lowlands. "So your lame mount will simply have to remain your problem, *torena.*"

Having concluded the conversation to her satisfaction, she turned and left the shrine.

It was a tremendous relief to her when Elelar left an hour later. Tansen was in a withdrawn mood afterward, brooding and ignoring them all.

He will never be free of her.

If it pained Mirabar to realize this, it positively tormented Basimar to know that Zimran had become completely—and exclusively—devoted to the *torena.* Mirabar found the Sister weeping in private that evening when she should have been preparing for tomorrow's journey, one which they all knew Tansen was unwise to make so soon. Feeling desolate and rejected, Basimar poured her heart out to Mirabar, telling her far more than she wanted to know about her former relationship with Josarian's cousin.

"But now he's in love with a *torena,*" Basimar sobbed. "Beautiful, elegant . . . younger than me . . ."

"She has . . ." Mirabar fumbled for words. "Men see something in her which . . . That is to say . . ." She gave up in the end and just let Basimar cry.

Darfire, sometimes she genuinely hated Elelar.

If Tansen still wanted the *torena,* then he was a fool who deserved the unhappiness she would surely cause him. And Mirabar would not demean herself by dwelling on those strange, exciting moments she had shared with him before Elelar's arrival. She would, instead, recall moments shared with the man who had never shown revulsion when looking at her, who had never backed away from her or avoided her eyes.

Cheylan's gaze made her feel appealing. His attentions made her feel appreciated. His touch was unmistakably that of a man courting a woman.

Verlon is my grandfather.

Mirabar still remembered her shock upon hearing those words.

"My mother's father," Cheylan had added.

Cheylan's aristocratic father had offered his ancient name and status to Verlon's daughter; and Verlon had offered the family a portion of his considerable wealth in exchange for the advantages of such a prestigious marriage.

Mirabar knew that such alliances were not unusual. In desperate times, an aristocratic family would do almost anything to save its estates and its prominent position. When the *toreni* couldn't find such salvation among their own kind, some turned to the Society rather than allying themselves with a Valdani family.

But for someone like Cheylan to be born to such a union! It was astonishing to learn that a waterlord's blood could run through the veins of a golden-eyed Guardian. Mirabar wouldn't have believed it had anyone other than Cheylan himself told her of his relationship to Verlon.

She had many questions, but had not been given time to ask them. Searlon had emerged from Lake Kandahar within moments of Cheylan's confession, and then Mirabar had been obliged to pay her respects to Kiloran. Cheylan, of course, had left then, heading east. And who knew when she would see him again?

Now she could only wonder in silence what sort of life his really was, and why his own grandfather had sworn a bloodvow against him.

If we both survive the war, Cheylan, she vowed, *then I will know your secrets.*

*　　*　　*

I KNOW HOW it can be done.

Elelar's heart pounded with conflicting emotions as she finished her letter to *Toren* Varian. Tansen was indeed as weak as Josarian had told Zimran. She'd had her doubts, for she knew better than to underestimate the *shatai,* despite what a *shir* could do to a man. However, a few minutes in his presence had convinced her that he had not yet travelled far enough away from death's door to return to Josarian's side any time soon. And Mirabar would not leave Tansen's side until he was well enough to defend himself against assassins. Even if the woman wanted to abandon Tan, Josarian had forbidden it, for he was worried about his bloodbrother's life should Kiloran learn of his current state of weakness.

For the first time since the Alliance had made their secret treaty with the Valdani, Josarian was not protected by either Tansen or Mirabar—his personal sword and shield. Together, they made his safety impregnable. Even singly, each was a force to be reckoned with, a defense which could not be easily breached. Besides, they were both too valuable to Sileria to be sacrificed along with Josarian.

The last of the hostage exchanges agreed upon in the secret treaty had been fulfilled by Kaynall's betrayal of Koroll. Elelar had just received word that, due to unexpectedly heavy losses in the west, the Valdani were surrendering Cavasar even sooner than planned. Unfortunately, Kiloran, rather than Josarian, would claim the city; but the *Valdani* would no longer have it, and that was what mattered most.

Nothing was left now except the final provisions of the treaty: Josarian in exchange for Shaljir. When they gave up Shaljir, the Valdani would withdraw the rest of their Outlookers from the rural fighting which was currently still going on—with devastating losses on both sides.

Josarian's life in exchange for Shaljir. In exchange for Sileria's freedom.

Dar forgive me.

Shaljir was a wealthy, well-defended, walled city protected by many thousands of Outlookers. Without the support the rebels had originally counted on from the Society, taking the city would cost thousands upon thousands of Silerian lives. The Kints and the Moorlanders were both locked in all-out war with the Empire; neither would venture far enough from their native waters to help the seaborn folk keep Valdani ships out of Shaljir's harbor. If the rebels besieged the city, then the Outlookers' supply of men, food, money, and weapons from Valda could go on for one year, two years . . . It could well last until the war on the mainland favored Valdania, thus freeing enough men for the Valdani to launch a new conquest of Sileria from their foothold in Shaljir.

Now is the time . . .

The prophecy of the Firebringer, Mirabar's visions from the Otherworld, and common sense all told Elelar that they must drive the Valdani completely out of Sileria, and they must do it *now.*

Josarian's life in exchange for Shaljir.

There would never be a better time. The Valdani were ready, and Tansen and Mirabar were not at Josarian's side.

I know how it can be done.

Zimran's voice interrupted her thoughts. *"Kadriah?"*

She looked up from the letter she was writing. She smiled—warm, welcoming, sweet. She had prepared the way with this man, but she had never in her life needed to be more persuasive than she must be now. He wanted her complete devotion more than anything else in the world, and she must convince him that only "Josarian's war," as he called it, prevented that. She hadn't bothered to tell him that her legal husband was not only still alive but, according to a recent letter from Shaljir, had also been released from prison. Ronall had reportedly entered the first tavern he could find and immediately proceeded to drink himself unconscious. Some things never changed.

There was too much at stake now to waste any more thoughts on her contemptible husband. Everything rested on Zimran. She rose to greet him as he entered the room.

"Yes, my love?" she murmured.

He eased his arms around her and buried his nose in her hair. "Hmmm. I thought I'd find you in here, writing more of your letters."

She nuzzled him. "If only the war could end soon," she purred. "Then I could give you all the time you deserve. All the time I long to give you."

"Why must we wait until the end of the war? Why not—"

"We've discussed this before. I'm a *torena*. I cannot turn my back on my duties."

"I know . . ." He sighed. He didn't like the argument, but he had enough awe for her traditional status to let the excuse stand.

"But the war *could* end soon . . ."

He shook his head. "Don't count on it, *kadriah*. The Valdani can hold on to Shaljir forever, if they want to."

"*Toren* Varian tells me they have repeatedly offered to give it up . . . on one condition."

"What's that?" he asked without noticeable interest.

"Oh, it's not something we could . . ." She bit her lip and turned away. "Never mind. I shouldn't have mentioned it."

Now he was interested. He didn't like her to have secrets from him. "No, tell me."

"It would only upset you."

"Elelar." He took her shoulders and forced her to face him. "What is it?"

"The Valdani will give up Shaljir in exchange for Josarian."

"Hah!" He lost interest again. "They must take Varian for a fool, if they're telling him that."

"You're right, of course," she said. "They can't be sincere."

"They just want Josarian."

She sighed. "Yes. They think his death would end the war."

"Hmph."

She let the idea sit with him for a few moments. She could never *ask* him to do it. She must guide him to the idea, let him believe it was his own.

When he spoke again, it was what she had hoped to hear. "Kiloran will kill him soon enough, anyhow. Even if what they say happened at Darshon is really true, no one is more powerful than Kiloran. No one."

"No . . . And it's too bad really."

"After the danger Josarian put you in at Golnar, you can say that?"

She smiled at him sweetly, sadly. "I just mean that if he's going to die anyhow . . ."

He stared at her. "You really think the Valdani would give up Shaljir in exchange for Josarian?"

She knew he didn't care what happened in Shaljir. She concentrated on what he did care about. "I don't know. I only know that the Valdani won't care if one Silerian— even Kiloran—has another killed in a personal bloodvow. In fact, it might encourage the Outlookers to strike while we're weak with internal feuding, renewing the fighting and dragging the war on forever. But if the Valdani take Josarian . . ." She ran her fingers along the seam of the costly tunic she had recently given him. He valued such fine things, especially when he took them as a sign of her devotion.

"Yes?" he prodded, listening intently now.

"They say they'd have something to bring home to Valda. Something to make up for losing Sileria in the end."

He frowned, his eyes dark with thought. "Do you really think that would end the war?"

"How could the war possibly go on then?" she asked artlessly. "Josarian is the war." It was no longer true, but she knew that Zimran believed it.

She knew she had him when he let go of her, almost forgetting about her while he wandered around the room, absently touching things as he mulled this over. "I don't think he would give himself up, Elelar."

"You're right, of course." She knew how he liked hearing those words. "It would have to happen . . ." She paused just long enough to set his mind on the problem, then shrugged and said uncertainly, ". . . in battle, I suppose."

"In battle . . ." He mused. "Or an ambush. A better one than they tried at the Sanctuary."

"Outlookers are so clumsy," she murmured.

"Such fools."

"And Searlon underestimated Josarian."

"Yes . . ."

"He wasn't clever enough to take him," she added.

"He didn't . . . know him well enough."

"And now Josarian's even more careful," Elelar said. "I don't think the Valdani will get another chance." She measured her words carefully. "Whether he stays alive or Kiloran kills him, the war will go on for . . ." She sighed sadly. "Years, I sometimes think."

"And us?" he asked, his dark gaze resting on her with almost brokenhearted longing.

"We have our duty, and it comes first, doesn't it?"

"Until the war ends . . ."

"It almost makes one wish the Valdani *could* take him now, doesn't it?"

He stared at her for a long, desperate moment. Finally he said, "Maybe they can, *kadriah.*"

IT WAS A glorious spring night in Cavasar. Scented blossoms perfumed the air, soft breezes swept in from the ocean, and water poured freely from every fountain in the city. Two full moons rose above Cavasar, casting their luminous blessing over the celebrations in the city's main square. The rebels had burned their honored dead days ago, after watching the last overloaded Valdani ship pull out of port. Now there was only joy in Sileria's westernmost city. Now fire-eaters, jugglers, acrobats, musicians, singers, dancers, and poets entertained the crowds day and night, celebrating victory, the end of martial law and curfews, the end of Valdani rule in Cavasar.

Right now, no one cared that it was Kiloran rather than

Josarian who had liberated them in the end. For now, people here cared only that no Outlookers would ever again patrol the streets of their city or carry them off to the mines. This evening, a newly freed people celebrated joyfully and turned their backs upon a thousand years of suffering and humiliation. Tonight in Cavasar, no one thought about what tomorrow might bring.

No one, that is, except Najdan the assassin. When the city fell, he had been part of Kiloran's personal escort here. Now he attended his master, who had set up temporary residence in the ancient fortress overlooking the city.

While Cavasar celebrated its freedom, Kiloran made plans. The Society had controlled many mountain villages and routinely extorted tribute from every major city in Sileria. Kiloran, however, was the first waterlord to ever achieve uncontested control of an entire city. The people of Cavasar did not yet know it, but they had a new master now, one that loved them no more than the Emperor had.

For now, Kiloran would let the people of Cavasar celebrate, enjoy their revels, and repeat his name again and again in their prayers, praises, and victory songs. For now, he would play the benevolent ruler and rebel liberator. Tonight, he would let them be free.

Soon, however, it would be time to urge the people to return to the business of living and the task of winning the rest of the war. Wars were expensive, Kiloran reminded his assassins, and therefore required tribute from the people, just as water did. The assassins would be expected to collect such tribute from Cavasar—and more efficiently than the Outlookers had. Power was a valuable commodity, Kiloran said, one he had no intention of sharing here in Cavasar with *toreni,* merchants, Guardians, or anyone else. Certain temporary concessions would be made to ease the way into a new age, to minimize protests from other factions in Cavasar, but the assassins must always remember that they ruled the city now.

Naturally, Kiloran didn't even need to add that he ruled them.

After gaining full and unchallenged control of Cavasar, Kiloran was most interested in developing a plan to gain control of the territory around distant Alizar. Yes, he had control of the mines themselves, which were still flooded with water cold enough to maim anyone who touched it. However, maintaining such control was a drain on Kiloran's energy, and the mines were a valuable resource going to waste. He wanted to get them up and operating again, enriching him as they had enriched the Emperor. This could not be accomplished while Josarian controlled all the territory around them.

This, however, was not Najdan's concern, Kiloran had informed him only today. Nor was Josarian his concern, for—incredible as it seemed—Kiloran had arranged for the Alliance to betray Josarian to the Valdani. The scheme would end Sileria's war and Kiloran's personal feud all in one fatal blow, and Josarian's followers would never even blame Kiloran for it. Indeed, without Josarian to lead them, many of them might even finally recognize the true master of their nation and come to Kiloran as wayward children eventually came back to their father.

Najdan's master had thought of everything.

Kiloran also thought about the troubles that would continue to plague him after Josarian's death. There was the *shatai,* for one. Tansen was hard to kill, as previous experience had proved, but no man was invincible, and that assassin-killing, father-slaying, son-murdering *shallah* upstart would someday be made to pay for everything he had ever done.

However, Kiloran said, this was not Najdan's concern either. The waterlord had a more difficult assignment for Najdan than assassinating Tansen. Najdan was one of his most skilled, trusted, and experienced servants. The assassin had proven his loyalty many times over the years—and been generously rewarded on every occasion. Now Najdan's abilities would be tested to their limit in an assignment for which Kiloran felt he was uniquely qualified.

"You know more about her than anyone except the other

Guardians," Kiloran said, giving Najdan his final instructions that night, sitting in the very chamber from which Cyrill the Valdan had once commanded Cavasar and its district. "You know her strengths and weaknesses, her habits and fears. You know where her ignorance sleeps and where her heart is hidden."

"Yes, *siran*," Najdan said.

Kill Mirabar.

"If you succeed," Kiloran promised, "I will reward you beyond your dreams."

"She is very powerful, *siran*. In case I do not survive . . ."

"Yes?"

"May I pay one last visit to Kandahar? I want to ensure that my mistress is prepared for what may happen to me."

Kiloran smiled, his cold eyes glinting with satisfaction. "Yes, of course." Fatherly, benevolent, a master who understood his men and their needs. "Take as much time as you need."

"Thank you, *siran*. I will leave first thing in the morning."

40

"EMELEN SENT A runner from Liron to Dalishar," Josarian told Tansen as they sat together in Basimar's Sanctuary.

Studying Josarian's expression, Tan asked, "Is the news bad?"

"It could be better," Josarian admitted.

Verlon, the most powerful waterlord in the east, had learned that Kiloran now had control of Cavasar.

"So now he's decided he'd like control of Liron," Tan guessed.

Josarian nodded. "Emelen says Cheylan is talking to him, but . . ."

"Verlon and Cheylan," Tansen mused. "There's something between those two."

"I know there was a bloodvow," Josarian said, "but no one seems to know what it was about."

"Imagine that."

The two men smiled wryly at each other.

"You're looking much better," Josarian commented after a moment.

"Well enough to go with you today," Tansen insisted. Again.

He was overruled. Again. "Not yet. When you're fully healed. When Basimar says it's all right."

Tansen sighed. The trip from the lowlands to the Sanctuary had taken more out of him than he liked to admit, though Mirabar's claim that it had nearly killed him was an exaggeration. He was training every day again, reacquainting his sore muscles and underfed body with the work of a *shatai*. He was getting better, but, no, he wasn't up to his usual speed and strength. His exercises exhausted him, and his wound continued to pain him.

Nonetheless, he was more useful to Josarian at half-capacity than most men were at full capacity, and he knew it. It frustrated him to be hidden away in Sanctuary, coddled by a Sister, protected by eight men and a Guardian, and left behind by his bloodbrother. Josarian was leaving today for Zilar, which was now under rebel control. He hoped to use the town as a base from which to plan the attack on Shaljir—the undoubtedly long and costly battle which would finally be the end of the Valdani in Sileria.

Tansen said, "I do not want to be left out of—"

"You won't be, but you're far too important to risk—"

"So are you," he interrupted. "Yet you're going off to Zilar without me. Kiloran will know you're there. He'll—"

"Tansen," Josarian chided, "I'll have thousands of rebels all around me."

"Any one of whom could be a traitor."

"I've got fifty loyal *zanareen* waiting outside for me even as we speak." Josarian paused and added morosely, "In fact, ever since the ambush at the Sanctuary, they're reluctant to leave me alone even long enough to relieve myself."

"Ten *zanareen* at once will be no use against Searlon, if he comes after you himself," Tansen pointed out. "They're not fighters."

"I also have Zimran."

"Zimran." Tansen didn't even try to hide his contempt.

"He's a good fighter."

"His heart is not with us, even now."

"You're wrong. He's changed since you were wounded."

Tansen had seen Zimran briefly upon Josarian's arrival here, and, unfortunately, he had noticed no astounding difference in Josarian's cousin. "He hasn't changed that much."

"He has scarcely left my side since the last dark-moon. I'm telling you—"

Tan shook his head. "You are blind to his faults."

"I'm not even blind to *your* faults." Josarian paused and added more gently, "Or to the fact that Zimran has something that you have always wanted."

Tan felt his face burn with embarrassment, but he kept his voice even. "She has nothing to do with—"

"Doesn't she?"

"I don't trust him."

"I do."

"Josarian . . ."

"He's my cousin, Tan."

"Let me come with you."

"No."

"But I—"

"You're not ready and you know it." Josarian shook his

head. "Even you can't recover that fast from a *shir* wound."

"I'll keep recovering at Zilar."

"The trip there will set you back, as the trip here did."

"Please—"

"No." It was the tone with which Josarian commanded thousands. "I forbid it. Unless you now mean to challenge my authority?"

Tansen looked away. He sighed—then winced at the pain it caused in his side.

Knowing he had won, Josarian's voice softened. "When you're better, I'll be waiting for you at Zilar."

He nodded. "All right . . . *siran.*" He glanced up through his lashes.

Josarian laughed. "Don't *you* start."

"Ah, are the *zanareen* making your life a misery?"

"Sometimes I think that if even one more man grovels before me or asks for my blessing or . . ." He sighed. "Ah, well. Didn't I once tell you I much preferred being a mere outlaw?"

"Too late now," Tan said. "That's what you get for jumping into a volcano."

Josarian grinned at him. "You have a rare gift for sacrilege."

"So Mira says."

Mirabar had left them alone earlier upon being asked by one of the *zanareen* to do a Calling. Zimran didn't disturb the two men either, since he had no more desire for Tansen's company than Tan had for his. Tansen wondered idly if Zimran was off reliving old times with Basimar, or if he was still being uncharacteristically faithful to Elelar.

Tansen also continued to wonder why Elelar had taken Zimran as a lover. Although he thought it likely that she had an ulterior motive, for he'd never known her not to have one, he was also aware that he was incapable of pondering the situation objectively, even when he tried to discern how the *torena*'s actions might affect Josarian and the rebellion. His thoughts were swayed by his *wanting* Elelar to have secret reasons for sleeping with Zimran, because he really couldn't stand the alternative—that she had simply preferred Zimran to him.

Darfire, his side hurt, and he felt light-headed from staying up all day due to Josarian's welcome presence here.

Yes, he was jealous. He was also tired and cranky. Maybe Josarian was right. Maybe Zimran had changed. Elelar had changed Tansen irrevocably, after all, all those years ago. She had swayed the bloodborn beliefs of an ignorant *shallah* boy, ultimately influencing him—however she denied it—to commit an unspeakable act of violence and betrayal against his own bloodfather, against possibly the most famous assassin ever born into the Society, against a man Tan had even believed to be the Firebringer.

If she could change me that much, who's to say she hasn't really made a rebel and a patriot out of that malicious, self-interested, woman-chasing fool?

No one in the world was better-equipped than Elelar to convince a man like Zimran of virtually anything, and despite her many faults, she was utterly and unconditionally devoted to the rebellion and the future of Sileria. Tansen supposed some of her commitment could have finally rubbed off on Zimran—especially considering how that woman could nag when she put her mind to it.

Tansen almost laughed as he realized that perhaps Zimran had returned to his cousin's side after all this time merely to get away from Elelar and her political lectures.

He still wished he were going with Josarian now, though. With both the Society and the Valdani after him, Josarian's life was in constant danger, and Tansen's worry wouldn't ease until he was once again at his brother's side day and night, protecting him. He knew Mirabar wouldn't go, either, for Josarian had made his position clear. He believed that Tansen was currently more vulnerable than he was. Kiloran had found a way to violate Sanctuary once before—by using Outlookers—so there was no reason to

assume that Tansen was safe from attack just because he
was in Sanctuary now.

"When you are well enough to protect eight men and
two women, instead of their protecting you," Josarian said
as he prepared to depart, "then you will be well enough to
join me in Zilar."

Josarian's farewell embrace was tentative and gentle, out
of consideration for Tansen's wound. As he watched his
brother leave, Tan reflected wryly that he'd finally grown
accustomed enough to Josarian's typically exuberant bear
hug to miss it on this occasion.

MIRABAR HAD LEFT Tansen alone after Josarian's departure yesterday, knowing that he would brood about being left behind. He was healing, but not as fast as he
wanted to, and he was full of impatience. Moreover, seeing
Zimran replace him at Josarian's side had clearly rankled
him, though he tried not to let it show. Zimran, who already had Elelar, after all . . .

Whatever had been on the warrior's mind that day in
the Shrine of the Three, when he had touched Mirabar in
a way she had never expected, he seemed to have forgotten
it since then. And considering the way he had fallen right
back under the *torena*'s spell, Mirabar had no intention of
reminding him of those moments.

Though Mirabar was vaguely aware that those two had
quarreled often in recent months, Elelar had practically
oozed charm that day at the shrine, as if reconsidering her
choices in light of Tansen's struggle against death. The
torena had played Tansen like a harp that day. And he—
a man unlike other men, a warrior of great skill and terrible
courage, a rebel whose coming had been foretold by
gods—had been helpless in the face Elelar's feminine sorcery, as the long-absent Beckoner had once warned
Mirabar he would be.

Now, as she wandered the mountainside gathering the
roots and herbs Basimar needed, Mirabar wondered what
Elelar was up to. Why hadn't she come again? The *torena*

must know where they were. Did she want Tansen for herself, now that she was free to choose? If so, why hadn't she given up Zimran? Or did she merely want Tansen to want her? And if so, then why? Did it feed her pride to know that a man she had once betrayed to Kiloran still longed for her after all these years? Had she sensed him slipping away and visited him at the shrine merely to strengthen her power over him?

It would almost be a relief to think so, but however much Mirabar disliked the *torena,* she knew she was not a silly woman. Elelar did nothing without a purpose, and while she might idly charm a man just to satisfy her vanity, she wouldn't truly exert herself without a reason. Why had she come all the way to that Shrine of the Three, soft-eyed, sweet-tongued, and bearing gifts?

Mirabar was still lost in such thoughts when a voice she had never again expected to hear called out, *"Sirana!"*

Najdan!

She turned to face the direction from which his voice had come. He wasn't close yet. She would have heard him moving through the brush if he were. Najdan was soft-footed, but Mirabar still had the senses of an animal.

She was on the verge of calling out his name when a chilling thought occurred to her. Since the beginning of Kiloran's feud with Josarian, assassins had returned to the old business of slaughtering Guardians; and any Guardian who hesitated to fight a former ally died instantly. In recent weeks, Mirabar had heard too many such stories being repeated in Sanctuary.

If Kiloran meant to send anyone after her, then Najdan, whom she had trusted for so long, would be his best choice. The assassin's shouting for her might seem to preclude a sneak attack, but Najdan knew how difficult it was to creep up on her. Tansen had managed it once, right here, but she had been weeping like a child and lost in misery at the time. She was not usually so easy to approach, and Najdan knew it. He'd be more likely to try to ease her suspicions first, and then attack when her guard was down.

"Sirana!"

He must know she was here because of his *shir;* it often quivered in response to her presence. His shouting would alert the sentries guarding Tansen. Should she wait for them? No, she decided; if Najdan had come to kill her, he wouldn't hesitate to kill anyone who tried to protect her. She didn't want to cause other men's deaths by avoiding the inevitable. She would face Najdan at once.

Najdan was one of Kiloran's finest assassins. Mirabar had spent too much time with him, seen too much, to doubt his skill. However, she had beaten Najdan once before, at Dalishar, and she could do it again. He had lost his fear of her after Kandahar, but she could rekindle it if she had to.

She wanted to weep, though. Najdan. He had been her shadow, her right arm, her trusted friend. She had missed him since he'd left her on Mount Niran, but she had known since that very day that it might well come to this. Assassins could not afford to have conflicting loyalties. When Najdan returned to Kiloran's side, he also returned to the way of life he had chosen many years ago, long before the war. He would do as he was bid, kill whomever Kiloran wanted killed, regardless of his personal feelings. She believed he would be sorry to kill her, but she knew he would not let his sorrow interfere with his duty.

Must it always be this way?

"Najdan!" she called, letting the sound of her voice lead him to her. "Over here!"

She sat down on a fallen tree trunk and blew a circle of fire into life as she formed her plan. She had never killed a man, and she didn't want to start with this one. Heart crying out in protest, she nonetheless prepared to slay her former friend.

She was surprised to hear *two* people approaching her moments later—and a donkey. She frowned. What was Najdan up to?

Her doubts and fears fled a moment later to be replaced by bemusement when he appeared in the midst of the forest. She had never seen a man who looked less ready for deadly combat. He was carrying a large satchel, leading a burdened donkey, and followed by a woman. The woman was attractive, expensively dressed, and about Basimar's age.

The woman's dark gaze flashed first to Mirabar, whose appearance often startled even those who had been warned about her, and then to the magical fire blazing away. She gasped in fear and moved quickly to Najdan's side. He put his arm around her and murmured something soothing. Mirabar heard him call her *"kadriah."*

His mistress.

Najdan wouldn't bring his mistress—or all that baggage—along with him if he had come here to assassinate Mirabar. In fact, she suddenly realized that he was unlikely to have known to seek her here. They were keeping Tansen's whereabouts, and consequently hers, very secret to protect him from Kiloran.

The explanation seemed pretty obvious: He was bringing his mistress to safety. He knew and trusted Basimar, hence he had chosen her Sanctuary. However, Kandahar was not threatened by the rebels, and Mirabar knew that Najdan had a comfortable house there. Why would he bring his mistress here, to a Sanctuary in the heart of Josarian's territory, to the protection of a Sister completely loyal to Josarian?

"Najdan . . ." Mirabar rose to her feet, her fears forgotten.

"Sirana." He crossed his fists and bowed his head. "I thought you would still be at Niran."

"No."

"I'm glad. I must be the one to tell you."

"What?"

"Well, first of all . . ." He met her gaze. "I have been sent to kill you."

"And?"

She thought he would say that he couldn't do it, that he had changed, that he had lied to Kiloran so he could get his mistress safely away from the vengeful wrath of the master he was about to betray. She could see in one glance at his face that it was all true. Yet he said none of that.

Instead, he stunned her by saying, "And Josarian is about to be betrayed."

TANSEN'S SIDE FELT like it was on fire as he hiked to the nearest place that had horses. He felt like he was going to be sick as he pressed the pace, his heart racing with fear. His wound felt like it was splitting open again, as it had during the journey to Sanctuary. He didn't care. It didn't matter if he bled to death, so long as he was able to warn Josarian in time.

Najdan had entered the Sanctuary with Mirabar, and after a chaotic moment when Tansen had gone after him with his swords and Mirabar had jumped between them, the assassin had betrayed his master and told them both what he knew.

A secret treaty between the Valdani and the Alliance. A series of hostage exchanges—*including Koroll.* No wonder the ambush had been so easy! A bargain to end the war in Sileria so that the Valdani could more efficiently pursue their wars on the mainland.

The surrender of Shaljir in exchange for Josarian's life.

They left Najdan's mistress behind with Basimar, with instructions that they were to go to a Sanctuary closer to Dalishar, just in case. Then, ignoring Basimar's protests about his condition, Tansen armed himself and took Najdan, Mirabar, and his eight *shallah* guards down the mountain with him. They would find horses and, travelling along main roads, they would catch up with Josarian.

"But how does Searlon know all the details of this treaty?" Mirabar asked.

"I wasn't sure at first," Najdan said, "but my mast . . . Kiloran told me more after we took Cavasar. Somehow, he is behind the treaty. He works through Searlon, but the treaty is his creature, though those who signed it may not even know that."

"If the plan succeeds, Kiloran gains everything," Mirabar said pensively, "doesn't he?"

"And loses nothing," Najdan added. "Even if it fails."

"They'll do it now," Tansen said, fighting weakness as they hiked. "While they know that Mirabar and I aren't with Josarian."

"The Valdani? But they'd have to find him first," Mirabar pointed out. "He's been very secretive about his movements since the feud with Kiloran began."

"He'll be betrayed by one of his own," Najdan said. "Who in the Alliance would know where he is now?"

Mirabar gasped and stopped suddenly. Her gaze flew up to Tansen's. He had guessed instantly, the moment Najdan had told him that the Alliance was involved. It had taken Mirabar a little longer to figure it out; but then, she didn't know the *torena* the way he did. No one did.

"Zimran is with Josarian. He would have told Elelar where they were going," Mirabar said slowly.

"Exactly," he confirmed. "And she'll tell—"

"Do you think Zimran knows?" Mirabar asked.

"Yes." He turned and continued walking, even faster than before. "I think he'll lead Josarian into the trap."

Mirabar stumbled to catch up. Najdan was right behind her. The other men were further back, still out of earshot as Mirabar said, "But why would he do it? How could she convince—"

"She can be very convincing when she needs to be," Tansen said bitterly.

Now he knew why she had come to the Shrine of the Three, had once again woven her spell around him. He'd been a fool to think, to hope, for even a moment that his near death had stirred her heart even a little. She had come to assess just how badly wounded he was, just how long it would be before he could return to Josarian's side to guard him day and night. Then she had replaced him with Zimran, who was now loyal to her rather than to Josarian, sending him back to his cousin's side after all this time.

Josarian's life in exchange for Shaljir.

Tansen stumbled and fell. He shook off Najdan's helping hand and pushed himself back to his feet. He followed the direction of Mirabar's worried gaze and looked down to see a fresh stain on his tunic. The wound had reopened.

"You must stop and rest for a moment," Mirabar ordered.

"No, I—"

"Yes. You will be of no use to Josarian if you die before—"

"I don't need—"

A strong hand forced him to sit down. "The *sirana* says you must rest. So you will rest." It was the warning of an assassin. "Until she says otherwise."

Despite everything, Tansen almost laughed. "I think you were less trouble when you were our enemy."

"This is Sileria," Najdan replied. "A man's friends are always more dangerous than his enemies."

Tansen met the assassin's gaze. "He'll want you now, even more than he wants the rest of us."

Najdan knew whom he meant. "I have betrayed my master. There is no worse crime."

Tansen had seen enough of Najdan to know he would never try to excuse himself for it, either. Nonetheless, he said, "You've made the right choice, Najdan."

"Yes," Najdan said dryly, "and I hope that knowledge is a great comfort to me when the White Dragon finally comes for me."

"You don't really believe in it, do you?" Tansen asked.

Najdan looked into the distance, as if remembering something from long ago. "I have seen enough of Kiloran's power not to doubt the White Dragon just because I have never seen it myself."

"Do you know anyone who has?"

The assassin faltered, "No, but—"

"It's just a story the waterlords made up to keep people obedient to their will," Tansen said.

"You've seen prophecy from the Otherworld and the birth of the Firebringer," Najdan said. "Your own destiny was foretold in visions which tormented the *sirana*. You, of all people, should know better, Tansen."

"I don't deny Kiloran's power," Tan assured him. "I'll never forget those tentacles that nearly drowned me, dragging me under the surface of Lake Kandahar. And I saw what Kiloran did to the well at Alizar . . . But surely such feats are what men have taken for the White Dragon?"

Najdan frowned, unconvinced, but he caught Mirabar's eye and dropped the subject. "You should rest, not argue with me."

His side hurt a trifle less now. "Elelar has convinced Zimran to betray Josarian to the Valdani, and somehow Kiloran is behind it. I've rested enough." He rose to his feet and continued down the path to destiny.

HE WILL DIE soon, anyhow. He might as well die to end the war. To free Elelar. To pay for what he did to her at Golnar.

Zimran returned his cousin's smile as they made camp at dusk somewhere along the road to Zilar.

If he must die anyhow, then it might as well be so that I can have my own life back at last.

Being loyal to Josarian was merely a habit, he realized, nothing more. His cousin's madness had worn out Zimran's heart long ago. Nothing was left except regret that it had come to this in the end.

Who had grown up with Josarian, sharing his boyhood adventures, discoveries, fibs, punishments, and rewards? Who had moved into Josarian's house to keep him company in the grim months following Calidar's death? Who had invited Josarian into a lucrative smuggling trade so that he might improve his humble position in life?

It certainly wasn't any of the *zanareen* who now fawned and groveled, clustering so thickly around Josarian that Zimran could scarcely get a single moment alone with him these days.

When Josarian turned an ordinary smuggling raid into a mad night of violence and murder, who had remained loyal

to him? Who had stayed by his side while he recovered
from his wound in Sanctuary?

Not Tansen.

The *roshah* hadn't even been in Sileria then.

Zimran had risked his own safety time and time again
to bring Josarian information and supplies during those
early days of outlawry. He had never faltered once. And
what was the thanks he got for it? The moment that two-
sworded stranger had shown up, Josarian had become loyal
to *him*, deliberately excluding Zimran from that day forward.

In fact, ever since then, Josarian had favored all of them
over Zimran—Lann, Emelen, Amitan, Falian, and many
more recent recruits. Even the demon girl had more privileges and respect within the rebellion than Zimran did!

Josarian has brought this on himself.

Angering Kiloran with his stubbornness, murdering Srijan, infuriating the Society, alienating Elelar and the Alliance . . . Alienating the cousin who had loved him, who
once had been more loyal to him than any man alive!

*I will mourn you, remembering you as you once were;
but I will not let you go on ruining my life.*

Watching the *zanareen* milling around his cousin now,
Zimran tried once again to believe that the ordinary boy
he had grown up with was the Firebringer. Even now,
though, he simply couldn't. He'd never believed in the
Firebringer anyhow, and *Josarian* . . .

Zimran had been with Josarian the first time he'd ever
gotten drunk, and he had held his head while Josarian
vomited it all up the next day. Zimran had seen him go all
calf-eyed and half-witted after meeting Calidar, who was
no different from any other *shallah* girl. He'd even seen
Josarian chased halfway through Emeldar by his wife's
vicious cow, for the love of Dar!

How could such an ordinary man be the Firebringer?

Zimran had toyed with all of these thoughts for days,
and it always came back to this moment. He knew what
he had to do, and he knew he'd be safe. No one would

ever know. No one would ever accuse him, Josarian's own cousin—certainly not when he would describe how he himself had barely escaped alive from the Outlookers' ambush. Josarian would lose the life he'd been throwing away for months anyhow, and Zimran would finally be able to reclaim his own life, with the woman he had chosen as his own, and return to a peaceful, profitable existence free of warfare, bloodfeuds, and bloodvows.

This evening, Zim wore the yellow tunic that would identify him to the Outlookers waiting on the other side of the shallow Zilar River; therefore, of the two *shallaheen* walking into their trap, they would know which one was Josarian, their enemy. They would know which one to kill. They would then take the body to someone who could verify that the dead man was indeed Josarian. Once satisfied, they would turn Shaljir over to the Alliance. Then it would all end.

The war will be over.

All he had to do was play on the sentiments of a man who still trusted him.

"Good hunting land," Zimran said casually to Josarian, surveying the countryside around their camp.

"Yes." Josarian glanced up. "Lann claimed he once—"

"Please, it's enough that I have to hear Lann's ridiculous claims from him; don't you start." He grinned when Josarian laughed. "There are still a couple of hours of good light left. Why don't you and I go get a stag? Fresh meat."

Josarian looked around hesitantly. "I'm not sure . . ."

"Come on. Come with me. How long has it been since we've gone hunting together?"

Josarian sighed. "Ah, too long, Zim."

He picked up Josarian's quiver and bow, holding them out like bait. "Well, then?" Seeing that he nearly had him, he added, "Just you and me. Just like it used to be."

Josarian met his gaze, hesitated for only another brief moment, then grinned. "All right. Let's go."

Zim smiled in response. "I think the land across the river looks best, don't you?"

41

THEY WADED ACROSS the shallow waters of the Zilar River, then stalked through the dense brush in search of game. Josarian suggested they separate, but Zimran wanted to stay together. They weren't out here for long before Josarian began to suspect that his cousin hadn't really wanted to hunt, after all. Normally a good hunter, Zimran was currently being as noisy as a whole pack of clumsy Outlookers, tromping around with heavy feet and speaking often and loudly.

Knowing they'd see no deer now, Josarian smiled tolerantly. He realized that Zimran had just wanted to spend some time alone with him, something they hadn't done in months. It saddened him that his cousin felt he needed a pretense to get his company for a few hours these days. Glad as he was to have Zimran back at his side, he had been too busy to pay any attention to him.

He would rectify that now, he decided, as the shadows lengthened and the forest grew dark. He slapped Zim on the back and slung his quiver over his shoulder, talking idly as they ambled along, now making no pretense at hunting.

Even after focusing his attention on Zimran, it took him a while to realize that Zimran was . . . *nervous*. It was now becoming increasingly obvious, though, as evening descended. Zimran was looking around as if he had come to this forest as prey rather than as a hunter. He jumped at every little sound. He seemed anxious and strangely impatient. Now that he had Josarian's undivided attention, in fact, he hardly seemed to hear a word his cousin said and contributed little to the conversation.

"Zim?"

"Hmmm?"

"Is something wrong?"

It was getting too dark to be sure, but Josarian thought his cousin's face flushed. "No."

He wondered if Zimran was just nervous about being alone out here with a man marked for death by both the Valdani and Kiloran. It was getting rather close to nightfall, after all. Perhaps they should turn back. Josarian said as much.

"No!"

The outburst surprised him. "Zim, I don't think—"

"We're not going back!"

He knew then. Even before he saw the first Outlooker, poorly disguised as a Silerian, descending from a concealed ledge in the rocks; even before he saw two Valdani appear behind Zimran or heard two more come up behind himself, he knew.

"*Zim.*"

It was there in his cousin's face now. The betrayal. The hatred. The guilt. The triumph.

It broke his heart.

Zimran? No!

The Outlookers ignored his cousin, as Zimran ignored them. Josarian jumped back and unsheathed his sword. He would not be taken alive. Zimran jumped back, too, a flash of fear in his face suggesting that he thought Josarian meant to kill him.

"Come for me," Josarian snarled at the hesitating Outlookers. "Come for me now!"

He saw that they were willing to ambush an unsuspecting *shallah,* but not ready to risk their lives bringing down an armed and fighting rebel.

They never changed.

He swung out at the nearest one, then whirled around, holding half a dozen men at bay, fighting with both his sword and his *yahr.*

Dar, let me take many of them with me as I die!

He heard thundering in the distance. Horses. Hoofbeats. More Outlookers?

"Josarian!"

He recognized the distant voice. Tansen!

He grinned wolfishly, seeing sudden panic take hold of his attackers. They were deep in rebel territory, and they had only come here to kill a single, isolated man. More Outlookers were emerging from hiding—there seemed to be at least a dozen now—but there were not nearly enough men here for a battle.

"Josarian!" Tansen called, closer already.

"Here!"

Two Outlookers came for him, intent upon killing him fast enough to escape from the approaching rebels. The ground shook as the riders drew near.

"No!" Zimran screamed. *"No!"*

"Tan!" Josarian called again.

He thrust his sword into the body of one attacking Outlooker, then struggled to yank it back out before someone killed him. He struck his second attacker across the face with his *yahr,* then braced his foot against the chest of his first victim to withdraw his sword.

Mounted riders thundered into the scene, separating Josarian from most of his attackers. He saw the familiar flash of Tansen's two blades, saw Lann cut a man down with the absurdly long Moorlander sword he favored, saw his friends sweep through the Valdani with violent energy and deadly intent. They launched themselves off their horses and entered the battle, howling their war cries as they rescued their leader from this trap.

Josarian ducked the whirling blow of a skillfully handled *yahr,* then met his cousin's hate-filled gaze.

"Zim, no!" he begged.

He parried a thrust of Zimran's sword. Ducked another swing of the *yahr.* Fell back several steps. Tansen had warned him never to fight defensively; he should always seize every opportunity to wound or kill. But he couldn't. Not this time. He couldn't kill this man.

I can't!

"Zim, *please . . .*"

He took another step back and ducked the *yahr* again. As boys, they had trained together in the use of the *yahr*. He knew every counter to every move that Zim knew, for they had shared the same teacher and had practiced together thousands of times. They were evenly matched with a *yahr*. But not with a sword . . . Zimran had never practiced enough with that new weapon.

"Please don't make me kill you," Josarian pleaded, parrying another thrust.

Sweating and gritting his teeth, Zimran snarled with rage and came at him again.

I can't. Please don't make me!

He fell back another step, knowing he would have to stop retreating. He would have to fight Zimran. He would have to kill a man he had loved his whole life. He must do it or die.

"How could you betray me? Why?"

Zimran paused for only a moment. Panting with mingled fear, rage, and exhaustion, he said in a low, unfamiliar voice, full of venom and bitterness, "I never wanted your war."

Josarian stared at him, everything forgotten except the dark heart now revealed to him. He had never foreseen this. He couldn't believe it, not even now that it was actually happening. He wanted it to be merely a nightmare, merely a mistake.

"Zim . . ."

He couldn't seem to raise his arm to defend himself, not even as he watched Zimran's sword come at him. Everything was happening in slow motion, and only the burden of his sorrow seemed real right now.

Zimran's eyes suddenly widened with astonished pain, and he dropped his sword as a blow to his legs drove him to his knees. Tansen stood directly behind him, blood-splattered, sweat-drenched, and breathing hard. His gaze was unyielding as he met Josarian's bewildered, tear-filled eyes.

"Bid him farewell, Josarian." Tansen's voice was harsh and breathless.

"Tan . . ." Josarian shook his head. "Don't. Let me talk to him."

"Make your peace with Dar, *sriliah*," Tansen advised Zimran, raising one sword.

"No!" Zimran screamed.

"Tan!" Josarian lunged forward.

Too late.

Tansen was faster. He had always been faster. He slit Zimran's throat with a single, merciless swipe. Josarian caught his cousin's body before it hit the ground. He held Zimran's gaze in his last instant of life.

Standing over him, gulping for air and holding the seeping wound at his side, Tansen said, "So die all who betray Josarian." His voice was hollow and exhausted. "There are . . . no exceptions."

Tears streamed down Josarian's face as he stared into the lifeless eyes of another boyhood friend who had died because of him.

"It could have been different," he whispered to Zimran. "I wish . . ." It *should* have been different.

Must it always be this way?

He had not known he could go on living with a heart this broken and battered. He cradled Zimran's limp body in his arms, oblivious to the screams of dying men all around him, and howled with grief as the hot flow of his cousin's blood poured over him in silent condemnation.

TANSEN AND JOSARIAN knelt side by side on the banks of the Zilar River, stripped to the waist, washing. A fire blazed in the forest behind them, begun by Mirabar, who now guarded it, burning the Outlooker corpses along with Zimran's body. They had kept one Outlooker alive. He was securely bound and under guard now. Later—perhaps in the morning—they would send him back to his masters with a message. Right now, though, neither of them could even think, let alone compose a verbal message for their enemies.

Bound by blood and brotherhood, Josarian had helped Tansen down to the river when the fighting was over; but he had not yet spoken a word to him. Not since Tansen had slaughtered Zimran even as Josarian begged him not to.

Feeling light-headed and weak, Tansen let the icy waters of the Zilar wash the blood off his skin, knowing that Josarian would continue to see it there long after it was gone. The *zanareen*, who had sent his rescue party in the right direction in time to save Josarian's life, now stood guard around Josarian, chanting, praying, giving thanks that the Firebringer was safe. He ignored them. They elevated Tansen in their praises, for he had come to save their leader. He ignored them, too.

Weak, exhausted, and in pain, he barely had the strength to sluice the bitterly cold water over his body.

"Here," Josarian said at last, his voice subdued, "let me. You're going to fall in headfirst in another minute."

"No, I—"

"Sit back," Josarian snapped.

He sat back.

Josarian soaked a cloth in the water and then wiped gingerly at the edges of Tan's seeping *shir* wound. "It looks worse again."

"Oh."

"You should rest."

"We must leave here."

"Tan—"

"Now." He winced as Josarian placed pressure on the wound, trying to stop the bleeding. "If those Outlookers were expected to report somewhere tonight, someone may come looking for them when they don't show up."

"Searlon?"

"I don't know." He couldn't bear to tell Josarian the whole truth. Not now. Later, yes. But not right now.

"How did you know?"

"I'll explain later."

"Did you know about . . ." Josarian's voice broke. He looked away for a moment. "Did you know he would be the one to lead me into the trap?"

"I . . ." He took a shallow breath, trying not to strain the wound. "Yes, Josarian."

"We . . . We were born only three months apart." Josarian dunked the cloth into the river again. "We shared everything as boys. As men, we . . ."

"I'm sorry."

I'm sorry he betrayed you. I'm sorry I had to kill him. I'm sorry.

A tear streamed slowly down Josarian's face, glistening beneath the brilliant light of the full twin-moons. "I know."

Tansen would not ask for forgiveness. He said only, "It had to be done."

"If only . . ." Josarian bowed his head and gulped for air. He scrubbed at his face and finally said, "We will meet again in the Otherworld. Mirabar says that our earthly concerns and quarrels will not matter there."

"Mirabar . . ." Tansen pushed Josarian's hands away from his wound and said, "She's been out there long enough." He rose to his feet.

"I'll get her. You—"

"No, you go back to camp. Tell everyone we're moving out *now*. And fast. I'll get Mira."

Josarian nodded and turned to don his shabby tunic. Tansen scooped his up and slipped it over his torso as he ventured into the dark forest in search of Mirabar, following the glow of her fire. At his insistence, she had stayed with the *zanareen* until the fighting was over. Few men could match her for courage, but she didn't belong in close combat with Outlookers.

Najdan was with her, of course. He was filthy from the recent battle, and his *shir* was practically leaping out of his *jashar* it was so agitated by Mirabar's funeral fire. His face was unfathomable as he watched Zimran's corpse burn. Considering that he, too, had just betrayed his leader, Tansen couldn't help wondering what he was thinking right now.

"Mira," Tan said, "we need to—"

A blood-chilling scream split the night wide open. It came from the riverbank. Tansen was already running toward the sound when he heard more voices—screaming, shouting, crying out. Above it all, there was a terrible *roaring* unlike anything he'd ever heard in his life, a sound which was so terrifying it made his hair stand on end and a clammy sweat break out on his skin.

His side was burning and his head was spinning by the time he reached the riverbank. What he saw there made him forget his pain, his exhaustion, his weakness. Made him forget everything but the horror confronting him.

It rose out of the river, looming over the shallow waters of the Zilar like some monster from a madman's worst nightmares. Tansen knew what it was even before he heard Najdan's hoarse, shocked voice utter the words: the White Dragon. A voracious, evil creature born of a magical union between water and a wizard.

It was huge, far bigger than a Widow Beast or even a dragonfish, and its fierce roar made the very ground tremble with awe. It shifted and glittered beneath the brilliant light of the moons, gleaming like the blade of a *shir,* shining like the diamonds of Alizar. Its long, serpentlike neck swayed and twisted, the sharp icicles inside its great mouth snapping at its enemies. If it had eyes and ears, Tansen could not see them, so he didn't know how it had found its intended prey—the Firebringer—with such unerring accuracy.

The White Dragon held Josarian in its grasp, its powerful, icy claws cradling him against its horrifically beautiful form as it roared at the *zanareen* and *shallaheen* who were screaming, waving weapons, and trying to find the courage to attack it. Josarian's face was distorted with terror. His frantic struggles didn't even seem to be noticed by the creature which held him in its deadly embrace. He was badly wounded, probably by those claws, and his blood mingled with the water that dripped off the beast, splattering the rebels and spilling into the current of the Zilar River.

Tansen ran forward through the shallow water, feeling its deadly chill. He had attributed the icy cold of the river to the time of year and to its source being high in the mountains . . . But now he knew the true source of that life-stealing cold. Now he understood. This was Kiloran's river now. The old waterlord had taken control of it without telling anyone, biding his time, awaiting his chance. He had given birth to this monstrous creature here in the heart of Josarian's territory, hoping that it would someday have the opportunity to fulfill the purpose of its creation.

The Valdani had failed, and so Kiloran now set his deadly monster free to devour Josarian.

"No!" Tansen screamed, running straight at the enormous, dripping beast, his swords drawn.

He swung at its haunches. His blade cut through pure water. He swung again, cutting, stabbing, slicing, thrusting. He circled the roaring beast, plunging through thigh-deep water, his flesh burning in a thousand places from the bitterly cold, ensorcelled droplets flying off the White Dragon. Each splash was like the touch of a *shir*. Tears streamed down his face from the pain.

"Josarian!" he howled, attacking the creature again.

An enormous claw came down and struck him. It was like being hit by a galloping horse. He flew backwards. The waters of the Zilar closed over his head as he fell. He lunged to the surface, still hanging onto his swords. The great dragonlike head lowered, following him, the hungry jaws snapping and seeking him. He swung a sword with an arm that felt heavy and numb. His blade scraped along the *shir*like fangs. The cold breath of the beast froze his wet flesh.

"Tan!" Josarian screamed.

A bolt of fire struck the creature in the head. It flinched

and turned away momentarily. Tansen scrambled to his feet and sloshed forward to attack again.

"It's *water*, you idiot!" Mirabar shouted. "Get back!"

Standing hip-deep in the river, she opened her mouth and extended her arms. Fire poured from her body. Sheets of flame swept into the White Dragon. Ribbons of lava encircled its head. A ring of fire floated atop the water's surface, surrounding Kiloran's evil beast with the ancient power of the Guardians.

The White Dragon bellowed with rage. It clawed at the flames, spat upon the fire, and fought the woman.

It glittered as it whirled in search of her, momentarily forgetting its hostage as it sought to destroy this new and greater threat. Sensing his opportunity, Josarian made another attempt to get away. The creature felt the Firebringer's struggle and returned to its original purpose, clamping both claws tightly around Josarian's chest. He grimaced with pain, crying out again.

The White Dragon now turned its back on Mirabar, hurrying to finish the work for which it had been born. It ignored the circle of fire licking at its shimmering body. Its head descended, and its great mouth closed over Josarian, its dripping fangs ripping into his flesh.

"No!" Tansen fought his way through the ring of fire, slashing wildly at Kiloran's creature.

Josarian's horrible screams tore the night apart and shattered his brother's soul.

"Noooo!"

A powerful blow from the beast sent Tansen flying into Mirabar, bringing the two of them down together. She screamed, too, and lost control of her fire. Her flames withered and died as she sank beneath the river's surface with Tansen. They clawed at each other, trying to rise again, trying to plunge through the water to renew their attacks on the White Dragon.

Josarian's agonized screams died the very moment he did, ending as his body disappeared into the gaping maw of Kiloran's hideous offspring.

"No!" Tansen fought Mirabar as she tried to stop him, to hold him back. "Josarian!"

"No, you can't help him now! Stop!" she cried. "It'll take you, too!"

He flung her out of his way as the great beast curled in on itself, devouring the last of the Firebringer. Mirabar clung to Tansen's legs, coughing and sputtering, dragging him down into the water again.

"Let go, damn you!" he snarled, hitting her.

The creature was just beyond his reach, hissing and sizzling as it started decomposing, its task complete, its goal achieved. Josarian was dead. Gone. Devoured.

"Josarian!"

Mirabar held onto Tansen's tunic, his hair, his harness—any part of him she could reach as he struggled to get away.

"No," she screamed. "It'll get you, too! Don't go near it!"

He raised his sword, intending to strike her with the hilt. She moved faster and punched him hard *right* where Koroll had stabbed him. His knees buckled with the pain and he fell back down. His head sank beneath the surface again, and he inhaled water when his pain-shocked body gasped involuntarily for air.

A strong arm—much stronger than Mira's—seized him by the hair and dragged his head up. Sputtering, choking, and gulping down air, his gaze immediately sought the White Dragon again, not even acknowledging the hands that hauled him upright and then held him prisoner. The creature was disappearing now, dissolving, melting back into the river which had given it birth. Dying after its brief, destructive life. Escaping before Tansen could avenge the man it had murdered.

"Josarian!"

He struggled to go after the thing, to try once more to kill something which had never even been truly alive.

"It's gone." Najdan's voice was breathless and quiet. "He's gone, Tansen."

My brother is dead.

"No . . ."

Mirabar surged to her feet, soaking wet, disheveled, bleeding. "We must . . . get away from this river," she said, panting hard.

"Josarian . . ."

"He's dead, Tansen. We must leave now."

My brother is dead.

He heard the terrible, heartbroken wailing before he actually realized that it came from him. Helpless, grief-stricken sobs shook his body as Najdan hauled him laboriously to the riverbank. The sorrow of his loss tore him apart with wracking cries of protest as Mirabar took his swords from his numbed hands.

Josarian is dead.

The mourning of the *zanareen* shuddered through his senses, their death chants lighting a fire that singed his soul. He heard Lann sobbing, heard the sounds of panic and horror and heartbreak all around him.

My brother is dead.

For the first time since that day, long ago, when he discovered his entire village had been slaughtered by Outlookers, for the first time since he had gazed upon the mutilated corpses of his loved ones, Tansen shah Gamalani broke down and wept like a child.

SO EXHAUSTED SHE could hardly keep standing up, Mirabar blew several small fires into life in the empty hours before daybreak. To ward off the menacing darkness of this endless night. To warm men chilled by grief and terror. To await the light of the most uncertain dawn of their lives.

Najdan dug food and water out of the supplies they carried and now forced it upon her. She took one bite and thought she would be sick. Hot tears slid down her face again. Grief renewed itself in her heart.

Josarian was forever in Kiloran's keeping now. He would never reach the Otherworld. He would never answer a Calling. He would never see Calidar again. That was the way of the White Dragon, a death far more horrible than anything the Valdani had ever devised. And until the day Kiloran finally died, Josarian's spirit would be locked in the agony it had entered last night in the jaws of that grotesque water-born creature that the old wizard had created for his enemy's destruction.

I will wait for you forever, Calidar had said.

Mirabar now saw that the words had been prophecy, not promise. Calidar's shade had known what becoming the Firebringer would ultimately cost Josarian, what it would cost them both: an eternity apart. *Forever,* as Calidar had said; and for Josarian, an agony that would end only with Kiloran's destruction.

"Sacrifice . . ." Mirabar's voice broke on the word and more tears streaked down her cheeks.

Josarian had believed more than anyone—in Sileria, in freedom, and in making sacrifices for both.

"Sirana?" Dull with exhaustion, Najdan now became alert again, observing her renewed misery.

"He gave everything," she said hoarsely. "And this is his reward." She met the assassin's gaze. "When his agony finally ends, what awaits him? Oblivion. Nothing more. For *this,* he gave his life and heart to Sileria, followed the prophecy of the Firebringer, fulfilled the visions of the gods . . ." Her voice faded as a painful wave of guilt swept across her. "And I led him to it."

"No, *sirana,* he sought his destiny, and you—"

"I led him to it, Najdan! I went to Kandahar and turned his bloodfeud into a revolution! I Called the shade that convinced him to go to Darshon! I—"

"Shh, *sirana.* He would not want you to do this to yourself."

Najdan abandoned his usual respectful reserve and wrapped his arms around her, holding her close as she wept brokenheartedly, blaming herself and railing against the gods.

"I will not serve them any longer!" she cried. "The

Beckoner can stay away forever! I will not . . ." Her lungs strained for air in the midst of her grief and outrage. ". . . serve such . . ." She gasped again. ". . . cruelty."

"Ah, *sirana.*" Najdan stroked her hair like a father comforting a favorite child. "I said that when I left Kiloran. But the gods, the Otherworld, the tides of destiny . . . Surely they are superior to a waterlord, and their will—"

"*No,*" she said furiously. "I will not! If the Beckoner ever comes again, I will not—"

"Shhh, you're tired," Najdan said. "Make no vows or promises in the dark, *sirana*. Always wait until dawn."

They had left the riverside as soon as possible after the deadly horror of Kiloran's revenge withered back into the waters from which it had come. Stumbling through the dark, they had travelled until they were simply too tired to go on. Tansen's howling grief had faded into a hollow-eyed silence that was even more disturbing than his unprecedented outburst. Wounded and battered, he walked as if propelled by some secret sorcery of his own. He refused any attention for the seeping *shir* wound, or for the deep cuts and heavy bruises he had earned in the recent battle for Josarian's life. He refused food and water, too, and he ignored any attempt to communicate with him. Now he sat alone, away from the fire, his gaze fixed upon the distant, moon-drenched peak of Mount Darshon, wherein dwelled Dar—the destroyer goddess.

He will both succeed and fail . . .

Is this what the visions meant? Tansen had been the catalyst for the rebellion. Without him, Josarian might well have died long ago at Britar. Without Tansen, Josarian would never have met Elelar or made a pact with Kiloran. Without the *shatai*, Josarian might never have left the small range of mountains to which he'd been born or sought his destiny as the Firebringer.

He will both succeed and fail . . .

Josarian was dead, but Sileria was not free yet. Not until the Valdani left. Would they do so now?

"The prisoner," she said suddenly, her mind now called

away from grief and set once again upon the path of duty.

They had brought their Outlooker prisoner with them. They had no plan or purpose, they had simply brought him along on their mad flight from Kiloran's river.

Mirabar pulled herself out of Najdan's comforting embrace and repeated, "The prisoner."

"What about him, *sirana?*"

Tan's quiet voice startled them both. "The prisoner . . ."

She turned and watched the warrior rise to his feet. He approached them as they stood beside the fire she had conjured, his steps slow, his face pale with pain. His eyes were shadowed and weary. His voice was calm when he spoke. Familiar. Shrewd and quick. Once again the voice of the man she was accustomed to.

Tansen met her gaze in the firelight and nodded. "We need him to tell the Valdani that . . . when the Outlookers failed, the Silerians killed Josarian themselves to . . ." His face twisted briefly with disgust. "To seal the bargain. To fulfill the treaty."

"So they'll leave Sileria," Mirabar said.

"Kiloran knew," Tansen said. He glanced briefly at Najdan, then turned his gaze to the fire. "He found out you had taken your woman away from Kandahar, and he knew what that meant. Knew that you would warn us. Try to save Josarian."

Najdan's eyes clouded with horror. His mouth worked for a moment, but no words came out. Even upon learning of Srijan's death, he had not looked so shocked. Finally, struggling to get the words out, he said, "Upon my soul, I swear I had no—"

"I know," Tansen said. "You couldn't have known. No one could have known, Najdan. I didn't even *believe* in . . ." He shuddered slightly. The silence was heavy with memories they all wanted to banish. "We did all that we could do. Josarian himself would . . . say so if he were here now." He cleared his throat.

"I think the prisoner's mind is a little unhinged now," Mirabar ventured. It wasn't surprising, really. They at least knew what that river-born thing was; the Valdan, however, had probably doubted his own sanity from the moment he'd seen the White Dragon rise out of the water.

"As long as he can remember what we tell him to say to Kaynall," Tansen said, "that will be good enough."

They hadn't bothered to bind the Outlooker after fleeing from the site of Josarian's death. He was too frightened to try to escape in the dark and too shocked to do much besides huddle pathetically amidst the *zanareen,* who chanted and prayed, wept and mourned. Mirabar had been surprised to discover the man spoke a little common Silerian; she supposed it was why he'd been chosen to join a raiding party going deep into rebel territory, where Valdan wasn't the most useful language.

The Outlooker was willing to cooperate with Tansen's orders, as long as no one tried to make him go anywhere alone before morning. Then he fully intended to go straight back to Shaljir and board the first Valda-bound ship leaving port, even if it meant being charged with desertion.

Tansen sighed. "Sometimes we're tempted to leave, too," he admitted, "and we *live* here. However, you mustn't leave until you've reported to Kaynall. After he questions you, I doubt you'll have much trouble getting back to Valda."

Once they were sure the Outlooker would do as he was told, Tansen questioned him about the ambush on Josarian. The Valdan didn't know who had arranged it or how.

"All I knew was that there would be two *shallaheen* at the ambush site near the river, and we were not supposed to attack the one in the yellow tunic." He brushed a trembling hand through his short hair and added, "Then we were supposed to bring Josarian's body back to Shaljir."

"To Advisor Kaynall?" Tansen asked.

The Outlooker nodded. "And Commander Cyrill. He's been in Shaljir since the surrender of Cavasar."

"How were they going to identify the body?"

"There's a Silerian who meets secretly with Kaynall. He

used to meet with Koroll, before the commander got killed
b—"

"What does this Silerian look like?"

"Tall, sleek, dangerous. Always well-dressed. He has a
scar on his face and speaks good V—"

"Searlon."

The Outlooker shrugged. "I don't know his name. I always had the impression that I wasn't even supposed to
know about those meetings."

Mirabar met Tansen's gaze as the sky turned pink with
the long-awaited dawn. "Kiloran," she said. "He means to
rule Sileria now."

"Then we will just have to stop him," Tansen replied.

When morning glowed bright and brassy all around
them, they gave the Outlooker a fast horse for his journey
back to Valda. Before he left, Tansen also gave him a
length of knotted, woven twine dotted with the rough
beads of a *shallah*.

"It's a *jashar*," Tansen told the Outlooker. "Show it to
anyone who tries to stop you between here and Shaljir."

"Is it some kind of spell?"

"It's a message, one which almost all Silerians can interpret. It gives you my protection to return to Shaljir as
a messenger between the rebels and the *rosh*—the Valdani."

The Outlooker studied it curiously for a moment, then
nodded his understanding and kicked his horse, setting off
on the long journey back to the relative safety of Shaljir.

They watched him leave, then Tansen turned to Mirabar.
"I want you to go back to Dalishar and—"

"No, I'd rather go to Niran," she said, thinking of the
way her head always reeled at Dalishar.

"No. It must be Dalishar," Tansen insisted. "Kiloran
can't hurt you there."

"If not Niran, then I'd rather return to Sanc—"

"Kiloran has used Outlookers to violate Sanctuary before. As long as there are Outlookers in Sileria, he might
do so again." He took her shoulders, shaking her slightly

when he could see she still intended to object. "He knows Najdan has betrayed him. He'll send someone else after you."

"I can—"

"Can you survive the White Dragon?" he snapped. "You saw what it did to Josarian, surrounded by a *shatai,* a Guardian, an assassin, and more than fifty men." He shook his head. "Go to Dalishar and wait for me there."

"She will go," Najdan promised. "I will see to it."

"But where are you going?" Mirabar asked.

He said nothing, only showed her the second *jashar* he had made after weaving one for the Outlooker. She recognized it instantly.

So die all who betray Josarian.

"The *torena,*" she whispered.

He nodded.

"You'll never do it," she said.

"I will." There was steel in his voice.

"I'm coming with you." She didn't trust him. Not where that woman was concerned.

"I want you safe at Dalishar."

"I don't—"

"After I ki . . . After I do this, we must destroy Kiloran. I can't do it without you, Mira."

He was right, she realized. She must concentrate her energy against the waterlord. "All right," she said at last, "I will wait for you at Dalishar."

"I won't be long."

"There's just one thing, Tansen." Now there was steel in *her* voice.

"What?"

"Don't come back until it is done." Her gaze was fierce as she held his, willing him to remember Josarian's death. "Don't come back to me unless you can show me Elelar's blood on your sword."

42

TANSEN ARRIVED IN the middle of the night, in the silent hours when even rebels were lost in the solace of their dreams. The sight of two sleepy sentries confirmed that the *torena* was in residence at the half-ruined villa she inhabited near Chandar.

The Valdani were already pulling out of the region around Elelar's ancestral lands. In another few days, she could have reclaimed the estate she had inherited from Gaborian. Now she would never live to see it again. Now she would die before the sun rose over Darshon once more.

He had left his horse somewhere down the road, overused and footsore. He had no wish to alert the sentries—or anyone else—to his presence before he killed the *torena*. He was too tired and injured to fight all the men who protected Elelar. He must do this quietly.

His seeping wound now hurt like the branding ceremony he had endured to become a *shatai*. His lungs burned from working so hard to make up for the loss of blood and the lack of food and sleep. His whole body ached from the blows of the White Dragon. His flesh burned in a thousand places from the drops of ensorcelled water which had dripped onto him from that voracious monster. The cuts from its claws were as painful as wounds made by a *shir*.

What a fool I was, not to believe.

He ignored the pain, the exhaustion, and the lightheaded dizziness as he crept through the dark and sought an entrance into the well-guarded villa. He shut out the ache in his heart as he thought of murdering the woman who had haunted his thoughts since his boyhood. He resisted the familiar longing which assailed him as he slipped through the silent shadows of her house and made his way to the chamber wherein she lay.

Soft-footed and shallow-breathed, he crept up beside the bed where she now slept alone.

The bed she shared with Zimran.

He slowly unsheathed a sword, controlling the soft whisper of sound the blade made when he did so.

The light of the twin-moon night poured through the windows and spilled across the bed. How lovely she looked, lying in her gossamer gown with her black hair spread across the pillow. The rise and fall of her soft breasts looked so welcoming to one who had fought hard, lost tragically, and come so far since dawn. Her fair, flawless flesh almost seemed to glow in the dark nest of her bed. The scent which arose from her sleeping form clouded his mind and filled his senses.

Elelar.

He whispered her name, as so many other men must have done in the night. She turned her head. A shallow sleeper. Would he ever again hate anyone this much? Would he ever desire another woman this desperately? What a peaceful heart she must have, that it did not—she had told him—ever hold two such feelings at once.

He lay his blade across her throat, observing how the cold steel caught the moonlight, capturing the deadly beauty of the moment forever in his mind.

He had never killed a woman. He had never imagined that he would. He wondered how long he could bear to go on living after killing this one.

He wondered how he had kept on going after seeing Josarian devoured by the White Dragon. He could scarcely remember the hours which had followed. He knew that he had broken down, wailing like a child; he also knew that Najdan and Mirabar were unlikely to ever remind him of it. Of the rest—the mad flight away from the river, the long trek through the dark, the decision to stop and await dawn . . . He remembered almost none of it. He mostly remembered the hollow grief of loss, the empty ache of failure, the disbelieving horror of Josarian's end.

His brother had never feared death because he had believed, with a faith which Tansen could envy but never emulate, that he would join his beloved Calidar for all eternity in the Otherworld. He had even expected to be reunited there with his worthless cousin, reclaiming the long-lost harmony of their friendship in a place free of the concerns, quarrels, and burdens of this world.

Now Josarian would never see Calidar again. He would never answer Mirabar's Call. Nothing awaited him but oblivion, and until Kiloran died, Josarian would be locked in the agony of his own terrible destruction.

Tansen closed his eyes, gritting his teeth as he tried to escape the memory of Josarian's agonized screams.

Focus on the task at hand.

"Elelar," he whispered again.

She had heard too many men whisper her name in the dark to be alarmed. She slowly opened her eyes. She didn't even tense when she saw a *shallah* sitting upon the edge of her bed.

"Zimran?" she murmured sleepily.

Elelar moved her head slightly—and felt the blade at her throat. She gasped and went very still. Then she focused her eyes on him and whispered incredulously, "Tansen?"

"Yes."

The moons highlighted him, too. He had some idea of how he must look. Hollow-eyed, clammy with feverish sweat, filthy, wounded, dishevelled, haunted, exhausted . . . and his clothes liberally stained with blood: his own, Josarian's, Outlookers', and Zimran's.

Her gaze travelled over him, then rested upon the hand holding a sword at her throat.

She licked her lips and guessed, "Zimran is dead."

"You've always been very quick." Even Kiloran's voice had never been as cold as his was now. "Make your peace with Dar."

Her breasts rose and fell with sudden agitation. Her

breath trembled as she tried to speak. "How did . . . did you know?"

"A secret treaty with the Valdani," he spat.

"Yes," she admitted. "To end the war."

"Hostage exchanges."

"To end—"

"Josarian's life in exchange for Shaljir!"

"To end the war."

"You betrayed him." *Do it now. Kill her now.*

"It was the price of our freedom."

"You betrayed the Firebringer to *free* us?"

"From the moment he murdered Srijan, he was marked for death," she said desperately. "You know that! It's why you wouldn't leave his side!"

"Did you arrange to have me wounded so that he'd be easier to kill?"

"No! I only . . ."

"What?" He pressed the blade a little harder against that soft flesh.

"I only saw the opportunity after . . . after I realized you were too badly hurt to return to his side."

"It's why you came all the way to the Shrine of the Three to see me."

"Yes . . . Please, Tan . . ."

"To tell your masters that you knew how my brother could be killed," he snarled.

"Before Kiloran could do it!" In her agitation, she moved too far. The razor-sharp blade pricked her flesh. She gasped, thinking *he* had done it. "He was going to die! No one could stop it! Not you or Mirabar or anyone! I wasn't going to let him die for nothing!"

"Next you'll be telling me you did him a favor!"

"Torena?" There was a loud knock at the bedchamber door, which Tansen had locked behind him. *"Torena!"*

Servants.

"Send them away," he whispered.

"Just a minute," she called. Then she whispered to him, "Put your sword away." Seeing him shake his head, she said, "If they know I'm not safe, they'll attack. You'll kill them all."

"What do you care? A few more deaths—"

"Tan," she whispered urgently.

He hesitated, then sighed and sheathed his sword. He stood by the bed while Elelar got up to answer the door. Faradar stood outside with the two sentries whom he'd slipped past. The maid, who knew him, gasped at his appearance, but apparently lost all concern that her mistress might be in danger. Elelar's brief, whispered explanation suggested that Tansen had come at this unconventional hour to mix business and pleasure. He noted wryly how quickly the *torena*'s servants accepted this explanation. Elelar closed the door, locked it again, and asked if he would object to her lighting the lantern.

"I can kill you just fine by this light," he said.

She sat on the edge of the bed and folded her hands. Moonlight and wavy black hair spilled over her shoulders. "The Valdani guaranteed complete and total withdrawal from Shaljir upon receiving proof of Josarian's death."

"And you believed them?"

"They have fulfilled the rest of the treaty." When he didn't reply, she said quietly. "In the end, Tan, Josarian's death was the price of Sileria's freedom."

He stared at her, appalled by her dispassionate assessment of her betrayal. "How could you have done it? How could you have betrayed him? How—"

"You can say that to me? You?" She jumped to her feet and stalked forward, her fear of him forgotten in her anger. "You, who murdered your own bloodfather?"

He took a step backwards. He should have just killed her, should have never given her a chance to talk. Now she was opening more wounds.

"Armian trusted you!" she cried. "He loved you. And you slaughtered him rather than—"

"It's not the same!" he shouted. "What you did—"

"It's exactly the same!" she shouted back. "Do you think

you're the only one who loves this land? The only one
who's made sacrifices to free it?"

"I didn't sacrifice the Firebringer!"

"Yes, you did!" she reminded him. "You thought Armian was the Firebringer, and you killed him anyhow."

His side felt like it was on fire. He was breathing like
he had just run all the way here on foot.

"No . . ."

"I was there," she hissed.

He felt dizzy. "It's not the same . . ."

"It's the *same.*"

He shook his head, swaying slightly.

She saw his weakness and pressed her advantage. "The
war would have dragged on forever, Tan. Maybe for years.
You saw the butchery. Koroll's revenge. Whole villages
slaughtered by night, one after another. Women, children,
old men."

"Like Gamalan . . ." He thought he would be sick.

"How long could we hold out? And at what cost to our
people? How long could the rebellion last once Kiloran
and Josarian went to war against each other? How soon
before the Valdani saw our vulnerability? They would
have stayed in Shaljir, waiting until the wars on the mainland favored them, waiting until they could reconquer Sileria."

He leaned weakly against the wall, shying away from
the onslaught of her words.

*Armian. A windy night. A deadly decision. The father
who loved and trusted me.*

"Josarian was doomed from the moment he killed Srijan.
I know . . ." She sighed. "I know why he did it. I know
how the *shallaheen* are. But he . . . he could never survive
Kiloran's vengeance after that."

*Josarian. A darkening forest. An ambush. The cousin he
loved and trusted.*

"No." He couldn't bear it. No one could bear this.

"Yes," she insisted. "Nothing and no one could have
saved him, not even you! Not even nine years of exile

would have saved Josarian. Kiloran would never rescind
the bloodvow. Their feud would have destroyed the rebellion, destroyed all of Sileria! We had to act fast to save
it."

*Daurion. A night in Shaljir a thousand years ago. A
deadly attack. The friend he loved and trusted.*

"The Yahrdan . . ." The room was spinning, the years of
blood and vengeance whirling around him.

"Who knows if he would have become Yahrdan, if he
had survived?" she said. "And if he had, Tansen, don't
you see how it would have destroyed us? The first Yahrdan
in a thousand years, the leader of the newborn nation, murdered by a waterlord . . ." Her hands balled into fists.
"Don't you see, Tan? It's exactly what made Sileria vulnerable to the Conquest in the first place." She paced along
the line of windows on the other side of the room. "Nations
are born like men, in blood and fever and legend. But they
must be ruled with strength and wisdom and power."

"Kiloran . . ." He struggled for air, suffocating beneath
the tragedy his own race brought upon themselves again
and again and again. Until now, until her words, he had
never known how deeply his own sins were woven into
its tapestry. *Daurion, Armian, Josarian . . .*

"No, it mustn't be Kiloran. It *won't* be Kiloran," she
said. "I have never wanted that any more than you do. But
it could never have been the man who murdered Kiloran's
son. Not while Kiloran lives."

Must it always be this way?

"You have given Sileria to Kiloran," he said bitterly.
"You and your precious Alliance have made us all his
slaves."

Her pacing stopped abruptly as she whirled to face him.
"Haven't you heard anything I've been saying? Now the
Valdani will leave Sileria, before every piece of it is destroyed by another year, two years, five years of warfare,
before people are starving in the streets, before—"

"In destroying Josarian, you have become Kiloran's
creature, just as Zimran was your creature."

"Kiloran has nothing to do with this!"

"Doesn't he?" He pushed himself away from the wall and stalked forward. "You don't know what happened to Josarian."

She was staring at him intently. "I thought you came here because I *do* know what—"

"I got to him in time to save him from the ambush."

"You what?" She sat down suddenly. "But I thought . . . Isn't he dead?"

"Oh, he's dead. I saw it myself. He's unquestionably dead."

She heard the change in his tone. The hatred. The horror. "If he didn't die in the ambush, then—"

"Kiloran. The White Dragon."

She shot to her feet again. "You are *lying.*"

"Am I? Ask Mirabar and Najdan. Ask Lann and the other *shallaheen* and some fifty *zanareen.* They were all there, too, and none of us could save him from that thing."

"The White Dragon? No . . . No, it's not possible."

She shook her head, backing away from him as she sought to deny his story. He seized her shoulders, holding her in a grip that he hoped hurt like all the Fires, forcing her to listen as he told her how Josarian had died, sparing her nothing, painting a picture he wanted her to remember for the rest of her life. He wanted her to hear Josarian's screams of agony forever, just as he would.

"No!" she cried, shoving at him, shaking her head as if to rid it of the images, the sounds, the memories he wanted her to carry as a burden until the day she died. "No! How would Kiloran even know where he was? How would he—"

"He knew everything about the treaty, every move the Alliance and the Valdani made together."

Her eyes flew wide open. "No, you're wrong! Searlon . . . Yes, Searlon was my guide, he took me to the meeting where we made the treaty, but he never came near any of us! He never even asked me what we discussed!"

He shook her, amazed that such a shrewd, scheming

woman could have been so stupid. "You knew Searlon was connected to this thing, and yet you never wondered—"

"The Valdani simply contacted the Alliance through . . ." She gasped and stared at him, her mouth hanging open. Her knees buckled and she leaned against him. "The Valdani . . ." she panted. "They came to us . . ." A sob escaped her. ". . . through Kiloran."

"And who had betrayed Josarian to the Valdani once already?" He forced her to keep standing, using his voice the way he usually used his swords. "Who do you think told the Valdani that the Alliance could be convinced to betray Josarian? Who had the most to fear from the Fire-bringer's strength?" He shook her hard. *"Who had the most to gain by Josarian's death?"*

"Nooo!" she howled. She broke free of his hold and fell to her knees.

Servants knocked again at the door. *"Torena! Torena!"*

"Go away!" she screamed at them. "Go! Leave me alone!"

"He used you." Tansen forced her to hear him above her howls of rage and grief. "He knew where you were weak, what you wanted to believe, and just how blind to all else you would be when you thought you saw your goal in sight."

Tears streamed down her face as she raged at Kiloran and destiny, beating her fists against the floor until she was too weak to move. In the end, she simply knelt there, staring at nothing while her shoulders shook and sobs tore at her throat.

She had shown no mercy to Josarian. She had shown none to Tansen tonight—*Armian* . . . And Tan showed no mercy to her now.

"You've paved the way for Kiloran to rule Sileria by helping him destroy the only man strong enough to oppose him after the Valdani withdraw." Every breath made his wound scream in protest. "We were all better off under Valdani rule than we will be now."

"No . . ." she sobbed.

"I gave nine years of my life to prevent what you've just done to us all."

"No!" she cried.

"Nine years, wandering foreign lands, living among the *roshaheen*, fleeing the bloodvow *you* encouraged Kiloran to swear against me . . . Nine years longing for Sileria, longing to come home. I killed my own bloodfather so that we wouldn't be ruled by the Society, and unlike you, *torena,* I loved the man I slaughtered for our freedom. Sometimes I miss him even now." He lowered himself into a chair, fighting the faintness, the darkness closing in on him. "Damn you, Elelar, did it never once occur to you that there's one person in Sileria even more clever than you?" He sighed. "No, of course not. Kiloran counted on your arrogance. You and whoever else signed that damned treaty."

She looked up at last, gazing at him through dark lashes which were spiky from her tears. Even in her grief and shame, she was still beautiful. It shouldn't move him, not now, not after all she had done . . . but it did.

"But Mirabar said . . ." She gave a watery sigh. Longing filled her tear-streaked face. "The visions. Mirabar said we would be free."

"Perhaps we will." How weary life in Sileria made a man. "But not yet."

"I . . . I have no right to ask, Tansen, but I am afraid, and so I will."

"What?"

"After you kill me . . . Will you burn my body?"

Kill her. Kill Elelar.

He should do it. He knew he should. He had vowed to do it. Mirabar would never forgive him if he didn't.

Don't come back until it is done.

He rose to his feet and unsheathed a sword. Elelar met his gaze for a moment, bidding him silent farewell. She showed more courage than her lover had in his final moments. More courage than most men did.

Don't come back to me unless you can show me Elelar's blood on your sword.

He should do it. He must do it. She had betrayed them all by betraying their leader, the Firebringer, his brother.

So die all who betray Josarian.

He hadn't spared Zimran, not even when Josarian himself had begged him to.

There are . . . no exceptions.

Who could say what Elelar would do next if he let her live? She had betrayed him once, too.

Daurion, Armian, Josarian . . .

The tender flesh of her neck was exposed. Her hands were neatly folded on her knees as she waited for him to strike.

He raised his sword. One Silerian killing another in vengeance over bloodshed and betrayal.

Must it always be this way?

"Are we no more than this?" he finally said aloud, his voice hoarse with sorrow. "Will we *never* be more than this?"

She glanced up, surprised, bewildered. "Tansen? I am ready."

"This is Sileria." He remembered the recent words of another traitor—one who had tried to save Josarian. "A man's friends are always more dangerous than his enemies."

"What?" she whispered.

He couldn't do it. He looked down at the woman who had inspired love, hate, desire, contempt, and a myriad of other emotions in his breast, and he couldn't kill her. He gazed into that unmistakably Silerian face, and he could not take the life that had shaped so much of his own. He looked down at the woman whose sins were so close to his own, and he found that he couldn't kill her unless he slit his own throat immediately thereafter—and he wasn't ready to do that. Not yet.

"We have work to do first," he said suddenly.

Prepared for death, she had trouble standing up, even with his arms to support her. "Work?"

"Kaynall was waiting for Josarian's body," he said briskly, leading her back to the bed. When she started trembling with reaction, he wrapped a blanket around her. "Searlon is supposed to identify it for him."

"B— B— But there will be no body. Not if the White Dr—"

"Exactly. I sent an Outlooker back to Shaljir to tell Kaynall that the treaty conditions have been met: Josarian is dead."

"You did *what?*"

"But I think it would be best if you go to Shaljir and pressure Kaynall to fulfill his part of the bargain and surrender Shaljir."

"Y— You want me to go to Shaljir?"

"Koroll's dead, and Kaynall has signed a treaty with you. You'll be safe enough. Besides," he added, "we can't have the Valdani changing their minds now, can we?"

She shook her head, teeth chattering. He found a flagon of wine on the table across the room and poured her a cup.

"Tell Kaynall and Cyrill that Kiloran is secretly part of the Alliance." He lifted one brow and added, "It should be a refreshing change for you, telling the truth."

"Very fu—fun—"

"Here." He pressed the cup against her lips and forced some wine down her throat. "Tell them that Kiloran finished what the Outlookers started. Find Searlon and convince him—I don't care how—to back you up when you talk to Kaynall. The one thing we all still agree on," he reminded her, "is that we want the Valdani out of Shaljir and out of Sileria."

"I thought . . ."

"What?"

"Wh— When Kaynall said we must give up Josarian, Varian convinced me . . . I convinced myself," she admitted more honestly, "that this must be Josarian's destiny.

This was how the Firebringer would finally drive them out. There is nothing in the prophecy . . ."

"That says *how* he must do it," Tansen concluded.

Elelar nodded. Tansen felt sorrow cloud his eyes.

Josarian.

"There will be civil war now," he said.

"Yes." She swallowed more wine. "I know." Tears streamed down her face again, but she did not break down this time. "At least now . . ."

"What?"

"For the first time in a thousand years . . . It will be just us. Only Silerians in Sileria."

"Free to slaughter each other at will," he said bitterly. "If we're going to win our own land once and for all, we must do it before any of the mainland powers become strong enough to attack us again. If they do it while Sileria is still in turmoil . . ."

"I will leave for Shaljir at first light." Her eyes sought his. "You are not well, Tansen. You should rest here until—"

"I have to go to Dalishar." And he would have to tell Mirabar he had spared Elelar. He'd almost rather face the White Dragon again.

"Your injuries," she protested. "You must re—"

"No one can rest now, Elelar."

As he turned to leave her, she said, "You were wrong about one thing."

He paused. "What's that?"

"There is one other man strong enough to oppose Kiloran." She nodded slowly. "You."

He held that dark, troubled gaze. "May Dar make it so," he finally replied.

Tansen left Elelar alone with her demons, knowing that his own would follow him. He ignored the wide-eyed stares of the *torena*'s servants as he passed them in the corridor, and he left her house without a backward glance.

He was unspeakably weary and in more pain than even a *shatai* could bear with grace. But he was right: No one could rest now. All of Sileria was at stake, and the Society had held sway here for far longer than the Valdani; they would be even harder to defeat. Now there would be civil war, and if he couldn't win it, Sileria would know slavery beneath the cruellest yoke of all.

He had killed his bloodfather to prevent it nine years ago. And if. he had to, he would take Josarian's place to prevent it now.

The night air was sweet and cool, perfumed by wild fennel and rosemary. The moon-streaked shadows invited him to lie down and sleep, and the serenade of a soft breeze sweeping through the trees soothed his senses. Sileria at her most enticing.

Tansen resisted her allure and, focusing on the task at hand, set his foot on the road leading toward Dalishar and his destiny.

Epilogue

"OUR WORK IS NOT YET DONE."

The Beckoner came for her in the night, while the others slept.

Here at Dalishar, the gateway to the Otherworld, his silent voice was very loud, reverberating through Mirabar's senses, storming the walls of her resistance, mocking her efforts to ignore him. Her head pounded so brutally with his insistence that she finally surrendered and acknowledged him.

"Go away. I will not serve you anymore," she said to the darkness.

Come, the Beckoner called her silently, urgently. *Come.*

She didn't want to wake the Sister who was sleeping near her in this cave, so she got up and quietly went outside. In the wake of Josarian's death, the rebel camp at Dalishar was heavily guarded; the usual number of sentries had been doubled. No one knew what Kiloran planned to do next, and everyone was afraid. Tansen had been right, though; if Mirabar could be safe anywhere, it would be here at Dalishar, a site sacred to the Guardians and steeped in their power.

Mirabar herself had brought the news of Josarian's death to Dalishar. Now the shocked rebels mourned him; but there was no body to burn and no hope that he would ever reach the Otherworld, so no one could decide what rituals to perform to mark his passing. No one knew what to do in remembrance of a victim of the White Dragon.

Slipping through the darkness, Mirabar encountered a sentry—who nearly jumped out of his skin before he recognized her and settled down. She could smell the fear on his skin as she passed him. What would Kiloran do now? Who would be next?

Come to me, come . . .

The Beckoning led her into the darkness, far from watchful eyes and curious ears. Mirabar followed it, also wanting privacy from the others at Dalishar, but her resolve remained firm. "Leave me alone. You are not welcome here."

Your work is not yet done.

"What work?" she cried. "What do you want? Why did you let him die?" A tear streamed down her face. Her throat filled with bitter hatred. "I did everything you asked of me. And you have betrayed us."

Visions filled her head, flowing through her blood, clouding the night with the will of the Otherworld. She fought it, but the Beckoner was more powerful, and so she saw what he wanted her to see.

"The Sign of the Three . . ." It lay smashed, the shattered ruin of what had once been a monument to the power and glory of the Valdani.

She didn't want to acknowledge it, didn't want to ask anything of the Beckoner. But she had to know. "They are leaving?"

Leaving Sileria forever.

"Then . . . he did free us."

When he died.

"When he died," she repeated. Her shoulders slumped with renewed sorrow. "But it was wrong. He should not have died. Not that way."

Your work is not yet done, the Beckoner told her again.

"No." She shook hear head. "I will not obey you anymore. I will not lead more good men to their deaths. I will not—No! Stop!" She screamed as he drove her to her knees, inflicting pain on her as he sought to bend her to the will of the Otherworld.

"*Sirana!*"

She heard sentries shouting in panic. They crashed around in the darkness, seeking her, ready to fight their enemies. The sky overhead turned black, blotting out the light of the moons, smothering all of Dalishar in velvety darkness. The shouts in the distance grew more frantic as powers beyond the rebels' understanding swept through the night.

Fire streamed across the sky, then curled and twisted until it formed a shape she knew well by now: the symbol of a *shatai*.

"Tansen?" she whispered, staring up at the sky.

You and he must prepare the way.

"I don't . . ." Her head pounded. "For what?"

The fiery symbol dissolved against the black sky, drifting and reshaping itself into two separate balls of fire. She watched as a face formed around those two glowing eyes. Like the symbol, she had seen this face before.

"Daurion," she murmured.

The voice which addressed her was a new one, not the Beckoner's. It filled the whole sky.

He is coming. Prepare the way.

"Who is coming?"

The sky exploded in flames, shards of firelight scattering into infinity to mingle with the stars. Mirabar shielded her eyes against the stinging brilliance, flinching against the thunder that roared through the heavens like a victor's triumph. It echoed through the night, then slowly faded, leaving her too weak to move.

She was still huddled on the ground when Najdan finally found her. "*Sirana!* Why didn't you answer? Haven't you heard us calling you?"

She looked up at him. The soft light of a twin-moon night once again crept through the shadows, and she could see the strain in the assassin's face. "No, I . . . Sorry, I . . ."

"Your screams woke everyone," he said, hauling her to

her feet. "And then . . ." Najdan shook his head. "I would not believe it had I not seen it myself."

"What?" Her legs felt weak and her stomach was churning.

"In the sky. It was . . ."

"A face?" she prompted.

"No." He took her arm and started to lead her back toward camp. "It looked like a fist."

"A fist?"

"Yes."

"A fist . . ." Her knees buckled, and she would have fallen back down if not for Najdan's support.

"What is it? Are you ill?"

"You all . . . saw a fist?"

"Yes."

"Daurion," she gasped. "A fist of iron in a velvet glove. We must prepare the way."

"Sirana?"

She had never expected to feel hope again. Now it flooded her, renewing her strength. "He is coming."

"Who is coming?" Najdan demanded.

"The next Yahrdan." She smiled tremulously. "Our work is not yet done."

About the Author

Laura Resnick won the 1993 John W. Campbell Award for Best New Science Fiction/Fantasy Writer for her short fiction. The daughter of science fiction writer Mike Resnick, she is also the award-winning author of over a dozen romance novels (published under the pseudonym Laura Leone), as well as *A Blonde in Africa*, a nonfiction book about her eight-month journey across Africa in 1993.